Discovery

Discovery

Volume I of the Dark Side Trilogy

William Hayashi

To order additional copies of this book, contact:
Xlibris Corporation
1-888-795-4274
www.Xlibris.com
Orders@Xlibris.com
56846

Dedication

This book is dedicated to absent family and friends.

May they all find their way back together one day.

ACKNOWLEDGMENTS

R IGHT OFF THE bat, I need to thank Michael Hall, who paid me the greatest compliment I had ever received once he read the extremely rough first draft of *Discovery*.

I thank my two editors, Mae and Linda. Without whom anyone reading this book would easily have concluded that English was not my first, my second or even my third language.

Thanks go out to Charlie, who has a great sense of style in putting together the cover of the book and the Web site graphics just from my description.

There are also host of people who I must mention who never seem to make it into the thanks given by others. For example, I must thank Joe and Diane, the owner and the manager of the building in which I live. Without their consideration during the writing of this book, I probably would have become homeless. I also have to acknowledge the great work of my physician, Eric, who manages to keep me healthy despite my benign neglect when other priorities push self-maintenance to the background of my attention.

Thanks must also be given to all the neighborhood restaurants that deliver, with special thanks to going to Glenn; may he rest in peace. Without them I would never have been able to stay at home (in my pajamas, or worse) for nine months typing, editing and agonizing over the fact that the characters in this story refused to do the things I wanted them to and insisted on behaving with minds of their own.

I also want to thank an unnamed NASA research librarian who helped me plausibly reconfigure one of their space shuttles to travel to the moon. I want to make it clear that there was no endorsement by anyone at NASA of the fictional situation I created, nor is it even technically feasible to do what I have suggested, but after all, it's just a story. Right?

And finally, I want to thank all my friends who answered their phones when I called, fully knowing (CallerID) it was me. They answered knowing that I was probably going to bend their ear for uncounted hours reading them something I had just written because I needed their encouragement and affirmation in order to keep going.

These are just a few people in my life who deserve mention and I want to thank and acknowledge any of you I left out for your having provided invaluable support resulting in this book.

INTRODUCTION

THE ORIGIN OF this story is somewhat lost to me at this time. I do remember the day I began to write this first volume. At that time I thought that this would be the only volume. Once the story began to unwind I realized that the characters who populated the story had more than a single books worth of life, a story that would span decades of time.

The day I decided to begin writing this book was a blustery, snowy day in Chicago, the snow instantly turning into heavy slush when it hit the ground. At the time I was Board Chairman of a social service organization operating in and around Chicago's famous Cabrini-Green neighborhood. I was sitting in a small office assigned to me because I was helping edit the various sections of a five-foot-long span of three-ringed binders that the organization had to fill out to reapply for accreditation to supervise foster children.

As I sat there, waiting for the next batch of paperwork, I realized that no matter how many stories I had in my head, they didn't exist until they were put to paper.

So, as a former software engineer, I opened up one of my technical drawing programs and created a flowchart of the plot of the story. Once I was satisfied with the various plot lines and where they would intersect, I put the drawing away and began typing; that was in February of 2001.

At the time, I set up a work schedule for writing: no matter what I was doing at 10PM, I would stop and sit down at the computer and either write or edit until 2AM. This went on for nine months until a Friday afternoon in November. I had never given any thought to what would come next, but the fact that I had finished writing my first book was a shock.

What stands above everything I felt about the process, the difficulties in managing the characters, the days of writer's block and the anxiety over wondering if this is really a good story, was the sense of accomplishment. This is a story that I enjoyed writing, and one that I'm sure will be cause for discussion; it has been for those who have already read it. I only hope that those who read it will be entertained and engaged enough to want to see how the story ends.

William Hayashi

Would you like to swing on a star,
Or carry moonbeams home in a jar?
Swinging on a Star
Written by Jimmy Van Heusen, performed by Bing Crosby

CHAPTER 1

A S WITH MANY discoveries, finding Asteroid 2005 XF13 was more the result of serendipity than hard work. After what seemed like a long, uneventful winter, Norma's discovery of the asteroid brought enough excitement to her life to propel her out of winter doldrums into spring.

Norma Lancaster was just finishing up her last year of study in astrophysics at the University of Chicago. She'd attended U of C for the last six years after graduating from a small suburban high school with straight As and a perfect SAT. She was extremely bright, but she had an easy way with people. Everyone she met saw her as warm and approachable, not your run-of–the-mill computer geek.

On this particular Monday she arrived at her small cubicle in one of the geological science department's laboratories, dropped her books on her desk and checked her weekend's e-mail. While her workstation was booting up she looked around and once again vowed to clean up her cubical. She could find anything she needed, but it made her look rather unorganized.

Norma had no new e-mail messages waiting for her. She turned her attention to the weekend run of digital images uploaded from the observatory on the edge of the Mauna Loa volcano in Hawaii. These pictures, negatives of the night sky, black dots on a white background, were the stuff of which her dreams were made. She lacked the patience to spend hours gazing into the night sky on her own, learning quadrant by quadrant, but she secretly hoped she would discover a new world or asteroid that would bear her name in perpetuity.

Instead of spending her nights in solitary contemplation of the sky, Norma had written a suite of programs that compared digital images of the sky and flagged items that appeared, moved or disappeared over time. The hardest part of her project was writing the programs to map the thousands of stars into her computerized sky so that images could be perfectly compared against each other. These search and comparison programs had earned her a grant from NASA in digital image processing, and were the precursor for an automated system for discovering and plotting new bodies in the sky.

"Hey, Norma, baby . . . what's shakin'?" came over the top of her cube. She looked up at the familiar face of research fellow Alan Richards, with his brown wavy hair wildly askew atop his head and warm, brown eyes twinkling in easy-going humor.

"Nothing yet, but as you know 'on any given Monday, anything can happen!'" they both finished together. Alan was a University of Chicago Fellow working on his own project and a very low-maintenance lab mate. He had no really annoying habits like humming to himself, or tapping his pen on the desk, or questionable hygiene. Most of the time, Norma felt lucky to share her space with him instead of some dense mouth-breather with overactive hormones and bad skin.

"What's up with you?" Norma asked. "And how is it that you beat me in the door on a Monday of all days?"

"Actually, I was in all weekend working on something I think is really hot," he replied. "I haven't been home since Thursday night." *Oh well*, she thought, *so much for the good hygiene.*

"What's got you so pumped up, if I may ask? Some new shoot-em-up computer game?" she asked sarcastically.

"Not this time, although I seem to recall you like playing those games almost as much as I do. No, this is a 3D mapping routine that just may make me some serious cash with the public planetariums out there." He paused, trying to decide whether or not he should spill the beans to Norma. It's not that he didn't trust her, after all they had been through their own cycles as colleagues, friends and very infrequent lovers. He wasn't sure he wanted to talk about it until he was closer to being finished, but plunged ahead anyway.

"Well," he began, "it's really a kind of a three-dimensional extension of the star mapping program you're working on. But before you get pissed off, it's not really the same idea at all. Instead, it's for displaying star maps, planetary systems and other astronomical objects in three dimensions instead of flat on a screen," he finished, watching her face for reaction.

"And just how are you planning on cashing in on this idea?" she asked.

"Instead of just seeing the sky pasted to the ceiling in a planetarium theater, the whole sky could be displayed in three dimensions using holographic technology!" he replied. "One could paint using lasers in three dimensions. And, if I can paste digital images of planets, moons and other celestial objects into the program, I can project three-dimensional renderings of the entire solar system and the nearby galactic neighborhood with built-in calculations to show movement over time."

Norma was silent for a few seconds rolling the idea around in her head, looking at it from all angles. Was she pissed that he stole part of her idea? Was it that he had taken what she had worked on for the last two years and added something so remarkable that became greater in magnitude than her whole life's work? Or, was it that he had seen a facet of her idea that she had never considered and ran with it without so much as a by-your-leave?

"Did I 'boldly go where no man has gone before' or are you thinking of some way of making me disappear in some South Side alley without a trace?" he finally asked.

"No," she answered. "I'm not exactly pissed. It's more that I didn't consider before how my project could be extended into the third dimension."

"Although, now that I think about it, you can't use this mapping program for detection of dark bodies because you would need simultaneous, offset observations to locate a body in the third dimension," Alan added.

"True," Norma said. "If you could plot anything in the sky immediately in three dimensions, you could calculate speed and direction in a much shorter time instead of waiting several days, or weeks, to perform serial observations. By the way," she asked. "Did you notice whether my latest uploads came in?"

"Oh, yeah. They started Saturday afternoon, hosing up my network bandwidth until around eleven o'clock last night. It looks like the whole set was about thirteen gigabytes of data based on the decrease in available server disk space this morning."

"Awwww, did little Alan miss out on his music downloads over the weekend?" she tossed over the partition as she started checking the coordinates of this latest batch of images. The demise of some of the shared music sites on the Internet a few years earlier had in no way kept Alan from stacking up a bunch of searches on Friday so that he could download and burn music off to blank CDs during the week. "What'd you get this weekend? Some thrashing, techno, grunge Gregorian chants?"

"Nope," he answered distractedly, "actually I was downloading a couple of classic movies."

"Porno?" she asked with a grin.

"Nope. One was *Some Like It Hot* with Tony Curtis and Marilyn Monroe, you know, the old black and white movie directed by Billy Wilder, and the other was *The Fifth Element* with *Die Hard* guy Bruce Willis." But even as he was answering, Alan was back into the depths of his dual-screen display, fingers flashing over the keyboard, mouse clicking away.

His project was the refinement of the underlying math behind the famous "unrestricted three-body problem" in physics. It had applications from astrophysics to molecular engineering, and finding its definitive solution had been on the table since Newton published his Laws of Motion. Since most of the equations dealt with motion in three dimensions, his project and Norma's slightly overlapped, enough so that they had had some pretty far-ranging, and heated, discussions on both.

Norma settled into her chair, pulled her keyboard into her lap, put her feet up on her desk and began supervising the computer's aligning and resizing of the uploaded images for comparison to her reference sky map. She noticed that this image set included Saturn in the lower right quadrant of the sky and she marked it to be ignored by the computer. Some of the edges of the images showed a slight distortion in the same spot; she was going to have to crop the pictures and send a note to the observatory to check for dirt or spots on the lens of their telescope.

When she was about halfway through the pictures, Norma looked up and saw that it was after two o'clock. She stood, stretched and peeked over the partition. Alan had fallen asleep in his chair with his head thrown back, mouth open and slumped down in that boneless slouch guys seemed able to achieve at the drop of a hat. She looked at his face thinking how much younger he looked when he was asleep. Her stomach broke the mood by growling in indignation over its long neglect.

Norma considered waking Alan to see if he wanted her to bring him something back, but nixed the idea, positive he needed the sleep more than anything. She grabbed her bag, slung it over her shoulder and headed out to one of the local restaurants, wondering what today's soup and sandwich were.

Late spring and early summer in Chicago's Hyde Park neighborhood often yielded exhilarating weather. One could see a hard, subzero freeze morph into tropical heat and humidity in the course of a day. Norma liked the panorama of the changing seasons, even the gray, oily slush of the Chicago winter, because the spring brought a renewal of hope and excitement each year.

The day was glorious, the temperature was in the high seventies, and the sun beat warmly on her cocoa brown skin. The wind blew her skirt around her long, slim legs and warmly caressed the toes peeking out of her sandals.

Today Norma could look all the way down the street, past the Museum of Science and Industry, to Lake Michigan and the deep blue water scattering the sun's rays. Walking through the door of her favorite hangout, she stopped for a moment to let her eyes adjust to the dimly lit interior of the restaurant.

Catching the eye of the greeter, Norma waved him off, letting him know she was just ordering something to go. She paid for her selections and, walking back to the lab, started to think about what plotting objects three-dimensionally in the sky would entail.

The first problem was determining location accurately. The second problem was finding the direction and speed of any nonluminous body at any distance from the sun. The amount of reflected light normally wasn't sufficient to directly view an asteroid without practically knowing where it was in the first place. The third was the complicated problem of plotting an asteroid's path through the solar system with any degree of accuracy given the effect of the gravitational pull of all the planets, moons and other large asteroids that would influence an object's motion.

Walking back into the lab, Norma saw that Alan was awake and prowling around in the middle of a low-voiced, heated discussion on his cell phone. She ignored his terse muttering and sat down at her desk to eat, occasionally glancing at her screen as the various images were resized and mapped. The speed and accuracy of her program had taken a long time and a lot of effort to accomplish. The sweat she had put into programming her computer to scan the sky reminded her of the process she had gone through to get to where she was now.

With the constant cutbacks at NASA beginning shortly after the last American left the moon in 1972, her proposed automated computer programs promised to keep watch on the heavens for inbound asteroids and do it much cheaper than human observers could. Once her computer images of the sky were resized and mapped, the differences could be marked for additional attention by human eyes. Since the entire NASA sky search budget was only sufficient to watch about two percent of the sky surrounding the earth, Norma's project was the only way those scant funds could be stretched far enough to seriously keep watch for that extinction-event asteroid everyone worried about. Any asteroid of sufficient size striking the earth would render the entire biosphere of the planet unlivable for years, just like the asteroid blamed for the extinction of the dinosaurs sixty million years ago. Proving that low-cost computers could watch the sky was the basis for the grant, and had been the focus of her last two years. Thinking over the progress she had made during those two years, and seeing the evidence of her efforts on her computer screen, had her feeling pretty damn good.

Finishing her lunch, she brought up the results from the batch of images from the observatory in Hawaii and ran the stats. *Hmmm*, she thought, *only about eighteen anomalies from the entire run. Not bad, assuming that they're from errors in mapping or positioning.*

She brought up the first tagged image and checked the circled region the computer marked for her attention. False alarm, she saw; it was the result of a little portion of the distortion she had noticed before. After cropping and resubmitting the image to the analysis queue she called up the next image. This one was from a different part of the sky just below the plane of Saturn's rings. The question here, upon closer observation, was whether this small blur in the picture could be an imaging artifact or a real object. Norma brought up the next image in the series. Again the computer had highlighted an object in almost the same location. She saw that the times the images were taken were about twenty-eight hours apart and the only difference between the two pictures was just this one blur.

Although not normally very excitable, Norma felt a tiny flutter in her stomach as she let herself imagine the possibility of catching an actual space-borne rock in motion with her program.

Typing quickly, Norma went through table after table of tasking coordinates trying to find a telescope or satellite that was scheduled to observe this quadrant of the sky in the upcoming weeks. Only two were, but she was in luck. One was a space-based x-ray telescope that had a powerful optical sighting system for precise aiming of the x-ray sensor array.

Norma sent off an e-mail message to the head of NASA's X-Ray Observation and Analysis committee who supervised the tasking schedule for the space-based x-ray observatory. She requested access to any visible light images downloaded from the quadrant of the anomaly. She then sent a message with the coordinates, time and estimated size of the object to the Planetary Registry Society, staking her claim to the registration and naming of the body.

Although cautious by nature, Norma entertained a singular thrill that she might finally discover a new, loose asteroid she could name whatever she wanted. She stood up, stretched and looked over the divider to give Alan the news. Unfortunately, he had gone away while Norma was off into her own world. Instead of waiting for his return, she isolated the blurred spot from the best of the two images, added an electronic circle to the picture and sent it to him through in-house e-mail with a note saying "Check this out!"

Checking the computer's calculations on the amount of sky that seemed to be occluded by the asteroid, Norma whistled in amazement. The computer's best guess showed a width of just over one mile and a length of four point three miles, although at that distance it was a shot in the dark. Preliminary mass calculations couldn't be completed so soon. However, if the asteroid was about twenty-five percent rock with the rest made up of frozen water and carbon dioxide, it could almost qualify as a small moon. Well, maybe not quite, but if it continued to get closer to the sun it could probably be seen by the naked eye in a matter of weeks.

Norma was so excited by the implication of her discovery that she needed to share it with someone, anyone, before she burst. She wondered where Alan was, vaguely remembering his agitated telephone conversation, curious with whom he had been talking.

Her overall ambivalence toward Alan was a defense against being hurt by men in general. Not that she was emotionally frail, she just never wanted a relationship to get in the way of her goals. The mysterious disappearance of her parents just after she started college as an undergraduate, and the self-imposed emotional isolation that followed, had stiffened her resolve to get everything *she* wanted from life. She still felt a great deal of bitterness toward the Georgia authorities for what she considered a shallow, nonchalant investigation into her parents' disappearance. No trace of a crime or any clue concerning their fate was ever uncovered.

Norma wanted to believe that not knowing what happened to them was better than finding out they were, indeed, dead. Her not knowing kept them alive to someday return. She was much too smart to really fool herself in her heart of hearts, but her little mind game kept the pain and loss compartmentalized enough for her to finish her degrees and sustain her through her doctoral project at the university. She had enough of her emotional self left to go around for several fulfilling relationships with men, and a singular lack of bitterness at the throw of the dice life gave her. One positive thing her parents' disappearance brought her was a small estate that paid for her education, but not much else. At least she wouldn't finish her doctoral studies with a huge pile of debt. Some of her fellow students, once they got their Ph.D.s, would have a debt load of well over a hundred thousand dollars, a daunting pile of cash to have to begin to pay back right out of school. One perk of graduating from the University of Chicago was that the starting salaries of its top graduates were usually half again as much as those graduating from lower-ranked schools.

Her on-again, off-again thing with Alan was more a matter of convenience for the both of them than a deep abiding love. They were both too driven by their respective studies and ongoing projects to be able to sustain a committed relationship. And they were both enlightened enough to not let each other's lovers be anything more than a source of entertainment. They knew each other so well that their on-again times were easy and very comfortable for Norma. She knew she wouldn't have to go through lengthy, painful explanations about her family or her lack of roots. Her practice of "out of sight, out of mind," remained a workable accommodation to the pain in her soul where the memories of her parents resided.

Norma loaded her best image processing software to see how much she could enhance the outline of the asteroid. She reveled in the fact that the software she was using was as good as anything the various spy agencies used to enhance their satellite photos, just a bit slower. After all, the government security services did get the very best in hardware, most of it never getting into the hands of ordinary consumers.

Norma set the program to apply normal adaptive sharpening to both images and left it to process overnight. The countdown clock in the program estimated the time of completion nineteen hours away. With the rest of her images flagged, cataloged and stored in her master database, she started a full system backup. Since Alan wasn't there he wouldn't bitch about slowing the system down backing up her data to tape and offsite storage. Norma was, if nothing else, a belt *and* suspenders kind of woman.

She looked around to see if she had forgotten anything that needed her attention. Finding nothing of import, Norma left the lab, locked the door and walked out into a perfect spring afternoon.

Getting into her car she headed for the lakefront, hopped onto Lake Shore Drive and began the drive downtown. On the way she called her best friend

Angela to see if she wanted to go get a bite to eat. What she really wanted was to share her discovery and for Angela to help her celebrate. If this piece of rock was what it appeared to be, it was proof positive that her project performed just as she predicted it would. Not that she had met any detractors on the decision train when she conceived the system, but getting any funding for research was becoming increasingly harder.

When Angela answered the phone Norma shouted, "Hey girlfriend, what's up?" above the wind blowing in through the car windows.

Angela answered, "Nothing! Get me out of here, it's so dead." Angela worked as a job costing accountant for a large construction company. She spent most of her time figuring the cost of the company's construction projects down to the last nail and screw before they went to bid. During the summer, when most of the jobs were in full swing, she could sit around doing nothing, often for days at a time. Fortunately, unlimited Internet access provided her at least some entertainment during the day.

"Did you drive?" Norma asked.

"No, I took the train in. Come get me. RIGHT NOW!" she ended with a yell.

"Okay, I'll be there in about twenty minutes, and then it's margarita time!"

Norma took her time driving downtown because the view of Chicago's skyline was most spectacular coming in from the South Side, something that Norma was sure well-heeled North Siders resented. The ride was great, and seeing the sailboats on the water reinforced Norma's decision to play hooky for the rest of the day. The only thing missing was a convertible.

Pulling up to Angela's office building, Norma saw that her friend was already waiting outside. Angela jumped into the car and gave Norma a big hug. "Thanks for rescuing me, there's only so much movie-watching I can do on the computer before I go nuts sitting inside the same four walls. All of the guys are on site, and everyone else was acting like they were some weird Stepford office workers. It seemed like they all were in some sort of trance all damned day."

"Just judging from the couple of visits I've made, the whole office could do with a personality transplant. So guess what?" Norma asked her friend.

"What, Alan got that sex change operation he so desperately deserves?"

"No."

"You bought me those electric undies with the built-in vibrator we saw in that leather shop up north?"

"Nooo," Norma answered with a laugh. "One more guess."

"Well, you can't get a raise, the Nobel Committee doesn't meet until October and I know you don't play the lottery. So give, what's up?"

"Okay, it's not for certain yet, but it looks like I've found one."

"One what, for Christ's sake?"

"I may have found an asteroid!!" shouted Norma.

"Using your programs and stuff? That's great, sweetie, are you going to be famous now?" Angela asked.

"Well, not exactly, maybe if it comes close to the earth it might get some news coverage."

"Hey, I'm sure it will, look how much press those two guys got when their rocks plowed into . . . what was it, Jupiter? They were interviewed for a couple of weeks on all the news shows," Angela gushed. "I can't wait to see you on television, maybe if they interview you at home I could be visiting as your best friend."

"If I get that kind of attention I'll be sure to have you over. Hey, where do you want to go for a margarita?" Norma asked.

"Are you hungry at all?"

"Not really, I ate around three, but we can get you something to eat. What do you have a taste for, Mexican, Greek, Chinese? How about we hit Halsted Street and get something from Greek Town?" Norma suggested.

"You know that no one over there knows how to make a good margarita. How 'bout heading over to Jesse's place, they've got sandwiches AND margaritas. What do you say?"

"Fine, just don't expect me to get totally polluted with you, I still have to drive home tonight."

Angela leaned over and tuned the radio to the smooth jazz station and sat back watching downtown Chicago go by. The tavern Jesse worked at was just outside downtown in Chicago's trendy Lincoln Park neighborhood. The three of them were pretty good friends, having met at a walk for breast cancer two years ago. They had all been in the same line to register and get their t-shirts when they struck up a conversation about whom they were walking for. Both Angela's and Jesse's mothers were cancer survivors and Norma was there for one of her peers at the U of C who had unfortunately lost her battle with cancer the year before.

The three of them made a striking trio. Norma was slim, with skin the color of milk chocolate, cool blue eyes and features suggestive of former Miss America Vanessa Williams. Angela had naturally curly, almost red hair, grey-blue eyes and a bigger build than Norma, but without any excess baggage (as she called it) to ruin an almost perfectly proportioned physique. Jesse was pale and willowy, with long, straight dark brown hair. Her calm, unflappable demeanor hid a smoky intensity that many men found startling, and most found intimidating. The three of them never failed to turn heads when they were out together, but more times than not their gang had little time for the nonsense most men visited on women win their attention.

Pulling up to the bar, Norma's parking mojo was with her; there was a space only a few doors down from the tavern.

Once inside, they found a booth and sat down. Moments later Jesse appeared on the bench next to Norma.

"Hey, you two, I was wondering when the three of us were going to get together again. What's up with you guys?" asked Jesse.

"We're celebrating," replied Angela. "Norma found a new planet and were trying to find a name for it better than Uranus."

"No shit? You found a planet? Where is it? Is it out past Pluto, or is it in some other solar system?"

"Hey, you know better than to listen to Angela. No, what I think I've found is an asteroid that may have originated around Saturn. My programs found it, but it's going to take a couple of days to confirm it," said Norma.

Jesse leaned over and gave Norma a big hug. "That's great, hon, no one deserves it more than you. Have you told anyone else? How about the rest of the gang in the department?"

"Not yet. I sent one of the pictures to Alan with a big circle drawn around it, but no one else knows yet. I did send an e-mail message to the Planetary Society to register it and if I'm the first to find it, I get to name it!"

"Or they'll name it after her," Angela added.

"That's great, this really does call for a celebration. How 'bout a couple of margaritas on me to start you off?" asked Jesse.

"You know that's why we come here. You go ahead and throw together whatever you think this party needs," Norma said.

As Jesse got up and headed for the bar Angela asked, "No bullshit, why's this kind of thing so important anyway?"

Norma thought about it for a moment, and began, "Well, it's really three things. The first and most important reason is the extinction event. That's where an asteroid large enough to change the weather for hundreds of years actually hits the earth. What happens is that a large enough piece of anything hitting the earth will throw so much debris into the air that sunlight and heat are blocked from reaching the surface. That causes a mini ice age for a couple of hundred years, or at least until most of the crap settles out of the air. The combined might of all the missiles on the earth couldn't do anything to deflect a rock even half a mile wide, and some of the asteroids out there are the size of Texas. So, seeing them as early as possible, especially if they are incoming, is important in terms of preparing for disaster. Remember back in the spring of 2002, when scientists didn't see a football-field-sized asteroid until a few days *after* it passed within seventy-five thousand miles of earth? That one, if it had hit, would have had the same power as several of our larger nuclear warheads. If it had hit land somewhere the results would have been spectacularly bad, no matter if it was away from a major population center or not. Seventy-five thousand miles isn't far at all in terms of the entire solar system, and even one that small couldn't have been deflected with our current level of technology. Essentially we're just sitting ducks."

Angela broke in, "Well, don't just beat around the bush or sugar-coat it Norma, tell me what all this really means."

"Okay, maybe I'm being a little dramatic, but this is serious stuff. It's why I got the grant in the first place. Anyway, the second reason for finding and identifying asteroids like this one, especially if a large portion of the thing is ice, is that the majority of the cost of any off-earth mission is lifting consumables like food and water into orbit. Getting even a gallon of water into orbit costs over thirty-five thousand dollars using current space shuttle technology. Imagine what it's going to cost to get that same gallon of water to the moon or Mars. If we could somehow grab a few of these chunks of ice and bring them into earth orbit and process them there, the cost of manned missions in orbit, or to nearby bodies like the moon, Mars or Venus, drops dramatically."

"But wouldn't grabbing these things and keeping them in orbit above our heads be just as dangerous as having them fly around loose?" Angela asked.

"Not at all. For the most part objects in orbit, at least high enough orbit so that the earth's atmosphere doesn't cause them to slow down, will stay in orbit practically forever, just like the moon. Besides, they would be getting progressively smaller and smaller as their mass was processed for water and air for space stations and shuttles between high earth orbit and the moon. And with some of the new propulsion technologies coming online, that same frozen water could be separated into hydrogen and oxygen and used for rocket fuel.

"The last part of this equation is this. Imagine how much manufacturing could be done in space if you could use a huge iron asteroid to produce steel for space stations or habitats on the moon. No lifting cost at all, just the cost of pushing it into earth's orbit so it could be made into whatever parts you need for building a space habitat. Some science fiction writer even wrote about making enormous space stations by heating huge iron asteroids until they're completely molten and then blowing them up with air like large balloons and letting them cool. The idea was to start out with a huge, empty sphere and build the habitat inside."

"Yeah, but it doesn't seem like we're anywhere near that kind of capability now." said Angela.

"That's mostly true, but it's not that far off in the future. The biggest hurdle to beginning something like harvesting any kind of asteroid is the cost of transportation, getting consumables off earth, and for propellant to push an asteroid into orbit."

Just as Norma finished her explanation, Jesse arrived with the two huge glasses on a tray. As she set down napkins and the glasses she asked, "Has Angela figured out a better name for it than Uranus? How about 'Her-anus?'"

The three of them cracked up. The two girls raised their glasses in Jesse's direction toasting their friend and host. Jesse blew them kisses and headed back to the bar.

"So what would we be able to do if one of these large rocks were going to hit earth, Norma?"

"Probably nothing. It's not like we could pull off something like in the movie *Armageddon*. There would be no mission to the asteroid to blow it up, we can barely lift a crew of six and a satellite with the current space shuttle. Nuclear missiles would have practically no effect on a solid iron rock, maybe melt some of the surface, but blowing it up is out of the question. I think the only practical thing we could do would to be to make sure as many people as possible could survive the impact and resulting change in climate. The best bet is to get them underground to escape the deep freeze to follow. But really, how many is that going to be? A few thousand, maybe. And, if it all goes to hell, you'll have chaos, vigilantes and masses of humanity trying to get underground, way underground, subways and basements won't do. You'd need to get far enough down so that you could get some heat from the earth's core, maybe build near active volcanos, but not near the fault lines, too unstable. I'm sure a hit like that would trigger quakes and aftershocks for quite a while after the initial impact. No, I think the lucky ones would be the ones who happened to be right under the thing when it hit."

"Jeez, Norma, not only is the glass half empty with you, it's cracked at the rim with fungus fuzz growing on it! I thought this was supposed to be a celebration."

"You're the one who asked what would happen. But you know what, you're right." Norma lifted her glass and said, "Here's to Lancaster's Folly, or whatever they name it!"

"Hear, hear! But no speech, no speech!" shouted Angela.

After the toast their conversation drifted off into more mundane subjects like Angela's work; when, if ever, Norma and Alan would be on again; Angela's imaginary lover (the one she maintained she really had, but whom Norma had never met); the weather; the news and anything else that came to mind. Things really deteriorated after ten o'clock when Jesse punched out and joined them. The three of them drank together until closing time.

Despite her best intentions Norma managed to get quite polluted after all, and wound up having to call a cab to take her home.

I Said Shotgun,
Shoot It For They Run Now
Shotgun
Written by Jr. Walker, performed by Jr. Walker & The All Stars

CHAPTER 2

THE WORLD PRESS only reported on the political and military situation in Iraq from the perspective of the West. At this time no one was the least bit interested in the embargo, the isolation, Iraq's economy or the no-fly zone skirmishes from the viewpoint of the Iraqis. Military duty at an Iraqi missile defense installation was burdened by danger from the Western allies and ambivalence over any death or destruction the West might visit on them.

American and British air-to-ground missiles were so devastatingly accurate that most soldiers who manned the stations didn't even light up their targeting radar for fear of drawing down a rain of death from the sky.

The only electromagnetic signals emanating from one particular installation on the southern edge of the northern no-fly zone were from normal commercial radar, the kind used by any airport in the world; hardly a threat to any aircraft flying through the area.

The radar operator sat back in his chair in the command trailer with his feet up on the console and a cigarette dangling from the corner of his mouth as he paged through a well-worn British girly magazine. Every once in a while he glanced at the radar screen when something showed at extreme range. But for the most part, he lost himself in his tired fantasies of the girls on the pages before him.

All at once a high-pitched tone started warbling from the console in front of him, signaling contact with an airborne intruder. The technician's feet hit the floor hard and the magazine was tossed unceremoniously aside. He reached for the controls of his console to refine the focus of the radar array outside, hoping to get a better glimpse of the size, speed and direction of the intruder. He debated the pros and cons of switching from search mode to targeting mode and immediately rejected the idea. What if the intruder was a Western fighter that had strayed into their zone and retaliated with a radar-guided missile because the pilot thought he was under attack? No, a higher-powered sweep of the search radar was the safest bet for now.

While he was trying to develop a better lock on the intruder, the site commander climbed into the trailer. "What have we got?" he asked, making sure the radar was in search, not targeting, mode. He too was a veteran of the kind of retaliation Western pilots dished out under the least provocation.

"Not much," the junior technician replied. "It's still pretty far away and is moving much slower than the Americans usually do. Maybe it's someone who drifted off course and is trying to get back into the zone," he added.

"What's his heading?" the commander asked.

"According to the computer he's angling in toward our location, but I can't get his height readout. He's not squawking any commercial or military identification and he's going too slow to be a commercial aircraft that's lost or off course."

"All right. Alert sector command and see if we've got anyone in the air who can run an intercept. Try to sound casual, I don't want them ordering us to do anything that arouses the Americans into sending a missile up our ass!" ordered the commander. As the technician was on the radiophone to command, he continued to watch the computer readout. The object didn't really look like a fighter at all. It wasn't lined up with any strategic target. No radar site or missile emplacements were anywhere near where the intruder was flying.

Putting the telephone handset back in its cradle, the technician informed the commander that headquarters had already received a report on the intruder and ordered them to keep a close watch.

"They also agreed that we should not adopt any aggressive posture against the aircraft," the technician added. "I think they too do not want us to cause an incident that gets our remaining equipment destroyed."

"Where is he now?" the commander inquired.

"Coming inbound, about thirty degrees off a direct course to this site," the technician replied. "Do you think we will have to engage him?"

The commander considered the options. "I hope not," he stated. "But I'm afraid that we may be ordered to try to shoot him down if he comes too much closer.

"Once he's in range, see if you can get a heat track on him," ordered the commander. "I'll check on the missile crew, they should be up by now. Call me if there's any change in the intruder's direction, you got that?"

"Yes, sir."

"And get rid of that magazine, you never know when we might get visitors," the commander threw over his shoulder on his way down the trailer's stairs.

The technician's computer had recorded the path the intruder had taken since it had been detected. Upon closer examination, the directional trace didn't really look like the flight characteristics of any known aircraft. Its speed was too low for a fighter and its altitude began much higher than most military aircraft flew. The object had dropped from sixty thousand feet down to less than twenty thousand feet in moments, and then leveled off with a forward velocity of eighty knots. No known fighter, or any other aircraft, could make that rapid a drop and level off at such a slow forward speed. Maybe the computer was wrong. The technician recalled that the computer had a hard time initially getting a good reading of the object's altitude. The Soviet-made equipment *was* over twelve years old, and since the fall of the Union replacement parts were getting harder to obtain. For the most part Iraq was forced to decommission older consoles and scanning equipment to consolidate parts for the newer.

Switching back to the live track, he noticed that the forward speed of the intruder was down to sixty knots, too slow for any conventional fighter to maintain flight. Only the British Harrier or the American V-22 Osprey could fly at that speed. It couldn't be an Osprey, they couldn't get up over twenty-five or thirty thousand feet, and the latest intelligence reports didn't mention any Harriers deployed in the area, although the term "intelligence" in this case was always suspect. No, if this wasn't an intelligence or computer glitch, this aircraft was something totally new.

As he watched, the intruder turned directly toward the radar installation. The computer started blasting the alarm recommending a change from passive to active tracking. The door to the trailer was thrown open and the commander and the offensive weapons officer charged into the command trailer.

"Status?" the commander shouted over the alarm.

"Intruder has changed track and is inbound directly for the installation," replied the technician.

"Estimated time until he's within the kill zone?"

"Eighteen minutes if he stays on track and at the same speed. Commander, the intruder's track has changed in ways that do not fit any Western aircraft flight characteristics. The computer cannot give better than an eighty-five percent predicted kill assessment." The technician paused and then continued, "Forward batteries cannot get a lock on the intruder unless we go active with targeting radar. Should we activate, sir?"

"How long do you need in order to acquire the craft?" asked the commander.

"From initial sweep to acquisition, about fifteen seconds, sir."

"Give it another thirty seconds and then light him up. Call the forward observers and see if they can spot the craft visually, or via infrared from behind," the commander ordered, crossing over to the missile operator.

Looking up, the missile operator stated, "All systems show ready," as he scanned the command console of the SA-10 missile launcher. This Russian-made mobile launch platform was comprised of four interlinked batteries, each holding four Grumble ground-to-air missiles, all pointed in the general direction of the aircraft. His radar screen in standby mode, the missile operator waited patiently to paint the incoming bogey with the targeting radar. He checked again that no stray signals were being sent out that might lead a missile to their location.

Their command trailer seemed to become smaller, almost claustrophobic with tension, as the three officers waited to find out what was inbound.

"Stand by," said the commander, counting down in his head. "Three, two, one. Light him up!" he ordered.

He waited while the radar swept over the intruder twice so that the computer could get location and velocity.

Once the computer had a lock the technician shouted, "Acquired and locked in, sir," as he shut down the transmitter. All three gathered around the screen reading the report at the same time.

"That can't be right," the commander shouted. "This craft is inbound at fifty knots and is still twenty thousand feet up?"

"No American helicopter would be so high up, they stay low down among the hills. And no fighter can sustain flight moving so slowly," answered the missile operator, who had the most recent training on Western battle tactics. "Are we sure that the equipment is operating properly?" he asked.

"Time to kill zone?" asked the commander.

"Sir, the intruder will not close to within fifty miles for another six minutes at present speed.," replied the technician.

"How long to run a diagnostic?"

"About three and a half minutes, sir. Although I would like to remind the commander that if the original track showing the craft over fifty thousand feet above ground was an error, or the Americans are jamming our signal somehow, it could be one of the American Marines' Osprey aircraft." The technician then added, "Why would the West send aircraft in this direction anyway?"

"I cannot answer that question," the commander answered. "Alert sector command and see if they have any information on other craft entering our air space."

While the radar technician was running his system diagnostics, the missile operator phoned in their status and inquired into any other activities along the border.

"All reports are negative, commander. Our bogey is the only aircraft showing along the entire front," reported the missile operator. "Sector command is sending up a pair of fighters to check out the intruder. Estimated time of arrival is around twenty-five minutes."

"By that time we'll have either shot it down or they'll be out of range. Even at fifty knots," mused the commander. "Status?" he inquired.

The radar technician replied, "Diagnostics almost complete, no problems reported, sir."

The radiotelephone buzzed. Answering, the commander asked, "No track at all? Are you sure?"

The commander slammed down the handset in disgust. The two techs exchanged glances, both thinking that this couldn't be good news.

"Both observation posts report seeing an object in the sky, but neither could see any exhaust nor get an infrared lock on the craft. They claim that there was no heat signature or engine noise at all."

The commander looked at the two of them and wondered aloud. "Perhaps this is some new kind of stealth aircraft, bringing in special forces to take out one of our strategic outposts."

The radiophone buzzed again.

The commander answered, stiffened and merely said, "Yes, sir."

After hanging up, he ordered the technician to bring up the targeting radar as soon as diagnostics were completed. Looking over at the missile operator he ordered, "Prepare the missiles for launch. Our orders are to take this intrusion as provocation to fire, and possibly as a prelude to invasion."

"Yes, sir," said the operator. "Preparing to bring radar to targeting mode, all missiles show ready."

"Any sign of jamming?" the commander asked the radar operator.

"Nothing, sir. No jamming, no transmitter aimed in our direction," he replied. "Except for its movement, for all practical purposes it appears dead. No ident, no radar, not even broadcasts on civilian frequencies."

"Switch radar to active, targeting computer on," ordered the commander.

"Yes, sir," they both answered.

Once active, the SA-10 FLAP LID radar needed almost no time at all to lock on. In two sweeps of the radar beam the missile operator had his firing solution. His first bank of eight missiles were locked on and ready to fire.

"Hold fire!" shouted the radar operator. "The intruder just lost altitude, he's dropping through fifteen thousand feet . . . thirteen thousand, twelve, eleven. Sir, intruder is holding at just under ten thousand feet. He has dropped his forward speed to less than thirty knots."

"He must be the US Marines, sir," stated the missile man. "Nothing else makes sense. The Osprey is the only operational aircraft that behaves like this."

"Are you still locked on target?" asked the commander.

Looking back at his screen the missile operator replied, "Yes sir, track is true, missiles are locked in."

"Fire one and two!"

The trailer rumbled as the launchers disgorged the two SA-10s.

"Missiles away," came the instantaneous report, "both missiles have lock and are traveling straight and true."

Out in the nighttime sky over northern Iraq, the twin missiles were flying at over mach one and still accelerating, each with its own trail of vapor drawing a line from the launchers to their target.

The foreign craft still flew at slightly under forty knots and was slowly descending below nine thousand feet. The lack of jamming or evasive maneuvers made this intercept little more than target practice. Both missiles, guided by radar, homed in on the object. The first, upon sensing that the target was within the kill radius of its warhead, exploded about twenty feet below the craft, sending hot metal completely through its undercarriage. The second warhead detonated just two-tenths of a second later, incinerating almost all of the remaining wreckage falling through the sky.

Both explosions were audible for miles and plainly visible from the stairs of the command trailer, down which all three crew members were running in an effort to get as far away as possible in fear of return fire. As the fireball fell to the ground they stopped and stood watching until the wreckage was out of sight.

The reality of the kill was frankly shocking. None of the three had ever scored a hit on any Western aircraft in the no-fly zone. The very idea was rarely even discussed in the ranks.

The commander jumped up with a whoop and began slapping the two technicians on the back in congratulations. The radar operator jumped up and down for a second or two before remembering his duties. Checking first for any visible sign of other aircraft or missile tracks headed in their direction, he climbed back into the trailer and sat down to scan for other bogeys.

The commander stuck his head in the door and asked, "Anything on screen?"

"No, sir, still no jamming and no sign of any other aircraft, sir," he replied.

Bidding the missile operator to remain outside and watch the skies for any more visual signs and any secondary ground-based explosions, the commander returned to the trailer and picked up the radiophone to report the shootdown. After giving the approximate location of the crash site, the commander hung up and fell into the missile operator's chair sighing with relief.

"Pending confirmation in the morning, we have been credited with our first kill!" he exclaimed. "Not only is section command delighted with the kill, they were greatly impressed with the fact that we did it with only two missiles!"

The technician knew from this news that their triumph would be complete, with no recriminations for wasting expensive armaments. Sometimes the lot of a soldier left much to be desired, even when he did his job properly.

"Are we to investigate the crash site, commander?" the technician asked.

"Sector command is going to send air reconnaissance over the site in the morning, but we'll probably be sent out to see if there's anything to recover. Once our relief gets here, you and I will take the truck and see what we can bring back," explained the commander.

"Yes, sir."

The commander got up with a heavy sigh, thinking about the one or two hours of sleep he would be getting this night. Although the excitement over the shootdown was abating, the events of the evening still had him keyed up. *Well,* he thought, *at least I'll be up for early morning prayer,* something he almost always missed when he commanded the overnight shift. He went outside, to check with the missile operator.

"No real visible signs, sir. There were no secondary explosions and there's no sign of fire on the horizon either," he reported.

"Very good, carry on. Oh, and write up the report for my signature in the morning. I want to look it over before I head out to the crash site."

"Yes, sir," snapped the operator. He went to arrange for a missile load-out crew to reload the two expended tubes.

Inside the trailer, the radar tech downloaded the data from the computer to be sent to sector headquarters with the commander's report, which the commander rarely wrote himself.

The rest of the night passed uneventfully.

The next morning, the commander, with the radar tech as his driver, took a truck out toward the low hills where the intruder had fallen. After about two hours they arrived at a burnt-off area of brush on the side of a hill covered with small pieces of metal reflecting the morning sunlight. Dismounting from the truck, the commander waved his driver back, telling him, "Wait until I photograph the hillside before you start poking around."

After about a dozen photos, they both advanced into the burnt area, kicking at larger pieces of metal looking for anything with markings on it. While they were quartering the area a slow-moving, propeller-driven plane passed overhead, banked, and came back over them.

The commander waved at the pilot who wagged his wings in reply, circled a couple more times and flew off.

"Sir, there are no large pieces left of the aircraft. I'm sure the only thing he could see from up there was the burn mark," shouted the driver.

"Keep your eyes on your work," the commander admonished. "I want something to bring back to camp, anything with Western markings will do."

"Yes, sir," snapped the driver.

After twenty minutes of searching the driver shouted, "Over here!" to the commander. As he walked close enough to see what was on the ground, the commander's stomach turned at the sight before him. It looked like a haunch of cooked goat, the smaller end wearing a man's boot. The pilot's foot had been severed and singed in the explosion. Looking around the immediate area, there were no signs of large pieces of the wreckage or additional remains of the pilot. The only remains they *could* see were finger-sized pieces of shiny metal and some charred, softer remains of the craft's interior.

Pulling a large plastic bag from his pocket, the commander kicked the charred foot into it and immediately zipped it shut.

"Keep looking for anything with Western markings while I radio in my initial report," ordered the commander. He walked off to the truck to make contact with headquarters.

The driver walked off the extent of the immediate crash site and made notations in his book. On his way back to the truck he saw the commander coming his way under a full head of steam.

"Find anything with Western writing on it?" the commander demanded.

"No, sir. I haven't found anything larger than my hand, and none of it with any kind of writing on it at all," the technician said.

"Did you look over to the south, where the craft came from?"

"No sir, I just covered the burnt spot."

"Hang on, we'll both go together. After all, you got even less sleep than I did," offered the commander.

After securing the burnt limb in the truck's cooler, and getting a drink of water, the driver led the way south. Although the way up into the hills was only slightly inclined, both soldiers were winded as they topped the first rise. Off in the distance the commander spotted a reflection of something metallic, a glint in the low, early-morning sunlight. The two split up and approached, flanking the object. As the driver got closer, he saw a mass of twisted metal about half the size of a man, with tattered fabric blowing in the light breeze.

The commander called a halt. "Don't get too close, it may not be safe." He sniffed the air then waved the driver closer. They both approached, noting that there was no sign of burnt foliage or any discoloration of the surrounding ground.

"This part must have been blown free, commander. There are some pieces over here that are only ripped apart, no sign of fire or scorching on the metal," said the driver.

"Do you see any markings on the pieces on your side?" asked the commander.

The driver lifted away a large, flat piece of metal, probably the outer skin of the craft.

"No, sir. There isn't a single bit of writing on anything. Not even on this piece of what looks like a circuit board. Not a single letter or number anywhere, sir."

"I am not familiar with any of the construction of these parts. No markings. This skin is so light, some kind of alloy that I have never seen before," the commander observed.

"Sir, does this mean that we're going to have to cart all this wreckage down the hill?" the driver asked, knowing the answer in advance.

"Unfortunately, yes. They won't send a helicopter unless we have a compelling reason for them to do so. When I report that this craft is something we've never seen before, I'll be questioned by those who will think I'm nothing but an old woman afraid to be decisive on my own. If I insist, they might dispatch a helicopter to confirm my observations. But, even you can see that there's nothing here that is recognizable as being of Western manufacture. The Americans mark all their parts. Even those they get from Japan or China have Western numbers on them. These pieces have nothing." He paused to consider, then continued, "Let's just bring a few of the larger pieces and mark the coordinates from the truck's GPS. Let sector decide whether or not they want to send a helicopter to recover this piece."

"Yes, sir," said the driver.

"Keep looking for more of the pilot of this thing, maybe we'll find dog tags or some other identification."

Pulling a canvas bag from his pack, the driver started picking up a number of the larger pieces, those that could be used for metallurgy or component analysis. The commander started pulling pieces from the main jumble of wreckage, trying to find something recognizable in the mess. He thanked Allah there was no sign of blood or body parts in the pieces he was pulling apart.

The driver, after putting a dozen or so pieces of wreckage in his sack, began to entertain a thought that raised the hairs on the back of his neck. This craft behaved like no military craft he knew of. Neither the Americans nor the Russians had an aircraft exhibiting the flight characteristics tracked on radar. If it was some kind of exotic helicopter or Harrier-type vertical-take-off jet, so far they had found no sign of an engine or blades. How was it powered? It flew above fifty thousand feet, dropped to under twenty thousand feet and slowed to under one hundred knots in a matter of moments. And furthermore, it emitted no form of radio, radar or infrared energy that he or the forward observers could detect.

If not for what looked like a foot in the wreckage on the lower hill, there was nothing that could even suggest that it was built on earth at all. The driver redoubled his search to find something, anything, to indicate this was an advanced craft sent from the West to attack his country.

Meanwhile the commander was entertaining thoughts of his own concerning the origin of the craft. He was thinking that if this was a Western aircraft of such an advanced design that the press, his government or even their slightly reserved former Russian allies knew nothing about it, he might be up for a promotion for shooting it down. The only drawback was that, because it was destroyed in the air, the remains would yield little information about its design. Perhaps that part would be overlooked should he produce proof that it was American, and that they were sending stealth craft to attack and invade his country. As one of upper ranks of the military, most of his actions were guided by a single purpose: "what's in it for me?" In this case he was hoping the evening's success would lead to a posting in Baghdad. Outpost duty left a lot to be desired.

For now, the commander and his driver were resigned to collecting as much of the wreckage as they could and getting it back to their base for analysis.

Different strokes for different folks,
And so on, and so on, and scooby, dooby, dooby
Everyday People
Written by Sly Stone, performed by Sly & and The Family Stone

CHAPTER 3

DETECTIVE JOHN MATHEWS had been working in the Atlanta Police Department's Missing Persons Bureau for seven years. Originally, it was just a temporary assignment after he got his detective's shield. All of the slots in homicide, where he originally requested to be assigned, were filled. As a result, Detective Mathews was relegated to the waiting list, biding his time in MP.

The temporary assignment grew into a permanent posting, partly due to circumstance, but mostly due to the results he got when other detectives on the squad hit a brick wall on a case.

Mathews was born and raised in a suburb outside Atlanta before the city's explosive growth in the eighties. After a stint in the United States Air Force as a helicopter mechanic, he was promoted to the position of crew chief, left the service and, with his education benefit, attended the police academy. After six years on the force as a patrolman he passed the detectives exam and received his shield. Atlanta had grown as the business hub of the South. Its growth opened up a lot of new slots at all levels of the department.

Detective Mathews was sitting at his desk shooting the breeze with a couple of the other detectives, waiting for some paperwork to get upstairs from processing, when Lieutenant Batterman, the head of Missing Persons, shouted for him to come into his office.

"Close the door and grab a seat, John," said the lieutenant.

"What's up, chief?" John asked.

"We've been asked to look into a missing person case over at Steddman College."

"Someone snatch a girl from over there? Or is this a case of someone shacking up with someone else and one of the someones has a connected parent?" Mathews asked warily. He'd had his share of false alarms and pissed-off parents not caring for the mate their son or daughter had chosen. Instead of dealing with the situation themselves, they used the police, mostly in hopes of stressing the relationship to the breaking point.

The lieutenant let out an explosive breath and glared at John. "What makes you think this is another political thing?"

"Well, you don't generally have us close the door when you call one of us in here. It's not as if no one knows something's up when you drag us in here and close the door," Mathews replied.

"All right, I'm busted. It is something like that, but not political this time."

"What do you mean, Lieutenant?"

"This case didn't come to me through the usual channels. I got a call from some Fed who wants us to do a quiet background check on the missing girl. He wants us to see whether or not she may have taken off with some guy and forgot to let anyone know where she was going. So your task is to do your usual sniffing around. Find out everything you can and report to this guy here," Batterman finished, handing John a telephone message slip.

"I'm guessing he doesn't want the usual case notes made available to the rest of the squad? I'm probably not supposed to mention the FBI angle, am I?"

"Until further notice, that's about the size of it. I'll square it with the chief, but no one is to know you're working the case for the Feds, got it?"

Looking at the area code of the telephone number, John asked, "How do I expense this?"

"Just bring me all the receipts and vouchers and I'll take care of everything. Oh, by the way, keep track of your overtime. I'm going to bill it back to the Feds first chance I get. And one more thing, if you find anything snaky that you think I should know about, call me, day or night. I want to know what these guys are really looking for."

John got out of his chair, memorized the number, dropped the message slip on the lieutenant's desk and left the office. As usual, as soon as he opened the door there was a sudden flurry of activity, as everyone in the room tried to look busy. Without the lieutenant shouting, no one had a clue as to why John was in there, or what, if any, consequences the conference might mean for him.

John avoided eye contact with the others as he made his way to his desk. He sat down and began to plan out the logistics of tracking a case without using the normal department resources. Sitting across from him was his friend, and sometimes partner, Jason Pickering. Pickering had made detective the year after Mathews. Early on they were picked to partner on about half of the cases that came their way. They were acknowledged as the best zebra partnership (Jason black, John white) in the department. Their diversity seemed to bring something extra to the table in solving the cases assigned to them, the whole being greater than the sum of its parts.

"Anything you want to tell me?" Pickering asked in a quiet voice that didn't carry past their desks.

"Nothing special," John replied. "The lieutenant dragged me in to go over my expenses for the last two weeks."

John wasn't ready to let on about the assignment yet. He knew he would tell Jason eventually; no cop goes into a questionable situation without backup, at least no good cop.

"He was pissed I had put in for reimbursement for dinner twice last week at Arnelli's and told me to date on my own dime."

"Fine, don't tell me," said Pickering.

John stood up and started to pull on his jacket.

"Where're you headed for lunch?" Pickering asked. "You want company?"

"Nah, I gotta go to the bank and head over to the garage. My grill lights don't blink anymore when I hit the button, they just stay on. The lieutenant doesn't want me to run over some citizen who can't see my unit's in hot pursuit." Besides, John thought, I can't call this Fed with you hanging around.

"Sure. Maybe tomorrow then."

"No problem," said John, on his way out.

When he got into his unit in the parking lot, John pulled out his mobile phone and dialed the number the lieutenant gave him.

After one ring a woman answered, "2112, how may I direct your call please?"

"Mr. Samuels, please." he replied.

"One moment, I'll connect you."

"Bob Samuels speaking, how may I help you?"

"This is Detective John Mathews of the Atlanta Police Department, Lieutenant Batterman gave me your number."

"Yes, detective, thank you for returning the call. I would like to meet with you as soon as possible to go over how you can help us with an investigation. Would it be possible for me to meet you first thing in the morning?"

"Yes, that'd be fine. I was told to give you my full cooperation. Could you give me a hint of what this is about?"

Samuels answered, "If it's all the same to you I would like to save the details until we meet. I can tell you that it is a missing persons case and it calls for a certain amount of discretion. According to Lieutenant Batterman you come very highly regarded and frankly, your record is above reproach."

"If there's some question about . . ." began John, getting a little pissed.

"No, no, no," interrupted Samuels. "Nothing of the sort. What I was trying to say, badly I see, was that with your experience I hope you'll understand if I am reluctant to discuss this case over the phone. I'm sorry if I gave you the wrong impression."

John cooled rapidly. "No problem. I'm just not used to being kept in the dark. Of course I'm curious about the circumstances of the case and why the secrecy."

"I promise, you'll have all the facts, and probably all the answers to your questions in the morning. Where do you want to get together, and may I suggest someplace where we won't run into anyone you know? It wouldn't help for us to be seen together. Tongues wag."

"Do you know the Atlanta area very well?" John asked, recalling the DC area code he'd dialed.

"Not too well. Give me directions from the airport, I'll be flying in around six forty-five in the morning."

John gave him directions to a small restaurant about fifteen minutes from the airport, confirmed the time and gave Samuels his mobile phone number. Once he ended the call, John decided to get some lunch and head back to the office. If I'm going to be working on a case for the Feds, he thought, I should probably put in as many appearances at the office as possible. Once back at the office, John finished off the day routinely, cleared his desk, checked out and went home.

The next morning John arrived at the restaurant about a half hour early, ordered coffee and began to read the paper. About five minutes after seven a voice asked, "Detective Mathews?"

John dropped the paper, nodded, getting ready to get up.

"No, don't get up. I'm Special Agent Samuels, but I'd rather not stand on ceremony if it's all the same to you. Just call me Bob."

"Call me John," John replied, "So, to what do we owe getting into such a quiet investigation with the Feds?" John said when Agent Samuels was settled in with a cup of coffee set in front of him.

"What started out as a series of missing persons cases scattered around the country has grown into a multidisciplinary task force investigation of a disturbing trend . . ." Samuels started.

"Before we go any further, is this the real story, or the smoke blown up my asshole story that I'll read about a few years from now in some exposé?" John asked with a smile.

"Okay, maybe we deserve that. The FBI has an unenviable record of lying to fellow officers and using them without regard to professionalism. But hear me out before you make up your mind. If you think I'm blowing smoke up your ass, I'll say no more and go away. However, I'll bet that after you get the whole story I'm going to have to kneecap you to keep you out of this investigation. Deal?"

Looking at the agent's grin, John replied, "Deal. So what's the story?"

"Over the past thirty or so years there's been an unusual trend that has just this year been identified," Samuels began. "The trend was masked by the sheer number of missing persons every year in this country. Even if someone had noticed it, probably nothing could have been done about it until recently. Buried in the numbers was a group of people who, after their disappearance, were never found or associated with any crime. These people couldn't be accounted for using any normal criminal profile. The group of missing stood out only when an extremely deep analysis of all national cases was conducted by computer.

"There was a demographic similarity to this group, a sameness that really jumped out at us when we understood what we were looking at.

"We found that a significant number of African American students, professionals, and intellectual types had disappeared in the last thirty-five or so years. In the beginning everyone assumed that most of the cases were the result of the KKK or other white supremacist activity here in the South. Up until now no one ever placed a high enough priority on finding a bunch of missing blacks, especially with little chance of identifying the perps, or convicting anyone without any evidence. Right or wrong, that's the way it was. Now everything's different. Washington's scared shitless someone will independently discover the numbers, do the math, and make a big fuss over the government's lack of concern over this many unsolved black disappearances."

"So what makes this case so important, and by the way, who disappeared?" asked John.

"A student over at Steddman College for Women. Her name is Jaylynn Williams and no, she isn't connected to anyone important. The only reason we got the heads-up before you did is that her boyfriend is a data center analyst in the Atlanta office of the Bureau. He asked one of our locals to look into her disappearance. He wasn't sure whether or not something had happened to her or if she was just avoiding him. I guess they had some kind of blow-up just before she disappeared."

"Is he a suspect?" John asked. "It's not unusual, we've seen it before. Something triggers a fight, some domestic thing that gets blown out of proportion and someone ends up dead. The survivor drops the body off somewhere and calls in a missing person report to throw off suspicion."

"And that's where you come in. Instead of us running the investigation and raising a red flag locally, we would like you to be the lead investigator in this case, even run it through your department. But as a courtesy to us, you can keep me up-to-date on the investigation on a day-to-day basis. Maybe even give me a call if something significant comes up before you have to make your regular reports.

"In return, I will give you all the assistance I can. Any resource the Bureau has will be at your disposal, confidentially though. You see, this will be one of the first times we will have been in on one of the profile-fitting disappearances we identified in the trend. I'm hoping that we'll be able to find some point of departure from past efforts that will lead us to a cause." Agent Samuels paused for a second and then asked, "Do you have any questions?"

"Who's going to be looking over my shoulder, you?" inquired John.

"If you want. I'm on sort of detached duty until further notice. I'm not going to insist on a ride-around, nor am I going to be hanging out at the station crowding your investigation. Your record shows that you're self-motivated and work best under minimal supervision. I'm not in the habit of fixing things that ain't broke, if you know what I mean."

"I appreciate it, but I wasn't worried about that. What I wanted to know was, how do you want me to keep you up to date, and how often?"

Samuels thought about it for a minute and then asked, "Do you have a computer at home, and an e-mail account?"

"Sure, and I actually know how to use it," John answered.

"What I can do is set up an account on the local Bureau host and a private storage area for any files you would like to keep online. I'll keep up with the investigation there. Also here's my personal mobile phone number, it's on all the time. Call me whenever you have anything you can't wait to let me know, or if there's something you need only I can get for you."

Jotting down a note on the back of his business card, Samuels added, "Here's the web address of our host, it doesn't appear on any search page. Before you log on I'll have to e-mail you a plug-in for your web browser that will ensure both ends of the connection are secure. What browser do you use?"

"I'm a Mozilla man myself. I stay away from that other stuff."

Samuels let out a huge laugh. "Great, just install the security plug-in I'll be sending you tonight. What's your e-mail address?"

"Here," said John, handing Samuels one of his cards. "I wrote my personal one on the back."

"I'll set up your account this afternoon. Your username will be your full name with no space and your password will be your high school I.D. number. Remember it?" Samuels asked with a smirk on his face.

"Touché, you prick, I guess my name didn't really just come up for this investigation, did it?" laughed John.

"I don't know what you're talking about, Detective Mathews!" replied Samuels with an innocent look on his face.

"Fine, just for that I'm not going to warn you about the food here," said John. "Look, if it's okay with you I think I'll get started with the preliminary groundwork on the Williams woman. Do you have anything on her you can give me?"

"Meet me in front of the Bureau around lunch time and I'll give you whatever we've been able to gather so far."

"How close do you have to keep the bigger investigation?" asked John. "Can I see anything on the demographics and particulars of people the computer spits out? It may give me some hint on what to look for."

"I'm not sure how much they'll let me give you. Even though Washington wants local blue to run the investigation, they still doesn't trust anyone outside the Bureau. Hell, the right hand still doesn't know what the left hand is doing most of the time. Let me see what I can shake loose. I promise, you won't be treated like a mushroom."

"Kept in the dark and fed shit!" they both said at the same time.

"Fair enough," laughed John, "I'll roll by your office about twelve-fifteen. By the way, how much of this can I tell my boss?"

"I ask that you confine what you tell him to the cover story of someone who knows someone wants special attention given to this case. It'll keep everyone satisfied if nothing high-profile comes out of your investigation. I personally don't want the trend data getting out to the press, I can't see how it would do anything other than drive those responsible for these disappearances further underground." Samuels then added, "Seriously, I really do want to find out what happened to these people. Just once, I'd like to catch someone in the act."

"Good enough, see you this afternoon." Getting to his feet, John asked, "Do you need a ride anywhere?"

"Nope, the office had a car waiting for me at the airport. I drove here on my own. Besides, how can I judge the quality of your personal taste without having breakfast here? I'll catch up with you later."

On his way back to the station, John prioritized how he was going to run the investigation. He was relieved that he wouldn't have to conceal any aspect of the investigation from Lieutenant Batterman, he could play that part straight. The lieutenant already knew about the Fed's interest in the case. All John had to do was report to him just like any other case, at least until something really sensitive turned up, then he'd have to clear everything with Samuels before making any substantive report.

As soon as he got upstairs, John went to the lieutenant's office, conspicuously leaving the door open as he sat down.

"Well, what do you want?" Batterman asked.

"I met with that Fed, Samuels, this morning," said John.

"And?" the lieutenant prompted.

"It's pretty much like you thought. Someone has a hardon for this girl's disappearance, he wouldn't say who, but it definitely sounds like either her parents or the boy's parents are connected to someone who wants special attention paid to her disappearance but doesn't want any unfavorable publicity. So, I'm going to give it the VIP treatment. High-profile service, low-profile exposure."

"Fine. Anything else I should know?" the lieutenant asked.

"Not that I can see. I'll let you know if this one looks like its going to be a problem."

"Great. Now get the hell out of my office and go earn your keep," Batterman growled, dismissing John with a wave.

At noon, when John rolled up in front of the FBI's office building, he was surprised to see Samuels in a jogging suit with a gym bag thrown over his shoulder. As he pulled to the curb, Samuels casually walked over, opened the door and climbed in.

"Nice duds," John remarked. "Casual Tuesday?"

"Not really," Samuels replied. "I'm supposed to be sniffing around a little myself. I'm heading over to the boyfriend's gym to ask around about his habits and friends. Here's a copy of all we have on the two of them. Oh, and a little background on her folks. Nothing out of the ordinary. Both sets of parents work, no record of unusual behavior on them or her. Her grades are almost perfect, and she's some kind of science major, botany I think. I also included a short summary of the whole list of missing persons cases in the back of the file there."

"Seems pretty normal. With her being at Steddman I assume she's black. I mean otherwise she wouldn't fit your profile, right?"

"Yeah, it's almost too perfect, the fit I mean. If it weren't for the fact that the distribution is almost equally spread between men and women we'd be looking for a serial killer/rapist. One distinction that stands out in the computer analysis is that all of the suspected victims are very well educated, almost too well educated."

"What did the computer pull up for a total number of disappearances that fit the profile?" John asked.

"Over eighteen hundred."

"Eighteen hundred! How the hell did that many fall under the radar with you guys? You keep the national data, someone should have seen this before now. What the hell have you been doing for the last twenty years?" John said in indignant dismay.

"Look, I told you, up until now no one put any sort of importance on the slight bump in the numbers of black folks mostly in the South. You know as well as I do what J. Edgar's priorities were, and that culture isn't entirely gone from the Bureau. Besides being a freak in a dress, he hated blacks, Hispanics, immigrants, and homosexuals outside his own cadre. Hell, he hated nearly everybody. You think that kind of thing doesn't trickle down to every man in the Bureau?

"Why do you think they assigned an almost translucent white guy to this investigation? It's not because I'm some kind of supercop. It's because I do my job and I keep my mouth shut. No black in the Bureau is in on this for fear that they'd go to the press and spill the beans about how this country still treats African Americans like second-class citizens.

"I hate the fact that we're more afraid of this seeing the light of day than the fact that somewhere, somehow, we've got someone, or someones, who's been snatching folks off the street or out of their homes without a trace for years.

"Look at you," Samuels continued, "you've been teamed with a black partner more times than not according to your jacket. How would you feel if he disappeared and no one really gave a shit? Oh, I don't mean your department, I'm sure you would leave no stone unturned getting to the bottom of a crime against a cop, any department would when one of their own's involved. But, in the case of a civilian, who's going to lead the charge? The Bureau has only just now identified the problem. Up until now it's been easy to pass off the isolated cases to relatives and friends as racially motivated.

"When you get online you'll see that I included all of the raw data in the mainframe, all the names of the ones we think belong to this group. When you get a chance to look closely, you'll see that over half of them aren't even from the South, and fourteen of them disappeared overseas. Take a look at the file and give me a call tonight. I left a card in there with the local number where I'm staying. Can you drop me a few blocks from the Paramount Gym? Know where it is?"

"Yeah, they've got amateur boxing there a couple nights a week."

"Thanks. Oh, and by the way, I'd appreciate it if you would try to report to me face-to-face or online, I hate the phone. I know it's a pain in the ass, just mark it down to a Fed's paranoia. Hey, is that Duncan Avenue up ahead? Let me off here, I don't want to roll up in front in an unmarked squad."

John pulled over and stopped just short of the corner.

Samuels got out, telling John, "Thanks for the lift," through the window.

John turned the corner and headed over to his favorite watering hole. Even though it didn't open until four, he knew the owner would be there cleaning up and getting ready for the after-work crowd.

Parking the squad around the corner from the establishment, John went into the alley to the back door. Walking in, he stopped, unable to see in the dim interior after the bright sunlight outside. Spotting Pete mopping behind the bar, he gave a shout and headed for a seat at the bar.

"How's tricks, officer, am I behind in my payoff this week?" Pete inquired with a grin, setting a frosty tumbler of iced tea on the table.

"Nah, today I'm representing the Board of Health. You're going to have to shut down and make about fifty thousand dollars worth of repairs and upgrades if you want to stay in business."

"Yessah, Mister Inspector man. Yo'all wants me to go and gets massah the money for yous and your friens?" said Pete, falling into his perfect Stepin Fetchit impersonation.

"Get the hell out of here, you reprobate. I just needed to sit somewhere inside to go over some paperwork. You don't mind, do you?"

"Hell no, John," replied Pete, flashing a blinding smile through his coffee-colored face. "Just let me know when you want a refill."

"Sure thing Pete, thanks."

John open the file and began to go through its contents. On top was Samuels' note with his address and phone number. Also, scrawled at the bottom, was a line letting him know where raw data was available online and how it could be sorted.

The first sets of information John began to review were the notes on the oldest disappearances. According to the chart, they started as far back as 1967. Nearly forty years ago. He saw that there were barely a handful of cases that far back. Just looking over the dates, and adding up the numbers in his head year by year, it looked like a bell-shaped curve with the peak sometime in the late seventies or early eighties. Things tapered off through the eighties and nineties and looked like they were beginning to pick up again around the turn of the century. Most of the victims were young, between the ages of twenty and thirty-five; some were older, but not many. He saw that a few sets of couples, married, middle class and seemingly solvent, belonged to the group too. Other than their color, nothing seemed to link these people except for the fact that none were ever found, dead or alive, and they all disappeared with no visible signs of foul play and were educated.

From the overall lack of further detail, the FBI must have massaged the numbers and only included cases that had all of the more obvious factors in common. This wasn't the raw data set, but it did give him a good starting point. Three of the cases in the last ten years were from the Atlanta area. There might still be info online at the department, saving him a trip over to the dead files storage warehouse and drawing undue attention to the investigation. The notes on the current case included Jaylynn Williams' grades, bank and credit card statements, telephone records and her medical and dental charts. How long was the FBI working on this, he wondered. He was impressed when he saw the date she disappeared: just last week. Awfully quick work. The file on the boyfriend was equally complete, including the report on a preliminary interview conducted over the weekend.

"Boyfriend states he and subject had a disagreement Monday evening over dinner at the subject's apartment. He further stated he left the apartment at nine-thirty and returned to his place of residence." The narrative picked up on the next page: "The boyfriend called the next day and left an apology on her voice mail (confirmed) and waited until Wednesday before attempting to visit. Boyfriend states he has no key to Williams' apartment and was unable to enter. He returned home and left several messages on Williams' voice mail and then asked for assistance in trying to locate her the following morning upon arriving for work at the Bureau's data center." John read on. "No evidence of violence in the girl's apartment, rug was swept for signs of blood, nothing unusual in either bathroom or kitchen drains, no signs of blood, etc, in Williams' or the boyfriend's automobile."

"How's it going?" asked Pete, startling John and breaking his concentration. "Sorry man, didn't know you were so deep into it," he apologized.

"It's cool," John replied. "Just trying to absorb a bunch of stuff for a case."

"New one, or something that's got you stuck?"

"Nope, a new one, a girl at one of the local schools disappeared." he said closing the file. Thank God Samuels put it in a plain jacket; all he needed was to have to explain to Pete or anyone what he was doing with an FBI case file.

Pete dropped off a refill of iced tea for John and went back to finish stocking the bar for the afternoon crowd. John hadn't even noticed he'd drained the first glass while he read. He decided the best way to start off the investigation was to interview the boyfriend and compare what he got against what was in the file. Nothing really stood out, except maybe a question clarifying just how close these two really were.

The file stated they had been dating for about nine months, plenty of time for them to have become intimate. According to the information given, the boyfriend didn't have a key to her place. He had no priors, just a couple of speeding tickets and a mention in a disturbing the peace complaint from a fraternity bar fight. The file indicated he'd been out of school for just under a year, had gotten his graduate degree in computer sciences, something to do with networking security.

It was two-thirty, too late to head back to the office. Besides, the lieutenant would want some kind of status report regardless of the fact he'd only begun that morning. At least he would be able to cover some ground during the afternoon.

John was looking forward to getting into the FBI mainframe; he had always wanted to lurk around in their systems, but didn't want to chance getting caught. He was a far cry from being a hacker. Other than some of the techniques he read about in the department files on computer fraud cases, his computer use was strictly mundane—a computer geek he was not.

John gathered up the contents of the file and drained his glass. Getting to his feet, he threw a wave at Pete and shouted, "Catch you later!" on his way out the back door. When he got to the car John decided to take a drive to Steddman College and scope out the lay of the land. Afterwards he might even take a quick drive by Jaylynn Williams' apartment.

Steddman College for Women was established nearly a hundred years ago in a single-room school house just outside Atlanta. It was the area's first all-black, women's college and steadily grew into the thirty-four-acre campus it was today.

Students lived in apartments on and off campus, many working in Atlanta proper and in other nearby suburbs. As he got farther away from the downtown area, John began to relax. The traffic density began to drop off. The surroundings transformed from a sprawling metropolis into more genteel, older neighborhoods.

The entrance to the campus was a traditional, semi-gothic gated driveway, through which visitors could see the administration building which looked more like a wealthy, old-money estate than an all-women's college turning out some of the most successful graduates in the country.

The slow drive to the administration building gave him ample opportunity to observe that everything seemed outwardly normal. Groundskeepers were trimming trees and, off in the distance, cutting the vast expanse of green lawn. Others were planting or replacing flowers that circled the outside of the administration building. A handful of students were walking between the buildings, sitting under trees talking or studying. Even the weather was conspiring to add its cast to a scene out of a college catalog cover photo. It barely even registered that all of the students in view were black, but now that he thought about it the only white faces he could see were a couple of the groundskeepers.

It was only three-thirty, plenty of time to get someone in administration to help him get started on the investigation, he thought, as he pulled into the parking lot. Getting out of the car, he pulled on his jacket, mostly to conceal the rig of his shoulder holster out of respect for the sensibilities of this quiet campus. He grabbed his notebook, walked to the administration building and entered the propped-open main doors. Once inside, he walked over to the smiling receptionist sitting behind the counter and pulled out his identification.

"Good afternoon, sir, how may I help you today?" she asked him.

"Hello, I'm Detective John Mathews and I need some assistance with an investigation. Could you direct me to someone who can help me with some information on one of the students here?"

"Yes, detective, that would be Dean Atkins on the second floor. If you like I can call upstairs and have her come down and meet you."

"No, that won't be necessary; however if you would check and make sure she's in and if it would be convenient for her to talk to me now, that would be very helpful."

The receptionist picked up the phone and dialed. After describing John and his business, she put down the phone and said, "Detective, she will be happy to see you."

"Thanks for the help."

"No problem. At the top of the stairs it's the second door on the left."

Climbing the broad, curved stairs, John couldn't help but draw the inevitable comparison between the building's sweeping staircase and the one in Gone With The Wind. The design of the entire building was one of quiet, understated elegance. Windows were covered with fine draperies, chandeliers were made of beautifully cut crystal and at the top of the stairs was a hallway that looked like something out of an older home, lined with doors more suggestive of bedrooms than offices. John walked to the dean's door and knocked twice before entering. The door opened into a small outer office tastefully appointed with contemporary furnishings, modern office equipment and a young, smiling assistant.

The assistant's desk held a flat-screen computer display, something John had always wanted for his system at home to help him reclaim some of the precious desktop that never seemed to be large enough to hold all the junk he accumulated. The dean's assistant stood and came around the desk. "Good afternoon, Detective, Dean Atkins will see you now. May I get you coffee, or some other beverage?"

"Thank you, no. I'm hoping to take only a little of the dean's time."

Entering the office, John was pleasantly surprised by the woman standing behind the desk. Dean Atkins appeared to be in her early to mid thirties with classical features; the mahogany brown of her face was a striking counterpoint to a pair of almost sea-green eyes. Her build was slim, athletic and tastefully attired in a deep blue business suit.

Gathering himself together, remembering why he was there in the first place, John walked over to the desk, and pulled out his wallet. "Good afternoon, Dean Atkins," he said, showing her his identification. "I apologize for dropping in unannounced. My coming here this afternoon was more of a case of fortuitous timing than design."

"Don't mention it, Detective, I'm more than happy to help you out." she replied in a warm contralto. "What kind of information are you seeking, and, if I may ask, what kind of investigation is this?" she added.

"Dean Atkins . . . ." he began.

"Please, my name is Sydney, or Syd. It wouldn't be a breach in departmental protocol to call me by my name instead of a title, now would it?" she stopped him, an amused twinkle in her eye.

"No ma'am . . . I mean Sydney, it wouldn't at all. And, if you'd return the favor and call me John, I'd appreciate the same. Anyway, we received a report that one of your students may have gone missing. And even though it may be a lovers' spat or an unannounced out-of-town visit, I still have to follow up on the case."

"I understand completely. May I ask why a detective from the city is out here running an investigation? Don't get me wrong, there won't be any nonsense about jurisdictional boundaries. I'm just curious."

John considered just how much to tell her, and then answered, "The initial call was made by the girl's boyfriend. He reported to the authorities in town and it got assigned to me. There may be a connected parent involved who greased the case to our department, but I really don't know the particulars." John continued, "The student is Jaylynn Williams, do you know anything specific about her?"

The dean stood and went over to file cabinet and pulled out a file. "Not too much, she's in her third year here, she's a science major . . . yes, here she is. She's a biology major working on her degree in the horticultural sciences, hydroponics, forced growth, hybridization and some related topics. Her grades are excellent and there's nothing here to indicate any past personal problems. Here, take a look, although I ask that you keep the contents confidential."

"Thank you," said John as he made a couple of notes on her class schedule, home address and telephone number, even though he had most of the information in the file from Samuels. It would have looked odd had he not taken any notes at all.

"Do you know her personally?" he asked the dean.

"We've met, of course," she replied. "I see all the students in their first year as a matter of course, and occasionally I'm called upon to supervise any student who develops problems with grades or personal problems. I don't teach any regularly scheduled classes, but I do substitute on occasion and, as Dean of Student Affairs, I monitor and supervise student activities on and off campus. I'm also one of three administrators who are responsible for the college's community outreach programs."

"It says here that Ms. Williams is involved in a government grant, what can you tell me about the grant itself?" John asked.

"The grant involves the hydroponic growth of oxygen–and food-bearing plants in low–and no-gravity environments. The obvious applications would be space-based botany, and the development of farming techniques on the moon and other planets. The assumption is that space travelers from earth are not going to be able to carry soil from home into space just to grow plants. The cost of lifting anything into space being as high as it is, bringing along dirt just isn't cost effective. It's been discovered that there is a vast supply of water in space in the form of frozen asteroids, on the moon buried under the regolith and more recently on Mars. Water, properly flavored if you will, is going to have to be used as the growth medium in situations where soil containing the proper nutrients is not available.

"The college has received a grant to study the means of accelerating the growth of fruit–and vegetable-bearing plants and maintaining the plants over the long haul. In many cases accelerated growth burns out some plants just as rapidly as they grow and they lose their potency and vitality. It's no good to have a tomato plant grow, bear fruit in a matter of a few weeks, and then wither and die after the initial burst of life. This is the A part of the grant Ms. Williams was working on. The B part was on the development of algae strains that could be used to produce oxygen and possibly recycle some kinds of liquid waste and produce oxygen, just as they do in nature. She's been developing a strain to be used in zero gravity over an extended period of time without spoilage."

"That's pretty impressive, this level of research being entrusted to an underclassman, or woman in this case. No offense to her gender." John apologized.

"None taken," responded Sydney with a laugh. "The English language is up to the task of gender-neutral description, it's just social inertia that makes us lag behind. We do have faculty supervision over all of the outside funded projects our students work on both here on campus and away. I think there are about fifteen or so projects currently underway, with about thirty more students working across the country on others. Most of them are at institutions like the National Institutes of Health or downtown at the Centers for Disease Control. Two are out in California at the Jet Propulsion Laboratory for the year as well."

"Do you know anything about her personal life?" John asked.

"No, I don't. Let me call her faculty advisor on the project. Do you have the time to wait for a minute?"

"Sure, would you like for me to wait outside?" John offered.

"Not at all. Hang on," she said, as she picked up the phone.

John got up and began to wander around the office, looking at photos on the wall and the handful of certificates and degrees hanging next to them. This woman obviously had some pretty impressive mental horsepower. Her undergraduate degree was from Steddman, but her master's degree and Ph.D. were granted in mathematics at the Massachusetts Institute of Technology. Somehow John began to feel somewhat lacking in the brains department, but was broken out of his reverie by the dean hanging up the phone.

"Well, her advisor says that she hadn't noticed anything unusual recently. She did confirm that Ms. Williams has been seeing someone pretty steadily, but there are no complaints on her lab performance or her class work. She also said she hasn't seen Ms. Williams since Monday of last week."

"Is that unusual, I mean for her advisor to not have seen her so often?" asked John.

"Probably not. Most faculty advisors see students as little as every other month, some more, some less. We pride ourselves here at Steddman in turning out, what I guess would be described as "well educated ladies of distinction." This includes promoting self-sufficiency and full accountability for their own actions. I'm not that old myself and I can't believe just how messed up our culture has become since the early nineteen-seventies.

"Most people my age were raised by parents who either didn't care about discipline or were afraid to apply any for fear of interference by misguided local authorities who are largely incapable of putting in the time and effort to make an informed determination whether or not children are truly abused or just being appropriately punished for unacceptable behavior. My parents were throwbacks who didn't have a problem showing me where I had behaved in an inappropriate manner, and their discipline was handed out fairly, and only when necessary."

"Yeah, but judging from your credentials you don't strike me as the kind of woman who started out as a problem teenager."

"Don't let the degrees fool you," Sydney said. "My parents blamed me, and my brother, for every grey hair in their heads. I think that's partly what drew me here in the beginning. All of the students I met while I was checking out the campus seemed to be entirely normal, well adjusted girls. But they seemed to also have a sort of underlying dignity and confidence; it was very compelling to want to belong to a group like that. Going to an all-girls school was a huge drawback, but given the proximity of the city and some of the all-male colleges around the area, I didn't see coming here as particularly onerous to my social life.

"From my initial impression, Ms. Williams isn't too terribly different from me in that respect. She dates, she does well in classes and her extracurricular activities are pretty normal. I would be hard pressed to point to anything that stands out as unusual. Would you like to talk with her advisor?" Sydney asked John.

"I don't think so, I'm sure she would have mentioned anything unusual if it had occurred to her. But if I do, I'll give you a call first, all right?"

"Thank you, that would be best. Here's my card, and I added my home number should you need to contact me after hours. And don't worry, there's no one else you'll be disturbing when you call," she said, smiling warmly.

Getting up, John held out his hand, Sydney rose and met his hand with hers and gave a businesslike shake before conducting him to the door. "By the way," she added, "do you have time for a quick tour of the campus? I can arrange for one of our guides in student services to take you around, or if you can wait a few minutes I could show you around myself. I have to return a couple of phone calls, but being so near the end of the day, I'd love to get out of the office a little bit early and enjoy the afternoon outside."

John considered the time and all the things he wanted to get done tonight, and decided that spending more time with Sydney would definitely fall on the plus side of his day. He didn't entertain any grand illusions. Though he was single, he had no idea what kind of entanglements she might have in her life. He'd automatically checked out the fact that she wore no marriage ring on her finger when he first came in the door.

"If you have the time, I'd love to take a look at the campus. All I saw coming in is just about the biggest lawn I've ever seen in my whole life," said John.

Sydney laughed, "If you only knew how much money goes into the maintenance of that lawn you'd faint. But the truth of the matter is that the school's appearance is just as important, at least in the administration's eyes, as the quality of the classes we teach. It also helps with those who are long-time benefactors, they seem to look at the grounds as an aesthetic oasis in otherwise pedestrian surroundings. You're welcome to drop your things off in your car and wait for me on the porch. I should only be about ten minutes or so.

"See you in a few minutes then," Sydney said, as she returned to her inner office.

John nodded to the dean's assistant on his way out and went back outside to his car. Throwing his binder on the front seat, he briefly considered leaving his jacket behind in light of the beautiful day. But he didn't want to have to suffer the looks he was sure to get wandering around with his shoulder holster visible, and he couldn't really leave it in the car while on duty. Oh well, he thought, the breeze was pleasant and the late afternoon sun was only warm, not actually beating down hot.

Climbing the stairs back to the porch, John sat down in one of four wicker chairs grouped around a glass-topped table. He made a mental note that if he ever did came back, maybe he could arrange to meet out here instead of in the office.

He then turned his thoughts to the dean. She was obviously smart, maybe even street smart, but John normally thought women who were in the intellectual elite were somewhat out of his league. She had the whole package, brains and looks, and she also seemed to be very comfortable with herself. No airs, no feeling of condescension came from her concerning his being a civil servant. She was definitely a pleasant surprise. Well, a man can dream, he thought.

Moments later she came out on to the porch and asked, "Ready?"

"Sure, where to first?" John asked.

"How about we take the counter-clockwise tour," she replied. "That's what we call the standard tour we give prospective students and their parents. It's a little different from the one we give prospective benefactors and donors. But it provides a better overview of the kind of educational environment we have here at Steddman. The name comes from the order of the tour; if you look at a map of the campus, the principal buildings form a lumpy circle. Starting here, if we follow the path off to the right as you come in the entrance, you would make a large circle and end up coming back off to the left there."

"I see. Well, lead on, MacDuff," said John.

"Shakespeare fan?" Sydney asked.

"Who, me? I must have picked it up from a commercial or something," he said with a grin.

As they began their walk, John took the opportunity to examine Dean Atkins a little more closely. Her spiel was interesting, the delivery natural, as if she was relating information from her own experiences rather than from some canned tour. Her gestures were not overly animated, again with that quiet elegance that seemed to characterize her every move. Her walk barely contained the energy of an athlete. Her shoes were not high heels, but not flats. John didn't know very much about women's shoes, but he saw hers as simple and sensible. They brought her height about even with his eyes. All in all, quite a nice little package.

He brought himself back to the here and now and inquired, "Is that the sciences building where Ms. Williams worked?" interrupting her spiel.

"Yes it is, would you like to go inside?" she asked.

"If it's all right. Maybe I could see her desk, peek into her locker if she has something like that. Does she have her own office?"

"No, the only offices in the life sciences building are for faculty. They're all upstairs on the top floor," Sydney replied.

They left the sidewalk paralleling the campus main driveway and crossed the lawn to a side door in the building. Going up the stairs to the double door, John stepped forward and opened the door for Sydney to enter first. "Not locked?" he asked.

"Not this time of day, most of the buildings open at seven in the morning and close around ten at night. The library stays open until midnight, and the student union remains open until one a.m. during the week, and two a.m. on Friday and Saturday nights."

As they walked down the corridor, John dropped his voice and asked, "What about visitors, do they have to check in before running around the campus? Do they have to be escorted after a certain time at night?"

"Well, as much as we would like to treat our girls like ladies, we do require a certain amount of supervision of their gentlemen callers. For the most part male visitors have to check in when they visit any of the girls' apartments. And overnight visits in the apartments are forbidden. We do have a hospitality house for out-of-town visitors, family members, prospective students and such, but girls who find the rules and regulations too restrictive generally move off campus. We require first year students to live on campus. The school has twenty-four-hour security guards, but they mostly handle lockouts, parking tickets, traffic control during on-campus events and helping the occasional drunk student home. The security staff are all screened before being hired, the groundskeepers are an outside contractor and the maintenance staff lives mostly off campus. I think an electrician and an engineer stay here around the clock in case of emergencies."

They turned into a double-doored entryway to the lab and stopped. The fluorescent fixtures hanging from the ceiling cast a bright, yellow-tinted light over ten water-filled tanks lined up in two neat rows along the walls. The tanks looked about three feet deep, each twice as large as two king-sized beds placed side by side. All of the tanks had air bubbling up from underneath the surface, adding cloying humidity to the air. The room's temperature was somewhere in the mid-eighties; several ceiling fans kept the air moving.

"These are the primary tanks that Jaylynn was using for her project. Off to the left, those are filled with your standard garden-variety vegetables and fruits. If you look closely there isn't a spoonful of dirt to be found. That slightly rotten smell in the air is coming from the tanks on the right. Those have algae in them and have both CO_2 and some kind of organic waste flowing through. The covers overhead gather the gas that exudes from the algae for analysis. And now that you have reached the extent of my knowledge of what goes on in here, what do you think?"

"Please don't judge me harshly, but I'm both impressed and surprised," answered John.

"It's the girl thing, isn't it," laughed Sydney.

"Well yeah. I know better, but old habits die hard," John replied, laughing himself.

"Okay mister liberated man. Let's go and let you take a look at her desk."

Sydney turned and went to a side door. Walking through the door, John saw a room about half the size of the lab, with several desks along the wall. Sitting at one of the desks by the windows was a single student typing away on her computer keyboard.

"Excuse me," called out Sydney, "Could you tell me which desk is Jaylynn Williams'?"

"Over there, Dean Atkins," replied the student, looking up at the dean, and pointing to the desk to the left of the door, returning almost immediately to her typing.

"Would you like her to leave the room while you take a look?" asked Sydney.

"No, I just want to see if she has a calendar showing what she was doing last week. Maybe she headed home or had some other trip planned."

"Let me make a call to the data center, I'll get her password so you can see her online scheduler. Go ahead and start her computer up, I'll call them from over here."

Sydney over to the other side of the room, picked up the phone and made the call. Meanwhile, John started looking for a daily planner or personal calendar, opening drawers and sorting through papers. Everything was neatly piled and sorted, but there was no sign of any personal planner, nothing on the hanging calendar from the local Horticultural Society. As a matter of fact it looked like Ms. Williams would be returning any moment; the only thing that even remotely implied she wasn't right around the corner was that her computer was the only one turned off when they walked into the room. All the others had screen savers running.

Her computer booted up and offered a login prompt for a user name. John looked over to Sydney, still on the phone, and raised an eyebrow in inquiry.

"Hang on, they're looking it up. Yes. Okay, I got it. Thank you very much," said Sydney hanging up the phone. She continued, "Her user name is JWILLIAMS and her password is BOUNTIFUL in lower-case letters."

John entered the information and waited for the network connection to be completed. Once logged in, he clicked on the calendar icon, bringing up Jaylynn's personal planner. He and Sydney both looked at the screen as he scrolled through the previous week's entries. Just the usual stuff, test dates, one reminder for a report deadline on the algae project, a dinner date notation for Friday, no mention of with whom, and a reminder for a dental appointment that she had for the following week. John printed her schedules for the preceding two months and for the next two before he clicked over to her electronic address book, printing the entire list of about fifty entries of telephone numbers and e-mail addresses.

John asked Sydney, "See anything that stands out to you?"

"No, it all looks pretty normal. My guess is her dinner date for last Friday was probably with her boyfriend, you'll be checking into that if I'm not mistaken."

"Yeah, I'll be talking to him in the morning."

John closed all the open programs and shut the computer down. Turning off the power to the monitor he asked, "Do students have lockers in this building or in the phys. ed. building?"

"No, all lockers over there are unassigned. When the girls use the gym they bring their own lock and grab whatever locker is available. Besides, it would be a little hard to let you into the locker room discreetly right around now, a lot of the girls use the gym in the afternoon. There's swim team practice too."

"All right then, I guess I'm done with the official part of my duties. Still have time to finish the tour?" John asked with a grin.

"Why Detective Mathews, you aren't interested in viewing a little eye candy, are you?" Sydney asked in mock indignation. "You're not some kind of pervert? My mother always did warn me about the quiet ones."

"No, it's nothing like that at all. I just appreciate the company of a good woman."

"Careful, detective, you just might turn my head. Actually, tonight I have a business dinner that may crowd our tour, but I'm perfectly willing to give you a rain check," said Sydney.

"I'd like that. Now that I think about it, it wouldn't hurt for me to hit the road a bit before rush hour begins. I have to head back into the city tonight myself."

"At least let me walk you back to your car."

"Deal!" said John.

The two of them left the science building and headed directly across campus toward the back of the administration building instead of following along the road. The late afternoon shadows had begun to lengthen and the air had cooled somewhat from the midday high, making the walk most pleasant.

They ambled back to the administration building parking lot, saying little of consequence, each enjoying the company of someone outside their normal sphere of friends and associates.

After Sydney promised to call John if she should hear anything at all about Jaylynn, and they said their goodbyes, John got into his car and pulled out of the lot. He looked back in the mirror to see Sydney watch him drive away. Food for thought, he wondered, or was he making a mountain out of a molehill? He definitely wanted to find a reason to see Dean Sydney Atkins again.

Working in a coal mine,
Goin' down, down, down,
Working In A Coal Mine
Written by Allen Toussaint, performed by Sam Cooke

CHAPTER 4

D EEP UNDERGROUND,
SOMEWHERE between
Boulder, Colorado and Salt Lake City, Utah, in a deep retreat United States
Army bomb shelter, Martin Harris, Ph.D. shivered slightly against the cold.
Infinitely recycled air blew across his back as he finished his work for the day. It
seemed no matter where he sat in the Shelter Fourteen complex, cold air would
blow across some part of his body, often leaving him feeling like he would never
be warm again.

He'd been told more times than he could count that the ambient temperature
and humidity were maintained at optimal levels for the computers and
communications gear, not, strangely, for the humans for whom the shelter was
built.

The Army had built the facility in the nineteen-sixties as a long-term habitat
for government officials and their families in the event of a nuclear exchange with
the now-defunct Soviet Union. The shelter began as a small set of natural caves
that were deepened and expanded into a multilevel, twenty-acre community
designed to provide a self-contained home for up to eleven hundred people
almost indefinitely. Now decommissioned as a shelter, the facility was utilized as
a research park for projects that could benefit from its unique living space and
isolated location.

For Martin, locating his project forty-four hundred feet under ground gave him the perfect environment for the study of his chosen specialty, gravity. This far below ground the only vibrations that reached out to disturb his sensitive test equipment were those generated by good old Mother Earth herself.

Earthquakes were a constant fear when he began living the better part of a mile underground. The dread of being buried alive had never darkened the door to his own closet of neuroses until he came face to face with the insurmountable climb he faced should the elevator to the surface ever fail. Now his nightmares mostly consisted of endlessly climbing in the darkness toward a light that never seemed to get any closer. When awakened from these dreams, his heart pounding, his pajamas and sheets sweat-soaked, Martin had long since given up trying to fool his mind into ignoring its underlying fears. Instead of unsuccessfully trying to soothe himself back to sleep, he would get up and go watch a movie, or if he was really agitated, just go back to work.

Martin's life's work was the detection, measurement and location of gravity waves. He studied quantum disturbances that passed through the earth leaving nothing behind but a tickle in the space-time continuum. So far he had discovered that the sun oscillates like an ever-ringing bell, flexing its gravity field in detectable harmony. He could also, with enough computer processing power, detect the wells of gravity surrounding the larger planets in the solar system. The nearest passage of Jupiter to Earth caused a change in the local gravity constants as Jupiter's huge gravity field gently drew the earth toward it as it passed by.

What Martin lived for was the detection of gravity waves originating outside of the solar system, the result of the near passage, in galactic terms, of a black hole or the cataclysmic violence of a star going supernova. Although gravitons were an imaginary mathematical construct outside of the theories of general relativity, Martin had found some compelling hints to substantiate their existence. Especially since gravitons were the only particles that were supposedly able to escape the crushing gravity of a black hole and pass through any physical substance virtually unimpeded. What secrets could gravitons reveal should he be able, not only to prove their existence, but utilize them to examine events and objects that until now could only be observed through visible light or x-rays?

Martin's main testing apparatus was a round platform, thirty-five feet in diameter, four feet thick, and made of a huge, vat-grown aluminum crystal. This crystal was the result of an underground construction project that rivaled in complexity the excavation and construction of the shelter itself. It was shock-mounted in the lowest level of the shelter and covered on its upper surface with a series of mirrors, prisms and four argon lasers. The laser array measured, to less than a single nanometer (one billionth of a meter), any change in size or shape of the huge platter on which they were mounted. The system was so isolated from vibrations in the surrounding rock and the machinery of the shelter itself that even the power supplies for the lasers were self-contained battery packs mounted on the top of the platter. The instruments were physically isolated from the rest of the laboratory's equipment and transmitted the data they collected by infrared laser to the same kind of sensors used to send and receive fiber-optic telephone calls. The entire apparatus ended up costing almost thirty-five million dollars to construct, a cost borne unsuspectingly by the taxpayers of America.

Dr. Harris initially got his project funded by convincing the Department of Defense that the development of gravity-related science would have a revolutionary effect on weapons research and long-distance surveillance and even begin the development of a reactionless propulsion system. The possibility of graviton-based detectors of sufficient sensitivity to locate submarines hidden in the depths of the ocean greatly excited the imagination of the Joint Chiefs of Staff. Graviton detectors could also be used to locate underground facilities, like the one in which the project was operating, by spotting large air-filled pockets in otherwise normal rock formations. Graviton-based detectors would render earth, water or any other substance transparent to view, a huge military advantage even during peacetime.

The process of detecting particles that didn't exist was, to say the least, difficult. Even trying to explain the concept of detecting gravity waves or gravitons in terms of strategic importance required the endless retelling of a Dick-and-Jane version of quantum physics to those who could scarcely calculate artillery shell trajectories.

The first hurdle was preparing a proposal for the average military mind that made the study of something that couldn't be seen or directly used as a weapon easy to understand. The entire project revolved around the detection of differing densities of objects by analysis of their effect on the gradient of the local gravity field. Just thinking about how many times he was going to have to describe the phenomenon almost made Martin give up the whole proposal and go teach physics at some midwestern, all-girls college. However, he kept at it, attending endless meetings in the first year trying to sell the idea to the Pentagon.

Unfortunately, he made little headway until he began to make the rounds of the Navy brass. The thought of being able to detect submarines anywhere in the world from a single installation, protected by the vast borders of the United States and out of harm's way, was an idea too good to pass up. After refining the proposal to focus on undersea detection, and getting final naval approval for a developmental project to be funded for five years, Martin was off to the races.

Because of the classified nature of the project, the Navy wanted it housed in one of their own research facilities. However, the need for isolating the proposed testing apparatus from any and all vibration directed the search for an isolated and reasonably secure location for the project headquarters away from the Navy's usual facilities. Housing the project in one of the Navy's own research centers would have had the added benefit of enabling Martin to draw resources in engineering and electronics from the Navy's own staff of high-powered braniacs. But finding an existing facility that fulfilled all of Martin's requirements proved to be nearly impossible. Then the Navy came up with idea of locating Martin's project in Shelter Fourteen, even though the shelter was under the supervision of the Army. The prospect of developing a completely new remote surveillance technology confidentially greatly outweighed normal interservice rivalry.

Based on the initial timeline, the first three years of the five-year project were to be devoted to the development of the experimental hardware needed to measure the direction and force of gravitational anomalies. The preliminaries began on the east coast at the naval academy. Once the initial math had been worked out, Dr. Harris and the engineering team turned to developing the hardware design of the detection system.

The design of the detector was the result of the efforts of a developmental team of six scientists working through the initial year and a half of the project. The construction of the unique solid metal crystal which lay at the heart of the detector had taken an additional year to finally get right. Two crystals were initially grown, the first one getting as far as being outfitted with the developmental team's detector equipment, but an internal flaw in the crystal matrix rendered it useless. The fracturing of one of the edges of the second crystal by a chance collision with the outside of the huge tank in which it was grown had almost sunk the project before it had properly begun.

The third time was the charm. This crystal had formed perfectly in the supersaturated solution in which it was grown and survived removal and transportation over seventy-five feet from the tank to the shock-mounted cradle in the lab. Once installed, it was outfitted with the optics and electronics without mishap.

While the crystals were being grown, Martin's math crew was working on the requisite calculations governing the placement of the laser array on the upper side of the massive crystal. These lasers helped detect changes in the density of the crystal whenever the distance between optical detectors changed by the smallest degree. These same deflections of the laser beams, due to the passage of gravity waves, helped establish two measurements, the amplitude of the change and the direction from which the gravitational change originated.

Martin often recalled something he had seen at a lecture by Rear Admiral Grace Murry Hopper, one of the original designers of the first commercial computer, UNIVAC. She showed everyone in the lecture hall a piece of wire about a foot long, then went on to tell everyone the length of that piece of wire represented the distance electricity traveled in a nanosecond. The visual stuck with him as an illustration of the snail's pace of light when compared to the speed of gravity waves.

In a vacuum, light travels just over a foot every nanosecond, and over 186,000 miles in a full second. In contrast, gravity had been theoretically calculated to travel thirty-seven million times the speed of light. Gravity also didn't appear to be slowed by the density of the medium through which it traveled, unlike light.

Because of the incredible speed of gravity waves, Martin's team had the unenviable task of trying to design a detector both sensitive and fast enough to register extremely tiny changes in the local gravitational field of the earth occurring in incredibly short spans of time.

Once the initial design of the detector was completed, the entire team moved into the shelter to prepare the lower level of the administrative area for the installation of the massive apparatus they had designed. The custom cradle and all of the support electronics were installed in the underground laboratory and tested while the massive crystal was growing in its special tank. The preparation of the new laboratory distracted Martin so much that the stark realization of where he was going to be spending the next few years of his life never really penetrated his innermost thoughts. Unfortunately, once the Navy's scientists drifted off to other projects or back to their home billets, the tons of rock between Martin and the open air began to weigh heavily on his psyche. Although other researchers visited from time to time, both from his original team and others who had technical contributions to make in support of his efforts, he was the only full-time member of the team living underground.

He had around a hundred and fifty others who shared space in the underground community. Some were involved in other research projects, along with a handful of military and civilian support personnel, all of whom he got to know pretty well in his first six months stationed there. The Army stocked a small theater in the installation commons with hundreds of movies. They also had cable television piped down from the surface, and of course everyone with a computer on their desk or in their room had wide-band access to the Internet.

Every day that passed became a victory over isolation and claustrophobia in Martin's mind and actually gave him a slight emotional lift, incrementally helping build his confidence in and acceptance of his life underground.

Martin had made it through another day without developing frostbite or pneumonia, both of which he was convinced were just waiting for his health to fail him, living as one of the community's mole people. He stopped by the vending machine alcove near his room and got a sandwich and milk in lieu of a sit-down meal in the commissary and headed off to his room to relax, catch up on his e-mail and read himself to sleep.

He woke much earlier than normal. When he turned on the light he realized that he wasn't even sleepy. What he really wanted to do was head up to the surface and walk around outside for the remaining hour or so until the sun came up. But though the underground facility was declassified, the Army didn't want the location of the shelter's entrance known to anyone without military clearance, or other government business, like Martin's. So they discouraged wandering around topside. Besides, he didn't really want to have to walk all the way over to the other side of the complex, take the thirty-minute ride to the top level and go through the security checkpoint to get outside.

Thinking he would get an early start on the day's work, he took off his clothes and pulled on his favorite sweats. Martin wandered over to the commissary to grab something to eat before heading downstairs to the lab.

As he took the keycard hanging from the chain around his neck, he once again thought how silly the military was about security this far underground. Having to use the card every time he wanted to get into his own lab could be one gigantic pain in the ass, especially when he forgot to bring it with him and had to go all the way back to his room to get it. He slid the card through the reader and opened the door into what he thought of as his lab. The automatic sensors, reacting to the motion and heat of his body, turned on the overhead lights and brought the ambient temperature up a few degrees from the environmental default. Originally designed to save energy and extend the life of the equipment throughout the entire shelter, some misaligned heat and motion sensors more than once caused their own set of mishaps for those sitting still for extended periods of time, especially in a few of the bathroom stalls.

On his way to his desk, Martin stopped at the small refrigerator to drop off the extra orange juice and the yogurt. Plopping down into his chair, he flicked his mouse with a single finger to bring up the latest chart of data, noting he was going to have to change the batteries on two of the four lasers some time that day. They only ran for about six and a half days before they had to be recharged. The strict rotation schedule that he'd set up in the beginning of the project had deteriorated to the change-em-when-you-had-to schedule he currently employed.

The detector's computer had been programmed to ignore the oscillations of the sun and the rest of the solar system's planets, and instead concentrate on detected incidents that originated from other quadrants in earth's neighborhood. Most of the ongoing research centered on the reduction of deviations in the data collection process that were caused by electrical anomalies – flaws in the electronic components causing detectors to give off erroneous signals due to voltage spikes and dropouts. Even the best electronic components couldn't maintain perfect current flow over long stretches of time, so what Martin spent most of his time doing in the lab was redesigning the circuitry that made up the detector so that it could record finer and finer observations without error over time.

Looking over the data collected the previous afternoon, Martin saw that there had been a spike and then an uneven decay in what the computer classified as a local gravitational event. He checked with the delivery schedule for the complex to see whether there were any trucks in the compound above and found nothing listed. So he began the long process of elimination, comparing the input from all three detector circuits to see if all of them showed the same event at the same time.

One of the improvements to the detector Martin was considering was cooling the electronics of the detector down to superconducting temperatures. Dropping the temperature of the metals so low that current flowed without resistance called for re-engineering the detector array so that the sensors could operate at such a low temperature. Those design changes would require a total overhaul of the entire system and end up sidetracking data collection for several months. Even though the project was funded for nearly three more years, Martin was loath to have to reconfigure the circuitry and design a housing for each detector that could be continuously cooled by liquid nitrogen or helium. Doing so would require a team of low-temperature physics experts on top of his original electronics team just to work out the overall feasibility of the idea. Something like that was going to seriously add to the expense of the project, and probably add a year or more to the time he originally estimated before a working prototype could be produced.

Martin put the design changes out of his mind and began comparing the data collected by the sensors side-by-side. Looking closely, he saw that all three detector circuits showed disturbances over the same period of time. Martin logged on to his account at the earthquake research center on the US Geological Survey's Menlo Park campus to check whether there were any earth tremors during the same period his detectors recorded yesterday.

Nothing had tripped the seismic sensors along California's various fault lines; the earth had been quiet for the last few weeks. Martin's next step was to dissect the data down to the microsecond to determine the location of the event.

So far none of the previous computer-recorded events had turned out to be anything Martin could use as proof of any perturbation of the local gravitational field. No black holes, no supernovas, nothing but the background pull of the moon, the sun and the other planets.

As he cross-checked the data, he began to get excited. As far as he could tell, some event had affected the local gravity constant. Mathematically, it seemed as if a massive object appeared spontaneously, affected the local gravitational field over a period of about ten to fifteen minutes and then disappeared.

Despite speculation in the more esoteric physics literature, there had never been any direct evidence of the spontaneous creation of a quantum black hole. A quantum black hole was a construct of almost no diameter, but with all of the other characteristics of its larger brethren existing at the center of the galaxy. This type, however, existed at the molecular level. Current hypothesis called for these quantum holes to disappear as abruptly as they appeared.

At first blush, this was what Martin hoped he had recorded. Based on the initial scan of the duration of the event, the data supported the spontaneous creation and disappearance of just such an animal, perhaps proving their existence once and for all. But before he broke out the champagne and e-mailed the data to those who sponsored his research, he wanted to make damn sure that what he got wasn't the result of a poorly soldered connection or a software glitch in his equipment. While the computer processed the huge amount of recorded data, he began to think about the various improvements in the experimental model he had originally conceived.

One of the next things on the project's agenda was to write or adapt some three-dimensional mapping software so he could display the positions and movement of detected objects visually. Martin's initial thought was to adapt the graphics software used in medical scanners or one of the more popular computer games, and merge the gravitational data stream with the graphics display to show relative positions of the sun, planets and moons within the local universe. He hoped to spot gravitational anomalies in real time as they occurred. He added the idea to his mental to-do list and continued tracing the detector's circuitry and the analysis of the raw data collected by the system's computer.

The operational problem in developing a real-time display of the local gravity field of the solar system was the massive amount of data that had to be crunched in order to even begin to plot anomalies instantaneously.

Checking the current data run, Martin was pleased to see that he would be able to plot the locus of this event in a matter of hours. What Martin did not know, nor would he find out for weeks, was that his detector had, in fact, recorded the malfunction and subsequent destruction of a UFO shot down in Iraq.

Your eyes had a mist
From the smoke of a distant fire
Smoke Of A Distant Fire
Written by Ed Sanford /Al Stewart / John Townsend
Performed by The Sanford-Townsend Band

CHAPTER 5

WHEN NORMA WOKE the morning after her night of celebration, her head felt heavy and her mouth tasted like something dragged in from the garbage. She felt even worse when she remembered that her car was sitting downtown in a metered parking space. She would have to hurry if she were going to jump on the train and pick it up before nine o'clock. She didn't want to chance getting any more tickets, or towed.

Dragging herself out of bed, Norma plodded into the bathroom and began her morning ablutions. As the shower woke her up, she became excited about the possible discovery of a new asteroid. If, in fact, hers was the first sighting of the body, she would definitely be able to name it, or leave it named after her as the discoverer.

By the time she was dressed and ready to leave her apartment, the effects of the previous night's drinking had just about disappeared, with the walk to the elevated train station brightening her disposition even more. The train was only partly filled with inbound commuters and Norma was fortunate enough to get a seat for her ride downtown.

Once she had retrieved her car, fortunately ticket-free, she hurried back to the South Side, stopping for coffee. She couldn't wait to see if she had received a reply from the Planetary Society. She also wanted to discuss the discovery with

Alan and maybe see how his new mapping program worked. Perhaps there was something she could add to it using her detailed map of the earth's sky.

Arriving at the lab, coffee in hand, Norma heard music emanating from Alan's workstation. Raising her voice over what sounded like a remix of Fifty Thousand Watts of Funk she shouted, "Hey, what happened to you yesterday? I was working on my stuff and the next thing I knew, you sneaked off to do God knows what."

Lowering the volume and popping his head over the partition, Alan smiled sheepishly and replied, "I had to cut out early and see this new girl I met. We had made plans to go see one of her favorite singers at the Park West and I forgot to get the tickets. So I had to scramble and try to find two tickets for a sold-out show."

"Smooth move. Did you have to go to a scalper?"

"Nope! One of the brokers had a set of four, I got two of them and only had to pay a service charge equal to three times their face value. What a rip."

"All I can say is I hope she's worth the effort. Hey, what'd you think of my little note?" Norma asked.

"If it's what you think it is, you just may get full funding for your project after all. I was thinking, with simultaneous views of the object taken a couple of a thousand miles apart I might be able to plot its location in relationship to us three-dimensionally. If I can get a similar set of observations a few days from now I should also be able to calculate distance and speed, plus or minus a five percent margin of error. Who else has a telescope looking in that direction these days?"

"The only project I could find was one of the x-ray telescopes in orbit. I already requested any visible light images they might have on file from the last couple of weeks. There's no way I can get any satellite tasked for my project, I've got no funding for that. The only thing I can think of to get a better view over time is if the thing is going to cross our orbit, or if it is going to intersect some other body like the Shoemaker/Levy impact on Jupiter."

Alan asked, "Do you think your rock is a comet, or is it something knocked out of orbit around Saturn?"

"I don't think we'll know until we can get a better look at it. I'm hoping that it's a piece of ice from Saturn's rings. If so, there may be enough interest in getting a sample of it that NASA will be willing to expend some resources for closer observation. It's going to take a pretty close passage for them to consider sending a probe up to get a closer look or to try to get a piece of it to study. Let me check my e-mail and see if I actually got credit for the discovery first." Norma said with a smile, "Let's try not to put the cart before the horse."

Norma immediately checked her e-mail. Moments later she whooped in triumph. "Yes!" she shouted.

"What'cha got?" Alan asked.

"Listen to this, 'Subject to independent corroboration, your discovery has been noted and recorded, please fill out the registration form attached to complete your application . . . . ' blah, blah blah. Hey they already gave it a designation, Asteroid 2000 XF13. Not a very exciting name though. "

"Have you given any thought to what you'll name it? You know, you could name it after me and ensure my name will live on in perpetuity! After all, without my constant support and personal tutelage you never would have been able to carry this project as far as it's gotten. It's the least you could do!" Alan said.

Norma snorted in derision and shot back over the partition, "I got your 'least you could do' right here, buddy. You're lucky I share my meager digs with you at all. If I wasn't so in need of comic relief on a daily basis you'd be out on your ass in a New York minute."

Norma opened her image processing application and saw that the first picture was finished and the second one was about fifteen percent complete. She loaded the first image and zoomed in to the area around her object, trying to make out what little detail the software had been able to ferret out. So far it looked like it was long and somewhat cylindrical, with two shiny spots near one of the ends, but it was still too far away for any great detail to be revealed.

"Hey, where's your 3D stuff stored? I want to take a look at what you've come up with so far," Norma said over the wall to Alan.

"It's off my root directory in the COM3D folder. You'll see the executable there, and the help file, such as it is, is in there too. If you get stuck let me know."

"Where's the data set for the mapping matrix?" Norma asked.

"I'm using JPL's realtime positional data for the solar system. I added all of their rotational calculations and built in a look-ahead buffer to run a simulation of the solar system out to about a year into the future. Any further than that and the thing loses accuracy because I can't get the gravity calculations to come out right. When I tried to add the subroutine that calculates the effect of gravity between objects, like when Jupiter and Mars pass close together, the whole thing crashes. With ten gravity subroutines running for all of the planets and the sun, feeding data back to each other, the whole thing grinds to a halt. There's just not enough computing power here to get it to run right."

"Can you steal clock cycles from some other facility for a trial run?" Norma asked.

"Not really, since the data has to be integrated in real time. Even using the University of Illinois mainframe downtown with the U of C mainframe here, and integrating the result using the mini here in the lab, I still can't get enough CPU capacity to do three out of the nine planets. No, what I have to do is find some way to preprocess the data so that a smaller data set can be used for the real-time display I want."

"Why not post a note on some of the research news groups asking for spare time on some of the other university systems in order to do your data? You might be surprised at the response."

"Yeah, I guess I could do that. It's just hard to find the time to put together the spec I need in order to let anyone else sift the numbers the way I need them," answered Alan.

"If the data set is pretty static, at least you could get a model of the planetary movement completed. Can't you do something like the SETI-at-Home group at Berkeley? They've got thousands of PCs all over the world processing their radiotelescope data in lieu of booking time on a supercomputer just by using a screen saver program."

"Yeah, but look how long it took them to get the word out. It took them years to make any sizable dent in the data they collected, and more pours in every day."

"That's true. But look, your data is pretty static, how about if you cut it off at ten years into the future and then take snapshots of the solar system every ten years after that, then you only really need projections for the current decade."

"Let me see just what kind of partnerships I can come up with before we make any big plans. Besides, what's your angle in this? Have you decided that since the original mapping project was yours, that entitles you to cut yourself in?" Alan asked.

"Not at all. Even though you may have used parts of my data, and maybe even part of my original idea, I'm a big girl. I can take care of myself. If you do make a big splash with this visualization model, I figure that I can use it for my project, with attribution of course. It may help me begin to build a truly representative simulation of all of the objects in the inner solar system. I also want to build a catalog of all of the comets that are currently known to the Planetary Society and be able to predict when and where any of them might pose a threat to earth.

"Furthermore, with my digital detection software, and your plotting application, the two of us have the best opportunity so far for putting together a real-time map of our neighborhood of the galaxy. Why not post a 'CPU Time Wanted' notice on the net and see what you get back, it can't hurt."

If he could latch on to some fast system that had excess capacity, he could at least complete the initial solar map through the next ten years. Alan thought about it for a while. "I don't want to let the cat entirely out of the bag though. Let's be honest, the last thing either of us wants is for someone else to steal the idea before we can cash in on it."

"Fine, let me know what you find out. If I can get images from any other observatory or satellite, I want you to try to use your program to plot my rock in relationship to Saturn first, and then its relationship to Earth. If you can get close enough to plotting speed and direction then I can project its path along the rest of its route."

"No problem," Alan replied.

He thought about what to say in his message. If he included the location of the data set, along with the algorithms he was using, it would save time and effort on the part of others who might be able to actually help out with the necessary processing. The first thing to do was to upload a data set to the public area of the lab's Web server, give outsiders read-only access to the files, and then include the address of the files in the message he was posting.

He began to segment a period of data for each of the ten primary bodies in the solar system. He included a ninety-day period because it was a small enough data set for test processing, but big enough to give everyone a hint of the size of the entire data set he needed processed.

Meanwhile, on the other side of the partition, Norma was filling in the information requested by the Society on her discovery, her current project and the status of her research. She was hoping the latter two items were for internal purposes only. She was also thinking about the possibility of collaborating with Alan on the finished product of their combined work.

His work was sponsored by the university and hers was a government grant; however this third project wasn't funded or controlled by either of their granting bodies. She would have to look at the restrictions on commercial exploitation in her grant to determine how to proceed. The last thing she wanted was a fiasco with the university or the federal government where anything she discovered, developed or created while on the grant belonged to either of them, leaving nothing for her or for Alan.

After she finished filling out the Society's questionnaire and sent it back, Norma checked the rest of her messages. Most were the usual crap, useless commercial solicitations, ads for adult Internet sites and offer after offer of get-rich-quick schemes. Nestled among them was a message from a Dr. Reinhold who, according to the header of the message, was the director of the archives of California's Jet Propulsion Laboratory. He informed her that her message to the x-ray satellite tasking board had been forwarded to him on the chance that he might have some images from the quadrant of interest. His message pointed her to an archive folder that might have what she wanted. He had also attached a set of forty thumbnails of the master images in that folder for her to preview to see if they were from the right location. The dates of the images were all within the last forty days.

If there was anything to see in these pictures, she might catch a better glimpse of her asteroid. At the end of the message, Dr. Reinhold wished her luck in her search and requested to be kept up to date on her discovery so that he could re-index the images with a reference to her project.

She opened another window in her browser and called up the directory of the JPL server on which the images were stored and examined the thumbnails in the e-mail message for their exact location. After examining all forty, she was sure that eight were of the location and time period in question and selected them for download. While she was waiting for them to transfer to her workstation, she got up and went over to the coffee and hot water pots to make herself some tea, something soothing for her stomach which was still a little sour from the previous night's drinking.

When she returned to her desk she saw two new messages in her in-box, both from the archivist of the x-ray satellite project, forwarding her an index of over a hundred images taken in her quadrant of space. However there were no thumbnails attached so she would have to download the entire set to view them. She logged on to their server and began the bulk download of the pictures.

"Hey, what gives?" asked Alan, "All of a sudden my bandwidth just dropped to shit!"

"Your bandwidth?" replied Norma, "Who is renting space from whom here?" she paused a beat and then continued, "Sorry, I just got wind of a bunch of images from the x-ray satellite group and I have to download them here to view them. The whole thing shouldn't take more than ten minutes or so. Did I hose up some streaming video of Amber, Jenna or any of your other dream dates?" she teased.

"No," he replied, "I was just grabbing a bunch of positional data that I had stored on the mainframe downtown. I think I've got the data set I want to include with my request for outside CPU time."

"What, you're going to send the data with the request? You know . . ."

"No, no, no," Alan interrupted, "I'm just putting it on the server here and including a link to the folder in my area of the project web server. I don't want a bunch of strangers logging into my account downtown just to get the data. Besides, I'm sure some techno-weenie in the IT department would flag all of the unusual access and put a hold on my account. You remember what happened when I stored all my music there and left it open to share, I couldn't log back in to the system for a week after they disabled my account."

"Got it. Well my download is almost done, you should be up to full speed in a few minutes."

Just then the phone rang. Norma answered, "Astro lab, Norma speaking. How may I help you?"

"Hey you, it's me, Angie. How'd you feel when you got up this morning?"

"Low and slow. But I had to hustle my ass downtown early and pick up my car before I got a ticket. Next time I'm parking in the lot, screw the sixteen bucks. What's up?"

"I was calling to see if you got confirmation on your comet or moon or whatever it is."

"Well, according to the Planetary Society I've got first dibs on it, and I will get to name it if no one claims to have spotted it before me."

"Have you decided what to name it yet?" she asked.

"That was the first thing out of Alan's mouth this morning too. Is that all anyone is interested in?"

"Well, it's not like we can go and visit your rock, is it? All you have, at least until it gets closer, is its name. According to you we can't even see it yet can we?"

"No, but I can e-mail you a picture of it taken by a satellite. Want it?"

"Hell yeah, I can't wait," Angela answered. "Can I forward it to all my friends?"

"Oh, I don't know. I'm not really sure if I'm comfortable with that yet. Let me get final confirmation of the discovery first. Then I promise, you can tell whoever you want, okay?"

"No prob. Hey want me to come down there for lunch?"

"Sure, why not? Mind if Alan comes along?"

"Yeah, all right. Maybe I'll spend the whole time teasing him about his inability to commit to a healthy monogamous relationship with my best friend."

"Hey, cut that crap out. Things are just fine the way they are. Besides, he's got someone new he's seeing. Just come down and you can torture him about anything else you like."

Angela laughed as she said, "Sure, but you're going to have to get the lowdown on his current squeeze so I can really bite down on him. I'll be there around eleven-thirty. Ta-ta."

"See you later."

"Hey criminal, want to go to lunch with me and Angela today?" Norma asked Alan after she hung up the phone.

"I don't know. What is she going to break my balls about this time? What was it she said last time? Oh yeah, that my research into the three-body problem was just an excuse to experiment with finding the perfect menage-a-trois. You didn't tell her I'm seeing someone new, did you?"

"I might have mentioned it," Norma answered with a laugh. "That's not going to be a problem, is it?"

"What in the hell did you tell her? I want to be able to prepare my defenses for her assault."

"I think I told her that your new sweetie was an underaged high school girl you lured into your car with candy," said Norma, laughing at his obvious discomfort.

"All right, anything she can dish out I guess I can take. Maybe I'll surprise her and give back better than I get for a change. That is if you keep your mouth shut and don't take sides, at least then I've got a fair chance."

"No guarantees, but since it's my turn to treat at least you won't be paying for your own execution."

"Fine by me, I should have just enough time to set up the server and get my request uploaded to the three message groups I've picked out."

"Three groups? Which ones did you pick?" asked Norma.

"I added two more that I know some of the government's astrophysics guys tool around on. They'll probably have the most in common with what we're doing, plus they have access to so much spare computing power maybe we'll get lucky and find an angel partner who can get a head start on processing a big chunk of the data."

"At least you're saying we and us. I hope this is going to be a real collaboration and not a kiss me, screw me and then you're out the door kind of thing, professionally speaking of course."

"No chance." Alan replied seriously. "What I really want is for this to take off and become the most comprehensive three-dimensional map of the heavens possible. Maybe we can make access to it a subscription service that will produce passive income for the rest of our lives!"

"Yeah, sure. Great words now, while I still have you by the balls. But what happens when you're done here and try to peddle the whole idea commercially?" Norma asked.

"Look, I'm not going anywhere soon so can you quit trying to buy trouble. Jeeze, if you're so scared of getting screwed you can always run me over with the car. Better yet, why not just feed me to Angela if I screw up, she's carnivorous enough to keep me in line. Tell you what, let me leave my testicles with you until this thing goes public. That way if anything doesn't go the way you want you can drop them into a vise or do whatever makes you feel good, okay?"

"Fine, I'll pick up a really tiny box to keep them in while we're out to lunch."

"Great, I can't wait. Now shut up and let me get back to work. By the way I think your download is finished, I'm back up to full speed over here."

"Thanks," said Norma. Turning back to her screen and taking a sip of tea, she made a face when she found it had cooled off during her conversation with Angela. She thought about heating it up in the microwave, but this close to lunch she didn't bother. Navigating to the folder where the JPL images were stored, Norma rendered each image into a small thumbnail so that she wouldn't waste time on those that had no relationship to what she wanted. But before she forgot, she sent the picture that she had enhanced overnight to the color printer so that she could sign it and present it as a souvenir to Angela.

Getting back to the pictures she had retrieved from both sources that morning, she began to load the higher-resolution images for quick viewing of the area around where her rock was first sighted. She started with the oldest image and moved forward in time, scanning through about a dozen before she thought she saw the object slightly off to the side from where her best picture showed it. This offset could give her an approximate speed of the asteroid in relationship to Saturn, so she kept this image in the background of her screen as she scanned through the next two pictures in the series. Both showed the object in slightly different locations. Although the deflection from image to image was small, Norma saw from the time stamps of all three images that they covered a span of about forty hours. Her heart began to beat a little quicker when she realized she could not only calculate the speed of the asteroid, but from these three pictures, along with the two she originally spotted it in, she might even be able to plot the direction in which it was traveling.

Norma cleared her screen and loaded the pictures into her mapping software. It automatically resized and aligned the five images and showed the largest object, Saturn, stationary in the middle right of the screen. Flipping through them one at a time, she could definitely see the track of the rock as it passed across the lower face of the huge planet and into the black background of space. She became more and more excited as she replayed the five images over and over. It still didn't quite suit her as there was a huge gap between the first three images and her last two. Then she had a brainstorm.

Norma open up some menus in her oldest applications and mentally high-fived herself when she located what she was looking for. Buried in the clutter of old software she had never uninstalled was an old morphing program. The software was used to do silly things like change one face into another or age a friend's face from a young adult into a very old person.

She loaded the program, calculated the time interval between the first three images and saw that adding some frames between each of them would smooth out the motion of the asteroid. Norma loaded the five images, added the intervals of time between each one and started the program rendering the in-between frames. She was so excited she could hardly contain herself. She didn't even want to tell Alan what she was doing, wanting it to be a surprise.

A few minutes later the sequence was done. Norma clicked on the playback button and watched the magic of morphing technology show a nine-second movie clip of "her" asteroid. At the end of the first run-through she jumped to her feet and gave a thunderous shout of victory, scaring Alan almost into crapping his pants.

"What the hell is wrong with you?" Alan shouted. "I almost shit myself. You scared the living hell out of me."

"Quick, get over here and take a look at this," Norma shouted. "Hurry up."

"What's gotten into you?" Alan said. "Give me a sec, I'll be right there."

"God dammit, I said now."

"What the fuck is your problem?"

"This is important, get your ass over here. Now, now, now!"

"Jesus Christ. Here I come."

Once around the partition, Alan just stared at the image on Norma's screen. As soon as she knew he was watching, she clicked the playback button.

As he watched in rapt fascination, he saw her asteroid moving across the screen over and over again.

"Holy shit! How did you do that?"

Norma described the process she went through to extract the images and produce the movie clip. Alan watched the sequence as Norma put it on automatic replay, completely blown away.

"You have to e-mail this to the Planetary Society. I'll bet it would be the first time something like this was received as an attachment to a sighting!"

"Yeah, maybe. And maybe they'll think I'm pushing too hard," said Norma.

"How about you release it to the press? Think about how much publicity you would get!"

"You know as well as I do the university policy on releasing anything to the press. It has to be submitted in triplicate to public affairs, and they call in the lawyers, and then end up telling you not to do, or say, anything. The only reason I even sent my application in is that it was stipulated in the grant that all sightings were to be reported as soon as the computer spotted them. I don't know if this really falls into that same category. Let's wait and see what the Society says. Although I think I will send off the clip. It's only four and a half megabytes, and I'll explain the entire procedure so they understand how much of the data is from original images and how much was rendered."

"Yeah, sure. Whatever you think is best. Hey, maybe they'll send it in to the press themselves. After all, the entire point of your project was to see if a strictly computer-driven detector could be used to spot incoming space junk optically instead of having to rely on deep-space radar or a bunch of insomniacs looking at the sky in between peeping in the windows of people across the way. The university should be tickled pink if another of their alums makes it big with a national project like this," Alan pointed out.

"You're right. I'll phone the dean of public affairs and see if he has time to stop by and look the whole thing over. Oh, and I'm sorry for scaring you like that, I would have burst if you hadn't come over right then."

"I know, and I would have ended up having to do something revoltingly sick and sappy just to get back in your good graces."

"Back? Let me let you in on a not-so-well-kept secret, you've never been in my good graces," laughed Norma. "So any time you want to begin that campaign let me know. I'm partial to Belgian chocolate and expensive champagne. Speaking of which, Angela should be here any minute."

Norma saved the rendered clip on her workstation and on the mainframe and sent it to herself via e-mail so she could have it at home. Just as she was finishing up Angela bounced into the lab shouting, "Waaazzzzzuuup! Geeks, let's saddle 'em up and head 'em out!"

"Hey girl, before we go take a look at this," Norma said.

"What'cha got? Hey, do you have my picture of your new planet there?" asked Angela.

"Even better, watch this," Norma said as she started the clip.

"Oh my God! How did you get that? Is there more, is there a satellite out there watching? How did they find it so fast?" gushed Angela.

"Whoa, slow down. It's nothing like that. I rendered the clip from five images that showed the object. It's all done with software."

"Have you shown it to anyone important yet?"

At that question Alan popped his head over the partition and said, "What do you mean 'anyone important' over there? What am I, chopped liver?"

"Not really. More like the parts of the pig that don't make it into the hotdog," replied Angela, smiling.

"Nice, you two. Can we call a truce and go get something to eat? I'm starved. Oh, and Angela, I've got something for you," said Norma as she ran over to the printer. "Here," she said signing the picture with a flourish. "Just for you. The first autographed image of, as you call it, my planet."

"Oh honey, this is great. I'm going to get a frame for it on the way back to the office and hang it above my desk," she said, giving her friend a hug.

Walking around the edge of the partition Alan said, "If you two aren't going to get it on on the desk, let's get the hell out of here."

"You really can't help yourself, can you?" replied Angela. "You always manage to live down to my expectations, worm."

"Hey guys, I thought we were calling a truce for the time being," admonished Norma.

"I'm game if he is."

"I could use a break in hostilities myself. Besides, I wanted to get an outsiders view of the three-dimensional mapping program. Someone with at least a triple-digit IQ," said Alan.

"Oh, you say the nicest things when properly motivated. Let's get out of here," said Angela, effectively closing off any further conversation.

CHAPTER 6

ONCE THE LOCAL Iraqi military had exhaustively examined the metal fragments from the unidentified craft, they knew they had their hands on something brand new. Using the best of the Soviet scientific instruments purchased during the cold war era, they were unable to determine the craft's country of origin, or who had built it. The only clue that might possibly help them was the foot found at the crash site.

Close examination clearly showed the foot was of human origin; the bones were the normal size and configuration of a man between forty and sixty years of age. The blood type was even the most common on earth, type O. Nothing else suggested any deviation from human norm.

The military was stumped. Given the advanced nature of the pieces of wreckage and the complete absence of markings, the craft had to have been constructed by one of the superpowers or a close ally. Even though the owner of the foot was a Black man, no one thought for an instant that the craft originated anywhere in Africa. At least the foot silenced any speculation that the craft might have originated from another planet with a resounding "no." In fact, that theory wasn't even mentioned in the resulting report from the laboratories or discussed by the scientists or the military.

As a result, discreet inquiries went out through Arab intermediaries asking for information on whether the western allies admitted to losing any of their aircraft in the area. Said craft quietly was described as an advanced, single-seat, experimental reconnaissance ship with unusual flight characteristics.

Unfortunately, this only served to prompt inquiries from the West on exactly what the Iraqis were talking about, and whether the inquiry was the result of some kind of disinformation campaign. The British, having the best intelligence assets in place, gathered as much information they could and forwarded it on to the Central Intelligence Agency with their own inquiry attached. They appended their offer to help recover any downed pilot lost or hiding out in the area, should that be the case.

When the report reached the Langley, Virginia headquarters of the Central Intelligence Agency, it was sent to analysis to see if any additional sources of intel could add to the British report before being kicked upstairs. Based on the billeting of the Iraqi officers mentioned in the report, satellite reconnaissance located the crash site with ease from the burn mark on the hilly landscape. Several of the satellite photos showing the area in question were included in the report along with a note describing the number of vehicle tracks around the area, indicating the unusual amount of activity for a location so far from any military garrison or town.

Robert "Bobby Boy" Bascomb was the analyst who drew the file sent in from the British. He was one of a dozen or so Iraqi intelligence specialists working full time to determine Iraq's military threat against its neighbors and the United States. Knowing already that there had been no alliance aircraft lost in Iraq, Bobby's curiosity was piqued over just who had crashed in the hills. He e-mailed a note to the satellite tasking group requesting a closer look at the crash site, and began to check on whether it might have been one of their own jets that corkscrewed into the ground.

Once he finished reviewing the file, Bobby entered everything that wasn't already in the computer and scanned in the original report from the British agent. He then looked up the next code name from the top of the list for his file, and entered the word "CARJACK" in the file name field of the index form.

Bobby had been an analyst for seven years and had truly grown to enjoy his work. The best part of his job was assembling each piece of intelligence data from every asset he could get his hands on into a completed picture. He lived for neat, complete reports that answered any and all questions on the topic at hand. He would have protested greatly if anyone advanced the notion that he was inalterably anal about his work.

Initially, this particular report didn't look like anything significant. His first guess was that the Iraqis had accidentally downed one of their own jets and were covering their butts with the claim of an allied shoot-down. He typed in his preliminary report and ended the entry with a note saying he was waiting for further intel to confirm the initial analysis. After closing the electronic file, Bobby grabbed the next report in his in-box and scanned the information.

Meanwhile, halfway around the globe in an Iraqi military laboratory, a senior technician was using a ordinary kitchen bag sealer to prepare the recovered foot for deep freezing. He had already prepped several sections of the skin and blood and concealed them around the lab, as he had done to a number of the tiny pieces of the wreckage. He wasn't sure where the samples were being taken, but it didn't pay to ask too many questions or give in to normal curiosity. Frankly, all he wanted was to continue his studies of these artifacts, despite orders to have everything removed from the lab and sent along with the courier on his way to Baghdad.

What he didn't know was that the frozen foot and the mysterious metal were being transported to one of original secret underground bunkers built just outside of Baghdad a decade before the Gulf War. The technician's reports had come to the attention of The Great One himself, and as a result, all pieces of the aircraft were to be brought to this most secret, and best protected, laboratory for analysis.

Though completely loyal to The Great One, the technician was burning with a need to know how the metal skin of the downed aircraft had been fabricated. Spectrographic analysis of the metal's composition showed steel, aluminum and titanium in an alloy not previously known. Getting those three metals to blend into the light, nearly impenetrable alloy with a melting point of over forty-one hundred degrees, six hundred degrees above pure tungsten, was beyond anything he had read about in European or American scientific literature. Given its characteristics, he was sure that this alloy was a strategic resource of whoever had constructed the aircraft.

Fortunately the scientist operated with minimal supervision. All he need do was deliver the organic and metal specimens to the courier and wait until he left. Then he could resume his analysis of this fantastic metal. The tissue samples from the severed limb were of lesser interest to him, but he was a cautious man by nature and had learned to hedge his bets. He also wanted to run toxicology screens on the tissue for metal residue deep within the cells. This might lead him to some small clue to the origin of the aircraft and whether the pilot had breathed or otherwise absorbed contaminants from the environment.

The laboratory staff knew that the samples came from an aircraft their own military shot down. The fact that their own army had actually shot down a Western aircraft was initially a source of great pride, especially given that the number of US fighters shot down since the no-fly zone was imposed could be counted on the thumb of a single hand. However, when no acknowledgment of the shoot-down was forthcoming from the Western press, and there was none of the usual caterwauling about the loss of a single US life in the fight for freedom worldwide, their enthusiasm was considerably dampened. Most of the Arab world saw the constant interference by the United States government into the sovereign affairs of the Muslim world as little better than state-sponsored racism targeted against those who lived and worshiped in any manner different from the Christian West.

It didn't take long for the laboratory staff to discover they had gotten hold of something completely out of the ordinary. Something that their former sponsor, the Soviet Union, lacked the technology to create during the height of its power, let alone since its collapse into financial and political ruin. No, the only possible source of this kind of technology was the West, either the United States or one of its European or Asian allies. The lack of any markings, no numbers or letters of any kind, was driving the entire research staff crazy. Many of the electronic components had somewhat recognizable uses, they thought, but were just slightly off. Many of the samples lacked the characteristics of mass manufacturing and looked custom fabricated. What had been identified as resistors and surface-mounted transistors stumped the Iraqi scientists, many of whom were educated and trained at some of the best universities and laboratories in the United States. The materials were sufficiently different from standard Japanese and Chinese components, used by every country in the world, to cast strong questions on their origin. Was there a new player in the electronics industry? Someone who had developed on-demand fabrication technologies? Someone under exclusive contract to the governments of the West?

When The Great One's courier arrived, the senior scientist had several hundred kilos of metal and electronics sealed in boxes, the whole collection shrink-wrapped on a shipping skid with the quick-frozen foot in an insulated cooler on top. When the lab was cleared, he brought out from hiding one of the metal samples and one of the portions of electronic circuitry he had held back.

He clamped the metal in a vise, and using a small rotary sander, ground off a small sample for detailed analysis. The diamond-faced grinding wheel slowly abraded tiny flakes of the metal and flicked them into the glass petri dish below. Once he had collected a dusting of the metal flakes, he removed the small piece of metal from the vise and placed it under the strongest optical microscope he had, wishing for the hundredth time for the kind of equipment a fully stocked, modern lab would have, like an electron microscope. The surface was visibly scored from the diamond grinding wheel, but under the highest magnification the edges of the abraded surface showed no sign of heat-related melting or deterioration. It had resisted puncture to over ten thousand pounds per square inch. He excitedly realized this metal was essentially bullet-proof.

Leaving the metal scrapings for a moment, the scientist turned his attention to the circuit board. Using the same techniques as he used on the metal, he prepared the sample for analysis by a gas chromatograph to determine the type of materials from which it was made. Leaving the sample to process automatically, he turned to the metal scrapings in the sample dish. With a sterile swab he collected a portion to be subjected to chromatographic analysis. Maybe this test would reveal some of the other elements in the metal and lead him to the technique used to create the remarkable alloy.

Now, all he could do was wait for the results. He decided to take the rest of the day off and spend some time in the local restaurant that catered to the military and scientific elite. Some of the less-advertised entertainments would greatly help pass the afternoon, and quite pleasantly too.

As he locked the door and left the laboratory, the scientist gave a nod to the guard. He informed him that he would be out all afternoon and probably wouldn't return until after dark.

This particular guard's loyalties were divided. His primary allegiance was to his military superiors and The Great One, but he also had grown to respect a quiet confidant in his village, a man who took to looking after the guard's family when he was assigned away from his home. This quiet man was discharged from the military when he received a disabling injury to his left foot in an engagement against a pair of United States fighters, rendering him useless as the fighter pilot he was trained to be. He barely drew any kind of pension at all, but instead existed on the kindness of his neighbors. He returned that kindness with repairs to their farm machinery, their home appliances and even the few working automobiles left in the village.

The man was simply known as Basra, the name of the city in which he claimed to have grown up. He proved himself to be an able engineer, very good with his hands. Many in the village had more than once depended on him to keep their vital machinery running. So, sharing the little they had was the best they could do to try to make sure he wanted for nothing. Sometimes he was pressed so hard to accept what others could little afford to give him that he would decline the gifts in embarrassment.

Though a past member of the military, Basra was one of the many Iraqis who were disaffected with the harsh, unforgiving rule of The Great One. Too many of his brother pilots had perished in defense of the corrupt leader. His own family barely survived at subsistence level until he was accepted into the Air Force. Only then did he see his parents, brother and sister have decent clothing, enough food to eat and, for his brother at least, the chance at an education. His mother and sister were still barely second-class citizens in Iraq's strict Muslim society, both constantly under social assault to conceal their faces and bodies, having to conform to the strictest Muslim rules.

Basra hated how the ruling class of his country had access to the best of everything, with no requirement to adhere to Muslim law, no restrictions on their dissipated behavior at all. He had come to the conclusion that for his people to have any chance to live free, to prosper in commerce, to realize true religious freedom, and to exist in a society where his sister could have the same opportunities as he, a change must be made at the top of the ruling class. The Great One had to be deposed, either by arrest or exile, or, if necessary, by death.

Once the decision was made, the next task was to plan the means to achieve this goal. As a former pilot he was entitled to some considerations, a meager pension and somewhat better food and clothing. All this would have been his due had he remained in Baghdad. Instead, he chose to wander the country until he found a small village seemingly plopped down out of nowhere in the middle of several military installations. Here he decided he could be of some help in slowly undermining the military infrastructure by passing defense and deployment details to several of his fellow countrymen. Some who, at various times, contacted him probing for any measure of dissatisfaction with how the military abandoned him once he could no longer perform as a combat pilot.

He knew immediately what they wanted, and almost reported them to the authorities just because their approach was so transparent and clumsy, and yet it gave him pause. Maybe they were a means to an end. Perhaps they could lead him to someone who did have the resources to bring about a better life for his people through his intelligence gathering.

He humored them, cautiously drawing them out, never committing to any overt act of defiance or uttering an incautious word. He watched and learned all he could about the personalities who sought his favor. Once he eliminated the also-rans and the hangers-on, he zeroed in on the one man who he believed to be a conduit to those who really mattered. While he was working his way up to those who were the real power in the underground movement, he was also becoming a part of the village's social landscape. He became a constant in the tapestry of village life, helping any and all without thought for what others could do for him. He never required a quid pro quo, always helping without comment or in judgment of others, and he paid exceptional attention to the families servicemen assigned to, and living in, the village.

It was in this way he became friend and confidant to the soldiers assigned to the laboratory and the missile installations located around the village. He never probed for any sensitive information, just listened sympathetically to their complaints. He was always ready to regale his fellow soldiers with stories of the mistakes and incompetence of his superiors while he served in the air force, and to sympathize with their own tales of woe.

Thus, Basra learned about the unusual activity at the laboratory, and of the special courier dispatched to pick up the wreckage and the remains of the aircraft's pilot to return them to Baghdad. He asked a casual question or two about the pieces of the craft; after all, he was a pilot, naturally curious about the exploits of those still flying. His interest in a new kind of aircraft flown by the Western Alliance was reasonable, as was his praise of the missile crew who had shot it down. How close had it come? How quickly had the missile crew reacted to the incursion? Questions anyone would have asked.

That afternoon, Basra noticed that the entire laboratory staff had been dismissed and were all in town partaking in its meager entertainment. His curiosity peaked an hour later when the head scientist himself showed up. What is going on? he wondered. He had to wait until he could talk to one of the guards to see what had gone on at the lab. He had already prepared the report on the aircraft reportedly shot down. If this had anything to do with the unusual activity at the lab, he wanted to be able to pass the information on to his Western contacts as soon as possible.

Later that evening Basra left his home, seeking out the head guard of the lab, slowly making his way to the few establishments the soldiers regularly patronized. He briefly considered attempting to break into the lab to have a look around while most everyone was off duty, however, he knew that at least one guard would be posted overnight, and getting around him would prove quite a trial even for a man not hampered with a bad foot.

He entered the last and most probable eating and drinking establishment, to see it was full of the local militia. He scanned the room through the heavy smoke and haze and spotted his quarry sitting with two fellow soldiers. Basra made his way around the hot, humid room, greeting those with whom he had more than a passing acquaintance, many whose families he had helped in the past. Passing by his target's table, he greeted him and his fellows and made as if he was just going to continue when the head guard invited him to sit a spell.

Dropping gratefully into a chair, he gave thanks for the respite from being on his feet most of a long hot day. He waved to the bartender and indicated he would be having what the soldiers were drinking. When he had taken the first sip he asked the head guard, "How is it that all of you get a holiday today? Is it the Great One's birthday and I've lost track?"

"Nothing of the sort, Basra. Great doings went on at the laboratory this morning, and because of our dedication to the cause of our country we were blessed with the reward of the rest of the day off," replied the soldier. "Besides," he added in a hushed tone, "all of the samples from the Western aircraft, and the remains of the pilot, were picked up by our Great Leader's courier, there was nothing further to be done." Despite the head scientist's admonition not to discuss the events of the morning, the guard never believed the restriction applied to this hero of the people. After all, this was Basra, the pilot who fought in the skies for the cause of their country, becoming crippled by the enemies of their people. Besides, the consumption of alcohol had definitely loosened his tongue.

"You mean there actually was a Western fighter shot down by our side? I though that was just a rumor, or maybe propaganda to keep the troops' morale high," said Basra.

"No, it's true. I saw pieces of the wreckage come in, and a thing wrapped up in plastic that I heard was part of the pilot, a foot they said."

"Is the wreckage still here? Maybe I can help examine it. After all, we pilots more often than not had to do our own mechanical inspections of our planes, for no better reason than our lives depended on it."

"I'm afraid you are too late, my friend. The Great One's courier took everything back to Baghdad late this morning and all but the chief scientist left for town right after the courier left." Dropping his voice the head guard said, "Shortly thereafter, even he left." Sitting back up straight, he continued in more normal tones, "However, he did say he would be returning this evening, for what I don't know. Even if he wanted to there's nothing left to experiment on. Everything left earlier today."

"Perhaps he just wanted to finish cleaning up," Basra offered. "Anyway, a day off is a day off, no?"

"You've got that right, my friend. Although, I half expect to have some of us sent back into the hills to see if we can recover more of the wrecked aircraft. It seems that this plane wasn't like anything our scientists or technicians had ever seen before. While we were helping box up the parts I overheard that there were no markings on the craft itself, and none at all on any of the parts. The electronics didn't even have Japanese or English letters or numbers like all of ours, and the Soviets, do."

"What, no English or anything printed on the components?" Basra asked.

"Not so much as a letter or a number. Very strange, if you ask me." the soldier said, taking another sip of his drink.

This sounds like a prototype or something experimental. They often do not have standard markings, everything is custom built, or jury-rigged for easy access and for making changes, Basra thought. "But to have no markings whatsoever is quite out of the ordinary," he said.

"As you say," replied the soldier. "I'm sure I don't have to tell you to hold this in the strictest confidence."

"No, no. Not at all. I am proud you boys were able to bring down one of the oppressor's fighters in defense of the homeland."

With half of his mind on the continuing conversation, Basra considered all of the facts at hand. They would have to be conveyed to his Western contacts, if for no other reason than the pilot's family should be notified of their loss. It would be no problem for the Western allies to identify the pilot; they knew who was assigned to each of their aircraft. If only he could get a look the lab notes on the wreckage; that is, if they hadn't gone the way of the wreckage and remains. What he had to do was to decide if the risk of getting caught where he had no business outweighed the benefit of getting to the bottom of whatever spooked Baghdad about this particular wreck.

Once Basra weighed the pros and cons he decided to do what any good military man would do, buck it up the chain of command. He set off for home to compose a message to his conduit to the West. What he didn't know was that the contact he thought of as a minor member of a low-priority cell of resistance was the deepest undercover agent of the CIA operating in Iraq, and would recognize the importance of the report he was about to receive.

The agent's report was encrypted, transmitted and placed on Bobby Bascomb's desk less than four hours after Basra had left it in the secret drop outside of town. When Bascomb picked it up he sat a little straighter in his chair. He opened the file he had started from the British intel received a couple of days before and appended the report from his best asset in the area. He also noted that two responses had been received by e-mail to his inquiry. Both reported that no Iraqi aircraft had been reported missing, nor did satellite counts of all the nearby Iraqi military airbases show any reduction in the inventories of fighters and reconnaissance aircraft deployed in the region. And, according to radio intercepts, there was no air-to-air or air-to-ground traffic out of the ordinary on the night of the crash.

The US Air Force E-3 Sentry Airborne Warning and Control System's (AWACS) command center round-the-clock surveillance of Iraqi military communications traffic recorded nothing that night except for the intercepted communications from the missile defense site to their command headquarters. Transcripts of both sides of the conversation, from the local HQ commander and the missile battery commander, seemed to suggest the threat was real. They definitely believed that the missile installation shot down a Western aircraft in their defensive zone, and that the aircraft was presumably going to attack their side of the no-fly zone.

Routine inquiries to the British, the only other air group operating in the area that night, turned up nothing missing from their side either.

He tried to put the entire affair out of his mind as he prepared to leave for the day. The last thing he did before locking up was pull up the profile of Basra. He noted that Basra's training was originally compliments of the Saudi Air Force, training on mostly older Western aircraft until he graduated to the Iraqi Advanced Air Weapons Group's MiG-23 Flogger and the MiG-25 Foxbat, one of the fastest combat aircraft in the sky. The report detailed his shoot down and the subsequent injuries that kept him from returning to the sky. The dossier showed an honorable discharge and a pension. There was no mention of family or relatives elsewhere in the government or the military, just two siblings. The whole picture was of a level-headed soldier, no hidden agenda in the transmission of his reports to his handler. He looked like just what he purported to be, a disaffected soldier fed up with the corrupt, oppressive regime sucking the life out of his fellow countrymen with no hope of positive payoff for their sacrifice.

Locking his desk, closing his personal safe and locking his office door on the way out, Bobby thought that a few hours in the gym, or maybe a couple of sets of tennis, would clear his mind. He needed a fresh start on ferreting out and assembling the various pieces of this particular puzzle.

His request for any associated information about the shoot down incident had made its way to the British liaison, who passed it on to their Iraqi division. Once there, Bascomb's opposite number retrieved their own files and began to comb through them for information relating to the aircraft shootdown. In the process he came upon a copy of the missile crew's report of the incident. Checking the source of the report, and the routing it took to get into their hands, he assigned a "very high reliability" rating before scanning, encrypting and electronically transmitting it back to Bascomb.

Sharing intelligence reports like this was fairly routine between the two groups, especially since both were tasked with the responsibility of keeping tabs on current events in Baghdad. The CIA had even given their associates across the pond unrestricted medium-level access to satellite imaging and AWACS intel. Bascomb's opposite number also appended his own request for a summary of the report when Bobby had something substantive.

After tennis, Bascomb showered and got into his car, fully intending to go home. But, when he saw where his mental automatic pilot was taking him he knew it was no use. His hindbrain needed to track down the origin of that aircraft. He wanted to know who might be active in the area besides those allied air groups specifically assigned to patrol the no-fly zone, if for no other reason than to be able to make an accurate threat assessment of any new players in the area. He wanted to try to determine just how they might affect the balance of power in the region. If the Iraqis, or anyone else, had new allies supplying them with advanced military support, this was of vital interest to him and, consequently, to the Joint Chiefs of Staff and the Secretary of Defense.

He knew his return had already been reported to security and, he thought sadly, it wasn't out of the ordinary to be returning to work this late in the evening. He checked in and made a beeline to his office.

At his desk, he saw that he had two replies to his inquiry. The first almost made his heart stop. He couldn't believe he had the actual intercept report from the missile crew, including the computer readout of the flight profile of the intruder. He ignored everything else in the report and concentrated on the initial location of the aircraft. From the tracking data he tried to match the flight characteristics to any fixed-or rotary-winged aircraft in the Allies' arsenal. Nothing that flew that high could reduce speed, drop several thousand feet and then continue forward at half the stall speed of a fully loaded Tomcat.

The only aircraft that was even close to being capable of the flight characteristics he was staring at was a British Harrier. Pulling up the deployment database of the region's assets, he could find no mention of Harriers in the deployed group, neither land-nor carrier-based. Besides, his British intelligence opposite number already confirmed they had not lost any of their birds during the campaign. No one in the region had any of the British fighters deployed. The closest allied fighter force with Harriers was in Turkey.

His interest definitely aroused, Bobby began to draft his report on the situation, adding the intel from the satellite photo, the missile crew's incident report, the two asset reports from his in-country contact and the original British report that started the inquiry. He was torn about what to put down in the recommendations section. The last thing he wanted to do was provoke a mission to extract further information, or samples of the wreckage, just so the aircraft could be positively identified. What stood out in his mind was the question of who had deployed the aircraft in the first place, and whether it was some kind of mistake.

He decided to recommend additional monitoring using their best Baghdad assets to try to locate the destination of the recovered wreckage. If so, there was a good chance to positively identify of the source of the aircraft.

He scheduled an all-staff briefing for early next week. He would be able to discuss his concerns with the rest of his team and give his best analysis of the data that had been dropped on his desk less than forty-eight hours earlier. He leaned back to stretch out the kinks in his shoulders and upper back. Now that he had a plan of action, maybe his mind would relax enough to let him get in some quality sack time.

He's a real nowhere man, sitting in his nowhere land
Making all his nowhere plans, for nobody
Nowhere Man
Written and performed by The Beatles

CHAPTER 7

ONCE JOHN MADE it home and parked the car, he considered walking around the corner and getting a six-pack to nurse through the evening's study of the FBI data on the disappearances. He nixed the idea, thinking a clear head was the better way to go. He also didn't want to sound fuzzy when Agent Samuels called.

John entered the house, opening a couple of windows to let in the cooler nighttime air, went over to his office alcove in the dining room and started up his computer. While it was booting up, he shed his sport coat and shoulder holster and then grabbed a can of soda from the fridge. He went back to the front door and picked the mail up off the floor, noting there wasn't a single thing in the pile he wanted to keep. Tossing the entire pile in the trash, he sat down to check his e-mail.

John opened the waiting message from Samuels and saw there was an attachment that would install itself on his computer. This little add-in would permit him to connect to the FBI mainframe with both ends of the connection encrypted to prevent any sort of electronic eavesdropping.

Once he installed the encryption software, he pointed his browser to the numbered address of the FBI host. The anonymous page showed just a login prompt, nothing to alert someone to the fact that it was a direct line into the

FBI systems. John entered the user ID and password Samuels had given him and waited while the two computers negotiated the encryption sequence and authenticated his session.

He was presented with a menu of half a dozen options. Only two, case files and Internet e-mail, weren't greyed out, indicating they were the only options accessible to him.

Clicking on case files, he was prompted for a case number. John entered the number Samuels had sent him and was treated to a list of folders sorted by last name. He clicked on the date header and resorted them from the earliest to the latest. He wanted to scan them looking for the pattern that the computer had caught, although he knew he wasn't going to be able to check them all in one night.

The earliest files dated back to the late nineteen-sixties, all with similar characteristics. The victims were of course all black, young, in their early twenties to mid-forties. Almost all were well educated, college level or better.

Some of the files included majors in college, but there was no discernable pattern there, maybe a slight leaning toward the sciences. All had disappeared without warning, as if they were just cut out of a picture, leaving behind a hole in the lives of everyone around them. Most had bank accounts never accessed after their disappearance, some had family that ended up claiming their effects and assets after the investigations had cleared them of any responsibility in their assumed demise. But to a man, or woman, none were ever heard from again and no trace of their bodies found.

Almost every disappearance was written off as a hate crime with racial motivation. In several of the cases from the South, John even found the phrase "uppity nigger" quoted in interviews from coworkers or neighbors speculating on possible motives.

Shaking his head, John realized just how short a time forty years was.

Jumping ahead to the last few cases, John saw they were spread around various parts of the country, almost evenly split between the North and South, hailing from cities and towns of all sizes.

As he was reading, a little window popped open on his screen, informing him he had a new message waiting for him. Clicking on the window, it opened up to reveal Samuels had left a note pointing him to a file folder with a map of the US showing the location of each disappearance. The message added that Samuels would be calling him around nine o'clock that evening. John closed the window and opened the folder with the case notes and map. He sent the map to his little color printer and opened the case file. He didn't see anything new added by any of the case officers. The file only contained the original notes of the cases that were seen as possible kidnappings, cases where the FBI had been brought in from the beginning. The rest only had local police reports.

Pulling four sheets of paper out of his printer, he taped them together to make the full map of the US. The location of each disappearance was indicated with a small triangle. The triangles were color coded by date, with the legend sitting in the Gulf of Mexico. John could discern no pattern by date or location. Most of the triangles were clustered around cities, but given the distribution of population in the US, that made statistical sense.

He taped the map to the wall over his computer and went to the kitchen to see what he could scrounge up for dinner.

John thought back to his afternoon with Dean Atkins. The dean impressed him with her quiet dignity, something that stood out in someone so young. She had the aura of an old soul around her. He wasn't given to mystical flights of fancy but he did believe he could divine something of the nature of a person just by close observation.

Sitting down to eat, John picked up the file on the Williams girl and reread the sections on her family and the interview with the boyfriend. Tomorrow he was going to drop by the boyfriend's job and try to get a read on him.

The phone rang right on time. John answered, "Mathews."

Agent Samuels said hello, then asked, "Do you have time to get up to speed on this right now? Otherwise we can hit it in the morning."

"No, now's fine. You want to do this over the phone or do you want to get together somewhere?"

"Have you eaten?" Samuels asked.

"Just a little while ago, but I'm game if you buy me a piece of pie somewhere."

"Where do you suggest? I've got an agency car and I'm getting the hang of getting around the city."

"Tell you what, I'll drive over near you. Four blocks north of your room is a restaurant called Kappy's or something like that, I'll meet you there in half an hour."

"Fine. You want me to bring anything?" asked Samuels.

"Nope, I just want to ask you a few things and bring you up to speed on my visit to the college today."

"Fine, I'll see you there."

John pulled on a pair of gym shoes and transferred his service automatic to his belt holster, which he parked over the crack of his butt, hidden when he put on his windbreaker. He grabbed his wallet and badge and headed out to his cruiser.

Arriving early at the restaurant, John waved at the owner behind the counter and walked toward a quiet booth in the back. The waitress brought over a menu and a pot of coffee.

"You by yourself or are you gonna have company?" she asked.

"Just one more," John replied.

"Coffee?"

"Sure, and what kind of pie do you have tonight?" he asked.

"We've got apple, cherry and blueberry in the fruits, and there's still chocolate cream and banana cream. Want something now?"

"No. I'll wait for my friend and order when he gets here. Thank you."

"No problem, I'll come back."

It wasn't five minutes before Samuels dropped into the seat across from him.

"Howdy," Samuels said.

"Hey, you hungry? The food's not bad here, they make a great soup," said John.

The waitress came over and took their orders.

As she walked away, John asked, "Find anything at the gym?"

"No. The guy seems to be just what he appears. He's a computer geek who does pretty much what anyone with a job his age does. He works, he goes out and his friends all come up normal too. There's nothing to suggest he isn't what he says he is, a concerned boyfriend. What did you come up with at the girl's college?" Samuels asked.

"Nothing out of the ordinary. She is a good student. She was working on an outside grant in hydroponics for the space program, and her grades were superb. I checked her office calendar and e-mail account and didn't find anything unusual. I also printed off all the contacts in her address book to check out later. I haven't been to her apartment yet but I'm guessing your crew turned up zero there too."

"Other than the messages on her answering machine there's nothing, absolutely nothing out of the ordinary."

Looking pointedly at Samuels, John asked, "Yeah, okay, now tell me, what's the real reason you guys called me in on this? I read a few of the files online and saw that local law called you guys in on most of these disappearances, and nothing was ever picked up out of the ordinary. So what's up? And please, start at the beginning, are you really the lead investigator on this thing, the special agent in charge?"

Samuels paused for a second, then made up his mind and began, "As far as I know I am. This whole thing started with a telephone call received on a talk radio show in Chicago. The evening host was spouting off about how the US still had to fight terrorism no matter where it struck. Anyway, the caller led the host by the nose and dropped what normally wouldn't have been the bombshell that it eventually became for us. He said, if the United States government, the FBI and all of the local law enforcement agencies in the country were really serious about eradicating terrorists wherever they operated, then when were they going to go after those responsible for the over eighty thousand deaths and disappearances of blacks in America since the 1820s. The host made the stupid mistake of saying 'Well, first of all, I doubt your figures.' and that's when things got ugly for us.

"The caller stated that the figures were compiled from FBI statistics going back to its inception and then from crime reports from the two hundred fifty largest cities in the country before the FBI existed. The caller went on to accuse the US of maintaining a policy where crimes against anyone who was not white, or wasn't a businessman operating from the US, were completely unimportant to the government, and had historically never been a priority since well before Lincoln freed the slaves.

"By then the damage was done, the rest of the callers who followed this guy were divided between the hatemongers who were saying blacks who were victims of crime were reaping what they sowed, and those who pointed to the first caller's numbers as proof that this country is little better than the South depicted in Gone With the Wind or Mandingo."

Pausing to take a sip of water, Samuels continued, "The next day the whole thing began to escalate. Someone at one of the daily papers called the local deputy at the Bureau and asked him to comment. Then our public Web site was inundated with hits in the historical stats sections from people trying to add up the figures themselves. Then, someone at the Washington Post called the White House press secretary and wanted to know what the official position of the administration was on the accusation."

"I'll bet that made a whole lot of folks happy out there, didn't it?" laughed John.

"You know how it is, everyone in Washington is so risk-averse it's a miracle anything gets done at all. So anyway, the thing quieted down when the Bureau issued a 'we'll get back to you on that' to everyone who inquired. Fortunately things heated up again in the Middle East, pushing this off the front burner. Meanwhile, we ran the figures ourselves and found about twelve percent more cases than this guy in Chicago was talking about, and that's only because we've got the raw data that comes in from the states every year. That's where we found our problem. The distribution of disappearances isn't concentrated in the South where we thought it would be. Actually, after about 1975 they weren't concentrated any more in the South than anywhere else. Also, the distribution was almost evenly divided between men and women. Before then the percentage was almost ninety percent male. So the long and the short of it is, at the top, they're worried about how it all looks, or what kind of hay will be made if the whole picture comes to light. For those of us down here in the trenches, we're worried about how a trend like this could get away from us and how it was missed for so long."

"Who at the Bureau really knows about the investigation?" John asked.

"There's only three of us besides the director and his deputy."

"Okay, here's the million dollar question . . ."

"The answer is, no. Before you even ask, the deputy did not want any of the black agents to know about the information uncovered, or the investigation. In some ways it's not that much different than it was under Hoover. Hell, you've seen the messes that Justice, ATF and the Bureau had to clean up in the past couple of decades. There's the Branch Davidians, Ruby Ridge and everything else the press has thrown back at us, pointing the finger of blame on the government. It's almost completely crippled us as a law enforcement agency. So the last thing the director wanted was one of our own running off to the press and leaking the fact that the FBI, and by extension, the current administration, isn't concerned with devastating numbers of unsolved crimes against African Americans."

"Did anyone find out who this original caller was in Chicago? Could it have been someone with a bone to pick with the FBI, or was it one of your own?" asked John.

"No, we got his name from the radio station's caller ID record. He's just a business consultant with no real political ties. He turned out to be a dead end as far as this investigation is concerned."

"And where does this leave us with the Williams investigation?"

"First of all, if she's at all connected with the larger number of disappearances then she's the freshest case we've got," began Samuels.

"Wait a minute. You sound like you've already made up your mind that these cases are related. Is that what you're really thinking?"

"You've seen the data If this were another time or place I would be looking for some kind of religious cult angle, like Jim Jones in Jonestown. But the victims left money, homes, cars, stocks, bonds, 401ks, everything behind and were never, ever seen or heard from again. We have no bodies, no wallets flushed out of any sewers, no briefcases floating to shore, nothing. It's just too clean, too perfect. This whole thing makes me check under my bed every night for boogeymen before I go to sleep. My only comfort is that I'm not black. We even kept all of the credit card accounts of the last twenty or so victims open just to see if we could trace any perp who might be killing these people, we left bank accounts open for the same reason. Not a single one was tripped. We ran surveillance of their homes, cars, vacation homes, none of them were ever so much as robbed. You would think that with a set of door keys and an address, someone would want to see if they could boost a car or home electronics. And, as for the white supremacist angle, those guys are dumber than dog shit. Someone would have spilled the beans by now, or at least tried to break into one of their homes just to steal the beer from the fridge. No matter how I look at it, nothing adds up, and it's driving me crazy."

"So, I guess the only question I have left is, why me?" asked John.

"You can keep your mouth shut, you always put the investigation first, and the other two times you worked with the Bureau you worked the case better than our own guys. I need someone I can trust, someone who doesn't have any issues with blacks and who gets results. Besides, isn't your partner black?"

"When I work with one, yeah. We get along fine, as a matter of fact his wife keeps trying to set me up with her single friends. She describes me as the 'white sheep of the family' to her girlfriends when she tries to hook me up," John answered, laughing.

"So, what I need is someone who can look at this with fresh eyes, someone who's immune to the political considerations my fellow agents seem to be saddled with," Samuels said.

"Lay your cards on the table. Who do you think is behind these disappearances? Is it some ultramilitant group without the gap-tooth, cousin-marrying, double-digit IQ baggage of the KKK?" John asked.

"No, that's the scary part, I don't know who it might be. However, almost two thousand people don't just disappear without a trace for no good reason, and I aim to find out why," Samuels said with a trace of heat.

"So where do you want me to start?"

"We need to go over the Williams girl's every step for the last few weeks and find out just where and when she disappeared. Since this is the only warm trail, insofar as it's less than a month since she was last seen, it's our best shot at finding out who or what may be behind these cases before another one happens."

John thought about it for a second or two. Just then the waitress brought their food to the table. Grateful for the break in conversation, John sat back and considered the possibility that there might be some heavy hitter behind such a long-lasting trend. None of the many serial killers he had researched in the past had ever operated over so long a time span, and no one had ever amassed anywhere near the number of people they were talking about here.

The worst example of this kind of serial murder around here was the Wayne Bertram Williams case in Atlanta, but that ended with twenty or so boys. These cases were all adults, and several were couples, not so easy to take down without a struggle. No, this was something completely different.

"How's the salad?" John asked, after a minute or two

"Not bad. Is this restaurant a hangout for cops?"

"No, it's kind of out of the way for most of the headquarters staff. But let me get back to the subject at hand. When I talked to the dean at the college she did invite me back if there was anything else I needed. I can start checking into the Williams girl's other friends and see if I can get a better picture of her schedule for the past few months. I'm going to need everything you guys can come up with, cell phone records, home phone logs, the ones that only the Feds can get. I also need the detail of her credit card transactions, not only where but what time of day they were made," John listed.

"Hey, anything you want, or can think of, just let me know. By the way, did you have any problem logging on to our system?" asked Samuels.

"No. I got on and found the files just fine. I printed off the map, since it didn't really have much in the way of identifying what it shows. It helps me think when I have something visual. If it compromises your security I can take it down and shred it."

"I don't think that's necessary. Be careful what you print off from the files though. Our system records whatever you print in a log file kept on the mainframe. Supposedly no one can access the case files and your account except the director and myself, but I wouldn't put too much stock in that. I wouldn't put it past him to have someone on the inside monitoring my progress," Samuels warned.

"Where are you going to be concentrating your efforts, if I may ask?" inquired John.

"The thing I'm really trying to get a handle on is whether or not there's some kind of inside help being given to whoever is behind these cases. I don't want to go as far as to call it a conspiracy, but damned if I can think of it as anything else if it's been going on for nearly forty years. Especially since no one twigged to the whole thing before now," replied Samuels.

"Are you back to the boogeymen thing again?"

"Hell yeah. Think of the resources it would take to snatch almost two thousand middle-class blacks off the streets of America without a trace, or any hint of who's doing it. What I want to know is why the data wasn't flagged before now. It's all sitting in the FBI's systems. It's been accumulating all these years, but it took some guy calling into a radio show to point out what's been staring us in the face for the past four decades. I can't help but wonder if there's some shadow group operating in the Department of Justice or the Bureau that keeps stuff like this from getting out, or at least holding down wider distribution. Besides, I'm trained and paid, poorly I might add, to be paranoid," Samuels finished with a laugh.

"Look, I still gotta finish up some things at the office after we're done eating. Here's my local cell phone number, it's a personal one that doesn't get reviewed by the office. Call me whenever you need something," Samuels said, pulling a business card out and jotting the number down on the back. "I'm jetting off to Chicago to check something out, I'll be back day after tomorrow. The number's national, so if you ring I'll still be able to get the call. Hey, try to stay out of trouble, I'm not sure if this investigation is going to lead to disaster or not. The last thing I need is for you to go missing. It's too much paperwork when a cop disappears, okay?"

Barking out a laugh, John put his mind to eating his pie while Samuels worked on his soup and salad. They chatted about baseball, weather, everything but the case. Samuels picked up the check saying, "I'll get it this time, I dragged you out of the house. It's the least I can do."

"Hey, thanks. When you get back I'll take you to a great Greek place I found," promised John, getting up from the table.

"You know, I forgot to ask, is this going to mess you up with your lieutenant?" Samuels asked as he pulled his jacket on.

"I don't think so. If I start catching some crap on the time I'm spending of this case I'll let you know. The only thing I can see that might change the situation is if the department gets a bunch of missing persons cases thrown at us, you know, runaways and such. That might crowd my time if I have to take up some of the slack, but until it happens let's not borrow trouble."

When they got outside and parted ways, John got into his cruiser and did something he couldn't remember ever doing since he'd joined the force: he checked the back seat for Samuels' boogeyman, swearing he'd never, ever, cop to having done so.

Leave your cares behind
Come with us and find
The pleasures of the journey to the center of your mind
Journey to the Center of Your Mind
Written and performed by The Amboy Dukes

CHAPTER 8

THE ONLY WINDOWS to the world above ground for Martin Harris were the Internet and cable television. He spent a lot of time on the Internet corresponding with colleagues, checking out other projects around the world, and sometimes even chatting online with women in an effort to maintain some sort of social life. So it wasn't any great coincidence that he ran across the University of Chicago Fellow's request for some high-speed processing help for his three-dimensional, real-time mapping programs.

Martin read the synopsis of the project and downloaded the data file information with the algorithms, and dropped them into a new folder on his workstation. He knew he had the excess capacity, and estimating the size of the sample data set this Alan Richards talked about online, he calculated that he could process the sample data in less than fifteen minutes. With the computing horsepower the military had given him for his project, it looked like he could finish the whole ten years of this positional data for the entire solar system practically overnight.

Loading his spreadsheet program, Martin constructed all of the equations Richards listed in his message. He then loaded the sample data set, parsing the columns of data for the equations, and started it calculating. While that was running, Martin sent off a message to Richards asking for additional details on his mapping program. If it really was a means of producing a three-dimensional display of the solar system, then he might be able to adapt it to be the visual display his gravity wave detector needed.

A few minutes later the computer completed processing the sample data into the refined and reduced data set Richards needed. Looking up the direct e-mail address of Alan Richards at the U of C, Martin sent the resulting data off with his own direct-dial telephone number, requesting that he and Alan discuss their projects and how they might be able to help each other out.

Once his message was safely on its way, Martin began writing a program to run a real-time analysis of Alan Richards' data set. To test the speed the system could achieve, he replicated the sample data one hundred times and linked all the files together. He started the program.

Opening another window on his computer, Martin revisited the data collected by the detector from the other day. After isolating and discarding all extraneous readings from the plotted data, he was still left with a trace showing that a gravitational anomaly had occurred in the local galactic neighborhood. If the detector's information was correct, the incident occurred well within the solar system, but because of a lack of really fine definition in the directional portion of the detector, the exact location was not possible to calculate. It looked like the detector's central crystal was not of sufficient size to triangulate anomalies as accurately as he needed.

According to Martin's subsequent calculations, he would need a crystal five times the size of the one that had been so painstakingly produced after two failures. There was no way anyone could grow a crystal like that on earth. Maybe in the weightlessness of space something that large could be grown without the stress of gravity distorting the matrix. Bigger was not going to be the answer.

All of a sudden Martin smacked his head in dismay, wondering how he could have overlooked so simple a solution to his problem. Visible light and radio astronomers had already conquered the same problem. To increase the light or radio signal received to pump up the density of the information they were interested in they didn't build bigger, they just used more mirrors or antennae.

The Very Large Array, one of the world's premier astronomical radio observatories, consists of 27 radio antennas in a Y-shaped configuration in New Mexico and could pull in signals thousands of times weaker than a single antenna. All Martin had to do was build a second detector and compare the readings between both detectors to better triangulate the location of any gravitational event.

Martin opened a blank spreadsheet window to calculate the minimum distance necessary that two detectors, operating in tandem, needed to be placed to accurately resolve the direction of any anomalies out to a distance of, say, just under fifteen light minutes. Anything further away and the data would be so old, in terms of the interval between occurrence and detection, that he wouldn't be able to do any significant real-time analysis. This increased resolution would more than satisfy the Joint Chiefs' requirements for the detection of submarines underwater and satellites in high earth orbit.

Finishing the calculations, he plugged in the conversion from wavelength to inches and saw that he could achieve the detection resolution he needed with a second detector placed just over three hundred feet away from the first.

Then the reality of the cost of what he would have to sell to the Pentagon hit him. A second detector would cost slightly less than the first; hopefully enough less that he would be able to convince the military to fund a second one. But growing another crystal in the existing tank and getting it across the complex to be mounted the necessary distance away would be impossible. None of the corridors were wide enough to allow the thirty-foot-wide disk passage. He had to disassemble the tank and reassemble it on the other side of the complex. To prepare the destination site, take the original tank apart, put it back together and monitor the growth of a new crystal, Martin figured he was already looking at around fifteen or sixteen million dollars in additional funding.

He picked up the phone and called his project's military liaison to request a meeting in Washington to discuss the breakthrough in the project. When his contact got on the phone, Martin described the detected event and explained that the concept of the detector had been validated, giving a quick overview of the incident and the resulting data. He suggested a face-to-face meeting about beefing up the locator portion of the system so that it definitely would be able to detect subs and underground installations to within a few feet.

The liaison officer was excited to hear that the detector worked as theorized and wanted Martin to fly out to Washington later that day. He told Martin he would make arrangements for a military transport to pick him up at the shelter and take him to the Colorado Springs airfield near the NORAD base in the mountain. A helicopter would pick him up from the base in a couple of hours, if Martin was sure he could wind up anything pending and get to the surface by then.

Martin assured him he would be ready in time and thanked him for getting him to DC so quickly. Hanging up the phone and sitting back in his chair, Martin began to believe he had a chance to get a second detector actually built. The officer, a lieutenant commander no less, had brushed aside all consideration of the cost of a second detector. He was only interested in the fact that the detector worked.

He copied and encrypted the various spreadsheets and notes he had been working on, along with the data and resulting plots from the detected event, burned them on to a compact disc and threw the disc in his briefcase. With only the CD, and a couple of pads of paper, his briefcase looked woefully undernourished. He added a couple of science journals to fill it out, telling himself that he would catch up on his reading during the flight east.

He remembered the data run for the Richards 3D modeling program, sat back down in front of his computer, printed the original message Richards had posted, and dropped it next to the journals in his briefcase and left his office. When he reached his room, Martin packed an overnight bag and changed into his business casual attire for the flight to Washington. He transferred his ID and access cards to his wallet, checking that he had enough cash to cover a meal or two until he could get to a cash station in DC. Locking the door behind him, he noticed he was actually excited at the prospect of getting up to the surface for the next couple of days.

At the bottom of the long elevator shaft, Martin once again marveled at the feat of engineering that had gone into the construction of the unique conveyance. The shaft itself was not a straight shot to the surface; if you looked from the bottom to the top, the view was obstructed by several bends in the path the car traveled up and down.

The car itself was the size of a small alpine gondola. It measured about eight feet by twelve, had benches along the walls and rode on wheels attached to the top and bottom of the car itself. Its speed wasn't spectacular; the trip from top to bottom took about twenty-five minutes and the trip back up added about ten minutes more to that.

The entire system was designed to get large numbers of people into the shelter as fast as possible. The bends in the shaft were designed to prevent a shockwave from surface detonation of a conventional or nuclear weapon from having a straight shot down the shaft. The bends had airflow disruptors that slowed and roiled the air in both directions, helping prevent overpressure from blowing out the doors and damaging the installation below.

Normally the car was kept at the bottom of the shaft to facilitate quick evacuation in case of an accident, and when Martin got to the elevator its doors were opened and the car was empty. He dropped his bags on a bench next to the door. He had mixed feelings about riding up and down alone. The time before the doors closed and the car began its trip always seemed like his last chance to bolt to safety, or freedom.

Martin closed his eyes as the car began the thirty-five-minute trip to the surface. He knew that the interior of the car was monitored by camera and microphone from the security office topside. This was something he found out once when he had sung a bunch of classic rock songs at the top of his lungs for practically the whole trip up. When the doors opened topside he had been treated to a standing ovation for his performance by about ten of the soldiers who manned the various offices in the compound. He took the ovation good-naturedly, gave them several bows and opened and closed the car doors to simulate several curtain calls before he finally exited the car red-faced in embarrassment. On his way past the security checkpoint, he asked the head of security if he would please erase any recordings of his performance, but was kindly rebuffed as the guard told him that his singing was going to be forever enshrined in the base's performance hall of fame.

Half an hour later, Martin opened his eyes and sat up. He felt the car slowing at the top of the shaft. He stood and grabbed his two bags as the sharp click signaled that the car was locked in place. The doors opened and he walked down the hallway to the security checkpoint to sign out. As he drew even with the wide window, he nodded to the soldier on duty who asked him, straight-faced, "What, no songs this trip, doc?"

"Thanks a bunch, Corporal. It's bad enough I didn't know you guys tape everything that goes on in there, but to not have the opportunity for any postproduction remixing, what'd'ya expect?" laughed Martin as he signed his name.

"I suppose so. At least knowing that the cameras are out there keeps you on your best behavior! When do you think you'll be returning, sir?" asked the guard. "It doesn't say on the routing orders for the chopper."

"I think it shouldn't be more than a day or so. Hey, you want anything from DC?"

"How 'bout a bunch of girls to keep us company?"

"Just as long as I get a copy of those tapes. Hey, have you caught anyone knocking off a piece in the elevator?" Martin inquired.

The guard smiled and replied, "I really couldn't say. Have a nice flight, Doctor."

"Thanks, I will."

Martin pulled his sunglasses out of his breast pocket and put them on against the brightness of the day. Walking down to the helipad, Martin was surprised to see a fully combat-configured Blackhawk waiting for him. He had expected one of the Bell Jetrangers that were stationed all over the United States by all branches of the military.

A flight-suited lieutenant jumped out of the side door and approached him, looking at a faxed picture he held in his hand. Satisfied with the identification, he stuck out his hand and said, "Dr. Harris, I'm Lieutenant Stillson and I'll be your flight engineer to the mountain today. Do you have any other bags that have to be fetched from inside?"

"No, everything I've got is in these two bags. Why the big guns? Is there something wrong that I should know about?" Martin asked, a little worried.

"No, sir. We were the fastest transportation into the area. We were dispatched to make sure that you wouldn't miss your connection in Colorado Springs, besides, it's much better than driving! Here, let me stow that for you sir. Is there anything you need to get out before I tie it down?" the lieutenant asked, heaving both bags into the side door of the menacing aircraft.

"I don't think so. I'm pretty psyched to be traveling in this thing. You know, I've seen them on TV or at air shows, but I never really thought I would be a passenger in one."

Making sure Martin climbed inside safely and after securing the door, the Lieutenant secured Matin's bags.

"Sir, if you just sit down over there, you'll be able to look out the side window and see a little bit out the front windows too. Please fasten the seatbelt and pull it tight, and don't unbuckle unless I give you the word."

Martin complied. The engineer checked the snugness of the belt, reached over his right shoulder and handed him a set of headphones with a boom microphone attached.

Pulling one earpiece away from his head and pointing to a in-line switch on the cable, the engineer spoke over the rotor engine noise, "If you want to say anything to me in flight just push down on the rocker switch here and speak, got it?"

Martin nodded and felt a momentary lightening of his body before it was pushed back down as the helicopter took off. Looking out the side window, he was treated to a circular fly-by of the compound before heading off toward the east. As the Blackhawk gained altitude and speed the vibration and noise somewhat abated. He heard a click in his headphones and a voice in the middle of his head said, "Welcome aboard, Dr. Harris, I'm Captain Simpson, along with my copilot Captain Christopher. We plan to have you in Colorado Springs in plenty of time to make your flight. You are booked on a military transport so there will be no security check-in lines or any of that other nonsense. If you have any questions press the talk switch and speak normally."

Martin pushed the switch and said, "Thank you very much for the lift, I don't know why I drew you guys, but this is about the best ride I've ever taken."

"If there's anything you need Lieutenant Stillson will be able to assist you, he'll even show you how the troops go to the can back there sir."

Martin nodded his overweight head and looked back at the flight engineer to see him pointing to a large can on the floor. Laughing, Martin shook his head and went back to watching the ground pass beneath them.

After about an hour, Martin heard the click signaling someone about to speak.

"Dr. Harris, we have been rerouted to Boulder. You're to pick up your ride there, it cuts about a half hour off the trip and I know my butt would appreciate a break, it always does. Do you have any questions, sir?"

"Am I still going via military flight or am I going to have to transfer to a commercial carrier?" asked Martin.

"You're still with us, sir. We're to see you to the door of one of our troop transports. They have you booked on one of the transports used for military dependents, your pass is being transmitted as we speak, sir," replied Captain Simpson.

All this "sir"ing was making Martin nervous, but his voice sounded fairly normal in his ears as he said, "That'll be fine, captain, just let me know if we're going to see any combat, I'll have to get my baseball cap out of my bag if anything serious breaks out." He heard the pilot laugh in reply

About forty-five minutes later, Martin saw the outskirts of a large city and when the Blackhawk began to drop lower he realized that off to the left was the Boulder airport. The Blackhawk approached from behind the one-story building that served as the staging area for the military passengers and translated in a tight one-eighty before setting down with hardly a bump. Crouching at the door handle Lieutenant Stillson held up his hand, palm out, indicating that Martin should stay seated. At some signal that Martin couldn't see Stillson pulled back the huge sliding door and jumped down with two sets of wheel blocks in hand.

Moments later, Stillson jumped back in and plugged his headset back into the system and announced to Martin, "We're not going to shut the engines off, we're going to lift off and go get refueled right away. What I'm going to do is grab your luggage and escort you to the terminal and see that you get on the transport. What I want you to do is to unstrap and wait until I'm on the ground before you get up and exit, got it?"

Martin gave him a thumbs up and was startled when a hand clapped him on the shoulder. Captain Christopher had gotten up to make sure he would stay put until called for. Stillson unstrapped Martin's two bags and dropped to the ground. Captain Christopher removed Martin's headset, hung it back up and directed him to the door. Speaking directly into his ear over the noise of the rotors Christopher said, "There's not much danger from the blades while they're idling but humor me and duck until you get to that yellow line on the tarmac, okay, sir?"

Martin gave him a thumbs up and stuck out his hand to the copilot. Shaking his hand and handing him out at the same time, Christopher made sure that their human cargo made it to the ground safely and then gave a wave goodbye. Stillson indicated that Martin was to precede him off the landing pad and brought up the rear-carrying one of Martin's bags in each hand. Reaching the yellow safety line Martin straightened up and looked back at his unexpected transport, smiling.

In the small terminal, Stillson handed Martin his two bags and told him to wait just inside the door. Stillson saluted a major sitting behind a desk and began talking in a low voice. The major cut Martin a glance, picked up an envelope from the desk and gave it to the lieutenant. Saluting again, Stillson did an about-face and returned to Martin, handing him the envelope.

"Here's your travel papers. They held up the flight for you, it was supposed to take off twenty minutes ago. Follow me."

Stillson and Martin walked in the direction of a rolling stairway parked against a Boeing 727 adorned with Army markings. Stillson bounded up the stairs two at a time and saluted the major waiting just inside the door, "Here's your VIP, sir, sorry we were late. This is Dr. Martin Harris and he has a meeting with the Joint Chiefs this afternoon."

Taking a look past what would have been the divider between coach and first class in a commercial flight, Martin was dismayed to see that the plane was practically filled. The entire flight had been held up just to wait for his arrival. He began to wonder if someone had made a big mistake about just how important he was. He had heard Stillson tell the major that he was meeting with a representative of the Joint Chiefs of Staff, but knowing that his project was in the preliminary stages of usefulness to the military didn't seem to jibe with the VIP treatment. Maybe this was just how the military got things done.

Sitting back in his first-class-sized seat, Martin closed his eyes to rest and was surprised to see when he opened them again that the plane was at cruising altitude. I must have dropped off, he thought. He began to organize the presentation for the Joint Chiefs in his head.

He planned to lead off with the data proving that the detector was working, first the data from the sun, then the local incident. Then he would segue into discussing the need for increased resolution of the detector in order to be able to better chart distance and bearing of gravitational changes. Then he would discuss the ability to focus the scanner so that it could be panned through the oceans, underground and through high earth orbit. And if he had time, he also wanted to see if he could bring this Alan Richards at the University of Chicago in on the development of the detector display system a little later on. That was, if this guy could pass the security check they would be sure to run on him.

Before he knew it, they were on final approach to the airstrip and the pilot gentled the jet in with hardly a bump. Martin pulled the travel documents from his pocket and opened the envelope. Inside were orders for him to get to the Pentagon by the quickest means possible, listing him as a consultant currently under contract to the Joint Chiefs weapons research division. The additional paperwork included routing orders permitting him to hitch a ride on any military transportation that could get him to the Pentagon soonest.

Not bad, he thought. As he collected his bags, lined up waiting for the stairway to be brought to the plane, a sergeant squeezed up the aisle and stopped beside him. "If you will wait at the bottom of the stairs I'll call for a car to take you to the Pentagon, sir," she said.

"Do you think that's going to be all right with everyone?" he asked.

"Your travel orders do say to get you to the Pentagon soonest, sir. That's almost enough to get you another helicopter ride, if you know what I mean," she replied.

"Does everyone know where I'm going and what I'm supposed to be doing?" Martin asked.

"Do you think a forty-thousand-dollar-an-hour military transport waits on the ground with engines running on the say-so of a chopper pilot an hour or so away? I hate to burst your bubble but someone out there, someone with plenty of juice, wants to hear whatever it is you have to say. Here's the stairs. You can just wait in your seat until the passengers disembark, or wait for me at the foot of the stairs if you want to stretch your legs. But don't wander away too far because you're really not supposed to leave the plane unescorted. You're supposed to be handed off personally from transport to transport. Officially speaking, you are under my care right now and I'm not supposed to let you out of my sight until your car gets here, sir."

Sitting back down, Martin was able to watch as the other passengers passed him in the aisle, and then again as they reached the bottom of the stairs. As the last few stragglers were passing by, he saw an Army sedan pull up next to the plane and watched as the driver got out and stood waiting at the bottom of the steps. Just then the Sergeant came back to his seat and picked up his overnight bag.

"Ready, sir?" she asked.

"Absolutely. I can carry my own bag, you know."

"Oh it's no problem, we carry much heavier on march," she answered.

She preceded him down the steps and introduced Martin to the waiting driver.

"Here's your VIP, Corporal. His name is Dr. Martin Harris and his appointment is listed as 'soonest,'" she said.

"Yes Sergeant." he replied. Reaching for Martin's bag, he said, "This way, sir."

Forty-five minutes later they were pulling into the main gate of the Pentagon. The driver handed his clipboard to the entrance guard, who opened the back door and asked Martin if he had any identification he could show him. Martin extracted his driver's license and the ID card issued at Shelter Fourteen.

The guard made a quick phone call and came back out to the car and said, "Thank you, sir. Here's your identification. The driver will escort you to your appointment." He then closed the door and waved the car into the parking lot.

Inside the world's largest building, he was awed by the sheer amount of humanity that this imposing structure housed, and further struck by the fact that the entire purpose of this structure was the management of the United States military.

Soon Martin sat in Lieutenant Commander Ames' outer office; he was surprised by how ordinary it looked. Not much to suggest it was manned by an officer instead of a civilian, maybe a little neater than your average business; a lot neater than your average scientist, he thought ruefully.

When the inner door opened Martin scrambled to his feet to finally meet the liaison officer with whom he had only spoken over the telephone. In stepped a black man around thirty, trim and with an intelligent-looking face. Accepting the firm handshake of Commander Ames, Martin said, "It's a pleasure to meet you after all of these months. I'm forever grateful to the Navy to allow me to pursue my dream project."

"Not at all, Dr. Harris, it is we who should be thanking you. Besides the military applications of your detector, the advancement in the understanding of the fundamental forces of physics would be justification enough for seeing this project through," Ames replied. "Come on in and have a seat. Can I get you coffee or something else to drink?"

"No thank you, your aide already asked."

"Well then, is there anything you need for the presentation? I can have a flip chart or whatever else you might need brought in."

"Do you have a conference room that has a projector hooked up to a PC? That way I can show you everything I brought with me."

"Let's go down the hall. We can set up there. Beside, if anyone else wants in on your show it'll hold more of us comfortably."

Commander Ames informed his aide he would be in the conference room for the next hour or so. Reaching the well-appointed room, Ames motioned Martin over to the computer on a small desk in the corner so he could get started. Once the PC had booted, Martin loaded his CD-ROM, entered his password for the files, opened up his first chart and began.

"Commander, this chart represents the earth's local gravitational field over time. This sharp blip shows a disturbance in the local gravitational field of the earth. Something within earth's neighborhood caused several ripples in the gravity field over a period of just under fifteen minutes. This trace does not reflect the gravity of the moon or any other astronomical body. Their effects have been filtered out to just show the strength of this incident right here. By comparison, here is a chart of the gravitational field of the sun. You'll see that although the magnitude is far greater than that of the incident shown in the first chart, the change in the sun's field is a rhythmic pulse that is quite steady. None of the measurements of the sun, or any other body, have ever shown this kind of sharply defined episode."

"Let me ask you this," asked Ames. "How certain are you that the reading on your first chart wasn't the result of detector error or faulty electronics or such?"

"I ran diagnostics on the entire system; the last thing I wanted was some sort of false positive to send me off on a wild goose chase. What made me as certain as I am is that all three detector circuits recorded the same event at the same time. As you know the circuits are on separate power supplies and share nothing in common other than their connection to the crystal itself. And, since there's never been an event like this recorded before, I'm sure that the crystal itself is stable. It's not prone to flexing or any kind of tick or pop that matter exhibits with changes in temperature, or when stressed. This slide shows all three of the detector's readings for the period in question. They all show deflection at the same time, although the difference in amplitude, though small, does show that they are not identical in performance. This is the result of the minute differences in the electronics, microchanges in voltage over time and various instabilities that are largely unavoidable. Given the overall readings though, the tiny anomalies can largely be ignored.

"This slide shows my attempt to focus on the location of the incident in three dimensions. This curve over here is a representation of the surface of the earth based on the center point of the earth's interior, the focal point of the earth's gravitational field. This large blob is the estimated location of the event and looks to almost intersect the surface of the earth. Unfortunately this illustrates the lack of resolution in the locator portion of the detector system; the size of the crystal limits the resolution of the detector," Martin said, pausing to see if Commander Ames had any questions.

"So let me sum up," began Ames. "According to the data gathered a couple of days ago, it appears that the system works for locating changes in the local gravitational field of earth. The system detected an incident where the local gravity field of earth was affected by something, but you don't know what. However, in order for the detector to be able to achieve the resolution necessary to locate in space the exact position of any incident that occurs, you need a more powerful detector. And, if I may extrapolate, in order to be able to focus the detector closely enough to be able to locate changes in gravitational field density to be useful in locating subs, installations buried underground or objects in space, the detector has to be larger and more powerful. Is that about right?"

"Yes, sir. What I have here, " Martin said as he cleared the screen and loaded some more charts, "are the calculations I worked out to determine the minimum size of detector needed to do the job. Looking at the formula here, the result shows that to achieve a resolution down to about two meters we're going to need a detector about five times the size of the current one. This is clearly impossible to achieve, there's no way to grow a crystal of that size on earth."

"Are you seriously suggesting that the project be moved into space?" asked Ames.

"Not at all," said Martin with a laugh. "The cost of doing so can't be calculated, nor do we have the space-based capability to construct something like this with current technologies. My idea is much simpler. This next set of calculations shows the resulting resolution if we build a second detector and place it about three hundred feet from the first one."

"Oh, now that's brilliant! Why the hell didn't I think of that?"

"I said the same thing when I did the initial calculations. The Very Large Array in New Mexico gave me the idea."

"What would it do to the accuracy of the entire system if you have a bunch of these things spread around the country, doctor?" the Commander asked.

"It would help increase resolution, but the problem then becomes the synchronization of the data stream. Locating changes in density of local gravity in three dimensions is dependent on the simultaneous acquisition and triangulation of data. Even leased lines change the timing of the acquisition of digital data if the detector is far enough away. What I would like to do is see if I can get the authorization, and the necessary funding, to tear down the original growth tank and reassemble it on the far side if the shelter. Then, we build a second detector to achieve the resolution we need. Here's my estimate of the cost of doing so in this spreadsheet," said Martin pulling up his calculations.

"Around two-thirds the cost of the original, I see."

"Yes, we achieve a smattering of savings from not having to completely start the installation from scratch, the rest of the savings are in reusing the equipment left behind from the original growth tank. The detector electronics are easy to duplicate and the computer that does real-time analysis can easily accept the additional data channels."

Looking at the screen the commander said, "Print that out right now and I'll pass it on. Can you leave that disc behind?"

"Sure, I'll write down the password for the files."

"And can you hang around for a few hours in the event anyone else wants to take a crack at you?" Ames asked with a grin.

"Commander, I'm at your disposal. If there's a cafeteria nearby I'll get a quick bite to eat and await word from you. I did bring some journals from the lab I can read, or if there's a computer connected to the Internet I can catch up on some of my work. Oh, that reminds me, " Martin said pulling the message from Alan Richards from his briefcase. "This guy may have already developed a three-dimensional mapping program that can holographically display relative positions of objects in space. Not just in outer space, but any three-dimensional space. His data is based on planetary bodies and includes a real-time motion component that might be the principal graphics engine I could adapt for the detector. Using what he already seems to have might help us avoid reinventing the wheel in the development of the display subsystem."

"Does he have clearance from any of the services?" asked Ames.

"I have no idea. I only saw the message in the news group and ran the sample data set he uploaded in his request for computer time. I do know that he's at the University of Chicago and it looks like he's a student. Anything else I was going to leave to you on how to proceed."

"Very well, leave me that message and I'll have someone make some preliminary calls," Ames said as he walked over to the computer. Holding out his hand for the CD-ROM and the message Martin had pulled from his briefcase, he gathered everything and left the room with Martin in tow.

Later that afternoon in the Pentagon cafeteria, Martin looked up to see a marine approaching his table.

"Dr. Harris?" he asked.

"Yes, can I help you?" Martin replied.

"If you would come with me, sir."

The Marine escorted Martin around the bend of one of the vertices that helped give the great building its name to a huge conference room and told him, "Please have a seat, sir, the others will be here shortly." He then stationed himself to the side of the conference room door, looking straight ahead. Martin marveled at how these guys could blend into the background so well it was like they had their own special form of indoor camouflage.

Moments later the door opened and the Marine straightened to attention. Through the door came Lieutenant Commander Ames, a couple of military aides and one officer with dozens of ribbons on his chest. Looking more closely, Martin saw two stars on each of his shoulders; this guy was an admiral. Martin got to his feet and waited until the admiral was seated before resuming his seat.

Lieutenant Commander Ames stood at the head of the table and began the meeting.

"Gentlemen, this is Dr. Martin Harris, he is in charge of the gravity detection project we've been funding for the last couple of years. All of us here know the strategic importance of holding the high ground in any tactical situation, and this definitely fits the bill. Being able to track submarines or stealth satellites from earth without having to launch corresponding surveillance craft reduces the resources needed on our side. As you know, this detection technology will allow us to locate underground bunkers and laboratories as well. Imagine how the search of the hills of Afghanistan would have been simplified had this technology been mature back then. I'm going to turn the meeting over Dr. Harris now. Dr. Harris?" Walking around the table, Commander Ames passed out folders with copies of the information Martin had brought.

Martin explained how building and using a second detector would improve the accuracy of the system in locating anomalies in three dimensions. He gave the cost benefits and detailed how building the second detector would cost far less than the first because the initial research and development costs would not have to be allocated again.

"Okay, Doctor. How long would it take for you to be able to duplicate the detector you already have?" asked the admiral.

"Well sir, it looks like it can be done in about eight or nine weeks. That's assuming that we can use the first crystal out of the tank. I have some ideas on improving the growing system that should yield a purer, flawless crystal using shaped magnetic fields the first time out of the tank. These modifications won't add any additional construction time to the project either," Martin said.

Turning to an ensign who was obviously his aide, the admiral asked, "Is there any problem with getting the original crew back working on this thing?" This question immediately got Martin excited because it appeared the admiral had already decided to go ahead with the addition.

"I don't see why not, sir. Most of the personnel we used in the initial project are still in the service and could be redeployed over the next two weeks. The engineers could be there by the end of the week to begin building out the second lab and disassembling the tank. The only thing logistics has to do is ship out the additional consumables for the crew and whatever construction materials are needed for the lab. Doctor, are there any additional electronics, computers, et cetera, that you might be needing? And will you require additional full-time staff once the second detector is on line?"

"Gentlemen, I could always use an extra hand or two. It would help if you could assign an electronics engineering team, at least for the first few months. I have a couple of ideas on cooling the interface between the crystal and the pickup down to superconducting temperatures to increase electronic stability and I'm on somewhat shaky ground in the low-temp studies. If I had some EEs who could help out in that area it will greatly move things along."

"Very well," said the admiral. Turning again to his aide he said, "Check with the advanced weapons group on this low-temp thing. They had a huge crew working on the rail-gun project and if I recall the entire launch system was a huge superconducting magnet." The admiral turned back to Martin while his aide scribbled almost a page full of notes.

"Anything else, doctor? If you don't ask, we can't fetch it along for you," the admiral asked.

"I don't think so sir. If it's all right with all of you, I'd like to get back to the lab as soon as possible to prepare a comprehensive materials and manpower list and e-mail it to the commander. Once I'm back there I'll be able to get a better idea of exactly what we'll need," answered Martin.

"Fine," said the admiral, getting to his feet. "Good work, Dr. Harris. It's always gratifying to get into a research project that actually pans out. Commander, a word with you before you leave for the day."

"Yes sir," said Ames as the admiral turned to leave the room. "I'll be there within the hour, sir."

The Marine snapped to attention and opened the door for the admiral and his aides and left the room closing the door behind him.

"Okay, Doctor," he began, "this project has just taken a bump in importance, and unfortunately for you, a bump in security. I'm going to have to ask you to sign additional papers that detail some new restrictions on your communications and discussions about what you're working on. They're not much more than common sense, if you have any questions about what you're going to sign just ask. I'll have the Marine escort you back to the conference room near my office, my aide will have the paperwork for you to look over in a few minutes."

"No problem, Commander," Martin replied.

"I'll see you shortly. Oh, did you have any other appointments for the evening?"

"Nope, I was hustled here so quickly I didn't have time to call anyone for dinner or anything else."

"Dinner's no problem, if you want to we can run into town for some good old down-home cooking. That is if you like soul food. It'll even be on me!" Ames offered.

Martin perked up and said, "That would be great. I've never really spent much time here the few times I flew in before the project started."

They both left the room, with the Marine directing Martin to follow him down the hall to smaller conference room.

Martin saw that the lieutenant commander's aide was already inside, holding a folder from which she extracted a sheaf of papers for him to sign. After he glanced over the papers and signed where indicated, the aide left the room just as Ames walked in, looking excited.

"Well, the admiral bought into the whole thing," he said to Martin. "And he wants me to go back with you so that I can help evaluate the site for the second lab and the accommodations for the construction crew and technicians."

"That's great," said Martin. "When are we heading back?"

"I'm thinking first thing in the morning. That way I can wind up a few things before we leave town. Still up for dinner?"

"That's fine. What about the guy at the University of Chicago?" Martin asked.

"I've got someone looking into that already. I really can't say until he's checked out, and I'm not really sure that it's in the best interest of the project to have a pretty important part of the program developed off campus, so to speak."

"I see. Well then, I guess the only question I have is, where do you want to eat?"

"Give me ten minutes and I'll be back to take you into town," Ames said, turning to walk out the door.

You got no money, you got no home
Spinning wheel, all alone
Talkin' 'bout your troubles and you never learn
Ride a painted pony let the spinning wheel turn

Spinning Wheel

Written by David Clayton-Thomas, performed by Blood, Sweat and Tears

CHAPTER 9

THE INQUIRIES THAT Middle East analyst Robert Bascomb had sent out started an entire machine of investigative assets overseas churning. US and British intelligence sources, once they read the summary of what Bascomb wanted, were equally capable of figuring out what kind of information he was after. What kind of aircraft was shot down in the area around the huge burn mark in the Iraqi countryside, and who did it belong to?

It took two days for one of the CIA's own in-country assets to get to the area and secure about half a kilo of metal fragments and debris from the crash site. It only took two additional days to get it flown back to Langley for analysis. Unfortunately the fragments of what was assumed to be the outer skin of the aircraft were too small to extrapolate the size or shape of the airframe. The pieces of what appeared to be electronics were not the recognizable work of any known commercial or industrial fabricator.

The substrate of the boards on which the electronic components were mounted was made of a composite that hadn't been seen before, and devices that performed the same function as transistors and microchips were built with a glass underlayer. All these products were familiar enough in construction that the tech could figure their purpose, but the construction and materials used to make them were largely new to everyone. They performed their functions better, with less heat, using less current and were better isolated and insulated than the same components manufactured in the known industrial world. Everything looked like parts from some kind of advanced prototype technology built just a few years into the future.

The more information Bascomb accumulated on the aircraft, the more perplexed he became. Spooks don't believe in time travel, they don't believe in men from outer space, despite whatever they have in Area 51, and they absolutely hate an unsolved mystery. He had personally visited the lab. He saw firsthand the excitement of the scientists over the properties of the alloy. Their methods, though a magnitude more comprehensive than those used by the Iraqi scientists, yielded the same results: high heat tolerance, very smooth at the microscopic level, and virtually puncture-proof.

At this point, the only thing more important to Bascomb than ultimately finding the origin of the aircraft was getting hold of the pilot's remains for DNA and other testing. Rumor was that the only portion of the remains the Iraqis recovered was a leg or foot. Since most of the Western countries took footprints of newborns, Bascomb was hoping that if it actually was a foot, a match of the footprint might possibly lead to the owner. Longer shots than that had panned out in the past. Sometimes there was no better investigative technique than wading through thousands of fingerprints to identify a dead body or perpetrator.

At the all-hands departmental meeting Bascomb called, the discussion eventually centered around the recovery of the wreckage and remains from the secret lab into which they had disappeared. For analysts who worked from comfortable offices, safe in the bosom of the United States of America, the complexity or danger of the actions they put in motion sometimes didn't fully register. For the most part the long-term consideration in the squandering of foreign assets for the sake of immediate, short-term gain was the battle constantly waged between analysts and the operations group. Bascomb's group wanted to find the secret lab and send out a raiding party to recover as much of the wreckage and remains as possible, period.

The first part of the problem was solved by going back into the database of satellite images taken over the area near the site following the crash. They were looking for any trucks entering the area of the tiny local lab, then following them back to the Baghdad area to see where they may have stopped and unloaded. This was routine work normally completed in-house. The second part of the problem was to get a ground level view of the probable laboratory site, locate the entrance and get in and out safely. This was the part that required the utmost planning and flawless execution. This was the expensive part, both in time and people.

Over the next two days photo-recon specialists studied satellite photos of every vehicle that had entered the target area and their destinations. They entered the routes and times into one master database that was able to display real-time tracking of the four trucks that might be involved in the transportation of the wreckage. When they were done, the map was uploaded to Bascomb's group and pored over until the group had satisfied themselves that they had the right truck and its destination spotted. Then it was operations' turn.

In the next day's security briefing for the Joint Chiefs and the White House, the director of the CIA brought to the attention of the group his analyst's belief that there was a new player in the Middle East. And furthermore, said player had access to technology far more advanced than anything the West was currently producing. This brought a shocked silence to the group for a few seconds while the implications sank in. Then everyone began to speak at once. Holding up his hand for silence, White House Chief of Staff Simon Masters waited for them to all quiet down and asked the director, "Could you elaborate on this startling news and bring us all up to date? Are we looking at a threat to the stability in the area, or is it something bigger?"

The director replied, "Here's what we have so far. About two weeks ago a missile defense crew along the northern border of the no-fly zone in Iraq shot down an aircraft that strayed over the line. The intruder exhibited unusual flight characteristics just before they fired a salvo of two missiles, practically destroying it in midair. The next morning the local militia was dispatched to recover enough of the wreckage to prove Western incursion into their airspace. They recovered parts of the aircraft and remains of the pilot. When they were examined by the local military, the report sparked something in Baghdad that made them send a courier to pick up all of the pieces along with the remains. Subsequent to this revelation we dispatched ground assets to the crash site, which we located through satellite reconnaissance. Imaging of the area showed the burn mark from the crash about fifteen kilometers from the missile emplacement. Pieces of metal from the area were returned to the states for analysis, unfortunately we recovered no pilot remains.

"The metal is an unknown alloy that's more heat resistant than anything we've been able to produce to date. Electronic components are of a design more advanced than anything even on the drawing board here. And, not a single bit recovered has any marking that identifies the country of origin.

"The final piece of this puzzle is that we have a fairly good guess where the wreckage and the pilot remains are being studied. It is the recommendation of the Middle Eastern group, and the entire laboratory staff, that we make a serious effort to recover as much of the wreckage as possible. Additionally, if the remains of the pilot actually consist of a limb of some sort, its recovery would enable us to try to determine his country of origin so that we can begin to backtrack the source of this technology. In a nutshell, that's it."

Air Force immediately spoke up. "None of our allies have lost anything in the area and all of our birds are accounted for. If this is something new, we need an immediate analysis of the level of threat the owners of this aircraft present to us."

NSA chimed in, "I concur with the Agency and Air Force, getting our hands on as much of the wreckage as possible in order to secure this technology would be my top priority as well."

Chief of Staff Masters asked the director, "Where does ops stand on the subject of a covert invasion and acquisition of the samples at the laboratory over there?"

"I would like to task a covert unit to plan an operation so we can get a handle on the level of exposure it represents. Invading Iraq isn't something to be taken lightly, we've got no one to support us in the area. If we plan our insertion from Turkey, that's a hell of a lot of ground to cover from the border to Baghdad, and operating so close to Baghdad yields a declining assessment of success at less than fifty percent. What I would like to do is get everyone in on planning the logistics, and see what we can come up with. The chances of this turning into one big cluster fuck are almost certain. If it weren't for the upside, I wouldn't even suggest wasting our time. But so far, the reports from our lab scare the hell out of me, they haven't even begun to figure out how the alloy was manufactured. Building a space shuttle out of this stuff would eliminate the need for the thousands of tiles it uses for a heat shield, practically ensuring us against a repeat of the Columbia disintegration on reentry. Also, fighters covered in this stuff would be totally bulletproof." Looking over at Navy, the director continued. "And, we haven't even looked into the implications for building a sub out of this stuff, how much further down could we cruise using it as a hull?"

"Who else knows about this?" asked the chief of staff.

"The British gave us about half of the intel surrounding the downing of the aircraft, and it was their agent who completed the recovery of the metal fragments we've been studying. It's a no-brainer that a second set of samples are in England right now. Since they have more feet on the ground over there, it might be a good idea to see what they can come up with around the Baghdad lab. I won't lie to you, I really want this stuff just for us, but they are an ally and they may have the only chance at getting in and out of that lab safely."

"Who's going to be lead on the invasion plan?" asked the chief of staff.

The Army, Marines and Navy all looked at CIA and nodded.

"I think the manner of insertion and extraction are going to dictate who gets the call," said Navy.

Army added, "If we want quick and dirty, a high-altitude, low-open air drop insertion just might be the best bet. However, other than making sure our guys get back safely, we all realize that the recovery of this technology is job one. I'm sure we'll be able to bypass the usual intramural competition with this one."

"That would be a welcome change from the usual dick-waving contest you're all so fond of having. If what the director says is even partially true, we may not be the biggest dick on the block any longer. That's a report I don't want to have to bring back to the president when he returns from Camp David, let alone be responsible for reporting to the congress or the American people. If this thing was a prototype, then we need to locate its source. If it's someone who has manufacturing capability we don't know about, someone who has been able to keep such a low profile that none of you have even caught a whiff of them until now, then that's just as much of a concern as their apparent lead in technology," said the chief of staff. "I want all of you to get together and have a preliminary operations plan for the president by four o'clock this afternoon, that's sixteen hundred hours for those of you who can't tell regular time anymore. Is there anything else, gentlemen?"

"Nothing that won't wait, sir," suggested Air Force.

"Okay everyone, until four o'clock," finished Masters.

The chiefs and the director hashed out which of their staff would sit in on the interdisciplinary group, then each went back to notify their staff. Naturally, the director appointed Bascomb as the leader of the team.

Later that afternoon the director traveled to the White House to brief the president immediately upon his return to the capital. He carried with him the satellite photos and all of the information Bascomb had been able to gather on the incident. He also carried the terse, three-page report summarizing the need for an invasion plan.

Inside the Oval Office, he noticed the director of the NSA was also attending the meeting. President James Bender, his chief and the director were all sitting down around the coffee table.

The chief began. "I brought the president up to speed on the preliminary report you gave this morning and I gave him the details of the technology we've recovered already. What did ops come up with on getting the rest of the wreckage?"

"Well sir, the planning group for this operation, now code named "Goldmine," has come up with this summary," he said, as he passed out copies to everyone. "The initial take is not good. Even if we could get a unit to Baghdad, and if they stayed undiscovered, if they could get in and out of the lab unobserved, and if they could haul the wreckage and remains far enough away from the city to be safely extracted, there's practically no way we can get air transport in and out without being compromised."

Looking over the operations summary, NSA said, "This shoots the hell out of my idea to get one of our top guys in there undercover."

"I doubt that we can get a special ops unit in and out safely, let alone specialists or support staff. I put in a call to British Special Air Services to see if they had anyone in-country who could help us out, but I suspect they've no better assets in the area than we do. They've got intelligence people on the ground, but no one with SAS training or even combat-qualified. They'll assist in any way they can. As for ground support for what amounts to an invasion, they can't help us out," the director said.

The president asked, "Just what level of threat does this technology represent to stability in the region, and, ultimately, to our national security?"

"The lab reports suggest that this craft represents research off the radar at even our best facilities. The metal alloy can't be duplicated by any known technique, and work on the electronics isn't faring much better. Somehow someone has managed to dope common glass with additional semiconductive compounds so that it outperforms anything we've ever seen, or are even close to achieving. I sent a couple of pieces to the lab in Area 51 to compare against anything they've worked with, but in the twenty-four hours they've had the samples I've received no report from them yet."

"What about the pilot's remains?" asked the president.

"The best we've been able to glean from the information we have at hand is that there was a lower limb recovered from the crash site. There was a single notation that the pilot was black, but this is not confirmed," replied the director.

"Well, can't we pin down his identity from a footprint?" asked the chief of staff.

"Sure. If his footprint was taken at birth as we do here in the US, and if we can locate his country of origin, and if it really was a foot that they recovered. Unfortunately, the probability of that single piece of information being correct can't be accurately calculated," answered the director. "For all we know the pilot could be an albino pygmy as long as the report is without attribution. If we can get our hands on a sample of the pilot's tissue, we can do a DNA workup and get some kind of idea of his or her genetic makeup. Even though it's a crapshoot, we can run the DNA sequence result through the FBI database on the remote chance that the owner is on file. And, if not, we have enough representatives of the world's races on file to get some idea of the genetic origin of the pilot, maybe even an idea of what he looked like."

The president spoke up again, "I'm very concerned about the fact that someone we don't know about is operating in the region. The last thing I need to worry about is anyone challenging us over there. We should draw up contingency plans on how to fit any new player into our strategic planning in the area, and pray to God that they aren't aligned with any extremists or fundamentalists.

"So what do we do now? The consensus here suggests we're going to launch a covert invasion of Iraq to recover as much of this wreckage as possible on the off chance that we'll be able to locate the source of the aircraft and the technology it represents. Does that about sum it up, gentlemen?" the president asked.

The others looked around, none wanting to admit that they were advocating the invasion of a sovereign nation, despite the fact that it was a nation the US waged an all but undeclared war on for the past two decades.

"Well?" prompted the president in the ensuing silence.

"Yes sir, that's about it," replied the director.

"What do you think?" the president directed at NSA. "Is it going to be worth the time, trouble, and possible exposure to obtain this technology? And, once we've gotten our hands on it, can we duplicate it in any reasonable amount of time? And, what kind of contingency have you developed in case we end up having to confront the original owners of this craft? Do we have the nads to pull off a snatch and grab, and make it stick?"

"Mr. President, the United States of America is still, hands down, the most powerful nation in the world. Yes, this new technology is considerable, but how much of it exists? If the builders have had to keep a low profile in the development of it due to scarcity of resources or even to keep someone like us from acquiring it and stealing their thunder, then I can't believe they represent an immediate danger to our national security. Admittedly, this is just a guess, but given the fact no one has reported even a hint of technology like this, I question the ubiquity of its existence. I advocate caution, but this level of technology could push the US right to the top as the king of the heap once and for all. I believe it is worth the risk to acquire the knowledge that built it, or at least the fruits of the technology itself, to ensure our strategic superiority for decades to come."

Chief of Staff Masters added, "I think we might be overlooking the economic ramifications of this technology. The trickle-down effects of advances in electronics, aircraft design, space technologies, et cetera, have pushed our economic power to the forefront of the world despite our lack of manufacturing capability here at home. We could conceivably reclaim the innovation absent from our shores in electronics, miniaturization, or medical technology, not just in weapons research. The possible list is endless. It seems short-sighted to believe the fruits of this knowledge should only be reflected in the development of military technology, sir."

"Good point. But the immediacy of the instabilities in the region make the case for proceeding with the operation on its own merit," began the president. "Gentlemen, I'm issuing a green light for the planning of Operation Goldmine, subject to my review before final approval. Are there any questions? No?

"Go get started on the mission plan and keep me up to date. I also want you to include the British in the op plan. More often than not, they come up with some creative solutions to some really hairy problems. Besides, it looks like they pretty much know where we are on this thing anyway."

"Very good, Mr. President," said CIA, rising to his feet.

After conducting the two men out of the office Masters sat back down, raising an eyebrow toward the president.

"What do you think our exposure on this is if our guys get caught?" the president asked.

"I'll tell you this, it's not going to be good. We're short on options. One, we don't want to use the Israelis on this at all. Two, we dare not ask the Saudis or any other of our partners in the area. What one knows, they all know. The operation would be over before it got started. And C, truth be told, we want to keep all of this to ourselves, don't we?"

"You're right about that. But plausible deniability is what we need here. That's one of the reasons I wanted to keep British intelligence involved. If this is a joint mission, we get to spread the blame around if something goes south, maybe even blame them if the shit hits the fan," the president explained. "Let's keep this close to the vest, I don't even want a distribution list on this operation. No briefing book, nothing. As far as I'm concerned the operation doesn't exist until I say otherwise, or the worst comes to pass and it blows up in our faces."

"Yes sir, I'll pass this on to the directors and the chiefs."

"Good. Now get out of here, you know how much crap I have to go over before tomorrow morning," Bender said with a grin.

"Oh, really? According to common opinion, the only reason you keep me around is so that I can translate all of your paperwork into 'see Dick run' briefing books for you!"

"Let's keep them guessing just a little bit longer, shall we?"

"You've got it. I'll check in before I head for home, Mr. President."

"Thanks, Simon."

The chief turned down the hallway to his office to make the calls on the short briefing list. He then checked the president's schedule to make sure that he could fit in a fifteen-minute briefing every afternoon for the next few days so he could be kept abreast of the planning of Operation Goldmine.

The wheels were turning. All the necessary assets of the intelligence and military commands were planning the invasion of another country. That brief, half-hour meeting set in motion an illegal invasion on foreign soil. No war had been declared, no crime had been committed against the American people, and Iraq had adopted no provocative posture against the US.

Once again the American people were ignorant of what their government planned in their name under the guise of protecting national security.

None of the meeting participants knew that what they had begun was the most self-destructive series of events in the history of the United States of America. What President Bender thought might be a slippery slope was, in fact, the precipice of disaster.

When you wish upon a star
Your dreams will take you very far
When you wish upon a dream
Life ain't always what it seems
Shining Star
Written and performed by Earth, Wind and Fire

CHAPTER 10

THINGS QUIETED DOWN for Norma after she returned her completed application to the Planetary Society. The dean had delayed her request for a meeting to discuss her discovery until he returned from taking a few days off away from the city.

So far, none of the other space—or ground-based observatories had come up with pictures of the quadrant of the sky she was interested in, so Norma returned to the more mundane processing of the normal stream of incoming images of the nighttime sky.

Almost a week after she requested a meeting with the dean she received an e-mail asking if she was free to meet later that same day. Norma called the dean's office to confirm and to find out whether he would come to her lab or would rather her to meet in his office. Waiting for his secretary to connect her, Norma couldn't help but have a renewed feeling of excitement over the prospect she'd be going public on her discovery. When the dean got on the line their conversation was warm, but short. He agreed to meeting at Norma's office so that he could review everything she had on the discovery.

Jumping up from her chair she spun around in a circle, trying to decide just where she was going to begin tidying up for the dean's visit. She also carefully looked at the entire lab with an eye toward how it would look on television, should the chance present itself.

"Hey Alan, we've got to get this place cleaned up. The dean's going to be here this afternoon and I want the place looking spic-and-span before he arrives. Besides, if I get to break this to the news I'm sure we'll both get to be on TV," said Norma.

"Why do I have to clean up? They're only going to want to see you, not your poor step-cousin of a researcher who languishes at the feet of the gods of theoretical math!" answered Alan.

"Maybe, but I still want to make a good impression on him. So can you at least hide all that stuff on your desk by this afternoon, and wash all of your dirty cups, and pull down some of your more obnoxious posters?"

"All right, already! You want me to order some fresh-cut flowers and essential-oil candles too?" Alan asked in irritation.

"Quit being an ass. Is it too much to ask you to straighten up a little? It's not like I'm asking you to give up a weekend to paint the place or something. Lighten up already," she replied.

Leaving off bothering Alan, Norma started to straighten up the lab, tucking things into drawers, standing books up properly on shelves and the like. It wasn't too long before she finished everything, even washing out all of the dirty cups and stacking them to dry. She then bent her efforts to collecting the various exhibits she planned to show the dean when he arrived for their meeting.

She printed out all of the documentation from the Planetary Society, the images she had originally received and the short movie clip rendered from the five images showing the asteroid in motion. Now she was screwed. She had done everything she needed to do for the meeting and still had three hours to go.

Norma almost decided to help Alan get his cube and surrounding workspace ready, but nixed the idea when she realized all she would be doing was meddling, which would only end up pissing Alan off. Instead, she grabbed her jacket, telling Alan she would be back, and scurried out the door.

Space is vast, and there are more objects out there that man knows, or can know about. Some of these objects are moving around in uncharted paths and at incredible speeds, sometimes bumping into each other. The evidence stares down at everyone on the earth whenever the moon is visible. Every crater, every dark pockmark on the moon's face is a testimonial to the pieces of the universe running into each other. Unfortunately, a piece of the universe large enough to make a moon-sized crater on the face of the earth would cost uncountable lives and rock the foundations of buildings, bridges, tunnels, nearly everything man-made, costing incalculable dollars in damage.

Looking at the earth from space, man could see the results of such collisions that had occurred through the ages. The meteor crater in the state of Arizona was the first crater identified as having been caused by an asteroid. Between 20,000 and

50,000 years ago, a small asteroid about 80 feet in diameter impacted the earth and formed the resulting 1.2 kilometer-wide crater. That was a meteor the size of two semitrailers end-to-end. The results of an impact from something several kilometers in size was what scientists call an extinction event.

Nobel Laureate Luis Alvarez proposed the theory that an asteroid about 10 kilometers in diameter, traveling over one hundred fifty thousand kilometers per hour, had struck the earth sixty-five million years ago, causing catastrophic changes in the weather and the greatest mass extinction ever recorded. This is man's greatest fear from the sky. Chicken Little was right; the sky falling spelled disaster any way you looked at it.

NASA, the world's lead agency in the study of such phenomena, could barely cover about two percent of the heavens in their efforts to discover any such threat to the earth; this included both earth-and space-based telescopes. What NASA wanted was a way to automatically search the heavens for moving objects that might pose a threat to the earth, using their scant resources. Norma's project demonstrated that one didn't need hundreds of stargazers employed around the world to watch for celestial visitors to the neighborhood. Her system of computers, using medium-powered telescopes, could keep watch in the sky to alert man to danger.

Computers didn't need sleep, didn't have to pay bills, never had their eyes water from the strain and didn't get distracted or bored. And best of all, Norma stated in her original grant, they were cheap. Fifty computers with the necessary optical systems cost the same as three astronomers for one year.

Norma wanted to create a master map of the entire northern hemisphere sky against which computers could compare any new image they acquired to see if new objects appeared or disappeared in the case of a star being occluded by some other object. This map would require a set of ultra-high-resolution images of the sky and a table of coordinates for the thousands of stars mapped in relationship to each other. Both tasks were daunting. Just obtaining pictures of the northern portion of the sky had taken well over a year. Mapping almost a million stars in relationship to her eleven hundred reference stars nearly ruined her eyes.

Norma initially programmed her system to map the twenty-one first magnitude stars, the brightest stars in the sky. Once they were plotted the computer began on the second magnitude stars, and so on until much of the sky had been completed. Once she was satisfied with the accuracy of the computer's placement of the stars and the calculation of their coordinates, she let the computer fill in and chart the locations of the remaining stars with minimal supervision. Norma wrote a "tell me three times" algorithm that told the computer never to add a star to the master map unless it had appeared in at least three different images.

This part of her project introduced Norma to hundreds of astronomers and astrophysicists at NASA and around the globe, mostly via electronic mail, in her effort to accumulate the tens of thousands of pictures she needed to build her map. In a few cases she maintained contact with some of those who helped her get started, gaining her own recognition and respect in the astronomy community for her unique project. She wondered how her new discovery would be received by many of them. After all, she didn't find this new asteroid, her computer did. Would the computer's principal role alienate those who spent countless hours in observation of the nighttime sky? She'd soon see.

Her registration of the asteroid with the Society would definitely leak out to the scientific community, and by serendipitous effect probably get her more pictures of that part of the sky from others who would want to confirm her observations. I'll just have to hope for the best, she thought.

At her favorite bakery she looked at the people around her. Norma wondered how her life might change if this asteroid attracted more than a passing interest outside of the scientific community. Would the increase in her visibility to the world, to the people she saw shopping and working in the stores, bring her any kind of fleeting fame? Would attention to her contribution to science, and to her own life, help give her the one thing she wanted with all her heart, but denied within her? Would fame and fortune lead her to find out what really happened to her parents, somehow focus attention on their disappearance so that this mystery could be solved? And, once she learned the truth would she feel better, or would the knowledge only deepen the hurt that she so carefully kept walled off?

Shaking off the beginning specter of emotional pain, Norma selected the cookies and coffeecake that would, in her eyes, be the perfect accent to her meeting with the dean.

She recalled how she had gotten on Alan's nerves about cleaning up the lab. She pulled her phone out and called the lab; when Alan answered she asked him if he wanted her to pick up something for lunch. Surprised and pleased, he declined, explaining that he was going to lunch with Rachael, his newest infatuation.

"Is she the one you almost didn't get the tickets for?" Norma asked.

"Yeah, it looks like we have more in common than I gave us credit for," said Alan.

"I hope it works out. She can't have any worse effect on you than you do on yourself," Norma said, laughing. "Anyway, try to get back by two, that's when the dean's stopping by. Maybe there's some way I can work your project into the conversation."

"What if he tells my advisor that I'm screwing around doing stuff that's not related to my project?" Alan asked.

"That's not true. Being able to visually display the effect of different mathematical models is one of the quickest means of determining if the math has validity," answered Norma.

"You are good! I never thought of that," Alan said, in frank admiration.

"You might want to load several animations of real versus calculated three-body movement. He might see something good enough that he'll mention you in a positive light. After all, he doesn't know you like the rest of us do!"

"Just don't let him get the skinny on me from Angela, I might be kicked off campus as some sort of pervert," Alan said laughing. "Can you get off my phone now so I can get something done before he gets here?"

"No problem. I'm bringing back goodies if you're still hungry later."

"Thanks. See you after lunch," said Alan, hanging up.

Norma picked up a bag of fresh-ground hazelnut coffee. It would be a pleasant change of pace from the "whatever was on sale" they normally drank, and it would make the whole lab smell good. On her way back to the lab, Norma did stop to pick up some flowers despite Alan's crack. It wouldn't hurt. And, they do look pretty, she thought.

Back at the lab, Norma printed out the best processed image of the asteroid on the high-resolution color printer so she could present it to the dean with the full press packet she had prepared. She gathered the entire package of materials into a binder and added a transparent cover on the front so that the picture showed through.

Norma tried to eat a leisurely lunch. She was keyed up about the meeting, but she forced herself to finish her food. The last thing she wanted was her stomach to start kicking up an embarrassing ruckus in the middle of the meeting. She tried to bury herself in routine matters like answering her e-mail and bringing her project paperwork up to date. She also cleared all of the saved messages on her voice mail, and probably would have built a deck off the side of the lab if she had had much more time to fret before the dean's arrival.

Just before two o'clock, Alan returned from his lunch with Rachael in a pretty good mood, so good, in fact, he didn't even make a crack about the flowers. As she peeked over the partition she was surprised to see he had already straightened up his side of the room. She kissed him on the cheek, thanking him for putting up with her case of nerves.

"I've got mixed feelings about this whole thing," she said. "I mean it's a fantastic opportunity to get the entire project funded by NASA, but I'm not sure that I want to devote the next ten years of my life to seeing the project through."

"What else do you have on your plate? Is the possibility of becoming some NASA bigwig for a while really so unpleasant?" Alan asked. "Or is it you think while you're doing a project like this something better might pass you by? Or, is it that there's no way you're going to find Mister Right among the geeks of NASA?" he finished with a laugh.

"No, knucklehead. I like it here, and I like the life I have now. I'm just not sure I want to have to make any big changes," said Norma.

"Well, sweetheart, until you really make it big, the question is moot," pointed out Alan. "And, even then there's no telling where you'll end up. It could even be at JPL out west, or better yet, out in the middle of nowhere at the Very Large Array. Hey, don't count your chickens before they're hatched."

Just then Dean Goodman cleared his throat at the door. "I didn't come at a bad time, did I?" he asked, smiling.

"No, Dean Goodman, we were just talking about the possibilities that might come out of this discovery," replied Norma. "Would you like to sit down by my desk over here so I can show you everything I've got on the asteroid? Oh, and would you like coffee and a little something to eat?"

"Coffee would be good. Is that hazelnut?" asked Goodman.

"Yes it is, I just picked it up this afternoon for a change of pace. Could I interest you in a cookie or cake?"

"Maybe just a small piece of the cake. I didn't have lunch today . . . thank you."

Dean Goodman was a familiar sight around campus, and on television. He served as the primary point of contact between the outside world and the university community, liaison to the press and often wrote articles in the campus newspaper covering the university's vast community outreach programs. Dean Goodman was young for the position, in his mid-forties, was universally liked, and it appeared he really enjoyed his job.

Goodman asked, "So, start at the beginning, what have you got for me?"

"Last week I received two images from around Saturn in my normal load. These two here. Here's what they looked like when they came in, and here's the section flagged by the computer. This small smear of light, here and here. The computer flagged the spots without any image enhancement and correctly identified the object as a bogey."

"So what you're saying is that the system works as you expected? That's great, NASA is sure to be happy with that," said Goodman.

"Yes, that's what I was thinking. I guess in the excitement of finding the asteroid I almost forgot this is what I was supposed to be doing."

"That's understandable, discovering a new asteroid is pretty exciting. It doesn't happen that often, and a number of other discoverers have been made into minor celebrities as a result. You should be very proud of your project. So tell me, what happened next?"

Norma pulled up the message requesting any images of the area and the application she filled out for the Planetary Society. "Here's the application I filled out. I guess it was a little selfish, but I did want to get credit for the discovery if I was the first to spot it. And I thought it wouldn't hurt the university if someone here was listed as the initial spotter."

"That's all right, Ms. Lancaster. There's no real downside to the university if it works out either way. Frankly, even if you were mistaken we could always characterize your claiming to see something that wasn't there as either computer error or the overenthusiasm of a young researcher."

"I see, I'm either brilliant or an idiot," Norma said, with a sick laugh.

"That's about the size of it," he replied, chuckling at Norma's chagrin. "It's not really as bad as that. But the university does have to protect itself. We've been had in the past. That's not the bad part, mistakes happen. The bad part is that everyone wants to latch on to anything negative and use it to paint everything here with the same brush, academics, sports, outreach, the whole organization. There are some things even a school like the U of C has trouble with, like falsifying data or academic mopery and dopery," he added.

"Now, what happened next? Did you get any answers with images from the area around Saturn?"

"Yes I did. These next three images came in from the archives of the x-ray telescope image database," she said, bringing the three images up on the screen. "If you look here you can see that they were taken later than the first sequence. These three showed the object, but no one must have seen them, or at least no one realized what they were. So now I had five shots of the same object but they were from two separate time periods, about nine days apart.

"I enhanced the first two images overnight. Then I thought about some old morphing software I still had. I loaded all five images into the morphing program and placed them along a time line approximately as far apart as they occurred in time. I then had the software fill in the frames in between. This is what I got," she said as she started the rendered clip.

Dean Goodman sat speechless as he watched the clip loop repeatedly. Over the first three run-throughs he sat spellbound as he saw something that, though real, was made even more real by motion. He looked over to Norma and asked, "Has anyone seen this yet?"

"Alan Richards on the other side of the partition here, and a friend of mine who came by for lunch yesterday. I was going to send it off to you but I figured it would be better if I explained every step of the way how I rendered it so that there would be no mistake about how it came about. I prepared an information packet for you in case you wanted the technical info to prepare a press release."

"Press release, hell! I want to call a news conference for four o'clock so that we can get five o'clock news coverage and maybe pick up some national exposure as well. Where's that info packet you were talking about? Oh, good, color pictures and everything. I'm going back to the office to get these copied and call the press. Can you stay late this evening just in case I need you, and is it all right if I bring the media here? You aren't working on anything else that they shouldn't see, are you? Oh yes, and how about Mr. Richards, was it?" Raising his voice, the dean said, "Young man, what are you working on over there?"

"Uh, it's a math project, sir," said Alan, peeking over the top of the divider. "Um, pleased to meet you, sir. I'm working on the refinement of the three-body problem and a visual interface to display the behavior of the bodies."

"Is there anything sensitive or classified to your project?" the dean asked.

"No sir. And just in case, I cleaned up for you and the press," said Alan.

"Sassy young fellow," Goodman said to Norma, "How much of a pain in the ass is he normally?" he asked, with a huge grin that Alan couldn't see.

"If it wasn't for the rent he pays, I'd have had kicked him to the curb months ago," she replied.

Getting to his feet, Dean Goodman shook Norma's hand and said, "Ms. Lancaster, you have done very well for yourself. And it looks like your discovery is not only going to bring a measure of honor to the university, but will probably make history in robotic monitoring of the heavens. I'll call you back within the hour. And good day to you too, Mr. Richards," he said, raising his voice so Alan could hear.

"Um, yeah. Goodbye, sir," Alan said to the dean.

Waiting for the door to close behind the dean, Norma ran over to Alan and wrapped him in a huge hug that he returned enthusiastically.

"Did you hear what he said?" she asked.

"Hell yes, you're gonna be famous!"

"No, we're going to be famous. You are going to have to set up Saturn and an estimated path of the asteroid in 3D, think how that's going to look on TV. Can you get it done?"

"Sure, I can grab some stock images of Saturn and the rings. I'm just not sure how I'm going to plot the path from those images you've got."

"You don't have to, at least not accurately. It's just for a dog and pony show. Once I get some of the other telescopes focused in on the asteroid you'll probably get that offset that you were talking about. Then you can plot it in space instead of just in the two dimensions my clip shows. Just get it mocked up for now. You've got about an hour or so until the evening news broadcasts, get it done, will ya'?"

"All right, let go of me and let me get to work."

Fifteen minutes later, Dean Goodman called and asked Norma to make a hundred copies of the sample media pack she had given him and told her that he was sending some undergrads to help bind them. He also said that they were bringing over the department's industrial coffee urn, cups and a lot of other refreshments.

"Hey, the dean said to expect about a hundred reporters to come through this evening, be sure to hide the good silver and lock up the valuables. He's scheduled the press conference in the big room down the hall and he wants individual interviews to be done here so that I can show the clip. Hey, how many blank CDs do you have over there""

Alan opened his file drawer and counted, "About forty, it looks like."

"How long would it take to burn a four meg file onto one?"

"A couple of minutes. What, you want me to burn the clip to a bunch for those who want to put it on the air?"

"Exactly, can you do it?"

"Sure, drop the file in the common folder and I'll start burning. I'm out of laser labels for them, though."

"Don't worry about it, they'll know what it is," she answered opening and closing her file drawers looking for regular mailing labels. Norma decided to push the table over to the wall under the windows to make more floor space for the crowd. Just as she was done rearranging, she looked up and saw a couple of students peeking around the door.

"Ms. Lancaster?" one of them asked

"That's me, but call me Norma," she answered.

"We've got the coffee urn and a bunch of other stuff in the car. Where do you want us to set up?"

The enormity of the whole situation came crashing down on Norma as she looked in the washroom mirror. She was representing not only herself to the members of the press, but the University of Chicago and NASA as well. All manner of doubts began to haunt her. Was she sure enough of what the computer found, and what of the logical conclusion of the validation of her project? Would she be able to make the commitment to deploy her network of sky watchers around the world? And more importantly, was her makeup going to look good on camera?

Norma focused on her presentation, the bullet points of her discovery and what it meant in terms of earth's future safety. She would point out that a few years ago an asteroid was discovered that was predicted to hit the earth in around the year 2800. True, that was the distant future, but detecting a rogue planetoid that might visit earth's orbit at thousands of miles per hour would give earth years of lead time and was precisely why her grant was funded.

Gathering her resolve, Norma left the washroom, determined to them the best she had to give.

Back in the lab, Alan came up behind her and quietly asked, "You all right?"

"I think so. It all seems kind of overwhelming. I'm definitely worried about how I come off. This pushes things over the line into the surreal. I guess I never really thought this far into how the project might evolve. At the beginning it was all about me proving that my idea would work, now it's so much more than me. Now there's a big ol' piece of the sky wandering around out there that will probably have my name on it. I hope like hell the thing isn't aimed for earth, that's all I need to top off the entire experience."

"With a bang, not a whimper?" Alan teased.

"Thanks! That's just what I needed, your firm grounding in reality, not some smarmy remark that only increases my anxiety."

Alan gave her a hug and retired to his chair. He had finished the simulation of the asteroid's motion with Saturn showing in the background three different ways; actually it was the same clip shown from three different perspectives. He had added the three clips to the CDs he was burning for Norma to give out to the press. He had also inserted her name and the U of C logo running along the bottom of each clip. Just to be thorough, he included her original image files in a separate folder. Alan called her over and displayed the four clips for her approval.

Looking over his shoulder she exclaimed, "Oh Alan, these are great! Why didn't you add your name too? This is great work."

"This is your moment, let it happen. Remember, none of this would have come about without you and the work you've done for the last couple of years."

"Thanks sweetie, I owe you," she said, hugging him from behind.

"Knock them dead, kiddo."

Moments later one of the undergrads came into the lab looking for Norma. "Ms. Lancaster, Dean Goodman is ready for you in the conference room."

As she walked down the hall, Norma knew she had come to a turning point in her life and that much of what she had been and done before would be irreversibly changed from here on out.

Well no one told me about her, what could I do
Well no one told me about her, though they all knew
But it's too late to say you're sorry
How would I know, why should I care
Please don't bother trying to find her, she's not there

She's Not There

Written by Rod Argent, performed by The Zombies

CHAPTER 11

JOHN REVIEWED EVERYTHING he'd read about Travis Woodson, Jaylynn Williams' boyfriend. He had been out of school for almost a year after graduating with a computer science degree. He was slated for the job at the FBI data center before he graduated through his work as an intern during his last year in school. His grades were above average, and though he had grown up in lower-middle-class surroundings, his grades in high school and college stayed consistently above average, a 3.75 GPA for the entire time he was in school.

John knew the type. What he was interested in now was whether Travis had become the kind of person who could murder in cold blood, and conceal the crime. That was the bottom line of the investigation. Who was responsible for Jaylynn's disappearance? Had she run afoul of someone who may have killed her in the heat of passion, and then, realizing what they had done, hidden her body to conceal the crime?

The fact was, most murders were committed by someone known to the victim, all too often a member of the family. John tried not to prejudge any aspect of the Williams girl's disappearance; it made for sloppy police work. He put aside any speculation until he had something concrete to work on.

Inside the federal building, he strolled over to the bank of elevators. As he waited he caught Samuels out of the corner of his eye, but before he could turn and wave he saw Samuels give an almost imperceptible shake of his head. Looking straight ahead, John got on the elevator and made a note to ask Samuels just what spook protocol he wanted him to follow under these kinds of circumstances.

He got off on the seventh floor, walked over to the glass security doors and pressed the intercom button.

"Who is it?" a disembodied voice asked.

"Detective Mathews of the Atlanta Police Department, I'm here following up on an investigation and I would like to talk to one of the staff in the data center."

"One moment please, I'll be right out."

Moments later a young woman appeared, opened the door and inquired, "Detective?"

Showing her his identification, he said, "Mathews, John Mathews. I'm with Missing Persons. I'm here to do a followup interview with Travis Woodson."

"Does he know you're coming, Detective?"

"Not specifically today, but he probably knows that we have to do a follow-up interview to be thorough. Would you be kind enough to let him know I'm here, ma'am."

"Agent Davis, detective, and if you will follow me I'll take you back into the data center."

Walking through a long, glass-enclosed corridor John saw rows upon rows of computer cabinets, most with nothing but blinking lights, but a few with tapes spooling back and forth. John wondered if one of them housed the data he had been looking at.

Using the ID hanging around her neck, Agent Davis opened the electrically keyed door and led John to a vast room filled with cubicles. They stopped short of the cubes as she called out for Woodson. A pleasant-looking young man peeked his head out of his cube.

"Travis, would you come into my office, there's something I would like to go over with you."

Agent Davis lead John and Travis into her office, stopped outside the door and told John, "Please feel free to use my office for as long as you need, detective. It's quiet and private. If you want me for anything just dial two, two, four, four and I'll pick up."

"Thank you, Agent Davis, you have been most helpful," John answered.

Closing the door behind him, John said to Travis, "Please have a seat, Mr. Woodson. I'm Detective Mathews from Missing Persons at the Atlanta Police Department. I was sent to interview you on the disappearance of Jaylynn Williams."

"Yes, sir. I'm the one who reported her missing. She hasn't returned any of my phone calls and her neighbors say they haven't seen her for the last two weeks. I know we had a fight, but it wasn't something that would make her just pick up and leave."

"Could you describe the argument you had, Mr. Woodson? Was it a violent exchange? Did either of you lay hands on each other?"

"No, there was nothing like that. I was complaining about her always keepin' me at a distance. Even though we've been together for almost a year, I always feel like she wasn't really committed to our relationship."

"Had you been pressuring her for sex?" asked John.

"No way. I mean we've been intimate, um, had sex. What I was talking about was more emotional, you know, things like moving in together and sh . . . stuff like that."

"Settle down, son. I'm not trying to pry into your private life, but I need to know as much as possible so I can get to the bottom of Ms. Williams' disappearance."

"It's cool, I understand. Sorry."

"That's all right. Now, would you please describe what happened the last time you two were together."

"Well, we were having dinner at her place, her apartment. And, we had been talking about, well everything, my day, her day and normal stuff like that. She was mostly listening to me rattle on about my day, you know, not saying much, but not sad or angry-like. After we had cleaned up the table and put everything away, we were watching some comedy movie. We were just talking, kind of holding each other when I brought up us livin' together. That's when she blew up and told me I had gotten on her last nerve. She got in my face about how I was always pressuring her, and that she was fine with the way things were between us. That's when I accused her of not caring about the relationship, that she was always holding back, like she had another agenda or something. I even asked her if there was someone else. That's when she told me to get the hell out."

"So, what did you do then?" John asked.

"I got my jacket and left. I slammed the door and went home."

"About what time was that, Travis?"

"About ten I think. I could probably tell you if I could get hold of the TV listings. I know the movie we were watching was a little bit over half over. It was an old film with Martin Lawrence and some white guy who was supposed to be his police partner. It came out a few years back, and he and his partner had just been kicked out of an airport. If that helps."

"We can check that out later. So then what happened?" John prompted.

"Well, by the time I got home I was sorry I had pressured her. I thought about how my parents would feel if I just moved in with a woman. You know, my dad's pastor of our church, that's what made me stop and think about what I was trying to push her into."

"Have your parents met her?" John asked.

"Yeah, I've brought her home for a couple of holidays. I also went home with her and met her folks twice. My folks love her, they think the world of her. Her mom and dad are a lot like mine. They're churchgoers, her mom sings in the choir and I think her dad's a deacon. We really are in love, Detective. I would never do anything to hurt her, sir."

"I see. So did you stay home that night, Travis? And if so, did you try to call her?"

"Yes, I did. I called, but her answering machine picked up. She wouldn't answer herself," answered Travis.

"Did you go back over to her house again that night, Travis? Maybe to try to reason with her, or to try to apologize?" John prodded

"No. Even though I was sorry, I was still angry that she wouldn't even talk to me about the whole thing. She just froze me out."

"So what happened next?"

"Well, I tried to call Jaylynn in the morning before she left for work, but she didn't answer. When I drove by her apartment after work, I saw that her car was there. I rang the bell but she wouldn't answer. I knew she was mad, but she never just wouldn't talk to me. She might not let me come by, but she always answered the phone.

"I gave her a couple of days and then I got one of her neighbors to buzz me into the building. I told her that I was worried Jaylynn was sick or something and I wanted to knock on her door. When I went upstairs and knocked, no one answered. When I listened through the door, it sounded like no one was there. So, the next day I asked one of the agents here if he could do something to help me find out how she was. I wouldn't have done that except she didn't even go to school. No one there had seen her since the day we had dinner," Travis finished with a sigh.

"That's the whole story, detective."

"Travis, are you willing to submit to a lie detector test so that we can confirm what you're telling me?" John asked.

"Will my parents have to know, or hers?" asked Travis.

"I don't see why they would, unless you've been less than honest with me. Have you? Is there anything you want to add to your story? Anything at all?"

"No, sir, everything's just like I told you. Could I have the test done here? At least that way I know no one will find out about it and think I had something to do with her leaving."

"I'll have to get authorization to be able to do that. It shouldn't be a problem, but you do know that your guys are tougher than ours," said John.

"That's no problem, officer. I know I didn't do anything wrong, besides the quicker I'm cleared the quicker you can get on to checking out everyone else."

"Is Agent Davis your direct superior here in the department?"

"Yes, she's head of the whole IT staff here in Atlanta."

"I'm going to call her back. You sit right here until she calls for you," John said as he dialed the extension Agent Davis had given him. Putting down the phone he asked Travis, "Did you have breakfast this morning?"

"Yes I did, why?"

"How many cups of coffee have you had today?"

"None. I don't drink coffee, but I did have a bottle of grapefruit juice. Is that a problem?"

"Not at all. Wait here until one of us comes to get you."

John waited just outside until he saw Agent Davis returning. He stepped away from the door to talk to her.

"Did you get everything you needed, detective?" she asked, stopping short of the office.

"Yes, and no. Procedure calls for a lie detector test to check over his story. I take it you were the one he asked for help with his girlfriend?"

"I am. I passed it on to one of our investigators. I think he might have gotten access to his girlfriend's apartment. If so he didn't share anything with me about it, he would have said something if anything was amiss. What did you think of his story?"

"You know him better than I do, but he appears to be just what he claims. He's got no record. His parents seem to have turned out one of the good ones as far as I'm concerned. I tend to believe him," John prompted.

"I would like the test results sent over to my office when you're done, assuming he comes up clean, that is. If not, I want to know about it immediately, and I would like you to hold him until we come and pick him up. He may still be a material witness to a homicide, maybe even charged with the Williams girl's disappearance, or death, if he fails the test," John explained.

"You can be sure we will not participate in shielding Woodson from the local law. Wait here, I'll call for an escort downstairs and order the test. Are you sure you wouldn't like to sit in?" Davis asked.

"I don't think so. I'm sure your technicians hate folks looking over their shoulders just as much as our guys do," John said with a smile. "Besides, I don't think he knows anything about her disappearance at all. He's smart enough to know he's the primary suspect. He was too worried about what I thought of their relationship, both of them being kids of church folks. The ones who act like they haven't a care in the world are the ones I watch out for. Here's my card. If anything else turns up could you give me a call?" John asked.

"No problem."

Opening the office door, John leaned in and told Travis, "Agent Davis will arrange for you to be tested here. If nothing comes up I probably won't be back right away, but stay close. No leaving town except maybe to visit the folks, keep Agent Davis apprised of any trips you might take. You might think about calling

Ms. Williams' family tomorrow and bringing them up to date if you haven't done so already. I'll be calling them myself today, it might help them out if you can answer any questions I'm sure they'll have for you."

"I will, sir. Hey, if you find anything out could you let me know?" Travis asked.

"Yes I will, when time permits, son."

"Thanks, thanks for everything."

John waited until he had collected his car and was out of the building before calling Samuels on his mobile phone. Samuels answered almost at once.

"I was expecting your call. I'm sorry about the cold shoulder in the lobby but I wasn't prepared to let on about our relationship yet. I hope you understand," Samuels explained.

"No problem, and if this is as bad as you hinted at it makes sense. That's not why I called though. Have any of your people called the Williams' girls parents yet?"

"No, I did send a field agent to watch their home to see if they could catch her come or go. In fact, the surveillance team still has it under observation. Why do you ask?"

"Someone's going to have to contact them and find out whether she called with any hint of her whereabouts. Maybe she went off to visit another relative while she cooled off?" speculated John.

"I don't think so, hold on while I close my door . . . . here's the scoop. I had taps placed on the parents, and the boyfriend's phones, as I did with hers," Samuels said in hushed tones.

"How did you get a judge to sign off on that?" John asked in amazement.

"I didn't," Samuels said, and paused, "and you know what that means. The truth of the matter is I'm not looking for evidence to use in court. An illegal tap gives me nothing admissible, but I'm not planning on going into court with what I find in any case. I want every possible line of information covered. This is the only case that even comes close to us being in on it so close to the beginning."

"The ends justify the means, Samuels?"

"You know God damned well that's not the issue here. Tell me, where do you think hundreds of blacks have gone without a single trace, without a single clue to their whereabouts? Well? How do you propose to find out anything at all without panic, anger, accusation and alerting the persons responsible for a forty-year crime wave? Tell me, because I really want to know!" Samuels said, hissing into the phone.

"Hey, cool down. I'm not questioning how deeply you feel about finding out what happened to these people, and finding those responsible. Look, let's get together tonight if you've got the time. Weren't you off to Chicago today? What happened with that?"

"I put it off so that I could make sure that all of the data you wanted on her credit cards, mobile phone and all the rest would be in your hands by tonight. Hey look, I'll call you around dinner so we can meet. As for the parents, go ahead and call, they're going to have to be informed about their daughter anyway, no point in putting it off. Their number is in the file, they live in San Diego. If you think you need it, I'll pull whatever the surveillance team has so far for you as well," Samuels offered.

"If they picked up anything of interest, add it to whatever you bring me tonight." John said.

"Fine, but let's make it at a more reasonable hour?"

"Call me later," John finished, and hung up the phone.

John learned nothing from Jaylynn's mother; he even tried a few aunts but came up cold. He began to think that this case was going the way of all the others. No clues, no smoking gun and no one who could provide any possible leads. He suddenly thought of Dean Atkins. Perhaps she could help out with records of phone calls made from the lab, something, anything that might point him in the right direction.

He gave her office a call. In moments he was put through.

"Good day, Detective. How may I help you?" she asked.

"Would you have time for me to stop by today? I would like to see if the college could help me out with some background information. I'm looking for her phone records, her e-mail for the past two months, things like that."

"I'm a little uneasy with that last request, the college doesn't access private student communications without serious need, or a warrant. We maintain the systems here on campus, and have the legal right. However, as a policy we respect our students' privacy. Let me make a call to the chancellor's office and get authorization for you."

"Thanks a lot. Is it still all right if I come by and do a little more looking around?"

"Only if you will allow me to take you to lunch, that is if your male ego can stand the strain?" she asked, an amused tone in her voice.

"Oh, I'm a big boy. I think I can handle it. How about I get there just before twelve?"

"That would be fine, I'm looking forward to it. And need I remind you that it's Sydney, not dean?"

"Only if you can the "detective" bit for the duration."

"I think I can remember that. Until this afternoon, John," said Sydney.

Pulling his car back into traffic, John saw he had enough time for a leisurely drive out to Steddman. He thought about where else he could look for anything that might point to where Jaylynn Williams ended up. He was beginning to see what Samuels said about boogeymen under the bed. The Williams girl appeared to have disappeared into thin air.

Assuming the boyfriend was cleared, there literally wasn't anyone else to view as a witness and interview. These people were either taken against their will by someone committing the perfect crime or else they had all gone off to God knows where cooperatively, living in complete isolation. John made a note to read about the Jim Jones cult's mass suicide, but the difference there was with that group the family and friends of the cult members knew where their loved ones had gone.

John concentrated on his driving. At college, he was again struck by the vast expanse of lawn that greeted, and soothed, the eye. At the administration building he was pleasantly surprised to see Sydney already outside with a sweater on.

"Right on time, John. Ready to go?"

"Absolutely, ma'am, and may I say you look extremely fetching in that outfit."

"Keep that up and you'll turn my head. Can we hit the road? I'm starving. You drive," she said to John.

"Where to?" he inquired, opening the door to let her get in.

After they were both settled, Sydney said, "Take a left out the of the gate and go down about two miles. The restaurant is on the right-hand side of the road. Do you want to begin telling me how I can help in the investigation now, or do you want to wait? So far no one here has heard from Jaylynn, I checked around yesterday and today. None of the other students have been telling tales out of school. It looks like most of them think she had to go down to Houston to bring NASA up to date on her progress.

"By the way, I received permission to download her e-mail for the last two months, and I also pulled her office long-distance calls too. She only called her NASA project liaison in Houston, we don't keep track of local calls. I'll give you the printouts when we get back to the office."

"Thank you. Does she have a pager or cell phone issued by the college?" asked John.

"No, the students all get their own."

Pointing out a driveway on the right, Sydney said, "It's right here. One of the area's best-kept secrets. You'll get some real Southern-style home cooking, interested?"

"A change from diners and bachelor cooking? Absolutely!"

Going inside and sitting down, the two began discussing each of their work backgrounds, finding common ground on their views of authority, government and bureaucracies. Overall, they both were pleased at getting along so well. The lunch came to a close far too quickly for either of their liking.

They rode back to campus in a comfortable silence, Sydney breaking it only when they had parked in the lot.

"Would you like to come up? Or if you're pressed for time I can have my assistant run the file downstairs to you."

"No, I'll walk you back to the office, that is if you don't mind?"

"I'd like that."

They walked up the stairs in silence, as if neither wanted to break the spell that had been woven over lunch. John laughed to himself when he realized he couldn't even remember what he had eaten. At the same time, Sydney was marveling at how easy John was to be with.

In her office, Sydney handed John the folder with the information he had requested. Taking the folder from her hand his fingers just barely brushed against hers and the touch was electric, an almost palpable energy passed between them. Beginning to blush furiously, John stepped back in confusion, "Excuse me I didn't mean to . . ."

"Oh silly, it wasn't just you. And just what should two people like us make of such a thing?" she said, smiling at his obvious discomfort.

"I'm not sure, under the circumstances maybe not too much. I'd hate to screw up what has been one of the best lunches I've ever had," replied John looking in her eyes. "I've enjoyed the time we've had together, and a more foolish man would go on to make so much of it that he would probably ruin the whole afternoon."

"Not to worry. I really had a much better time than I suspected I would. Thank you. Perhaps we could see one another outside the bounds of business? If it doesn't shock your sensibilities to have a woman ask you out, that is?"

"I'm flattered, but let me get a handle on this case first."

"Just let me know when you have the time, I'll be looking forward to your call."

"Thanks. I promise I'll get back to you in the next few days for sure. I'll talk to you then."

"Goodbye, John, and good luck."

"See you soon," John said, giving her a firm handshake, one that was not too long, but not too short either.

Driving back downtown, John found himself in an almost obscenely good mood. He cranked the radio and sang along with the light rock he used as background noise when he drove.

Pull yourself together you fool, it was only lunch. Besides, a woman like that has better to choose from than a city flatfoot, he thought. And yet, he couldn't deny that spark, that momentary instance of simpatico they both felt in her office. Although he was far from a wide-eyed child experiencing his first puppy love, his feelings were not a whit less significant for their sudden onset. He would have to take great care to not squander this opportunity.

Back at the station house, John checked in the office for the lieutenant but found he was out. Looking around he noticed that most of the squad was out.

John decided to bag it for the day and go see if anything new had been added to the FBI online files. Maybe the surveillance stuff on the Williams girl's parents was available. He then saw that Agent Davis called.

When he returned the call an operator asked him to hold while she located Davis. Moments later she came on the line. "Sorry for the wait, they had to find me in the car. Any luck yet?"

"Nothing so far, I guess that our boy passed?"

"Sure did. Mostly, he's feeling pretty guilty about the reason she might have taken off, but after going over him for two hours he came through like a champ."

"I want to thank you for handling the test for me."

"No problem. If I may ask, when are you going to call us in officially on the case? I know someone in the bureau passed it on to you even though one of ours reported her missing first."

"That's true, but if you'll check I was given the case to get things rolling. Let me get my feet under me before I bring you guys in. It's not going to get away from me before I ask for help, my ego's not that big. Don't worry, I don't have the kind of prejudices against the bureau many of us in blue do. Maybe it's because I've always been treated with respect as a fellow law enforcement professional, ma'am."

"Okay, I give! You don't have to lay it on so thick. I'm not trying to crowd you. Just keep in touch so if anything breaks bad I can be the one to tell the kid, that alright with you?"

"I don't have any problem with that at all. I'll keep you posted," promised John.

"Thanks. The results of the lie detector test should be on your desk by the end of the day. Oh, and don't worry, I checked into you, and I don't have any worries about you being the lead investigator on the case."

"I appreciate it, goodbye."

John realized that he had exactly nothing to go on. Unless Samuels had something new, all he had was the legwork behind the numbers on Jaylynn's phone bill, the credit card purchases or maybe something that might turn up in the folder of e-mail Sydney had given him. He wasn't going to give up, he wasn't a quitter, but unless he found some direction to take, he was afraid the Williams girl was going to be the latest member of this unbelievable batch of crime statistics.

That night at home, John entered all of the information he had so far into a single spreadsheet, his preferred method of recording case information. Telephone numbers and dates of calls on one page, e-mail addresses and dates on another, and the credit card receipts on a third. From the FBI system he retrieved Jaylynn's cell phone bill and added the numbers to the entries from her home and office calls.

John could still see no discernable pattern. All of the people she had called were either friends or local businesses. There was a call to her parents almost two months ago and a call to NASA from her home phone.

He turned to the list from Sydney. Under the last page of listings was a handwritten note with her home number, saying "Call me when you have a chance, Sydney."

The note brought John back to their lunch together, the thrill of discovery, the feeling of quiet comfort he found in her. John was getting it bad. He put her number into the directory of his cell phone but resisted calling her, knowing that although he couldn't really think of anything to say, he would probably be on the phone with her most of the night if given the opportunity. Trying to put Sydney out of his mind, John uploaded his spreadsheet to the FBI case folder with the other data and erased it from his home computer.

While he was searching around the Internet for the kind of software that would clean all traces of Internet usage from the computer after every use, the phone rang. He was glad to find that it was Samuels on the other end of the line.

"Please tell me that you have something good to report," John began.

"Why so? Did you have bad day?"

"No, just unproductive as far as the investigation is concerned. Did you see that Woodson passed a lie detector test over at your office?"

"No, I was out all day. Digging into something that might pull several of these cases together."

"In a nutshell, Woodson looks like he didn't have anything to do with the girl's disappearance, but he sure as hell feels guilt and remorse for the fight they had. You can look up the results at the office, they sent me a copy to look at in the morning. So give, what did you find out?" John asked.

"I began doing a check of the last thirty or so cases and over half of them were engaged in studies or industries at the leading edge of their individual specialties, just like Jaylynn Williams' project with NASA. She's been working on the newest hybrids and hydroponics in low-gravity environments, over half of the others were somehow doing the same kinds of high-level research," Samuels said.

"Wait a minute, which way does this lean? Is someone knocking them off to prevent advances in black businesses and industry, or are they being harvested for some super-secret project for a black-only paramilitary group somewhere in the US? Or is this some other country harvesting them for their own purposes?"

"Either way you slice it, it's still going to be a huge problem. If, in fact, all, or most, of them have been snatched to create some kind of advanced African American think tank, all of whom are at the bleeding edge of technology, the question becomes, why? Why is someone doing this? Is it some ultraseparatist group fed up with the treatment of blacks in America out to get their own? Or is it something even more sinister than that?" posited Samuels.

"What kind of research? Weapons, nuclear physics, genetics? What are we talking about here?" John asked.

"Listen to what I dug up this afternoon: hydroponics, botany, electronics, nuclear physics and reactor design, propulsion systems, environmental engineering, animal husbandry, animal cloning, hybridization of food-bearing crops, entomology, water purification, biological weaponry, psychology, sociology, telecommunications, encryption, the list actually goes on for another page and a half," said Samuels.

"Did I catch a bioweapons reference in there? Are you suggesting some kind of threat to the country? Remember, there have always been those on both sides of the fence who have advocated separate but equal here since the Civil War. There have even been books about insurrections by African Americans wanting their fair share of America, most maintaining it was built on their grandfather's backs. We never moved on the reparations issue either. Believe me, there are issues out there almost as volatile as those between Israel and Palestine, we're just used to them."

Samuels was silent for a moment, then replied, "I'm not really sure how to proceed, now. So far, you're the only one I've told about this. How do you think we should go on from here?"

"Hey, I'm labor, not management. Frankly, this is getting so much bigger than the two of us, at least down here. My problem is that including anyone else in our circle just increases the chance that something will leak about the investigation. If what you suspect is true, what's the next move? Try to find out where everyone went? Try to flush them out of the woodwork and get them to go public? I just don't know. If they've been doing this for several decades, then I'm sure they have their game down pat. That probably includes how to deal with anyone who might spill the beans. So far isn't that just you and me?" asked John.

"For all practical purposes. Who knows where they may have their eyes and ears focused. By the way, I locked out everyone from the files on the mainframe except you and me. I even changed the system that they're stored on, even Washington won't be able to find them without my help. My boogeymen are beginning to scare the shit out of me, and the last thing I want is this getting out to the press. There's no upside to going public, we either look like shills for the likes of white supremacists or bleeding hearts who are the puppets of some liberal group acquiescing to the weakening of America.

"I'm going to have to think about this for a few days. Maybe something will jump out after looking at it for a while longer. You still want to grab a bite?" Samuels asked John.

"I guess so. I was waiting to hear from you before settling on what to eat," answered John.

"Let me swing by and pick you up. I definitely need to get something to eat, I've been running on empty all day. Give me about half an hour to get over there."

"Fine, you have the address, I presume?"

"Yeah, no sweat. See you in a few."

Hanging up, John felt a chilly sweat breaking out in the middle of his back. If Samuels was right, John was more than a little uneasy about participating in the investigation. If whoever was behind these people disappearing found out he was investigating them, what would they do to keep the whole thing quiet? Short of a skin transplant, he probably wasn't going to be invited to join them, especially if they were engaged in something criminal.

In terms of Jaylynn's disappearance, if she had indeed left town, a two-week-old trail might be impossible to resurrect. Since she hadn't used her credit card or written a check for a ticket, John would be reduced to trying to find an agent who might have sold her ticket for cash or see if any of the one-way car rentals out of the city could have been her. The legwork was insurmountable or, if someone came and picked her up, close to impossible.

On impulse, John gave Sydney a call at home, half hoping she wouldn't be there, until she answered and he heard her voice. "Hi, it's me," he said.

"Hey you. I'm glad you called. I wanted to tell you I really had a great time this afternoon. I thought about it for the rest of the day," Sydney said.

"Me too, but only part of the afternoon, the part when I was breathing. Otherwise, I was too busy!" he said laughing. His heart thrilled hearing her laugh along with him.

"You bear watching, Detective Mathews. This must be a sample of your good cop routine, I'm sure."

"Nothing so sinister as that. I just like how comfortable today was. But to tell the truth, I do have a business-related question I have to ask you."

"Fire away," she said.

"Has there been anyone unusual hanging around campus? More specifically, someone around the science departments who doesn't belong, some outsider?"

"I don't think so. We've had nothing reported that I've heard, but I will check with security. I don't think any strangers have been reported on campus since a bunch of guys from an across-town college tried to pull an old-style panty raid at the school," she said. "You don't think it was a stalker or something like that, do you?"

"I don't really think so, but I have to check out every possibility. Having an all-women student body, has the college ever had any serious problems with date rape or anything like that?" John asked.

"No, not really. But considering this incident, I regret that I didn't have any contact with Jaylynn prior to her disappearance. I can't help but think that I might have seen something that could point us in the right direction. This incident has put the college on notice about better student oversight. Even though we pride ourselves on treating our ladies like adults, doting on them isn't any kind of imposition on their maturation, or their freedom either," said Sydney.

"I never thought about how fine a line it is to try to promote the best judgment in a student and yet have to watch them make a mistake or two so they build their own self confidence and life skills. I guess it's like raising children, isn't it?" John said with a chuckle.

"You don't know the half of it. Too bad you've never been through it. Your time will come, I'm sure of it, and when it does, you have to let them go out on their own. That's a ball buster, I think they call it!"

"Yeah, maybe. Being a cop doesn't exactly give you the kind of view of the world you want a kid to have to learn about. It's hard enough being an adult. Anyway, on a lighter note, what are your plans for the weekend?"

"Oh, I don't know. Why do you ask? You have any suggestions?" asked Sydney.

"Well, let me give it some thought. I might be able to come up with an idea or two."

"You have a couple of days, give it your best shot," she challenged.

"I will, thanks for the info today. And if you find anything out that might shed some light on Jaylynn's doings before she disappeared, give me a call?"

"I will, and thanks again for coming by for lunch. I had a great time."

"Me too, I'll give you a call in the next few days."

"Good night, detective, and do try to stay out of trouble."

Hanging up the phone, John logged back on to the FBI system to take a last look at the data he entered into the spreadsheet. He went back to Jaylynn's outgoing phone calls to see who he could contact next to try to get a better idea of who she might have seen, or what she'd done just prior to her disappearance. The long-distance calls were all accounted for, so he turned to the cell phone calls. These would probably be more revealing anyway, people had a habit of making more personal calls on them these days, in many cases even more than their home phones.

Paging through the numbers and matching them in the reverse directory, he filled in the names for study later. As he filled in calls closer to the day she disappeared, John came across a number that chilled his blood. Checking his own mobile phone directory to be sure, he compared the number twice before he could believe what he was seeing.

He then pulled up Jaylynn's original mobile phone bill to make damn sure he wasn't making a mistake on the number. What John was seeing were two calls, each over ten minutes long, from Jaylynn's mobile phone to Sydney Atkins' home in the week before she disappeared.

John was stunned. He couldn't believe his eyes, but he knew the information had to be correct. He replayed his conversation with Sydney earlier in the day and distinctly remembered her stating that she had not had any contact with Jaylynn in the weeks before her disappearance. She'd also stated the same thing just a few minutes ago. He didn't know where to begin to fit this new information into the case before him. Was everything that passed between them today a lie? Was she part of this conspiracy Samuels was certain was behind all the missing group? If so, how did she fit into the picture? And, the sixty-four thousand dollar question, was what he had felt with her at lunch based on a superb performance designed only to manipulate and deceive him? Was it an act played only to gave rise to the feelings he felt that day?

Just then the doorbell rang. Startled from his funk, it took John a moment before he remembered it was probably Samuels coming to take him out for a bite to eat. Answering the door, John invited the FBI agent inside for a few minutes while he shut down the computer and changed his clothes.

While he was changing his pants and shirt, John debated whether or not to inform Samuels of this startling development. Withholding any information in an investigation was one of the worst no-nos anyone could commit in his book and here he was seriously considering doing so himself.

He really wanted to believe he would be doing so to give Sydney a chance to explain herself. He harbored a small hope that she had some kind of logical explanation for her deception, but for the life of him he couldn't imagine what it could be.

The more he thought about it the more his ambivalence began eating him alive. On the one hand, he had to tell Samuels what he knew, on the other he couldn't bear to think he had been played so well that he never suspected a thing. He felt worse than ambivalent, he felt like a fool. Being played a fool only served to make John angry, and an angry John was a very dangerous man to mess with.

Finishing changing his clothes, John decided to keep his own counsel until he got to the bottom of this mystery. Once he did, he'd come clean to Samuels and let the cards fall where they may. Feeling better for at least having made up his mind, John put thoughts of Sydney aside and prepared himself to make nice with Samuels over dinner.

Come on down to my boat baby
Come on down where we can play
Come on down to my boat baby
Come on down we'll sail away
Come On Down To My Boat
Written by Wes Farrell & Jerry Goldstein, performed by Every Mother's Son

CHAPTER 12

RETURNING TO HIS underground lab with Commander Ames, Martin was of two minds for a change. His dread of going back into this deep hole was overwhelmingly overshadowed by his excitement over the fact that the Navy had agreed to build a second detector. Ames was impressed with the engineering of the elevator. He became more animated and excited the farther underground they traveled.

Arriving at the shelter level, Martin showed Ames to one of the guest rooms so he could drop off his bag. He then escorted the commander to the room housing the detector. Once the lights came on, Martin stood silent, letting Ames take it all in.

"This thing is huge!" said Commander Ames, breaking the silence. "I knew it was large, but seeing it all put together, dominating the whole room, it's pretty impressive."

"Even though I live with it night and day, I sometimes have a problem grasping the enormity of it myself, commander."

"Look, we're going to be working together pretty closely for a while, call me Jim will you?" Ames said with a smile.

"No problem. Everyone down here either calls me Marty or Doc, either's fine by me. So, where do you want to begin?"

"Can we go over to the other side of the complex and scope out the location for the second detector? I want to get a handle on the number of engineers and techs we need to do the reconfiguration of the space."

"Sure, let me show you the room with the growing tank on the way. I have an idea or two on how we can tilt the odds in our favor for producing a perfect crystal the first time up by modifying the tank itself."

"That's great. Can I stop in my room on the way and change into something more comfortable?"

"No problem, while you're doing that let me go have security program the system to let your ID card open all of my laboratory doors. It's a silly requirement but it does cut down on casual wandering in and out."

After taking a quick look at the original tank and then changing his clothes, Ames began making his list of recommendations with Martin for the incoming construction crew and compiling the skill sets Martin thought the expanded project needed. By the time they were done the clock was showing midnight.

They both called it a night and agreed to meet at breakfast. In his own room, Martin saw he had received no telephone calls while he was away, but he had over thirty e-mail messages; unfortunately none were from Richards at the U of C. Fatigued from the day's travel, Martin fell into a deep, dreamless sleep.

The next morning he woke well rested and ready to tackle the day. He found the commander, already finished with his morning meal, talking with several of the soldiers stationed down below. Martin grabbed a rare breakfast of eggs and sausage and made his way over to the group.

Martin sat down to the chorus of "Hi docs" and waved a general hello.

"Hey Doc, the swabbie here says that you're going to redecorate the joint, that true?" asked one of the permanent support staff.

Talking around a mouthful of eggs, Martin answered, "Looks that way. You boys are going to have to really get this place cleaned up just in case any visiting brass stop by."

"So we're looking at what, maybe fifty newbies here for a while, Doc?" asked another of the Army staffers.

"That's about right. If I were you I'd be marking the cards and loading the dice for when the Navy invades. The least you can do is show them that you guys don't completely waste your time sitting around."

The whole group laughed good-naturedly over the rivalry between branches of the military, and yet Martin felt like the outsider among the easy camaraderie of the soldiers and sailor.

Back in Martin's lab he cleared a desk for Ames to use and set up a user account with a temporary e-mail address to use while he was there. Martin began drawing up an inventory of the electronics and other supplies needed to support a second detector. He took advantage of this boon to add some new components to the design that might give him an additional magnitude of accuracy in the directional component of the system. With what he had learned so far from his prototype, Martin believed he would be doubling the efficiency of the circuitry and the sensitivity of the laser array that made up the critical, central component of the detector.

When he was largely done compiling components for his list, Martin got up, stretched, and went over to make fresh coffee. He saw that Ames was on the phone, yet again, with someone in procurement. Instead of bothering him, Martin went to splash some water on his face to perk himself up.

He returned to his desk feeling better and opened up his e-mail. Some of it was spam, a couple from someone in the Joint Chief's office and one message from Alan Richards.

The message started out thanking Martin for taking the time to process the sample data and informed him that the results checked out fine against Richards' own calculations. Martin read with interest the summary Alan had sent along on his project, detailing his progress in refining the three-body problem mathematically. Alan included the basic concept of the three-dimensional mapping program he had written to visually display the mathematical results of the complex equations with which he was working. Richards explained that he was considering expanding the inputs for the program to enable it to display all the planets in the solar system, and, if he could harness enough processing power, he could add moons, comets and asteroids.

The more he read, the more Martin's interest rose. This looked like exactly what he wanted in a visual display for his gravity anomaly detector. Since he only needed to plot a handful of objects at a time to display the source of any local anomaly, this sounded perfect. Martin saw that Ames was off the phone, and asked, "Jim, I just received a message from Richards at the U of C, do you have any idea how long it will be before we know if he can help out or, better yet, join the team?"

"I'm not sure yet, why?" asked Ames.

"He's already written a beautiful suite of programs for three-dimensional display of planets and stars that's perfect for adaptation to the detector."

"Are you sure?"

"Pretty sure. As sure as I can be without calling him and tipping my hand."

"If you're that hot to get a look at his stuff, let me call Washington and light a fire under Intelligence to get a move on it," said Ames.

"Great. I would also like to get those superconductor experts here ASAP, if it can be done."

"Since they're all naval personnel it shouldn't be too much of a problem getting them reassigned in a few days. Just let me finish the manpower estimates for the construction crew and I'll get Washington on the phone and set as much in motion as I can," Ames finished distractedly, turning back to his computer screen.

Martin added, "I'm sorry for being so impatient, it's just that I feel like I'm turning a corner here and everything else we want from here on out is only a matter of getting it done."

Ames turned to look at Martin and said, "Look, I know exactly how you feel. It's just like before a battle you've been planning for weeks, or months even. All you want to do at that point is to just get on with it. Pace yourself, the Navy'll take good care of you. Tell you what, why not draw this guy out and see if you can get some details about the software, like what platform it was designed to run on and what the space requirements are for his entire data set. Then I can make sure you have adequate capacity and a compatible system to run the thing. If he's going to be helping you out, the least we can do is run his data for him."

"Yeah, that makes sense. I'll send that out to him but play it coy about exactly what's going on here."

"Fine, that's all I ask."

Martin looked back at Ames typing away at his keyboard. Somehow he knew that Ames would definitely finish everything on his plate before the day was out.

Soon Martin's message was wending its way through the Internet to Alan Richards' inbox. It just so happened that Alan opened it almost immediately, seeing who the message was from, and couldn't wait to see what his prospective benefactor had to say.

Alan saw that Dr. Harris wanted to know if he could run Alan's programs locally in his office, definitely not what Alan wanted to hear. The last thing Alan was willing to do was to let his baby out of his hands and into the computer of a complete stranger. On one hand he was flattered someone took such an interest in his programming project; on the other, he wasn't about to let anyone bring it to market before him and lose such a profitable opportunity. And yet, in order to render the solar system and surrounding space in any kind of reasonable real-time manner, he had to have access to a magnitude more computer processing power than the university would give him.

Alan couched a cautious reply to Harris' message, asking what Dr. Harris wanted in return for processing the celestial data runs, other than access to his source code for the programs. He proposed they form some sort of formal collaboration to see a successful product sold to the public. When he was content that the message conveyed just enough about the specifics of his personal project without revealing too much, he sent it off to Harris.

Alan had a lot of time on his hands while Norma was on the talk show junket being interviewed and photographed every other day. Oh, he enjoyed the initial furor when various representatives of the press were in and out of the lab. Norma made sure he got credit for his animations of the asteroid against the backdrop of near Saturn space, which got him a good deal of attention as well.

Just when it seemed they knew everything possible about the asteroid, JPL plotted its path and determined it might intersect the orbit of the earth. Not that there was any immediate indication it would collide with earth, just that it would travel the same highways and byways as earth and the moon. The speculation in the press of a possible collision refocused the public's attention on Norma's discovery and brought on a new spate of interviews for the young researcher.

To say that everyone involved with Norma's grant was happy with the state of affairs was an understatement. The University of Chicago got an immeasurable amount of good press as the home of Norma's project, and NASA saw a renewed interest in all things in space. The intense interest had President Bender proposing the deployment of Norma's computerized sky watcher network as soon as possible.

For his part, when reading about the newly discovered asteroid, Martin hadn't made the connection between Norma Lancaster and Alan Richards until he downloaded the movie clips of the asteroid from the Internet and saw the fancy three-dimensional clips showing Alan's name as the artist. Martin suspected what Richards had done was import digital images of Saturn and render them three-dimensionally, then dropped them into the clip. The result was pretty compelling. He wondered how much credit the Navy would give Richards should he end up a part of the development team for Martin's own project. That might be an additional inducement he could toss on the table in the attempt to get Richards' software adapted for his own use.

Later that afternoon, Martin reviewed the data collected while he was in Washington. He was disappointed to see no further incidents. Martin began to refine the calculations of the original incident that governed the positional element of his software. He adapted the whole system to accept the additional data channels a second detector would add to the data stream. He mentally made a note to increase the computer system's disk storage capacity tenfold to accommodate any future demands the twin detectors might impose if recording a long-term event.

Ames got up from his chair, stretching to get the kinks out of his back and shoulders, then asked Martin, "Is there some kind of gym down here?"

"Yeah. It's on the top floor past the commissary. However, getting a good massage is almost out of the question down here!"

"Thank you very little," said Ames, "I was considering getting an hour in on the machines, I usually run but I didn't think that would work unless I went outside."

"Actually, there is a track down here. It's a quarter-mile oval. Most of the soldiers use it in the morning so it should be free now if you want."

"I suppose missing my run for a day or two isn't going to make that big a difference, I was only checking in case I got up the ambition to do road work in the morning. What I could really go for is a nice, juicy steak, seared over a really hot, charcoal fire. A salad and a baked potato would top the whole thing off nicely," finished Ames, his expression wistful.

"Your wish is my command, great and wise one," said Martin. "If you can wait about forty-five minutes, I believe I can conjure up just what the doctor ordered."

"No shit? How do you do that, delivery, or military drop shipment?" Ames asked with a feral grin.

"Nothing so complicated. The supplies are in the upstairs commissary and we can use the outside picnic area grills for the steaks. If I sweet talk the kitchen staff up there they'll even start the charcoal when we head up. How's that sound to you?" Martin tempted him.

"You're not bullshittin' me are you? Does the staff mind?" asked Ames.

"Not if I don't make a habit of it. I think everyone needs a break in routine to keep from going stir-crazy. More often than not, when I ask them to fire up one of the grills for me someone else gets the same idea, so it usually ends up being an impromptu picnic. Let's do it. It may be the last chance I get to be outside for quite a while if we're actually geared up by the end of the week. Besides it'll give us some time to talk about phase two, and make sure I'm on the same page as the Navy on all this."

"Sounds like a plan. Make your calls, I'm going to get a jacket and I'll meet you at the elevator. Should I bring anything?" asked Ames.

"You got a good bottle of red wine?" joked Martin.

"'Fraid not. I'll see if they've got some red Kool-Aid, how's that?"

"That'll do fine. Meet you at the elevator in ten minutes."

Martin made his request at the commissary, adding that there would be two eating this time. The cook asked jokingly where Martin had dug up a date down there, and then proceeded to really ride him when Martin told him it was the commander. Oh well, he thought, at least it wasn't as bad as the crap I took for singing in the elevator.

After the ride up, and subsequent cooking preparations, their lazy dinner stretched out well past sunset, and the resulting feeling of contentment greatly contributed to the relaxed conversation between the two.

As the stars began to show against the darkening evening sky, Ames asked out of the blue, "If you get the detection of gravitational anomalies perfected, do you think your work could lead to conquering gravity, or at least being able to manipulate it on a local level?"

"What? You mean like antigravity?" asked Martin.

"Exactly. Do you think we'll ever be able to control the pull of gravity, or even negate it enough to be able to float off the ground without jets or blades?"

"Maybe eventually. But this monster of mine only looks for differences in the local field. I can't yet see where I can translate my detection work into finding the fundamental basis for the law of gravity. As one of the so-called weak forces in physics, I'm not sure we can even approach the control of gravity without the math and understanding of the relationship between all the forces, electromagnetism and the nuclear forces. So far we have a satisfactorily unified theory of three of the four known forces, but in spite of the immense efforts of the last few decades, gravity still doesn't fit in perfectly. The three unified forces are all brought together under the mathematical umbrella of quantum mechanics, whereas gravity is still explained in terms of Einstein's general theory of relativity."

"So what you're saying is that our lack of any useful theories covering the control of gravity is pretty much because we lack a handle on the fundamental principles of gravity itself. Sort of like trying to build a car without knowing anything about internal combustion?" asked Ames.

"Pretty much, why do you ask?" Martin inquired.

"From a strategic perspective, imagine what an aircraft using the manipulation of gravity to get from A to B would mean to the military. No traditional propulsion plant, hopefully no need for carrying massive amounts of fuel either. I'm guessing the thing would be damned hard to detect in flight with no heat trail from jet propulsion, probably silent too."

"I see what you mean. Unfortunately I can't yet see how. However, I do know how to nullify the pull of gravity on you here on earth, it's a teaser professors ask in class."

"How's that?" asked Ames.

"Just suspend a mass equal to that of Earth directly above you. Then the pull would be equal and you end up floating between the two."

"Very funny, Mister Wizard. As far as I know there's no one any closer to achieving antigravity than you are. I was only speculating on the ramifications of such technology becoming accessible to the military. I'm wondering if we'll see anything like antigravity for at least another fifty to a hundred years," Ames said.

"The one thing that just boggles my mind about gravity is how fast it propagates. I still can't believe how much faster than light gravity appears to travel. The effects are instantaneous in local terms. The hardest part about detecting gravity waves was developing a detector that reacted fast enough to catch the rise and fall of something that travels over thirty million times faster than light. Think about it, suppose we found a method of transmitting data using gravity waves? We could communicate across galactic distances, even through suns and planets. Local communications would benefit. Imagine, communicating from earth to any of the other planets in the solar system instantaneously.

"A remote probe on another planet could be controlled in real time, no radio lag at all. What it saw, the controller would see at the same moment. And, given the density of the gravitational medium, the bandwidth would be enormous. Unfortunately the only way physicists can think of to achieve that kind of communication would be to somehow capture and manipulate a microscopic black hole. Don't get me started on the level of technology that would take, let alone the task of finding or creating such a thing. Right now this detector is about the only way we'll be able to see if these microscopic black holes truly exist," said Martin, taking a sip of coffee.

"I see what you mean. You know, the first thing some nut job in the military would want to do is try to use one as a weapon. I think some of these kinds of technologies need to remain undiscovered until we grow up enough to use them wisely. I don't agree with every line of research the government is following or has tried to develop in the past. Remember the so-called Philadelphia experiment, trying to mask a destroyer or aircraft carrier using huge electromagnetic fields? How about when they were putting those soldiers in trenches just outside the blast radius of an atomic explosion, or infecting my predecessors with syphilis? No, from what you've just explained I can't see how the mastering of gravity could happen without the abuses that we seem destined to repeat time and time again."

They both sat silently for a while, enjoying the gathering darkness. When all trace of the setting sun had disappeared, they gathered up the dishes and trash. Ames doused the coals with the rest of their water and stirred the ashes to be sure no hot spots remained.

"That was great. I could get used to this pretty easily."

"Don't get your hopes up, commander. I doubt if I get up here once every other month. With the hours I keep, by the time I get to thinking about eating it's too late, and my ass is too tired to go through the hassle," warned Martin with a laugh.

"Well, it was worth a shot. I'm going to let you off the hook babysitting me tomorrow, I've finished everything I needed to get done so I'll be taking off. I'll probably be back in a couple of weeks to see how the crew's doing. Don't worry though, I'll be checking in frequently to see if we've forgotten anything. If you think of anything call me."

"How about making sure that the engineers and techs are all women? Any chance of pulling that one off for me?" Martin asked.

"Yeah, you and the entire contingent downstairs no doubt. No promises, I'll see what I can do for you, but don't hold your breath," said Ames, dropping their garbage in the trash can.

Inside, Martin dropped off their dishes while Ames called for the elevator.

"The first thing I'm going to do is check on this Richards at the U of C. I saw his handiwork on those animations for that new asteroid. Intelligence should have filled in his file by the time I get back. If everything checks out I'll call you right away. My personal preference is to haul him down here to help you. At least then he'd be somewhat contained."

Martin frowned and asked, "Is there that much paranoia in the service or are you some kind of control freak?"

"Yes, and yes. One of the first things the admiral said to me after your presentation was that this project was to be kept as quiet as possible. The soldiers who are stationed here at the hole will be getting additional orders sometime tomorrow on upping the security. Nothing that's going to make them have to put in extra time or effort, just a little closer scrutiny and elimination of some visiting below. I guess the closest thing in civilian life would be no more conjugal visits for the duration."

"I hope you're right about not ruffling any feathers. It's enough of a pain in the ass for most of us without having security checkpoints in every corridor. Hell, carrying around the ID card just to get in the door all the time is hassle enough," said Martin.

"I know it is for you, but just remember that those of us in the service put up with worse at some time or another in our various postings. Besides, you want the truth?"

"Yeah, that'd be nice," answered Martin.

"Once the security gets ratcheted up around here, the guys will be walking taller, taking a little more pride in themselves, because they'll know that instead of babysitting here in the hole, they are charged with the responsibility of watching over something important," Ames explained. "These guys know that there're a couple of projects other than yours that might pan out, but basically it's babysitting. Tomorrow, that all changes. Hell, they might even give you your audition tape and lose the original from the database because the change in security is for your project."

Martin reddened slightly and said, "Oh, they told you about that one, did they?"

"Yeah, but don't get your knickers in a bunch. These guys respect the kind of hours you put in and they also know that you don't get out much to see family or a girlfriend. They told me all that this morning. They respect anyone who is about getting the job done. We've all been through the shit storm America throws at us for the six-hundred-dollar hammers and the eighty-dollar toilet seats. These guys also see the big industrial firms that get billion-dollar contracts from the military and don't produce squat for the money. Just because they don't say anything doesn't mean that they won't stand up for you, remember that."

While he was talking the elevator arrived carrying a couple of the security staff.

"So anyway, enough with the speeches," finished Ames, getting on the elevator.

"Hey, look. Thanks, for everything. I mean it," said Martin.

"Martin, it's no problem. I'm just happy you seem to be on the right track," Ames finished, as the car began its descent. The two of them remained silent on the way down, each consumed with their own thoughts.

At the bottom, Martin bade Ames good night and went off to his room thinking about what he would do if he could harness a quantum black hole for experimentation.

Ames went off to the lab to make one more call to Washington to see if he could have a psychologist secretly included in the bunch of incoming crew to evaluate Harris for his file. He wasn't really worried, just being thorough.

Even after the long day, Ames headed for bed fully intending to get up at oh-dark-thirty to spend an hour in the gym before he left for Washington.

CHAPTER 13

NORMA REVELED IN the quiet familiarity of her own bedroom.

Her favorite parts of the entire publicity tour were the photo shoots for the covers of *Scientific American* and *Ebony*. Both issues would be on the newsstands at the same time. What a dichotomy, an American science heroine and an African American role model, all in the same week.

She hadn't been back to the lab in a week. She was glad that tomorrow she could at least *try* to have a normal day.

Musing over the interviews she sat through, especially those for television, her balance sheet came out on the positive side of the ledger. After a few fits and starts, Norma became quite comfortable talking about her project and what her discovery meant in the larger context to science and to earth. Only a couple of the interviewers attempted to delve into her personal life. They weren't trying to dig up any dirt on her, nothing remotely like that, they were just trying to bring out more of who she was. At least after a few print articles pointed out the facts about the unexplained disappearance of her parents, no one was crass enough to ask her about them again.

One of the serendipitous results of all the publicity was a handful of really great job offers for when she finished school, a couple of them pretty lucrative too. But, if Norma was ambivalent before her newfound fame and about what to do with the rest of her life, the previous week only pointed out just how hectic and tenuous things can be at the same time.

Dropping off to sleep, the last thing through Norma's mind was Alan, how he had fared in her absence.

The next morning dawned bright and clear. Norma almost ran through the door of the lab, and was disappointed that Alan hadn't made it in yet. She *was* reassured to see his cube was still a mess and that his screen saver was running. She dropped her bag on her own immaculately clean desk and sorted through the huge pile of mail sitting in her In box. Most of it was letters of admiration, a couple invitations to speak at, or to attend conferences, and a handful from elementary and high school students who wrote to express their pride in her accomplishments. These she tacked up on the walls of her cube, promising to herself to send replies as soon as she could.

Norma tackled her e-mail next. Unfortunately now that her name and e-mail address were public, she was bound to get every freak ad and spam mail the Internet had to offer. She saved about a dozen messages from colleagues, a few with directions to image databases from the same portion of the sky, and a couple of observatories that were not currently focused on that portion of the sky, yet promising to forward pictures to her should they change their focus to it. She was happy to see a handful from friends congratulating her on the discovery, checking to see how she was weathering the publicity. She picked up the phone and called Angela at work.

When Angela answered, Norma said, "World Travel Incorporated, may I send one of your friends to far-off places?"

"NORMA!" she shouted, "How the hell are you, girl? Where are you? Are you in town? Where've you been? Why didn't you call? Don't you love me any more?"

"Whoa, slow down. Give me a chance," Norma began.

"Why didn't you call? Jesse and I were worried about you. We thought since you were rubbing shoulders with the country's elite you'd just kick your regular friends to the curb."

"Didn't you see me on TV? It seemed like I was on every channel out there."

"Yeah, you looked great, Norma. We're both proud of you, girl. Can you go for lunch, or do you have too much to catch up on?" asked Angela.

"Can you come here so I don't have to be gone too long?"

"Sure can, let me see if Jesse is up and around, we'll meet you about eleven-thirty. That sound about right?"

"Sure thing, sugar. I'll see you then," said Norma, hanging up the phone.

Soon she heard Alan's familiar tread coming down the hall. When he came in the door he dropped his backpack and ran over to give her a hug.

"Why didn't you call and warn me you were coming, I would have baked a cake!" he said into her neck. "How are you doing, kiddo? I hope the trip didn't drain you of vital juices or anything."

Laughing, Norma replied, "No, nothing like that. Why, did something happen between you and that Rachael? And please, let's leave my vital juices out of the conversation!"

"Well, we sort of broke up. If I were an honest man I would probably point out my obvious emotional shortcomings and their negative effect on all of my past relationships, but it's really that I just don't have what most women want," said Alan.

"And what's that?" shot back Norma sarcastically.

"A fat wallet and twelve inches," said Alan with a laugh.

"You got that right on both counts, pig. Hey, I'm going to lunch with the girls in a little while. I'll tell you everything when I get back."

"Sure thing. Oh, wait! I think I found someone who I can partner with on the 3-D thing. At first it looked like he was only interested in getting the source code, but it turned out he was checking to see if the code could run on his system."

"Who is he? Where does he work?" asked Norma.

"Some Ph.D. named Harris, he's doing some project for the government, at least that's what it looks like from his e-mail address. If he's on some high-powered project he might have the kind of horsepower I need to get my data processed, and to test all of my three-body equations too," he finished.

"Sounds promising, keep me posted."

"It's great to have you back, I never thought I would miss your mug around here. Oh, Dean Goodman stopped by and left this envelope. I think it's the bio and head shot they want to use in the *Maroon* newspaper. Some of the eggheads want to know if *Scientific American's* doing a centerfold on you this month. If so, I want mine autographed, you hear?" Alan said as he went around to his side of the partition.

Before long Angela and Jesse showed up to take Norma out to lunch. Throwing a goodbye over the wall to Alan, Norma left to eat and bring her friends up to date on everything she'd been through over the last few weeks.

Meanwhile, Alan read the application from Dr. Harris to work at his facility on an associated project. According to the details, he would be paid for his time and the university would be compensated for his absence with a grant from Dr. Harris' benefactor. *Not a bad deal,* Alan thought. He would actually be paid to continue his own research and collaborate on the 3-D display programs. He couldn't believe his luck, a win-win for everyone.

He forwarded the application to his faculty advisor for approval. His acceptance should be a no-brainer. Moments later his phone rang and Alan was surprised to find, at long last, the famous Dr. Harris on the other end of the line.

"Wow! I've been wanting to talk to you for a while now," said Alan.

"As have I," replied Martin.

"Thanks for processing that first set of data, the results were exactly what I needed. Do you think that the rest of the stuff I have can be done in a reasonable amount of time?" asked Alan.

"I don't see why not. But I wanted to talk to you in more detail about working here for a while so we can collaborate a little more closely."

"Just exactly where is 'here,' may I ask? I'm a little hazy on that," said Alan.

Martin laughed. "I wondered when you would get to that. 'Here' is a little research facility between Salt Lake City and Boulder. It's a military installation that houses several civilian projects like mine, mostly research done on Uncle Sam's dime."

"Do I have to pass some kind of security check and give my fingerprints to get in?" Alan asked with a little trepidation.

"You'll have to be printed when they issue you your ID card, everyone does. It's not much different from working at one of the Fortune 500. Just blander colors everywhere and the support staff are a lot more polite. I promise, you won't have to salute anyone while you're here," Martin said with a laugh.

"I just now sent back the application and forwarded it to my advisor."

"I know," said Martin, "I got it a second ago. As for your advisor, he has already given his blessing for you to temporarily relocate your project down here. I hope you don't mind the impertinence but we are somewhat pressed for time."

"Um, I guess that's cool. When did he say I could leave?"

"Well, given that we're going to be paying the university, there's no time like the present. How soon can you leave?"

"Damn, I guess I could wind everything up and leave by the end of the week."

"Oh, don't worry about your rent and utilities, we'll take care of them. But I would suggest you empty your fridge, otherwise you'll probably return to a pretty nasty science experiment when you get back. I've see it happen and it's not pretty," laughed Martin.

Alan couldn't decide if he was more excited or apprehensive. He didn't want to admit that he might be unsettled about walking – well, flying – into a situation that might be bigger than he was. He knew that his software was something new and he just didn't want to get screwed out of any profitable venture built around it.

He looked at the various pictures of Norma he had collected from the newspapers and magazines of the last couple of weeks. She hadn't seen his shrine of honor yet. He didn't want her to make too big a thing about it, he was just proud of her accomplishment and felt lucky to count her as a friend. He sat, waiting for her to get back from lunch.

Shortly, Norma returned. She came around to Alan's side of the room and stopped with her mouth open, staring at all the articles and photos of her on the wall.

Blushing furiously, Alan immediately began to protest. "I just collected them so you'd have them for your scrapbook. Don't make a big thing about it."

"Anything you say." She beamed at him. "Hey, why the hangdog expression when I came in here? Bad news?" she asked.

"On the contrary. I just got offered a job, and I get to continue my project, apparently with all the computing power I could ever ask for. The bitch of it is I have to go out to the Southwest to do it."

"What kind of job is it? And why out there?" she asked

"It has to do with the 3-D stuff I've been working on. The guy who processed the sample data says that his and my projects are so similar that it would be better if we worked together out there. I'm going to be paid about twelve hundred a week and the department gets some kind of grant for the trouble of sending me away."

"Are you sure you aren't going to end up someone's sex slave in the desert out there?" Norma asked, laughing at his stricken expression.

"You know, I never thought about that. I'm going to need an extra footlocker to haul my best toys with me!"

"Well, good lookers like you with such cute little asses *are* in high demand."

"Thanks a lot. If it makes any difference to your glass-half-empty view of the world, my advisor talked to this Dr. Harris and got the background info on the project and gave me his blessing," Alan said.

"How long are you going for?" asked Norma.

"I'm not really sure myself. I'll know more when I get there. Don't worry, I'll be in touch by e-mail, and, unlike some people, I'll call when I can. Besides, you can call me too when I get settled."

"I know, I really did miss you when I was on the road. But hey, I *am* happy for you. I hope this all works out. If you're out there for a long time maybe I'll take a road trip to see you." Norma paused for a second and got serious. "And, I want to thank you for these pictures and clippings, I haven't had time to gather any on my own yet," she said, giving Alan a hug.

Squeezing back, Alan said, "I'm going to head home and straighten up before I leave. I'm going to have my mail forwarded out there as soon as I know the address, but could you stop by over the next few days and pick up what comes in?"

"No problem. Anything you need, let me know."

Alan gave her a kiss on the cheek and headed for home. It would probably be weeks before they got to see each other again. But in that intervening time they both would be entirely too busy to give each other much more than a passing thought.

Touching down at the helipad at the Shelter Fourteen installation was an anticlimactic moment for Alan. The buildings of the complex looked pretty normal from the sky, small even for the kind of projects he imagined were conducted there. He finally greeted Dr. Harris in person, who, helping with Alan's bags, conducted him to the security office. He was fingerprinted and photographed and issued his security card with a lanyard to hang around his neck. Martin explained that he would have to sign a secrecy oath before he could be allowed to proceed any further.

"I don't remember you saying anything about this secrecy stuff," Alan objected, beginning to feel railroaded into something he might not want any part of.

"I'm sorry, I couldn't tell you the whole story before you arrived. The military requires a degree of confidentiality concerning the work here. Not because of any great concern for national security, but because some of the projects are sensitive and could be misinterpreted. If you don't want to sign you will be immediately conducted back to Chicago, no questions asked. The decision is completely yours. Although, I'm betting you want to see what were working on more than a quick trip home. Take your time, and read the oath. I'll go and get us coffee," Martin said.

"Do you have some kind of cola somewhere around here?"

"I think I can scare something up for you. I'll be right back," Martin said, leaving the room.

Alan was relieved that Dr. Harris left the door ajar. He wasn't locked in and he didn't see anything that looked like a one-way mirror. He noticed that there were no restrictions on his travel in the contract, just on disclosure of the project(s) at the facility. Nothing extreme, except that any unauthorized disclosure would be treated as a federal offense, punishable by a stay in an unnamed federal facility.

Well, in for a penny, in for a pound, Alan thought as he signed his life away.

Moments later Martin reappeared. "Now that the unpleasantries are completed, would you like a rundown of what I'm doing here?"

"That would be a good start," replied Alan.

"Tell you what, I can waste time giving you an overview of the project here in this office, or if you can wait about twenty-five minutes I can blow your mind." Martin suggested.

"Uh, well, I'm not sure which I want. If it's not going to hurt, or negatively impact my sex drive, let's go for the 'blow my mind' thing," Alan answered with a smile, warming up to the obvious enthusiasm in Dr. Harris' manner.

Martin showed him to the elevator.

Looking at the larger-than-normal doors, Alan asked, "What kind of elevator is this? Where exactly are we going?"

"You aren't in any way claustrophobic, are you? Your medical records said nothing about a fear of enclosed spaces."

"What the hell were you doing with my medical records?" Alan challenged.

"Okay, time for full disclosure," Martin said as the doors slowly closed. "You've been checked out by naval intelligence six ways from Sunday and here's why. My project is funded under the strategic research division of the Navy and this Army facility used to be one of the deep shelters the government built back during the cold war. It's decommissioned as a bomb shelter and is now used for research projects that benefit from its unique location. We're heading just short of a mile underground. My project detects and measures gravity waves, so I need my instruments isolated from vibrations and any sudden changes in temperature. And, my new young friend, I need you to help me design and build the display subsystem for the detector."

"So that's why you wanted to know what system my programs ran on. FYI, it's all written in low-level assembler code that uses the X-system for screen display," explained Alan.

"All of the bigger systems here are either Unix or Linux-based, we're not big on proprietary systems," Martin said.

"Cool. About this gravity detector, how sensitive is it? Are you looking for distant events like supernova explosions or black holes?" Alan asked.

"Actually no, although that's what *I* ultimately want to be able to do. The Navy is interested in detecting submarines underwater by sensing the difference in density of the hull and the water surrounding it. There is a definite change in the local gravity gradient at the interface between such unlike materials."

"So they could find tunnels and aircraft, even satellites, no matter how they might be concealed or stealthed, right?" asked Alan.

"Exactly. You've hit the nail right on the head. I need you because I have no experience in the development of graphical display systems. Yours is almost exactly what this detector needs. It can place objects in three-dimensional space in real time, and apparently with a good deal of accuracy too," Martin stated. "In return, I can place at your disposal more computing power than the entire University of Chicago has on campus. I don't think that the increased horsepower will divine the solution to your classic three-body problem, but it will let you eliminate dead ends quicker than you might in Chicago. Still interested?" asked Martin.

"Hell yeah, I'm in! Hey, how often do you get out of here and go into town? Is there even a town to go in to?" Alan asked.

"To be honest, I generally don't go out. I don't have much in my life but my work, and, other than a theater with hundreds of movies, I generally stick close to the base. The food's pretty good and the soldiers don't really get in the way. You'll have your own room. Only your ID opens the door, it'll also open all of my laboratory doors. You'd better get in the habit of wearing it all the time.

"Right now there're about sixty extra personnel from the Navy building out a second lab. I can introduce you to a few of them over dinner. You should probably get moved in first though. I'll drop you off at your room and come back by in about forty-five minutes and we can get a bite to eat," suggested Martin.

"Sounds great."

"Other than the fact that there's no beer, wine or other spirits on base, it's pretty much like dorm living, without the excess testosterone and incipient stupidity. If you do strike up a relationship with one of the women posted here, keep it to yourself. The military won't do anything to you, but she might get discharged for misconduct. Oh yeah, some of the common areas are under scrutiny by security cameras," Martin finished as the elevator touched down.

Showing Alan to his room, Martin pointed out the main features of the underground community. Alan felt better seeing so many other inhabitants down there, many giving him and Dr. Harris a friendly nod as they passed. It helped him feel less isolated. His room was a delight; the bed was a king and he had his own bathroom. It didn't take him long to unpack, and he was pleased there was a network hookup right at his desk. He connected his laptop and let the networking software automatically connect to the Internet. He sent a short note to Norma letting her know he had arrived safely, and asked her to return a rented video he had forgotten.

He also noticed that the bandwidth was fast enough that he could transfer the bulk of his data from Chicago in a reasonable amount of time.

A second later Martin knocked on his door.

"Up and at 'em, let's get some grub," invited Martin.

"Lead on. Hey, are we really formal down here, not you, but, like the Army guys? Do we have to call them by their rank and stuff?" Alan asked.

"Not really. You only have to worry about rank when the brass visit. I'm Martin, or Marty to just about everyone; most of the soldiers call me Doc. I hate to say it but I'm sure you're gonna pick up some kind of nickname before long. Let's just hope it's something you can live with.

"Normally it's not this crowded, most of these people are helping in the expansion. You'll meet them over the next few days."

"No time like present. Just drop me into the fire, Doc, we'll see what I'm made of quickest that way."

After selecting and collecting their food, the two made their way to a table with four naval personnel. Martin introduced Alan as a programmer specializing in graphical display technology and mentioned that he was also the research mate of the discoverer of the new asteroid.

Martin added, "As a matter of fact, if any of you saw the clips of the asteroid with the shot of Saturn in the background, that was Alan's work."

"That was pretty cool, how'd you put it together?" asked one of the engineers, starting Alan off on the story of Norma's project and the events leading up to her discovery. Everyone at the table listened with undisguised fascination at Alan's description of the software Norma had developed for automating the search of the sky. They wanted more details about her. What was she like? Were the two of them close? One of the techs even asked if Alan had planned on inviting her there for a visit, based of course on how she looked in her pictures and television segments.

Laughing, Alan told them he suspected that the university and NASA would probably be occupying her time for a while.

When Alan and Martin finished eating, they made their way to the exit and Martin led them to the original lab. As soon as Alan got in the door, he stopped dead in his tracks getting his first glimpse of the detector.

"Holy shit! What do you call that?"

Martin laughed until his eyes watered. "'That,' is the operational portion of the detector. I've never heard anyone express himself quite like that. In your defense, though, everyone else who's been down here knew what to expect."

"The damn thing is huge! What's it made of, concrete or something?" Alan asked.

"No, it's one enormous crystal of aluminum. It's so massive that it has to be grown in place. The molecular matrix of the crystal flexes as gravity waves travel through it. The array of lasers on top there measure minute changes at the molecular level and the computers off to the side there collect the data.

"I couldn't pin down location finely enough, so what we're doing is instead of trying to grow a bigger crystal, we're adding a second detector, just like they do with radio astronomy," Martin explained.

"So that's why they're tearing up the rooms on the other side? They're putting in another detector for you?" Alan asked.

"That's right, for the next seven or eight weeks."

"Holy crap, Marty, this project is huge. Hey, where do you want me to set up in here?" Alan asked.

"I cleared off the desk over here. Did you see the network pop in your room?"

"Yeah, I set up my laptop and got e-mail from home. Thanks. Was there anything you wanted to start on tonight?"

"Heck no, let's head over to the other side where the second detector is going to be and then call it a day. Oh, before we leave try your card in the door, I want to make sure it's programmed right."

"No problem. I'm gonna wear the thing around my neck wherever I go, sort of like geek jewelry."

"One more thing. Look in the center desk drawer in your room, there's a blue folder with the emergency procedures of the shelter. The Army wants you to read the damn thing and sign and return the bottom sheet."

Despite his excitement, Alan was wrung out and ready for bed. He never suspected that his tour of duty underground would be the hardest of his life, and that he would do it with nary a beer in sight!

Shout, shout let it all out
These are the things I can do without, come on
I'm talking to you, come on
Shout
Written by Roland Orzabal and Ian Stanley, performed by Tears For Fears

CHAPTER 14

J OHN WAS LOSING sleep. He wasn't eating right, and if you asked his fellow officers what they thought of their friend's recent behavior, they would have simply shrugged their shoulders and said that whatever it was, John would spill when he was damned good and ready. More than a few suspected that John's self-imposed grief was over a woman.

No matter how he looked at it, John couldn't imagine any reasonable explanation for Sydney lying to him about her contact with Jaylynn Williams. He replayed all of their conversations in his mind. She denied any contact with the girl prior to her disappearance, and had gone out of her way to state that she barely knew the girl at all. And yet Jaylynn's mobile phone bill showed calls to Sydney's phone number twice in the week before the woman's disappearance, both calls over ten minutes long.

The truth of the matter was John did not intend to confront Sydney until he knew there was no other way to ferret out the facts. He dug into every fact, every nuance of Sydney's life. Hopefully, if she was somehow linked to the disappearance she would lead him to any others involved.

He was engaging in behavior he loathed in any cop, concealing evidence from Agent Samuels and his own boss, the lieutenant. His behavior was inexcusable and constituted an obstruction of justice. He rationalized that until he could uncover the motive behind Sydney's lies, premature exposure would only alert her and whatever accomplices she might have.

John and Sydney had spoken by phone twice since his startling discovery. Both calls had been brief, light and non-engaging: just a hello, how are you, keeping them in touch. He was certain she suspected nothing but was uncertain how to proceed with the larger investigation without tipping his hand to the FBI. Asking for a wiretap on Sydney's line required a judge's signature, and getting one illegally meant either calling in Samuels or finding some nefarious local who would one day demand a *quid pro quo* from him. Neither was an option at this point.

John got copies of all of Sydney's long distance bills for the last three months from his local contacts in Atlanta. He also ran the standard queries on every person in the Williams e-mail address book. Most of them were outside of John's jurisdiction, so he turned them over to Samuels and his people. Unfortunately the one thing John couldn't get was the detail of Sydney's outgoing long-distance calls from her office. Quiet inquiries into how the college's internal phone system worked showed that calls made from the administrative and faculty offices were lumped into a single bill, not separated by office or department.

In the meantime, Samuels was pursuing a separate line of investigation in Chicago and was in sporadic contact with John by phone. Most of their communications took place via the electronic messaging system on the FBI's mainframe. John had long since removed the two suspicious calls from the master listing, hoping no one would notice so small an anomaly, all the while feeling he had dirtied himself beyond redemption.

John began to distract himself studying Sydney's life. He saw the level of excellence she pushed herself to live up to. Behind her calm countenance was a woman driven to succeed, no, to conquer all that stood in her way.

Her undergraduate and graduate school records painted a picture of a woman who never settled for less than her best. He began to see she didn't compete with her peers. Instead, she was compelled to always beat her personal best. John knew that most people who got on this kind of treadmill almost always burnt out, sometimes even blew up. Any machine governed by positive feedback oscillated out of control, and yet Sydney made a successful accommodation to her obsessive drive to perfection. Her personality appeared almost completely and diametrically opposite of her earlier student incarnation. John could barely recognized anything of the student Sydney in the one he was poised to arrest as a material witness to a possible homicide, completely fall in love with, or both.

For the last few years she had been a frequent flyer. Each year she traveled to more and more cities, no longer just her parents' home in Michigan. But her job at Steddman explained this away. John could see that a dean of student affairs would visit high schools across America to persuade outstanding high school girls to consider Steddman College as their first choice destination after graduation.

John decided to go back several years and compare Sydney's travel itineraries against the long list of disappearances He entered the dates Sydney had made trips away from Atlanta into a new spreadsheet, and discovered no obvious pattern; the trips seemed almost random. He pulled up the FBI database of disappearances and began tediously entering the dates and locations of every case into the new spreadsheet. After about forty-five minutes of painstaking cutting and pasting he sorted the two lists together by date, hoping against hope there would be no overlap.

As he went over the two lists, John began to smell a rat. Of the thirty or so people who disappeared in the years in which Sydney was traveling for Steddman, four had gone missing within four or five weeks of Sydney's visit to their cities. The number was just about what one would statistically expect, but not quite.

John noted that each of the victims were young women between the ages of twenty and twenty-eight. Adding Jaylynn Williams to the group made it a bona fide trend. John pulled the four case files. The first woman worked in computer control systems, specifically in advanced environmental controls for a national heating and air conditioning contracting firm. She specialized in the environmental control of the most modern commercial and industrial complexes in the country. Sydney had visited her town three weeks before she disappeared.

John looked at the second case. Sydney's visit to this woman's city predated her disappearance by a little over four weeks. The woman was the oldest of the bunch at twenty-eight and was a child psychologist specializing in displacement therapy. The facts surrounding her disappearance were nearly a carbon copy of Jaylynn Williams'.

Samuels' suspicions were making more and more sense as John compiled background details on the various cases. Maybe the people who had been previously seen as victims of heinous crimes were, in fact, squirreled away somewhere, alive and kicking.

John scanned the background of the third woman. She was twenty-five, single, and employed as a private pilot with a charter jet company in Nashville, Tennessee. She received her initial pilot training from the Air National Guard, but had learned to fly in high school from her father, a former fighter pilot in Vietnam. She had taken her first solo flight at seventeen. Her grades in school were a perfect 4.0, she had graduated with honors. She had disappeared over a weekend in the same manner as the others, without any notice. Life around her was unchanged and unaffected, her mail had still been delivered, her credit cards and bank accounts remained untouched. Her boyfriend, who had an ironclad alibi, sensed nothing in her manner or behavior that led him to forecast her disappearance.

The fourth woman was the oldest of four siblings, divorced with no children and employed as an entomologist for a chemical research facility specializing in the development of commercial-grade fertilizers and pesticides. Sydney had visited her town barely two weeks before she had vanished. Unfortunately, there was no way of knowing who or where Sydney had visited during her stay other than the high school from which she was recruiting.

If he were a betting man, John would have to say that he was on to something. Yet the timing of Sydney's visits to these four towns was circumstantial at best. It wasn't proof of any kind, but if a mistake like Jaylynn's telephone records was overlooked, there would probably be others. Most successful conspiracies were made so by a combination of ignorance on the part of the public and concealment of the most obvious clues to its existence. John believed that if he was persistent, he would uncover the web of clues that would expose the entire mystery to him.

John wondered how Sydney had become involved in recruiting, kidnapping or murdering young, bright black women. When did she begin, and who might have initially contacted her? She couldn't have been involved as far back as the sixties, she wasn't old enough by more than a decade. Almost every member of the FBI's group were near the best and the brightest of their vocations. The range of specialties read like a vast think tank devoted to solving the most complex and important problems a modern civilization faced. Looking at the whole group in this new light, John wanted to get hold of Samuels and discuss the ramifications should the disappearances not be a case of foul play. If the victims had all been spirited away to live in some sort of secret community, if there was any chance at all that this might be true, it opened a much bigger can of worms. If these hundreds of African Americans left their lives behind to go off someplace where they had not been heard from, or discovered, in the last four decades, where had they gone? Where in America, or even the world, had almost two thousand people gone without a trace, and more important, what had they been doing all that time?

John logged on to the electronic messaging section of the FBI system and left word for Samuels that he needed to talk to him as soon as possible. The mere possibility of these people living completely hidden from view, and recruiting others to join them, had crossed the line of what John was willing to investigate without any kind of backup or safety net. The enormity of the situation came crashing down on him. The possible connection between Sydney and these five women could only be investigated with additional manpower. He wanted to orchestrate a brute-force investigation into every long-distance phone call to and from Steddman College and retrace Sydney's footsteps for the last five years.

And what of his growing feelings for her? At least *he* thought they were real, but what about her? Was she deliberately manipulating him to conceal a crime or conspiracy? Could he, should he, confront her, risking the chance of scaring her off? And the ultimate question was, could he conceal his suspicions from Sydney if he was asked to draw her into some kind of confidence that could blow the case wide open? Could he be just as calculating and manipulative as he suspected she was and pull it off with the same elan?

John was getting a headache. He had to shake off the mood he'd put himself in so he began to clean up after his evening's research. He logged off the FBI system and deleted all of the temporary files from his computer. The FBI files all went into his personal shredder. He even took the map down off his wall and shredded it as well. By the time he was done there was no trace of the investigation to be found in his home.

John decided to walk to Pete's to clear his head. A few minutes later he was startled out of his quiet contemplation by the vibration of his mobile phone.

"Mathews," he answered.

"Hey, it's Samuels returning your message. Find something?" he asked

"I think I may have, how about you? Are you still in Chicago?"

"No, I'm en route back to Atlanta. Can you hold what you found until I get there? I should be on the ground in about an hour," said Samuels.

"Yeah, but you're going to want to hear this right away."

"Can you give me a hint?" inquired Samuels.

"Let's just say that your boogeymen are beginning to scare me, and leave it at that," John replied.

"Shit . . . I'll call you as soon as I touch down."

John was walking slowly and deliberately. This case was getting worse and worse. The first woman he had made a connection with in years might be involved in a forty-year-old conspiracy, and this very case was the first he had ever worked that might directly threaten his own life.

What do I do now, he thought, *not go home? Get someone else to start my car from here on out? And what about Sydney?* He was going to have to speak to her sometime in the near future, if only to keep from alerting her to his suspicions. John was going to have to confront his own feelings, straighten up his act and get his mind right.

Nearing Pete's, John made a concerted effort to put Sydney and the case from his mind as the sidewalk traffic picked up.

Walking past several bars, he listened to the snatches of music drifting out to the street, jazz here, rhythm & blues there, even a little country to round out the night's selections. He absorbed the evening's flavor as he made his way to his own destination, watching the people sharing the night with him. He couldn't help but wonder if any of the men or women he saw in the night would go the way of those hundreds missing, or if anyone he saw on the street had knowledge of any of those who had disappeared. Then the willies caught up with him. He began to entertain the quiet fear that one of those passing in the night might be watching him for signs of his knowing their secret. He almost tightened up and began to scan the streets for anyone who took an unhealthy interest in him, but deliberately shook it off. There was no way he could acknowledge their attention anyway.

The music of the Ramsey Lewis Trio drifted around the corner ahead. John was relieved to finally get off the street. He was thinking how even imaginary boogeymen could drive one to distraction.

In the cooler, less humid air of Pete's Place, John felt some of the tension drain from him. He blended into the familiar, into a place that was his private home away from home. He never saw any others from his squad here; truth be told he never mentioned the place to anyone.

Pete, when he purchased the business, ripped out the ceiling, the walls and the bar, and rebuilt the whole thing around an audiophile-class sound system that was unmatched by any other establishment in town, perhaps in the country. And as good as the sound system was, Pete had made no effort to advertise the fact; he just played the very best in jazz and blues recordings every night.

Pete's was also equipped with one of the largest computerized music systems in the country. He converted his vast music collection on compact disc, and albums, to tens of thousands of digital music files stored on one gigantic computer system, giving him control over every minute of music played every night. Pete could pick out a custom play list in the morning that would pace the musical mood of the evening from when the doors opened until he closed up for the night.

John had helped Pete with the installation of the huge computer system in his upstairs office, though such help consisted of handing Pete components when Pete pointed his finger. He built a ten terabyte raid array connected to a dual CPU system to feed the digitized music to the sound system downstairs. And with the wide-band connection to the Internet, Pete could even play blues or jazz radio stations broadcasting over the Internet from virtually any location in the world. The entire system was controlled by a laptop computer mounted above the cash register behind the bar. When he understood what his friend had built, John couldn't help but think that computers really could do virtually anything.

John walked to the end of the bar, grabbing an open seat, and waited for Pete to notice him. He liked the fact that Pete's drew a quiet, adult crowd that never caused the kind of ruckus most places serving alcohol and playing dance or hard rock music seemed to draw. John couldn't see any of the ever-present smoke and stink that nearly every other bar and tavern left on their patrons. The music was crisp, the instruments were never muddy and the sound created an vibe that flowed through his soul, leaving him energized. Patrons who were there for the unique atmosphere didn't drink as much as those in noisier bars and dance clubs, and yet the prices weren't inflated to compensate for what John was convinced was a lower return on investment. Pete obviously knew what he was doing, so John let it alone.

Seeing John at the end of the bar, Pete lifted a glass and pointed to the chilled tea in a pitcher. John nodded and reached over to grabbed his own coaster.

"What's happening with you, man?" asked Pete dropping off the glass decorated with a sprig of mint and a thin lemon slice.

"Not much, I had to get out of the house," he answered.

"The same thing you were looking at the other day, or something else?"

"No, it's the same one. I needed to lose myself in something else."

"Cool, you want to hear anything special? I can drop in a few requests if you got 'em," Pete offered.

"How do you expect me to improve on perfection?" laughed John. "It sounds like tonight's theme is live tracks, am I right?"

"You hit it right on the head, if you hang around long enough there's Les McCann and Eddie Harris coming up, a little Brubeck, some Herbie Mann and a live cut of Wes Montgomery. You like?"

"You bet. When are you going to hook me up like this at home?" John teased.

"Foolish man! If I hooked you up with the setup I got here, how would I get to separate you from your money if you kept your pale ass at home all the time?" laughed Pete, as he moved down the bar to fill an order.

Sipping from his glass he watched Pete work the crowd at the bar. John couldn't help but wonder what his friend really thought about their relationship, he white, Pete black, both with similar military backgrounds. He knew that as much as they might find in common, a love for jazz, no patience for fools and no tolerance for childish behavior from those who should know better, their differences were so fundamental that no amount of explanation could bring understanding to the other. What could possibly induce his friend to abandon his life and seek out a place where he would never have contact with the life that made him the man he was? What could make anyone do so? If Jaylynn Williams had decided to leave behind everything she owned, every friend and family member, and whatever future she would have had with NASA and with her boyfriend Jason, what had beckoned so strongly that she had felt compelled to give it all up?

The thought was more than vaguely disquieting. John had seen alcohol and drugs take people away from their lives. He had seen crimes of greed and passion also lure people away, causing them to leave behind everything for the empty promise of all they believed could be. But, even then they still had some connections to the past. Most returned when they crashed and burned, or when they reached the end of the line of their fleeting dreams. The more fortunate ones even gloated when they reached a plateau that permitted them the luxury of a look back.

Could it be the promise of the grand adventure of a lifetime, or the hope for a life so gratified, so fulfilled, that the choice, though difficult and fraught with remorse, could deny the prospect of saying no? If the hundreds of those extracted by the FBI computer had chosen a lifetime of exile, with no connection to the lives that made them the people who they were, where had they gone? *That* was the question. That was the sum of John's fears. What can compel a man or a woman enough so that they would give it all up, so that they left parents, brothers, sisters and lovers behind to their loneliness, their pain and emptier lives to go on without them? *Great idea going out to get away from it all, eh,* he thought. Fortunately the vibration of his phone derailed his musings.

"Mathews," he answered.

"Hey, it's me, Samuels. Am I interrupting anything?" he asked.

"No, I'm out looking at a change in scenery. What's up?"

"You called me, remember? Something important . . ." prodded Samuels.

"Yeah, you're right. Where are you? I'll grab a cab and meet you somewhere."

"I'm heading in from the airport, want me to pick you up?"

"Not here. How about the same place we had breakfast? You remember how to get there?" John asked.

"No problem, I'll wait for you there."

John hung up, drained his tea and slipped a twenty under the coaster, knowing that if he tried to pay he'd only insult his friend. He knew Pete would probably drop it into the waitresses' tip jar.

Back in the sultry night air, John walked in the direction of the restaurant, watching for any empty cabs cruising by. The walk helped. He organized his thoughts for his meeting with the FBI agent and felt better realizing he was, in fact, going to spill everything about Sydney. Samuels needed to know about the overlap in her travel and the five women who might have met with her just before their own disappearances. Sharing his burden would lighten it, and he would deal with his feelings toward Sydney when the time came.

He saw an empty cab coming down the street and flagged it down. Watching the city go by he felt himself become a cop again, and was actually proud of the work he had accomplished. The realization pulled him out of his depressive funk.

At the restaurant, he immediately went over to Samuels' booth and sat down. The FBI agent looked exhausted. He had dark circles under his eyes and was pale and unshaven. "You look like shit. What the hell have you been up to?" John asked.

"Later, I want to hear what spooked you enough that you couldn't give me any kind of heads-up before I got here."

"Here's the short version. I think we caught a break. It's weak, but with the right assistance I think I can make a pretty good case," John said.

Waiting a beat for John to continue, Samuels growled, "Give it up, Mathews, I'm not in the mood to play twenty questions."

"Easy now, pardner. Here's what I've got so far," he began, and related the whole story from the telephone calls made from Williams' mobile phone to the coincidence of the dean's trips. John also enumerated the steps he wanted to take in segmenting all of the cases to see if any further connections could be made to the dean's travel itinerary, or through her home or work telephone records. As he got deeper and deeper into his story, John saw Samuels become more and more excited. His exhaustion seemed to melt away the more John told him, and he made suggestions on how to accomplish the prodigious amount of legwork the investigation called for. Samuels took out a pocket organizer and entered notes as John continued. When John had run out of ideas he asked, "Do you think that anyone else should be brought in on this yet or are you still wanting to keep things just between us?"

"I have pretty broad discretionary authority up to but not including disclosure of the demographics of the group involved in the crimes we're investigating. I will get someone working on the kind of background information you focused on, but I'm not going to let anyone in on the dean's involvement, that responsibility is yours. Can you handle it?" Samuels asked John, eyebrow raised in question.

"I think so. What I want to do is get closer to her and see if there might be any travel in her future. If she does leave town can you get someone to blanket her door-to-door without tipping her off?"

"That should be no problem, there's a squad that specializes in team surveillance, she'll never know they're on her. The thing I'm worried about is that there might be a fox in among us chickens. If they get wind of our interest in Atkins, she may get tipped off and we'll end up losing her *and* everyone else involved. That's the bulk of what I was doing in Chicago. I had a research group going over some of the dossiers of the middle management segment of the Bureau looking for anything that didn't ring true. What we've uncovered so far were a bunch of errors and omissions that led nowhere, and, I'm afraid, only alerted several higher-ups something is up. That's what's had me burning the candle at both ends."

"Have any of the other agents tumbled to the racial aspect of the investigation? In other words is this about to blow up and become a public relations nightmare, and maybe end up alerting our quarry that you're on to something?" John asked.

"I'm hoping not. I put as tight a lid as I could on the internal investigation. The group in Chicago has been led to believe that we're looking for a mole who may be passing intel to the mob. That way the inevitable leaks and rumors should lead everyone off in the wrong direction."

"Christ, this just gets better and better. Are you going to update the director on the direction you and I are going to take on the conspiracy angle?"

"I'm scheduled to meet with him in two weeks for a status report. In the meantime I'll get someone on the telephone records of the women who fit the profile of the ones you dug up and see where it'll take us. What do you plan to do about the dean?" inquired Samuels.

"I think I'm going to ask her out to dinner," John replied.

You may be right, you may be crazy
But it just might be a lunatic you're looking for
You May Be Right
Written and performed by Billy Joel

CHAPTER 15

A N ENORMOUS AMOUNT of planning was going into the covert invasion of Iraq. The CIA was the lead agency in planning and preparing the operation, and held responsible for getting their operatives in and out of the country safely. While the planning was going on in the CIA's Langley headquarters, Western operatives were trying to gain information on the layout and defenses of the laboratory near Baghdad where the wreckage and the pilot's remains had been delivered for analysis.

The few agents already in place had found the entrance to the facility, but could get no information on the floor plan, nor what invaders would face in terms of security or defenses. So far, attempts to identify and suborn anyone posted to the lab had met with complete failure. The British, who controlled the best available local operatives, had not given up, and continued searching for any chink in the armor of silence surrounding the hidden facility.

Back in Langley, the planning group settled on the size of the invasion force and were screening candidates for the strike team from the ranks of the CIA, Army Special Forces group and the Navy SEALs. Insertion was to be via a high-altitude, low-open (HALO) parachute drop from a stealth bomber just outside of Baghdad to keep the chance of discovery to a minimum and to reduce the time US operatives spent in the air and on hostile soil.

From any perspective the operation was ill advised, and illegal to boot. The only recourse for the administration should any of the team be caught or killed was complete denial. The entire intelligence apparatus of the US was involved in planning the insertion and extraction of the team to minimize any prospect of mishap.

The director of the CIA was early for the morning's national security briefing at the White House. As he entered he saw Chief of Staff Masters talking to one of his aides, so he gave him a nod and moved off to the side of the room to wait. Crossing over to talk privately, Masters asked, "You have something that you don't want to cover with everyone in the meeting?"

"Yes I do, I got the op plan this morning. Does the president have any time right after the meeting or do you want me to come back this afternoon?" the director asked.

"Give me the highlights."

"Four men, dropped from a stealth ship from fifty thousand feet. In and out in a matter of hours."

"Extraction?" prompted the chief.

"It looks like it will be either north to Turkey or south through Kuwait. I should have that by this afternoon," the director replied.

"Fine, nothing on this during the meeting. I'll clear a half hour this afternoon for you. Do you need to bring anyone else over?"

"No sir, I've got it covered."

"It'll probably be after five, his schedule's full until then."

"Very good, sir. Thank you."

Returning to his office, the director called for Bascomb to stop by and bring him up to date on the extraction plan for the operation.

"Sit down, Bobby, I want to ask you a few questions on the plan so that I can give a detailed overview for a briefing this afternoon at the White House," said the director.

"Yes, sir. Does this mean that the plan is going to be greenlighted today?" Bobby asked.

"I can't say. The president is really worried about getting hammered by practically everyone in the world if this thing blows up in our faces. We can't afford anyone getting caught or killed on this one."

After his meeting with the director, Bobby called everyone in his group into the conference room to inform them the director was going for a green light that afternoon. First, they had to get with the MI-6 liaison officer and nail down the details on the extraction plan. The US had covert assets in the Persian Gulf area that could be called in if needed, but nothing like what MI-6 had on the ground in Iraq and Iran. Bobby immediately had a satellite tasked for super-high-definition photos of the area around the secret lab, the entire path east to the Iranian border and along the southeastern route along the border to Kuwait.

While Bobby arranged for the necessary support services for the operation, other members of the planning group were compiling data for the briefings the members of the multinational team would have to attend. And so began the extensive task of collecting every piece of intelligence the team had to master before their trip to the Middle East. On the director's orders the US team was placed on detached duty to their own group. One of the planning team ordered the false documents needed in Iraq and Iran on the off chance any of the operatives were questioned on the ground.

The planning team prioritized a list of objectives for the covert break-in, beginning with the collection of as much wreckage of the aircraft as the team could safely carry. The head of their own laboratory wrote up the protocols on how to handle and store the samples of metal, glass and any other pieces and an FBI forensics specialist sent over the methods for handling and storing any biological samples from the pilot.

Of course these procedures were the best-case methods that might or might not be used, depending on the circumstances surrounding the actual penetration of the lab. The myriad details for the operation were compiled at a fantastic rate, all to be collated and organized within the next two days so the US and British team members could begin training for the operation the moment they arrived.

That afternoon, when the director returned to the White House, he was conducted to the Oval Office where the president received him alone. The director noted the president was reviewing the operations summary he'd left with Simon Masters that morning.

"Good afternoon, Mr. President," he said, extending his hand to Bender.

"Mr. Director. Have a seat and let's go over what you're proposing here. I'm sorry I don't have a lot of time, I have to fly to New York shortly, but I wanted to look this operation over before I left. From what I've read, we're going to put a four-man team down just outside Baghdad to gain entry to the lab. Unfortunately, I don't see how you're going to get our guys out safely. I hope you have a better devised plan than what the chief gave me."

"Yes sir, we do. First of all we're going to be sharing the team personnel with MI-6."

"Wait a minute. I wanted them in on the planning, but I thought we were only going to use our own guys," the President said, interrupting the director.

"We were initially, but they offered one of their own teams, one of whom has direct knowledge of the area around the lab. And they already know what we're after, so there won't be any additional exposure. They've also agreed to detach their team, putting them under our direct command," the director quickly filled in. "Besides, they are supplying the logistics needed to get the team safely out of the area and back stateside, sir."

"How's that?"

"The plan calls for them to make their way east to Iran . . ."

"Oh, that's just perfect. You're telling me that we're going to be trespassing on *two* hostile countries just to get a peek at what's in this lab?"

"Yes, sir. But the beauty of the plan is that no one will be expecting the team to be heading toward Iran if the break-in is compromised. MI-6 is providing an extraction team for us at the border who will then conduct the team south to Kuwait. Once there we can pick them up by chopper and get them to a carrier in the Persian Gulf."

"What's your estimate of success for the op, and more importantly, can we do it without losing any of our people?" asked the president.

"The lab itself is an unknown sir, we haven't been able to get any information on the site at all. We do know that there are about twenty-two regulars who work there six days a week. They're in the lab mostly during the day, with a few sporadically working overtime, presumably on special projects like the aircraft wreckage. There are normally four guards to contend with at night, two at the entrance in this cinder-block building here," the Director show him on an overhead photo, "and two who patrol the area in a jeep.

"We know the building houses some minor government offices, something to do with the Ministry of Health, and the entrance to the lab is somewhere toward the back of the structure. If you look at the floor plan the British intel guys drew up by looking in the windows, the stairs going down are in the back corner of the building right next to a small freight elevator located about right here. Our team will be avoiding the elevator and using the stairs, they're probably not secured with anything more than locks on doors. At least that's what we hope. We will get the team inside the building after midnight, bypassing the guards at the front of the building and, if they can get downstairs without being discovered, that should allow them an hour or two to get what we need and get out. No one begins their work day in the offices or the lab before seven in the morning. MI-6 thinks that their agent in place will be able to secure a truck for the bulk of the trip to the border. Frankly, we doubt anyone will be out that way looking for thieves in the night, sir."

"And you endorse this plan? Fully knowing what the discovery of our guys over there would mean to foreign policy and to this administration? You're that confident that you and MI-6 can pull this off with no exposure?"

"Look, I won't shit you, Mr. President, there is no promise of a happy ending. But if we can recover anything from this lab that will point to the source of the metal we recovered, that alone is worth the risk. We need to get our hands on every piece of this new technology we can. What we have already proves we are no longer the best and the brightest. It's a question of this country maintaining its scientific and military superiority, and our place on this globe as the one dog whose yard no one wants to trespass into under any circumstance, Mr. President."

"I understand your concerns, I want to make sure that the risks are well outweighed by the strategic benefits." He paused, looking severe, then continued.

"I'm giving you a green light for the operation, subject to final review before you deploy the team. How long before the team is ready?"

"Two weeks sir. The SAS team is on its way stateside now."

"Where are they going to be training?"

"We're going to do everything in-house sir, we want to keep exposure to a minimum."

"Very well, I'll expect a final plan in ten days. Thank you for bringing me up to speed, Mr. Director."

"Not at all, Mr. President. Thank you, and have a pleasant trip to New York, sir."

When the director had gone, the president called the Simon into the office. He considered the ramifications of the operation while waiting for the chief's arrival. Simon Masters and James Bender had been friends for thirty-six years, beginning when they met as interns at the same law firm in Boston over one long, hot, muggy summer. Their friendship had blossomed over beer and chasing the same group of Bostonian socialites during their summer hiatus from their respective colleges. They kept in touch through their undergraduate years and, when they both eventually graduated, they took off for Europe together to let off steam.

Masters had been drawn to his charismatic friend, seeing how easily Bender was able to make and maintain genuine friendships with virtually everyone with whom he came in contact. He respected the commanding presence Bender had in his burgeoning political career as a state assemblyman, sensing Bender was destined for greater things. Bender always sought Master's counsel in matters of political and business strategy. Simon easily evaluated the most convoluted relationships with ease. The two made a formidable pair at the apex of the most powerful country in the world, making and implementing policy in a seemingly evenhanded, unstoppable fashion.

Masters entered the office, sat down across from the president.

"I greenlighted the operation, but I have reservations about the downside if it all breaks bad."

"Is that why you had me wait down the hall while the director was here?" asked Simon.

"Would you believe I was giving you plausible deniability if the worst comes to be? When do we leave for New York?" Bender asked.

"The chopper is scheduled to leave at six-fifteen, you'll be getting in to New York by seven-thirty and at the hotel by eight. Ready?"

"Yep. I got the notes for the speech right after lunch, I'm sure I'll be a hit. Besides, no one but the press really listens to what I've got to say," replied the president.

"What do you really think about this invasion. Is the technology they're talking about really worth the risk to you?" Simon asked.

"I read the lab report on the metal, and I also looked over the analysis of the electronics. We're nowhere near being able to duplicate what's there, even with samples to play with. It's like Thomas Edison seeing pieces of a laptop computer. Would he be able to duplicate it? Absolutely not. The technological infrastructure didn't exist for him to build a computer even if he knew how. That's how I feel about the little bit we have so far, and yet someone out there already has it. That's what drives me to push for an operation that's breaking dozens of US and international laws. Whoever the owners of this technology are, they scare the hell out of me. I need to know who they are and what their agenda is. I will not go down in history as the president who let some other country steal the march of technological or military superiority away from the American people."

"Very good sir, working on the reelection already?" quipped Masters. "I think the rhetoric is just right, and your delivery was spectacular. Now if we can work on your hand gestures, I think we have a hit," he finished, sardonically.

"All right all ready, I get your point," Bender replied quietly.

"All rhetoric aside. I know you want to be able to secure this technology for the US, and you know I've already picked our favorite friends we'll want to pass it along to when we get it. I hate it when you feel the need to blow smoke up my ass, or more insultingly, when you believe it's going to work. I don't approve of the invasion, but I'll support it, that's not my problem. Let's agree to call it what it is: someone else has it, we want it. No more, no less. We'll do what we have to."

"Fine, but remember, if we end up going head-to-head with whoever built this aircraft, how will we stack up against something from a decade or more in our future?" Bender shot back, more than a little irritated with his longtime friend.

"I'm not saying you're not right. Just don't try to convince me that the shit you stepped in really smells sweet. Now I'm going to get everything ready for the trip, is there anything else?"

"No, I'm going upstairs to get ready. I'm sure we'll revisit this issue again."

"Yes sir, Mr. President. I'll meet you at the chopper."

The next morning, Chief of Staff Masters drove through the Virginia countryside for about twenty minutes before he saw the sign directing him to a county park with a small picnic area beside a large pond. The director's car was already there. Pulling in and parking, the chief saw the director was sitting at a picnic table next to the pond.

He rose and shook Simon's hand. "I checked around, we're alone here. You want to tell me what's so important that we had to meet out here?" the director asked.

"I'm very sorry. I just wanted to cover a couple of things away from my office, and yours. I apologize for the inconvenience, but I'm concerned with the possible political fallout if any part of this operation ever comes to light. We aren't talking about a Senate investigation, we're talking about the worldwide ramifications, not only from our enemies *and* friends in the Middle East, but from the owners of the craft as well. Eventually we're going to confront them and I want you to plan just as hard for that confrontation as you are for the invasion of Iraq. You, and everyone else in intelligence, had better plan for it, it's going to happen. I'm not here to mince words, or to worry you about the political ramifications of the invasion, I don't give a shit. But you and all your buddies in intelligence, and at the Pentagon, better have your shit ready for the fight of your life. Can you win a fight against bulletproof fighters? Can you win a fight against weaponry and defenses from the future? Well, can you? Because that's what you're going to be up against."

"You're serious about this. Is there something you and the president know about that you've not mentioned? Does he even know you're here?" the director asked.

"No he doesn't, and he never will. But what you and he haven't thought about is the coming storm when the shit hits the fan, and my best guess is that it will. If we get the wreckage from Iraq, and if we can get it back to the US, and if we can keep our operation a secret, we still have to face the fact that someone out there is better than we are, and they're slick enough that we have no idea where they are. Not scared yet? Well, you better be. You have just been relegated to the junior varsity on planet earth. And, based on the samples we've already gotten, we aren't even on the same field as the varsity squad. I want to impress upon you, and those in the military, in the global dick-waving contest the US has just come up short."

"Anything else?" asked the director, frostily.

"No, but until you hear different you better be making contingency plans in case the owners of the aircraft want their parts back, because I don't think we'd be able to stop them even if we wanted to. I'm sorry to be so blunt but I don't want to waste your time, nor do I want the American protectorate caught with their collective pants down."

"I'll take it under advisement. But you really didn't have to come down so hard, I can also take direction, my job hasn't been quite as political as some. And, unlike most of my predecessors I believe I'm capable of putting the country first."

"I'm hoping so. Look, I'll work the defense contingency planning from the White House side, but it would help if you could get the Joint Chiefs on the same page. These guys haven't fought a *real* war since Vietnam, and you know how that ended up."

"Look, I'll pass the word as soon as I get back. And I'll keep you posted."

"If anything comes in to the White House from overseas I'll call you immediately. I don't want anyone getting behind the eight ball on this one."

"Fine, I'll see you at the briefing tomorrow morning."

"Thank you. And thank you for listening to a scared old man."

"Don't start to get all mushy on me now. You really should have used the 'this is going to hurt me more than it's going to hurt you' approach, then I would have had some idea of what I was in for," the director said with a warming smile. "Just between you and me, the reports on the samples haven't left me able to sleep well at night. My own people have said that we're probably two or more decades from beginning to achieve the level of technology the samples demonstrate. Let me see who I can scare today, I'm sure someone is going to bring it up."

"Come on, let's get out of here. I'll be back at the White House around midday if you need me to play bad cop to any of our friends."

The two shook hands and returned to their respective cars and drove out of the park, taking off in different directions, Masters driving toward the harder of their two jobs. Convincing the president of the military threat that everyone seemed to want to overlook in their haste to get hold of the advanced technology the wrecked aircraft represented, and making sure whatever recovered got to the right people, was going to take some serious slight of hand.

The following evening the SAS team arrived at Langley and met immediately with Bascomb and the two CIA team members. Bascomb got the meeting started right away.

"Malcom Stiles, Geoffrey Linden, meet David White and Todd Kahill. The four of you have a lot to cover before the drop, so we've prepared some homework for tonight. We plan on an early start in the morning. Do you have any questions?" Responding to a hand half raised, Bobby said, "Yes, Mr. Stiles, what can I help you with?"

Getting to his feet Stiles asked, "Yes, sir. First of all thank you for having us over to this side of the pond. Anything we can do to help just ask. We're prepared to get in and make a night of it. What me and Geoff would like to know is if there's a respectable pub here 'bouts where a man can get a decent pint?"

Stifling a laugh, Bobby replied, "I'm not sure if we have something like that nearby, but you can get a beer or two downstairs in the commissary. You'll be bunking right here on the grounds for the time being. Sorry men, those are the director's orders."

"At least there's imported beer here, maybe we can even get some at room temperature for you lads!" kidded White, the older of the two CIA operatives.

"Listen, I hope this hands-across-the-water thing ends up working out. I'd hate to think that a little thing like the Revolutionary War is going to come between such well-regarded professionals," Bobby interrupted.

"No worries! We'll do whatever it takes to get the bloody job done, even if me and my mate here have to hold back so that you Yanks can keep up."

All five laughed easily, melting any tension in the room. The four team members would spend a good amount of their training testing and observing their counterparts, but all four knew that they represented the top percentile of their profession and should readily trust each other's skills and judgment. Their only hurdle was getting to know each other well enough to make sure they meshed tightly as a team.

Bobby handed folders out to the men and reminded them that the contents were classified, and that the folders were to be kept in their possession until they returned to the morning briefing. Dismissing the four team members until then, Bobby accompanied them downstairs to a van waiting to take them to secure quarters on the agency's grounds. On the way, the four traded insults on country, culture and language, getting to know the men on whom their lives would depend and subtly taking measure of their mettle. The ride was short, and the small dormitory room the driver conducted them to already contained their luggage.

"Nice and homey," said Todd Kahill, looking around and poking through the dresser drawers.

"At least there aren't any of those bloody double berths," added Linden, the younger of the Brits.

"Well, you're the guests, pick any bed you like. It'll be yours until we leave for Germany," offered White. "And, as for rank around here, let's forget about it for the duration, if we can't work together as a team then this mission is not going to work at all. You blokes are reputed to be bad-ass hombres in your own right, and frankly Todd and I are looking forward to working with you. Hell, we might just learn a thing or two from you. And, that offer to hunt down something decent to drink is still good, what about it?"

"I don't know about young Geoffrey here, but I'm all in. I'm still running on the wrong side of the clock, I'm going to lay back and go over the intel your Bascomb gave me. However, if the three of you want to knock down a few, I'll stand guard over your files until you return. I'll just stuff them under my mattress and sleep over them, that ought to be safe enough," offered Stiles.

Both Americans looked at each other and shrugged their shoulders. Kahill said, "If either of you want something to eat or drink I'll make the run and bring it back. I sort of forgot the time zone thing myself."

"I'm just going to wash up and look over my file. Even though I'm the younger by seven months, Dad over there still treats me like a student in middle school. But I'm done in as well, thanks for the offer," said Linden.

White said, "That's probably not a bad idea, let's all take a rain check on the drinks until the mission is over, and I'll buy. I want to get a good start in the morning too. You boys like a little run in the morning?"

"Nothing like a good brisk-five mile stroll first thing. You have a track around here?" asked Linden.

"That we do. There's also a path through the grounds that's marked off in quarter miles. What say we hit the bricks at oh six hundred?" asked White.

"Suits me fine," said Stiles, nodding at Linden. "Just be sure to keep an eye on Linden in the morning, he always tries to get in an extra five if I'm not watching. Besides, after the trip over we could use a stretch before breakfast."

"On that note, let's call it a night, gentlemen," suggested White.

Making up their beds and unpacking toiletries and clothes, the four settled in to read their files. As each one finished for the night they tucked them under their pillow or mattress, turned off their light and dropped off to sleep, blissfully unaware of the global maelstrom their mission would initiate in two weeks.

We, so tired of all the darkness in our lives
With no more angry words to say can come alive
Get into a car and drive to the other side
You babe, steppin' out, into the night into the light
You babe, steppin' out, into the night, into the light

Steppin' Out

Written and performed by Joe Jackson

CHAPTER 16

D ETECTIVE MATHEWS AND Agent Samuels had to call in an FBI computer analyst to help with the sheer number of telephone records for the four women in the target group.

The analyst had to pass Samuels' rigorous background check back to his day of birth before being allowed in on the investigation. Their young analyst was an expert in data mining, the practice of locating, organizing and reporting data collected from multiple computer sources. Special Agent Jeffrey Minor had an almost sublime ability to pull together invisible threads of information and expose relationships and convergences that more often than not led to case breakthroughs. All this was despite the dismal condition of the information technologies of the bureau, most systems still character-based, many older than the analyst himself. The two lead investigators required him to whittle down the herculean task of collecting long distance, home and work telephone records from each of the four cases identified by Mathews, for a period of several weeks before their disappearances. At the very least, he would have to collect and compare the home, work and mobile telephone records of Dean Atkins to try to find any connection between the women and the dean.

Initially, Samuels was careful to keep the scope of the investigation away from their new teammate. Agent Minor was a child prodigy in the use of computers to process and store the massive databases on which the business world relied. As a student attending Stanford University, Minor almost single-handedly converted all of the university's stored data and programs to Y2K compliance two full years before the over-hyped stroke of midnight at New Year's Eve in December of 1999.

He had publicly scoffed at the predictions of doom in the press and the opinions of his instructors who sounded their own lofty predictions for months before the fated deadline. Despite his reputation as a wise-ass on campus he was recruited by the bureau right out of school. He turned down several extremely lucrative offers by members of the Fortune 500 to do so.

In Atlanta, Minor was stashed in the temporary office assigned to Samuels. There, he could directly utilize the resources of the FBI systems and be protected from casual scrutiny when he bent the laws protecting citizens from particularly onerous invasions of privacy by their government.

Minor began immediately by downloading the records from several long distance and cellular telephone carriers from over twenty different systems around the nation. Samuels didn't inquire into how his young charge got access to those records, he was only interested in results.

Meanwhile, John took the bull by the horns and invited Sydney out for dinner and a show. He wasn't sure if he could carry it off, but his relationship was the only means to observe her up close and personal. His unexpected invitation seemed to genuinely please her. John thought dinner and a movie would allow for casual intimacy in conversation and yet keep enough emotional distance for him to feel safe.

As he drove to pick her up, John was excited to see her again. Her street was typically suburban, quiet and slightly upscale. He pulled into her driveway and saw a nice, larger-than-bungalow-sized house with its own garage and a well-manicured front lawn. He got out of the car, walked up the steps to the front porch and saw that her door stood open, letting a light, airy jazz composition permeate the porch. He knocked on the screen door and got a "just a minute" in response. A moment later Sydney appeared at the back of the house and came walking down the hallway toward the door. She was wearing a shimmering green dress, subtly hinting at the form beneath.

Sydney opened the door to let John in and reached up and gave him a peck on the cheek, immersing his head in a light floral scent. She turned back into the house saying, "Hang on a minute, I'll just get my coat and we'll be on our way."

Her home was decorated with contemporary furniture and modern art. From his vantage point, he saw a well-appointed kitchen at the end of the hallway. When she reappeared, Sydney wore a light wrap that complemented her dress and her eyes. John wholeheartedly approved of her look, nearly forgetting the fact that she was a material witness in his investigation.

"You look kinda good to be out with a lowly civil servant, ma'am. Are you sure you want to be seen with the likes of me?" John asked.

Returning a warm smile and taking his arm, Sydney replied, "And miss out on the first date I've had in months? You must be out of your mind. You wouldn't be having second thoughts would you, detective?"

"Can the 'detective' stuff and I'll take you anywhere you want!"

"Right now I need to be taken somewhere to eat. How about you, hungry?" she asked.

"I have a great seafood place I'd like to take you to. You're not allergic or anything, are you?"

"No, I'm not 'allergic or anything,' seafood is fine. Do you think you can relax and think of me as someone you've known most of your life, or whatever it takes for you feel comfortable?" Sydney asked, laughing. "I'm sure you're not nervous with the criminals you have to question, are you?"

"Well, not exactly. But you're nowhere near the kind of perp I deal with at the station," John replied. "Besides, I'm a little rusty with this dating stuff. I seem to not quite get what's going on, if you know what I mean."

Laughing lightly at the apprehension in John's face, Sydney moved quickly to reassure him and said, "I'm not holding all the cards with this getting-to-know-you thing either. Most of the men I've dated have either been put off by the fact that my IQ is in triple digits, or that I don't feel the need to immediately jump into bed to validate my self-worth. I don't treat sex as a commodity or my looks as bait. Are you going to talk me to death or can we get a move on?" Sydney asked, gently pulling him down the walk to the car.

Once in the car, Sydney asked, "How's the investigation into Jaylynn going? You didn't mention her the last couple of times we spoke. I hope no news is good news."

Sitting up a little straighter, John replied, "There's not much to talk about. We've developed no new leads; if we had something, anything to report, something that might indicate any kind of threat to the students at the college I'd have called immediately. Since there's no clue to what she did the day she was last seen, and since her boyfriend, family and friends have no idea where she went, I've got nothing to go on. Have you thought of anything, no matter how remote, that might give me a hint where to look?"

"Of course not, if I had I would have called, even woken you up if need be. The administration is concerned because there's been no word from her, and your telling me that you haven't found anything to explain her disappearance underscores the unsettling nature of bad things happening to good people. We're all afraid something did happen to her. Even some of her fellow students are beginning to believe something unpleasant has befallen her," she finished.

"I know exactly what you mean. Too many times I've had to tell some parent or spouse someone they love is dead. The only time it doesn't seem so bad is when the missing person has been gone for a long time. Then it's more like I'm bringing some measure of closure to an open wound. It's too bad you and Williams weren't any closer, you might have known something of what she was up to, something that you could look back on that could give us some idea of what happened to her."

"Me too. I often think about how my being more involved in her life may have made a difference, somehow prevented her disappearance," Sydney said.

John rolled her words around in his head, hampered by the fact that he couldn't easily look at her face while he drove. He wanted desperately to take her at her word, to believe she had nothing to do with the missing woman.

"Let's change the subject, otherwise I don't think we're going to have much of a good time tonight," he suggested. "Besides, I didn't ask you out to talk about my job. I'm guessing that there might be something else we can occupy our time and conversation with, you think?"

"I couldn't agree with you more. Do you mind if I turn on the radio?"

"Not at all, pick anything you like," John answered.

They drove the rest of the way to the restaurant without further conversation. It was a comfortable silence, the sound of blues coming from the radio. John was somewhat surprised, and pleased, that she appeared to enjoy the same type of music he did. After a couple of songs Sydney was humming along with Billie Holiday, and the tension seeped out of him despite himself.

Reaching the restaurant, John passed by the valet stand and parked the car himself.

Answering her raised eyebrow, he said, "There's police stuff in the trunk that I can't take the chance on losing."

"Ah, thumbscrews, manacles and such?" she asked, with an impish grin. "I'm beginning to think this date is going to be a lot more interesting than I thought."

John gave an easy laugh. "A man's got to be prepared for anything with the modern woman of the twenty-first century."

He took her arm and led her to the restaurant.

"This is very nice, I like the decor," Sydney said. "Do you come here often?"

"Not really. I don't go out to dinner very often, I really hate to eat out alone."

"If you don't mind my asking, why aren't you married? Have you even been? And if not, why not at your age? Is there something about you I should know about?" asked Sydney.

"First of all I'm forty-four, not a doddering old man by any means. I've never been married but I've lived with two women in my sordid past. Both times my job got in the way. The first time it was my not allowing her to smoke pot around me. I know plenty of cops who do, it was just me. I can't see doing this job operating under a set of situational ethics that says it's fine for me, but not those I bust. The second woman was always worried that I would end up getting killed out on the street, so she pushed me to get a desk job, or leave the force altogether. It got so that every time I left the house she tried to start a fight.

"I sometimes get together with someone who wants to go to some specific event, sometimes one of the women officers will be looking for someone to go out with, but nothing steady."

"So why me?" prompted Sydney. "What is it about me, because on the surface most people wouldn't even think of throwing the two of us together. Let's count it off, you're white, I'm black. You're a cop and I'm an academic administrator. You're a former soldier and I'm an avowed peacenik, and I'm guessing here, but I don't think you have a Ph.D. yet. How am I doing so far?"

"Can we just write it off to opposites attracting? It's true, you're completely different from anyone I've ever been out with, but I can't lie about being intrigued by and attracted to you.

So far you're a pleasant blend of contradictions."

"How so?" she asked.

"You're young, and yet you have the aura, so to speak, of an old soul. You have an exterior of deep calm, but you're driven to succeed at almost any cost. I think you live cool and burn white hot just below the surface, and you top it off with a comfortable sense of humor. You don't play any childish games with me. You're not falsely coy, you don't come off with a 'what have you done for me lately' attitude. You haven't crowded me, and it is a combination tough to resist."

"What if I'm only playing a grown-up version of hard to get behind all of this measured cool?" she asked, pinning him with a stare.

"If you are, it's a game I can play. Is there a home version?" he asked, his answer breaking her up in surprise.

"We'll see, officer, as long as there are no tacky lines about frisking for weapons or strip searching and the like, I'll consider it."

After they ordered, John asked, "So why me? I showed you mine, now you show me yours."

"Fair enough. I liked that you didn't come off like a typical cop. There was none of the usual verbal bullying they seem to perfect so well. You treated me like a person, not a position, or someone expected to do your bidding. And you don't appear to have any unpleasant racial baggage. You speak well, you listen to what I have to say and actually consider things before you answer. Your eyes are kind, but firm. You drive with a quiet confidence, and I noticed your radio was set for the same station as mine. You're only a few years older than me, but that entails a certain experience in life that my contemporaries have yet to acquire. And, you have a nice butt," she finished, watching him closely for reaction.

John began to cough as his ginger ale tried to flee his body through his nose. When he had control of his breathing he looked up to see her eyes dancing with laughter at having so successfully caught him by surprise.

"Oh, there's no doubt you have a great sense of understatement, and an even better sense of timing. Remind me to pay you back sometime. Now what's a nice academic like you doing looking at my butt in the first place? I would have thought that your endeavors were loftier than the examination of a public servant's ass."

"As a well-educated person, I have learned that accurate analysis of anything requires examination of the whole subject, not just the one or two primary points of interest. Besides, there's nothing wrong with looking at your butt, it's the last thing I see whenever we're together. I can't help it. Maybe now we can have a nice, quiet dinner and calmly get to know each other. What do you think the chances are of that happening?" she asked.

"I'm game if you are. Tell me a little about yourself, have you ever been married, or otherwise encumbered?" John asked.

"Not so far. In some respects I'm your typical career woman, one who wants to secure her position in life before marriage and children. I am aware of my biological clock ticking away, but I'm just not ready yet. My job at the school is very engaging and fulfills much of the nurturing part of my soul. As for men? In my experience there are several things that put me off dating any particular one. First of all I don't like superficiality. I can't abide a man who can't talk to me like a person, or who treats me like a trophy. There are cultural differences between black and white men, frankly both have attributes that diminish the dating experience. I want to befriend a man who wants to relate to me, the me that matters, not the dean, or the Ph.D., or the wrapping of the package with no interest in the person inside.

"I'm pretty comfortable with myself. I can be off alone just as well as out with others. That's not true of most of my girlfriends, there's still the stigma of a woman somehow not being quite complete without a man.

"What I want is to see better treatment of women in general, and black women in particular. Despite having gone through the liberation movement and increasingly independent trends in employment, sexual equality and the like, things are still pretty bad. At Steddman our graduates are not only of demonstrably superior intelligence, but they are well schooled in the psychological sciences of manipulation and self-reliance. They are not, by and large, going to 'settle' for whatever they are given. Part of the process at Steddman teaches them that they too are entitled to the benefits and aspirations of the American dream."

"Yeah, but aren't you somehow alienating these women from men in general?" asked John.

"Not at all, what they end up doing is demanding a better class of man. Unfortunately, there aren't too many of them out there. As long as some male lawyer can utter the words 'but your honor, she was asking for it, look how she was dressed' in any court in the country and not be jailed for contempt, this culture is still sick and in need of a radical cure. Women are constantly under assault, when they walk down the street, when they go out together, and when they're at work. Although you, as a man, may not believe it, women are still largely treated like property in American culture."

"I never looked at it from that perspective."

Sydney reached out and covered his hand with hers, "How could you? You, and everyone else are a part of it. How is someone not sensitized to such a perspective going to suddenly see it?"

"So how do you prepare your girls for life among us neanderthals? Is there some special self-defense course against American culture in the curriculum?"

"No, nothing like that, but I think we do manage a good balance between exposing them to some of the unnoticed discrimination women face, and the institutional racism directed toward blacks in America in general. When you add the two together, our girls are made very aware of the scope of what they have to overcome."

"And yet, here you are, having dinner with a member of both the oppressive, dominant culture and sex. Am I the recipient of some sort of reverse affirmative action?" John asked.

"Stop it! If I thought at all you were steeped in any of the attitudes I'm talking about, I would hardly waste my time with you. Remember, by and large we don't settle for less than exactly what we want." she answered, smiling.

"Well, is it out of line to ask what you want with me?"

"To tell you the truth, I haven't decided. But don't get me wrong, you aren't some kind of grand experiment in interracial relations. Simply stated, I like you. You treat me like I want to be treated, and remember, there's that nice butt thing too," she said with a wink.

"If it's all right with you, can we table the discussion of my ass for the duration? I mean I can't very well talk about your butt without living down to all the bad things you mentioned about our culture in general, and men in particular."

"When you put it that way, I guess I haven't really been fair with you, have I? But to satisfy my own curiosity, what *do* you think about my ass? Or haven't you noticed?" she asked as she took a bite of her salad, her teeth flashing in a quick smile.

"Um, as far as I can tell, there's nothing wrong with it at all," John answered, blushing. "I will state for the record that there's nothing wrong with the whole package from where I sit. Anything else will have to wait until the opportunity for closer examination."

"Touché. At least you give back as good as you get. I like that about you too."

"I've got an idea . . ." John began.

"I'm sure you do!" broke in Sydney.

Laughing, John said, "No really, instead of going to a movie can I talk you into going to one of my favorite places in the city? It's owned by a friend of mine and is probably the best place in town to sit and talk."

"Sounds nice. I'm curious to see what makes it such an attraction for you."

"Great," he said, and began to relate how he had discovered Pete's, and how he helped Pete remodel the lounge. Over the rest of their excellent meal they spent nearly the whole time talking jazz and blues. They discovered as many shared likes as dislikes in artists and styles. So much so John was able to put aside his reservations and to really enjoy the evening.

Later, when they arrived at Pete's, Sydney asked, "How does your friend Pete keep this place a secret? If I had known about it I would have told everyone in town about this joint."

"That's one of the things he doesn't seem to care about. It's almost like he doesn't want to become mainstream, having a huge crowd every night. I'm guessing if it ever gets to that point, he'll probably lose most of his regulars. Come on over to the bar, I want to introduce you."

Pete came over and slapped hands with John, and then noticed Sydney standing by John's side.

"Pardon me, ma'am, is this man bothering you? I can have him thrown out on the street if he is," said Pete, holding out his hand to her.

Laughing and returning the handshake, Sydney replied, "May I take a rain check on that? You never know how things may turn out."

"Just so, ma'am. You just give me the high sign and he's out on his ass."

"Are you two finished? Pete, I'd like you to meet Sydney Atkins, a new friend of mine. And you can shut off the charm, I told her everything about you already."

"All lies I'm sure. What's your pleasure, Sydney? I can't get Mr. Man here to drink anything stronger than iced tea," said Pete.

"Do you have a nice light Chablis? That would go down very well with the tunes in here."

"No problem, you two go and find a seat and I'll have your drinks brought over to you," Pete answered, smiling in delight.

"Thanks Pete, we'll be over there in the corner booth," said John.

When they had seated themselves in the booth, Sydney was surprised the music was no louder or softer wherever she turned. "How does he get the sound so clear without blasting it across the room?" she asked.

"Pete told me that he installed, and tuned, over forty speakers in here: I don't think there's a bad seat in the house."

"I'm surprised to see so few singles in here, it's almost all couples and groups," Sydney observed.

"It's not that kind of place. Pete's help isn't on the make, and you'll never hear a top forty song played in here. The atmosphere is all wrong for that kind of crowd. Perhaps this is the one place where a woman might not feel under assault when she goes out with friends. Although, I've rarely seen groups of women in here. Who knows, maybe they go out in packs for safety in numbers from us guys with only one thing on our minds," he finished, grinning.

"And just what is on your mind, John? Anything you want to share, any hidden agenda I should know about?" she asked.

Looking at her face for any sign of where she was going, John remembered why he was there. He answered carefully, trying not to give himself away, "I'm really not sure. Naturally I want to get to know as much as possible about you. I like you. I'm more than casually attracted to you, and I would like to end up counting you among my extremely small circle of close friends. I don't trust people easily, it comes with the job. So I play my own cards pretty close to the vest. If I seem reserved I guess it's just my nature. Anything you want to know just ask, because for tonight only, I'm an open book. But only for tonight."

"Why just tonight? Do you turn into a pumpkin later? You can't be a vampire, I saw you in broad daylight when we met," she said.

"After tonight you're going to have to work for it just like anyone else. Consider it your one free taste to get you hooked, then once you can't do without me, I've got you."

"Damn!" she exclaimed. "That's the same game I was going to run on you! Now I've got to rethink my whole strategy!"

John let out a laugh. Then he looked her right in the eyes, leaned over and kissed her softly on the lips, ecstatic when he saw her leaning in to meet him. When they pulled back they both were silent. A threshold had been crossed, and both knew where this would lead.

John took a long pull of his tea, looking over the lip of the glass at this enigmatic woman before him, wondering how long it would take for him to really get to know her, how long it would take before he could trust her?

Sydney sat back, looked across at John and thought about how many firsts this relationship represented. This was the first man who had disarmed her elaborate defenses. This was the first white man who interested her at all. This was the first man, since she was a teenager, that she thought she wanted to touch, to feel his weight pressing against her body, to feel his skin against her skin, to have him leave his scent on her. The feeling was as unexpected as it was primal. It touched something deep within her and was all the more disturbing for its power. It was the first time she ever considered letting a man have power over her.

She would never have admitted to anyone what she was feeling, not because it betrayed the sisterhood, but more a matter of deep privacy. Sydney was not in the habit of discussing her feelings. It had been a point of contention in her past. She was interested in how this one would play out. Could she, would she, ever change? Or was she on a merry-go-round leading nowhere? She drained her glass of over half of its contents, savoring the quick warmth that spread from her belly, hoping it would obscure the heat that was already there.

John saw how quiet she had become and worried that he had gone too far. Looking at her in mild concern, he asked, "Is everything all right, was that the wrong thing to do?"

"That's not it at all, John. I'm thinking about how *I'm* going to handle this, you, me, everything. It's just something I need to think about, but don't worry, it's not you, or anything you did. I like you. I like how you make me feel, and so far it's all good. It's too bad there's no dancing here, I want to feel you up against me, but just dancing. I'm not ready for anything else yet. Is that okay with you?"

"Sydney, anything you want is fine with me. Would you like to leave and go somewhere else?" he asked.

"No, this place is now a part of you to me, let's just stay here and be together. Do you mind?" she said, as she nestled into his side under his arm.

"Not at all," he answered.

CHAPTER 17

NORMA HAD SETTLED into a much saner schedule now that the initial furor over her discovery had died down. It was quiet, and somewhat lonely, with Alan gone. Her phone still rang once or twice a week with calls from the media or science groups about panel discussions or lectures on the astronomical sciences, or her own discovery.

It hadn't hurt her personal life, at least in generating the interest of men from nearly every walk of life. Reporters, scientists and academics all sought her attention, vying for her time all along her whirlwind media tour. A few invitations she accepted, but nothing became of any of their efforts.

The best aspect of the ordeal was that she had hundreds of additional photo resources at her beck and call. She received daily e-mails pointing her to repositories of pictures of her asteroid. JPL even gave her access to real-time radar scans of the many radar arrays they monitored, alerting her whenever they would point in her asteroid's direction.

In the day's e-mail she saw a high-priority message from one of her new contacts at JPL. It was short and to the point: her asteroid looked like it was going to pass within five hundred thousand miles of the earth. The data was preliminary, but after a month observing and calculating the path of her asteroid they concluded that it would intersect the orbit of earth in around thirteen weeks.

JPL had more closely studied Norma's piece of the sky, finally locating the object just outside the orbit of Mars, about one hundred eighty million miles from the sun, traveling sixty thousand miles an hour. The e-mail included a graphic showing the asteroid crossing earth's orbit on its way toward the sun. The message also cautioned her against revealing the information until its path had been further refined by their computers.

Norma began to worry. She clicked on the link in the message and was brought to the page at the JPL web site with all of the information on her asteroid they had to date. It measured just over three miles long by just under one mile deep. Spectrographic analysis showed that it was composed mostly of frozen water and carbon dioxide and the remainder was iron. At its present speed, if it should impact the earth, it would devastate the entire world's ecosystem for years.

She called Dean Goodman and relayed the information from JPL. He assured her that there would be no negative repercussions to the university, or her project, if her discovery was discussed in the press in a less than positive light. Dean Goodman asked her for the number of the JPL group tracking the asteroid, thanked her and hung up.

This new revelation elevated the amount of attention Norma's asteroid received not only by NASA and JPL, but observatories around the world. At any given time of day, at least one major telescope was directly observing the asteroid in real time. Some observatories ran spectrographic studies to determine the exact composition of the rogue object, while others refined its path to resolve whether or not it posed a threat to earth.

That morning's White House security briefing included the asteroid's estimated path. The president's science advisor, Diane Churchill, gave the probability of a collision at about two hundred to one. When asked what options, if any, NASA had as a contingency should the rock hit, Churchill replied, "Loosen all restrictive clothing and kiss your ass goodbye!" There was no defense against something that large impacting the earth, location was irrelevant. The amount of debris thrown into the air would effectively cut off heat and light from the sun for years.

The president ordered his science team to put together contingency plans in the unlikely event the Lancaster asteroid, as they all had taken to calling it in the press, would impact earth. The president had an ulterior motive for assigning the project to his science team. Hopefully it would distract anyone from probing too deeply into any leaks about the Iraqi operation. Also, discussion of the studies and preparations his administration was undertaking would look extremely presidential to the American people.

Norma was invited to join the special presidential commission on astrophysics to analyze the resources needed to fully deploy her detection network around the world and make recommendations on what it would take for the US to spearhead the installation of a global early warning system. They would also discuss the issues surrounding the asteroid itself. The commission would meet every month, but most interim meetings would be conducted via video conference. NASA equipped Norma's computer with a camera and headset that would allow her to fully participate in these online discussions and talk, face to face, with anyone else on the video network. They also gave her special encryption software developed by the National Security Agency to insure that there would be no eavesdroppers on the line.

The first time Norma had an opportunity to try out the new system was during a test call after NASA's IT guys installed and tested her camera and computer's sound system. About five minutes after they left, a small window opened up on her screen announcing she had a call from the president's science advisor's office. Quickly pulling on her headset and uncovering the lens of the camera, Norma clicked on the "Answer Call" button on her screen. Almost instantly the window widened out to cover about half of her screen and a pleasant-looking woman's face appeared on screen.

"Ms. Lancaster?" the caller asked.

"Yes, I'm here. Can you see me?" Norma answered.

"If you could point the camera down a little bit your face will be better centered in the window," the woman answered. "A little more . . . right there! Hi, my name is Diane Churchill. I'm the president's science advisor and will be your primary contact when the commission gets together or holds these electronic conferences. I see your people didn't have any trouble installing the hardware and software on your system. Do you have any questions while I have you on the line?"

"Not really, none that I can think of . . . oh, wait. How do I originate calls from here, is there a directory included with the software that was installed?" Norma asked.

"Tell you what, first of all call me Diane and I'll call you Norma. And let's see what your project coordinator in Houston is up to. Click the options menu at the top of the window you see me in. Now click "Add another person" and you'll see the directory on our video conferencing host here in DC. Do you see your Dr. Milton under the Ms? Click twice on his name."

Norma followed the directions and watched as the window with Diane's face became smaller and a second window opened next to hers. The word "Calling" blinked in the middle. About ten seconds later the window opened up showing the face of her project sponsor in his office in Houston.

"Norma! Glad to see you hooked into the network. Nice to see you too, Diane. To what do I owe this embarrassment of riches?" asked Milton.

"I was just showing Norma how the system works, I hope I didn't interrupt anything important."

"Not at all, I was going over the latest on Norma's asteroid. The figures are still a little too speculative to make any real predictions right now, but I'll tell you what, we may have a close enough passage to hit the thing with a probe," Milton said. "The only problem we see so far is that it's going to take a hell of a lot of delta-v to accelerate a probe fast enough if we want to soft-land on the thing."

Diane asked, "What do you guys think is doable in three months?"

"We can toss a camera in its path, maybe shoot a projectile into it, but soft landing anything on it is going to be a bitch. Hey Norma, you holding up all right with the fame thing? You know when the news breaks that this is going to pass really close, you're going to be right back on the publicity junket."

"So far, so good. I'm just hoping that we've gotten past killing the messenger when bad news arrives," Norma replied.

"Don't you worry, Norma, as far as the administration is concerned, we have you to *thank* for developing a system that actually worked as it was designed. There's no telling when we might have seen this particular asteroid if your system hadn't detected it so early," Diane reassured her. "Look you two, I have to run. I only wanted to get Norma checked out on the video conference network. I'll be talking to you both soon."

In Utah, Alan was totally involved in mating his display software with Martin's detector. First he learned how Martin's detector output the calculated coordinates of detected anomalies. Alan was fascinated with how fast the detector plotted the incoming gravitational changes in real time, and then computed the direction and probable distance the anomaly was from the detector. Alan was so busy he hardly thought of anything but the programming he wanted to accomplish to give them best display system possible.

Martin couldn't believe his good fortune. Alan was the kind of superstar programmer to which all of Silicon Valley pointed whenever they brought any project in just under the wire. Alan would have worked twenty-four hours a day, seven days a week, pausing only to eat and sleep in the office, not even bothering to get up out of his chair and go the few hundred feet to his room. Bringing Alan up to speed took less than a week. He also appeared to fit in fine with the underground community of scientists, soldiers and support personnel. His appetite for mastering the nuances of each and every computer system in the facility was phenomenal. For once, Alan was truly happy. He had no worries, no bills to pay, no shopping to do, and all his compensation from Dr. Harris' project went right into his usually anemic money market account. He even forgot all about his desire to explore the nearby towns topside. His entire being was focused on the unprecedented computing power now at his fingertips; he had even tightened up Martin's original software code so that it ran almost twice as fast as before. The naval programmers and technicians were in awe of his boundless determination to conquer the detector's programming and bend it to his will. Privately they were impressed with how large a sponge his brain was, taking in all manner of theoretical mathematical formulae and immediately applying them to the tasks at hand. Alan Richards bore watching, the naval programmers and technicians thought. Someone was bound to snag him for their own use once word got out about the contribution he was making to Martin's work.

Martin received a new level of respect from the staff of the underground installation, partly as a result of his project being enlarged to accommodate the second detector, partly because of an underlying excitement the project imbued in the personnel directly working with him. They had moved the growth tank without a hitch and reassembled it in less than a week, even with Martin's new additions. They cleared the second lab of extraneous partitions to make space for the crystal's cradle, and reconfigured the external hallways and doors for the new floor plan.

Just before the second crystal was due for extraction from the tank, an inquiry came to the commander of the shelter facility topside from the office of the Joint Chiefs. They were requesting a summary on utilization of the below-ground facility, number of personnel based below, and an estimate of how many more people the shelter could hold as currently configured. This request came completely out of the blue, coming as it did, right after they had authorized the additional floor space for the gravity detector project and the additional construction and engineering personnel. The base commander called Washington for clarification, and was informed that the request came from the White House. He was also told the president was interested in all such facilities currently under government control, and that was all he needed to know, thank you very much. Puzzled, but complying immediately with the request, the commander filled out the summary, appended a room and bed count to the report and e-mailed it back to the Pentagon. The figures from the report were compiled with all of the other inquiries and delivered to the White House in time for the next day's security briefing.

NASA sent the latest figures on Norma's asteroid to the White House as well, stressing that the object's passage would be close in astronomical terms, although there was still no indication that it would impact earth. The administration was hedging its bets, planning to preserve the American way of life in the event everything went to hell from a meteor strike. Every facility like Shelter Fourteen would be populated with top government officials and America's privileged. As in any survival of the fittest scenario in America, it all really boiled down to survival of those with the most influence.

The President and his top aides were concerned with how many of them, and their family members, would be able to hide out from whatever hellish disaster the rest of mankind would have to endure, little concerned that they fell so woefully short of being America's best and brightest. In the sixteen such facilities spread across the country, there was only room for forty-eight thousand people. Ten years to hide underground and emerge into what? What kind of life would be left above ground after the freeze? Many of the plants would come back, life undersea would largely survive, but how much of man's vast infrastructure would survive to bring civilization itself back to life?

The rest of America was ignorant of any of this planning. The dumbing down of America worked in this administration's favor just as it always had. Few citizens, if any, paid much attention to speculation that an asteroid could be aimed in earth's direction. Those who might have taken particular notice of said possibility were almost universally of a mind that no matter what, the government would take care of everything.

This bit of mental gymnastics was blissfully performed by the average American despite daily reminders that the United States government couldn't keep the trains running on time, couldn't deliver the mail with any kind of regularity and never managed to collect and spend their hard-earned taxes effectively on the health and well-being of the American people. As long as they were able to replace their disposable automobiles every other year, could feed their sports utility vehicles gas without lines and rationing, and could get their free porn and music on the Internet, life pretty much marched on without comment.

The massive collection and mining of the long distance and mobile telephone records of the previous four female disappearees and Sydney Atkins proceeded slowly. The computer expert Agent Samuels brought in slowly hacked into the various long distance and mobile service carriers in all four cities, adding the huge amounts of captured data to the growing list for comparison with Steddman College's phone records and Sydney's home and mobile numbers. So far there were no matches. The outlook seemed bleak.

Samuels was off to Washington, DC to report on the progress of the investigation to the director. His report began with the original call into the Chicago talk radio station exposing the crime figures the FBI had overlooked for so long.

"So far it appears the caller is in no way connected with the case, he has some political contacts, but most are at the local level. His parents were political activists in the sixties and seventies, and he himself led a student boycott in 1971 in high school that led the school system to remove armed police officers from school grounds." Samuels paused, waiting for the director to comment.

The director nodded. "Good enough, so how's the investigation going in Atlanta? Are you getting the help you need from the locals?"

"Quite so. I think we've struck the mother lode with the local detective there."

"How so?" the director asked.

"He identified a possible connection between one of the missing girl's school administrators and a handful of the other missing women."

"What!? And you waited until now to tell me? I hope you have a good explanation, I'm not at all happy being the last one to know significant details about major investigations."

"It's not that sir, I wasn't holding anything back. There's simply nothing to report yet."

"So, what's the connection?"

Leaning forward in his seat, Samuels explained what Detective Mathews discovered.

"Hot shit! This is good, *really* good. Do you need any additional help following this up?" asked the director.

"Not yet. I still want to avoid any possibility of leaks. I'd like to keep it confined to my small handful, although I did grab one of the computer analysts and stashed him in the office in Atlanta."

"What's he doing for you? Does he know what he's working on?" the director asked, ever mindful of the political repercussions should word of the investigation get out.

"Not directly."

The director thought for a few seconds. "I'm assuming that you've sought no local search warrants for the data searches?"

"That's right. I am still following your directive to keep this as close to the vest as possible. My thought still isn't to acquire information for future prosecution. I'm more interested in getting to the bottom of the whole sordid mess. Was I wrong, sir?" asked Samuels.

"Not at all, Bob. I want you to keep me posted on this dean, and whether or not we need to crawl up her ass with a microscope." The director got up and went over to his desk. "Are we secure as far as the data we're storing online? The last thing I want is for some hacker to get hold of what's in there."

"Well sir, I've done the best I can to keep prying eyes from getting in there. I even moved it from the system here to one of the other mainframes on the network, and I'm going to keep moving it around every few weeks until we finish the case."

"Good idea. You're sure there's nothing else I can send your way to help you out?"

"Nope, between Detective Mathews and me we're doing just fine."

Samuels got to his feet.

"When all this is over, I want to meet this detective," said the director. "We could do far worse than recruiting a few more like him. These college boys need too much training and seasoning before they're any use to us. I think we should rethink our policy about recruiting cops."

Lean on me, when you're not strong
And I'll be your friend, I'll help you carry on
For, it won't be long, 'til I'm gonna need
Someone to lean on, lean on me

Lean On Me

Written and performed by Bill Withers

CHAPTER 18

THE MEN TRAINING undercover at the CIA's secret operations facility came together well as a team. The Americans were impressed with the close-in weapons skills of their British counterparts. They had to catch up in their informal competition on the shooting range and the simulations they ran on mock-ups of the ground-level plan of the installation.

On the shooting range all four of the team scored practically the same inhuman level of accuracy with their Sig Sauer P-226 pistols, each able to group nine-millimeter rounds in holes no bigger than a half dollar, each hoping those skills would not be called upon in the mission ahead.

The only specialized training that they all underwent was jumping out of an aircraft fifty thousand feet above ground traveling just below mach one, the speed of sound. Although each of the Anglo-American team had numerous jumps to their credit, this particular HALO drop would stretch their skills considerably, and called for a unique delivery crew to get them to the drop zone safely.

The aircraft to deliver them to the outskirts of Baghdad was a modified B-2 Stealth bomber, specifically configured for the deployment of covert, advance personnel into hostile areas. With the B-2's operational range of over ten thousand miles, the team could deploy to Baghdad from a US-controlled airbase in Germany.

The bomber could then return to the staging area in Germany without anyone in the Iraqi military knowing their airspace had been compromised.

The major modifications to the airframe consisted of replacing the clamshell doors that normally concealed the rotary ordnance launchers with a rear-facing deployment ramp. The hydraulically controlled ramp was designed to quickly lower itself into the air slipstream and provide the means of egress for the jumpers. The ramp was equipped with composite side curtains to create a small pocket of slower air into which the jumpers would inject themselves while maintaining as much of the stealth characteristics of the aircraft as possible by deflecting and absorbing the energy of high-frequency radar beams. Unfortunately, as soon as the ramp was deployed, the radar profile of the B-2 was increased almost a hundredfold over its normal flight configuration. The engineers who designed the modification made sure the ramp could fully open, allow jumpers to deploy and reseal in under sixty seconds.

Leaving the aircraft in flight was a tricky proposition at best, requiring a jump well above the height where man had enough oxygen to survive. Contending with an airflow nearly the speed of sound added immeasurably to the danger involved. The teams familiarized themselves with their survival gear, the insulated jumpsuit and breathing system necessary to keep them from passing out as soon as the cabin was depressurized. The jump suits were custom fitted to each wearer with radar-transparent fasteners composed of composites.

None of the gear had any kind of label or insignia identifying the country of origin, although it wouldn't be hard for anyone to guess where they had been manufactured. Almost all of their equipment, weapons, ammo, and other gear, would be stashed in a belly pack, leaving their backs free for their primary and backup chutes, and a small plastic canister for oxygen. Each man would be loaded down with around sixty pounds of gear, some of which would be discarded and concealed upon landing.

Once each man's suit and breathing mask had been fitted and tested, the men personally inspected their own parachutes and supervised loading by the Air Force HALO specialists assigned to their mission.

They made several practice jumps from a standard C4 cargo hauler. All four team members were fully outfitted for the HALO drop, less their weapons gear, which was replaced with sand-filled bags to simulate the extra weight. Here, the American team had the edge in training and experience, although the SAS duo caught up in quick order.

Although stationed at Whiteman Air Force Base in Missouri, the Air Force deployed an entire support team for the B-2 and placed them on detached duty at Andrews Air Base for the training phase of the mission. The entire support team would precede the team to Germany when the mission began. The CIA had assigned one of their Virginia safe house estates as the practice drop zone for their training.

To aid in targeting the landing zone, the open area off to the side of the estate's mansion and garage was equipped with four infrared beacons that bracketed the safe area for touchdown.

On their first jump from the B-2, all four were excited, and more than a little apprehensive. They had all been drilled in the tightly held, tucked position required to safely leave the plane, how long to hold the tuck and the hard arch they had to achieve in order to stop their tumble and orient them to the ground as quickly as possible. Each team member was outfitted with a combination GPS locator/altimeter that could place their location anywhere on or above the earth within two meters and standard night vision goggles to help see details of the landing zone in the dark.

"At least we get to play with some of you Yanks' new toys," said Linden, the younger of the two Brits. "Contrary to what Q cobbles up in the James Bond movies, we don't always get the latest and greatest in expensive gear like you boys do."

The Air Force Special Operations Group training team had good-naturedly given the CIA and SAS team a hard time over their lack of experience, and in the case of the Brits, their lack of a common language. But, when it came down to the drop itself, they were all business.

"That's too bad," replied the jump master with a grin. "But don't get excited. We just ran down to the local toy store and grabbed these for you blokes. You didn't think we'd let you two play with the real deal, did you? Those are expensive, and surely too hard for you boys to learn how to operate in such a short amount of time."

The four of them were trained to program the instruments and use them to supplement their own eyes during the drop. With the coordinates of the CIA estate preloaded to compensate for any lateral drift due to the high winds at the upper altitudes, they were finally ready. After going over their gear with a fine-toothed comb and confirming that their breathing systems were operating properly, the jump master led them up the tight little ramp to the benches in what would normally be the bomb bay of the stealth bomber. The airman strapped each of them in and checked their equipment for the second to the last time, secured the ramp, and double-checked the door seals. Then, plugging in his combination mask and headset, he notified the pilot they were ready for takeoff.

On the way up there was little conversation. They sat quietly with their thoughts, doing whatever mental exercises prepared them best for the ordeal ahead. At the five-minute countdown, the red light on the partition between the cargo section and the pilot's cabin turned yellow.

"Everyone, unstrap!" the jump master shouted out before securing his breathing mask to his face; from here on out all signals would be made by hand.

Moments later he flashed six fingers and a closed fist letting them know they had one minute before the ramp was deployed. The team members felt the B-2 throttle back its engines, reducing its airspeed for the jump.

When the airman signaled thirty seconds to go, they felt the pressure and temperature drop in the cabin. The door seals were withdrawn and the ramp lowered into the airflow.

The team stood and moved to the end of the ramp and the airman moved to the rear bulkhead. He counted down from five, and when his hand made a fist, the four moved to the very end of the ramp, tucked their heads down around their knees and rolled off, immediately disappearing into the night sky. The airman delayed closing the ramp as he made sure his charges had safely exited from the high-flying jet.

As last man out, David had come out of his tumble and acquired visual contact with his teammates. He was glad he had held such a tight grip on his legs, clutching them to his chest with his chin tucked tightly in. The turbulence from the passage of the huge plane through the cold, thin air almost tore the breathing mask off his face. He arched his back hard, and waited for his tumble to die. Soon David begin his face-down drop through fifty thousand feet to the CIA estate below. The wind creeping into the tight-fitting hood made a quiet whistling sound. He checked his location and height above the ground. Pressing the radio transmit contact in the palm of his hand, David sent out a quiet, "Everybody make it out all right?"

The two Brits both gave an "affirmative," and a "What does someone have to do to get out of this lousy outfit?" came from Kahill. Their communications gear was low-powered and digitally scrambled against eavesdropping, but as a safety precaution the actual drop would be made under radio silence.

Jumping from a perfectly good aircraft was considered daft by most right-thinking people. To do it under potentially hostile circumstance was considered the height of lunacy by most. For the members of this team, the anxiety of the jump, though a matter of the most serious business, still managed to get their adrenaline punping. Unlike sport skydivers, the most dangerous part of the jump often happened *after* they landed.

"Equipment check, by the numbers," he called out. "GPS/altimeter?"

"Check," they all answered.

"NVGs?"

"Check."

"Sir, we should think about some IR flashers strapped to our suits so we can see each other on the way down," Linden suggested. "I can't see anyone up here at all."

"Yeah, chief, he's right. If one of us has a problem we still have some time before we deploy the chutes to make sure we don't bump into each other on the way down," added Kahill.

"Coming up on fifteen thousand," interjected Stiles. "I can see the beacons, I'm on target," Stiles added.

"Eyes front, men. Anyone not see the strobes?"

Everyone turned their eyes toward the ground and prepped to deploy their chutes. At eight thousand feet they pulled their primary chutes. Once fully deployed, they vectored in on the large square inside the infrared beacons. Within a few hundred feet of the ground they saw each other and all four adjusted their glide paths to avoid collision. It was a testament to the skill and training of the team that all four landed on their feet, killing their remaining forward velocity with a brisk run, turning to collapse their chutes seconds later.

"Down," each one called out through their comm sets. Once they all collapsed their chutes and gathered them up, a pair of jeeps turned on their headlights and drove into the landing zone to pick them up.

The two older members of the team were quiet as they changed into their street clothes; the younger two were still hopped up from the ten-mile drop, They made suggestions on how they could improve their chances of a safe landing in hostile territory.

When they returned to the barracks, White excused himself and put in a call to Bascomb's office. He asked for a brief face-to-face about the mission as soon as possible and let Bascomb know that the drop went well but he had a couple of concerns about the insertion plan. Bobby told White to wait for a car to bring him over to headquarters.

"So what's up?" began Bobby once they both had coffee and were seated in a small conference room. "Are they any problems with the team I should know about?"

"Nothing like that. I'm afraid that I just don't want to take a chance on landing safely in the dark on unfamiliar terrain. I know we've got the satellite photos of the site but shit, it was like dropping into an endless well tonight. I afraid of what might happen to anyone whose GPS goes on the fritz. If it weren't for the beacons, and having walked the LZ from ground level, we wouldn't have made it down nearly so easy."

Blinking his eyes while he processed this new datum, Bobby paused and then asked, "So what do you suggest?"

"Look, it's four days from the drop. Is there any way we can get someone on the ground who can mark the LZ with even one IR beacon?"

"Whoa, that's a pretty tall order. How the hell are we supposed to get the thing in-country on so short notice? If we could do that we probably wouldn't need the four of you, we'd have the assets already in place."

"Yeah, that's what I figured. I just don't relish hauling any of us overland if someone breaks a leg during the landing."

David looked at Bobby quietly, waiting for the analyst to pull a rabbit out of his hat.

"Let me get to work on this. You go back and keep to the schedule and I'll see what we can do to even up the odds for you. Is there anything else you think we overlooked?" Bobby asked.

"You mean like a floor plan and photos of the interior of the complex? Something like that maybe?" David said, grinning like a fiend.

"Yeah, just like that," Bobby answered.

Once White had left, Bascomb pulled up the operation file. He carefully reread all of the information on the players they had in the area of the drop. He decided to try a long shot and sent off an message to his opposite number in Britain's MI-6, requesting a secure telephone conference as soon as possible, no matter what the time.

Bobby had given his analysts the problem to see if they could come up with something he might have overlooked, hoping for a breakthrough.

He pulled up a chart of naval assets in the area. Surprisingly there was no problem transporting an IR beacon into the area, there were several vessels that were so equipped. The problem was getting one into friendly hands, along with instructions on how to use it. The main drawback was that the beacon might expose the incoming team to compromise, in effect telegraphing the exact time and location of their arrival. Outside help for the team, especially from personnel who had not been vetted and screened for their loyalty, was precisely the kind of thing that wrecked operations before they got off the ground.

In their quarters, White, Stiles, Kahill and Linden finished going over the analysis of their first HALO drop. White remained quiet about his request to Bascomb. They all decided to make at least two more HALO jumps before leaving for Germany.

During the discussion White asked, "How does everyone feel about trying the jump without the IR beacons, just using the GPS tracker and NVGs? It's what we're going to have to face over there on the real drop."

"I'm game if you are, chief. Although I would like to open my chute a little higher to hedge my bets on hitting that flat spot in the dark," said Kahill, pulling his file out from under his pillow.

"Too right, mate," added Linden. "I don't fancy having to look at your lab boy's toy on me wrist most of the trip down. Besides, the dial light is too bright for the NVGs. Flippin' back and forth to try to see the ground's not going to be easy."

"Good point, let me see if I can get the boys to darken the dial so you can see the directional arrows and the numbers without having to flip back and forth. Anything else?"

Stiles stood up and said, "I'm more than a little concerned with the possibility that unfriendlies might be in the immediate area. We're essentially dropping with little more than a pistol until we hit ground."

"Another good point. I'll have the armorer see if he can stitch up a cross-chest harness to fit over the suit, then you can carry the machine gun on the outside. I'm not concerned with being spotted on radar with the extra metal exposed, we'll be dropping too fast for anyone to pick us up. But remember, we're shooting, pardon the pun, for a zero body count on this mission. My preference is that no one in-country even know we've been there. In and out like the fog."

"We get you, David," answered Stiles. "No one wants to hurt anyone on a trip like this. Even though we don't operate by the Marquis of Queensberry rules in intelligence, our job is the acquisition of information, not the execution of scientists or civilians. As far as I'm concerned there's to be no collateral damage if we all do our jobs right, eh mate?"

"Well said," answered Kahill. "All I'm interested in is getting what we came for and getting mom and pop Kahill's favorite son back home, unharmed and in one piece."

"Alright everyone, give me your GPS units and I'll run them over to the shop to have the backlight dialed down. Is there anything other than the altimeter and the directional arrows that any of you need to see?" asked David.

"Not as far as I'm concerned," replied Stiles.

"Fine. Why don't the three of you go over the land at least a kilometer or two from ground zero just in case any of us drifts too far downrange. I'll be back as soon as I drop these off."

The rest of the team gathered around the table and laid out the satellite photos edge to edge, showing the ground immediately around the target site.

David called the operator and requested transportation to the tech lab as soon as possible, thankful they could make it a short night.

Across the grounds, Bascomb was on his fourth cup of coffee in less than an hour, still wrestling with his end of the problem. He was trying to shade the odds for a problem-free insertion in the team's favor when his phone rang in the short staccato rhythm of an outside call. Bobby waited through the five seconds of digital handshaking tones between his caller's instrument and his own. Once the line cleared, signaling a secure circuit, Bobby said, "Bascomb speaking."

"Bobby, good to hear from you. It's Walters at MI-6, I got your message and took a chance at you being in. What can I do for you? Are our blokes working out over there?"

"Thomas, you old sly dog, that they are. As a matter of fact our boys have a healthy respect for their training, especially in weapons. Thanks for sending the best."

"No problem, my boy. Now just what is it that has you still in the office after midnight?"

"Our boys are requesting some ground support on their insertion, they'll be dropping in under cover of night and they want someone to mark the LZ."

"How are you going to do that, you get anywhere near Baghdad with a transport and your boys are going to be spotted, aren't they?" asked Walters.

"We've got a modified B-2. They'll be doing a HALO drop from fifty thousand feet. They just want to see if someone can light up the LZ with an infrared beacon so they can vector in without mishap."

"Bloody ingenious. What's the radar profile of the thing when they exit? I'll bet the stealth characteristics go straight to bloody hell with a door open, something about the metal that becomes exposed in flight, right?"

"True," replied Bobby. "But when no one is looking for you, spotting the thing in the few seconds it takes to get them out takes a miracle. But all that aside, do you know of any way we can get someone on the ground who you trust to activate a beacon for their landing?"

"I'm not sure. Doing so raises the chances of compromise before their delivery vehicle goes feet dry. Do you want to take that chance?" Walters asked.

"So far I'm just looking into the options. I'm just as reluctant as you are to let anyone else in on this op. I'm wondering if we can borrow the asset who got the original metal samples from the crash site to mark the drop zone for us. What do you think?"

Walters thought about it for a few moments before answering. "Let me get back to you on this one, I have an idea or two I want to explore. I'll call you back in a few hours."

Halfway around the world, Basra was surprised to see the chalk mark on the door across the street from his modest home, the signal that an important message waited for him from his contact with the West. He continued on his way without noticeable pause and made his way around town, checking to see if anyone needed his repair services. Along the way he stopped to rest on a bench under a tree. He reached under a loose board in the seat and dislodged the small, folded piece of paper he knew would be there. Basra palmed the folded scrap and shoved it into his pocket. Basra sat quietly, waited a few more minutes, and, seemingly rested from his brief break, he resumed his rounds.

Once he finished his meanderings he stopped off at the usual establishment in which he spent most of his free time drinking with his friends in the local militia, as if just another day. He ordered a glass of the house's special brew, excused himself, went to into the toilet and latched the stall door behind him. He excitedly pulled the paper out of his pocket. He read and mentally decoded the obliquely worded message asking for his help in Baghdad. It informed him where to pick up the rest of his instructions should he decide he could safely make it to the vicinity of the capital.

Hands shaking with emotion, Basra tore the message into tiny pieces and flushed them down the toilet. He left the stall and washed his hands, looking in the mirror for any sign of the thoughts racing through his head. Was the request for his help a precursor to an invasion, or could he be needed to aid in the overthrow of the Great One's rule? Something prompted the West to think about him, which gave him a degree of contentment. He hoped his efforts would improve his fellow countrymen's lives.

Back in the main room, he returned to his usual table as the barkeep placed a full glass in front of him. Basra waved away the proprietor's objections and insisted that he compensate him for his wares. He greeted each of the patrons who passed his table, until a group of four servicemen entered, looking around in the gloom. Waving them over, he signaled the barkeep to bring four more of the same for his friends.

They took a moment to savor the cool bite of their refreshments. When they began to relax from the tensions of the day Basra casually asked if they knew of anyone heading to the capital in the morning with whom he could catch a ride. Basra told them that he had gotten word that his father was ill and that his mother needed help for a few days until his father was better.

"I'm not sure if there's a truck scheduled to head that way or not, I can check for you right now. It's the least I can do for a hero of the people," the eldest of the soldiers replied. "Wait here while I check," he said, strolling over to the bar to use the owner's phone. A few moments later the soldier announced, "You're in luck, there's a truck leaving around midday. I made arrangements for them to bring you as long as you get off before they reach their destination. Will that suit your purposes?" he asked Basra.

"Of course. I am forever in your debt."

"Nonsense, it is nothing, much less than you deserve. You should have your own driver, and be taken care of for the remainder of your days, given your contribution to our defense against the West," he answered to nods of agreement from the others.

"You exaggerate, I did what I could until I could do no more. But I accept your kindness, and am in your debt." Basra stayed only long enough to finish his drink, said his goodbyes and made his way home.

In the morning he woke feeling purposeful and excited at the prospect of finally doing something useful, something he hadn't felt since he had been shot down. Basra looked at his modest surroundings, wondering if he would miss living there should he never return.

Basra set out for the supply depot, knowing it would be hours before the truck's scheduled departure. He set out on a leisurely stroll, tracing a different path than the day before. He paused to rest on a different bench in a different part of town, concealing the small bit of folded paper containing a coded message to his Western contact.

Continuing his walk to the supply depot, he stopped frequently to chat with various soldiers with whom he had passing friendships before he checked in at the dispatcher's office. Basra engaged the office staff in light conversation, mostly asking after their families. He commiserated with their lot as soldiers keeping the local military emplacements stocked with supplies that never seemed to stretch far enough.

Soon enough, the dispatcher informed Basra that the truck was ready to depart and offered him food and drink for the trip, which he gratefully accepted. When he reached the truck, the driver motioned him to join him in the cab, and once Basra was settled, set off on the road to Iraq's capital. Fortunately for Basra, the two exhausted their conversation barely half an hour into the drive and he leaned back to try to get in a nap along the way. He wasn't sure what he faced when he picked up his instructions so he wanted to be well rested, prepared for any contingency upon arrival.

Around the time of Basra's arrival in the outskirts of Baghdad, the coded message he had concealed in the bench was transmitted by secure satellite connection to MI-6, informing them where and when he could be contacted in his parents' neighborhood. Thomas Walters got Bascomb back on the telephone to discuss what could be done in support of the insertion of the team.

"I only got this a few minutes ago. This fellow seems to be pretty resourceful, look at how quickly he made his way into Baghdad. I've had two of our guys rotating on him every since we left the first message asking for his help. There was no sign of a tail on him, other than our boys, the whole way to Baghdad. I'm inclined to trust him with helping the team out, both on getting them to ground safely and getting them east to the border. This, at least, lets me keep my other assets out of it if something goes sour," Walters explained.

"I've got no problem with you wanting to keep your boys under cover. There's no sense in risking their exposure, they're just about the only effectives in the entire sector, Walter. What I would like to figure out is how we can get a beacon to the guy in the three days we have left," Bobby said. "What are your thoughts?"

"If the team has NVGs they'll be able to see something as bright as automobile headlamps from quite a ways up, right? If so, how about having Basra get one of the local's autos, or even a truck, and have him signal from the ground? The timing's going to have to be spot on, but that shouldn't be too much of a problem for your transport."

Bobby was leaning back in his chair, tapping his pen on the blotter in front of him as he considered the pros and cons of the idea.

"True, but what if something does happen, and someone sees your boy signaling? I don't want the B-2 to send any signal whatsoever to announce its presence, and they'd have to if they're early or late. Leaving the beacon on the ground and letting it strobe for a couple of days would be ideal, then no one would be the wiser on exactly when our boys would be showing up. It's bad enough someone in-country will know our team's inbound as it is."

"What about his faking a breakdown? Is the LZ far enough outside of town so he wouldn't look too suspicious if he built a fire and seemed to be waiting for daylight to try to get help?" Walters asked.

"Maybe, but what if someone happens on him and offers to take him into town, or tow him into town?"

"Can't say 'bout that. How's the cover? Is there somewhere he can hide out by day?"

"Not really, that's why we chose the spot. The land's clear for quite a ways, and mostly flat. I'll be honest with you though, the idea of having a safe ride close to the objective is looking pretty good, especially if they can use the same means to get the hell out of Dodge when they're done."

"I get your meaning, my boy! By the way, it wasn't one of our blokes who was afraid of the dark, was it?" Walters prodded in an amused tone. "It doesn't sound like Stiles or Linden to worry about a little thing like a sprained limb when they land. I'm thinking it must have been one of your boys, eh, Robert?"

"I don't think so, it was more like my boys just didn't fancy the prospect of carrying one of yours for the whole mission because he was just short of terminally clumsy. Anyway, I've checked to see if we can get a beacon to him some how and so far I've come up empty. Any ideas?" Bobby asked.

"What about one of those laser pointers? I'm sure that one of the news boys over there might be able to dig one up. That should be visible from quite a ways up to NVGs, especially if someone's waving the thing around," Walters said, please with himself for thinking that one up.

"Yes, but we've still got the same problem with timing."

"In that case your truck's just going to have to make their delivery on time. What's the advert say, *When it absolutely, positively has to be on time!* Well, this is one of those times. Look, if we have to get your equipment in-country to make this work, where is the nearest supply point?"

"I can have one at the northern border of Kuwait in six hours. Anything over the border is a crap shoot."

"Can one of your flyers drop the thing to one of our boys on the ground? Then they could place the thing without tipping our hand to this Basra and still ensure the boys get off to a good start."

Bobby answered excitedly, "Now that's doable. If we can drop the thing just this side of the southern edge of the no-fly zone can you arrange to have someone place it in a shallow hole in the landing zone before the drop?"

"I'll get back to you on that within the hour, Bobby. Give me the coordinates of the LZ and I'll see just what can be done," Walters promised.

When he hung up the phone, Bobby felt confident they could pull this one off. He went out to the common area to get another cup of coffee, knowing that he was going to pay for the deprivations of this, and the following, week once the mission was over. As he was filling his cup, Bobby calculated that even with all the sleep he had caught up on between operations, he was only up to his sophomore year of college in reclaiming the sleep he had missed in his years at school.

CHAPTER 19

A GENT MINOR WAS working like a dog, compiling the nearly fifteen million mobile and long distance telephone call records of the women in Samuels' target group who had vanished in the previous ten years. He set up an analysis program that sorted all of the numbers by date into one massive list. Against this list, Minor ran a comparison of the telephone numbers the missing women had called from their homes, work and schools against the dean's office, home and mobile phones. It was a massive data mining operation.

Minor was further hampered by having to do the entire job without his normal FBI computer resources. Samuels had instructed him to keep all of the downloaded records and the rest of his notes on the computer in their private office. He wanted none of it stored on any of the FBI mainframes.

Although curious, Minor did as he was told. He advised Samuels that being relegated to using the PC in the office would slow his analysis down, but he did the work in electronic isolation as he had been instructed.

Despite the huge amount of work this project represented, Minor was having the time of his life. He didn't know exactly what Samuels was looking for, other than investigating a number of missing persons cases, but if there was something significant to be would find it.

Minor had written a program that compared each of the numbers on which the target women could have received a call against all the numbers Dean Atkins could have called from. Watching the progress of the electronic comparison he calculated that barring any additional data being added to what he already had, the entire process would take about two days. In a second window he started another sorting program comparing every outgoing, long-distance call from the target group against not only the dean's work, home and mobile numbers, but every hotel or motel the dean had stayed in during the last ten years as well.

Minor knew that she could have made calls from any number of pay phones using a common calling card, one that she paid for with cash at a grocery store for example. She could have called collect from virtually any pay phone in the various airports she traveled through over the time period in question.

Minor pulled his laptop from its case. He was looking for a program he had cooked up when he was reviewing some of the National Security Agency memos that crossed his supervisor's desk. One particular memo discussed the NSA's ability to break one hundred and twenty-eight bit encryption almost at will using the supercomputers they had buried under their Fort Mead headquarters. It further stated that until consumers begin to commonly use Internet browsers and e-mail programs using built-in one thousand twenty-four bit encryption, they could read anyone's messages with impunity. As a result, Minor and one of his buddies wrote a program that used four thousand ninety-six bit encryption, just to piss off anyone who wanted to try to read the messages they sent to each other. It was a poorly kept secret that the NSA kept close watch on all government communications, supposedly to help keep them secure, but who was really to say what their motivation truly was?

Whatever the reason, their little encryption program was perfect for keeping the data on this computer safe from prying eyes. Minor set the system to encrypt all the data and notes on the PC the next time the system booted up, which he would do as soon as the initial runs were finished. Until then he was camping out in the office to make sure no one got a peek.

John was thankful for the opportunities his infrequent visits to the Steddman campus gave him to drop in on Sydney. Often he timed it so that they could go to lunch together and advance their understanding of each other.

Investigating Jaylynn's life prior to her disappearance wasn't revealing anything of substance. He was going to have to concentrate on Sydney and everything about her life to see where the disconnect between her statements about not having contact with Jaylynn and the two phone calls made to her from Jaylynn's mobile phone occurred.

John checked the time and saw it was only two-thirty. He told one of the other investigators he was going downstairs to grab a sandwich should anyone call. In the stairwell he checked up and down for anyone else within earshot, pulled out his phone and called Samuels' office. Minor answered.

John asked, "Hey hacker, how's it going?"

Keeping deliberately vague, Minor answered, "Not bad, the data's in and I just started running the analysis. It looks like it's going to take a couple of days. I know I'm not supposed to know too much yet, but how's by you? Making any progress?"

John smiled ruefully. "Can't say I'm really making much progress yet, other than the two things you already know about."

"Too bad. Heard from Samuels recently? He hasn't spent much time in the office."

"I got a couple of messages from him, but nothing on what he's working on. Hell, I don't even know what part of the country he's in most of the time," replied John.

"Me either. Hey! Did you know that I qualify in weapons better than ninety-seven percent of the field agents we've got on the street? Actually, I'm better with a pistol than a keyboard, but no one except the armorer at the range really knows it because no one ever looks in my jacket for that kind of information. They only want to know if I can get launch capability at NORAD from my home computer or if I can transfer funds out of banks electronically without anyone finding out."

"Really? How 'bout I take you to the range tomorrow so you can get in some rounds? You can also bring me up to date face to face."

"Say, that'd be great. Where can I pick up some nine-millimeter rounds before we go?" Minor asked.

"Don't worry about it, I'll sign for a couple of boxes at the range. That way you won't have to give out your ID and possibly raise some questions about us hanging together. Want to shoot for beer?" suggested John.

Minor laughed. "Just how good do you think you are?"

"Look, it's only beer, don't sweat it. You are old enough to drink, aren't you, kid?" John asked with a laugh.

"I'll show you my fake ID when I get there. What time and what's the address?" asked Minor.

John gave him directions to the department's range, and arranged to meet him just outside so that he could escort him in.

John went to the cafeteria and grabbed a sandwich and coffee and took them back upstairs to eat at his desk. As he wandered by, Lieutenant Batterman called out, "Anything I need to know about, John?"

John stuck his head back in the door and replied, "Maybe a single thing I have to run down, but nothing of substance yet."

"Just keep me informed. How're they treating you over there?"

"No complaints, they're pretty much letting me do things my own way. So far so good, boss."

"Any expenses I need to send over for reimbursement? I don't want to get too far behind and then end up having to get medieval on them."

"Not really, all I've racked up are a couple of meals. If I have to buy a new car or something like that I'll let you know."

"New car my ass, if it ain't in impound, you're not getting it from us, you hear?"

John laughed as he waved to the lieutenant and went over to sit down at his desk to eat. While he was looking over the sports section in the paper and finishing his coffee, the phone rang.

"Missing Persons, Detective Mathews speaking."

"I'd like to report a missing person, do you think you might be able to help me out, detective?" Sydney's voice said over the phone.

John laughed. "The subject wouldn't be about six feet tall and just short of getting middle-age spread of the butt, would he?"

"How did you know?"

"I'm sorry Syd, I've been tied up with the Williams investigation and trying to keep up with the regular stuff too. How've you been? Are the wheels of academia still turning at the South's finest finishing school for refined young ladies?" John asked.

"My, my, you do have a way of turning a phrase. A mouth like that should be put to better use than playing bad cop in an interrogation. I just might have a position available for you if you're interested."

"We'll have to discuss your offer, for sure. What do you have in mind?" John asked.

"Actually, I called to see if I could persuade you to come by Friday night for a home-cooked meal. Interested?" Sydney asked.

"You bet. What can I bring?"

"Nothing at all. I'll take care of everything. You just be there on time, how's seven sound?"

"I'll be there with bells on!" John promised.

Sydney let out a low, throaty laugh. "This I've got to see. Is there anything else you want to let me know about you? You don't give Fruit of the Loom any new meaning, do you?"

"You'll just have to wait and see. Worried?" John asked.

"Not at all, I was a Girl Scout. We're always prepared. See you tomorrow night."

"I can't wait. Bye." John hung up the phone and caught his face reflected in the glass of his picture fame. He saw that he was grinning like an idiot. He knew that he had a credibility problem with Samuels, that he had some ground to make up in fully winning the FBI agent's confidence in light of the relationship that had grown between him and the only person who might have substantive information on a decades-old string of crimes.

That afternoon, driving to Pete's place, John called Agent Samuels' direct mobile number.

"Samuels, what can I do for you, John?"

"I'll keep this brief. I just got invited to dinner at someone's house. Are there any special toys you might want me to leave there?"

"Hang on a sec . . . I'll meet you at your house tonight at nine. That work for you?" Samuels asked.

"I'll be there," John said, and hung. He parked the car around back and walked into the cool, dim bar. John went directly to the bar and sat down across from Pete, who was washing Martini glasses to put in the freezer.

"Hey dude, you look like a man with a problem biting at him. What's up?" Pete asked his friend, pouring a frosty glass of tea and setting it on the bar.

"It's not much I can talk about, really. I'm wondering if I'm being played for a fool by someone."

"That same chick you brought in here? She looked like she was way over the end of your skis."

"Yeah, she has class in spades. She's also got more brains in her pinky than I've got in my whole head. I just can't tell if what we're doing is real, or if she's just too good for me to tell she's playing me. She invited me to dinner tomorrow night at her house, and frankly, I don't have a clue what to bring." John shook his head and grabbed the glass Pete set down in front of him.

"Did she say to bring wine or dessert?" Pete asked, with one raised eyebrow. "That would make it easy, I've got a great, full-bodied red and a crisp, light white that you could take. You know, depending on what she's serving."

"I suppose that would work. Even though she said she had everything under control."

"Yeah, but John, you could still bring it as a gift. It's what neighborly folks do, and you don't want her to know your true clueless and cheap nature, do you?" Pete clapped John on the shoulder and went to the cooler to grab the bottles of wine.

"Now that the smokescreen is out of the way, what's really bothering you? This is Pete you're talking to. We may not be family, but I know that if my back gets up against it like it did during the divorce, I can always call you for help. At least give me an opportunity to do the same."

"I'm having a hard time trusting this woman and I'm not sure if it's the job that's coloring my judgment, not being able to trust anyone I meet because they might have their own agenda talking to a cop, or if she's not being straight with me."

"You think she's pulling a scam on you? She's kind of high-class for that sort of thing, at least she looked like it. What's she do?"

"She's a dean over at Steddman College and has a wall full of degrees," John answered.

"Well that explains it, she's slumming. You know, seeing how the other half lives."

"What the fu . . ."

"That's right, get it out of your system. Now that the worst it could possibly be is on the table, look at what you two have said and done so far and see if the worst fits. If not, then what have you really got to worry about?" Pete watched John with concern, waiting to see how he took the poke in the eye he had dished out.

"Yeah, you're right. She's not slumming. I can't help but wonder what she's doing with the likes of an Atlanta flatfoot." John took a long pull from his drink and looked at Pete across the bar.

"One of the reasons we get along like we do is that for a white guy, you're straight with me. You seemed to have avoided the kind of closet KKK baggage that most of you Southern boys carry around like a good-luck charm. You saw it in the service just like I did, you see it on the streets in police profiling. You care for people regardless of color, that's why you never took a spot in Homicide when they opened up. I know you, once they're dead no one can help them.

With runaways there's still a chance of fixing what's gone wrong. Besides, you're one of the only honkies I know who understands that affirmative action isn't reverse racism. That, asshole, is probably what she sees in your pale ass. Go figure? How she could want some lowly civil servant with a melanin deficiency like you over a prosperous, entrepreneurial brother like myself?

I'm thinking she's got some kind of crippling mental problem. Yeah, that must be it."

John burst out laughing, feeling some of the weight fall from his heart. "I give up. So I'm the great white hope and I'm dating a color-blind schizophrenic who's trying to buy her way into heaven by befriending less a fortunate like myself?"

"In a nutshell. But if you doubt her at all, just look in her eyes. Damn it, John, you've got the skills, you know what to look for."

"You're right. I just don't reason right when it comes to her." Shaking his head, John continued, "Hey look, thanks a lot. Sometimes I have a hard time dealing with *myself,* let alone someone who I like and want to keep around."

Pete stuck out his hand to John and said, "No problem man, it's all good."

"I've done enough damage for one visit. What do I owe you for the wine?" said John, reaching for his wallet.

"Get the fuck out of here before I really get pissed off. When I want something from you it's going to be something worthwhile. Man, just enjoy her, enjoy the wine and above all, try to relax and trust your instincts. I'm betting they won't disappoint you, or her. Try to have a good time, and just let the evening happen, no expectations and you'll have no disappointments, cool?"

"Yeah, I got you. Just try to live in the moment." John picked up the bag and slapped five with Pete. "I'll drop in on Saturday and let you know how everything went."

"Hey, if everything goes as well as I think it might, try to get me some pictures, you hear?" Pete asked.

"That'll be the day. Hey, stay frosty, I'll see you over the weekend."

"You too, man, I'll catch you later."

Wir fahr'n fahr'n fahr'n auf der Autobahn
Autobahn
Written and performed by Kraftwerk

CHAPTER 20

M ARTIN WAS AMAZED at the skill with which Alan took his painstakingly developed programs, tore them down and rebuilt them to perform faster, more accurately and even more elegantly than before. The University of Chicago obviously had no idea what they had let go of when they let him come to the Southwest to live a mile underground for the duration.

The speed and accuracy of the detector had been increased by over a magnitude through the refinement of the underlying code that controlled the collection of the lasers' minute deflections. With the entire system running so much faster, the accuracy of the directional component had been increased as well.

As for Alan, he had never been this happy in his whole life. He had the most powerful computers he had ever used at his beck and call. He also had something else he had rarely experienced in his brief career as a research fellow: the visible respect of his new peers and his sponsor. Martin considered him an equal in the development of the project's various systems, and often deferred to Alan when the Navy's technical team had questions or suggestions in the reworking of the lab to accommodate the second detector. Once he fully understood the scope of the entire project, Alan adapted his three-dimensional display routines to the detector's configuration nearly overnight. Alan worked like a man possessed, and yet he never lost his calm manner when he ate with the soldiers and shelter staff, or when he was cooling out in the complex's common areas. He had a natural ability to multitask around the clock. His mind always seemed to be cooking up some newer or faster approach to collecting the minuscule traces of local gravity fluctuations and turning them into usable data. If he kept up this pace Martin was sure that Alan's efforts would keep the project on track in terms of the initial single detector time line, and save the American taxpayers hundreds of thousands of dollars.

Upon waking this particular day, Alan wanted to test out some of the operational specifics of the refined software, but he had no idea when another gravitational incident would occur. That was the only part of the project he considered a negative in his tenure underground, that there was no way to predict when something would show up in the detector's monitors so he could test his changes in the various software systems.

Later that morning, seeing Alan leaning back in his chair with a deep scowl on his face,

Martin asked him, "You look like someone shot your dog. What's up?"

"Uh, what? Oh, yeah. Hey, Marty. I was thinking that there's no way to really test the improvements we've made in the detector's analysis routines without a black hole or something dropping into the neighborhood. Look at this projection here. From the figures it looks like we're going to be able to place anomalies within a sphere of about ten kilometers, even without the second crystal hooked into the system, but I've got no way to test it out until something really massive gets within about eight million kilometers of the earth."

"Does the data have to be collected in real-time for you to run your test?" Martin asked the frustrated programmer.

"I'm not sure what you mean, do you have some way of planning an occurrence to detect, some kind of Acme Black Hole Maker or something?"

"No, but I'm wondering if you can run the data I collected a few weeks back with any degree of accuracy, or was the earlier collection routine too crude for the refinements you've added since then?" asked Martin.

"What data? Oh yeah, the first anomaly you detected, right?"

Pushing off with his feet, Martin rolled over to his desk and began to type on his keyboard, sending the location of the stored data to Alan's screen. "Run this through the sieve and see what you can come up with for a location. If you need the raw numbers they're on the mainframe in the archive section, you'll see it when you log in."

"No problem. I'm probably not going to get better than within about ten or twenty kilometers with this data set, but that should be plenty close enough for government work," Alan finished with a smirk.

"Fine, I'll leave you at it. I'm heading out to get something to eat, want me to bring you something back?"

"Just the usual, one blond, one redhead and a case of imported beer," Alan answered distractedly, already preparing to run the raw data through his new and improved location algorithms.

In the commissary, Martin got in line behind a group of technicians. He was surprised when they informed him that they would probably be finished about a week earlier than they had originally planned.

"Why so?" Martin asked the CPO in charge of the team.

"It's two things. Your changes to the growth tank have not only improved the stability of the crystal's matrix, but it looks like it has increased the overall growth rate between five and ten percent, I can't tell for sure yet."

"How'd that happen?" asked Martin.

"We're not really sure yet. I'd have to grow a handful of the things and mess around with your settings and the original specs we came up with a year ago."

"That's great news in any case. How's the lab coming?" queried Martin

"So far, so good. There have been no real snags, except pulling that center wall out and bracing the ceiling to compensate for the lack of support. Given that the floor above was reinforced concrete we really didn't *have* to do that, but I was just being cautious. You never know if any shift on the rock down here might slide the floors one way or the other. Just *thinking a*bout an earthquake down here gives me the willies," the CPO finished with a shiver.

"Well, it all sounds good, and I couldn't have done any of this without your crew's help," Martin said with genuine warmth.

"Don't mention it, that's what we're here for. How's the kid doing? It seems like it takes an act of Congress to get him away from that computer screen. We've been missing him here during mess. He working out all right?"

"You have no idea," said Martin. "He's already put me ahead of my original schedule by a few months just cleaning up my original code. The damn thing runs hundreds of time faster than before and for the life of me I never would have seen the shortcuts he wrote into the system."

"Yeah, he really knows his shit, the only bad part of him burying himself in the lab is that we'll probably never get to meet his friend the asteroid lady. Looks and brains are something the guys definitely appreciate! Try to remind him to invite her down here again, and see if she has some friends who might want to come along on a road trip."

Laughing as he picked out his and Alan's lunch selections, Martin said, "I'll be sure to remind him when I get back. You know what? He did call her using the video conferencing setup we have here. I might be able to talk him into giving her a call when you guys are working on our side of the lab, you might get to see her up close and personal."

When Martin returned to the lab, he was assaulted by the music of Robert Cray when the door opened. Alan turned down the music and jumped up to help Martin with the tray of food.

"Sorry about that, Doc, I was just letting off a little steam and celebrating a little," Alan said sheepishly.

"Don't worry about it, what's with the celebrating? You get married while I was gone?"

"Nope, I just finished running the data."

"How? I just left you a few minutes ago. How'd you run it so fast?" Martin asked.

"Well, when I took a look at the raw numbers, they were pretty close to the format that we're using now. So I ran a first pass to even out the three sets of numbers and then I put them through the current detector routines. I did sort of cheat by combining the data into one stream instead of doing each one separately. I guess that's how I did it so fast."

"I see what you did. So spill. What's the celebration for?"

"Doc, you won't believe it. According to the results that the computer spit out, the earth was hit, or grazed, by the opposite of a black hole!"

"A what? What the hell is the opposite of a black hole?" Martin asked, the food completely forgotten. "Show me."

"Look. Here's what was recorded. There *was* a deflection in the earth's gravity field. As a matter of fact the data shows that the incident was caused by an oscillation of a foreign gravity field, but the amplitude is one hundred and eighty degrees from that you would expect from a black hole. See here? The data shows a lessening of the surrounding gravitational constant, not an increase like there would be if an enormous increase in gravity had occurred."

"Did you check the original data? Could it have been integrated out of phase, or somehow mirrored itself from some programming screwup of mine?"

"I don't want to hurt your feelings, but that was the first thing I checked. According to the version of the detection software you were running back then the numbers are correct. The signs, plus and minus, are all correct."

Martin thought about the enormity of this discovery. He had never considered that there would be an anomaly that could *reduce* local gravity. He was completely nonplussed; he had no theoretical idea what the opposite of a quantum black hole would be, or what could cause a lessening of the local gravity field except for a correspondingly massive object juxtaposed to the earth.

"Alan, I have to think about this for a few minutes."

"Yeah, it hit me like that too. I have no idea what the opposite of a black hole is, but maybe you just discovered one, something no one else has ever even speculated on!" Alan was obviously excited over the discovery of something no one had even thought of, let alone might have seen or detected.

Sitting down at his desk, Martin was stunned, in the equivalent of intellectual shock.

"You don't mind if I look over your calculations, do you, Alan?"

"Hell no, I'd be happy as shit if you can find something I overlooked, I know I've been looking at this stuff too long to be able to see something as simple as a reversed operand. If there's no such thing as a "white hole," for lack of a better term, then somewhere I added or multiplied where I should have subtracted or divided. Anyway, this is a perfect time for a break. Hey, you're not forgetting about your food are you?" Alan asked.

"What? No, I haven't forgotten. Here, grab your stuff. And could you put mine in the fridge for a minute while I take a look at this?"

"Sure, no problem. Thanks for making the food run."

"No problem . . . I'll be right with you . . ." Martin trailed off as he began to trace the convoluted calculations that he used before Alan had arrived. Ninety minutes later, lunch completely forgotten, Martin looked up and saw that Alan had fallen asleep on the small couch by the door. Martin had satisfied himself that the original data was collected and stored correctly, there was no inversion of the raw numbers that would account for the strange results Alan's modifications had produced. Pulling up the streamlined code Alan had revised, Martin began to painstakingly trace the formulae the software was using in the analysis of the detector's data stream.

Hours later, Martin had found nothing out of the ordinary other than a calculation that seemed to skip two steps getting the answer but produced the right result. He opened his web browser and searched for gravitational phenomena that might hint at what the data seemed to suggest. After reading around forty abstracts of papers submitted by the most advanced researchers in the field of gravity, Martin was whipped. Nothing had ever been published, or even speculated on, from anyone, anywhere on any kind of white hole phenomenon.

Before he shut down his workstation, Martin began to compose a message to Commander Ames, carefully asking him if he was aware of any experiment in propulsionless locomotion underway and sent it off, grateful Alan had failed to make the mental leap that the opposite of gravity was antigravity. That was most assuredly something everyone would be interested in at the Pentagon.

The next morning Martin and Alan ate breakfast over small talk with the engineers. Once they dropped off their trays and began the walk to the lab Alan began pumping Martin for what he had held back in the cafeteria.

"So? What were you not saying back there? Did you find something that explains all this?"

"No, what I did discover, as you put it, was something you may think is completely nuts," Martin answered.

"Don't leave me hanging, what are you talking about?" Alan hissed, looking up and back down the corridor.

Martin paused to swipe his card through the lab's door, then led the way inside as the lights automatically came up to full brightness.

"Alan, as far as I've been able to see in the most advanced abstracts online there's no such thing as the opposite of a black hole. A white hole, for lack of a better term, is a theoretical construct that spews forth matter from a pin-prick hole in our universe, it has nothing to do with the opposite gravitational effect of a black hole's event horizon."

"So what do *you* think the data shows?"

"Keep this close, but I think what was recorded was something that used antigravity as a means of propulsion," Martin said, as he watched his young friend for reaction, and he wasn't disappointed.

Alan's face was a study in conflicting emotions as he absorbed the implications of what Martin suggested. Alan collapsed into his chair as he tried to formulate his response.

Martin continued, "So, if what the data suggests is correct, then what we have here is a recorded event where something is using the manipulation of gravity on a local scale."

Alan was stunned. "That's the stuff of science fiction, I mean there's not been a hint of anything like this in the literature I've read. Is it something secret that the government is working on?"

"I can't tell you that because I just don't know. But be advised, I did send off a message . . ." Martin broke off as the phone rang.

"Hello." Martin answered, covered the mouthpiece and mouthed "Speak of the devil" to Alan.

"Commander Ames, it's good to hear from you. No, everything is going well, how's the weather in Washington?"

"Everything here is just fine," said Ames. "You know why I'm calling. Your message last night was both exciting and disturbing. Have you anything more you want to tell me?"

"Alan and I just got in, we were going to go over the data and the software down to the last byte before we confirm anything. Why do you ask?"

"Are you serious? Something like this is explosive, that is if you guys aren't pulling a cold fusion on me."

"What? Oh, I see. No, but before we go further I want to check everything out."

"At least tell me this, can you tell me where the locus of the anomaly occurred?" Ames asked.

"What? Damn, I didn't even ask. Hold on . . ." Turning to Alan, Martin asked, "Hey, were you able to plot the location of the incident? Ames wants to know."

Alan looked up in surprise, and then turned to his terminal, his fingers flying over the keys.

"Hang on, Jim, he's checking."

Alan looked up and said, "According to my calculations it looks like it happened somewhere in or around the Middle East. I can't get any finer than a globe about two hundred kilometers in diameter with this original data."

"You hear that, Jim?"

"Yes I did, and what was the exact date and time?" Ames asked.

Martin read off the time stamp of the incident to Ames and then let him know that the work on the second detector was actually running ahead of schedule. Ames answered distractedly, and ended the conversation wishing Martin and Alan luck in debugging the software and promising to get back to them soon.

When Martin hang up the phone Alan asked, "Was that your head Navy dude?"

"Yes it was, he seemed kind of distracted."

"Was that who you sent off the message to last night?"

"Yes it was," Martin answered.

"Look, let's get started on the code, maybe this whole thing will turn out to be a screwup on my part." Suiting actions to words, Alan opened up several windows on his screen and began tracing the math and code Martin had used in the original version of the detector software.

Martin logged on to his own computer and began to do the same with Alan's current iteration of the software.

Hours later, having worked through lunch, Martin stood up and stretched. "Hey kid, find anything?"

"Nope. I even ran a third of the data through your original formulae to see if I got the same results as the number-crunching subroutine, and I got the identical results. If you made a mistake, it's not affecting the results. Maybe the original equations are hosed, but the software matches your original math."

"Damn, I was afraid of that."

Just then the phone rang. Martin and Alan looked at each other. "Want me to bar the door?"

Martin was surprised to hear the warbling tones signaling an encrypted call when he picked up the phone, but wasn't surprised at all to find Commander Ames on the other end.

"Martin, can you guess why I'm making this call?" asked Ames.

"We're betting that the news isn't good."

"Is the kid there with you? If so, you might as well put the call on speaker, he's going to need to hear this as well."

Pushing the button on the phone, Martin gestured Alan closer.

Ames began without preamble, "So, guys, I'll make this brief. From now on this incident has been classified top secret by the Pentagon. It's not going to be much of a change for the two of you though, you just can't discuss the incident with anyone not cleared by my office. Do you have any questions, gentlemen?"

Alan looked at Martin shaking his head. "No, commander, I believe we understand the situation just fine. Is there going to be any additional paperwork for us to sign?" Martin asked.

"Would it make any difference? No, if I can't trust you to give me your word, then what's the point?" came the commander's voice over the speaker. "Doctor, if needed could you put together a summary of your, and Alan's, findings just in case anyone here would like you to make a presentation of the facts?"

Alan nodding his head excitedly.

"That would be no problem. With Alan helping me I'm sure we could cobble up something that covers the facts," Martin answered.

"Very good, gentlemen. Today's Thursday, I doubt if anything will happen before the weekend, I'll call you Monday either way. And do me a favor . . ."

"Anything," said Martin.

"Could you *really* go over your facts before Monday? I hate to ask you to work the weekend, but I don't want a simple math or programming error to be the root cause of this brouhaha."

Alan broke in, "That's what we've been doing all day, sir. Is there anything you can tell us? Is there something in the works that could explain what we recorded?"

"Son, even if there were, do you honestly think I *could* tell you?" Ames asked Alan.

"No sir, probably not."

Martin wrapped things up. "We'll keep checking our results, and if anything does turn up I'll call you first thing."

"Thanks, Marty. And thank you both for putting in the extra effort. I'll talk to you Monday."

Martin looked at Alan and asked, "Well, son, you didn't have any hot dates scheduled for tomorrow night or over the weekend did you?"

"Sir, no, sir!" Alan shot back, snapping a salute in Martin's direction. "Before we start round two, can we get a bite to eat?"

As they made their way to the commissary, neither of them were the least bit put out that they would be spending the next three days checking code, and rechecking math. As a matter of fact, neither of them would have had it any other way.

CHAPTER 21

J OHN GOT UP bright and early for his shooting competition with Agent Minor. While he was microwaving something to eat, he quickly disassembled his Smith & Wesson semiautomatic to check for any dirt or grime. He wiped down each part with oil and reloaded the magazine to work the spring, then reassembled the pistol and snugged it into his shoulder rig. Satisfied he was ready for the shooting range, he pulled out his egg sandwich and left the house.

John saw Minor standing just outside the shooting range door carrying a small unmarked duffel. John shook Jeffrey's hand and led him inside.

John signed them in and asked Minor what kind of rounds he would like.

"Maybe a box or two of something easy, like Remington nine millimeter, a hundred and thirty grain load if you've got them," he answered.

The armorer reached back and grabbed a couple of green and yellow boxes and handed them to John. "No problem. Standard Qs for you guys?" he asked, referring to the targets nicknamed for the shape of the area where the human heart was on the target.

"That will be fine."

"Why don't you take lanes nineteen and twenty at the far end. And don't forget to pick up your brass and put it in the buckets, fellows."

John pulled a small case from his pocket and removed two small, silver sound suppressors and placed one in each ear. Minor pulled his own ear protectors from his bag and also put on a pair of shooter's glasses that cast a yellow hue to the skin around his eyes.

"Ready?" John asked.

"Lead the way," Minor answered.

The faint echo of early-morning shooters became a series of sharp reports that they could feel in their chests as they walked behind the lanes of the other officers.

They both laid out their weapons and spare magazines. John watched as Minor pulled a Glock 17 from his carrying case and loaded two spare magazines.

"How do you want to do this?" John asked.

"Your turf, your rules," answered the FBI agent as he slid shells into a magazine.

"How about groups of fives? Standard scoring?" suggested John.

"At what range?" Minor said with a leer, as if he couldn't wait to display his mastery over John.

"Why not start at ten yards and go from there?"

They both activated the motors that brought their targets up from the back wall. John brought up his hands and took a half step back with his right foot into the standard Weaver stance. Minor nodded in respect as he watched the police officer's form.

John then fired off five evenly spaced shots and then flicked down the safety lever on his weapon.

"Looking good detective, nice form. How's the grouping?" Minor asked.

Hitting the switch, John brought his target up to the line for them to check out. All five of his shots were grouped inside the target's Q in a ragged circle about four inches in diameter.

John looked on in satisfaction and pride at the results.

Patting John paternally on the back, Minor walked around the divider to his lane and relaxed. Facing down the lane, he burst into action, simultaneously dropping his foot back, bringing his hands up and firing all five of his shots in a span of less than two seconds. All the other shooting in the range came to a halt.

John looked on in amazement at the keyboard jockey, and before he knew it Minor hit the switch to bring his target to the line. When the target came to a stop John just about shit a brick when he saw a single hole in the center of the Q that could be completely covered by a silver dollar. Just to be sure, John looked closely and saw that he could discern at least four indentations around the small hole, proving that at least than many rounds had penetrated the paper. Minor just looked at him with a smirk.

"Not bad for a geek, eh?"

"Jesus Christ, do you sleep with that thing?" exclaimed John.

A couple of the other officers drifted down to their end of the range to see what all the commotion was about, and one, looking over John's shoulder gave a quiet "Holy shit," which only served to gather the rest in closer.

Seeing the attention that Minor's shooting was drawing, John said, "All right boys, there's nothing to see here. Just mind your own business."

"Who is this guy, detective?" asked one of the others stationed in John's precinct.

Facing the fact that the FBI agent's identity wasn't going to remain a secret easily, John replied, "He's an FBI agent who said that we flatfeet couldn't shoot worth a damn and challenged me to see who really has pissing rights here in town. Anyone want to take him on?" said John, figuring in for a penny, in for a pound.

John then said, "Well then, back to work boys, and let a couple of guys shoot in peace."

Watching everyone drift back to their own lanes John faced Minor and said, "I expect you're just as good at thirty yards. Just how good are you, Jeffrey, is there any point in continuing?"

"Well, I haven't been beaten by anyone other than the Quantico armorer in the last year. How about we just shoot for fun? Believe it or not I'm a little rusty." Minor released his pistol's magazine and replaced the five cartridges he had expended and slapped it back home.

After almost an hour of shooting, and advising some of the other of the officers on the range, the two begged off staying any longer, citing the work both had to do that day. They cleaned and oiled their weapons in the lounge and chit-chatted about the investigation.

"So far, " Jeffrey began, "I haven't really seen anything that is a definite match, but when I looked closer into the Atkins woman's travel I found four other possibles. Mostly places where the target group members lived and where she had traveled just before they disappeared, so I added them to the search."

"Shit, so it looks like, circumstantially at least, a connection exists," said John.

"Maybe, maybe not. If you know much about statistics, you know that this sort of data isn't too significant. At least we're trained not to hang a case on something as thin as this. But what it does do is give us an indication where we should be spending our time trying to establish more significant evidence.

"Samuels mentioned that you have some kind of relationship with the woman. Are you close enough to be able to find some other hard connections that are more than circumstantial?" Jeffrey asked.

"Not yet, maybe after tonight I will."

"You're not seeing her socially, are you?" Jeffrey asked with concern.

"Sort of, that part got started before I discovered the phone records. If I'd just cut things off it might have spooked her. Samuels knows about it, and so far trusts me to do the right thing if that's what you're worried about."

John sleepwalked through the rest of the morning, spending most of it buried in the brainless task of filing his foot-high pile of casework that had accumulated over the last few weeks. The lieutenant watched in bemusement as John appeared completely consumed with his task, knowing that something was weighing on his subordinate's mind. He also knew John would spill as soon as he reached some kind of substantive resolution to the problem at hand. At the end of the day John drove home to shower, shave and get into a clean shirt and tie for his evening out.

He retrieved the wine and left the house. His heart began to beat a little faster and he suddenly developed a flutter in his stomach. He felt a huge weight in his jacket pocket where he was carrying the four listening devices Samuels left in his care, although he still wasn't sure if he would to be able to secret them in Sydney's home. Even if he could conceal the bugs, what did the fact that he was considering doing so say about him? John decided that the best thing for him to do was to just play it by ear and put it out of his mind.

In front of Sydney's home, John gathered himself. As before, the inner door was open, this time the sounds of the Count Basie Orchestra drifted out to the porch. The smells of down-home cooking also wafted past his nose.

John rang the bell and Sydney emerged from the far end of the hall. She stood on tiptoe to give him a warm kiss on the lips. Surprised, John barely had time to gather her to him and return the kiss. Unfortunately, with his hands full he missed the opportunity to acquaint himself with her form.

"Come on in," Sydney said. "I've just got to put something in the oven. Go on in the living room and sit."

"I know you said that you had everything laid out for dinner, but I brought wine just in case," said John. "Actually I brought two, a red and a white, because I wasn't sure what you were going to prepare."

Turning back, Sydney asked with a twinkle in her eye, "And what else did you bring, detective? Some of those things you carry in the trunk of your car perhaps?

"Here, let me take the wine. Would you like a glass before we eat?" Sydney asked.

"Tell me first, what are we having for dinner?"

"Can you tell by the smell? I made gumbo, that's not going to be a problem is it? Perhaps I should have asked, but I didn't think anyone who lived alone would mind some good old down-home cooking. Was I wrong?" asked Sydney.

"Hell no. I love all kinds of Southern cooking. About every other year I get down to New Orleans for no other reason than to eat. That sounds great! But with sausage and seafood in the mix, just what color wine is proper for gumbo?" John asked.

"Just between you and me, I prefer the white."

"Why don't I open the bottle and pour while you do whatever it is you're doing out there?" John suggested.

"Come with me." Sydney led John into the kitchen and pointed to a drawer where he could find a corkscrew. Sydney brought down two glasses and passed them over to him.

John asked, "What do you suggest we toast to tonight?"

"Hmm, this puts me on the spot. I could go safe and give you a 'down the hatch,' or I could go commercial and try 'here's to good friends, tonight is kind of special,' but I hate banality. How about if I just say, 'to beginnings,' and let it go at that," she said watching John's face.

"Now the pressure's on me, is it? After that I don't want to spoil the moment with my usual 'sometimes you feel like a nut, sometimes you don't,'" John said, eyes sparkling. "How about, to beginnings?"

They both smiled and touched glasses and drank. "Not bad," said Sydney, setting her glass down on the counter as she checked the rolls through the oven door. "Did you pick this out yourself? I didn't see you as a wine drinker, not in a bad way though. I don't see the pretension in you that seems to permeate wine culture."

"You busted me, actually Pete made the selections. I really can't take any credit for the choice, but the sentiment is from the heart."

"That's all that counts. Dinner will be ready in about ten minutes. How about some music? Would you like to hear anything special?" Sydney asked.

"Sure, I'd like to hear what you were listening to last," John requested.

"You're an easy man to please, John Mathews," Sydney said as she went into the dining room. Moments later John was rewarded with the sounds of the Modern Jazz Quartet.

Returning to the room she asked, "Does that suit you?"

"Absolutely," John answered.

"So tell me, what does this music tell you about me? That is why you had me play it, wasn't it?" asked Sydney.

"Well, sort of. But this way I knew that whatever you played would be something you liked. It's not a test or anything, I only wanted to get to know your likes and your moods."

"You may be biting off more than you can chew. What if you discover that you don't like what you find?"

"Is that so bad either? Wouldn't that let me, and you for that matter, know that we might not be suited for each other? Although at least with music there's hopefully room for compromise.

"But seriously though, I do know that there are just some things that are too big to overlook in trying to build a relationship with someone. Fooling oneself is the most common cause of people breaking up when a little honesty in the beginning would have saved everyone a whole lot of trouble," John suggested.

Gesturing John to a stool at the breakfast counter, Sydney took the seat across from him to better see his face as they talked. "Perhaps, but how many people know themselves well enough to be able to properly or honestly decide what's going to work and what's not?"

"You have hit on the central problem to this whole man-woman thing, or man-man or woman-woman, what have you. The process of getting to know oneself isn't taught, there's no instruction manual on self-exploration other than crap, pop books that come out every year claiming to have the inside scoop on how to get along with others by knowing yourself. Christening some new psychological paradigm like understanding your inner child or some such bullshit is always all the rage. Most people learn about themselves by living, by exploring the things they experience and seeing how those experiences fit into their lives. Unfortunately these days the process usually stops at 'if it feels good, do it.' I think that's why there are so many people our age who just feel adrift in life and can't seem to get a handle on who they are."

"Yes, but don't you think that in general there's no real opportunity for younger people, late high school through college or so, to even begin the process, and by the time someone gets into real life it's largely too late?" Sydney asked.

"I don't know, but there is a way to help kids develop the requisite skills they're going to need for the rest of their lives and it just might help them develop that moral compass everyone is always so high on, and that's to just tell them the truth, and tell them the truth all the time, not just when it's convenient.

"As a cop, what I see as the biggest failure of our culture is not the availability of drugs, not premarital sex, and not the so-called alternative lifestyles, it's the complete lack of basic honesty." John flicked a glance at Sydney's eyes as he spoke those words, seeing if he could read anything untoward, but saw nothing in her face other than interest in what he was saying.

"Parents aren't honest with their children, teachers aren't honest with students, politicians aren't honest with anyone, the list is endless. Kids know very early on how to discern truth from lie, that's part of why two–and three-year-olds are so hard to handle. Parents try to manipulate them by shading the truth or lying, thinking that their kids are gullible, and they're not. When you constantly lie to a child all you're teaching them is that the truth doesn't matter, that the end justifies the means. After that, they're forever lost, the opportunity is gone to help them become something other than a poorly conceived caricature of a lying politician.

"Then, more times than need be, they end up coming into my jurisdiction. Worse yet, they become so frustrated or emotionally disenfranchised they withdraw into some kind of substance or emotional abuse, or they are so ostracized that they get their father's or grandfather's guns and take out a bunch of innocents." John paused to take a sip of his wine. "Sorry, I guess I have issues myself about a lot of things."

"One of the things that draws me to you is your passion for the way you think things should be and your frustration with the way they really are. I also like the way you haven't grown cold over life in general like so many policemen do. They see so much misery and deal with so many subhuman personalities many seem too inured to live.

"So let's get back to man-woman relationships. What is it you look for in a woman to see if they will pass the first round of eliminations and get on to the talent or swimsuit competition?" Sydney asked.

"The one thing I hate in a woman is selfishness, any inability to consider someone else completely turns me off. That's an immediate deal breaker because anyone who is so into their own self, to the exclusion of anyone else, is largely a waste of skin, at least for me. There are some men who like that because they always know what they've got, and that if they keep the wallet open then the girls will keep coming back," said John.

"That's a horrible way to think. What can those men be really getting out of a relationship based on that level of greed?" Sydney asked in disgust. "And what kind of woman would that be?"

"I look at it as a straight business deal, you get what you pay for."

"Enough about the great unwashed masses, what does John want other than an ability to consider someone else's needs, wishes?" Sydney prodded.

"It's like this. I'm pretty comfortable with myself, I can be alone without feeling like I'm missing out on something. Frankly, my work doesn't throw me into very many situations where I'm liable to meet someone normal, if you know what I mean. That's why I was both surprised and pleased when we met."

"Such a sweet talker, go on."

"I like that you have high standards for yourself, but you don't seem to look down on those who don't have your drive, your capabilities or your expectations. You were comfortable with me even though I'm a cop, many women aren't. And there's a good deal of flattery *of* me with your interest *in* me. You know what I mean?" John asked.

"I think so. My interest in you was both a surprise and a delight to me as well. The surprise is that though we have each chosen very different vocations to pursue, and we come from such different backgrounds, we've connected on an unexpected level. The delight comes from the unexpected manner in which we do seem to be getting along. It's more than the similar taste in music and that neither one of us is prone to rattling off words all the time just to be saying something. It's comfortable without the normal stress that dating always seems to bring out." John let the words hang out there for a few seconds before asking, "So, where does that leave us?"

"Would you believe, ready to eat?" Sydney said, breaking the spell.

John sat back abruptly, as if someone had tweaked his nose, as Sydney jumped up and got a potholder to remove the pan of rolls from the oven.

"Is there something I can help you with?" John asked.

"Why don't you get the wine and bring it to the table while I put these in a basket. Go on. I'll bring your food in to you."

Sydney came into the room carrying two bowls filled with rice and gumbo, set them down on the table and went back for the bread and her glass of wine.

"Do you say grace before meals? If so you may do so, I generally don't."

"I'm a longtime bachelor, I'm lucky if I even see my food on its way down. Tonight's dinner represents a number of treats for me. I get to miss eating alone, the food didn't come in a microwavable pouch and there's no one in the world I'd rather spend my evening with."

"That's close enough to a blessing for me, you old smoothie. Let's eat."

Once they dug in, for the most part the conversation centered on the meal, how it was prepared, how Sydney had learned her culinary skills.

Before he knew it he found that he had eaten his fill, pleasing Sydney with his appetite through three helpings. While she cleared the dishes she offered dessert in the form of either sherbet or Key lime pie. Declining pie in favor of the lighter fare, John helped clear the table while Sydney dished up the sherbet and brought the bowls to the table.

"So, where do you think we should go from here? After all we're far from being two lovestruck teenagers, and I don't demand, nor require, formal courting," Sydney said.

"Is there any reason to hurry things along? Not that I won't, but is there a need that I don't know about?" he asked in return.

"Not at all. But I'm not unaware of the power of the raw, male sex drive," she began smiling. "And I'm not some blushing virgin either. Frankly, sex can be a great way to divine the true nature of the man, much of what his character is made of shows through quite handily."

Feeling the warmth rise in his face, John asked, "You really enjoy seeing me squirm, don't you?"

"Not really, I'm just very comfortable with my own needs and I have no problem expressing them when the time is right. As for your discomfort, I apologize. I suppose I do take a tiny measure of joy at shocking your sensibilities, but you're so easy a mark. Much of your charm is in your honesty and in the ease with which I can set you off."

"Leave me at least some part of my dignity, and quit reading my mind, if that's what you're doing!"

"But John, it's so easy and so much fun," Sydney said with a soft tinkle of laughter.

"Well, knock it off. How would you feel if you were laid bare in front of someone?"

"Bare, John? Or naked?" she said softly.

"See, there you go again. I give up, you've won. Just be gentle, I'm only a man after all," John said, raising his hands in surrender.

"Tell you what. Go in the living room and choose some music while I put the dishes in the dishwasher, I don't really need help with the few things left."

Getting up and leaving the dining room, John paused at the computer, and feeling guilty, looked to see if there was any safe place he might secrete one of Samuels' devices.

Unfortunately Sydney kept things neat and tidy, although he couldn't tell whether she was always this neat or if she had straightened up for his visit; probably the former. John selected and loaded a mix of the Crusaders, Billie Holiday, Count Basie and B.B. King, just to mix things up a little. Once the music began to play, John perused Sydney's collection of books. The range was incredible. Her books were a mix of fiction, science, biography, travel (of which he took special note), and a full two shelves of larger books on art.

"See anything you like?" Sydney asked as she entered the room, wiping her hands on a towel and sitting down on the couch curling her feet underneath her.

"You have such a wide range of subjects here, are you partial to anything in particular?" John asked.

"Not really, although I admit that most of my explorations these days are through the Internet. I can pull up abstracts in math, stories from new authors, or even travel anywhere in the world just like reading a book, but more immediate, up to the minute."

"I know what you mean. I do the same myself, the Internet has really broadened the range of what I'm interested in too," said John, coming over to sit in the chair beside the couch.

For the next two hours they traded stories about work and about their teenage years, but very little about their own feelings. With all the conversation taking place in the living room John had little opportunity to find a place to hide the listening devices that Samuels had given him. In fact, he had completely forgotten about them. He was far more interested in adding to his picture of this woman who so completely enchanted him.

As for Sydney, the more she learned about John and the events that shaped him into the man sitting across from her, the more she wanted him. Though appearing calm and collected as they talked the evening away with the ease of longtime friends, Sydney was almost consumed with that deep-down heat that being with John set ablaze. No amount of wine was going to cover up the warmth that emanated from her midsection, and yet something she saw in John's demeanor held her back from revealing what she felt, from acting on her desire.

She saw the genuine shyness in John and the compassion he had toward those for whom he truly cared. The real John, the John that seemed unaffected by the job he had, even though he dealt with the vermin who ruined the lives and robbed the innocence of the young runaways they corrupted. He was still capable of love and compassion unsullied by the work he did. That was the John she wanted to hold, to feel against her. Her inner musings so consumed her she didn't hear the question that John must have just asked.

Seeing the blank look on her face John asked, "Is there something wrong? Was it something I said?"

"No, I was somewhere lost in thought, it wasn't you at all. What were you saying?" Sydney prompted.

"I said that I read a definition of love that really fits my own feelings."

"What was that?" Sydney asked.

"I've found that I'm truly in love when someone else's happiness is essential to my own," he answered.

Sydney was silent, absorbing the simplicity of John's answer. A moment later she asked, "So where does my happiness fit in your life right now?"

"I think I would love to be the one to make you happy, I'm just not sure if I can do the job properly," John said quietly. "I would ask that if you think I might be the one, could you give us a little more time to see if I'm right?"

Sydney got up from the couch crossing the single step separating them and bending over, she kissed John gently on the lips. Pulling Sydney into his lap, without breaking contact, John kissed her back with barely contained passion, feeling the warmth of her breath in his mouth as her lips parted with a soft moan.

The kiss seemed to go on forever as Sydney's tongue parted John's lips and rubbed slowly against his own. And, just before they both reached the point where there would be no stopping them from consummating the very act they both craved, John pulled slowly away. Opening his eyes, his breath ripping in and out of his throat, John pulled Sydney close to his chest, holding her tightly until his breathing calmed.

Sydney lay against the front of his body, feeling the physical manifestation of his arousal below, assured that it was she who caused it, reassured that it was she he wanted. And reaching up to the side of his head, she held her hand on the side of his face, feeling the warmth of him as the speed of his breathing slowly subsided.

"My God, Sydney," John asked, his voice barely above a whisper.

Waiting for her heart to calm, and her voice to return, Sydney answered, "If you only knew how long I've waited for a man like you. Your happiness, right now, is the only thing I'm interested in. Whatever you want, anything I can give you, is yours. All you have to do is ask me," Sydney said, flexing her bottom against his lap.

"Will you understand if I ask for just a little more time because I need to be convinced I can be everything you need me to be? So that I don't make the mistake of disappointing you because I hurried instead of considering whether or not I can deliver everything you deserve?"

Fighting her disappointment, and yet beginning to love this man even more for his frank nature, Sydney sat up and whispered in his ear, "Of course, take all the time you need. Just remember, everything I have is yours for the asking."

She then kissed him gently on the corner of his mouth and uncurled from his lap, light-headed from the depth of emotion she had plumbed.

Standing, and unconsciously straightening his pants, making a slight adjustment, John took Sydney in his arms and hugged her tightly.

"I need to go, you've given me so much to think about," John began. "I want to be a man who doesn't just go through the motions, a man whose every word or deed is conscious, well thought out, and makes a difference in your life.

"And, I am sufficiently honest with myself to question whether or not I'm equal to the task. That's why I ask for the time. Is that so bad?" John asked, hoping that he hadn't gotten in the way of himself.

Sydney was silent, her heart beat with unaccustomed feeling, and her eyes welled up hearing the naked honesty coming from this man, so different from any reasonable expectation she could have had the first time they met.

Realizing that she was wetting his shirt, Sydney pulled her head back to look into John's eyes and said to him, "You take all the time you need, I'm not going anywhere," and kissed him gently on the lips.

Slowly letting her go, John said, "I've got to go now. May I call you tomorrow?"

Sydney answered, "I have to go out first thing in the morning, but I'll be home by two. I'll be waiting for your call."

John said goodnight and kissed Sydney one last time.

Sydney watched through the livingroom window as John got in his car and slowly drove off, feeling as if she had run a marathon, tired and yet suffused with a euphoric endorphin high that helped gentle her to sleep.

CHAPTER 22

THE FOUR-MAN INCURSION team had flown to Germany by military transport to meet up with the B-2 team who had arrived a day earlier. Having completed six more jumps before leaving the Virginia countryside, the last four made using GPS instrumentation without benefit of landing zone markers, the team felt more than ready for their insertion into Iraq.

Arriving at their secure quarters on base, the team was surprised to find waiting for them satellite photos barely eight hours old, and a sealed packet from MI-6 for Malcom Stiles containing everything British intelligence had on their in-country contact, Basra.

Assigning the two younger members of the team to unpack and inspect their equipment, White and Stiles went over the information in the packet.

"Great stuff our fellows put together here, eh, David?" said Malcom.

"I'll say. Looking this over though, what's your take on how far we can trust this guy, Basra?" White asked. "Do you think he's on the up and up?"

"That I can't say, but the fact of the matter is his assistance in getting us to town from the landing zone will be invaluable," Malcom answered. "Is there anything in the packet on the escape route?"

"Hang on. Yes, there is, the whole route east is photographed, and most of the route south, although there's no telling if we're going to stick to the direct route once we're in the thick of it. Take a look at these."

"David, why don't you study the route east, and I'll take the route south to the Arabian Sea, and let's have Kahill back me up and Geoffrey can double your route," Malcom suggested.

"Good idea. How's our equipment look, boys? Is anything missing?" David said raising his voice.

"So far, so good, chief. They even included local duds for on the ground," answered Kahill. "Does it say when we drop, sir?"

"The latest communique says 'at our discretion,' what do you all say?" said David, putting the question to the rest of the team.

"If it's all the same to you older blokes, my feeling is that there's no time like the present," suggested Geoffrey.

"Is there any reason we can't go tonight, sir?" asked Kahill.

Looking at Malcom, and receiving a nod of agreement, David said, "Let me get with the B-2 crew and see if logistical support can get them a tanker deployed for tonight. If so, then we drop at 01:00, local time. Malcom, give MI-6 a call and have them signal Basra to stand by for confirmation of our 'go' for this evening. Kahill, Linden, you two take these photos and study the escape route. Geoffrey, take the route east, and Todd, you memorize the route south through Iran."

David then left to arrange for the B-2 to fly the mission that evening, and to notify Robert Bascomb that the mission was on.

After sorting out all of the gear, separating each team member's equipment and putting everything on their assigned beds, Kahill and Linden began to systematically memorize every feature of ground the recon satellite photos revealed.

David, reaching the visiting crew's billet, went in to try to find any of the B-2's crew. Seeing the jump master reading a book in the lounge, David walked over and sat down.

The Sergeant said, "You need me for something, sir? Is something missing?"

"No Sergeant, we want to go this evening. Will that be a problem for you guys?" asked David.

"Uh, no sir," the Sergeant said, jumping to his feet. "I'll go and find the colonel and get things rolling." He then hurried off to gather the rest of the crew and make arrangements with the base commander.

David made his way to the base commander's office. After flashing his agency ID to the airman at the desk, David showed the commander his identification and said, "Sir, I have need of your secure telephone to the States."

"And that would interest me, how, Mr. White? We don't let just anyone use our private lines on their own say-so. Convince me why I should care."

"If you insist. For all practical purposes, commander, *I* own that B-2 sitting inside the hanger over there. You're welcome to contact the colonel who drives that bus and ask *him* for confirmation, I'll wait outside. But try not to be too long, I have some work of my own to get back to." And turning his back on the commander, David walked out of the office and sat down in the small waiting area.

Not more than three minutes later the door burst open and the commander shouted, "Airman, get that man back here . . ." and broke off, seeing David sitting patiently by the door.

"Belay that, airman." The commander then said, "Sir, if you would be so kind as to step in to my office, I'm sure that whatever you need can be taken care of."

David waited for the commander to close the door and sit down behind his desk. The commander, at least having the good manners to look chagrined said, "I'm very sorry, sir, I had received the orders for the billeting of the B-2's crew, and that they were to be flying a special mission, but I had no idea that a civilian would be the mission commander, sir."

"That's to be expected, commander. There was no way you should have known ahead of time, the nature of the mission is, shall we say, classified," answered David. "Now would it be all right with you if I made that call, sir?"

"Of course. If you have the number, just dial directly on the blue phone. I'll just be outside, sir." The commander got up and gestured to his chair, and without a backward glance he left the office, closing the door carefully behind him.

Chuckling to himself, David picked up the phone and dialed Bascomb's office. He was amazed with the clearness of the connection once the two instruments had established a secure connection, for his part David only three words, "Go for Goldmine," and waited for Bascomb's "Understood," before he broke the connection.

David's short code phrase put in motion a plethora of preparations by the Navy, Air Force, several intelligence services and more than a handful of secret operatives, most of whom the team would never meet. His call also initiated the retasking of eight of the US's one hundred eighty spy satellites to provide overhead coverage along the team's escape route.

Back at the barracks, David saw all their gear neatly stacked and ready for deployment.

All three turned to look at David as he came through the door.

"Well, mate?" asked Stiles.

"The mission is go for tonight. I suggest you rest up, we're all still on Eastern time, which for a change works to our benefit. Is all the gear checked out?" David asked.

Receiving nods from the others, David asked Malcom, "Will your boys be able to alert the asset in time?"

"That's affirmative. He's supposed to be in the area from eleven forty-five on."

"Why don't we all take a quick stroll over to the hangar and check out the equipment. I want to go over the flight plan with the colonel and make sure everything's squared away before we grab a couple of winks," said White.

They jogged over to the hanger housing the specially modified B-2. Once there, they occupied themselves inspecting every fitting, strap and seam of their chutes and suits with their jump master and the support team. They then tested and topped off their breathing systems and checked the calibration of their GPS/altimeters; everything was ready. Once their inspection was completed and David confirmed the flight plan to the landing zone just outside of Baghdad, the four headed back to their room to try to get some last-minute rest.

Just after dusk, David woke those who were asleep and told them to gather their equipment and load it into the Humvee parked just outside the door. The driver brought them to the side door of the secured hanger to unload. Seeing them pull up, the air police guard stuck his head inside the door and moments later a handful of the B-2's support crew came out to help unload.

To a man, the mission team members were treated like royalty, with two airmen assigned to outfit each of them in their jump gear and check equipment stowage. Now that the mission was a go, everyone was all business, the crew just as concerned with the success of the team's mission as the four of them.

Even the pilot, Colonel Mason, conducted his own detailed inspection of the men. He too wanted to shade the odds of success in the team's favor in any way he could. Satisfied that he would find nothing amiss, especially in light of the master's attention to detail, the colonel shook each of their hands and bade them good luck.

The team stowed their gear and strapped themselves in as if they had been doing so for years. The easy way the team moved and chatted spoke well of their mission preparation. They were loose, but not careless.

As the flight engineer secured and sealed the ramp, they all felt the B-2's engines start, brightening the cabin lights to a cool glow. Before long they felt the plane taxi out of the hangar, able to tell when they cleared the massive doors by the decrease in engine noise as the B-2 left the protection of the huge enclosure, rolling out into the open outdoors.

The B-2 must have been cleared directly to the runway because in less than five minutes the engines hit maximum thrust and hurled the modified bomber into the darkening sky.

The flight was fairly quiet, with each member of the team consumed with his own thoughts on the mission ahead.

David unstrapped and moved across the ramp to sit next to Stiles, buckled in and asked Malcom over the noise of the engines, "What do you recommend if this Basra turns out to be working the other side of the fence?"

"Good question. MI-6 says that our other two agents in the area have been ghosting him since he arrived in town. Other than his family, he doesn't seem to have made contact with anyone else in the area since he arrived. There's been no additional deployment of troops in the landing zone, no sign of surveillance in the area at all. Barring any indications to the contrary, I'm willing to give the lad the benefit of the doubt," said Malcom.

"We should all stay on our toes in any case, wouldn't you say?" asked White.

"Too right."

The team spent the remainder of the flight in silence. Kahill even dropped off to sleep. As they penetrated Iraqi airspace the B-2 pilot throttled back to lessen even further the tiny heat signature of the high-flying jet.

The defensive systems operator noted that no active radar was pointing in their direction, and the upper atmosphere in which they flew was sufficiently dry that they were leaving no vapor trail behind that could be used to locate them.

Checking his instruments to verify that no detectable lights or electronic emissions emanated from their aircraft, the pilot announced over the intercom that they were twenty minutes from the drop zone and for everyone to stay sharp. He knew that their location was being monitored by an E-3 Sentry AWACS surveillance control aircraft, whose combination of ground, air and satellite communications systems were the only ones capable of monitoring any American stealth aircraft deployed over the entire Persian Gulf region. The E3 had the only means of vectoring in the orbiting tanker tasked to refuel the B-2 once it was safely out of Iraqi airspace, or any Western alliance fighters to support the B-2, should it get into any kind of hostile encounter.

When the pilot signaled ten minutes to go, the jump master began his final inspection of the team members' equipment, testing straps and topping off oxygen bottles for the last time. When he had completed his inspection he signaled them to secure their breathing masks, unstrap and attach their individual equipment packs for the jump.

Each team member removed his pistol from his pack and chambered a round before securing it to the sewn-in holster in their insulated jumpsuits. They checked each other's load-out and signaled their readiness to the jump master, who flipped the interior lights from normal to a dim blue. Moments later the light on the bulkhead between the hold and the flight deck changed from yellow to red. The team felt a lessening of pressure in their ears and the temperature of the air as the jump master equalized the air pressure in the hold to that of the atmosphere outside.

The jump master signaled them to their feet and lined them up for deployment. When the team was ready, the lighting was reduced to a dim glow along the floor, so when the ramp was deployed no light would show to anyone on the ground below. When the bulkhead light blinked yellow two times, and then turned a cool green, the jump master activated the hydraulics, dropping the ramp into the jet's slipstream and saluting the team members as they, one by one, disappeared into the nighttime sky. Once the last man was out he immediately closed and sealed the belly door.

The shock of the exit from the jet lasted only a few seconds and White, the last man out, came out of his tuck, arching his back as hard as he could to halt his tumble and orient him to the quickly approaching ground. Once face down, White clicked his mic switch twice and received three double-clicks in response. The rest of the team was fine. Looking at his GPS/altimeter, he noted that they had exited the B-2 within half a click of the LZ.

The team's descent went completely unnoticed by anyone on the ground. Even Basra, had he been looking, would have seen no sign of their delivery craft or of them against the starlight that faintly illuminated the wide expanse of ground below.

Free falling through fifteen thousand feet, the team all flipped down their night vision goggles, searching for features of the up-rushing ground.

White lifted his head to see if the infrared strobes attached to each team member's suit were visible, located them all, and was satisfied that they were all vectoring in to the right corner of the open countryside.

David saw that he was still on target and about to fall through six thousand feet above ground. Bracing himself, he pulled his ripcord and grunted in satisfaction as his chute deployed, jolted his entire body, and slowed his descent from over a hundred and fifty feet per second to a gentle glide toward the ground. Double clicking his radio once again, David was relieved to hear the three responses signaling everyone's chute had deployed successfully.

Now less than a mile above ground, each member of the team scanned the ground, picking their spot to land, making sure to avoid trees, larger rocks, and each other.

Moments later they were all down and, gathering up their chutes, they converged under the largest tree in the area. The shed their suits and breathing gear and unpacked their equipment from their carryalls. Each team member dumped his chute, jumpsuit, breathing gear and everything that they were not going to be taking along into a heavy foil bag Kahill was holding open. When everything was gathered in the bag, Linden quickly dug a shallow hole. Kahill tossed a small black device inside the bag and then dropped the bag in the hole. The four then threw the dirt back into the hole. Five seconds later a small gout of smoke puffed out through the dirt covering the bag, filling the area with an acrid smell. The bag's contents were burning under intense heat below the thin layer of dirt.

With their guns and equipment secured about their bodies, they filled in the resting place of their destroyed discards, trying to make it indistinguishable from the surrounding landscape.

Moving away carefully, the four spread out and began to walk to the southeast, heading for their rendezvous with Basra. After a brisk, two-kilometer hike they approached a road running to the east of the open expanse where they had touched down. David saw an old Mercedes pulled far off the road under an aged, gnarled tree.

Everyone stopped and, approaching slowly, Kahill stood a little straighter and walked up to the rear of the car as if he were just out for an evening stroll. Along side the passenger window, he bent down and asked the sole occupant, "Could you spare a traveler a cigarette?" in Arabic.

Startled by the man's sudden appearance, Basra almost forgot the proper answer to the man's query, but pulled himself together enough to say, "I'm sorry, I cannot. I smoke a pipe myself."

Kahill then walked around to the driver's door, opened it and asked Basra, "Would you mind stepping out of the car, please?"

Keeping his hands in plain sight, Basra complied with a smile. "Would you like to take a look in the trunk as well, sir?" he asked in barely accented English.

"Quiet please," Kahill answered in Arabic, and pumped his hand twice above his head.

The other three ran up and examined the car inside and out, visually and with a small, handheld instrument as Kahill quickly and efficiently searched Basra, finding nothing of note. Once the were satisfied the car contained no explosives or obvious transmitters, David went up to Basra with hand extended and said, "Thank you for putting up with our little bit of drama here. We have to be quite careful."

"I understand perfectly. May I be permitted to move now?" Basra asked.

"Of course. May I ask what your plans were regarding our getting to the outskirts of town?"

"This car has been borrowed from a friend of mine who owns a restaurant in town. He is known for his travels at all hours buying provisions for his business, food, drink and such. He has many brothers who use this car for driving friends and important clients around town as well. I thought that driving you into town would be the fastest and safest means of getting you where you are going, no?"

"That sounds good. Shall we go then? The quicker we get started the better," answered White.

He and Basra got in the front seat as Stiles, Linden and Kahill piled into the back. The car started immediately and pulled back on to the road. David asked Basra, "Do you have any new information on the objective that will help us getting in and out?"

"Unfortunately, no. No one in my family's circle of friends works in the Great One's lab, nor do any of them work in the maintenance crew or in the guards." Basra pulled out a handwritten note from his shirt pocket.

"Here is a drawing of the main lab floor that an old acquaintance who had visited there on deliveries drew for me. He's not sure that any of this is still accurate, it's been over seven years since he has been inside, but it's something, no?"

"It is indeed. We were not able to obtain any information on the interior of the lab, the actual entrance inside the building or the floor plan of the lower levels," said David.

"I can tell you this. After midnight there are rarely more than two people in the entire complex. There will be a car driving around the neighborhood patrolling with armed soldiers, but once you're inside they will be of no consequence."

"Do you have knowledge of alarms that we might face getting in?"

The question provoked a laugh from Basra. "The way things are now, even the best of the Great One's installations are running short of parts, and in many cases those not directly in the military, like the scientists and technicians, are not being paid regularly as it is. I suspect that you and your team can penetrate the upstairs entrance to the lab with no difficulty, but avoid the elevator. It logs the trips up and down, and is rumored to have a camera that activates by movement in the cab."

"Is there anything else you can think of that might help?" David asked.

"I have nothing else that would be of help; however, I think we should talk of after. I believe I can secure a small truck whose absence will probably not be reported until morning. Your people were not inclined to inform me of your escape route, but I'm sure that you want to get as far from the city as possible before daylight. Even I cannot hide you once your break-in is discovered.

"I will show you where the truck will be parked before I drop you off, although I will not risk exposure for you, or anyone else. My getting caught with you will serve no useful purpose," Basra said, regretfully. "I will wait for ten minutes after I drop you off in the event you have to abort, then I will leave to get the truck."

"Thank you for your help, and be assured that our appreciation is genuine. By the way, your English is excellent, where did you study?" asked David.

Basra paused to look over at David before replying. "My student days included two years at the University of Wisconsin in your city of Madison. There were many of us from places outside of your country and most were treated well. There are times when I consider living my remaining days somewhere in America. Unfortunately my neighbors would be completely ignorant of anything that happened away from your news cameras.

"Retiring to the US would be a vacation until the end of my days, but I want more than that. I want my people to have a better life here. Do not get me wrong, I understand that things must change within the powers that rule here, but eventually the United States must stop playing favorites throughout the world."

David asked Basra, "If you feel this way, why do you risk helping us?"

"Because I too want to know who built the aircraft whose parts you were sent to retrieve from the lab. Do not be surprised that I know. There was no other conclusion to draw from the requests made by your people, although I suspect that MI-6 has more of a hand in the information I pass on and receive. Their touch is lighter and less obtrusive. If there is a new player in the area or something new has escaped from the old Soviet secret labs, I too want to know what it is. I am first a pilot, even with this useless foot.

"I support your effort here because I want better for my family and friends. I will help you get away from town if I can. But take this message back to those who make the policies in your government for my country," asked Basra.

"Yes?" David prompted.

"Tell them that when they prop up some weak, small-minded agent to do their bidding, they are obviously forgetting their own history. Every one of the men your country has backed in an effort to promote their agenda in the Middle East has either taken their money with little return, or in the case of Bin Laden and others of his ilk who you train and set loose like rabid dogs to rid you of your enemies, remember that rabid dogs have a habit of biting their owners."

"In other words, try to play nice outside our own yard?" asked David.

"Essentially. Not that you really have a say in how your country does business, but at least *I* feel better," Basra finished, laughing, getting a chuckle from David as well.

Suddenly they all fell quiet as the lights from the city became visible ahead. Slowing and turning around in his seat, Basra directed his words to the two Brits and David. "If you speak little or no Arabic, do nothing if we are stopped. I will get out and handle all the explanations. Everyone understand?"

All four nodded, but they all checked their hand weapons and concealed them out of sight, ready for immediate action. Within minutes the car was traveling among homes and small businesses, all closed and dark in the middle of the night. As they approached the lab, Linden pointed out buildings and streets that he recognized from before, helping orient the rest of the team with the surrounding lay of the land. On two occasions their car passed military patrols of a couple of soldiers in open-topped jeeps. When they encountered the first one Basra turned the radio up loud enough to be heard by the passing patrol and waved as they passed. The soldiers waved back when they recognized the car.

"See, it's not so bad, is it?" Basra said to David.

Just then Linden tapped David on his shoulder and pointed down a side street, "There's the building, the one with the lit window, sir."

"He's right," said Basra. "Are you sure you've never been here before?"

"No, just good at remembering the maps," answered Linden.

"Where are you dropping us off?" David asked.

"On the other side of the lab, where you can come up on it from the rear. It's also darkest there. You'll be about fifty meters from the back of the building." Basra made a right turn away from their objective and turned again to bring them down the next block over.

"When I stop the car, just wait for my signal before you follow, understand?"

"Why are you getting out of the car? I can't let you do that and leave the four of us sitting ducks. What's this all about?" David said as Kahill cocked his pistol, the noise a deadly punctuation to the background noise of the radio.

"No, no. I'm just going to make sure that no one watches. If you are worried you may keep weapons on me, I will be less than two meters from the automobile, just wait."

Looking back at the three in the back seat, David gestured to the dome light and Linden unscrewed the exposed bulb, and as the car slowed Kahill and Linden released their door catches and held them closed until the car came to a stop.

Stiles grabbed Basra's shoulder from behind and said, "Do be careful mate, I wouldn't want anything to happen to you out there, if you get my meaning."

Basra nodded and slowly got out from the car, leaving his door open and the headlamps on. All four removed their weapons from concealment, cocked them and sat tensely as Basra walked around the front of the car, crossing through the light of the headlamps. They watched as he stopped next to the back of the building on the passenger side of the car.

David almost laughed out loud when he saw Basra fumble with the front of his trousers and then let out a stream of urine to splash against the wall of the building. Casting glances left and right, Basra nodded his head signaling the men to get out of the car. As they passed him to get under cover around the corner of the building Basra whispered to David, "I'll pass by here in exactly ten minutes, and then at twenty minutes. If you are not here I will return the automobile and see about the truck."

"How do we signal you when we're ready to go?" David asked.

Tucking himself back into his pants and pulling up his zipper, Basra pointed up the alley.

"Go this way for three blocks, you will see a restaurant with a green awning. I will be waiting around back in a dark red bakery truck. If I am not there, wait until 04:00. If I do not come then you will have to make your way east out of town and hide in the hills until nightfall. If I cannot find you I will at least inform my contact that you have, how do you say, gone to ground and hope for the best."

"We'll see you at 04:00 at the latest," David said.

"Go with God," Basra said, quickly driving off into the night.

"Psst, over here sir," came a whisper in the night. Good thing too, David could see no sign of the others.

Hurrying into the gloom David saw the other three looking at the hand-drawn diagram that Basra had passed on to them under the glow from a hooded pocket light.

Malcom pointed at the rear office in the diagram and said, "This looks like the best bet here. If there's nothing in front of this window we should go in through here."

"All right, let's go take a look. We have less that two hours to get what we came for and get out. Move out gentlemen," David ordered.

Moving from shadow to shadow, they were one building away from the concealed laboratory when they heard a vehicle coming down the next street over. They sought the darkest cover they could find and waited to see if they would be discovered. Fortunately the noise moved off into the distance.

Kahill and Linden inspected the frame and inner surface of the window for alarms or trip wires. They saw only a magnetic alarm switch along the upper edge of the window, so Linden applied a strip of magnetic tape to the surface of the frame right below the switch while Kahill drilled a small hole in the glass so he could push the broad, flat portion of the window lock with a probe. The window unlocked without any visible damage to any curious passers-by.

Linden quickly slid the glass up on its track to allow Kahill to climb inside. No alarms went off. Inside and crouching low, Kahill made an initial sweep of the room and, seeing no sign of threat, he tapped twice on the glass.

At Kahill's signal, Linden stepped back and gestured to the shadows that were Stiles and White. He quickly following him through a second later. As soon as he was in, Linden silently closed and locked the window.

At the alarm switch, Linden ran a jumper wire to ensure that their exit would be just as quiet as their entrance.

They moved silently into the hallway outside the office. White could see the lights were out all the way to the front of the building. Watching for trip wires or any other sensors in the hallway, he led the team to the stairwell adjacent to the elevator. He signaled Kahill forward, moved off farther down the hall as lookout, and waited patiently for Kahill to scan the door for alarms.

Kahill was completely focused on checking for any electrical current in and around the stairwell doorframe and as far as he could tell there were no operating electrical or electronic devices attached to the frame of the door. He pulled a small LCD monitor from his pack and quickly attached a fiberoptic camera cable to the monitor and turned it on. Satisfied it was working he handed the camera end to Linden who, watching the screen in the corner of his eye, slid the camera and cable under the crack in the door. Linden adjusted the focus of the camera turning the small guide midway down the cable and slowly panned it around the inside of the door. Linden could feel cooler, less humid air blow past his fingers near the floor. He whispered, "I've definitely got conditioned air coming from downstairs." He paused for a moment when Kahill signaled him to back up, but began to laugh soundlessly as he pointed out to Linden that the hinges of the stairwell door were on their side.

Stiles and Linden pried the hinge pins out and slowly pulled the locked door away from the frame from the side opposite the handle. They stopped briefly to allow Kahill to inspect the inner surface of the door. Then the two Brits pulled the door the rest of the way out of the frame and, once free, brought the hinged side back so Kahill could replace the hinge pins.

When they were all in the stairwell with the door safely locked behind them, White led the way down the stairs. The air became cooler and less humid as they descended. They dropped over a hundred feet before reaching the first door. White signaled Linden to wait there and watch their line of retreat. Then, further down, they found a single exit at the bottom of the stairwell. Kahill checked the unsecured door for alarm currents and pronounced it safe.

"Kahill, go back upstairs and check out that level with Linden. Malcom and I will take this level. You have fifteen minutes, if you find something that merits our attention, click twice; and do be careful."

White waited until Kahill was at the landing above before he nodded to Stiles to try the door.

Stiles saw that the hallway into which the door opened was dimly lit with no one in sight. They moved the corridor, checking inside each door as they passed, making sure they had the floor to themselves before looking for the wreckage from the crash.

White and Stiles moved through the larger rooms on their floor of the complex looking for any sign of parts that resembled the objects in the photos at Langley. Looking quickly, White and Stiles found nothing of the aircraft or its pilot.

Upstairs, Linden and Kahill came to an isolation lab that held the kind of equipment used for experimentation on hazardous materials and biologicals. Kahill looked over the papers in the immediate vicinity to try to determine what the isolation room contained. Fortunately the clipboard hanging just outside the door showed who had checked into the room and the samples they were working on. Looking backward through time Kahill saw that scrapings were taken from "a foot, male, African" for toxicology.

"Linden, over here!"

"What have you got mate?" Linden answered.

"They've got a foot in the freezer inside. The briefing includes the fact that the pilot's foot was recovered at the crash site, looks like we hit paydirt." Kahill clicked his radio two times and waited.

"What have you got up there?" White replied over the radio.

"I think we've found the pilot's remains, sir. There's a foot on ice up here. Find anything yet, sir?" Kahill asked.

"Negative. You need any help?" White asked.

"No, sir."

"Carry on." White nodded to Stiles, who had stuck his head in the room listening to Kahill's report over his headset, and they continued their search.

They found nothing in the lower level. White and Stiles ran up the stairs to join their juniors. White called on the radio, "What's your twenty?" requesting Kahill and Linden's location.

"Northwest corner, second to the last door," replied Linden.

Stiles asked, "Where's Kahill?"

Pointing over his shoulder, Linden hooked a thumb toward the isolation lab. "He insisted on going in and getting the foot. Said that if we can get a DNA sample and a print we might have a chance of finding its origin."

Through the observation window the three could see the Kahill in an isolation suit looking through the various glass-enclosed freezers and coolers inside. Triggering his radio White asked, "Kahill, can you hear me?"

"Affirmative, sir."

"Have you lost your mind? Do you even know if you got the suit on properly?"

"Shit, sir. If *they* can get in 'em, how hard can it be? Besides, Geoff helped me with all the seals and I set the air system on overpressure to make sure that nothing gets in."

"Dammit, Kahill, get your ass out here. What if the lab's wired? They could be heading down here right now." At that declaration, Linden slid out of the room to watch the corridor and elevator. Stiles checked the other isolation compartments throughout the room, looking for all the world like miniature mutant octopuses with their gloves sticking out of all sides of the cases.

"David, I've got something here. Looks like some larger pieces of electronics, only made out of glass," said Stiles.

"Are any of them attached to anything or in isolation?" White asked.

"No, they're on the bench over here in the open and have leads running to some sort of computer interface."

"Damn, that computer's too big to hump all the way back. Can you remove the hard drive and bring it with the piece they're working on?" David asked.

"Half a tic . . . No worries, I can slide the drive right out," Stiles answered as he took off his pack.

White crossed over to the side of the lab where Stiles was loading diagrams, parts and computer disks and tossed his bag to Stiles to fill as well. "Linden, see what's taking Kahill so long. I want us out of here ASAP!"

"You know, David, as soon as someone gets in here in the morning they're going to know someone was here," Stiles pointed out quietly.

"I know, I know. Fill up my bag and head out into the corridor, I'm going to grab Kahill, even if I have to go in there and drag him out."

He crossed over to the airlock of the isolation room, to see the outer door opening. He grabbed the package Kahill was carrying, pushed the door closed and made sure the status lights on the panel turned from amber to green.

"What's this you handed me?" asked White when Kahill removed his suit's helmet.

"I put the foot in an insulated storage bag. Actually, I triple-bagged it and poured liquid nitrogen into the second bag. That ought to keep the thing frozen until we get to the coast."

"Why the hell did you do that? All we needed was a DNA sample!" hissed White.

"Look sir. I don't know about you, but I'm dying to know who this guy was, and if he was flying some new kind of stealth craft then the chances are good that he's from one of the industrialized countries," said Kahill as he stripped off the suit and put his shoes back on.

"So?" challenged White.

"So, there's a pretty good chance that his footprint is on file somewhere. The DNA test should give us his country of origin, the footprint just might nail down his identity," answered Kahill, unwilling to back down.

"Shit, Todd, I didn't even think about that. All right, get packed up and get outside. Where's your pack?"

White watched as the blood drained from Kahill's face. "Fuck, I left it inside. I'll just nip back in and grab it."

"We don't have time for you to suit up and go back in there. We are out of time."

"David, you know if they find that pack they'll know exactly who was down here. Look, I can just run in and out without the suit, I promise I'll hold my breath the whole time."

"No fuckin' way. That's just nine kinds of stupid, now get out in the hall. We are leaving."

Kahill ran over to the door and triggered the opening sequence, saying to White, "I'm willing to take that chance, get to the stairwell and wait for me. Two minutes, sir." Before he could protest, White watched helplessly as Kahill closed and sealed the outer door.

Running to the corridor, White told the two Brits to get into the stairwell and wait there for him and Kahill. "If we aren't back in three minutes, get upstairs and outside to cover our exit."

Stiles and Linden went back into the stairwell. Linden ran up to the top of the stairs while Stiles waited on the landing below.

White fretted as he watched the inner door open, and Kahill run into the isolation chamber to grab his pack. Seconds later a loud staccato horn began wailing as the panel on the door began to flash red.

Triggering his radio White nearly shouted, "Kahill, what the fuck is that? Did you trip the alarm?"

Checking the matching flashing panel on the inside of the lab Kahill answered, "Sorry, chief, it looks like I triggered the temperature sensor, my body heat is too high. The door is locked down and it's not going to open until the entire system is reset. Get out of here, David, I'm sure someone is coming down here to investigate. Get out."

"Stand back, I'm going to shoot out the glass," warned White.

"STOP!" shouted Kahill. " It's too thick, the ricochets will kill you."

Just then they both heard Linden broadcast, "Jig's up boys, someone's just come into the building and they're headed for the elevator, I think it's about four persons. What do you want me to do? I can hose them before they get in the elevator and the door closes."

"Stand down, we'll be on our way up the stairs in a moment. When the elevator doors close go and check the alley," ordered White. "Stiles, can you hear the elevator coming?"

"Yes, sir, it's not very fast. I think you have just over a minute."

Kahill broke in and said, "All of you get out. I know what to do, I'm not going to let them get anything out of me. Go, get that stuff back home."

White gave a single look back at his partner and then ran to the stairwell. He couldn't watch his friend take his own life. As White ran out the door Kahill reached into his breast pocket and dug out the small injector included as the last resort. Just then a thick mist shot out of jets in the ceiling, chilling Kahill to the bone. He felt his breathing become labored and his chest constrict as the billowing fog engulfed him just before he passed out.

The percent that you're paying is too high priced,
While you're living beyond all your means,
And the man in the suit has got a new car,
With the profit he's made off your dreams.

The Low Spark of High Heeled Boys
Written by Jim Capaldi and Steve Winwood, performed by Traffic

CHAPTER 23

THOUGH NOT TRAVELING nearly as much as she had just a few weeks ago, Norma was still in demand as a speaker and interviewee. She participated in video conferences with others on the presidential commission studying the problem of interplanetary debris striking the earth. Unfortunately she had little time for her friends lately and had heard from Alan only twice since he had disappeared underground in the Southwest.

She felt detached from what she considered her real life, the life she had before her discovery. Norma wanted more than anything to take a week off just for herself, but she couldn't. Too many responsibilities weighed her down, things that demanded her time, if not her attention.

What she did like about her newfound fame was the wealth of information that was hers for the taking. Daily updates and pictures from JPL, low-level briefings e-mailed to her by the White House, and the scores of messages from her new friends at NASA made her feel tapped into an awareness of events and information not available to the public; she felt in the loop.

She checked her e-mail and saw she had accumulated over fifty messages overnight. Norma opened the first message from JPL, giving her an update on her asteroid. She sat up straighter as she absorbed the information on the screen. It showed that her asteroid had altered course on its way inward toward the sun.

The preliminary calculations on its new course showed that the new track didn't bring it any closer to colliding with the earth, but the change clearly puzzled the scientists. Had the rock changed course by colliding with another piece of space debris, bumping it into a new trajectory? Or had a pocket of gas forced its way out of the interior of the rock and pushed it on to a new course like the maneuvering jets used to change course on the shuttle?

Not sure whether all the people on the commission were on the JPL distribution list, Norma forwarded the message to the entire group. She logged on to the JPL in-house network and called up the raw numbers on the change in course. She speculated that if the aspect change was the result of a collision with another object, the object that it had hit was either very large or relatively small but traveling at a hell of a clip, many multiples of the speed of her piece of the sky. However, a closer look at the figures showed her that the aspect change was not instantaneous; it had occurred over several hours, which made the case for out-gassing the better hypothesis.

Norma deleted the obvious spam and began a leisurely look through the rest of her e-mail. Of the new spate of messages she received daily, the ones she especially enjoyed were messages from students around the world, nearly all of which she gave special attention to in her replies. Some wanted her to send pictures of the asteroid. Norma had collected and dressed up a good selection of the hundreds she'd already accumulated. A few even wanted her to send the original animation she had created from the first images.

Just as she was queuing up a load of replies, her computer gave a soft beep and a window popped up letting her know she had an incoming video call. Norma accepted the incoming connection.

Diane Churchill was at the other end of the call.

"Good morning, Madam Secretary, to what do I owe this call?" Norma asked.

Churchill answered, "Ms. Lancaster, I just received your forwarded message. What I need to know is who else you forwarded it to?"

"Uh, did I do something wrong? I only sent it off to the distribution list of other committee members," Norma said as she got a sick feeling in the pit of her stomach.

"Not exactly. I'm just calling to caution you that some of the information you are now privy to is not exactly for public consumption. As much as you may want to disclose to your friends or colleagues information shared with you on the commission, it is in everybody's best interest that you keep commission business confidential," finished Churchill.

"I will be more careful in the future, I didn't really think about the whole security part of the commission."

Laughing easily, Churchill said, "Don't worry yourself too much, the people who really do the worrying for us in governmental service are so paranoid. You should see how they behave here in Washington.

"Not only are they overly paranoid, they're also schizophrenic. They talk about how they value secrecy so much, but with the exception of the Secret Service, leaking secrets to the press or disclosing confidential information to their colleagues who are not in the loop are major pastimes around here.

"Ms. Lancaster, just be careful in the future and we'll say no more about it. Besides, I wanted to discuss this latest message you forwarded. What do you think about your asteroid changing course the way it has?" Churchill asked.

"Well, there's only two ways I know that could cause such a large object to change direction like this. The first is a collision with another object about the same mass of the asteroid or a smaller one moving at much greater speed, or a freak outgassing of a portion of the asteroid's own mass, a pocket of gas shooting out like a rocket engine, pushing it off its original course."

"That's my assessment too, Ms. Lancaster. Could you do me a favor?" asked Churchill.

"Anything at all, just ask," Norma answered.

"Could you be my lead investigator in determining the probable cause of the course change? If it was another piece of rock that hit, could you find out if we have any means of spotting it? And, if it was not from a collision . . ."

"But it wasn't, Ms. Churchill."

"What do you mean, it wasn't? What wasn't?"

"The course change occurred over a period of several hours; it was gradual, not the result of a collision," said Norma.

"Are you sure?"

"Absolutely, I looked at the raw data from JPL and it shows that the change happened gradually."

"Can you forward the data to me with a short summary of what you believe it shows?" asked Churchill. "And only me?" she added with a smile.

"Yes ma'am, I'll have it off to you within the hour," Norma promised.

"Norma, the president and I thank you very much for everything you've done, and I want to thank you personally for your help in this matter."

"Don't mention it," Norma said, waving her hand with a dismissive gesture.

"I'll be in touch soon," Diane said, as she broke the connection.

Norma cut and pasted the JPL data into a message to Diane, highlighting the numbers showing the course change occurring over time. She also added a short narrative stating her interpretation of facts surrounding the data.

In Washington, Diane was in the middle of handling two different issues, the asteroid and a query from someone in the Pentagon concerning possible experiments in antigravity. She had to get a handle on both before a two o'clock briefing with the president.

Less than fifteen minutes after her call to Norma, Diane received the data she had requested Norma forward to her. *Quick work,* she thought favorably, and was further pleased when she saw that there was little she would have to add before she presented it to the president and his chief of staff.

The other issue was puzzling. She knew that a number of universities and colleges around the country were engaged in the study of gravity, but the bulk of their research was on the nature of how it fit into the theory of general relativity. But she knew of no one at the point of negating gravity's effects, let alone controlling it. She was going to have to get to the bottom of the inquiry. If it was bullshit she didn't need the continued hassle, she had enough on her plate today. As it was, rearranging her schedule because of the president had ruined her own day.

At the White House things were in an uproar. The cause of the current flap was the news that the covert op team in Iraq had lost a man. The loss was reported almost immediately through a relay from MI-6; there would be no details until the team itself had transmitted their preliminary report once they had made it over the border into Iran.

The president's special meeting with his national security team was tense. The first item on the agenda was the briefing from the director of the CIA, bringing the team up to date on the mission and the facts surrounding the missing man. Masters began by asking, "I thought this was going to be a quick in and out, what the hell happened?"

"According to the preliminary report, the man down is one of ours, the number two American member, the Brits and the team leader got out and away from the lab without mishap," the director stated.

"What happened to our man?" asked the President.

"It appears that he was caught inside some kind of isolation or containment room, and to ensure the rest of the team made it out with the information we were after, he forced them to leave him behind. The team leader reported that the trapped man was not going to be taken alive, but was not able to visually confirm his disposition."

"Well, is he dead, or isn't he?" asked Masters.

"The team leader's assumption is that he is dead by his own hand. However, there was a single bag of equipment left behind that the team was not able to recover. Nothing in there is marked. The arms they all carry are from different countries and the downed man's clothes were manufactured locally over there. I'd have to say given that a dead man can't be questioned, our exposure is low," stated the director.

"Can any of the items in the bag be traced back to us?" asked the president.

"Not directly, sir. Of course the team's very presence in the area is probably going to be immediately blamed on us, or maybe the Israelis, but my advice is that we take a hard line and deny everything."

"What about the items they managed to get out of the lab?" asked the Chairman of the Joint Chiefs. "I'm more interested in who's got the military capacity to develop the sample alloy brought back and where they're getting their technology from."

The director of the NSA asked the director of the CIA, "Do you know if any of the other technology was picked up as well? Specifically, were they able to get samples of the electronics?"

"I'm not exactly sure, there is mention of computer data. I can't tell if it's in the form of removable media or documentation. Their report was understandably short."

"How long before we get them out of the area?" asked Masters.

"Barring any other complications, they should be able to be picked up and on board our carrier in the Arabian Sea by tomorrow morning," answered the director.

"Gentlemen, I want a contingency plan and prepared statements should the Iraqis decide to go public and accuse us of operating in their country. And for God's sake make damn sure the Israelis are completely frozen out from any of the details of this mission. No one, I mean no one is to know about our involvement from anyone in this room. Additionally, if you can't trust the people under you to keep their mouths shut then all of you had better reevaluate your departments and staff. I'm sick and tired of reading about what goes on here in the press," finished Bender.

Masters looked around the room to take in the expressions of the others. Then the director of the CIA dropped his second bomb. "By the way," he began, "we were able to recover the foot of the pilot of the craft."

The room exploded in babble as everyone began to talk at once.

"How in the hell did they do that? More importantly, is it going to be of any use by the time it gets here?" the president broke in above the voices of the others. When everyone quieted down the director answered, "The man who was left behind managed to wrap it in an insulated bag. Their message reads, 'foot appears to be of a black individual, sex undetermined. Little or no tissue damage, appears to have been protected by boot.' That's all I have for the moment. "

The director of the FBI spoke up. "If we do indeed have the foot of the craft's pilot, then DNA testing can narrow down his country of origin, we can even do some tissue testing to determine some things about diet, the air he or she breathed and, although it's a long shot, we could maybe get a match of the footprint to a birth record if the pilot's from one of the industrialized nations."

"Good thought," said Masters. "Make damn sure no word of this gets out. I'm not so worried about the Iraqis, but if the owner of the craft retains some attachment to their pilot, and I have no reason to believe they wouldn't, let's not start off on the wrong foot, pardon the pun, with them. The last thing I want is to start any kind of discussion or conflict with anyone capable of forging the skin of that craft, having to apologize for grave robbing, so to speak."

President Bender stood up and asked, "Is there anything else we need to cover before we conclude, gentlemen?"

Seeing nothing but shaking heads, Bender concluded with, "Thank you very much for coming, we'll reconvene at tomorrow's regular meeting. Could you stay behind for a few minutes?" he asked the director of the CIA.

Once the room was cleared, President Bender picked up everyone by eye and led them back to the Oval Office. He turned on the director and said, "How the hell could they let this happen? You had me convinced this was going to go as smooth as silk. The last thing I need is for this thing to become my Bay of Pigs, you get me?"

"Yes, sir."

"And as far as I'm concerned, if this gets out and threatens to drag this administration down, you know what's going to happen don't you?" President Bender threatened.

"I do, sir. However, with a dead body, and nothing to identify his country of origin in his clothes or the other equipment he carried, I firmly believe our exposure is minimal," the director assured the president and the chief.

"Get hold of MI-6 and see what else their people can find out about the man we left behind. I want to know what to expect before it spirals out of control," the president ordered.

The two nodded.

"When you get any further information from the team, I want a call, day or night!"

The director nodded and turned to leave the office. When the door had closed behind him the Bender looked at Masters and said, "What do you think, Simon? Is this thing going to blow up in our faces?"

Seeing the real worry in his friend's face, Masters said, "I see two real dangers to you in this one; both could drive you right out of here if we're not careful.

"The most immediate problem comes if the Iraqis toss this guy's body into the face of the world press. You and I both know that it's not going to take a rocket scientist to determine where this guy's from, his dental work alone will probably give him away. But this isn't what I see as the greater danger. If the owners of this craft decide that our interference is a danger to their own existence, do we have the wherewithal to stand our ground and go toe-to-toe with them? That's the real question."

President Bender looked at Masters and said, "I wonder how many of those in the meeting even thought about that possibility? Honestly, I didn't really consider it seriously."

"I know, that's what I've been trying to quietly impress on everyone, but all they're interested in is getting the technology. Their only real concern is what economic or strategic advantage this new technology represents, *not* that it, so far, belongs to someone else who might not want to share it with us.

"What if our actions result in the owners of this aircraft aligning with someone against us, the Iraqis for example? Do you want to get into a pissing contest with someone who can build bulletproof fighters? Who knows the extent of the technology we may face? This is what I've been trying to insulate you from.

"Your administration has been hawkish on the buildup of the military, on spending more on the intelligence services even though we have a policy of not hiring the best and the brightest because they don't automatically fall in line and keep their mouths shut. We have systematically eroded our lead in science, technology and the rest of the associated industries because we devalue brains in favor of compliance, and all this country panders to is building wealth for our privileged friends. Look how we're obligated to maintain access to those who paid our way here.

"Now I'll never utter those words outside of this office, and never in front of anyone who matters, but that's the last fifty years in a nutshell. So before we act without regard for anyone other than our country club buddies and friends in business, you better wake up to the fact that the builders of this aircraft have left us in the dust. That includes our friends in the military-industrial arena, so now's the time to consider thinking with something other than your dick, because in the global contest we are now number two; an ignorant number two. We don't even know where these people are. That alone should scare the shit out of you," finished Masters.

"Look, Simon, I know I'm not the sharpest tack in the box. Hell, my own father told me that anyone who wanted this job had already demonstrated their unsuitability to hold it. The last thing I want is for this country to come in second in any race. I still believe this is the greatest nation in the history of man and I will not be the man who's responsible for suffering any setback that adversely affects its people."

"Nice words, Mr. President, still working on your reelection campaign?" Masters shot back.

"God damn it, Simon, even if you don't respect the way I'm handling this issue you have to respect the office," said the president.

"No, Jim, I don't. And that's where you keep getting in trouble with the public. Respect is earned. You're going to have to continue proving yourself worthy of the job every stinking day, and most every single day, when you wake up in the morning, you're going to have to start from scratch all over again. It's a shitty job, Mr. President, but right now it's *your* shitty job."

"So how do you think this should be played?" Bender asked.

"I think we're starting off just fine. Be prepared to deal with the dead agent, but we have to keep to whatever story we start off with. Changing stories in midstream is what gets everyone in trouble. Besides, we can mount a better disinformation campaign than any amount of truth they might throw in front of the press."

"And the builders of the aircraft?"

"That's more difficult to predict. We'll probably need several contingency plans in place depending on what we find. I'm not confident at all that we would win any contest if it came to a showdown with these folks." Masters got up and got himself a drink of water. "Can I get you something, Jim?"

"No, I'm good. Who else do you think we should bring in on this one, Simon?" asked Bender.

"I think we better get all of our best researchers working on the composition of that alloy. Being able to fabricate it in-house would allow us to decisively move ahead of everyone else in military technology if we started to cover our jets, ships and subs with the stuff. Not to mention the civilian applications, artificial joints, heart valves, construction, transportation . . . everything we have will get some sort of benefit from alloys that don't wear out."

President Bender sat back, considering the broader implications. Masters sat down across from him and said, "This is so much bigger than just one man, even if he is the president of the United States. What we have here is unprecedented, let's not blow it, that's all I'm suggesting, Jim."

"You just keep looking out for me and I'm sure everything's going to work out," said the president.

"From your mouth to God's ear, Mr. President."

"I also think we should begin to activate phase one of the shadow government contingencies. Where's the vice president today?" Bender asked.

"He's in California until tomorrow morning. Then he's scheduled to make a stopover in Florida, returning the day after."

"I want Vice President Lane to be briefed on all of the events to date and for him to stay out of DC as much as possible. Be sure that he is no more than an hour or so from one of the Deep Shelter locations from now on. If something happens to me or the White House, or if Washington comes under attack, I want him safe." Bender sat back and rubbed his eyes in fatigue. "Advanced military technologies that have not been evaluated are not to be taken for granted. If this aircraft has stealth capabilities, we have to update our defense plans to take that into consideration."

Looking at Simon, President Bender said, "Make a note for me to prompt the Joint Chiefs to begin thinking about how they could defend against our own F-117 stealth fighters. That should be a good start, maybe light a fire under some of them."

"Very well, Mr. President, it will be on tomorrow's agenda."

The two finished up, chatting about the minor details of the day's schedule, now rearranged after the morning's emergency security meeting. Masters agreed to meet back in the Oval Office a half hour before the general meeting.

At the Pentagon orders were cut, directives followed, policies executed; pretty much business as usual, except for the unease Commander Ames, Martin Harris' liaison officer, had been feeling since his late-night call from the good Dr. Harris.

All weekend he had expected a call from Harris sheepishly informing him that he and the Richards kid had made an error in their calculations or in the software accounting for the startling revelation dropped in his lap.

Antigravity was so out there he could scarcely give it serious consideration. Commander Ames saw that the time was approaching midday in Washington, two hours earlier at the shelter. Ames picked up the phone and dialed, then hit the scramble button. He called directly into Dr. Harris' lab, assuming he and Alan would be there working out whatever bug had flipped the equations and given a result that was too unbelievable to consider.

The phone on the other end was answered almost immediately. Ames heard the beginning of a hello before the two ends of the connection broke up with the tones of the scrambling circuitry synchronizing the connection. Seconds later he heard a tentative "Hello" from the other end.

"Hello, Dr. Harris?" he asked.

"No, it's Alan, hang on while I get him from next door. Who should I say is calling?" Alan asked.

"Would you let him know it's Commander Ames." Ames then heard the phone drop to the desk as Alan ran off to get Harris.

Moments later the phone was picked up and Martin said, "Jim? That you?"

"Yes, it is. How's the debug going?" Ames asked.

Martin laughed and said, "So far it's a good news, bad news situation right now, Jim. The good news is that the detector is working hundreds of times better for the improvements in the software Alan has managed to wring out down here. The bad news is that he seems to have covered every base in his software improvements; he even cut out about fifteen percent of the real-time calculations that the software was performing at the beginning. In other words, there's no error in the calculations that we've been able to uncover. Believe me, we looked."

"Son of a bitch. That's the last thing I needed to hear, Martin. All right, can you put everything together for me and fly up this afternoon?" Ames asked.

"Does this have anything to do with the electronic hash at the beginning of the call? Alan told me about it and I figured you kicked in the scrambler."

"Just being cautious. Look, I'm going to make the call right after we hang up, I need everything you've got, including the current rev of the software. What the hell, bring Richards too."

"When should we expect to be picked up?" Martin wanted to know.

"I'll have someone call you within the hour. Better pack for a day or two. Are you going to be bringing a laptop or any removable media?" queried Ames.

"Alan will probably bring his laptop and I'll burn everything else on to a CD. Don't worry, I'll encrypt it."

"Good, don't let either out of your hands on the way in. See you this afternoon."

"Right, Jim," Martin said, and then heard two beeps and the line went dead.

Martin turned to Alan, who hadn't moved during the entire call. "You look kind of spooked there kid. You feeling all right?"

"I guess so. This whole experience has taken on a level of reality that I'm completely unprepared to deal with, I think. The only thing that I've ever had come close to like this was when one of my girlfriends said to me, 'I'm late.' That's about where I'm at right now."

"Pull yourself together young man, go get cleaned up and pack for a couple of days. We've been summoned to our nation's capital."

"Why do they want me to come? I haven't done anything, it's your project, they don't need me for anything," Alan said, starting to work himself up.

"Whoa, boy. Calm down, you're not in any trouble. What would make you think that?" Martin asked his troubled friend.

"First of all you had me sign that secrecy thing, then we had to go through every line of code over the weekend, then the scrambler, and now we have to go to DC. It's almost like I was on double secret probation or something," Alan said, worried about events that threatened to sweep him up and carry him along despite anything he would want.

"Let me put your mind at ease. The reason we're going to Washington is that, just like two heads were infinitely better than my one down here, three or four heads in DC are going to be better than two. Your insight, and your knowledge of the entire detector system, will be invaluable to those we're going to meet. So would you calm down and get yourself together for the trip?" Martin asked quietly.

"Yeah, sure. What should I bring?" Alan asked, quietly getting himself back under control as he bent his mind to the task at hand.

"I'll be bringing the data and all of the equations for review. Why don't you replicate the software, at least the analysis portions, on your laptop and bring it along?"

With that said, Alan dashed out of the lab, barely allowing the door to open to let him out, leaving Martin smiling at Alan's paranoia, misplaced guilt and youthful enthusiasm all rolled into one big ball of neuroses.

On his way to his room to pack, Martin grinned to himself when he realized he had a treat in store when Alan saw the way the Pentagon transported those they wanted to see "soonest."

Soon the two made their way to the elevator to the surface which stood waiting for them, one of the soldiers from topside waiting outside the lift door.

The security guard got them underway immediately. The soldier used a key from his belt to open a locked panel in the elevator and he pressed and held down a blinking red button. Moments later the car doubled its speed topside.

"Sorry about that, Doc, I just got a call from the Pentagon that said 'soonest' for you two to get underway. Would both of you remain seated until the doors open? The braking up top sometimes gets a little bumpy."

Alan cast a worried glance to Martin, as if to say I told you so, and then tried to relax.

Martin grinned back and then turned to the soldier and asked, "How often do you get to use second gear in the elevator?"

"As far as I know, doc, we've never used it. Hell, I didn't even know there was a second gear until twenty minutes ago. What's up? If you can tell me, that is," he asked.

Martin paused to consider and then said, "There's not much I can tell you. We're supposed to go and explain some data to someone out there. I think the big rush might be so we make our connection east."

"That's your story, and you're sticking to it, eh?" the soldier said with raised eyebrow.

"Hey now, Sergeant, cut it out. You're scaring the kid," Martin said with a laugh.

"Aw, bullshit," said Alan. "It's probably a military panty raid and they're calling me in as a technical advisor."

At the top, the door opened to two soldiers standing outside, obviously waiting for their arrival. They stepped inside and grabbed Alan's and Martin's bags and immediately headed off to the helipad.

Alan looked on in wonder until the sergeant tapped him on the shoulder and said "Move out, son," in his ear.

They followed their luggage out to the waiting helicopter. Martin was not surprised at all to see the same Blackhawk from his last trip out.

"Holy shit!" Alan exclaimed. He asked Martin, "Is this how you get around on this project?"

"Alan, I cannot tell a lie. I always travel like this when summoned to Washington."

But before Martin could add that this was only his second trip out, Alan was off to check out the Blackhawk up close and personal.

When they finally touched down at the Pentagon, Ames led Martin and Alan to a conference room with six other naval personnel already seated, each with their own laptop, and a small network hub in the middle of the table connecting all of their computers.

"Sit down, gentlemen. I've gathered a few of our eggheads together to help go over your calculations and code before we scramble the subs and launch the fighters. Please don't be offended, Dr. Harris, we're not here to pass judgment, or anything like that. We just want to make sure that everything is as it seems.

"Everyone, this is Dr. Martin Harris, he's in charge of a gravity-related project out in the Southwest. And this is his programming assistant, Alan Richards, from the University of Chicago.

"Between the two of them, Dr. Harris and Mr. Richards have written the software you'll be taking apart to make sure the subroutines match the doctor's original equations. The reason he's been brought here is that we need to debug, if that's what it turns out to be, the code as soon as possible so the doctor and Alan can get back to work. Any questions? No? Great.

"Dr. Harris, you're responsible for parceling out the duties here, you are the team leader. Everyone's here to help you and Alan get whatever you need done. Alan, is there anything you need?" Ames asked.

"I don't think so. Oh yeah, is there a projector I can plug into my laptop so I can display stuff to everyone?"

"Sure. This is Chief Petty Officer Peoples, she'll make sure that you have whatever you need. Also, the network on this table is not connected to the outside at all, if you need anything from the Internet or back at the lab you'll have to use this workstation in the corner here.

"Martin, if you need me, here's my extension. If I'm away from my desk someone will page me. I'll be onsite, but I'm going to stay out of your hair. Good luck, everyone," Commander Ames concluded.

While Alan hooked up his laptop to the projector and configured it for the network in the room, Martin got the names of their six helpers. When Alan was connected to the other laptops he sent copies of code to each of the other laptops and displayed the flowchart of the analysis program so everyone could get an overview of the underlying structure of the code.

They all bent to the task of dissecting Martin and Alan's code.

The group worked through the night, drinking uncounted cups of coffee, working through every line of code, every equation and every shortcut Alan had made. By midmorning they had all come to the same conclusion. Alan's modifications were ingenious and they were all correct. There was no deviation from Martin's original equations in the code, and according to the literature and reference materials accessible on the Internet, the whole system performed just as Martin had originally hypothesized.

When Commander Ames was summoned back to the conference room and told the news, he thanked the naval team and released them, giving them the rest of the day off. He then showed Martin and Alan to a private room around the corner and told them they could freshen up there and rest a bit until he called for them.

Alan was pleased to see his bag sitting on the bureau. He got up, grabbed his shaving kit and headed to the adjoining private bath to shower and shave.

Martin laid down on the other cot and stared at the ceiling, thinking about the implications of their evening's effort. If his equations were correct, if the software was true to the equations, and if the detector worked as specified, then the inescapable conclusion was that the detector recorded an incident resulting in a lessened gravitational effect on, or near, earth. This information, if true, would stand the entire scientific community on its ear, or head, or whatever, Martin was too tired to care at the moment.

Judging by Commander Ames' interest in the phenomenon, the military implications had not gone unnoticed either. Moments later the telephone rang once. Martin found Ames on the other end.

"Marty, can you, preferably you and Alan, attend a meeting with some of the Joint Chiefs' upper-level staff? I know you've been up all night, but this is pretty important," Ames requested.

"I'm willing, let me check with Alan when he gets out of the shower. How soon do you need us?" Martin asked, as he opened his bag and dug out a clean shirt and a tie.

"Can you make it in half an hour?"

"No problem, I'll be ready."

A half-hour later Martin and Alan were deposited in a different conference room. They were not disappointed when they saw the brass arrayed around the table, and even more startling was the fact that the Navy *and* the Air Force were represented.

Ames immediately opened the meeting by introducing the two to the rest of the attendees. He then launched into a brief overview of the nature of the Martin's project. He quickly related the incident Martin's equipment had recorded and the subsequent upgrades underway. He then handed the meeting over to Martin to explain the implications of what the detector had recorded.

With Alan pulling up the equations, charts and data on the large screen at the end of the room, Martin was able to give a comprehensive overview of the underlying science used in the project, and when he got to the specifics of the incident in question, several of the brass sat up straight in their chairs and leaned forward in rapt attention.

When Martin paused one of the highest ranking Air Force officers asked the inevitable question, "Are you absolutely sure of your conclusions here, doctor?"

"Yes, sir," Martin replied, "However, the conclusion is only half of the puzzle we have before us. Alan, would you bring up the positional plot slide please."

When the image came up on the screen you could have heard a pin drop, even on the thickly padded carpet of the conference room.

"As you can see, the incident occurred in fairly close proximity to the surface of the earth, and according to Mr. Richards' calculations on location, date and time, we've estimating that the locus of the incident was somewhere in the neighborhood of the Middle East on the date shown. Are there any questions?"

No one said a word. The silence grew uncomfortably long. Finally, Commander Ames stood up and said, "Thank you Doctor, Mr. Richards. Thank you both very much for your presentation. Could the two of you return to your room? My aide will escort you."

Puzzled at the sudden level of frost in the room, Martin and Alan were happy to put some distance between them and the meeting that continued after they left.

When they were settled back in their room Alan declared, "Jesus Christ, Doc, did we step on someone's duck back there?"

"I don't think so. I think we just witnessed some of the most powerful men in the world scared shitless by what we presented. Which, by the way, scares the living crap out of me. If they're that scared, then I'm inclined to just climb back down into my hole and go back to the hard sciences. The last place I want to be is here."

In the conference room Commander Ames was fielding questions about the veracity of the project, and both Martin and Alan. He also described the security of the project's underground location in terms of public exposure to the technology Martin's project represented. He assured them that the Pentagon was completely in control of any and all information about the project.

Ames then tackled the bull by the horns and said, "We all know what this data suggests. Someone out there is experimenting with, and may have found a way to control, gravity.

"This, gentlemen is what we're looking at. So instead of chasing our tails here, my suggestion, with all your permissions, is that we adjourn to think this over and schedule a meeting with the Joint Chiefs at 05:00. That way they can decide whether or not to take this to the White House. Does everyone agree?"

Seeing the heads around the table nod, Ames added, "Then why don't we all go make whatever calls necessary to make it happen. I'll take care of Dr. Harris and Mr. Richards. Does anyone think they will be needed for the morning's meeting? My opinion right now is the less they know the better. No? I'll set up the meeting with the Joint Chiefs and then I'm going to send our two guests home under guard."

You could climb the mountain, you can swim the sea,
You could jump into the fire, but you'll never be free.

Jump Into The Fire
Written and performed by Harry Nilsson III

CHAPTER 24

TUESDAY MORNING
DAWNED clear and sunny in
Washington, DC. Scarcely a single resident of the nation's capital knew the entire government was going to be turned upside down that day.

The first salvo was fired in the Joint Chiefs emergency meeting at 5 A.M.

Commander Ames simply stated, "Gentlemen, we are facing a crisis that surpasses any other this country has faced since the Second World War. By now all of you have been briefed by those who heard Dr. Harris and his assistant take them through the facts surrounding the discovery of someone or something employing the manipulation of gravity.

"According to everything we've investigated, the incident occurred in the Middle East a couple of weeks ago. Beyond that we have little to go on. Even if there was some kind of math error everyone overlooked, the only change in the information I've given you in the summary you received this morning would be that who ever it is who's reached this measure of control of the fundamentals of gravity has been able to decrease the force of gravity locally. Either way the significance, and threat, is undiminished.

"Being able to increase gravity locally is just as potentially a powerful strategic weapon as being able to decrease it. If gravity could be increased to the quantum levels, to the point of that of a black hole, the game's over, gentlemen."

"What would they be doing in the Middle East for Christ's sake?" asked the Army chief of staff.

"That's the question, why *would* they be operating there? The only thing I can think of is that it's one of the few places where we have practically no one on the ground working for us," Ames answered. "Who are they, and what is their agenda? Until we answer those questions everything else is moot.

"My recommendation is that this be brought to the White House as soon as possible. This level of technology affects the balance of power for the entire globe. Nuclear weapons are toys compared to the focused manipulation of gravity."

"Where are the two researchers who brought this to your attention, commander?" asked the commandant of the Marines.

"Don't worry, I've stashed them a mile underground in their lab out in Utah. They won't be spilling what they know to anyone. Steps have already been taken," Ames answered.

The secretary of the Navy then asked, "Jim, can their detector be used to reliably locate the source of this research or the base from which these people are operating?"

"I'm way ahead of you, sir. I'm dispatching a technical support crew to man the detector twenty-four/seven. Unfortunately for Dr. Harris, his project has been moved from theoretical to strategic operations. I'm going to travel out there this afternoon to supervise the changeover. I'm only waiting until you've briefed the president just in case any of you think I'll be needed here in town."

The secretary of the Navy said, "That's a great idea. I would like to recommend that the commander present this information at the security briefing, he's obviously got the full picture."

The chairman adjourned the meeting and sent Ames off to get whatever he would need to bring along. Upon reaching his office, the chairman called Simon Masters and brought him up to date on the fact that he had something of immediate concern to national security.

Simon thought, *what now*, but promised he would prepare the president for a longer than normal session. He became instantly concerned when the chairman suggested that everyone sit in on this one.

Masters assured him that he would make all the calls, hung up the phone and told his secretary to gather all the senior members of the national security staff and to get President Bender on the phone in the residence.

When Bender answered, Masters said, "Mr. President, we may have a situation here."

"Something from the op?" he asked.

"No sir, this is coming from the CJCS, he's on his way in for the regular national security briefing, but he requested everyone, sir."

"Look, I'll trade jobs with you for the day. I'll even throw in five bucks," Bender offered.

"No deal. I'm going to prepare everyone to clear the rest of your day just in case it's something bad."

"Thanks, I'll be right down," the President said, and then hung up.

Half an hour later, when all the heads of the various military, security and law enforcement services were assembled, President Bender said, "Mr. Chairman, it's your meeting."

"Thank you, Mr. President. What seems to have been uncovered yesterday is a situation that, if true and accurate, completely changes the balance of power in the world forever. I have here with me Commander Ames from the naval weapons research division, I'm going to turn the meeting over to him and let you be the judge." The chairman sat and gestured to Ames to begin.

"Thank you Mr. Chairman. Mr. President, everyone. Please dim the lights . . ."

Ames gave his presentation to a silent audience. When he finished everyone waited for President Bender to start the ball rolling.

"Commander, do you have any idea who is in control of this technology?" the president asked.

"No sir, we only have a possible location. If you will look at this next slide you'll see that the incident occurred very close to the surface of the earth. Due to a lack of resolution in the detector, we can only pin the probable location to within a bubble of about a hundred miles. But the locus is somewhere in the Middle East."

Surprised at the response the revelation evoked, Ames was asked by the director of the CIA, "Just when did this incident occur, Commander?"

Ames gave the date and time from the detector's raw printout, and was shocked when the CIA shouted "Son of a bitch!" bringing everything to a halt.

Looking at him in surprise, President Bender said, "You want to share your thoughts with the rest of the group?"

"Sir, may I suggest we clear the room of everyone below cabinet level."

At the president's nod everyone who wasn't a director or cabinet-level appointee got up and left, and two Secret Service agents came and stood beside each door into the room.

"All right, spill. What's on your mind?" President Bender prompted.

"Sir, this incident occurred at precisely the same time the Iraqi missile battery shot down the unknown craft," the director said, letting the statement just hang there.

"Commander Ames, you are now on a very exclusive list. I need not remind you that everything you hear now is classified top secret," said Masters.

"Yes, sir."

"What conclusion may we draw from these events?" asked the president.

"If the commander's information is correct, and there's nothing to suggest anything to the contrary, the coincidence is too great. I now believe that the Iraqis shot down some completely new kind of aircraft. One propelled by manipulating gravity," he answered. "If this proves out, the most important task at hand is to obtain as much intel on the craft as possible. I would like to request that our boys be brought directly to Washington for debriefing as soon as feasible."

Nodding to Secret Service Agent Sam Bishop, assigned as his personal protector, the president said, "Would you get my science advisor in here right now? I want every angle covered on this."

The agent whispered into his hand mic, knowing that wherever Diane Churchill was, nothing would impede her getting to the meeting as quickly as possible.

"Mr. Chairman," President Bender directed to the chairman JCS. "Since you thought enough of the data to bring this here directly, what is your take on our defensive capabilities against someone with the power to control gravity? What level of threat does someone like that present to the country?"

"Mr. President, if we are threatened by someone who can increase or decrease the effects of gravity at will, we are essentially helpless against attack."

"What about being able to launch an attack, say against the control center of this technology?" asked President Bender.

"Mr. President, if they can control gravity nothing can be sent against them that would have a prayer of hurting them. Missiles could be deflected into space, or dropped short of their intended target. Men on foot could be made too heavy to walk or breathe, or be reduced in weight so much they fly off into space.

"The commander is correct in his assessment. This technology renders all other weaponry obsolete. We couldn't even hit the thing with a laser if we wanted to. Any launch or aiming platform could be disturbed sufficiently to prevent it from aiming properly, whether it's in space or on earth," the CJCS said quietly. Just as he finished speaking, both doors opened and a squad of Secret Service agents came into the room as Agent Bishop appeared by his side.

"Mr. President, we will be moving you downstairs now. Would you please come with me? The rest of these people can follow as soon as you are clear, sir."

"Are you out of your mind, on whose authority are you moving me out of here? Stand down, Sam. I'm not going anywhere, unless you're prepared to carry me."

At that statement four agents stepped forward as the rest of the agents gestured everyone else to the side of the conference room clearing the way to the door.

"Don't make me give that order, Mr. President. Please come along quietly and we can straighten everything out once we get you downstairs, sir," Bishop said, praying he wouldn't have to give the order to have the President of the United States of America trussed up and carried away like so much baggage.

Simon quietly spoke up, "Go on, Jim. He's just following orders. We'll wait here for the all clear and be downstairs shortly."

Seeing the determination in the young, black agent's face, President Bender got to his feet, straightened his jacket and made his way out of the room surrounded by a phalanx of agents.

Everyone else in the room let out a collective sigh of relief, but stayed where they were until the two remaining agents gave them the all clear.

Gathering up their pads and papers to move the meeting down to the situation room, everyone was startled to see Marine One landing on the lawn outside. Normally it wasn't that strange to see the chopper come and go; what *was* unusual were the four fully loaded Apache Longbow combat helicopters hovering above the lawn.

Moments later the president's wife and daughter, along with their dog, were herded into Marine One, and once it was airborne, the five aircraft vanished rapidly out of sight.

Down in the underground command center, the president waited until he was alone with his personal agent before he turned on him and demanded, "God damn it, Sam, what the hell is all this about? Has a direct threat been made against Washington? Is there something going on I need to know about?"

"I'm sorry, sir. When I relayed the information about the CJCS's assessment of the level of threat being discussed I got the scramble code and everyone dropped whatever they were doing to get you down here and your family under cover."

"What! My family's gone? Get me the fucking head of the Treasury right now, I want to get to the bottom of this. What else has been put into action without my knowing?"

"Sir, Vice President Lane is being moved to one of the alternate command centers, along with about a fourth of the cabinet. The CJCS just deployed an additional E3 into the Middle East and the military has been brought to DefCon 3." Just as he spoke the Defense Condition indicator above the huge world map display blinked twice and changed to DEFCON 3.

"Sir, the Secretary is inbound, as are the command center staff. Chief of Staff Masters is also inbound with everyone else from the meeting," he said as he moved to his position at the side of the door so he could cover the President and keep an eye on everyone else when the room began to fill up.

Once everyone had made their way into the room, President Bender said, "Now where were we before we were so rudely interrupted?" getting several nervous laughs around the room.

"Mr. President, the Secret Service and the military have upgraded their defensive postures only with regard to protecting national command authority. No other changes in alert status will be going out to our allies, or be reflected in our defensive posture toward any hostiles.

"Commander Ames, could you give us a rundown on the capabilities of Dr. Martin's project insofar as it may be used as an early warning system, for lack of a better term?" queried the CJCS.

"First of all, we have to get the resolution of the detector higher so we can refine the focus down to better than the hundred-mile sphere we get now. To that end the Navy already authorized the construction of a second detector about three weeks ago. Dr. Harris came up with the idea to augment the sensitivity of the system by adding the second detector.

"Once this second system is operational, and I believe it's going to take at least four more weeks to get it up, Dr. Harris believes he will be able to achieve the necessary resolution to be able to place anomalies within about six feet, with a range well past near earth orbit. Once you get farther out, the accuracy is going to fall little by little."

"What if we build a network of these detectors and link them together?" President Bender asked. "How much range could we get, and how fine can we get the focus?"

Commander answered, "If it were possible, I would think the resolution could get jacked up pretty high. Unfortunately at this time it's not going to be feasible to get such a network up and running in real time sir. The problem rests with the extremely close tolerances the system requires in processing the data stream. Detectors too far away would not be able to synchronize their data stream with the primary computer system.

"Dr. Harris informed me that gravity's effect propagates at millions of times the speed of light. We have no way to be able to send data between widely scattered installations with any measure of success in synchronization with each other electronically."

"Do you have any other suggestions that might help us ferret out the source of this technology, commander?" asked the president.

"Not at this time sir. I'm hoping that if the director of the CIA is right and the source of the gravity readings was some kind of aircraft, our boys might get enough hints so that they might be able to duplicate what these people already have operational."

As the commander finished speaking, Diane Churchill entered the room looking rushed and confused as she walked over to the table to take an empty seat.

"Good morning, Diane, I apologize if I pulled you away from something important, but as you may have guessed we have a situation here. Commander, would you give Diane the short version please?" President Bender asked.

Ames gave Churchill a brief but complete rundown.

Looking at the president, and then at everyone else, Churchill said, "And this is somehow posing a direct threat to national command authority and that's why we're meeting down here?"

"The Secret Service is just taking precautions, Diane," the president answered.

"So what do you need from me, Mr. President?" she asked.

"Do you know of anyone who even comes close to this level of research here in the US, or anywhere else?" asked President Bender.

"No sir, I don't. Someone left me a message yesterday morning about that very same question, but I haven't had the time to dig the answer out."

"That was me, Madam Secretary," said Ames. "Yesterday it was just a hunch, today it looks like someone has made a breakthrough. Do you know of anyone who we can call in to help in evaluating the implications of this discovery?"

She thought for a moment, then replied, "Actually I do, but you probably won't like the answer. My advice is to grab a few of the better hard science fiction authors and use them to examine the possibilities. At least the idea won't be brand new to them," Churchill suggested.

The director of the FBI said, "Wasn't that idea used in one of those aliens invade the earth sci-fi books a couple of decades back?"

"Yes, it was, Larry Niven and Jerry Pournelle used the idea in their book *Footfall*. The premise was that in order to get the best ideas from outside the box you get unconventional thinkers to help plan strategies, ferret out contingencies and even formulate policy.

"The only problem with the idea is that those creative types tend to rub military types and bureaucrats the wrong way. Mr. President, I'm not sure how they would fit in, but I think they're the best short-term resource you might have, no offense to anyone here at the table."

"None taken, I'm sure. What does everyone else think?" President Bender asked.

"Well sir, I think we have a good start already. Dr. Harris was the first one to suggest the idea of antigravity to me from the beginning, and the addition of unconventional thinking would only help at this early stage," began Commander Ames.

The CJCS rolled his eyes and said, "I don't see any need for bringing anyone from the outside in on this. The quieter it's kept the better. Mr. President, allow me to go back to the Pentagon and pull together a threat team and have them begin brain storming on this one before you go and bring a bunch of, no offense, Madam Secretary, anarchist types into the fold."

"That's not what I said, Mr. Chairman, don't put words in my mouth . . ." Churchill began before anyone could cut her off.

"Please, you two," said Masters. "This is neither the time or place. What we need right now is a plan of action based on reasonable and reliable assessment of the threat this technology could, operative word could, represent against the interests of the United States."

Getting a nod from the President, Masters continued, "Is that understood, everyone? I want everyone to have something substantive tomorrow morning at eight. Diane, try to find out who's the best person in the country on gravity research and see if we can get them here for a few days."

"Thank you all for coming," said President Bender.

As everyone gathered their things and left for the elevator, the President stopped Commander Ames and drew him aside.

"Commander, what are your immediate plans?"

"I was on my way out to Dr. Harris' lab to see what I can do to get the second detector online quicker. I was also going to assemble a team to man the current detector around the clock. Why, sir, do you have use for me here?"

"Not specifically, it's just that your presentation was dead on. You have a gift for simplifying and explaining this whole issue so everyone understood the implications."

"Thank you, sir. If you want me to stay I will arrange for someone else to cover the lab," Ames offered, then laughed as the reality of the situation hit him. "Sorry sir, of course you can give me whatever orders you want."

President Bender laughed too, "I guess I can at that. No, I don't want to derail what you've accomplished already. You seem to be the one with the best grasp of the situation. See if you can pump this Dr. Harris for anything we might be overlooking too."

"Yes, sir. I'll route anything I find out to you through your chief of staff."

"Oh really? You heard I couldn't read either? I'm really going to have to plug that leak," the president said.

Ames swallowed and didn't say a word. Seeing his discomfort, Bender said, "Lighten up, I was just kidding. The one thing this job gives you, besides prematurely grey hair, is thick skin. Do you read any science fiction?"

"Sometimes, sir."

"Would you pick a couple of books that you think may broaden my horizons for dealing with this? I think Diane's idea is a good one despite what our General Kaminski may think."

"Very good sir, I'll have a couple of books sent over for you before I leave."

"Thank you very much, I'm looking forward to reading them," the President said, dismissing Ames with a smile.

Looking around, Bender saw that the only remaining attendees were Simon and Diane Churchill talking quietly in the corner and a major sitting next to the door who carried a locked briefcase affectionately called the football. The case containing all the release and launch codes for the country's nuclear arsenal was never far away from him no matter where he went.

Bender sat down and began to organize and prioritize the next steps his administration should take. Moments later the head of the White House Secret Service detail, Special Agent Daniels, walked into the room, nodding to Sam on his way over to the President.

Every time the president set eyes on Daniels he was struck by how nondescript he looked. Daniels had a face so plain and unremarkable, Bender bet himself that no one would remember the man even if he introduced him face to face.

Indicating the chair next to him, President Bender hit him with a terse, "Just where do you get off having me hustled out of a meeting like that?"

Meeting the president's anger with a calm, level expression, Daniels said, "I'm sorry Mr. President, but we acted in response to the possible existence of a direct threat to your life, sir."

"What threat? The possibility of someone dropping a black hole into the conference room? Or maybe sending a flying saucer to land on the south lawn? And where in the hell is my family? I hope you didn't scare my daughter!"

"We tried very hard not to, and according to Agent Downs she's just fine at bunker five. Right now she's playing on the computer with the vice president's daughter. They both were very excited to be participating in a drill and don't seem any worse for the wear. Both of their personal agents are very good with them, Mr. President. Try not to worry."

"We'll see about that. So what do I do now? Hide down here until our own people can develop anti-antigravity?"

"No sir, what I would like to do is ask that you remain here when you're in the White House for the next few days."

"I've got news for you, *Special Agent* Daniels, there is no defense against someone who can control gravity, that's the bottom line. So, the quicker we dispense with the drama and get back to normal the better," said Bender, with some heat.

"I beg to disagree, sir. If they can't find you, they can't harm you."

"I can't be ducking and dodging and staying out of sight forever. Hell, I've got a dozen appearances through the end of the week and at least two trips out of town."

"We're working on that, sir. Let my boss and the chief of staff work out the logistics while you concentrate on keeping the country running."

"You can quit patronizing me any time now," the president said, more than a little irritated.

"Then let everyone do their jobs, sir. Believe it or not, we're really good at it, honest. I personally haven't lost a president yet!" Daniels quipped.

Just then Diane and Simon broke up their conversation and came over to the president.

"Sir, Diane has an idea where we can get some outside expertise that's already somewhat under our control. She's suggested that we double up with some of the Asteroid Commission people, they're mostly from academia, research and homeland defense."

"What about the secrecy requirements?" Bender asked.

"That's what were going to work on today. Diane's going to put something together for this afternoon and get back to you."

"Fine. Thank you, Diane, for coming on such short notice."

"Not at all, Mr. President. I'll be in touch."

As she left, Bender motioned Simon to the seat on the other side of the table. "Agent Daniels is of the mind that someone with control of gravity can't hit what they can't see. So if the President of the United States is out of sight he's going to be a hard target to get to. I have a problem with hiding from anyone, let alone someone who's presented no threat to the country, me or my family."

"Agent Daniels, what's the Secret Service's official position here?" asked Masters.

"Until we have made a thorough threat assessment we're not going to take any chances. And until we have a better handle on this situation we vigorously insist that the president remain under wraps."

"I'll stay down here for the rest of today, and that's it. You and Simon come up with a better plan than burying my butt under the White House just in case some imagined danger might rear its ugly head. And I want the op team flown directly here once they reach the Arabian Sea, pass that along to the CIA as soon as you get upstairs, Simon. I want answers on just what we do face, not vague guesses, and more importantly, I want to know what happened to our man over there."

"Agent Daniels, would you implement whatever the plan is that temporarily moves me down here for the day? I might as well try to get some work done while I'm here."

"Already underway sir, your secretary and her staff are on their way down now, and the national security support team will have the consoles on the floor manned in about fifteen minutes. Since the military has moved to Defensive Condition Three, additional security will be arriving at the White House momentarily and we will have direct, encrypted communications with your family and the rest of your cabinet before lunch.

"Sam and two other agents will comprise your personal detail for the duration, and of course no one comes in or out without proper clearance."

When Diane Churchill got back to her office, the first thing she did was go through the list of scientists currently serving on the various White House subcommittees and commissions. Her plan was to put together a core group to begin the analysis of the broader ramifications of direct manipulation of gravity. Her selections cheated toward the young and more unconventional thinkers, believing their insights would be less apt to discount the impossible out of hand. She'd already seen enough of that in the military.

The director of the CIA, once he returned to his office, immediately called Bascomb and demanded a status report on the team's progress to their rendezvous with the carrier group in the Arabian Sea. He was told the team was still en route, probably still on the Iranian side of the border in their way south, but their exact location was unknown.

He then told Bascomb to put in a call to MI-6 to see if they had any movement with their in-country assets on the disposition of their downed man. Frustrated with the lack of useful intelligence, he concluded the call, telling Bascomb that when the samples got to Langley, to make sure that the pilot's remains were hand delivered to the FBI lab for detailed analysis.

By the time Martin and Alan had returned to the underground installation major changes in operations had already been implemented.

The security station topside was fully manned by armed soldiers, doors usually blocked open were now closed and locked. Martin and Alan had to use their ID cards to pass through each door in order to get back into their home away from home.

Once they had reached the waiting area just outside the last checkpoint, and before they could catch the elevator back downstairs, their bags were subjected to an apologetic, but thorough, search.

What greeted them when the elevator doors opened down below caught them completely by surprise. Across from the elevator was a fully manned emplacement with a floor-mounted twenty-caliber machine gun surrounded by sandbags, and just outside the elevator, out of the line of fire, was a heavy steel desk manned by an armed soldier who asked them to sign in before they could pass.

"Holy shit, Doc. You don't think we're the reason for all this, do you?"

"No, we're not the reason, we were just the messengers. It'll be interesting to see just how things are going to change around here."

Halfway around the world, it was dusk on the road south in Iran. Hidden in the back of a produce truck, the special ops team was relieved that their journey was proceeding without a hitch. Unfortunately this gave David ample time for recriminations over losing his partner and best friend for the last six years. The two Brits did what they could to try to relieve David of the burden of leadership and give him the space he seemed to need.

Basra, good as his word, had gotten them over the border into Iran where they were met by a second MI-6 operative. Their transfer to the second truck was accomplished quickly, and when they were ready to depart, Basra promised David he would find out whatever he could about his friend's body and get the information to him. David thanked Basra for his help, and for his consideration, and told their new driver to move out.

The drive south was pretty much a straight shot, and if all went well they would be on the shore in a handful of hours, allowing them to be picked up under cover of the early morning darkness.

Checking the frozen foot, Linden remarked, "This thing isn't going to stay frozen too much longer. The liquid nitrogen finished boiling off an hour ago."

"Should we take the chance and try to find some ice?" David asked.

"If we have to go to ground for one more day, definitely. Otherwise I'm hoping your boys on the carrier will have something to keep it close to freezing. Having it thaw and freezing it again will damage the tissue."

"Those things carry enough meat for a couple of thousand guys for a year, I think. I know they have a deep-freeze. Would dry ice do?" David asked.

"That would be more than adequate. If the trip back to the states is quick, we'll have no problems." Linden then removed his outer jacket and wrapped it around the bag as an extra layer of insulation and sat back in fatigue. They were all tired; the difference in time zones between Langley and Baghdad was taking its toll. They were content to just be along for the ride, hoping against hope that their trip south would end without incident.

None of them knew that while they made their way to Iran that morning, the laboratory staff had arrived to work, and it wasn't until one of them had dressed and entered the isolation room, stumbling over Kahill's body, that they knew that an unauthorized someone had been in the lab at all.

The director assumed he had a dead body on his hands. He immediately ordered everyone to begin checking for signs of theft and also put in a call to the local militia to alert them to the fact there had been an invasion of the Great One's laboratory.

The director was dismayed when informed of the loss of most of the exotic electronics, and the irreplaceable data on the missing computer hard drive.

A technician went through the pockets of the body he had dragged out of the isolation room. He then gave a shout, "This man is still breathing!"

Kahill was transported to the garrison's infirmary and secured to the steel frame of the hospital bed. Once the soldiers had satisfied themselves that the prisoner could not easily escape should he awaken, they left him to the ministrations of the doctor. He drew blood samples, took swabs of the insides of Kahill's nose and mouth for analysis and started an intravenous line to keep the patient hydrated and nourished. The doctor could find no physical injury that would have caused such a deep coma.

The doctor stepped into his small office and prepared the samples to send to the small medical lab with his nurse. He was just on his way back to take a closer look at his patient when the telephone rang. Picking it up, the doctor was surprised to find the director of the secret laboratory on the other end of the line.

"Doctor, have you had a chance to look over the thief?" the director asked.

"Nothing more than the preliminaries. Why do you ask?" the doctor answered.

"The monitors here show that this thief set off the supplementary cooling system while he was in the isolation room. He must have breathed the coolant fumes."

"Yes, go on," prompted the doctor.

"This coolant was mixed with an anesthetic gas to tranquilize test animals should they escape their cages. If test animals get out of their cages, the room's sensors trigger the gas to keep the temperature steady and bring down the animals to assist in getting them back under control," the director finished.

"Do you know the effects of this mixture of gases on humans if breathed over a period of several hours? Is there a fatal dosage that we may be dealing with here?" the doctor asked.

"That, I do not know. We have no data on the long-term effects on human subjects."

"Oh really," the doctor said ironically. "None whatsoever?"

"I understand what you are saying, Doctor. You have my word that *I* personally have no information that can help you. I recommend that you put him on oxygen to help flush as much of the anesthetic out of his system as possible. Other than that there is no known antidote, if that's what you're getting at."

"Very well, thank you for calling. I will inform you immediately should he awaken, if you so desire."

"I would like that very much doctor. I'm anxious to find out just who sent him and possibly glean the whereabouts of his compatriots."

CHAPTER 25

D EEP UNDERGROUND IN their remote parcel of Utah, Martin and Alan were pleased with the amount of support the office of the Joint Chiefs was throwing to their project. The computers were upgraded and hardened against electromagnetic pulse effects of air detonation of nuclear weapons. The complete lack of protection against the effects of gravitational attack such hardening represented was source of great humor to them both.

The expected operational date of the second detector was now almost three weeks ahead of schedule. Martin was surprised to find out that Commander Ames planned to grow two more crystals and have them kept in reserve should something happen to either of the detectors. When he discovered Ames' plan, Martin went off to confront him, not out of anger but out of curiosity, given the lack of available space for the installation of two additional detectors. Martin found Ames in the commissary.

"Mind if I join you, commander?" he asked.

"Not at all," Ames said, kicking out a chair for Martin.

"Let me ask you this. What happens if there's no repeat of the incident we originally recorded? What if the director of the CIA's speculation was correct, that the aircraft shot down was the only such craft in existence? Do we stay perpetually on guard?" Martin asked.

"Yep, this is it. Want out?" Ames asked, looking Martin in the eye.

"Hell no. I'm in it for the duration. Just the chance to study the effects of this technology will revolutionize quantum physics. The practical applications for manipulating gravity are endless.

"One thorny question is, what are the power requirements to be able to zero out the earth's pull on a gram of any substance? What happens to mass? Is it changed or altered in any way? How do you propel something that has had its weight altered within a gravity field like earth's? The questions are endless, but with what we have here maybe some of the questions might be answered. If they, whoever *they* are, manage to do it again, we'll be watching this time." The excitement was clear in Martin's face, and actually the nonmilitary part of Ames was just as curious about those same issues as Martin was.

"Martin, the truth is what has been done can never be undone; in other words we will never be able to return the plague to Pandora's box.

"The US will never rest until we have whatever these people have, or until we destroy the technology and those who developed it."

"That's criminal! Jesus, you can't be agreeing with that kind of thinking. What . . . if we can't have it, no one can? What kind of childish playground bullshit is that?" Martin asked with a shout, their conversation beginning to draw attention from the rest of the diners.

"Settle down. I didn't say I agreed with it, did I? All I'm saying is that the entireNational Security Council has its shorts in a bunch.

"I don't know about you, but if someone came into my yard with a bigger stick than I had, I'd find some way to make friends," Martin said, much quieter. "I'm sick and tired of this country's shoot first and ask questions later attitude."

"Is this going to affect your level of commitment here? If so, tell me now before you find yourself in too deep.

"I'm not going to even suggest that you try to take our perspective in any way, shape or form. As a matter of fact, you're of more use to me just as you are. I'd hate to have to put you in irons and keep you here under duress." Ames' eyes were sparkling with laughter as he took another bite of his sandwich.

Not quite sure if Ames was serious or not, Martin decided to pretend he wasn't, just so he could retain whatever measure of dignity working for the military had left him. To take the sting out of Martin's realization that he was essentially a very highly paid employee of the navy, Ames invited Martin to go with him check out the progress of the second crystal and to look over possible locations to store the backup crystals he planned to grow.

Across the country, at CIA headquarters in Langley, Bascomb's Middle East team had been putting on a full-court press putting together a strategy to build up their assets in the region.

Bascomb had been working very closely with his opposite number in MI-6 to aggressively increase the scope of the direct US assets in the region, especially in light of the search for the source of the technology whose discovery had so alarmed the national security command.

In Iraq, Kahill was still being held incommunicado in a locked treatment room in the barracks infirmary, fewer than a dozen people knowing he was being held there, still alive but completely unresponsive. The threat of the Great One finding out about the penetration of the lab and the subsequent theft of the remains and wreckage samples insured that everyone who knew anything about the incident would keep their mouth shut for fear of reprisal.

Detailed examination of Kahill's dentistry and appendectomy scar told the doctor that his country of origin was probably the United States or Canada. The damage to his brain might be too extensive to ever allow him to awaken.

Ever since the morning after the laboratory thefts, Bascomb and his team had pored over satellite photos of the region in an effort to see where the fallen man's body had been taken, but could discern nothing. All vehicular traffic to and from the lab appeared normal, with lab staff and military personal coming and going in the same manner observed in the days and weeks prior to the covert operation

Bascomb's crew, and Britain's MI-6, were both attempting to backtrack the flight of the advanced intruder, starting at the crash site, continuing along a direct line out of the region. This was a long shot, but for now it was all they could do. No new installations had been detected, even going back five years, that could support the fabrication of something as large and complicated as an aircraft. And given that the aircraft was airborne when first discovered by the missile battery, locating the country of origin proved to be impossible.

The CIA and Air Force labs couldn't determine anything about the craft's range, or flight capabilities, nor did they have anything in hand that gave a hint of the power source or propulsion plant that moved the craft through the air. The experts couldn't even agree on the shape of the aircraft.

When they received the data Dr. Harris' project had recorded on the effect the aircraft had on the local gravity, they matched that data second by second with the intercepted radar track from the Iraqi missile battery. They observed increases and decreases in the local gravity seemingly in direct relationship to changes in the flight path. Plotting all the data together showed that decreases in power saw corresponding drops in altitude and reductions in forward velocity. But other than those effects, all the sources of data were insufficient to provide clues to the basic nature of the technology the aircraft contained.

The president of the United States, once the Secret Service had exhaustively analyzed all the possible direct threats gravity manipulation posed to their charge and the members of his family, had returned to a more normal protective posture and schedule, if what the president did on a daily basis could be called normal.

The White House command center continued to be manned and ready, with all but a handful of the staff involved in the heightened state of readiness completely ignorant of the nature of the threat.

As a matter of fact, even the allies of the US were questioning the heightened state of readiness of the US military. They made indirect and direct inquiries into the reasons behind the seemingly aggressive posture but received nothing more than blanket denials.

Diane Churchill had her plate full. Every waking hour was consumed with trying to effectively manage the various confidential, secret and strategic projects under her supervision. She was constantly balancing the commission on the study of the asteroid, the confidential commission on gravity research, pollution, nuclear waste disposal, cloning, bioterrorism and the need for the normal Dick-and-Jane explanations of science to career politicians. Diane had a brief bit of excitement when the folks at JPL alerted her to a second change in course of the Lancaster asteroid; this time it appeared the change would bring it within two hundred and fifty thousand miles of the earth, well inside of the moon's orbit.

This new fact renewed interest in the asteroid in the press, once the information had been cleared for release to the public, putting Norma back on the press circuit. She also appeared in Washington for two separate commission meetings and found attending so much more fun in person. Truth be told, she liked being treated like a celebrity.

Norma was picked up by limousines, put up in A-list hotels and never had to pick up a tab, anywhere. Even though she loved every minute of her extended fifteen minutes of fame, every now and then she felt guilty for the commission billing the United States taxpayer for her room and board. But the excitement of being in on the planning of a possible fly-by mission to the asteroid kept her mind so occupied she seldom had time for guilt, and the excitement more than made up for the time she was forced to spend away from home.

The current session of the asteroid commission had been called to discuss the possibility of lifting a probe with a high-definition camera to take photographic and spectrographic images of the incoming asteroid. Although there was serious debate about what was causing these gradual course changes, high-definition photographs detected no other object colliding with or causing a shift in direction. Nor had those images revealed any sign of gaseous emissions that should be seen as a result of large gas pockets shooting out of the surface of the asteroid. No calculated gravitational effect from other planets or the sun provided an acceptable explanation for the changes in direction the asteroid had twice made in its journey through space.

The second directional change had also happened gradually, this time over a span of several hours. The asteroid would be visible to the naked eye in a couple of weeks.

When the day's meeting opened, the surprise guest speaker was one of the lead astrophysicists from JPL, Dr. Andrew Page, the man responsible for the current orbital calculations on Norma's rock.

"As all of you can see from the handouts, we have an unprecedented opportunity to study one of the larger pieces of our solar system to come this close to the earth since we've had the ability to travel into space. According to the latest tracking data, this asteroid is going to pass just under two hundred and fifty thousand miles from earth. That's inside the average orbital distance of the moon, and easily reached via current satellite probe technology.

"And, as of this morning's run of the trajectory data, there's a thirty percent chance it might impact the moon. The data's raw, and since we've already seen two course changes since Ms. Lancaster's unique project brought it to our attention, we simply cannot get any better accuracy than that."

Diane Churchill, chairing the day's meeting, said, "Thank you, Dr. Page. May I ask just how much longer do you think you'll need before you and your colleagues will be able to reach a consensus on the asteroid's exact path through our neighborhood?"

Looking at something off to the side of the camera, Dr. Page said, "I'm sure we'll be able to have a better track over the next four or five days. The closest passage to earth should occur in twenty-three days and some fifteen hours. That's more than enough time to get a probe configured, prepared and launched, but only just. If the commission should decide to pursue this course of action it would behoove us to make the most of the time available."

"Thank you for your observations and recommendations, doctor, we will be taking everything you've shared with us today into serious consideration. I invite you to remain online for the rest of the meeting if you have the time," Diane said.

"Thank you, Ms. Churchill, I would like that very much."

"Well then, does anyone have something they want to add? Yes, Ms. Lancaster?" Diane prompted.

"I'm still curious what everyone else thinks caused the course changes in such a massive object. Has anyone come up with any explanation for the gradual aspect change, a change in both cases that occurred over several hours?" Norma inquired.

"If I may, Ms. Churchill?" asked Dr. Page.

"Please, doctor, be my guest."

"Ms. Lancaster, this is the central mystery that we're trying to investigate here. Ever since the first course change we have had at least one telescope pointed at the asteroid at all times to try to capture evidence of gas or vapor shooting out from the surface of the rock. If that were the case there would be ample evidence in the form of illumination changes or increased radar cross-section as the ejected gas or vapor traveled along at the same speed of the asteroid until it had time to dissipate into space, but none of that has been observed."

Diane broke in and asked, "Dr. Page, is there any other explanation, no matter how far-fetched, that would account for the behavior of the asteroid?"

"Yes, there is. The simplest explanation for the asteroid's behavior is that it's path through the solar system is under direct control of some outside agency. That some kind of external force is responsible for the aspect changes."

Breaking the momentary shocked silence, Diane asked, "Doctor, are you trying to imply that there is someone guiding the path of the asteroid?"

"Not directly, but you asked what the most likely explanation was for the behavior of the asteroid, not necessarily the correct one. Until we can observe it much more closely, we cannot say with any reasonable degree of certainty why it changes course. The composition of the mass is largely ice with some heavier metals mixed in. It's actually the perfect way to carry along the consumables necessary to sustain life and provide fairly good protection against collision with micrometeorites over time. I think that the commission should at least consider the possibility, if for no other reason than to be thorough in the contingency plans you may be developing.

"However, I would not place the probability too high on this scenario, especially since the probable origin of the asteroid is from Saturn's rings or somewhere else within our solar system. The velocity of the rock is too low to escape the sun's gravity and travel out of our planetary system. Our guess is a chance collision pushed it away from one of the gas giants, and with its high concentration of ice, Saturn is where we're putting our money."

"Dr. Page, you have given us a lot to digest."

"I hope I haven't upset anyone's applecart, Ms. Churchill. I do think the question deserved an honest answer. As always, I am at your service. If you have no further questions I have another meeting that I'm scheduled to attend shortly."

"I think that's about it, Dr. Page, thank you for your kind assistance."

"Don't mention it," said Page, as he disconnected from the conference.

Norma's NASA liaison, Dr. Milton, then said, "Diane, if there's any chance that this thing is under voluntary control, some of us should be looking into putting down on paper the kinds of contingencies the country, hell, the rest of the world too I guess, should prepare for. Dr. Page is right in that in most cases the simplest explanation is most often the one that turns out to be the correct one.

"I believe the military say that once is happenchance, twice is coincidence and three times is enemy action. What if this thing does have intelligent life riding along on its journey toward earth? I'm sure the military will want to get a plan or two in the can. We're better off looking stupid than getting caught with our pants down."

Diane, experiencing a feeling of déjà vu, had just assembled a threat team for the president to study the various possibilities of gravity manipulation and the means it could be put to as a weapon of mass destruction. Now the same scenario was being suggested in conference by the asteroid commission.

"Thank you for the suggestion, Dr. Milton, I will bring it to the president. Are there any other suggestions or issues we need to discuss?" Diane asked the assembled group. Nodding to another of the commissioners with her hand raised, Diane prompted, "Yes, doctor?"

"Are we tabling for the time being development of the contingencies for preserving as many people we can in the existing long-term shelters should this asteroid make a change in direction that does put it on a direct course for earth?"

"Good question," Diane answered, "My immediate reaction is no, I think we should still complete that part of the recommendations, anyone else?"

Dr. Milton spoke up, "Indeed we should, if not for Norma's asteroid, but for the next one, and the one after that. Eventually, something large is going to hit the earth, there's no reason not to be as prepared as possible just in case we have no other technological alternative to being hit."

Reaching consensus on the work ahead before the next meeting, the commissioners and advisors began to hurry off to their next appointments.

Norma had a chance to share a cab with Dr. Milton. On their way she asked, "What do you think about the possibility that the asteroid is under voluntary control? The idea seems pretty far out there to me."

"Norma, a wiser man than I said, *not only is the universe stranger than it seems, it's stranger than we can imagine.* I think that regardless of how your asteroid gets here, it offers us a tremendous opportunity to broaden our knowledge and the scope of our reach as puny creatures on a single, insignificant planet in a backwater neighborhood of our galaxy.

"However, to answer your question, I tend to think not. The other answer breaks down into two different alternatives. The first is, if your rock is under voluntary control then we're looking at some sort of alien entity. That's exciting no matter how you slice it.

"The second alternative is that if it's under voluntary control, as you put it, then maybe man has a hand in its control. This option begs the question, who are they and why haven't they revealed their capabilities to the world at large?

"So, my personal preference is that we get to see something so unprecedented that it changes the entire fabric of our civilization. However, I'm afraid what we're going to really find is some boringly normal physical phenomenon that we've all overlooked that accounts for the behavior of your rock."

"So once we submit our recommendations to the president, what happens next?" Norma asked.

"Normally the committee will go along on a reduced meeting schedule. Some of us will be called to Congress or in front of other committees to present or discuss the findings and recommendations we come up with in committee. The icing on the cake for me is the chance that if we do decide to send a probe up there, in some small way we get to be a part of it. There is a measure of continuity in the work, and the possibility of increased funding."

Norma thought about what the long-term implications for her might be in terms of government service and the attendant loss of privacy and time with her friends at home in Chicago. Seeing some of this on her face, Dr. Milton said, "It's not as bad as you might think. For me the biggest pain in the ass is that I don't get to spend as much time with my children as I want. But the perks, and the stipends for serving, have made sure that their college educations are completely taken care of.

"As for how significant our work really is? That remains to be seen. By the very nature of the kind of recommendations we're putting together only one or two, if any, are ever going to be implemented. Your asteroid is either going to pass by or hit us. If it's under someone's control they're going to be either human or not. We're either going to be able to launch a probe or not. The decision tree is going to whittle down to a single branch no matter what the final disposition of the events we're studying."

Norma asked with a frown, "That's kind of cynical, isn't it? I mean if what we're doing is some sort of political and mental masturbation, what's the point?"

"The point is, my young and impatient friend, that we're paid to do the thinking that our betters cannot. Can you imagine the president of the United States having any clear idea of what to do with an alien visitor to Silver Springs, Maryland, for example? Or selecting the proper imaging protocol for a space probe to use to look at your rock? The simple answer is that he can't, his only expertise is in getting elected to office. They're all like that, Norma."

"So we're the drones who really do the thinking and get the job done?"

"Yes, that just about sums it up. Hey, what're you doing for dinner? I'm dining with Diane Churchill around eight, we're going to go over who we think should be on the threat team. You interested?"

Norma paused, "I guess so. I would like to be kept in the loop. Where should I meet you?" she asked.

"Tell you what, I'll swing by and pick you up at your hotel at seven-thirty. Bring an appetite, Diane said it was something special."

"Are you sure I won't be a third wheel? Maybe she wants to talk confidentially."

"I'll give her a call when I get to my room, if there's a problem I'll call you back and cancel."

"Great! Actually it will give me a chance to wear something other than a business suit." Milton smiled as they pulled up to Norma's hotel and the doorman opened the taxicab's door.

"Well then, barring Diane saying no, it's a date."

Norma was waiting outside her hotel at seven-thirty on the dot when Dr. Milton's cab pulled up. The cab driver pulled out into traffic, and sped off toward

Georgetown. Dr. Milton was dressed in a dark blue blazer with matching pants and a clean, pressed dress shirt and tie. He looked Norma up and down and gave a low whistle.

"You sure do clean up nice, ma'am," he said.

"You're not so bad-looking yourself, Doctor."

"Do you think you could find it in your heart to call me Paul for the evening? Even though we may be talking business, I propose that informality be the rule for the night. That doesn't upset your sensibilities, does it, my dear?"

"Of course not, but I may have a problem with Ms. Churchill, after all she is a cabinet member on the president's staff," said Norma.

"True, but I've known her for about a dozen years now. That's partly why I get on these commissions every other year. She's really just like regular folk. I think this evening will give you an opportunity to get to know her better. Give her a chance," Dr. Milton suggested.

When they pulled up to the awning of the restaurant, they both got out and went directly inside, neither really noticing the name of the establishment, just happy to get out of the overly warm and muggy Washington summer air.

After ten minutes of chit-chat about the various issues the commission faced, Diane breezed into the bar. They both got to their feet and followed Diane and the hostess to their booth.

Diane said, "Thank you for coming, Norma, I've been looking forward to getting to know you a little better. And Paul, it's always a pleasure. I'm sorry that my schedule hasn't been able to accommodate us getting together these last few months."

"Think nothing of it. If the two commissions I'm on are any indication of what you have on your plate right now . . . you've got your hands full."

Looking at Paul sharply, Diane asked, "No offense, but you haven't discussed anything from one panel with members of the other, have you? "

Quickly moving to reassure her, Paul said, "Not at all. I do understand my responsibilities."

"Sorry, Norma, some of the country's best and brightest, like Paul here . . ."

"Oh Diane, you say the sweetest things," Paul broke in with a smile.

"Quiet, you. Anyway Norma, guys like this are called on to serve in many different projects and people like me try to make their tasks as difficult as possible by making them schizophrenic about to whom they can talk to about what."

"Sort of what you called me to remind me of when I forwarded the data from JPL?" Norma asked.

"Exactly. Only in Paul's case the two major commissions he's on have taken a jump in importance since this morning. That's one of the things I wanted to talk to both of you about tonight." Diane paused to take a sip of her wine.

"Well, don't keep us in suspense, Diane!" Paul said.

"The president and the National Security Council are facing two huge issues that need immediate attention. Paul, you know what I'm talking about. Norma, what I am about to tell you is classified a couple of steps above your clearance. However, since I want your help, you'll need to know at least some of the particulars before you make any kind of decision. Are you interested in hearing me out?" Diane asked.

"I think so. Are we talking about a kind of 'if I told you, I'd have to kill you' sort of thing? If so, I can grab a burger and go home. Otherwise, you've got my undivided attention." Looking around, noting that the hostess had not seated anyone within earshot, Diane leaned in and said quietly, "The president needs to put together an effective threat team for two different situations dealing with science and technology issues. The first one you already know about. Your asteroid has him worried for two reasons. The first is that a collision with the earth would be devastating no matter where it hit, and the second reason is the two changes in its flight path with no discernable cause.

"The second issue is classified top secret, but a good friend of yours is already working on the project," Diane said.

"We have discovered the fact that someone has managed to develop the means to control gravity, and your friend Alan Richards is right in the thick of things." Diane watched Norma's expression as she absorbed what she had been told.

Norma took several swallows of water before she could think of something to say.

"So, antigravity. Is that what you and the rest of the president's people think is changing the course of the asteroid?" Norma inquired.

"Holy shit!" muttered Paul. Looking at Diane he said, "I never put the two together, Diane, has anyone else speculated on that?"

Diane, although far more practiced at concealing her thoughts, had just as startled an expression on her face. Looking at Norma she asked, "What made you think that gravity manipulation could be the cause of the two course changes, Norma?"

"I didn't think about it until you mentioned both things just now. I thought that's what you were getting at." Norma was beginning to become worried. Both of these two people were so much more in the know than she, and yet something so obvious to her hadn't even occurred to them. She watched as Diane pulled out her mobile phone and held up her hand gesturing them to silence until she was done.

"Hello, Simon? I have to see you ASAP. No, nothing like that, I just had someone bring something up that we've been overlooking, something important. No, we can be there in fifteen minutes. Dr. Paul Milton and Norma Lancaster. Yes, that's her. We'll be leaving right now."

Disconnecting the call, then Diane said, "I want to apologize in advance for ruining what could have been a delightful dinner; however, I believe I can offer a dining experience that might be a little more memorable for you two, if you're game. How do you feel about getting a bite to eat at the White House instead?"

Norma was speechless, and Paul just grinned like an idiot. Diane gestured to their waiter and when he arrived she told him that they would not be dining there that night, and to take the sting out of the announcement she added that they had been called to see the president of the United States. Asking him to charge the drinks to her account, she got to her feet and led them out to her limo waiting just beyond the awning.

Norma's shock lasted until the car pulled up to the White House gate. She asked Diane, "This is real, isn't it?"

"As real as it gets, Norma. Have you ever visited the White House before?"

"No. Well, almost. I was going to have a photo op with the president when I was on my first press tour, but he had to leave for New York and it didn't work out."

"I dare say you are in for a treat then."

As the limo pulled up the rear of the building a Secret Service agent opened the door for them and led them into the entrance. Greeting all three by name, the agent asked Norma to place her small pocketbook on the x-ray machine and asked Dr. Milton to empty his pockets before walking through the metal detector. Once they were all cleared, a second Secret Service agent led them directly to the Oval Office to await the arrival of the president and his chief of staff.

When they had seated themselves the agent who accompanied them asked if they would like a beverage while they waited. Paul and Norma were both too excited and declined. Diane informed the agent that they had skipped dinner and might want something a bit later. The agent nodded and went to stand beside the door to await the president's arrival.

Moments later the door opened and President Bender entered, followed closely by Chief of Staff Masters. All three shook hands with the president and Masters, and waited until President Bender was seated before they too sat down. They all waited while the official White House photographer took several pictures of the group, with the president asking Norma to stand and pose with him in a two-shot in front of his desk before the photographer left them to their meeting.

President Bender began with, "I understand from Simon here that the three of you have something to bring to my attention?"

"Yes we do, Mr. President," began Diane. "As you know, Ms. Lancaster and Dr. Milton serve on the commission you convened to study the asteroid Norma discovered, and Dr. Milton is serving double duty on the other, confidential commission, sir.

"The three of us met for dinner, mostly for me to offer Ms. Lancaster the opportunity to serve with Dr. Milton on both commissions. When I broached the nature of the confidential commission Norma said something that, frankly, just about left me speechless.

"By the way, she was the source of the briefing information that I brought to you on the first course change of the asteroid, the data showing the rock's aspect change happening over several hours, not abruptly as it would have had it been impacted by another mass out there. So when I described the focus of the commission on gravity manipulation, she asked me if that was what we thought was the cause of the asteroid's course changes. In other words, was someone using the manipulation of gravity to change the vector of the rock?"

Simon said, "Damn. We completely overlooked that possibility."

President Bender then asked, "Ms. Lancaster, what was it that led you to make the connection between the two?"

"First off, Mr. President, I couldn't think of anything that would change its course over a period of several hours except some sort of jet-like reaction. The only thing that matched the data was if there was a huge gas leak that had pushed it off axis, not a collision with another object. When it happened a second time, I thought, like everybody else, the cause was some sort of natural phenomenon that we just didn't know about yet."

Looking at Masters, President Bender said, "Let's see if we can get our folks out west looking closely at this piece of rock."

"Right away, sir. What about the two teams Ms. Churchill is assembling? Perhaps we should combine them, and maybe keep them under wraps. We don't want this getting out before we're ready to break the news ourselves."

The President asked Diane, "Where are we in setting up this group?"

"I've identified eleven additional people who fit what we're looking for. Other than Dr. Milton here, I haven't approached anyone yet. I don't think it's going to be easy getting a group together who will acquiesce to being away from home, and restricted in the manner they can, or in this case, cannot communicate with their family and friends.

"Ms. Lancaster, if the President asked you to serve on a committee that would be sequestered away from friends, family and your project in the name of national security what would you say? What issues would you have under these conditions?" Churchill asked.

"I guess the first thing that occurs to me is, what would I do with my apartment? How would I pay my bills? What would NASA say about me going on hiatus with my own project? And, what exactly do you mean I would have my communications with my friends impacted? Would I be paid? Would I lose my standing at the U of C? Where would . . ."

"Whoa, whoa there," President Bender began, laughing. "We would never suggest that your service to the country required you to endure hardship that negatively impacted your quality of life. If what Diane has told us is true, we need your kind of thinking around here. Our best thinking comes from a completely different perspective than here in Washington. Here we have an entire industry focused on getting reelected, of currying favor from whomever happens to be holding the reins at any given moment and trying to buy access and influence.

"The military has its perspective, the House and Senate have theirs, the industrialists have theirs and on and on. It's people like you who hold the key to effective and creative planning. If you don't want to give us an answer right now, I understand. I'm sure it does look, and feel, like we're piling on, but believe me when I tell you it's just working out this way.

"You're the first person to suggest a connection between the discovery of the ability to control gravity and the behavior of your rock. This is a very serious issue for my administration, even more so for the possibilities it represents in terms of the safety of the American people. All I ask is that you give it some thought," Bender finished.

"I will, Mr. President. I don't want to seem selfish, and I'm extremely grateful for everything that has been offered me because of my seat on the commission, from the beginning of my project through tonight. It's just a little overwhelming all at once." Norma paused to look at Dr. Milton. "I don't want to let anyone down, least of all the people in this room. I guess if it's important enough to bring me here to ask, the least I can do is give it my best shot."

Smiles broke out around the room, and Dr. Milton leaned over and squeezed Norma's hand.

"Diane, see to it that Ms. Lancaster has whatever she needs to make this happen. Ms. Lancaster, I want to personally thank you for your consideration. Dr. Milton, how much of a hardship will it be to your family for you to be absent for a while?" Bender asked.

"Mr. President, my wife doesn't work and we do pretty well with what NASA pays. And, with the supplemental income from the various commissions and outside lectures I give, I can spare a little time to devote to helping advance the concerns of the country. I'm in."

"Would you like some help in getting together a team to work these issues?" Milton asked Diane.

"Thank you, I'd like that very much. However, if you'll excuse me, I have to make a couple of phone calls," Diane answered.

President Bender stood up and said, "Now that we've taken care of that, Ms. Lancaster, Dr. Milton, would you like a quick tour and maybe get a bite to eat? I have the time, and it seems the least I can do for having interrupting your dinner."

Upon answering in the affirmative, Norma, Dr. Milton, the President and his personal Secret Service agent set off on a half-hour tour of the better-known parts of the White House. President Bender filled the role of tour guide quite well. After his so-called ten-cent tour, they were treated to the company of the First Lady, and after Diane eventually rejoined them, they were treated to a lovely dinner.

Afterwards, on the drive back, Norma was so excited by the day's events she talked almost nonstop until she was dropped off at her hotel. Norma settled in under the covers with a smile of satisfaction as she recalled that a copy of their picture together with the president would be delivered to her hotel in the morning, personally signed and framed to commemorate their meeting.

Her last thought before she drifted off to sleep was that it would be good to see Alan again and finally get to find out what he had been working on for the last few weeks. Besides, it would be quite a kick to show him her latest picture to add to their collection.

Everybody's got a pistol, everybody's got a forty-five,
The philosophy seems to be, as near as I can see,
When other folks give up theirs, I'll give up mine.

Gun

Written and performed by Gil Scott-Heron

CHAPTER 26

J OHN HAD SPENT nearly every waking minute thinking about his feelings for Sydney. He, at least, had a reprieve from the disquiet of his feelings since both of them were uncharacteristically busy with their respective jobs and didn't have the opportunity to get together.

Sydney was out of town attending back-to-back regional college fairs, one in San Diego, the other in Minneapolis, and only managed to talk to John on the phone twice since dinner at her house.

John had been busy helping Agent Minor sift through the immense amount of documentation covering the whereabouts of the last dozen or so women who had disappeared in cities where Sydney had traveled in the weeks prior to their disappearances. The computer search of the millions of telephone records had been a bust. There were no matches from any of the last dozen women in Samuels' group. They were forced to continue the investigation the old-fashioned way. As a result, John was treated to bad airline service, crappy food on the go and the kind of fuzzy dislocation one gets when one does five cities in six days.

John tracked down and interviewed old neighbors, friends, coworkers and boyfriends of the women, asking for information on anything unusual they may have observed prior to the disappearances. In every case the story was the same; there had been absolutely nothing unusual that stood out in their minds, and when John showed them a picture of Sydney, none could recall having ever seeing her before.

Every day he spent working on the investigation, John's guts twisted tighter and tighter.

His only consolation was that there was no evidence Sydney had been involved with the other women in any way he or Minor could dig up, but that did little to resolve the ambivalent feelings he had towards her. Nor did it explain the two cell phone calls from Jaylynn Williams.

Agent Samuels was spending more time in Washington working from FBI headquarters with the satellite analysis team, searching for possible locations of any isolated community that might be home to his group of missing persons. Working from infrared surveys of the more remote regions of the United States, the analysts were identifying hot spots in the nighttime photographs and matching them against known towns and settlements. Any location showing up in the infrared photos, and not recognizable as a known town or unincorporated settlement, required a closer look from the ground.

So far, none of the questionable locations bore fruit. Given the size of the continental United States, this was truly a brute force approach to trying to find the group Samuels was convinced was out there.

The troublesome question in all of this effort was the basic question of why? Why would anyone choose to completely sever all contact with their past to begin a new life devoid of roots, essentially repudiating family and friends? The thought of what had led these people to do so frightened Samuels. His gut feeling was that whatever this group of African Americans was up to couldn't bode well for the country.

Part of Samuels' job was not only to solve crimes and bring responsible parties to justice, but to uncover the motives and actions that led up to the commission of the crime. This was just as important in understanding the criminal mind, and a vital component of the investigation.

In this case, since every member of the missing group was black, race was obviously a factor. But how *did* race fit? Were the members of this group, assuming of course that there were alive and well, part of a new ultraseparatist group fed up with America's racist baggage? If so, were they a threat to America? In other words, would they seek retribution for over four hundred years of wrongs perpetuated on them because of the color of their skin?

Samuels wondered if the institutionalized racism still prevalent in America was strictly a holdover from slavery, suggested by the kinds of hate crimes still popular in the South, or was it xenophobia against people visibly different from their pale brethren? Culture plays its part, his training and the crime stats bore that out. But, even as a member of the dominant race, Samuels saw the hurdles, the glass ceilings, the lowered expectations, the institutionalized slights and insults his black contemporaries in the Bureau faced, day in and day out.

Samuels put the finishing touches on his status report to the director, including his strong suspicion that the members of the group were not the victims of a criminal conspiracy that had left them dead, but were instead members of a different kind of conspiracy, one that could potentially pose a threat to the security of the United States of America. The report included every piece of substantive evidence collected so far and a mention of the only lead to date that could uncover the disposition of the missing group. He did leave out Dean Atkins' name for the time being; he didn't want anyone else to jog his elbow, so to speak, and spoil any progress Mathews had made so far.

When he completed the sixteen-page report late in the afternoon, and had gone over it several times to make sure nothing had been left out, Samuels forwarded it on to the director, flagging it "eyes only" and encrypting it for added security. Samuels notified everyone that he was returning to Atlanta the next morning and left headquarters for the remainder of the day.

In his car on the way back to his apartment, Samuels dialed the number of the office in Atlanta where Agent Minor was stashed. When he got Minor on the phone he said, "Jeff, it's Robert. How's it going?"

"The good news is that there's nothing new to report, the bad news is that there's nothing new to report."

"Smart ass. Where are we right now?"

"Well, John's off to Nashville to do some background checking into the woman pilot's last few days before she disappeared. The phone records were a bust. My guess is that if Atkins is involved with these other women they were far more careful than Miss Williams. Those two calls from her were a fluke that someone overlooked."

"What about any other convergences between the woman's travels and others of the group?" Samuels asked.

"Sorry boss, there're actually four more candidates where there might have been an overlap, but the time between visits and disappearance is six months or longer, more like a statistical correlation than something I could take to a grand jury," Minor answered. "When are you going to head back down here?"

"I'm booked on a flight tomorrow morning. Why, is there something I should know about?"

"Not exactly. I have a nagging concern about our friend the cop, but I don't want to make a big deal about it."

"Oh? What's up, Jeff?

"He seemed different after he went over to her house for dinner. Nothing I can put my finger on, but there's definitely something on his mind."

"Hey, the guy was falling for the woman before he even suspected she might be a material witness. I'm thinking that he's just having problems walking that line, keeping the friendship on track so that she doesn't suspect, and trying to dig anything out that will help us get to the bottom of this case. I've got nothing but sympathy for him. Why, do you think he's in danger of blowing it with her?" Samuels asked, with a trace of worry in his voice as he mentally reviewed his report to the director. He was reminded that the pickings were slim indeed, and that the Williams girl's phone calls to Atkins were their only clue to date. Losing their best avenue to finding out the information the investigation needed would not help at all.

"No, I don't think so. Both of them are out of town on trips, she's in Minneapolis at some college fair. What I wanted to ask you is if you wanted me to arrange for her house to be wired while she's gone?"

"At this point, I don't think I can get a court order for that. If she's actually got a line on where these folks ended up, and there's criminal intent, then our shit has to be squeaky clean."

"What about the wiretaps? If I'm not mistaken, they're not entirely kosher, are they?" Minor asked.

"True, and anything we get from them won't be admissible, but that wasn't my intent. I want information on the whereabouts of these people, pure and simple. Once I know where they are then I'll worry about what's admissible," Samuels answered, hotly.

"Hold on, chief, I'm not criticizing, I don't want anything to come back and queering a solid case on this one. If two thousand black folks are out there with an agenda that puts the *pigmentally* challenged on notice, then I want to have every advantage possible on my side. Do you really think it's possible they're out there, planning to do something to the rest of the country?"

"I'm looking into it. Personally, I don't know what to think, but that many well-educated and well-trained people disappearing without any trace is inhumanly impossible from a criminal conspiracy standpoint, unless they themselves are directly involved. Look, I'll bring you up to date when I get there, and I want you to take a look at my report to the director to see if anything in it gives you something I overlooked. I'll see you late in the morning."

"Damn, now I have to spend the rest of the day cleaning up the office. Do you remember where the fire hose is on this floor?" Minor asked, laughing.

"No, I don't. You just make sure I don't get any cooties when I sit down at my desk."

"Right, chief. I'll see you in the morning."

Back at FBI headquarters, the director returned to his office from a meeting with the president, getting a briefing on the joint commission members President Bender's science advisor was drawing up as the administration's threat team. The president requested a summary of the issues the director wanted the threat team to consider in terms of security on the home front.

The president also wanted an update on the analysis of the recovered foot brought back from Iraq and whether or not the FBI had determined the pilot's country of origin. Unfortunately little had been found so far. Analysis of trace elements in the skin and the fibers burnt into the ankle hadn't yet yielded any substantive information.

A print from the sole of the foot had been taken directly and scanned so that the resulting pictures could be used to try to match it against those usually taken at birth. The problem was the FBI had no idea yet in what country to begin the search.

The director checked his telephone messages and returned two calls, and once finished, turned to his computer to check his e-mail. He began to scan through the various status reports, inquiries and administrative paperwork. Seeing the message from Special Agent Samuels and noticing it was encrypted drew his immediate attention.

He scanned the contents rapidly. Then the director stopped and reread the section where Samuels detailed the reasoning behind his speculative conclusion. Going back to the beginning of the report, he began to read it more carefully, now with an eye toward how much of it he would pass along to the White House in the morning's security briefing.

He cut and pasted portions of Samuels' report into a new document, filling in the framework of the report he was going to present at the briefing. As he typed he considered who would be at the briefing and to his relief he realized that not a single person at the meeting was African American. The last thing he wanted was to create an issue polarizing twelve percent of America's population into any further mistrust of the administration. Strangely, the director thought nothing of the fact that President Bender's administration was almost completely white, although HUD and Health and Human Services were headed by a Hispanic and an African American respectively. Coincidentally, the leadership of the various branches of the military had fallen to whites this time around as well.

As he completed his report for the morning, the director was beginning to feel the first quiet pangs of anxiety. It didn't take a rocket scientist to make the connection between forty years of highly intelligent, and capable, African Americans disappearing without a trace and the discovery of an advanced aircraft using futuristic technologies whose pilot was black.

He told his secretary to get Agent Samuels on the phone as soon as possible. It wasn't many minutes later when his phone beeped twice to let him know Samuels was on the line. He asked without preamble, "Are you on a secure phone?"

"No, sir. If need be I can get to one or come back to the office," Samuels answered.

"That won't be necessary. What I need to know, man to man, is how certain are you that what we're looking at is not a case of serial murder or something similar?"

"Sir, I'm almost completely certain. If I'm wrong then we're looking at something unprecedented. No one is that good, and I don't believe in alien abductions, and that's the only alternative I can think of that fits the facts."

"You didn't go into detail here, what's your next move?" the director asked.

"The satellite search is still underway, and I'm returning to Atlanta to look further into the woman in question."

"And how is your local help working out?"

"He's doing just fine, sir. He's established a relationship with the woman and is actually doing as well, or better, than I would under the same circumstances."

"I'm moving this to the front burner. I'm not going public yet, but things are happening that make getting to the bottom of this investigation a top priority. If there's anything else you need in the way of support call me directly."

"No problem, sir. Is there anything else?"

"Be careful. If what you suspect is true, you might be putting yourself and the rest of your team at risk. Anyone who could pull this off for almost four decades is no piker!"

"I'll keep that in mind. You'll hear from me the minute anything breaks," Samuels said and hung up.

The director sat back, suddenly feeling exhausted and wrung out.

He picked up the phone again and dialed the forensics lab where the pilot's remains were being studied. Getting the laboratory director on the line he asked, "Have you been able to determine what kind of diet this guy had before he separated from his foot?"

Taken aback, the director of the lab said, "No, sir. At least he didn't eat anything so different from a standard American diet that anything stands out. The only thing that is unusual at all are the length of the telomeres in the cells."

"The what?"

"Telomeres, sir. Telomeres are the structures at the ends of your genes, they are kind of like extra genes at the end of your chromosomes that most researchers believe somehow control the aging process in your body. The longer the telomeres, the younger the cell, and the longer they will last in terms of how many times they can divide. Older cells have shorter telomeres and younger cells have longer telomeres.

"From the length of this guy's telomeres we would normally estimate his age at about ten or eleven years old. However, when we look at the ends of his bones and the thickness of the skin on the sole of the foot, his age appears closer to that of a forty–to fifty-year-old."

"So what are you telling me?" the director asked.

"He either grew physically far faster than normal or he would be extremely long-lived compared to an average man," he answered.

"How much longer?"

"Based on our measurements, maybe thirty or forty years longer than the average African, about twenty to thirty years longer than the average African American."

"Is this verifiable?" the director asked.

"Not given the level of secrecy you've clamped down on this. I haven't consulted with anyone outside of the Bureau about this at all."

"Type up what you've got and walk it over to my office. I need it for a meeting in the morning."

"Very well, give me about an hour or so and I'll have it over to you."

"Thanks, I'll be waiting," said the director and hung up the phone. First antigravity, now extended life spans. If they were looking at this group as the source of these new technologies, what else had these people managed to cook up?

He perused the index of the missing persons in Samuels' report and their areas of expertise. The list was chilling. These people were the cream of the crop in science, math, nuclear research, theoretical research, weapons design, biological warfare, and on and on. A veritable wish list of specialties for anyone who had a serious bone to pick with someone big, someone like the United States of America.

The director began to compose a document that he never in his entire career thought he would have to draft. His report would state that it was his considered opinion that there existed a group that was not only clearly superior to the US in their level of scientific expertise, but that the FBI had no idea where they were located.

He added that these same people had demonstrated their superiority in metallurgy, electronics, propulsion, biological sciences and the concealment of their location. And, until this investigation into the circumstances of their disappearances, no one had even suspected they existed. The director wanted to call the White House immediately and spill what he knew and suspected, but realized that the proper forum was in front of the entire NSC team. That way he would only have to tell the story once. Who knew, someone else just might have something to add that he had overlooked.

He ruefully thought back to the events that had put them on the path they traveled now, that single phone call to the talk radio program in Chicago and the resulting furor over the crime statistics against African Americans throughout the twentieth century. If anyone doubted blacks in America had serious issues about the treatment they receive in their own homeland, they had to be blind or deluded.

What if this group decided to pressure the country into changing domestic policy, or granting special privileges to their kinfolk? Who would have the stones to say no and make it stick? With the control of gravity and the tantalizing hints into their medical technologies, who could stand against them? How do you overcome people who can not only outgun you, but simply outlive you?

How was he going to run any kind of investigation when the nature of those they were looking for was discovered by the public at large? The Bureau was populated with its fair share of African Americans who probably harbored resentments over slights, imagined and real. How would they react to the need to locate and possibly prosecute a group of their own? Would they cross over to the other side?

Hopefully, he was putting the cart before the horse. Maybe there wouldn't be any need for any kind of criminal prosecution at all. Unfortunately, given the current climate in the US, the administration was not about to allow any one group to harbor the kind of technology this group had already demonstrated. The threat they represented would push the Administration into trying to negotiate control of their technologies away from them, or more likely just steal them. Neither prospect was good. Someone who could cancel the pull of gravity could float the White House off the surface of the earth.

Hitting the intercom button, he told his secretary to go home, that he was staying behind to wait for a report from the lab. He dimmed the lights in to office and sat in the quiet of the coming night. He sat alone with his thoughts until his solitude was interrupted by the director of the forensic lab with the lab report on the stolen foot.

Looking the report over, the he became even further depressed. The public would be split between those clamoring for their fair share of the largess and those who would cheer the fact that for once the shoe was on the other foot.

This was one time he just wanted to lock up, go home and get drunk.

The next morning dawned hot and muggy in Washington, making for an unpleasant start to another oppressive summer day. The members of the National Security Council were all inbound to what they thought was just a normal status briefing. The director of the FBI had barely gotten two hours of sleep, after working well into the night at the office trying to anticipate the questions he would be called upon to answer. When he had gotten home, he spent most of the wee hours of the night worrying the problem of conducting an investigation into a group of blacks with an integrated Bureau. The extent of the kind of domestic investigative team he would have to assemble was daunting. He had left a message for the Secretary of the Treasury to be sure to attend so he could get the Secret Service up to speed as soon as possible.

Remembering that the president's own personal agent was black, he was unsure of how to approach the whole problem. He knew that calling Simon Masters at three in the morning wasn't the best way to begin to formulate strategic policy. Somehow the administration was going to have to make damn sure that whatever they decided to do wouldn't plunge the nation into a race war.

He waited until morning to call Masters' private number. To his good fortune for a change the phone was immediately answered.

"Masters," came the quick, no nonsense greeting.

Identifying himself, the director got right to business. "Simon, we have a problem."

"Shit, what now?"

"I'm bringing in a bombshell this morning and you deserved a heads-up. We have a situation that I'm not sure how we're going to handle. The aircraft shot down in Iraq was just the tip of the iceberg."

Masters broke in, "Thirty seconds, I've got something going."

"Here's the short version. I have strong evidence that the source of the technology we're trying to locate is right here in the US, was developed and is currently being held by a secret group of black separatists."

"Son of a bitch. This is just what we don't need. Did you call Treasury?"

"I left him a message to be sure to attend. What about the president's personal agent?" the director inquired.

"Fuck! I'll call you back in five. Are you inbound?" Masters asked.

"I'm in the car, call me here or I'll catch you when I get there."

Masters just stared at the phone for a second before he burst out of his office.

"Where's the president?" he asked the Secret Service agent stationed in the hall.

"Still in the residence, sir."

"Who's head of the detail today?" Masters asked.

"Sir, Special Agent Daniels is on duty. Do you need to speak to him?" the agent asked with a frown.

"Right away, and I mean now."

Lifting his cuff to his mouth, the agent passed along the order. Less than a minute later Agent Daniels came racing down the hall.

Jerking his head toward the office, Masters led him in and shut the door.

"We have a situation," Masters began. "The FBI says that the people responsible for the aircraft shot down in Iraq are black separatists based somewhere secretly here in the US."

Had situation not been so serious, Masters would have burst out laughing at the expression on Daniels' face. Then the agent's expression turned grim.

"What the hell? Do you want me to pull Bishop, is that what we're talking about?" Daniels asked. "And everyone else on the detail who's black? God dammit, what the fuck is going on Simon?"

"You tell me. How do we assess a situation like this? What's the level of threat? Who do we trust? Hell, I don't know what to do with this. The director is inbound now, he's already called SecTreas, but I wasn't sure if he got the word."

Getting up from his chair and pacing back and forth, Masters asked, "Is Bishop upstairs now?"

"Damn straight, and unless you have a damn good reason, he's staying right where he is. I'm not going to turn my detail upside down on something this flimsy. We've got nine black agents on the detail today. What do you expect me to do, give them all the day off telling them that it's Martin Luther King's secret birthday, and then send someone to watch over them? Give me something better to go on, will you?"

"Dammit, Mike, I don't have anything else. The NSC meeting is going to start in fifteen minutes. What do you suggest?"

"Even if I pull Bishop, whoever I replace him with is going to hear what's said in the meeting. That's not going to stay under wraps for long, and there's no way you can have the meeting without coverage. Besides, any such absence is bound to be noticed."

The head of the White House detail watched as the chief of staff walked over and looked out the window.

Daniels stood up and said, "I'm going to go handle this before the meeting gets started."

"What are you going to do?" Masters asked.

"You'll know as soon as I do," Daniels said as he opened the door and left.

Charging back down the hall, giving a dismissive wave to the inquiring look from the agent stationed outside the door, Daniels called Bishop over the radio and told him to meet him in his office.

Five minutes later Bishop was knocking on Daniels' door.

"Come in. Sit down, Sam."

"I heard the call a few minutes ago, what's up?"

Getting up to close the door, Daniels returned to his chair and sat down before speaking.

"Sam, we have a situation that I don't know how to resolve. The director of the FBI is inbound with evidence that the source of the technology recovered in Iraq is in the hands of a secret group of black separatists based somewhere in the US."

Looking his superior in the eye, Bishop said, "And?"

"And, I want to know how you think we should handle this. I want any suggestion you have on how to approach the what can rapidly become a pretty shitty situation," Daniels said.

"If there's a question about those of us on the detail, I'll get everyone together, wait outside for our replacements and we'll go back to Treasury and wait, sir." Sam answered and stood up, pulled his sidearm from its holster, and removed the magazine and ejected the chambered round. Placing the pieces on Daniels' desk, Sam turned and left the office before Daniels could even get a word out of his mouth.

"Dammit, Sam, get back in here," Daniels shouted at Sam's back, and then heard over their command circuit Sam's call to the rest of the black agents to assemble. As they came into the squad room, Sam instructed them to disarm, hand their weapons over to the two white agents standing there dumbfounded, and then led them out the rear entrance to await their replacements.

Daniels followed the group outside, pulled Bishop aside and said, "Dammit, Sam, why are you doing this?"

"Look, sir. If there is any doubt about our loyalty, then we cannot do our jobs. The fact that the chief of staff ordered you into his office tells us just how serious this is. It's better for everyone if we remove ourselves from the situation." Agent Bishop looked away, and then moved to stand with the other eight African American agents, agents sworn to protect the president and his family with their lives now under a cloud of suspicion over nothing more than the color of their skin.

When Daniels stormed back inside, the two agents manning the entrance watched as their superior made his way slowly back to his office to await the replacement agents, and to work out the details of their individual postings. As he made the necessary calls, he was just itching to confront the Secretary of the Treasury as soon as he had the opportunity. This was not right. This would not do. He was going to have to draw a line in the sand. He picked up the assignment sheet and left to await the arrival of the secretary at the West Wing entrance.

Meanwhile Masters had already informed President Bender of the gist of the FBI report, and stood silent under the verbal assault from the commander in chief, dressing him down for having taken unilateral action to bar the black members of the detail from their posts.

When he got himself under control, President Bender left the residence and headed downstairs to the NSC meeting due to start in just a few minutes, with Masters almost having to trot to keep up.

President Bender was even angrier when he noted Bishop had been replaced. Walking into the conference room, President Bender sat down in his chair, impatient for the meeting to get started. When Masters started to say something, President Bender raised his hand, silencing his friend without a look.

Masters subsided, and took his own seat as the rest of the cabinet made their way into the room, grabbed coffee and took their seats. As soon as the door closed President Bender said without preamble, "All right everyone, settle down. Today everything gets turned upside down whether we like it or not. The director of the FBI has a report for us that I can't wait to hear. Mr. Director?"

"Thank you, Mr. President. Good morning, everyone. Yesterday I received a report form one of my field agents involved in a confidential investigation that I believe will seriously impact national security, probably forever."

He recounted everything from Samuels' report, including crime statistics, the specialties of those missing, the satellite recon efforts, to the telomeres of the cells in the antigravity aircraft wreckage.

Pausing to look around the table, the director concluded quietly, "It is my belief, based on the kind and number of people missing, the length of time they have managed to remain hidden, the test results on the pilot's remains, and the data received from the Navy's gravity detection project in the Southwest, that we are looking for a group of black separatists who have no intention of letting us know where they are, what they're doing or what their goals are until they're ready to do so. And, after being successfully dug in for forty years, they're going to be a bitch to dig out."

The president looked around and said, "There's one other thing. One of the members of the commission studying the issues surrounding the near passage of the asteroid, in fact its discoverer Norma Lancaster, offered a hypothesis that is quite disturbing. She speculated that the reason behind the two changes in course of her rock might be someone applying gravitational pressure to guide its course. If this is so, then we are looking at a level of threat that is literally impossible to defend against. By the way, for those of you who may have forgotten, Ms. Lancaster herself is African American, just in case anyone wants to inject some additional drama to worry about in time for the next meeting."

Everyone was silent. Looking around the room, President Bender said quietly, "So, gentlemen. Where do we go from here? I've been told that all of the black agents of the White House Secret Service detail turned in their sidearms and have absented themselves from the premises. My own personal agent led them out and recused them from the detail because they felt we wouldn't trust them because of the color of their skin. Is *this* what we have come to? If so, I won't stand for it.

"How long do you think it's going to take before this gets out?" Looking over to Treasury, President Bender said, "I want those agents back on post before this meeting is over, and I want them to meet me in the Oval Office so I can apologize to them personally for the behavior they fell victim to."

He looked directly at Simon as he finished and caught the replacement agent speaking quietly into his mic out of the corner of his eye.

"I want to know what these people want and what their agenda is just as much as anybody, but I'm not willing to start a race war in the process. So far, the people we are looking for have only managed to show themselves in the Middle East, nowhere around the US at all. They may not even be within our borders," said President Bender.

The Chairman of the JCS interjected, "Why operate over there? What would they be doing in the region, and what really caused their aircraft to be shot down? Anyone who can manipulate gravity can surely avoid detection from radar, what was going on with that aircraft? We need to understand all of these questions to best assess what we're up against."

Simon cleared his throat and spoke next.

"As I see it we have a couple of issues to develop strategies for. The first is, what is the best way to go about locating these people, if in fact they exist? The second issue is, how does the makeup of this group affect the administration's and the nation's policies in the near term?"

"I am not going to have a Japanese internment-like debacle because of this. We're talking about twelve percent of the population here, one in eight. We can't treat them all as suspects. Despite the fact that everyone in this room is white, I expect you all to operate with the utmost sensitivity. I don't want a repeat of what happened with the detail in the rest of the government, or the general population."

"Mr. President, what if this group has agents who they report back to on what we're doing? How do you propose we deal with that possibility?" asked CIA.

"You know what, boys, that's your problem. Deal with it. Now is there anything else?" Looking over to the director of the FBI, the President asked, "What kind of help do you need in locating these people?"

"Mr. President, I'll coordinate with the CIA on some help in satellite tasking. I also have a possible material witness to the latest disappearance down in Atlanta. We're working that angle now, but I don't think we need any help yet."

Masters then said, "I would like to recommend we begin to assess the need to begin moving African Americans out of critical positions in this investigation. I don't think the question of there being moles inside the government should be overlooked."

"Simon, what in hell makes you think that a group like this, a group of people who obviously don't want any contact with their former lives, would leave anyone behind, especially in some dead-end job in government?" President Bender asked.

"Mr. President, that's not the idea. The purpose of this precautionary measure is to make damn sure that whatever we plan is not prematurely exposed to a possible enemy, or to the press. I'm not concerned with what the American public thinks. The fact is we have a known group that has demonstrated their technological and, according to the FBI lab, their biological superiority over the best this country has to offer, including, I might add, all of our secret projects. I for one do not want to count on their benign nature to keep them from becoming major players in the balance of power around the world. What if they align themselves with someone potentially hostile to the interests of the United States? If they're operating in the Middle East what's to prevent them from helping out an interest against Israel? What then?

"I'm not willing to see this administration go down in flames because we counted on this group's benevolence or neutrality and ignored the potential harm. Mr. President, we have to make serious plans right now, and whether we like or dislike the things we put in place, we must always remember we're working for the common good of this country. We have a obligation and a duty to keep it secure."

Everyone waited to see if President Bender was going to respond to Simon's remarks.

The director of the National Security Agency spoke up. "Is there anything we can do to assist your investigation?" he asked the FBI. "Is there any electronic coverage that we can put in place that might help your folks out?"

"That's a good thought. Let me find out what kind of computer communications or Internet usage the subject is currently using. Maybe if you can siphon off the subject's e-mail and any real-time sessions they might engage in, we might get some kind of a clue. I'll get with you on that later," said FBI.

"If they're using standard software we can drop right into their computer when they're online, they'll never know we're there," added NSA.

"Can you strip the hard drive remotely?" FBI asked.

"Yes we can, but if they're using a modem the process would take forever. We're better off skimming off a copy of the entire system and picking through the files and looking at the ones we're interested in."

Nodding, the head of the FBI said, "Good, we'll get you the information by this evening."

President Bender asked, "Is there anything else we need to look at?"

"I think that Churchill's threat team should get together under wraps as soon as possible. I want to add representatives of the armed forces and one member each from FBI, CIA and NSA," said Simon.

"Fine, make it happen. Anything else?"

"Sir, I'm sorry if it seems like I'm beating a dead horse but what about the black members of the threat team, those stationed at the Navy's project in Shelter Fourteen and those in the security forces posted topside at the Southwest site?" asked Masters.

"God damn it, Simon! Put that shit on ice for a minute, will you? Look, everyone go back and put whatever we need into place, *and* give the racial aspect of this problem some serious thought. I want everyone back here this afternoon at . . ." President Bender looked at Masters.

"Five-thirty," Masters answered.

"Five-thirty it is. I want each of you to have an action plan, and a full set of recommendations for review. Is there anyone else who should be included this afternoon?" Bender asked.

The Chairman of the Joint Chiefs, who until now had been uncharacteristically silent, cleared his throat and said, "Do you consider the United States to be confronted by an imminent threat, Mr. President? And if so, what kind of military response do you wish the armed forces to formulate given that we have no identifiable target, no theater of operations and no central authority?"

Shaking his head, Bender answered, "General, as of now we have no concrete facts to go on or targets of opportunity we can identify. Hell, we don't even know if they are operating here or abroad. At this time I want no change in our defense condition, nothing that would tip our hand to anyone here or even to our allies. Right now this is at the investigation phase and will stay that way until further notice. Is that understood?"

"Yes, sir."

"Good, is there anything else, gentlemen?" Bender asked.

"Sir. I think it would be appropriate to have Diane Churchill here, her group is going to have the lead on developing some of the contingencies we're going to want to put in place," said the FBI.

"I'll see to it. Anyone else?"

CIA spoke up and said, "I'm going to put together a plan that assumes the people we're looking for are not operating within our borders, and based on that assumption, the best way to search them out. Sir, what about our allies? Do we share this with them yet?"

"No. It's bad enough that the whole Secret Service knows it already." Looking over at Agent Bishop's replacement he asked, "Are the rest of the detail back on site?"

Cutting a glance over to Treasury and getting a nod, the agent said, "Yes, sir. They're just waiting for the meeting to break up."

"Good, I want them waiting for me in the Oval Office *before* I get there. And if I catch anyone here making that kind of mistake again, I'm definitely in the mood to make an example of them. Does everyone understand my position on this?"

Seeing everyone nod, Bender said, "Good, now let's get out of here, I've got some fences to mend." He immediately left the conference room with Masters and Bishop's replacement in tow.

Stopping just outside the side door to the Oval Office, Bender turned to Masters and pointedly said, "Why don't you wait in your office, Simon. I'll call you when I'm finished."

"Very well, Mr. President." Without a backward glance the chief of staff left.

Opening the door, but not entering the office, Bishop's replacement said very softly, "Thank you, Mr. President. I'll wait outside for you to finish," and stuck out his hand. Bender took it and nodded his thanks before he entered the office.

All nine of the Special Agents stood against the fireplace, well away from the two entrances to the office. The president immediately said, "Ladies and gentlemen, please be seated."

Looking at each other, the members of the detail were unsure how to react.

"I mean it. Please, sit," Bender repeated. "First of all, I want all of you to know that I had nothing to do with this shameful incident, and as long as I'm here it will never happen again. Not one of you have done anything to merit any lack of trust in your commitment to your duties here. I am personally apologizing for any impression that anyone may have conveyed to any of you that the White House – that *I* – don't have complete confidence in each and every one of you.

"What happened was a misunderstanding. Masters overreacted. The only thing I can say in his defense is that he is responsible for helping me with every facet of the presidency. It's not pleasant, but it is a continued reality that has to be attended to almost as much as everything else that goes on here.

"Sam, what you and the rest of you did was in the highest tradition of the Secret Service, and I want all of you to know that I understand *what* you did, and *why* you did it. I can't say enough about your integrity and commitment."

Agent Bishop stood up and said, "Mr. President, we understand the chief's concerns. We all know what the job entails, some of it even better than you do because it's our job to keep you from knowing or worrying about it. We also understand how Washington works. We have to in order to do the best possible job of protecting you and your family. If it becomes necessary for us to be reassigned, we understand, sir."

"Sam, if that becomes a necessity then it's my feeling that the battle is lost. I don't want to be the president of a country that puts anyone in that position. Have you all had your sidearms returned?" Bender asked.

"No sir. They offered them to us when we came back, but we wanted to see what you had to say before we accepted them," Sam answered.

"Well how in the hell are you going to protect me and my family if some KKK/Nazi/skinhead nut bursts in here and tries to stab me in the heart with a burning cross?" Bender asked, actually getting a few chuckles at his weak attempt to lighten the mood.

"Very well, sir. We'll get right on it."

The agents got to their feet and were surprised when the president came over and shook their hands, apologizing to each and every one of them.

When he led them to the door and opened it to let them out, Bender was pleased to see that all of their sidearms were piled on his secretary's desk, and that the three white agents stationed outside his office were grinning from ear to ear, the detail's pride and honor restored.

Bender waited until Agent Bishop had replaced his sidearm and taken his accustomed place outside the office door. He then closed the door, motioning the Secretary of the Treasury to the couch.

"Mr. Secretary, I don't want a repeat of this incident to ever happen again. Is that understood?" he said when they were seated. "And I damn sure better not hear about it from anyone out in the street."

"Yes, Mr. President. But it was the agents themselves who took it upon themselves to leave the detail. Daniels tried to stop them but they wouldn't listen."

"Yes, I know, but they never should have been put in the position in the first place. If you were one of them what would you have done? You fix things with your people on your side, I'm going to have a talk with Simon about his behavior. Make sure that your people know that I'm serious about them having my complete trust.

"Changing the subject here for a minute let me ask you this, how much money would you think it would take for a group of a couple of thousand people to completely outfit the best research facility in the world, conceal it from scrutiny and provide for their living needs? Aren't we talking about a substantial amount of money just to get the equipment to set something like that up? Could we possibly get a trace on their whereabouts by looking into unusual lab equipment purchases over the last few decades?" asked Bender.

"That's a good idea, Mr. President. Let me make some calls, that could be a good avenue to help begin tracking these people down."

"Good. Bring anything you think of back here this afternoon."

"I will, sir."

As the secretary exited the Oval Office, President Bender realized, like it or not, he was going to have to strike a compromise with his chief of staff. Masters was right in thinking that the administration had to have in place *all* of the pieces of their strategy for dealing with the potential firestorm a racially divided nation was going to ignite. He crossed the office and sat down at his desk. President Bender put in the call to Simon's office and asked him in to discuss the distasteful issues they were going to face in the upcoming weeks, planning to step on him hard so that another debacle like the Secret Service flap never happened again.

Time has come today,
Young hearts can go their way,
Can't put off another day,
I don't care what others say,
They say we don't listen anyway,
Time has come today, hey.

Time Has Come Today

Written by Joe & Willie Chambers, performed by the Chambers Brothers

CHAPTER 27

THE FBI NAMED the investigation Operation Tenacity. Their efforts were divided between two main groups. The first was concerned with finding the location of the people in question; the second investigative team was focusing on trying to determine the scientific and military capabilities of that same group.

Like any investigation, its start was full of furious activity getting the assets in place, developing the investigative team's organizational structure and setting up the intelligence data collection methods.

The FBI was the lead agency in the investigation and tasked with the coordination of the data collection effort, and by secret presidential decree, the issue of race, vis-a-vis who was to be excluded from the investigative effort. President Bender decreed that until turning up evidence to the contrary, no African American in any of the investigative agencies was to be excluded, reassigned or dismissed under any pretext. Instead, each agency was to implement a tell-me-three-times means of verification. Information that was developed as a result of their efforts was to be independently confirmed by two additional sources before being added to the massive database.

Added to the total of over a billion dollars, the cost of the increased military defense posture after Dr. Harris' discovery was the cost of including every other law enforcement and security agency, branch of the military and research facility in Operation Tenacity, with no end to the spending in sight.

Diane Churchill put the finishing touches in compiling the members of the science analysis team. President Bender had them posted at Shelter Fourteen where Dr. Harris' detector project was housed. Their isolation was mandated for two reasons. The first was a matter of secrecy and security; the second was to put them right where they could observe firsthand any data gleaned from the detection of any additional antigravity aircraft. The team was composed of a group of leading scientists, Army engineers, an Air Force flight instructor, and two special agents from the FBI and CIA, respectively. Thrown into the mix were Commander Ames, Dr. Harris and Alan Richards.

Alan was speechless when he happened upon Norma lugging her bags to the room she had been assigned, but he quickly managed to get over it, gave a whoop, ran down the corridor, picked her up and spun around in circles.

"Put me down, you reprobate! I don't want the other guys here to think I'm already spoken for," she said, laughing in joy at seeing her lab mate after so many weeks.

He let her down and gave her a lung-crushing hug. He held her out at arm's length and said, "Hmm, what happened? I was sure by now all the worldwide attention would have at least doubled the size of your head."

"It's good to see you too. Hey, nice digs. Do we get issued a machine gun once we get checked in?" she asked.

"I know what you mean. But don't worry, the Army guys are pretty cool. Except for the stuff they *have* to do, like guard duty and checking IDs, they're pretty much just like regular people. Why didn't you tell me you were coming here? Come to think of it, why the hell are you here? You slumming or something?"

"The short answer is I'm on the presidential commission studying my asteroid and the thing you and your Dr. Harris discovered," she said quietly, making sure no one was eavesdropping.

Alan said, "Here, let me help you get your stuff to your room. You have your ID card? Just swipe it here and it unlocks the door."

Alan closed the door and said, "We had to go to Washington, to the Pentagon. You should have seen the uproar Dr. Harris' data caused."

"So how are things down here? That ride down was sure a bite in the ass. Nothing like having a half-hour ride to hell to make you realize just how isolated you are from the real world. What's the food like? Although given the way you eat you probably haven't given it much thought," Norma said.

"Au contraire, my newly arrived compadre. The food is great, as is the entertainment."

"Is that so? Come over here and let me see the callouses on your right hand. Rubbed yourself raw yet, or have you found suitable male companionship?" Norma asked.

"Very funny. For your information, there's about twenty-five women stationed down here in my age group," Alan said with a sniff.

"Is that so? And how many have given you the time of day?"

"Not counting you . . . um, none. They're all pretty much spoken for, or if they're in the Army they don't want to risk doing something that would get them gigged or discharged. To be honest, I haven't really had the time to miss women much. The stuff they have me working on is phenomenal, and next to you, Dr. Harris is just about the easiest person I've ever worked with. Hey, what's happening in the clean world back home? I don't really get to see the news at all. Well, sometimes I catch WGN on cable."

"Chicago's very own, eh? Chicago is the same, I checked your apartment before I left, nothing's changed. Angela and Jesse are the same, although Angela's getting stale because she hasn't been able to sharpen her wit on you for a while. My asteroid has changed course twice . . ."

"What? How? Did something deflect it off course?" Alan asked.

"Do they listen in on us in our rooms here?" Norma asked.

"Not that I know of, if they do no one's said so."

Over the next hour the two caught up on what each had been doing since Alan left Chicago. After a while, Alan suggested Norma get her things squared away and suggested they eat dinner together.

Alan said, "I'll be back at five-thirty."

"See you then."

Norma turned to putting her clothes away.

Alan stopped by to escort her to the commissary. When they arrived, their entrance caused a slight buzz, mostly because she was new to the small community and everyone was naturally curious. However, when she *was* recognized, several of the naval engineers actually got up and insisted she join them at their table, not taking no for an answer.

When she made her way to their table, the engineers let her sit down and then introduced themselves. Alan gave them an overview of Norma's project and when they couldn't wait any longer, the engineers questioned her on the details of her system and the thinking behind her system design.

Raising a questioning eyebrow toward Alan, Norma just got a shrug in reply. She thought she was being accosted because of her sex, so she was surprised to find that they really were interested in the scope and details of her work. When she described the image processing portion of her system. Alan could see that they shared a real kinship, the same kind he had developed a few weeks ago. The whole table was filled with geeks. Norma saw that her time underground could add some new insights to her project and might even improve her overall design. It didn't hurt their enthusiasm that she was probably the prettiest woman posted underground.

The discussion looked like it would go on for hours until Alan reminded them he and Norma had to attend an orientation meeting in a few minutes. The engineers sent them on their way, extracting a promise from Norma to show them as much of her project as she could.

"They seem like a pretty cool bunch of guys," Norma observed.

"Here we are," Alan said, pulling open one of a set of double doors.

Norma was surprised to see a room that was no different than one of the larger lecture halls of the university. Seats stretched left and right, and the screen was actually larger than those at the bigger multiplexes where theater owners tried to cram ten screens in a building really only big enough for three or four.

The seats were about a quarter full. Most of the occupants clustered near the front. Alan looked around to see how many of those already there were familiar and saw only a handful. A few minutes after seven o'clock, an attractive woman in her forties came out and took her place behind the podium.

"Good evening, ladies and gentlemen, my name is Diane Churchill, I am the president's science advisor and the administration liaison to this committee. I would like to extend an official welcome to Shelter Fourteen and hope that all of you new to the facility were able to get settled in reasonably easily.

"I would like to begin by thanking all you again for consenting to put your lives on hold to come here and serve on this commission. We will do everything we can to ensure your time down here is as small a hardship as possible. If there are any special needs you might have living here I will introduce you to those who will be more than happy to help accommodate you.

"Now if I may, I would like to begin this briefing. Many of you know pieces of the overall picture I'm going to present and I ask that you bear with me. Not everyone knows the whole story and I ask that any questions be held until my initial presentation is finished."

She began to recount every detail known about Norma's asteroid and the project Dr. Harris was working on. She also included the details about the aircraft shot down in Iraq as well as the secret mission that recovered the samples from the foreign laboratory.

She had to bring the audience to quiet more than a few times when a particular item she presented triggered comment or discussion; the information about the presumed pilot's cellular anomalies drew the loudest outburst. Only the promised question and answer session when she concluded her presentation brought a measure of quiet to the crowd and minimized the crosstalk between commission members.

When the questions began to wind down, Diane introduced Commander Ames and Dr. Harris to the crowd. It wasn't until she made Norma stand up to be introduced that the crowd applauded like she was a rock star, so much so that the blush of embarrassment on her face easily showed, to the audience's delight.

"Everybody, since we've all had quite a day of travel, I'd like to call it a night after we finish here. So, are there any questions you might have? Yes, you there.

And everyone who has something to say, would you please stand up and introduce yourself to everyone here before you ask your question? Go ahead."

"David Blain from the Jet Propulsion Labs. Ms. Churchill, how certain is anyone that these course changes by the asteroid are due to deliberate means?"

"Dr. Blain, we're not sure at all. Ms. Lancaster herself speculated that manipulating local gravity fits the circumstance that your people outlined in their analysis of the flight characteristics. I believe that the principle of Occam's razor might certainly apply here, that the simplest explanation is probably the most likely. If you have any other scenario that might apply, this is the group charged with developing theory and response. Anyone else? Yes?"

"Hi, I'm Dr. Susan Roscoe, Massachusetts Institute of Technology. As an African American, will my participation be compromised in any way given the FBI's assertion that the people in control of these advanced technologies are also black? Frankly, I get enough of that bullshit at home in Boston and I'd just as soon as skip it here and go home if that's to be the case."

"Dr. Roscoe, if you see anything like that down here, you may call me personally and I will have the offender escorted directly to prison for treason against the United States of America."

The crowd audibly gasped at Diane's promise. They immediately quieted when she continued. "I can't express strongly enough how little tolerance I, and the President of the United States, have for that kind of crap. Do I make myself clear to everyone here? Due process is suspended as far as racial discrimination is concerned down here. And for the record let me ask, is there anyone here who thinks that they cannot conduct themself in an adult manner in matters concerning race? Don't be shy. No one? Good. From here on out all of you are on record as having affirmed that you will not be bringing any racist baggage to this commission."

Diane paused and looked down at her notes and then continued, "Before we get bogged down in a lot of things we're going to cover in the morning sessions, let me suggest that everyone take the rest of the night off, get to know the complex here and let's get started in the morning. Tomorrow's session will let everyone meet each other and begin drawing up preliminary work groups. I will be on site until tomorrow afternoon just in case we've overlooked anything that might be needed.

"You are all free to get together tonight and get to know one another if you've got the energy. I would like to ask that you be somewhat careful what you say to people down here not on the commission, even the soldiers and engineers. Otherwise you are free to go."

Alan looked at Norma and shrugged his shoulders. "What do you want to do? I'm open, Dr. Harris said that we'd be free tonight."

"I don't know. What do you think about that black separatist bullshit?" Norma asked.

"I don't know what to think. And what's all that about them being hidden for forty years? If they were hidden that long how do they know anything about them now? Wait a minute, you're black! I can't discuss this with you!" Alan said, with a shit-eating grin on his face.

"Just how do you feel about military-style prison, pretty boy? All kidding aside though, they sound pretty serious. I don't think this is one of those bullshit sociology experiments where they test in-group/out-group dynamics."

"I don't think so either. Hey, quick, get up. I want to introduce you to Dr. Harris before he leaves."

Jumping to his feet, Alan led the charge over to Dr, Harris, who was shaking hands with Dr. Milton and Diane Churchill. Diane said to Norma with a grin, "So, is this your Alan Richards, who you tried so hard to get rid of back in Chicago, Norma?"

"Yes, it is. Alan, I'd like to introduce you to Diane Churchill, the president's science advisor, and this is Dr. Paul Milton, you've already heard all about him."

"All lies, young man, I assure you, and call me Paul," said Dr. Milton, shaking Alan's hand.

"Nice to meet you as well, Mr. Richards. The president is very impressed with your contribution to Dr. Harris' project," Diane said.

Alan blushed and answered, "I just do what little I can to help. Oh yeah, Norma, this is Dr. Martin Harris."

"Ms. Lancaster, I've been looking forward to meeting you for quite some time, both for your scientific accomplishments and your restraint in not strangling Alan here. The way he describes his work at the U of C he must have been quite an handful."

"Alan's not so bad. Boys will be boys, and all that."

Diane asked the group, "Is there any reason why we can't all grab a seat in the commissary and get some refreshments while we get to know everyone?" Seeing everyone nod their heads, she then said, "Dr. Harris, if you would lead the way."

They chose a table out of the way and Diane started off by saying, "Look at all of you. You four are probably the root cause of everything that's brought the government to appoint this commission." They looked at each other in various degrees of wonder.

"That's right. Dr. Milton was responsible for Norma getting her grant. Norma's system was the first to spot the incoming piece of rock. And Dr. Harris here developed the means of measuring gravity that now seems to have been the right invention at just the right time. And according to Dr. Harris, Alan's streamlined software was responsible for us determining that the amplitude of the effect was negative instead of positive. Who would have thunk it?"

"Ms. Churchill, are you suggesting that you and/or the president are responsible for getting us all together down here?" Norma asked.

"I'm just a bureaucrat, it's all of you that I'm in awe of. Yes, Norma, besides having proven your brains, the president and I thought if you have the time, and the interest, you would like to see this through from start to finish."

"It's good to be the king!" Alan said, breaking up everyone at the table.

Paul then asked Martin, "When can we get a look at this detector you've built? It's not classified, is it?"

"No, not really, but I would ask that you look at it through the glass outside of the room, we've got wires and equipment strewn all over. I don't want anyone to get hurt," answered Martin.

"That would be fine. I'm fascinated that it's able to measure something like gravity in the first place. How'd you come up with the design?"

"Let me explain tomorrow when I take you over there. Did you know the Navy authorized building a second one?" Martin asked.

"No kidding. Is it for backup?"

"We're going to use them in tandem."

Norma asked, "Like the radiotelescopes?"

"Exactly. With Alan's refinements to the software we should be able to detect the locus of a gravitational event down to about two meters in all three dimensions," Martin said.

"That's great, how did you get the thing funded in the first place?" Paul asked.

"Can I get back to you on that? I'm not sure how much of that part I can discuss."

"No problem. I understand," answered Paul.

Diane then said, "Let me get to why I suggested we all get together before tomorrow's session. Along with Commander Ames, who I had hoped might be along by now, I would like to ask the four of you to be my eyes and ears down here. Not to spy on anyone or anything like that, but more toward trying to see where things might be getting off track or if there's something I've overlooked like people with certain specialties or expertise, that sort of thing. I'm not going to be able to be here very much. I'll mostly be in touch by phone or video conference."

"Diane, I'm sure I speak for the rest when I say we'd be happy to help you out keeping an eye on things. Personally, I want the deliverables from this commission to give you and the administration the tools necessary to help the nation through whatever it's going to face," said Milton.

Looking over at Norma before he spoke, Martin said, "I just hope there's no backlash because of what you said about African Americans being responsible for the manufacture of the antigravity craft."

"I meant every word I said. Norma, if you see any sign of that kind of behavior down here I want to know about it, is that understood? President Bender also ordered Commander Ames to keep his eye out too, both as an officer and as an African American sensitive to the possible issues ahead of you." Diane said.

Nodding her head, Norma answered, "I'll keep an eye out. I haven't been dumped on as much as maybe someone like Dr. Roscoe, but I've seen my share. It'll be nice not to have to deal with it for a change."

Just then, Commander Ames wended his way over and pulled up a chair. Diane introduced him to Paul and Norma and gave him a thumbnail sketch of the conversation so far. When he was brought up to date Ames said, "I've been looking forward to working with the entire group, but I especially wanted to meet you, Norma. The system that discovered your asteroid sounded remarkable when Alan described it. He's gathered quite a fan club among my engineers, they can't wait to pick your brain. But I'm not really going out on a limb when I say your beauty might also have something to do with it."

"Better watch out for this one, Norma, he's probably got quite the reputation back in Washington," Diane warned. "Getting back to the subject at hand. What the president and I want is for the commission to develop contingency plans devoid of political baggage, contingencies that don't pander to either political party, the money that backs them, or any other influence group or lobbyists. We want well-conceived plans that are based on irrefutable science and nonpartisan decisions on what course to take.

"President Bender hasn't shared this goal with anyone in the cabinet, nor directly with the military. I've decided to trust the five of you with his true mission because I want your complete cooperation and need your help doing this right. You don't have to share this with the rest of the group. As a matter of fact it will probably be better if you don't. Commander, can I count on you to keep undue military influences away from the commission? You've had almost a week to think it over, I need your answer now."

Commander Ames replied almost immediately, "As long as what is required does not violate my oath of service and is not a clear violation of the law, I can agree to your terms."

Visibly relieved, Diane continued. "Good. What I would like for all of you to do over the next week is to get to know each other as well as possible. In the final analysis you five are the true leadership of this commission and it's no exaggeration to say that the hopes and safety of an entire nation rests on your shoulders."

Looking at her watch, Diane drained her coffee and announced, "Now, if you'll excuse me, I have to go and make some phone calls before I turn in, I'll see all of you in the morning."

Halfway across the country at the Pentagon, the Chairman of the Joint Chiefs was meeting in closed session with the heads of the combined services.

"Gentlemen, the purpose of this meeting is to draft a plan of action designed to infiltrate a community of about two thousand individuals and completely denature any form of resistance. The objective has strategic military value in the form of scientific knowledge, materials and principles that are unavailable to us at this time. This proposed strike team must go in, pacify the citizens, capture and hold the sources of their technology, probably in the form of some sort of lab or fabrication facility. It is essential that everything they have be taken intact, along with their top people who can explain whatever our boys in development need to know."

The commandant of the Marines said, "Do we have any idea whether or not the objective is within US borders, or are we looking at having to plan an assault overseas?"

"So far, the FBI is concentrating their efforts in remote locations in the lower forty-eight states. The aircraft was shot down in the Middle East. Right now there's no good intel on where they may actually be based."

The CJCS pulled out a reduced map of the US. "These areas here have been covered by the joint FBI/CIA analysis team working from satellite photos and infrared scans. If what we're looking for is an underground or underwater installation we may never find it unless we manage to get some kind of inside information."

"Sir, when the president greenlighted the planning for this operation . . ." began Army.

"Let me make something clear to all of you. President Bender has not approved any op plan yet. What we're doing here tonight is preplanning to get a jump on the situation. I don't want to have us deployed at the last second without the best possible preparations in place. Think of it as a planning exercise until we actually get the green light.

"Now, due to the sensitive nature of the makeup of the group we seek, we have a serious need to keep this planning away from the African American members of your staff. We especially don't need any blacks on the strike force. I don't want to have to face the issue of anyone having divided loyalties," said the CJCS.

At this revelation everyone in the room froze. Without looking at each other, no one seemed willing to break the silence.

Finally Army spoke up. "But sir, how do you reasonably expect us to plan an operation like that? Concealing it from rank and file members of our senior staff, putting together and training a strike force with blacks excluded is not going to be easy to accomplish. Mr. Chairman, how do you propose we do this?"

"Look, I didn't ask for the situation to play out this way, but this is how it's going to be," the CJCS responded. "I want preliminary action plans from each of you, even Navy, on the framework of a pacification plan and estimated personnel for a strike group. The racial requirement stands, gentlemen. Is that going to be a problem for any of you?" Pausing to look at each officer, the chairman continued. "Good, we'll get together at the end of the week.

"Oh yes, one more thing. The Air Force spy satellite that's scheduled for next week's shuttle launch may be bumped for an instrument package for rendezvous with the asteroid. I want an update from NASA on rescheduling the spy satellite's deployment as soon as possible. We'll all meet back here Friday afternoon, I expect everyone to have something substantial by then. Dismissed, gentlemen."

And so it begins, thought the chairman, as they all filed out of the office. He was old school, he came up through the big one, World War Two, then Korea and Vietnam. The son of Polish immigrants who had moved to America shortly after his birth, he still remembered the segregation of the troops in WWII, and like it or not the chairman advanced through the ranks under officers who adamantly believed that President Roosevelt had moved too quickly in pushing to integrate the troops. Having grown up in Tennessee, where his immigrant father found mechanical work in a manufacturing plant, he had seen first hand how his contemporaries maintained that the Negroes were just not prepared for the rigors of war, especially serving as officers.

His induction into the Army at the age of seventeen occurred at a time when basic training was completely segregated. Having been born outside the US, he was indistinguishable from those with generations of prejudice fueling their perspectives. The only Negroes stationed at the base were in the kitchen or on the custodial staff. They certainly were not holding noncommissioned officer rank or higher there, or anywhere else except the segregated bases where Negroes were trained away from their white peers.

It was a long time before the upper military echelons had grudgingly admitted that the Negro's time had come. It wasn't that they were overtly racist, especially given the universally acknowledged accomplishments of such military notables as Colin Powell. General Kaminski had acquired his views from the constant exposure to the values of the South, and to a lesser extent, the attitudes of his parents. Their view of the Negro in America came out of newspapers.

Facing the fact that a black separatist group might have access to this obviously advanced technology, and that the members of the target group all had better-than-average qualifications and personal achievements, was a stretch for the general to believe, even now. Unfortunately, he couldn't quite bring himself to believe that there wasn't someone else behind them, someone white, or worse yet, someone from another country using African Americans to forward their own agenda. With, or without the blessing of the Commander in Chief General Isaac Kaminski was preparing to go to war and he was willing to do anything to protect his family's adopted country from any invader, foreign or *colored* domestic.

INTERMEZZO

THINGS WERE BEGINNING to ramp up quickly at NASA and all its far-flung associated space exploration partners. The Air Force had donated one of their older reconnaissance satellite prototypes to NASA to modify for the purpose of a fly-by rendezvous with the Lancaster asteroid. JPL's latest and greatest figures were dissected and calculated. A supplementary fuel supply for the maneuvering rockets was attached to the probe to provide the extreme thrust needed to match speed with the asteroid as it sped by.

The satellite would undergo final assembly in orbit. Astronauts would attach the massive fuel tanks being modified in Houston. NASA was quickly preparing a shuttle crew for the mission. The final assembly would be completed at the International Space Station; the Russians would get the auxiliary fuel tanks for the satellite into orbit using one of their own unmanned launch vehicles. It would rendezvous with the space station prior to the arrival of the satellite being carried aloft by NASA shuttle.

The satellite was outfitted with an upgraded digital imaging system to enable it to take super-high-resolution pictures, an infrared camera to look at the heat signature of every inch of the rock to help determine its mineral and chemical composition, a spectrographic scanner and a high-powered projectile system to attempt to hit the asteroid with a metal bullet to find out even more about its origin. Unspoken by NASA was the portion of the mission profile concerning the attempted location of any outside agency that could account for the changes in direction the asteroid had taken to date.

Both NASA and JPL were working on the exacting calculations the rendezvous called for. This in itself was causing great excitement because the figures showed the asteroid, in addition to passing closer than two hundred fifty thousand miles of earth, looked like it had a fifty-fifty chance of colliding with the moon. This tidbit alone was fuel for a great deal of excitement within a number of different branches of science, including astrophysics and geology.

If the Lancaster asteroid did impact the moon, scientists would be in a position to see something that hadn't been observed in modern times: the formation of a new crater. With the moon always showing the same face to the earth, there had been scant opportunity for a large inbound bogey to pass close enough to the earth to miss and yet impact the moon's face.

The attendant publicity had created an instant demand for Norma to make the media circuit once again. She temporarily had to leave the day-to-day sessions of the commission to make the rounds of the morning news shows, the cable news outlets and several press conferences. This time she had more cachet than the last junket. Now she was a Special Presidential Commission member, giving interviewers a wider range of questions to ask, including those about meeting the president and the commission's findings.

She became an apostle for the entire scientific community. She was pretty, bright, and handled herself well. President Bender's couldn't be happier having her on point, selling his administration's plans to the American public.

She still looked back at her previous life with a measure of regret. She missed just working on her grant and having some sort of life of her own, and even though she wouldn't admit it to herself, she was lonely.

About halfway through her media junket, Norma received word that NASA had calculated her asteroid had an almost eighty percent chance it would impact the moon. When the word hit the press the flurry was unbelievable. Her demand, already high, became astronomical.

Her own excitement over the possibility of a collision was infectious. Although upon reflection, realizing that her asteroid was about to land instead of flying through the heavens in perpetuity left her with a measure of sadness and impending loss.

Based on the latest orbital figures on the future locations of earth and moon, and the refinement of the projected passage of the asteroid, NASA began to retask the satellite they were sending up for orbit around the moon, a much simpler trip to plan and program. The additional fuel that the Russians were sending up would allow the probe to remain in orbit around the moon for years if necessary, and to make numerous orbital and attitude adjustments. The extra delta-v would give NASA the opportunity to further map and study the moon not available to them since the close of the Apollo program.

In Utah, Dr. Harris' research group had seemingly accomplished the impossible. The second detector had been completed in record time and all of the improvements they had installed on the newer system had been replicated on his original system as soon as detector two was operational. They should be able to resolve the location of gravitational anomalies within a six–to ten-foot sphere, and several million miles from the earth.

A few of the naval team were informed that they were to continue on detached duty at the shelter for the duration to help with ad hoc improvements to the system and to maintain a military presence in support of the Army contingent already stationed there.

The naval engineers and electronics experts were frequently invited to participate in some of the commission's strategy sessions. Commander Ames had integrated them into the threat team and the technical projections group smoothly, without the usual rancor that traditionally existed between the more creative, liberal science community and the military. It didn't hurt the proceedings that the news was full of interviews of their most famous team member on the media circuit.

The personnel who manned Martin's detector around the clock were under orders to instantly inform the Pentagon of any new gravitational anomalies. The control room for Martin's detector was directly wired to the NORAD base in Colorado Springs and to the situation rooms at the Pentagon and White House, making it an integral part of the nation's first line of defense.

At the White House, President Bender was caught up in the contingency planning the military was undertaking at the Chairman of the Joint Chief's direction. More than once he was called upon to mediate between seemingly well-meaning conservatives who wanted to restrict the responsibilities of members of the government based on racial profiling of the ugliest kind. Already, word of proposed profiling was leaking out of the highest offices of the government to some of the better connected members of the Washington press corps. President Bender knew it was only a matter of time before he was directly confronted by the question of the administration's policies in public.

He found himself bouncing ideas off of Agent Bishop more and more often in an attempt to understand the unique perspective this group might have on any formal relationship with the US government. The President found Agent Bishop's answers and advice to be thoughtful and insightful. He was beginning to see America through the eyes of a black man.

Bascomb had requested a temporary transfer from the Middle East Intelligence Group to become the liaison with the search team at the FBI, helping them locate and download the satellite photos they requested in their search for the hundreds of missing blacks who were, in fact, still alive. Bobby was one of the few intelligence officers who knew the racial makeup of the group the FBI sought, and he appreciated the delicacy of the domestic investigation and the firestorm of controversy the hidden colony was sure to ignite.

Bascomb had taken it on his own to examine the more remote locations of the globe, searching for the same kinds of indications the FBI sought within US borders. He searched hundreds of remote islands, the extreme northern and southern latitudes and the remote expanses of uncharted jungle for signs of habitation that just didn't fit.

An objective observer would conclude that all of America's security services were chasing their tails. There was no clue to the whereabouts of those they sought; evidence of the group's actual existence was still largely circumstantial. There was no evidence of the commission of any crime by the missing. And yet, they were the subject of the largest collective law enforcement manhunt in the history of modern civilization.

Dance with me, come on dance with me baby
Dance with me, come on dance with me baby
Dance with me, come on dance with me baby
Dance with me, come on dance with me baby
I want you,
And you want me,
So why don't we,
Get together after the dance
After the Dance
Written by Marvin Gaye and Leon Ware, performed by Marvin Gaye

CHAPTER 28

A FTER THREE STRAIGHT weeks of school-related travel, Sydney came home to a quiet, slightly musty-smelling house. She had a lightly browned lawn in need of some serious attention and a huge pile of mail on the floor inside the door waiting for her. Sydney opened an unmarked envelope and was pleasantly surprised to find it was from John. The card simply said, "Because I was thinking of you, John."

Sydney thought about the guileless nature of this man. John was obviously a good cop.

He seemed very dedicated to his work. His feelings for her appeared uncomplicated and straightforward. He was a man of deep feeling, and a small part of her felt guilty for teasing him so often, but it was only in response to *his* more serious nature.

Her feelings for John were far more complicated and she hadn't managed to resolve them. *This* man was so unexpectedly right for her and had managed to understand and accept her as she was. She thought with a smile that she should warn John what he was getting into. It had been over a year since she had shared her bed with someone else, there was a good chance that her appetite and her need might overwhelm him. She shed all her clothes and went into the bathroom to take a quick shower.

Sydney turned around and let the water drench her hair and flow down her narrow back, down her legs and out the drain, hopefully washing away whatever fatigue and tension she had accumulated over the last few days. Soaping up her short hair and slowly massaging her scalp, Sydney thought about John. She entertained speculation on just how his touch would feel on her skin, what kind of pleasure his skin, his fingers and his mouth would provoke in her body.

She closed her eyes and recalled his voice and his scent as the sensation of her hands, slick with soap excited the nerves of her skin as she touched, caressed even, her chest, stomach and thighs. Shaking away the vision, coming back to the here and now, Sydney laughed out loud at just how much John had come to consume her thoughts and fantasies. She briefly considered taking matters into her own hands, but decided that anything she did in the shower, or even later in bed, would only blunt the delicious need she felt, and most assuredly be just a pale comparison to the real thing.

She went downstairs to rustle up something light to eat. On her way into the kitchen, she turned on her computer. She logged on to her college e-mail server to see what she had missed. She saw not too much going on; the summer sessions were light, nothing of consequence. It seemed the school barely knew she was gone.

Sydney then checked her personal e-mail, hoping for something else from John. She scrolled through the advertisements that were the bane of any Internet user's existence and stopped short when she saw a familiar return address.

Sydney opened the message and read the few words, words that sent a chill through her and opened an emptiness inside. Her mood plunged from happiness to be home to dread over what this message conveyed to her. She deleted the message and logged off; then got up, her food forgotten, went upstairs to her bedroom, laid down, and began to think, her mind in turmoil.

When Sydney reopened her eyes she was surprised to see that the light coming through the windows was the muted shade of dusk. She had fallen into a dreamless sleep and felt strangely energized, as if her batteries had been recharged by the unexpected nap she'd taken.

She got up and drank a glass of water in the bathroom before she went back downstairs. Sydney picked up the phone and dialed John's number, hoping he was back from his travels. She got his answering machine, so she left a quick hello, missed you, call me when you get home message. She saw the congealed mess her waffles had transformed themselves into and rejected the thought of preparing something for dinner. Instead, she decided to go out and grab a bite. In a strange form of denial, Sydney refused to revisit the implications of the message she had received.

Dressed casually, Sydney grabbed her wallet and hit the bricks. Her favorite neighborhood restaurant was only half a mile away, and the evening air filled her lungs with an energized tingle. The familiar sights and smells of her neighborhood reinforced that she had truly come home.

At that same moment John was sitting in a window seat of an American Airlines Boeing 737, about a half hour out from Atlanta's Hartsfield Airport. He was bone weary after asking the same questions and tracking down countless friends and coworkers of the missing women, trying to get them to recollect events and circumstances years old. Despite his efforts, John had found nothing of note. He looked forward to getting home and sleeping in his own bed. He would upload most of the notes he'd taken in the morning once he checked in with the lieutenant. John had not been able to check the FBI mainframe to see if he had any messages waiting for him from Samuels or Minor. What few updates on the case he got from Minor by phone, with whom he tried to check in at least once a day. He'd be able to see Samuels in the next day or so since they'd both be in town.

John wondered how the investigation was going away from Atlanta. He wasn't sure how he felt about Samuels' assertion that the missing members of the group were not victims. If Samuels was right, then where were they and how had they managed to stay under cover for so long? If they got wind of the investigation would they want to do something to those on their trail?

John hoped not. After all, what better way of tipping everyone off than bumping off those investigating you? No, anyone who could spirit away hundreds of people without a trace for four decades probably wasn't the least bit concerned with his efforts. But, John thought with a pang of guilt, if Sydney was involved with the group, were they aware that Sydney was under suspicion? Did they overlook the fact that Jaylynn Williams had made the mistake of calling Sydney at home on her mobile phone? Which brought John right back to his feelings toward Sydney. John sat back and tried to relax for the final approach and landing.

On the ride into town, he gave calling Sydney a thought. He had dropped a card in her mail slot. It was an impulsive gesture, to let her know he was thinking about her, and to let her know that he was okay with everything, especially since he had walked out of her house so abruptly. The last thing he wanted was for her to think he was upset with her, that there was some kind of problem between them that would preclude them from becoming closer, to keep them from becoming lovers.

John had thought frequently about the roiled emotion of his evening at Sydney's and why he had been so disturbed by the intensity of the moment. The truth of the matter was that he was shy, and not the least bit impulsive by nature or training. Not an award-winning combination for attracting and interesting a woman of intellectual depth, a woman of impulse, a woman of playful passion, in short, a woman like Sydney.

Pulling to a stop in front of his house, John gave the driver the fare and tip. He went straight to the fridge and grabbed a beer. He twisted off the cap and drank most of it down at once. He looked at his answering machine. Not too popular these days, he thought. He wasn't surprised to hear the first message was from the *Atlanta Business Chronicle* trying to get him to subscribe. The second was from his partner. Thinking that the third message was another telemarketer, John almost skipped it and erased the tape. When he heard Sydney's voice his heart began to flutter. When the machine gave the day and time at the end, he saw she had returned today as well.

John picked up the phone and tried her at home, but was disappointed when her voice mail clicked in. He left word that he had just gotten in and was happy she called. He debated for a second, and then added that if she got in before midnight, and wasn't too tired, to give him a call.

John booted up his computer. and went immediately to the FBI mainframe and logged in. As soon as he was connected, three messages from Samuels and one from Minor appeared. Taking the three from Robert in order, the first was an inquiry into any progress he had made with Sydney. The second was a note informing him that the investigation had been changed from kidnapping/murder to conspiracy by the director. It warned him that if this was the case, then those he was investigating were alive and to take precautions.

What precautions? He'd already caught himself checking the back seat of his squad car more than once and looking around the side of the house when he came home.

The third message was a request for John to give Samuels a call as soon as he hit town. The message from Minor invited John to dinner.

The phone rang. John picked up the phone and said, "Hello?"

"Hey sailor, in town for long?" said the voice on the other end.

"Maybe. Is your husband home?" he asked.

"Not until the tide goes out," Sydney said, laughing. "I missed you, why couldn't you stow away in my bag so I could drag you out and play with you at night?"

"There's no rest for the wicked, Syd. Besides, you have the youth of America to recruit into your secret Amazon conspiracy. By the way, how's the conquest of the male species going?"

"John, if I told you, I'd have to kill you. How was your trip? Where'd you go?" she asked.

Remembering just in time, John answered, "I was all over. We have to go out and do backgrounds and interviews with parents of runaways who end up in our jurisdiction, or might be headed our way. It was just my turn, I guess. How did your trip turn out?"

"Not bad. I think I interviewed about a hundred and fifty girls for the college and set up about fifty trips down here for parents and such. I've done it enough that it's not really hard work, it's just time-consuming and after a while I get confused about what city I'm in. By the end of the tour all I want is to be able to take a nice long bath in my own tub, and sleep late in my own bed. It looks like we may actually end up with between fifteen and twenty of the girls I interviewed, not a bad month's work.

"What are you up to?" Sydney asked.

"Just organizing my notes from the trip, sort of unwinding, I'm not really tired yet."

"I just got back from getting a bite to eat. It's only a little past ten, you want to go out for dessert? To sweeten the deal I'll even drive up that way," Sydney offered.

"Are you serious? Don't you have to get back to the office first thing in the morning?" asked John.

"Not especially, no one's going to care if I come in after lunch. There's nothing on my schedule through the end of the week. So John, what do you say? You hungry?" Sydney persisted.

"Sure, let me grab a quick shower and I'll meet you wherever."

"Will you need help washing up? I'm told I have superior grooming skills, and for friends I don't even charge."

Laughing into the phone, John said, "I'm sure you don't! I'm just afraid that if you start washing anything of mine we're not likely to get anything to eat."

"Speak for yourself," Sydney said with a sly snicker. "I really liked Pete's, does he have dessert stuff to eat there?"

"Sure, he's got some kind of pastry shop or bakery that delivers there every morning. I'll clean up and meet you there in about forty-five minutes or so."

"You're on, officer. I'm really looking forward to seeing you. Bye now."

John hung up the phone grinning like a fool.

On the way to Pete's, John had to consciously slow down when he saw that he was going fifty miles an hour down a residential street. *Jesus*, he thought, *I'm acting like a love-struck sixteen-year-old*. Slowing down to a respectable thirty-five, he made it to Pete's without mishap, stopping at every stop sign and red light along the way.

John saw that Sydney had beaten him there and was sitting at the bar talking to Pete. He walked up behind her, shaking his head at Pete to not let Sydney know he was coming. He bent over and whispered in her ear, "Hey lady, know where a sailor could go to have a good time?"

Sydney squealed and jumped off the stool to give him a breathtaking hug and a warm kiss on the lips. Pete asked, with a woeful expression on his face, "Just what does a guy have to do around here to get that kind of attention?" Breaking into his trademark grin, he highfived John and said, "The joint's missed you, white boy. Where've you been hiding yourself?"

"Pete, it's been rough. The last time I saw this woman she put me in intensive care. Too much of that could get a man killed!"

Laughing, Pete said, "What a way to go. And you know, no one would feel the least bit of sympathy for your ass if you did."

"If you two are quite through impugning my virtue, *I* came here for dessert. You didn't get me here under false pretenses, did you, sailor?" Sydney asked.

"Hell no, it's been my experience that a well-fed woman is so much easier to handle."

"Oh, so now you're trying the handle me?" she asked in mock indignation.

Trying to save his friend from digging himself deeper in the hole, Pete said, "What's your pleasure, Miss Sydney? Pay no attention to the philistine, ma'am, he's hopeless."

"Do you have something bad for me like cheesecake?" she asked.

"I have chocolate, strawberry and a caramel thing they call turtle pie. What sounds good to you?"

"I'll have the strawberry."

"You go sit down and I'll have it brought right over. And for you, Sarge?"

"I'll have the same. Thanks, Pete."

"Don't mention it. It'll be up in a minute."

By unspoken agreement Sydney and John made their way to the same booth they'd sat in the last time they were there. This time John sat directly across from her so he could watch her face without having to turn.

"Playing it safe, sailor?" she asked as he sat.

"Nothing of the sort, I just like watching you."

"So, did you miss me at all? You know a girl likes to know these things."

"I can honestly say that you were never far from my thoughts almost every minute of these last couple of weeks," John answered truthfully.

"How is everything going with you?"

"What do you mean?" John asked.

"I mean, are you all right with the dinner at my place? I'm not blind, there was something weighing on your mind and I want to make sure we're okay."

The waitress picked that moment to arrive with their dessert. Once she set everything down, she withdrew without saying a word.

Sydney continued, "I'd like to know what was wrong at dinner. Did I move too fast, maybe shock your sensibilities?"

"No, it wasn't anything like that. I couldn't have asked for anyone better than you to come into my life, but I have nagging concerns that I have to work out on my own. It's not you in any way; just thinking about you does things to me."

"Oh really? What kinds of things?" she asked.

"Never you mind. What has usually gotten in the way in the past is what I do, day in and day out. I'm a cop with a cop's attendant responsibilities, sometimes they involve getting in harm's way. But that's not what was on my mind the other night. What surprised me was the intensity of what I felt, and the obvious power of the connection between us. At least that's how it was for me."

"For me as well. It's not just you."

Sydney took a bite of her cheesecake and closed her eyes in ecstasy. "Ummm, now that's a taste sensation. Try yours, this was definitely worth the price of admission."

Suiting action to words, John took a healthy bite. When he swallowed he said, "You're right, that was definitely worth leaving home for in the middle of the night. But it wouldn't taste nearly as good if I were eating it alone."

Sydney got up and walked around the table, took his head in both hands and gave John a smoldering kiss that tasted all at once of strawberry, of cheesecake and of woman, hot, luscious, willing woman. In all his life John couldn't remember tasting anything like this before.

When his eyes stopped spinning and he caught his breath, he saw that Sydney had already resumed her seat and was once again eating, savoring every bite. Her every motion, her eyes and her expression blended into a smirk. "How's that taste now, sailor?"

Looking around the room trying to find his voice and his equilibrium, John caught Pete's eye and got a wink from the bar.

Fortunately, as they continued eating their conversation drifted off into less intense territory for John. They revisited their ongoing debate on music, fed constantly by the selections Pete's computerized system played through the night, pausing their conversation only to listen to Roberta Flack's rendition of *Reverend Lee*. John was happy he had exercised the foresight to sit more than an arm's length away from Sydney. He truly feared for his life, or at least his dignity, had she continued her unintentional *and* intentional arousals.

As the night wore on, fewer and fewer patrons remained scattered throughout the bar, and Pete started the two waitresses tidying up the tables already empty of customers. Soon, only John and Sydney were left.

Pete strolled over to the booth and said,"Hey pretty lady, Sergeant. I hate to interrupt what looks like a night that could last forever, but I'm bushed."

Surprised at the time, they thanked Pete for a great evening and said their warm goodbyes.

The next morning John went to the FBI offices. When he reached the office assigned to Samuels and Minor, John discovered Minor inside by himself. He greeted the sharp-shooting hacker and inquired into Samuels' whereabouts.

"He's around here somewhere, he didn't go far. He said something about kicking the surveillance on Atkins into high gear, I guess something happened in Washington that's putting the investigation on the front burner. I looked over your notes, didn't find anything new on the trip, did you?" asked Minor.

"Nothing out of the ordinary in the interviews, and no one could recall seeing Dean Atkins either, at least not from the picture I had."

"Was there something wrong with the pic?" Minor asked.

"Not at all, your surveillance guys got me a really good one, I just don't know if she looked like that back then."

Just then the door opened and John got up to shake Samuels' hand.

"Jeff says that the investigation is moving into high gear, what's up?"

"Kid, you wait here while I bring our friend up to date. John, let's take a walk."

Samuels led John out of the building. When they were a block away from the office Samuels said, "Thanks for waiting, I'm not sure if the office is bugged or not."

"I thought maybe you didn't want Minor to hear what we were going to discuss." John steered Samuels over to a hot dog vendor and paid for two dogs and a couple of cans of soda.

"So what's the story?" John asked when they had found an open bench and sat down.

Samuels took a bite and said around the mouthful, "Washington has made the investigation a top priority, whatever we need they'll provide. I'm going to tell you some classified information that I wasn't specifically told to pass on, but if you are going to stick with the investigation you have a right to know what's up.

"Let me start with some background information you don't know about. About a couple of months ago the Iraqis shot down what they thought was a new Western stealth craft that had strayed out of the no-fly zone on to their side of the line. They hit it with two missiles and pretty much destroyed the thing. From the pieces left, the Iraqis, and subsequently our labs as well, were not able to place the origin of the craft. The skin was of an alloy we don't know how to make and the electronics, if that's what they call them, were based on semiconductor technology that is barely recognizable by our best guys.

"The only human remains they found at the crash site was the foot of a black male about forty years old. Getting the picture yet?"

John nodded and said nothing.

"What has the administration and the armed and security services wigged out is that the craft was powered by some kind of device that controls gravity. The owners of the craft have found a way to decrease or eliminate the effects of gravity."

"No shit? I'll bet Washington is spinning in circles knowing that someone has something like this and we don't. So who made the connection between the group we've been investigating and the makers of the aircraft?" asked John.

"Well, I think I may have started them on that path when I reported I didn't believe any of our group were dead, but that they were hiding out somewhere instead. The other group working on the case under me are quartering the remote areas of the country via satellite infrared scans to try to locate where they might be. So far, nothing."

"So what's going to change down here? Do you still want me in on this, or have you gotten the word to send me back to chasing runaways?"

"Nothing of the sort. You don't get off that easy. What I may ask you to do might not be pleasant." Looking at John, Samuels raised an eyebrow.

John bit, saying, "You must be talking about Sydney. I can safely say that I have not made any mistakes in my relationship with her, especially nothing that will compromise your investigation. I can't help how I feel, though. Maybe you *should* consider pulling me from this case."

"Normally I would, but I'm willing to let it play out. Besides, it might not be a bad idea to have you close to her, if you know what I mean." Samuels balled up the hotdog's wrapper and his napkin and tossed it in the trash can behind the bench.

"What we have to do is to find out what Atkins knows and get that information back to Washington, ASAP. Where do you think we can start, John?"

"Short of kidnapping her and shooting her up with truth serum, I'm at a loss. Was there any talk of suspending due process or extraordinary powers being granted for the time being? How much latitude do you have, Rob?"

"The director didn't give the president any specifics on the investigation as far as I know. No names were discussed so we wouldn't bump into any of the other services snooping around. That's not to say that someone hasn't twigged to what we have down here, but I'm thinking we have a week, two at the most. Last week I authorized real-time monitoring of her online sessions and, no offense, her house is now wired from top to bottom. If you have something private to say to her, don't say it there."

"Jesus, is my house wired too?" John asked peevishly.

Looking John straight in the eye, Samuels said, "Don't think I didn't consider it. If she's over at your place, and she spills something significant I want to hear about it, no ifs, ands or buts. Do you understand?"

"Hell yeah, I understand. If you feel better wiring my place up go right ahead, you have my consent. It really doesn't matter to me since I don't expect anything to go on there that I wouldn't want you to hear."

"Thanks for the offer, but I think with her house, car and office covered we have a pretty tight lock on her. Surveillance said that you two closed down that jazz joint last night, anything I need to know?" Samuels asked.

"No, although I can tell you this, she's sharp, maybe even sharper than we are. Nothing gets by her, and she can read people like she's in their head peeking all the time. Obviously she's not been in on this for the last forty years, but she's not likely to make some obvious slip-up. What do you suggest I look for?" John asked.

"Shit, if I knew that we would have this entire affair wrapped up by now. Let's head back, I want to see what, if anything, Jeff's come up with since last week."

When they returned to the office, Minor pulled up the playback of Sydney's e-mail session, and showed the other two what had transpired. Samuels put a hand to

Minor's shoulder, stopping his playback when he reached where Sydney had logged on to the public e-mail server and took a look at the message on the screen.

Samuels pointed to the words and said, "Does that mean anything to either of you?"

John shook his head and looked at Minor, who was also shaking his head.

Samuels read it aloud. "'School's out, is anyone looking for a summer job? Save lost souls, no one needs to show you how.' Doesn't suggest anything to me. Who's the sender, Jeff?"

Minor scrolled backwards through the screens and pointed to the sender, "Cletus."

"See what you can find out about this Cletus. I want to do this without having to ask anyone's permission, got it?" Minor nodded his head. "I'll be shuttling between here and the search team in Washington to keep track of the overall investigation, and to keep everyone else off your asses. If I reveal anything more about the woman I'm afraid someone is going to get a bug up his ass and take her into custody. Then, all bets are off."

"So what's stopping them? If the administration and the law enforcement agencies are committed to getting to the bottom of this, why aren't they on her like white on rice?" asked John.

Getting to his feet, Samuels led John outside the building once again.

"John, the reason she hasn't been picked up is that they don't know who she is. I concealed her identity initially because I was told to trust no one; we have no idea who might see the information and run with it, or alert the very people we're seeking. Now, the last thing I need is some pinhead blowing the only lead we might have. So my man, it's all up to you, me and Jeff.

"For your part, I want you to be careful what you say to us on the phone. You might as well assume that the NSA is recording every call and screening it for the White House. I'm also going to assume that they can crack the encryption we use to connect to the mainframe, so you might as well forget about logging in from home. Mind you, I'm not trying to obstruct justice or anything like that, I'm just making sure no one jogs my elbow, messing up our work."

Samuels stopped just outside the lobby door.

"I can't stress enough how serious this has gotten. Everyone is scared shitless that these people will try to exact their measure of retribution from America for the last four hundred years. Watch your ass, John. You may not be able to tell who's trying to screw you first, those we're looking for or those we are supposed to be working for."

"I got it. Let me give some thought to how to try to get something out of her," said John. "Tell Jeff I'll catch up with him later, I'm going back to the station. If anything comes up, call me on my mobile."

"No problem. Don't *you* go missing on me," Samuels said before he turned and walked back into the building.

You may be an ambassador to England or France
You may like to gamble, you might like to dance
You may be the heavyweight champion of the world
You might be a socialite with a long string of pearls
But you're gonna have to serve somebody
Yes indeed you're gonna have to serve somebody
But it may be the devil, or it may be the lord
But your gonna have to serve somebody

Gotta Serve Somebody

Written and performed by Bob Dylan

CHAPTER 29

THE ATMOSPHERE AT the White House was tense. The daily security briefings brought no progress in the effort to locate the builders of the aircraft or the suspected group's hidden home. For two weeks every morning was the same. No movement from any phase of the various investigational fronts.

Already a number of senior African American staff members of all branches of the armed forces were grumbling. President Bender was afraid that the same mistake Simon had made with the Secret Service detail was being revisited throughout the military. Bender had assumed that, being the Commander in Chief, his orders would naturally be followed. Unfortunately, the Chairman of the Joint Chiefs was a stubborn son of a bitch who would just as soon sabotage the President's orders if he truly believed there was a creditable threat to his adopted homeland.

So far, President Bender heard nothing of discrimination at the FBI or CIA. He knew his stock with the Secret Service was at an all-time high. The members of the rank and file acted like they were an elite family, a family whose members trusted each other like no other. The fact that he directly went to bat for their team members only reinforced their *espirit de corp*s. The real battle was going to be with the American people when the separatists were finally found.

President Bender was going to have to prepare for the prospect that these people were not willing to share in their bounty. If found, would they gift the world with what they were holding? And, if not, how would they stand against a world demanding their share of their wealth in the form of life-improving technologies?

The sequestered commission had sent the preliminary report detailing their assumptions on the scope of the capabilities of someone having a practical means of controlling gravity. The summary alone was awe-inspiring or terrifying, depending on one's perspective.

Gravity could be used to control weather on a global scale if properly manipulated. This capability alone was a double-edged sword that could mean famine or bounty for any area of the globe just by controlling the amount of rainfall a region received. Using gravity, one could manipulate the effect of the sun's rays by actually bending the rays of light or by suspending some sort of opaque cover over any given region of the earth.

The report described how wholesale irrigation or flooding could be accomplished by changing the flow of waterways, or lifting fresh water out of a lake and depositing it directly over land, and the same could be said for transporting soil, sand or rock.

As for grossly larger effects, something the size of Norma's asteroid could be used as a doomsday weapon to devastate whole countrysides or cities. Large enough water strikes would affect weather for years, plunging the earth into a mini-ice age.

As President Bender read through the secret report he became more and more convinced that a head-on confrontation with these people would be in the worst interest of the American people. He saw the projected horrific effects of a known weakness in the earth's crust, like one of California's fault lines, being manipulated by increasing or decreasing the weight of one side of the fault against the other. Thankfully the report wasn't all negative.

The benefits of gravitational technologies had far-reaching implications in space exploration, the transportation industry, waste management, medical treatments, industrial production, construction and on and on. President Bender saw that the possibilities were endless. Every industry in the country would want to get their hands on this technology. Every lobbyist in Washington would be giving money to Congress on the one hand and expecting preferential access on the other. The president knew that none of those on the gimme list were the least bit interested in giving fair market value to those who owned it in return for the financial boon the technology represented.

Taking it away from them wasn't going to be easy, regardless of what the Chairman of the Joint Chiefs of Staff believed. President Bender knew he had to keep a tight rein on General Kaminski if he was to prevent out-and-out war.

President Bender saw that he had almost an hour before his lunch with the leadership of the Senate Intelligence Committee. He called Masters to his office for a quick rundown before his meeting. The plan was to give them an overview of the investigation underway and some of the details about the antigravity aircraft's existence. He and Masters would go over the final briefing paper containing information, he would impress upon the committee that the information it contained would reach the media only if they *all* wanted to spend the next twenty years in prison.

Looking up when the door opened, President Bender was glad to see Masters in a good mood. Bender had wondered how their relationship might change over the Secret Service detail debacle. Simon seemed to have accepted his mistake, even going so far as to apologize directly to Special Agent Bishop and ask him to convey his apologies to the rest of the members of the detail.

"So how do we handle the leadership today, Simon? How much do we tell them?" Bender began.

"I think we face two problems, Mr. President. The first is that this is one time where we cannot afford to have anybody leak our situation to the media, or anyone else for that matter. The second is the question of how the good senator from Georgia is going to react to the news that a group of his fellow African Americans are the target of this interagency investigation."

"Damn, I had completely forgotten about him. Are you sure we really need to have this meeting? Isn't there some way we can put it off?" Bender asked, hopefully.

"The reality of the situation is that members of Congress already know something's up. Normally I would counsel secrecy over disclosure, but with every branch of the military and all the security services working on contingencies for a meteor strike and defenses against an attack by gravity manipulation, it's only a matter of time anyway, Mr. President," Masters said.

"All that's true. However, I damn sure don't want to go public until we have their location. Until then there's no mobilization of the troops, nothing concrete anyone on the outside can specifically point to. I want to keep it factual and straightforward. Then I'll ask the senator if he might have some insight into what these people might have as an agenda, bring him directly into the process, so to speak. I'm not expecting him to offer anything substantial. However, I do want him firmly in our camp before the shit hits the fan. Until we know any better, the committee has to act on the assumption that we are facing a threat to the United States. We're going to *have* to plan accordingly."

"Yes sir, Mr. President. I'll get a summary ready for your approval within the hour," Masters said, then left the office.

Once he was alone, President Bender returned to the threat team's report. He began reading the summary section on biological sciences. It was speculated that the target group had the means of manipulating organisms at the genetic level, implying a faculty for gene splicing or genetic engineering in advance of the best experimental labs in the U.S. The report went on to say that the treatment the pilot appeared to have had would have meant higher resistance to disease due to a more robust immune system. This benefit, along with the speculative results of having increased telomere length, suggested those who underwent the cellular modification procedure would remain vital right up until natural death. There would probably be little in the way of debilitating weaknesses or systemic deterioration that normal humans experienced over the final twenty or so years. It was all speculation, though if any of the speculation was true, there would be angry demands for access to such treatments from the public.

Bender was at the point of wishing the FBI had never discovered these people existed. But stuffing everything back into Pandora's box wasn't possible at this point. Neither was calling off the search or trying to pretend none of this had ever happened.

The country was already sliding down a slippery slope into confrontation with these people. Any such confrontation must end with America getting everything these people had to give, even without the provocation of aggressive action against the US.

Bender called Simon and told him to set up a meeting with General Kaminski that afternoon. Masters said, "Sir, you'll be happy to know that the Navy and Dr. Harris have put the second gravity detector into service almost three weeks earlier than planned. They are calibrating the two detectors to work together and hope to be fully operational within the next few days."

"That *is* great news, perhaps they'll be able to locate these people from the detection of another aircraft like the one shot down. Do we know what the effective range is yet?" Bender asked.

"I don't have that information, sir. The full report won't be ready until calibration is completed," answered the Simon.

"Fine, keep me posted," Bender said and hung up the phone.

The naval engineers stationed underground were constantly stimulated by ideas and conversations with the commission members. They discussed ideas they probably never would have considered on their own. The commission itself was given the opportunity to quiz their military counterparts on the capabilities and internal workings of the armed forces in developing their contingency plans or threat assessments.

Alan and Martin had more help than they could use. They had the best possible sounding board for theoretical discussion and analysis they could ever hope for.

As for Norma, she felt like she hadn't had more than four hours sleep at a time since she had returned to Shelter Fourteen because of the excitement generated by the highly charged group. She'd never had the opportunity to brainstorm with so many sharp thinkers in her life. She grew to respect nearly everyone there regardless of their roots. Here was the true essence of a think tank.

The most exciting part for her, and probably for most of her contemporaries on the commission, was the speculation surrounding the probable level of technology the hidden group possessed. Dreaming up the kinds of problems they could solve with gravity-based technologies was the best part of everything they did.

Today, Norma's panel was discussing the wide-ranging implications of the biological advances implied by the test results on the pilot's foot. Their focus was on threat assessments and the panel was small; Norma, Paul Milton, Susan Roscoe from MIT, Dr. Stephen Pitts, neurobiologist from the Centers for Disease Control and Lieutenant Davies, one of the naval engineers helping Dr. Harris' project in the area of electronics.

Paul led the discussion with the implications of longer-lived humans separated from the regular garden-variety type of man, as he put it.

"As I see it, we have a bigger public relations problem once this information makes it into the public than any threat. However, what kinds of technologies have all of you dreamed up based on the the the lab results we saw on the pilot's remains?" began Paul.

"The first thing that comes to mind is the probable gene splicing techniques being used to create biological weapons," answered the lieutenant. "If that's the case there are really no practical limit to their capabilities. To accomplish something like elongating telomeres gets right down to the lowest level of cellular mechanics. Unless this pilot had two heads or was a chance mutation, this change was made artificially and accurately, which is phenomenal."

Dr. Pitts spoke up. "If the technology to rework the ends of genes has been perfected then there is little doubt in my mind that fully manipulating genes is well within their capability. So, essentially what we face is people who can create bugs, microbes and viruses with a faculty we can't possibly match. And matching their capability is what we'll have to do if they decide to infect a population center with a weapon.

"The defense projections we update monthly for the Pentagon plot the rate of contamination by different disease vectors like insects, or mammals like birds or dogs, or chemical dispersion via lower-atmosphere air currents. We're well aware of the vulnerabilities that exist in the US. Biological warfare is ugly business. The scariest kind of pathogen we worry about is one that has a long incubation period with fatal results. In other words, something that can infect a person and not have them displaying any symptoms until they have substantially contributed to the spread of the disease. That's generally the worst-case scenario we face," Dr. Pitts finished.

"So essentially we have little defense, or recourse to offer the president other than the effective isolation of infected areas and the 'no-exception' kind of enforcement this brand of terror calls for. Does that about sum up this line of investigation?" Paul asked of the others.

Lieutenant Davies added, "There are some simple precautions most of the population can take if the existence of such a disease is known, but I think we have plumbed the depths of what can be done prophylactically. I can say this, though, the best way of keeping the population from becoming infected with some kind of biological weapon is to keep it from being deployed in the first place."

"So what are you suggesting?" asked Susan, sitting up in her seat. "Is this the advocacy of a preemptive strike philosophy? That's bullshit. From everything I've heard, these people, if they exist, haven't made any kind of threatening gesture toward anyone. Just because they have better technology than we do they are provoking attack? Or is it something else, Lieutenant? Is it because of their color that you feel entitled to rape them?"

"Hold on there, Susan," Paul broke in putting a calming hand on her arm. "I don't think the lieutenant was suggesting that these people deserve to be destroyed, at least that's not what I heard him say. I think what he meant was that should we become aware of a such a threat that our only recourse might be a preemptive strike of some sort to save lives. The thought is ugly, even abhorrent to me, but we are charged with reporting all our findings, no matter how distasteful."

The lieutenant quickly said, "I'm sorry, Dr. Roscoe. I really didn't mean to suggest that we shoot first and ask questions later. I was only talking about saving lives. And as for the other accusation, I don't even want to dignify it with a response. A third of my team here is African American, and I trust my life to every single one of them. Not being in the service you have no idea how we gauge someone else. It's not a matter of color, or religion, it's a matter of trust."

Norma took this opportunity to interject, "As much as we would like to ignore the issue, especially in light of Diane's warning about racial problems rearing their ugly head, it does exist. I'm hoping that we can all show a little sensitivity without anyone flying completely off the handle."

Susan threw up her hands in surrender. "Look, everyone, I'm not mad. I just want some sort of balance to be struck in any plans we discuss or any possibilities that exist. The old way of doing things has probably brought us to this point to begin with. I'm dying to know what is motivating these these people to repudiate their lives and conceal their existence. And, to be honest, maybe I am a little pissed that I wasn't invited to join them. My guess is that they don't want a thing from America. And yet, here we are, treating them like sworn enemies just because they have things white folks don't," Susan said, sitting back and crossing her arms.

No one wanted to be the first to venture into the silence until Paul said, "Well, we can sit around and participate in a glaring contest or we can continue. I don't have any unpleasant baggage I need to bring to the table. Susan, can you relax enough to believe that we can all rise above the racial subtext and work together?

Or would you rather go home? Frankly those are your only two choices. To be honest, I'm not sure the president would even let one of us go home at this point. Did any of you consider that?"

Norma chimed, "Hey, that's right. Diane only said that anyone leaving early for stirring up trouble would spend time in a military prison, she didn't say anything about us going home. Lieutenant, what do your orders say? Is there a time limit, or schedule on them?"

"No ma'am. Mostly, all we're told is where to go and what to do, almost nothing about what comes next. Our business is saving lives and protecting America from enemies outside our borders, and within. I'm not a warmonger, I'm a soldier who fights when the US government decides that the application of force is necessary to protect the security of our nation.

"It's a job. But, unlike yours, or Dr. Milton's or Dr. Roscoe's, my responsibilities are absolute, and not subject to casual dismissal if I don't feel like it that day. We are held to the ultimate level in job accountability. I'm proud to be what I am. But don't anyone ever question my views on race or my commitment to the serious work we're doing here," Lieutenant Davies said, his voice getting louder with barely suppressed anger, as he began to rise.

Pulling Davies back into his seat, Paul said, "My suggestion for now is that we take a break and come back in half an hour. Susan, if you can find it in you to join us, I for one would appreciate your participation. How about the rest of you?" he asked, looking at the lieutenant.

"Yeah, whatever. I'm fine with that. I think a break is a good idea, I could use something to drink."

Susan said, "Me too. Who do you have to kill around here to get a beer?" getting a laugh from all present. She made a point of grabbing Lieutenant Davies' arm and, putting it under her own, she marched them off to the cafeteria.

On the other side of the complex, Alan was trying to synchronize the data streams from the two detectors so that the computer could process them at the same time without having to expend the overhead to ensure the data was processed in step. He had worked through the night with the entire technical crew from the Navy. Martin called a halt to their efforts and told everyone to take a break, as no one had really eaten or slept for more than a hour or two for the last forty-eight. They would start fresh in four hours.

Alan tried to stay behind, but Martin walked over and with an affectionate hand on Alan's shoulder, shut off his monitor.

In response to Alan's reproachful look, Martin said, "I'll make a deal with you. Come and get some breakfast with me and you can discuss where we are so far, deal?"

"Sure, but I'm positive I can lick the timing problem if I can just go over the code, alone, one more time," Alan protested.

"Fine, then the answer will be there when we get back."

They collected Commander Ames and a few of the engineers on the way to the commissary, and ran into Dr. Milton's group when they arrived.

Once the engineers saw Norma they loudly invited her to join them. Why is it, Martin wondered, that the company of an attractive woman could banish all signs of the ordeal they had just put themselves through and give fresh life to the young?

They pulled several tables together to accommodate the group. A few of the engineering crowd were paying attention to a discussion between Norma and a young electronics technician, but the rest continued hashing over the work of the last two days.

Paul got everyone's attention, and turning to Martin's group, asked "Does the synchronization signal have to be generated locally?"

"I'm not sure what you mean," Martin replied. "Are you asking could we use an external clock to try to get the degree of synchronization the computer needs?"

"Maybe, but I'm wondering if you could use something like the gravitational perturbations of the moon or that oscillation of the sun you mentioned to synch up the two detectors. They're close enough together that the detectors would read the sun simultaneously, but they're still far enough apart to triangulate local incidents in local space. If the detectors have the resolution, I'm thinking that if the sun's gravitational changes can be measured simultaneously by the detectors, then you have an external signal both get simultaneously."

Paul sat back and waited for his idea to be shot down because he had missed something obvious. As no one immediately spoke up, he began to feel pretty good.

Commander Ames finally broke the silence, "Holy shit! An external timing signal. We were thinking too small, we were looking at a timer we could build that could accurately split time down to a billionth of a second, generating a timing tick the detectors and the computer could synch up to."

Then Alan chimed in, "So if we focus a portion of both detectors' bandwidth on the sun's native oscillation, they could automatically synchronize themselves to the same time-stamped picosecond and then . . ."

Martin finished the thought, "We could use the detectors themselves to produce the timing spike that the computer would need!"

Two of the engineers jumped up and demanded paper from the kitchen staff. They brought a roll of white butcher paper to the tables, along with several pencils and began to sketch math, program code and logical diagrams of the proposed system.

Norma and her group, completely forgotten by the engineers and Martin's staff, watched in amazement at the flurry of notes and drawings that seemed to magically appear.

No one noticed as Paul led Norma, Susan, Davies and Pitts out of the room and back to their own aborted discussion. When the engineers had produced yards of drawings, equations and notes scrawled across the huge pieces of roughly torn paper, they decided that they could work more effectively back in the lab. That's when Martin called a halt to the exodus, reminding them that they were not to return to the lab for another three hours. He said that he wanted them all to get cleaned up and squared away, ostensibly because he couldn't get any work done in the lab anyway with them smelling the place up. He looked at Commander Ames for backing, who then ordered the naval team not to return to the lab before fourteen hundred hours. Under orders, the group left the room in small groups, chatting over their new challenge.

Alan turned to go to his room but Martin grabbed him by the collar and said, "Not so fast, youngster. I'm going with you to your room and confiscating your laptop for the duration." He laughed at the stricken look on Alan's face. "Don't worry, I'll have it back to you this evening." Before Alan could frame an argument, Martin softened his voice and added, "It's for your own good. I can't afford to have you burn out on me."

Flattered, but not particularly happy, Alan's shoulders slumped as he resigned himself to the inevitable. The two left the commissary together so Martin could make good on his promise.

In Atlanta, Mathews, Samuels and Minor all felt like they were drilling a dry hole. Their prime suspect was conducting her day-to-day activities with no sign of change.

John had managed to squeeze in a brief lunch with Sydney. They talked about safe topics, nothing too emotionally charged. Her laugh was music to his ears, and when she reached over to hug him, it was so comforting, so familiar that his heart ached to think that what he was doing for the FBI could deny him a lifetime with her.

John sensed that she was somewhat distracted, as if she had something on her mind that kept her from completely focusing attention on the matters at hand. But he just couldn't be sure.

Sydney was quite content in John's presence. She felt a certain quiet calm, a familiarity that made the time pass quickly without any undue effort on her part. It was what made her feel so free to spar with him, which never alienated him, but drew them closer together.

After lunch John dropped her off on campus and turned the car downtown to check in with Minor and Samuels. At the FBI agent's office they were stepping through someone's Internet session. Looking closer, John noticed the sites were almost all news oriented, concentrating on national and international stories.

Samuels invited John to sit down and watch the proceedings with any eye toward discovering what the sequence might mean. Tapping Minor on the shoulder, John asked how many sites were they talking about.

"About seventy, it looks like she was searching for something specific in the news."

"This is another session Sydney had online?" John asked.

"It is. There's nothing new from her phone conversations so we're snagging her online traffic at home and at her office." Minor turned back to clicking though the screens.

"My guess is she's either a news junkie, or she was looking for a story on some specific event. If you look at the dates of the stories, they go back over two months and move forward in time to the present," said Samuels, sitting back in his chair, stretching. "Even this is probably a dead end. It probably doesn't have anything to do with the investigation at all. I'm at a loss as to where we should go from here.

"John, look, we're running out of time. Sooner or later the president is going to force me to pull her in and apply persuasion to get whatever she knows out of her. The director will have to go along with him now that this has been upgraded to a national security matter. I don't know what else we can do."

John sat back and exhaled with a hiss. "So what are you saying? The Constitution is suspended for the duration? Do we have yet another crisis that lets the government stomp on people's rights in the name of political expediency? Let's check the tote board, shall we?

"In World War Two it was the Japanese. This time the profile is 'black and breathing,' right? Christ, when are we ever going to learn?" John said, jabbing his finger toward Samuels chest.

Minor remained silent.

Samuels pressed on. "Pretty damn soon my hands are going to be tied, and we'll all be out of options."

John asked, "How long do you think we've got?"

"The last I heard, the administration was bracing for some kind of ultimatum when the asteroid passes. Someone thinks it's under voluntary control and may be used as a threat quite literally held over our heads," Samuels replied.

"Son of a bitch! Is that true? Has there been something to substantiate this or is this just normal paranoia raising its ugly head?"

"President Bender assembled a threat team to oversee this entire investigation. They've been turning out recommendations, contingencies and projections based on their assessment of the probable capabilities of this level of science. Someone in that group had originally speculated that the cause of the asteroid's changes in course were the result of the application of gravity manipulation.

"The Lancaster asteroid is due here in a matter of days, although it's looking like it's not going to get any closer than about two hundred and fifty thousand miles from earth. No one is taking any chances."

Rubbing his eyes with the heels of his hands, John asked, "How much time do you think we really have?"

"Probably no more than a week. My reports have been truthful, and noncommittal, basically saying that we have made no further progress To be honest, *I* don't want to see her taken into custody. If she's not involved, no one is going to believe her until after they wring her dry. A distinctly unpleasant prospect at best," Samuels said, apologetically. "Maybe it's time to show your hand. We've just about run out of options, and I don't want to see her hounded."

"Is this why you didn't want me to break off the relationship from the beginning, so you could use me to get to her later? Jesus Christ, I hate this job . . . and I'm damn sure not happy with you either," John said, as he glared at Samuels.

Minor began to get up, but John shoved him back into his chair and said, "Stick around, Jeff. I may need a witness later to substantiate the fact that I didn't kick Robert's ass around the room after he informed me that I was his bitch." As he uttered those words, all three men jumped to their feet.

John watched as Minor's hand crept toward the phone, and to forestall any escalation of the emotion in the room John said, "Don't worry, Jeff, I'm not going to do anything stupid, but neither am I going to be pushed into something I don't want to do by the likes of you two.

"You may want to consider what might happen if Sydney gets word of what you're about to do. Then where are you and the rest of the federal investigative apparatus going to be if she ends up disappearing like the others? Don't push me, boys, I may be just a city flatfoot, but I'm no one's fucking patsy."

Samuels sat down very slowly, and nodded at Minor to do the same.

"Sit down, John. I'm not here to try to push your buttons, *or* because all I want out of you is a means of controlling or spying on Atkins. If it weren't for you we wouldn't know as much as we do. You're not my bitch, or anyone else's for that matter. You've already proved your worth in this investigation. All I was trying to convey was that she's going to picked up whether she knows something or not. I can't keep her name a secret for much longer, I need your help in figuring out how to get to the bottom of this mystery and save the girl in the process. Isn't that what you want too, John?"

John rolled Samuels' words around in his head, slowly sat down and then said. "I didn't sign on to be a spy, I don't like the position I've been put in.

"What galls me the most is none of *you* have been able to find out anything more than what I've already turned up, isn't that right? So what's the FBI bringing to the table? Or anyone else for that matter? I'll tell you what they bring, nothing! Not a damn thing. You figure this group is hiding out there somewhere because there's no sign of foul play, no clue to their whereabouts, nor someone who could have been responsible for their disappearance. Some advanced aircraft is shot down halfway around the globe, and because the pilot's foot shows that he's black, there must be some kind of connection to the missing hundreds. Where's the proof of any connection whatsoever? There isn't any.

"The state of the government's investigative and intelligence services is abysmal. You can't deliver any additional clues in this investigation so the only recourse is to squeeze someone who *might* know something. Does the name Richard Jewell mean anything to you? How about Wang Ho Lee? The FBI's record for the last two decades sucks. Two isolated instances, you say? Not even close. And you wonder why you don't get any respect from guys like me. Well figure it out, respect is earned.

"You feds, you just run over anyone you think is in the way regardless of the circumstance, respecting no one but your own. Up until today I thought you were different, but you're not. You're just like all the rest when it gets down to it, aren't you?"

Looking at the younger agent, John said to him, "Watch and learn, Jeff. You'll do well in the service of your country if you follow Samuels' fine example here. This is textbook FBI here, none finer. What you and everyone else in the government always seem to forget is that collective ignorance is still ignorance."

John stood to leave the office. "Don't worry, I'm not going to blow your cover, yet." Looking at Samuels, he continued, "Thank you for the lesson in running an investigation, and reminding me just why I was in on this in the first place, I won't forget it." He opened the door and left the office without a backward glance.

John moved under a full head of steam as he left the building's underground garage; he felt ill-used and dirty. He should have seen it coming but he hadn't. He was ashamed, letting himself get into the position to be used in the first place. Driving through the city with no destination in mind John felt lost. He had nowhere to go. The investigation had him boxed in from both sides; he couldn't confide in Sydney, he couldn't even discuss what was going on with his best friend on the force because Jason wasn't cleared for the FBI investigation. The pisser of the whole thing was that up until now the best divination rod he had had was Samuels.

He saw he had been unconsciously driving in the direction of Pete's place. He laughed when he realized where he was and he gave in to the inevitable and parked the car around back.

When John stormed out of his office Samuels let out a huge breath and asked Minor, jokingly, "You don't think he was pissed off or something, do you?"

"Man, I thought I was going to have to get in between you two for a second there. Thank God my medical is all paid up. Still waters run deep, huh?" commented Minor.

"The thing of it is, I never planned for things to go this way. John's damn good, better than most of the agents I've worked with since I joined the Bureau. And you know what, he's the most genuine person I've met in this business. Now I have a major fence to mend that just might be irreparable. Fuck!" Samuels exclaimed, as he stalked out of the office.

Later that night he pored over every page of every report he had forwarded to the director looking for any specific reference to Atkins. He knew it was too late to redact her name from the reports he already sent, but he wanted to know just what level of exposure they faced if the investigation was taken away from him.

He felt bad about how he and John had left things. He carried more than a little guilt over how John's situation had played out, knowing that John's accusation was true.

Manipulating and using people was part of Samuels' training, and achieving the desired outcome was usually the only consideration during an investigation. But his relationship with John had been different, and the trick he tried to pull made Samuels feel dirty too.

For now, he was closeted in the office with Minor. Barely a word had passed between the two agents since John left, and Samuels knew that as loyal as Minor was to the Bureau, he didn't approve of what had gone down with John. Samuels' crude attempt to force John to do his bidding, in a circumstance where the situation clearly didn't warrant the effort, was everything John had intimated. It was indeed the worst of what many agents did in their so-called search for the truth.

To make it up to him, Samuels was trying to minimize the possible consequences and repercussions John might face if he and Minor were pulled off the investigation and someone else took over. He was doing his best to shield John from the worst of what the Bureau could pull in a rush to judgment, ever mindful of the collateral damage these investigations so often left strewn behind. He knew he was going to have to face John and apologize to him for what he'd done.

Us, us, us, us , us, us, and them, them, them, them, them, them,
And after all we're only ordinary men
Me, me, me, me, me, me, and you, you, you, you, you, you,
God only knows it's not what we would choose to do

Us And Them
Written by Richard Wright and Roger Waters, performed by Pink Floyd

CHAPTER 30

"GOOD MORNING, EVERYONE," said Dr. Milton. "I would like to thank all of you for your continuing efforts on behalf of the commission. Today we diverge from the usual discussions about the possible threats or harm from the technologies we've been discussing over the past couple of weeks. Today we are going to center on the beneficial aspects of the core technologies we've covered previously, and what effect they will have if brought to market, or become readily available to industry, medicine, anything else we can think of.

"You are free to take notes. However, this session, just like all the rest, will be recorded and a transcript extracted for posterity. Let's break up into groups of about six or so and I'll jot down the area each group should concentrate on so we don't all end up covering the same ground."

Martin ended up in the same group as Paul and went off to the smaller dining room off of the main cafeteria.

When everyone was seated, Paul let them know that they had drawn the discussion on exploration. The group excitedly began to segment out the various ways being able to manipulate gravity would help facilitate exploration of the earth, nearer planets and even under the sea. The session was full of ideas, and everyone took notes on everything they covered, not wanting to overlook anything that might be of use in the afternoon session.

The rest of the groups were equally busy with their assignments. By the time lunch rolled around they all had no lack of enthusiastic ideas to present at the afternoon session.

When Milton reviewed the written summaries of the sessions for the day, he immediately recognized the wider implications of reports. The uses that the control of gravity could be put to were magnificent in their scope. He saw just how America's capitalist system would be driven to obtain these capabilities at any cost. It was the first time he truly understood the primary reason the White House was so interested in locating the source of this technology. The innovations and predictions they had brainstormed that afternoon were nothing short of revolutionary in every field of industry, science and technology and represented wealth immeasurable by any estimation.

If history was any gauge, the chances of these technologies, if acquired, directly benefitting Americans without a select few getting filthy rich first were slim. But, what to do? To discuss his growing fears with anyone there wasn't really an option, but he needed at least one other perspective, if only to satisfy his own paranoia. He was going to have to choose his confessor very carefully. In his mind, the idea of the powers that be rationing the largess merely to heap more wealth on those who already had more than their share was more than disturbing, it was disgusting.

Milton saw that it was only eight-thirty. He went in search of Dr. Harris. On a hunch, he headed over to Martin's lab, hoping to find him available to chat for a while.

Milton found the lab door propped open with a stack of books, presumably to facilitate the almost constant traffic in and out by naval research personnel. Peeking inside, he saw Martin in close conversation with Alan.

He saw they were discussing something on the screen. Not wanting to interrupt, he waited patiently for a break in the conversation before he cleared his throat behind them.

Martin and Alan looked up and Martin's face broke into a smile when he saw who it was.

"Dr. Milton! To what do we owe this pleasant surprise?" he said, getting to his feet. "Slumming?"

Laughing, Milton said, "I hadn't really been over here much, so I though I'd drop in and see how the other half lives. I also wanted to see if we could get together when you have some time. And it's Paul, even in front of young Richards here."

Alan smiled self-consciously at being noticed and remembered by the NASA scientist, nodding his head in acknowledgment.

"Actually, we were just winding up here. Alan promised me he'd try to get a good night's sleep, didn't he?" Martin replied, directing the last at Alan.

"Yes, he did," Alan answered, as he printed out the data on his screen. "I'm just going to leave this on my desk so I can get started on it first thing in the morning. Um, goodnight Dr. Milton, doc. I'll see you in the morning."

He waited for Alan to get squared away and leave, then Martin asked Paul, "So what's up? Something from earlier today, or something new?"

Casting a glance around at the few naval technicians still working, Paul offered, "How about I buy you a cup of coffee?"

Martin raised an eyebrow in question, and receiving a single, slight nod in reply, said to the nearest naval technician, "I'm going to knock off for the day. I'll see all of you in the morning."

They left the lab amid a handful of "goodnights" and strolled off to the cafeteria. Although curious, he held his questions until they both drew cups of coffee and retired to a quiet corner of the room.

As they sat, Paul started off with the classic, "You're probably wondering why I called you here today."

"Your meeting, your agenda. What's up?" Martin asked.

"I was looking over the summary of today's session and thinking about the commission's directives. How we were instructed to cover the weapons and threat angles first, and only now the impact on industry and science. It got me thinking about the administration's goals, what they want us to achieve here and how they might truly respond during their first meeting, or confrontation if you will, with these people. If history is any guide, I assume that there's no intention on the part of the government to treat these people as anything other than adversaries."

"And you think this is the wrong tack for them to take, I gather?" Martin asked.

"Not exactly. If I read the situation right, the president and the Joint Chiefs are gearing up for a conflict with these people once they are located and in their minds it's a reasonable precaution. But is it wise to begin with such an aggressive posture against a group that is segmented by race with an apparent desire to isolate themselves from the rest of the world?

"And, if I read the situation right, your detector may be the only means of locating these people if they have any additional gravity-based technology in place. Is that correct?" Paul prodded.

"That's true. If there is another aircraft that uses gravity to get around the chances are pretty good that we'll be able to detect it and hopefully follow it home," Martin answered. "So you think the military is going to use that information to attack these people without warning, is that it?"

"Pretty much. I keep thinking about history. Are we facilitating slavery at best, and selective genocide at worst, by giving the administration the means of finding and maybe attacking people who have made no aggressive move against us?"

"Paul, anything done in the name of science can be perverted. The people we seek have the means of destroying nearly anything on the face of the earth. What do you think about their possibilities for doing harm? Do we leave ourselves open to mishap by ignoring the threat?" Martin put it to him.

"No, but that's not my point. Think about this for a minute. As soon as the connection was made between the incident your machine recorded and the crash of the aircraft in Iraq, what happened? They wasted no time militarizing your project to the extent that they are in control of the detector twenty-four hours a day.

"I'm uncomfortable with a number of things that seem to be in the works, but I have little control over anything the administration or the military might do. I don't look favorably upon the prospect of standing on the sidelines and watching the military shoot first and ask questions later. Much less giving them their heading. What about you?" Milton asked. "All we really know about them is that they don't want anyone to know where they are. So what do we do? We prepare to hunt them down and steal their stuff. Sound familiar?"

"And so?" Martin asked.

"And so, I just want you to think about the issue of unannounced aggression against someone who, for all practical purposes, hasn't bothered anyone. Nothing more seditious than that," Paul said, trying to reassure Martin.

"I understand what you're getting at, and it doesn't make me feel any better about what purpose my project is being put to, but I'm clueless as to what I can do about it. You're not talking about sabotage, are you? I couldn't possibly be in on something like that, no matter what you want. There's no practical way of doing so short of destroying the detectors themselves. No, it's out of the question."

"Martin, look, that's not what I want at all. It's more along the lines of what Enrico Fermi and Einstein did when they sent letters of objection to President Roosevelt during World War Two concerning the use of atomic power for war. Something like that. Hell, I don't really know *what* I want. I just don't want to be a part of exterminating a group of African Americans who have expressed no desire to engage us at all, just because they have better toys than we do. It's just not right no matter how you slice it," said Paul.

"Look, Paul, you've given me a lot to think about. But, I hope you don't expect me to do anything in a vacuum here. So far, there's no evidence that a second aircraft exists using the same technology the one in Iraq did, nor any other sign of gravity-based technology. Did you know that we're monitoring the Lancaster asteroid to see if gravity manipulation will be used to change its course? I didn't think so," Martin informed him.

"There's a full-court press on to find these folks, and I don't see anything wrong with doing so. Like you, I don't want the US to invade, imprison, kill, destroy, or anything else along those lines. But I am a scientist just like you, and as such I'm dying to see just what kinds of things these people have managed to create.

"Also, like you, I hope that America's penchant for shooting first and asking questions later, as you characterized it, will not be the policy that the president or the Joint Chiefs follow in this case. I agree, it's time we stop treating everyone who's not under our thumb as an enemy, especially in this case where we face someone who so outstrips our capability. Let me think about all this and let's talk about it later," Martin concluded.

"Remember, I'm not trying to stir up trouble, I just wanted to see what you thought about the broader implications of our master's, so to speak, setting up the commission with the military contributing so much assistance to your own project. By the way, while I've got you here, tell me something. Just how fast does gravity propagate? When we do orbital calculations the computers treat it as instantaneous for all practical purposes," Milton asked.

"That's the shit, Paul. At almost every level except at the quantum, it is instantaneous. Looking at it closely, the latest research shows that it really propagates at over thirty million times the speed of light."

"That would indicate that this force exists outside of normal Newtonian space, and that the theories of general relativity don't apply, since there's no real radiation component as with electromagnetic forces," Milton stated.

"Exactly! One of the most exciting prospects in this line of study is the possibility of instantaneous communication between say, Pluto and Earth using modulated gravity waves. So far, conventional thinking suggests that in order to accomplish this we're going to have to be able to harness the capabilities of a quantum black hole. That means capturing or creating one, and controlling it enough to induce it to oscillate and produce modulated waves that could be picked up just like radio waves. Hang on," Martin said, as he got up to get the pot to refill their coffee.

When he returned, Martin continued. "Light from the sun takes eight minutes to reach earth; light continuing past the earth takes another nine minutes to reach Mars. So if we send another probe to the surface of Mars, and want to control it in real time, the operators have to think ten minutes into the future when they navigate across the landscape using conventional radio. Using a gravity-based communications system, operation of the same probe would be instantaneous regardless of where Mars would be in its orbit around the sun in relationship to the control center down here.

"Hell, we wouldn't even need communications satellites anymore, gravity waves penetrate the earth without delay or deterioration. No more need for satellite television dishes, gravity-based radio wouldn't require antenna towers. And say we can get the technology small enough, mobile phones would have global coverage."

Paul continued, "Just this one breakthrough could make everything in the telecommunications industry obsolete."

"That's what I'm really after with my studies. I wanted to be able to detect and study instantaneously created quantum black holes as they passed through our universe on their way to other dimensions, if that's what they do. Locating them is the first step in trying to capture one."

"It's going to take a hell of a strong magnetic or gravitational field to attract and grab one of those things," said Paul.

"True. I'm hoping to find a way to generate a quantum black hole at will. There are three hurdles that we have to overcome. First, we have to figure out how to generate one of these things. Second, we have to be able to contain it. And finally, we have to be able to control it, to bend its power to our will.

"If these people the administration is hunting have these capabilities, they could advance science decades from where we are now. That's *my* agenda. I need to know how they manipulate gravity, how they gained the capability, what hints led them to where they are today," Martin said excitedly. "I've never given anything else a thought. Sorry for the blinders, but I guess I've been living with this project so single-mindedly for so long I kind of forgot about the nature of man."

"Don't sweat the small stuff, eh? I'm sorry, that's not entirely charitable, but I too have a problem with seeing the forest for the trees when I'm back in Houston. My biggest problem is that no one realizes the contribution space exploration has made to medicine and the everyday conveniences that the average person takes for granted. My entire existence now is consumed with the realities of politics. That's why I think the administration isn't going to play it straight with anyone, especially those of us here. Just keep it in mind, that's all I ask," Paul said. "Now I'm off to try to catch up on some of my correspondence before I turn in. I'll see you around."

"Wait a minute, Paul. Why the question about the speed of gravity?" Martin asked.

"Along the same lines as what happened with atomic power, I was thinking about what kind of devastation a gravity-based weapon could cause. Sending out compression waves, for example, that compressed matter down to the quantum level. If I can think of something like that, imagine what they're thinking about at the Pentagon . . ."

With that said, Milton got to his feet, took his cup to the conveyer belt feeding dirty dishes and silver back to the kitchen, and left. Martin stayed behind, thinking about their conversation.

He reviewed the entire history of his project, and its early militarization well in advance of the proposed ability to scan for submarines underwater or underground installations. Now that the seed had been planted, Martin was no longer sure his research would be allowed to continue given the strategic importance the Joint

Chiefs now placed on its use. A thought that made the whole issue much more personal to him.

The next morning's security briefing at the White House was a troubling repeat of the day before, and the day before that, and the day before that. The FBI and the CIA had made no further progress in their efforts to locate the home of the aircraft builders. With the entire world to search for two thousand people to find, the lack of progress was pretty much expected, but that still didn't sit well with anyone in the room.

President Bender summed up the various efforts. "So far, we have three different fronts on which we're still looking for this group. The CIA is concentrating their efforts into looking for a low-profile settlement that doesn't quite fit into its locale. The FBI is investigating the alleged last member of the group to disappear. And finally, Dr. Harris' project is on the lookout for any disturbances around the earth, or anywhere near the Lancaster asteroid, just in case this technology was the cause of the course changes."

Masters added, "And, with NASA getting ready to launch the probe, we might have a chance, albeit a small one, of catching on film any space-based craft or installation on the asteroid itself."

Looking at Diane, the president asked, "Is the asteroid still on course to impact the moon?"

"Yes, it is Mr. President. The latest figures from JPL show that if it remains on course, the asteroid will impact the moon in just under four days, placing the point of impact well out of sight of earth, on the lower half of the back side of the moon."

"And that's for certain?" asked President Bender.

"As close as we can tell," replied Diane.

"How soon before we can get that probe up and around the backside of the moon to get us images of the impact zone?" Bender inquired.

"The shuttle launch comes about forty-eight hours after the time of impact. Boosting it around the moon using the additional delta-V in the auxiliary tanks can place the probe in lunar orbit in about five and a half days. Figure a week after we boost it away from earth it should be in a position to relay images of the impact site."

"Good. How's the commission working out? Have any racial problems raised their ugly head out there?" asked the president.

"No sir, nothing that's been brought to my attention. But I've heard that's not the case at the Pentagon. Two different sources have come to me inquiring about your position on the exclusions of African American officers from some of the higher-level strategy sessions over there. My guess, Mr. President, is that if I'm getting direct inquiries then the actual situation over there must be close to getting out of hand," Diane finished.

President Bender nodded to the Simon to make note of what Diane said, he wanted to get on top of that situation *before* it blew up in their faces.

Masters accompanied the president back to the Oval Office to discuss the Pentagon situation.

"I knew that son of a bitch Kaminski would make this into a problem for us, I should have stepped on him harder from the beginning." President Bender was royally pissed at having yet another unnecessary crisis to deal with. "And where was he today anyway?"

"He's out of town for the day. I don't think there was anything else you could have said to him, Mr. President. He's always had a reputation for doing pretty much whatever *he* thought was right. Unfortunately, in this case he's a political neophyte. I don't think he's got the stones to deal with what the political realities are, let alone be smart enough to not step directly in it," Masters said, shaking his head. "I will say this though, if it comes down to a direct confrontation, he's about the only one who's going to have a chance of pulling off any kind of victory."

"Damned if I do, and damned if I don't. Give some thought to how we're going to play this one out in the press if it comes off with a bang, not a whimper.

"I'm also not happy with the lack of progress in finding this group. Dammit, it's like trying to push against air, we have nothing on which to base any of our contingency plans. How do you plan a military solution to a problem that has no shape, size or location? It's infuriatingly frustrating," President Bender lamented.

"I know," Simon said softly. "But this single situation, if we do finally find these people, is probably going to define your presidency. The situation is unprecedented in the history of the United States. What ever conclusion emerges is pretty much your contribution to history."

Just then the telephone rang. After picking up the instrument and listening, Bender just said "Shit" and hung up. Grabbing the remote control off the desk he turned the television on.

The network's talking head was reporting on breaking news from the Pentagon.

"Unnamed sources in the Pentagon have confirmed that upper level African American officers in all branches of the armed services are being reassigned to less sensitive posts, or are being outright excluded from any operations covered under national security directive. It was further stated that the Joint Chiefs are developing invasion and pacification plans against an, and I quote, unknown community of African Americans living in isolation from the rest of America, unquote. So far there's been no comment from the White House . . ."

Just then the President's phone rang again; this time Masters answered.

"Our official response at this time is no comment. The president does not respond to anonymous sources regardless of how much the press is screaming for a response," and without waiting for an answer, hung up.

"Well sir, the proverbial shit is hitting the fan. What else did they say?" he asked, seeing Bender switching from one news channel to another, looking for similar reports.

"Not much, they didn't have anyone to interview on camera so it's pretty much just rumor and innuendo. Get me that son of a bitch, I want him here this afternoon," said Bender, referring to the chairman.

"Mr. President, you have a trip to New York this afternoon to speak about continuing ethical issues in corporate business practices and accounting."

"I don't care, have him meet me on the plane then. I am the Commander in Chief, aren't I? Then tell him I ordered him to be there, I've had enough of his pissing on my parade."

"Yes, sir. Is there anything else, Jim?" Masters asked, mindful of his own dressing down on the issue of race.

"Is my speech ready? I want to look it over before I get there. It's bad enough that I have issues of my own to face, but constantly having to keep cleaning up after someone else's crap is a pain in the ass."

"I'll check on it right away, sir."

Masters got to his feet and made his way back to his own office. When he reached his desk he called the White House press chief and let him know that there would be no statement from the president concerning this latest flap at the Pentagon. He also passed along that there was to be a news blackout on the chairman riding along to New York with the president that afternoon.

Masters called Diane Churchill's office and left word for her people to send him the travel itinerary of Norma Lancaster. It wouldn't hurt to have the president seen with the young scientist. It might be a good idea to see if he could have the leadership of the Congressional Black Caucus make the appropriate statements in support of the president's appointment of Lancaster to the commission.

By now dozens of telescopes were continuously trained on the incoming asteroid, with new pictures posted daily in the news and on the Internet. The CIA had even retasked several of their better spy satellites to track the object, trying to catch anything unusual in its immediate vicinity.

All the attention made Norma's life a never-ending series of interviews, only this time the demands of the foreign press were just as onerous as those from her native land. Asteroid fever climbed to a nearly hysterical pitch as the hours to impact counted down.

The US Air Force had also secretly raised its own alert status in the event the asteroid were to take a turn for the worse and alter course toward earth. Most administration-level officers privately thought the whole exercise in preparedness a complete waste of time, given that no weapons technology on earth would make the slightest difference against a piece of rock that large.

Fortunately for the president, the furor over the impending collision with the moon was *the* top news story around the clock, pushing everything else off the front pages and the top of the hour news broadcasts.

NASA had managed to push the launch of the shuttle up by almost forty-eight hours in an effort to get the probe underway that much faster. The four scientists currently stationed at the International Space Station had completed unpacking and preparing the outboard fuel tanks for the probe the Russians had sent up earlier in the week. Everyone seemed as though they couldn't wait to see the probe safely on its way.

Inside Shelter Fourteen everyone was just as consumed with the impending collision as the rest of the world. The fact that the impact was going to take place on the back side of the moon, out of direct sight of observers on earth, made their isolation somewhat more bearable. And yet, they were just as excited about the impending event given their unique ability to track the asteroid's progress using Dr. Harris' detector.

Alan, along with the rest of the naval programmers. had begun his own side project to display the local space around the earth in a three-dimensional format on the high-definition television screens scattered throughout the complex. This same picture was transmitted in real time to NASA, JPL, and various departments and agencies throughout Washington, DC.

There was an added bonus to using Alan's display to monitor the event: the information was received instantaneously. There was no waiting for the round trip of radio signals, no lag in downloading digital images from satellites and having to decode and render them for transmission and display around the world. Even though Alan's display didn't actually show Norma's rock, or the cratered surface of the moon, it was still like something out of some kind of science fiction movie. It was somehow more compelling for all its immediacy.

The players in the investigation centered in Atlanta were also watching the events taking place in space, each from their own perspectives. Samuels was hoping that the asteroid wouldn't end up as some kind of axe literally held above the earth's head. Detective Mathews was watching pretty much as one spectator out of billions, seeing galactic history pass before his eyes. And both men were left to wonder from what perspective Sydney watched the events unfold in the sky.

She and John hadn't managed to spend much quality time together between Sydney's trips to college fairs around the country and John's travel out of town to retrace investigations of the last few people to disappear.

Agent Minor was happy to still be working on the investigation. He felt that with persistence he would somehow find that one little piece of evidence, that one overlooked clue that would give them their 'aha' moment. His primary focus was tracing back the sender of the cryptic e-mail message to Dean Atkins, trying to find the actual person behind the seemingly blind account. He set up a tracer, a small program that would inform him whenever the owner accessed the account, either reading or writing a message.

He hadn't seen John since his confrontation with Samuels. He missed John dropping by and thought about sending him a message asking when they could make good on their dinner plans or go shooting again, but Minor felt bad about how Samuels had tried to use him. He wasn't quite sure if John lumped him into the same bag as Samuels. He wondered if his call would be answered or returned.

Sleight of hand
Hands of fate
Chance you take
Life's a snake
And it's all in the draw, of the cards
Draw of the Cards
Written Dave Ellingson, Bill Cuomo and Val Garay, performed by Kim Carnes

CHAPTER 31

THE DAY OF the collision between the Lancaster asteroid and the moon dawned bright and clear in Houston.

In Washington, the air was still warm and humid as the wheels of the government were coming up to speed. But even in the capital more than a handful decided to miss work to watch the all-day news coverage of the asteroid hitting the moon.

Nearly everyone in America and most of the rest of the world were just putting in time until the hour when the two pieces of the heavens were destined to meet.

The busiest people that day weren't on earth at all; they were the engineering crew on the shuttle Atlantis, assisting an engineer and a scientist stationed aboard the International Space Station making a rare space walk. They were currently in the middle of the most crowded EVA in history. A full five astronauts were suited up and out in space assembling the probe and attaching the outboard fuel tanks sent up earlier by the Russians.

For safety, the crew gently maneuvered the probe several hundred feet away from the space station and the shuttle, awaiting the command from Houston to trigger the probe's rockets. When the countdown reached zero, the shuttle command crew treated everyone on earth to a close-up of the probe's rockets firing from the camera mounted in the window of the command deck.

Though the probe appeared to leave the area quickly, becoming just a tiny reflection against the tapestry of space, the trip to the moon would still take over three days.

On earth, several cable television stations were broadcasting a split screen showing the virtual display from Dr. Harris' lab on one side and the real-time view of Norma's asteroid from the International Space Station's telescope on the other.

The scene switched to President Bender standing in front of a podium with a number of NASA's earlier rockets pointing skyward over his left shoulder.

"My fellow Americans. I come to you today on the eve of this historic occasion to celebrate several triumphs of American scientific know-how, and to celebrate the ingenuity and the persistence of the American worker. This address is coming to you from NASA headquarters here at the Johnson Space Center in Houston, Texas, the nerve center of our efforts to document this momentous occasion and extend our knowledge, once again, beyond the boundaries of planet Earth.

"It was here that the beginning of a project that led us to discover this traveler coming to our neighborhood was conceived. The fruits of this project, born of the imagination of a young scientist who took an idea and made it into a reality, are the reason the whole world has been captivated by tonight's events in the heavens.

"This young scientist who we have all grown to know in the past few months should be an inspiration to us all. Ms. Norma Lancaster, the discoverer for whom this visiting piece of our solar system was named, is the best example of the kind of 'right stuff' we Americans are made."

At the mention of Norma's name by the president nearly everyone in the theater at the shelter stood up and cheered, drowning out his words for almost a a minute. Just as the crowd calmed down, the camera panned and briefly centered on Norma as her name was flashed at the bottom of the screen and the cheering began anew.

Mercifully, the president's address was short, and then the coverage moved on to the NASA probe and the cooperative effort of the United States and Russian space programs. Unexpectedly, there was a brief mention of Alan Richards' role in the original animation of Norma's asteroid and as the source of the real-time graphical representation of the asteroid's position in relationship to the moon's surface. Whoops of laughter and jeers erupted from the entire assemblage as Alan's high school graduation picture briefly flashed on the screen.

The underground party kicked itself into full swing until shortly before the impact. As the majority of the partygoers settled down to watch the news coverage on the screen, Alan, Martin and the commander slipped away to the lab to monitor the collision site using the high-resolution mode of the new and improved detector.

Alan began setting up the computers connected to the detector to sweep the moon and the closing asteroid for any changes in the gravitational fields.

Looking at the news feed, Ames pointed to the screen and said, "Look, the asteroid has passed behind the moon. It won't be long now."

Alan widened the detector's focus to include scanning the data from the incoming piece of rock. As the data was streaming by, Alan noted that the countdown calculations showed that the impact would occur in just under six minutes.

"Anything unusual there, Alan?" Ames asked.

"Nothing so far. The acceleration due to their mutual attraction is increasing and the asteroid's speed has increased by almost four percent. It won't be long now." Alan's entire attention was focused on the display before him.

Meanwhile, Martin had pulled up his own display, showing the raw numbers of the force of the gravitational constants of the moon, and the much lower gradient of the asteroid itself. He switched his computer to record the data, much like a VCR, for analysis later.

Alan switched his display to the large screen at the end of the room and the three of them watched as the two objects grew closer together. When the asteroid was about three minutes from impact, Martin's computer began to beep.

He rolled across the room to his workstation and shouted, "Son of a bitch! Take a look at this!"

Alan and Ames both ran to see what the commotion was all about. "The gravitational constant between the asteroid and the moon is dropping. It's actually reversing, the rock is slowing down!" Martin punched in a bunch of commands, as the alert lights began to flash above the laboratory door. "Shit, the monitoring room team's seen it too," he said.

Ames stood up abruptly and said to Martin, "What else do you see? I need to get on the horn to Washington, ASAP!"

"The asteroid is still going to hit, it's just losing much of its momentum. The impact will probably result in less than twenty-five percent of the inertia the asteroid carried with it. Go on, I'm recording everything I can and so is Alan," Martin said getting a confirming nod from the young programmer.

Just before Ames went through the door, Alan asked, "Should I cut the feed to the news channels?"

Ames stopped and thought for a second. "Martin, is the feed showing anything that indicates what's going on with gravity up there?"

"Nope, it's just the positions, commander," Martin answered, fully aware of the complete change in Ames' demeanor.

"Leave it go, if we shut it down everyone's going to know something's up." As Commander Ames cleared the room a number of scientists and staff were making their way quickly to Martin's lab, anxious to see what was going on. Leading the charge was Paul Milton, pulling his reading glasses out of their case in preparation for action, like a knight girding his loins for battle.

"Martin, we saw the alert lights, what's going on with the asteroid? What's happened?" Paul asked.

"It looks like it's slowing down instead of speeding up. According to the data we have here the gravitational constants in the immediate vicinity of the moon and surrounding the asteroid itself have been reduced and in some way reversed, slowing the forward progress of the rock."

"Is it still going to hit?" Paul asked.

"Oh, yeah. It's not going to reverse its path, at least not with the relatively small gravitational effect we're seeing here. But I'm afraid the geologists are going to be disappointed, there's not going to be anywhere near the impact they expected. Impact in about seventy seconds," Martin announced.

In the monitoring center Commander Ames was on a conference call with the watch commander at NORAD and General Kaminski explaining what the data indicated.

"It still looks like impact in just over a minute, and no, I don't think there is any direct threat to the US or anyone else on earth. What we're seeing is someone, or some thing, effectively dampening the forward progress of the asteroid so that its impact will not, I repeat, will not have the force previously expected. Stand by, are you watching the feed?" Ames asked.

The whole world watched as the two objects on the screen merged into one. One of the technicians had counted down from ten, just before the asteroid touched down.

The rest of the naval monitoring team listened as Ames continued. "No sir, it is my opinion that raising the defense condition will only yield unnecessary attention, letting both our allies, and enemies, in on the fact that we observed something snaky in this event. No sir, I can be in Washington in five hours if you send someone to pick me up, do you want Dr. Harris to tag along? Yes sir, he *is* the best we have at the moment."

Ames was silent, obviously listening to a long list of instructions and admonitions, if his frequent "yes sirs" were any clue. Hanging up the phone, he looked at the curious technicians who had obviously heard that something important was up. "Gentlemen, nothing of what you observed here, nor anything of my conversation, leaves this room. Is that understood?" he asked quietly.

The naval technicians stood and saluted.

Commander Ames returned a salute and said on his way out the door, "No one without authorization is to be in this room for any reason whatsoever. And someone shut off that damn blinking light," he said, pointing to the alert light flashing over the door.

Around the world, everyone watched as the two objects merged into one, feeling let down that there wasn't some sort of explosive payoff at impact.

In Houston, President Bender was in mission control watching the graphic showing the impact when Agent Bishop tapped him on the shoulder and whispered in his ear, "Flash traffic from the Pentagon, sir. We have a room for you to take the call."

The president followed Bishop and was himself followed by two others in the Secret Service detail. Reaching a small conference room, the President saw an air force signals officer holding the receiver of a telephone connected to a metal suitcase.

The Captain handed the phone to the president and saluted.

"The is the president," he answered.

"Mr. President, this is the CJCS, I have an alert for you. Are you prepared to copy?" he asked.

"Go ahead."

"Mr. President, we have direct evidence that the asteroid's path was affected by parties unknown who were able to manipulate the speed of the asteroid by changing the gravitational attraction between it and the moon. So far we have no location of the person or persons responsible. However, I recommend we up our defensive posture, sir."

"Is there any reason to believe that whoever affected the asteroid poses a direct danger to the security of the United States?"

"Mr. President, at this time they have demonstrated capabilities beyond anything we currently have under development. That alone presents a potential danger to the security of the United States, it is my recommendation that we upgrade our forces to DefCon 3."

"And that will accomplish what, general? With nowhere to direct our forces, isn't going to DefCon 3 going to announce to the rest of the world that something's up? And doesn't that, in all likelihood, include those we seek?" President Bender asked pointedly.

"That's a chance I believe we need to take, Mr. President. I cannot stress enough the importance of maintaining a higher state of readiness in the event that these same people decide to threaten or attack this country or any of its interests."

"General, I am giving you a direct order to have the military stand down. Do not, I repeat, do not upgrade the defense condition of the military at this time. I will be returning directly to Washington and will need a detailed briefing on the events as they occurred. Also get me someone who can discuss the implications of what happened up there."

Handing the receiver back to the captain to forestall any further dialog with the CJCS, President Bender told Agent Bishop that he needed to leave immediately, not realizing Bishop had already put the traveling detail and Air Force One on notice.

On the way to Air Force One, Simon made the call to the White House informing the president's personal secretary to call the entire national security team into session upon the his return. He then sat back with President Bender and watched the streets of Houston go by in silence, thinking with sad amusement that none of them had the least idea what their country faced as a result of the events in the sky.

Ames and Martin sipped coffee in a large conference room at the White House, waiting for the arrival of the president and others on the national security team. Ames directed Martin to set up his laptop computer at the far end of the table and showed him where to connect the cable that would transmit the computer's screen display to the larger television screen at the end of the table.

Thankful to have something to do to occupy himself with while they awaited the arrival of everyone else, Martin began to organize the various pictures and charts he had hastily compiled on the way to Washington.

Martin called Ames over and the two of them composed a presentation that more or less covered the data the shelter's gravity detector had collected. While they were working, they heard a helicopter in the background and no more than five minutes later President Bender and Simon Masters entered the room, followed by Agent Bishop.

When they all had coffee and had taken their seats, President Bender said, "Well, boys, just what did you see down there that has the general trying to heat up the missiles and launch the bombers? Just give me the quick rundown before everyone else arrives."

Deferring to his colleague, Ames let Martin begin.

"Mr. President, everything was going along fine. We were able to track the asteroid with no trouble. Then, at just under three minutes from impact, the gravitational attraction between the asteroid and the moon began to, well, to dissipate, for lack of a better way to describe it. The force of gravity that was drawing them together had been reduced effectively to zero, and then reversed. The two objects began to repel each other, not enough to make the asteroid fly away from the moon, just enough to reduce the impact to a fraction of the force there should have been. Even with the reduction in velocity, the asteroid still smacked into the moon with a hell of a whack, but nothing like the crater-popping force we were looking for." Martin waited for the President and Masters to absorb what he had said.

Masters then asked, "How much power do you think it took to do what you've described up there?"

"I haven't a clue. The asteroid weighed millions of tons and was moving thousands of miles an hour with the moon's gravity pulling it faster and faster to its surface. To reverse the inertia of that much rock and ice would probably take the combined output of every power generating plant in the United States for about twenty years, maybe. But that's only a guess, it could have taken fifty years' output, or a hundred. I have no real idea." said Martin, as he began to scribble furiously on the pad of paper in front of him.

Commander Ames, forgetting himself, said, "Holy shit!" Then remembering where he was, immediately said, "I'm sorry, Mr. President. It just slipped out."

"No problem, Commander," President Bender said with a smile, "you just saved me the trouble. Dr. Harris, was there any way you could determine the source of the power that was used to accomplish what happened?"

"I'm sorry, sir. There was no way to trace back the source. We don't even know what to look for. The power to do this has to be something we've never encountered before, I don't even think it's nuclear-based. That sort of thing would be pretty hard to conceal no matter where it was."

"Commander, what do you and the rest of the commission think the overall level of threat this technology presents to the security of the United States?" asked Masters.

Cutting a glance at Agent Bishop standing next to the door, Ames decided to speak his mind.

"Mr. President, given the fact that these people, if it's the group everyone seems to want to suspect, have never threatened the lives or interests of the US and that they've protected their privacy so well for decades, I estimate the level of threat is low.

"From the summaries I read from the FBI, we're looking at somewhere between fifteen hundred and two thousand people, African Americans exclusively, who have never revealed themselves to their families or friends once they disappeared. For all practical purposes they were content to let everyone believe that they were dead. Now all of a sudden we believe they aren't dead. As far as we can tell, they have isolated themselves from American society, wanting little, if anything from us. My question has always been, just where is this threat everyone's so afraid of? I would think that demonstrating that they can throw something the size of that piece of rock would give them the credibility to demand pretty much whatever they wanted. And yet, we've heard nothing."

Ames sat back and shrugged his shoulders. "Why is everyone so anxious to classify them as hostile and attack them or, worse yet, invade their homes and steal what they've got? I still haven't heard a single voice of reason expressing a desire to open a dialog with these people when they're found; just preparations for war. If you'll excuse me for speaking plainly, sir."

Bender cast a significant glance to Simon, which wasn't lost on Agent Bishop, and replied, "I mostly agree with you, commander. I don't want to stir up trouble where none exists. But, let me tell you what's lined up against the live and let live philosophy you obviously would like to see played out.

"At the head of the line is General Kaminski. He has stated he will fight to his dying breath, that he will protect his adopted homeland from any and all dangers, foreign and domestic. He doesn't see that as a cliche, it's what he lives and breathes. In his zealousness to keep America secure he has polarized every branch of the military by shoving African American officers out of the chain of command just in case they *might*, mind you, *might* have divided loyalties.

"You have the rest of the command staff of the various branches chomping at the bit to get their hands on the unprecedented power these technologies represent to convert into better weapons of mass destruction, *and* they want to make damn sure that the fall only into the hands of the United States military, not in the hands of any of our enemies, or even our friends.

"You have well-meaning people here in Washington," Bender began, again cutting a glance at Masters, "who are so short-sighted and shallow they would just as soon tar everyone of a group with the same brush as the worst of them until proven otherwise. Hell, I'm surprised you're still at the helm of the Dr. Harris' project given the colorful circumstance of your birth, if you'll excuse my bringing up the obvious.

"You have thousands of corporations throughout every industry in America clamoring for the next big thing that will ensure their continued accumulation of great, and in many cases, unearned, wealth. Not to mention their lobbyists and business friends who have influence in congress, spreading around cash and favors to insure preferential treatment somewhere down the line.

"You have millions of Americans who'll demand any largess gleaned from these people as their birthright, regardless of whether or not they earned or deserved it.

"And finally – please don't take offense at this Dr. Harris – you have the scientific community and the intelligentsia who believe that scientific knowledge, any and all major discoveries, should be shared freely, regardless of the source or sweat it took to uncover. I don't believe I've left anyone out.

"So now you know on just how sharp an edge we balance whenever we try to decide the best way to proceed. I think you'll get a bird's-eye view of what I'm talking about in about fifteen minutes once this meeting begins." The President measured the look of the two men, and found that he liked what he saw. They both had quite a bit of starch in them, though coming from very different worlds.

Martin and Ames started the meeting with an overview of the events that occurred on the moon. Someone else followed with a summary of the capabilities that the technology suggested. The final minutes of the meeting quickly became a polite argument about the responses the various departments of the government should undertake. The more vocal arguments were dominated by the stubborn insistence of the chairman that the defensive posture of the country should be elevated "just in case."

Martin got an eye-opening view of the highest level of the most powerful nation in the world getting things done. He saw everyone acting like an advocate for their own department or special interest group. The argument over what to do, who to exclude and how to deal with the racial backlash continued for quite a while. Everyone bent over backwards to be politically correct in their arguments in deference to the commander and Agent Bishop's presence, so the mood of the room remained cordial.

As far as Martin could see they were at an impasse, and he was letting the discussion go in one ear and out the other until he heard General Kaminski state disgustedly, "I don't care whose feelings we hurt. These people, if they are indeed able to operate out past the moon, have established a beachhead on the highest ground possible. I'm not going to have the entire military of the United States of America stand by and do nothing, becoming sitting ducks to a bunch of niggers in space."

The room went silent. Everyone looked first at Ames and Bishop then to President Bender, waiting for his reaction to the chairman's remark.

"General, do you want to spend the next twenty years in Leavenworth?" the president asked quietly, drawing gasps from more than one person seated around the table. "Do I have to have you taken into custody right here and now for actions taken against the best interests of the United States of America and refusing to take orders from the commander in chief?" President Bender asked, noting out of the corner of his eye Agent Bishop whispering into his microphone.

To his credit Kaminski didn't actually piss his pants; however, most of the color drained from his normally florid face. It was almost as if those sitting on either side of the chairman had taken one giant step away from the man's seat, leaving him alone in the spotlight of President Bender's glare.

"Absolutely not, Mr. President. My aim was not to disobey any direct order, but I just didn't want the country caught with its pants down. I'm trying to save lives *and* protect the country, sir."

"I understand that part of your intent, and have no problem with you voicing your concerns. What I am referring to is your remark concerning the nature of the group we face. I am well aware of the problems you've created behind my back with your directives at the Pentagon, not to mention they've already been leaked to the press. I am also well aware of your own personal opinions regarding the role of African Americans in the armed services. It's a shame that someone born in another country could have learned so well the worst of what this country has to teach. African Americans are as much a part of this country as you and your parents, even more so because they have scores of generations of blood, sweat and tears invested in this great land, General. I will not tolerate that kind of behavior from you or anyone else in my administration, or any other department of the government, again.

"At this point I can't control what you think, and frankly I don't give a damn. However, if you can't behave like you love each and every American living in this, or any other country, I'm having your ass thrown in Leavenworth. Do you understand me?

"Oh, and don't think a resignation will shield you from my wrath. If you think you're going to leave this administration and get away with saying a single word against African Americans, against me, or against any actions this administration undertakes in this situation, I will personally hunt you down and have you locked up for the rest of your natural life. Do you understand where I'm coming from, Mr. Chairman?" President Bender finished, his voice barely above a whisper.

White as a sheet of paper, the chairman answered, "Yes, sir. I'm very sorry sir, it won't happen again. I also want to apologize to the rest of you for my remarks, especially to the agent at the door and Commander Ames. What I said was indefensible, and will not be repeated."

"Thank you, General. Now, if no one else wants to act like an ass for our entertainment, I suggest we get back to the business at hand. Here's what I want from all of you, simple and to the point: I want these people found."

Looking directly at FBI and CIA, the president said, "I want any clue run down, I want anyone who could possibly lead us to these people squeezed. I want to find this group before they come knocking at our door. Where are you with this possible contact you've got in Atlanta?" Bender asked the FBI.

"So far sir, we've got nothing. The initial evidence was so circumstantial that the Special Agent in Charge hasn't been able to develop anything further, but he does have someone on them just in case. Unfortunately, it looks like it's a dead end."

Looking at Martin and Ames the President asked, "Dr. Harris, Commander, is there any way to back-trace the source of the gravitational manipulation, no matter how remote? Do you need any further support down there? I need *something* that's going to lead us to these people."

Martin shook his head and placed his hands flat on the table in surrender. "All the way here I was racking my brain for any way to locate the source of the effect. I can't even imagine the means they're using to generate gravity fields. I mean are we talking warp power, or antimatter? Hell, science fiction is just as good a place to start as real science at this point.

"Right now, my people back at the lab are running high-resolution scans of the impact area on the moon and over every square inch of the surface of the earth looking for any unusual gravitational signatures. This is about the only way I can think of to locate the source."

"Dr. Harris, are your people also scanning underwater and underground? If these people can slow millions of tons of space debris, there's no reason they can't build some kind of base whose construction is completely unprecedented," added the CJCS.

"We already thought about that. I believe our people are not excluding anything down to about five miles below the mean surface of the earth and oceans and up through every mountain range. If they aren't currently using any gravity-altering technologies, they can avoid detection for quite a while," answered Commander Ames.

"But if they do, we've got them, right?" the President asked.

"Yes sir, I believe we do."

"Good." Looking over to the Air Force, Bender asked, "How long before we get that probe around to the back side of the moon?"

"Actually, sir, I checked on that before I came. If we trade longevity for speed we can cut down the remainder of the trip to just over two days. Orbital insertion at the higher speed is going to be trickier, but NASA says it's doable, they've got the fuel. The probe just won't be able to maneuver for as long in orbit if we deplete most of the fuel getting it there quicker."

"Do it," ordered Bender. "I want eyes up as soon as possible. Someone wanted the asteroid to crash into the moon in the first place. I don't know why it was directed there, no one has claimed what happened as a demonstration of their superior capabilities, but I'm betting no one sends something that large careening around the solar system on a whim. I suspect there might be something going on back there and I want to know what it is."

"Yes sir, as soon as the meeting concludes I'll alert NASA to reprogram the probe for a high-speed insertion," confirmed Air Force.

"Do we have any backup in case this one goes south on us?" Bender asked.

"Not so far, the shuttle Atlantis is due back in Houston in two days, Endeavour can be ready to launch in about fifteen days. We have nothing in the works in the form of a single rocket lifting system, no missiles, nothing in waiting. I'll check with the Europeans, the Russians and anyone else who can lift something into high orbit, but quietly of course, sir."

"Very good," said the President. "Can anyone think of anything we've overlooked?"

Diane Churchill, who up until now had been silent throughout the meeting, spoke up. "Has anyone given any thought to the idea that these people might not be operating on earth at all?"

"Are you serious?" asked Masters. "Do you honestly think that someone has their own space station out there? How'd we miss it for so long?"

"We're only thinking near-earth orbit. What if they're in the L4 or L5 Lagrange orbit positions?"

"What do you mean, Diane?" the President asked.

Getting up and pulling a flip chart over to the table, Diane began to draw. "Look, here's the sun," she said, drawing a circle in the center of the page, "and here's earth," adding a second circle in the twelve o'clock position. "The L4 and L5 positions are here, and here, about one sixth ahead and behind earth, in the same orbit as earth," drawing Xs in both positions.

"Anything lifted into orbit and placed in the advanced or the trailing position in the earth's orbit will tend to stay there because these points are what we call metastable. The gravitational forces are in balance there. Additionally, there would be almost no chance of detection because we rarely look in those areas."

Without warning Diane began to laugh.

"Something strike you as funny?" the president asked.

"I was going to say that putting a space station out there in that orbit would take a hell of a lot of delta-V, but if you can control gravity that question is moot," she answered as several of the others laughed along with her, the president even managing a grin.

"Commander, Dr. Harris, would you direct your scanning team to check those coordinates when you get back? Thank you. And thank you too, Diane. Anyone else have something to add?" Bender asked, looking around the room.

"Nothing? Fine. Dr. Harris and Commander Ames, thank you for coming here again on short notice. If the two of you think of anything you need that will help your efforts at the lab, call me and it's yours. By the way, would you please leave all of your data behind so some of our people here can take a look at it?

"Mr. Chairman, are we on the same page regarding keeping our military at DefCon 4?" Bender asked the general.

"Yes, Mr. President. I will continue to have the services draft those contingency plans should these people be located here on earth," he said. "And as to the CNN coverage of the other issue, I'll draft a statement and begin immediately to see what can be done to smooth things over."

"Thank you very much, General."

"Everyone, let's all get the hell out of here and go earn our pay."

As everyone was getting to their feet, President Bender signaled for Kaminski to stay behind. When everyone but the chairman had left the room, Agent Bishop walked out into the hallway and pulled the door shut behind him.

Bender motioned the general to the seat beside him. "This country has gone this way before, and each time we got bit in the ass when the dust cleared.

"When the word officially gets out concerning the makeup of the group we seek, it's going to polarize the country, probably even the world. I want what we do to be completely aboveboard and above reproach. I owe you an apology as well. I used you to make a point with everyone else at that meeting. However, make no mistake, I will prosecute anyone who uses the investigation to discriminate against anyone else.

"I've already had to kick Simon's ass back in line and I'm tired of having to deal with this whole issue, especially in my own house."

"Truly, I understand, sir. It won't happen again," said Kaminski. "I will smooth things over back at the Pentagon."

"I'm sure you will. Thank you for your help, General. I'll see you in the morning at the regular briefing."

"Thank you, Mr. President."

The chairman took his leave and Agent Bishop accompanied his charge back to the Oval Office.

"Sam, may I ask you a personal question?"

"Any time, sir, you don't have to ask first," Bishop answered.

"Do you think I came down too hard on the chairman?"

"I don't want to talk out of school, sir, but from what I've heard from other agents, he has some hangups that are just as much a part of his military upbringing as anything else. I think what you did probably will make him think things over before they get out of hand. I really can't say much else, sir."

"Yeah, I don't know either. I'm just going to have to wait and see," President Bender said, shaking his head.

Smiling faces, sometime pretend to be your friend
Smiling faces show no traces of the evil that lurks within
Smiling Faces Sometimes
Written by Norman Whitfield and Barrett Strong,
performed by The Undisputed Truth

CHAPTER 32

A TLANTA WOKE UP the day
after the anticlimactic meeting of
the Lancaster asteroid and the moon pretty much like any other day. John called
Sydney's office to see what she was doing for lunch. Reaching her voice mail, he
left a message for her to call him if she found herself free around noon, leaving
his mobile phone number for her to call him back.

He decided to bite the bullet and accept Samuels' overture to recoup their
friendship, or at least a more harmonious working relationship. He called over
to the FBI offices looking for Samuels, but was connected to Minor instead, who
informed him Samuels was back in Washington. John shot the breeze with Minor
for a few minutes and hung up, somewhat at a loss for what to do with himself
for the remainder of the morning.

John decided to get out of the house and grab breakfast somewhere
downtown. As he walked toward his car, he was startled to see Samuels pull up
to the curb and gesture him inside. Puzzled, John got into the sedan which quickly
moved back out on to the street.

"Jeff just told me you were in DC, what's up?" John asked.

"I just got back a half an hour ago. Jeff doesn't know I'm back. Something
happened last night that's changed everything," Samuels answered.

"What do you mean by everything? Are you talking about the investigation or do you really mean everything, as in someone's found who we're looking for"? John prompted.

"Tell you what, I'll let you decide. I didn't take you away from anything important, did I?"

"No, we were on call last night at the station, I'm not due in until noon or so."

"Good. Let me start from the beginning." Taking a deep breath, Samuels began.

"Yesterday, before the main news coverage of the impact began, parts of the military were on high alert, just in case something went wrong with the incoming asteroid. Although what they could have done wouldn't have amounted to much, but you know how they are. Anyway, everything was fine until about three minutes before impact and then that's when the shit hit the fan."

"What happened?"

"The gravitational attraction between the moon and the asteroid reversed!"

"Reversed how? As far as I saw, the thing still crashed into the moon. What do you mean by reversed?" asked John.

"It slowed the asteroid down so much that it just about soft-landed on the moon instead of blasting a huge hole in the ground up there, or at least that's what NASA thinks."

"How do we know? Did someone see the thing go down?" asked John.

"No, not yet at least. NASA launched a probe a few hours before impact, but it's not scheduled to be there for a couple of days yet. The thing is, one of our secret project installations was able to somehow detect a change in gravity as it occurred. And get this, their measurements showed that the power necessary to do what was done was more than we generate in a decade." Samuels took his eyes off the road for a second to see John's reaction, he wasn't disappointed.

"Son of a bitch! That's huge! Do we have any clue where that power came from?" John asked.

"That's the thing. There was absolutely nothing that could be traced. The military's going apeshit, even though the President wants the discovery to stay extremely low-profile."

John whistled. "So let me take a guess. What's happened now is that the group we're looking for is believed to have access to power sources that cannot be duplicated by us, and they most definitely have capabilities that make our biggest and best technologies look like children's toys. And, that means finding these people has become job one."

"Absolutely, that's why I beat feet to get back here ASAP. So far, from the way I've written my reports, the director believes Atkins is a dead end, basically more coincidence than substance. What I want to know from you is, do you think we have any chance at all of getting something from her? The time's come to lay all the cards on the table because everything's about to change for the worse and I can't keep the hounds at bay forever. Things are getting desperate all over."

"Honestly, I don't know what she's got to give us. I still want an explanation for the two phone calls from Williams, but other than that and the circumstantial travel overlaps, I've got nothing. What do you think the president's likely to do?" John asked, more than a trace of worry in his voice.

"I'm not sure. The director told me that General Kaminski is already turning the military upside down, moving black officers out of sensitive posts and cutting them out of contingency planning, and it's only going to get worse as time goes on. The director's not going to follow the general's example, but he's asked me more than once whether or not I was completely sure that my conclusions on the investigation down here, and the covert background checks I ran on everyone up there, were cogent. He asked in no uncertain terms whether or not I'd stake my life on my findings."

"Jesus, you're not in the soup for this, are you? Does he think you're concealing something here?"

Shaking his head, Samuels answered, "I don't think so, but he's had to pass summaries of my reports, along with the results of the tests on the pilot's remains, to the president."

"What pilot?" asked John.

"Shit! Uh, I guess I can't ask you to forget I just said that, can I?"

"Hey, don't worry about me, I didn't hear a thing."

John stared straight ahead out the windshield, wondering just how much he didn't know about the investigation he was supposed to be such an important part of.

"Here's what gone down. But remember, I'm only telling you this so that you can better gauge the quality of the subject's responses to questioning if you cover information in this area, you get me?" said Samuels, his tone telling John exactly how to play it should the two of them get into hot water later.

"Yeah, I understand. So, what pilot?" asked John.

Samuels told John everything about the aircraft shot down in Iraq. "When our boys got there they discovered that a part of the pilot had been recovered, a foot, and they put it on ice and got it back to the states. Guess what? It was from a black man about forty years old."

"And everyone thinks it's from someone in our group, I take it?" asked John.

"It was definitely discussed. Most of the cabinet-level people seem to want to discount the possibility, but it's not a big leap to make. So now our forensics people are trying like hell to find out anything they can about this foot."

"So what did the director tell you to do now?" John asked, dreading the answer Samuels might give him.

"That's where he began grilling me on what our suspect might know, and were we really working that angle or was there something keeping us from putting the screws to them. I'm telling you, everyone's running around acting crazy in Washington. No one wants to face the possibility that if we end up having to go toe-to-toe with these folks, we're going to come out second. Think about how much power it would take to get a mile-wide piece of rock to move, let alone slow the thing down from traveling thousands of miles an hour in seconds."

"I know I'm probably pointing out the obvious, but is anyone running down the footprint from the pilot? Hell, if we only have about a thousand men in our group, how hard would it be to get their birth records and do a comparison to the infant footprints on the actual hospital birth document?" John asked.

"Son of a bitch . . . . son of a bitch! I completely overlooked that little tidbit. The guys in the lab don't know about this investigation so they probably said screw it trying to compare the print to every black man in America around the right age." Samuels stopped the car in the middle of the street to angry squeals of brakes of the cars behind him and made a U-turn, heading back in the direction of the FBI offices.

John barely kept up with Samuels as they quickly made their way from the garage to the office. They arrived at the door to see a greatly surprised Minor. John listened as Samuels told Minor to pull out the list of men from their group and break it down by age. Samuels had Minor e-mail the list, along with each subject's city of birth, to the director of the forensics lab in Washington. Once the list had been sent, Samuels picked up the phone, dialed and then waited for the lab director to come on the line.

When he answered Samuels said, "I've just e-mailed you a list of probables for the owner of the limb you received from overseas. No, I can't tell you how I know.. That's not important right now, but I do suggest you send for the birth certificates of these men and do a match of the prints. Yes, I'll do that. Thank you." Samuels said to Minor, "Our man in blue strikes again. You just made a molehill out of a mountain!"

"So kiss the guy and get it over with," Minor said sarcastically, grinning at John as the three of them laughed. He was glad that, at least for now, the detective and agent seemed to be on better terms.

"How long do you think it's going to take them to run down those records?" John asked when their laughter died down.

"Less than a week is my guess. It's not like they'll be able to do anything with a match other than know who we're dealing with. Good call, John."

At that moment John's phone rang. "Mathews speaking," he answered

"Hey, yourself," he said, as he held his hand up to quiet the others. "No, I was just talking to a couple of associates about a case. Sure I'm still free for lunch, what time can I pick you up? One o'clock is fine, see you then." He disconnected the call and put the phone away.

Before he could say anything, Samuels spoke up. "I don't want to screw anything up between the two of you, and what I said before still stands. I'm sorry for coming down on you before, if you want out as far as she's concerned I'll understand."

"As far as *I'm* concerned, that's behind us. It's not that I don't want to get to the bottom of this whole thing, I do. I just don't know how to get anything out of her without showing her what a double-dealing bastard I've been *and* possibly alerting the rest of the group, if she's involved, to our interest. If she's innocent of any involvement then I've blown the best thing I've had since I can remember, but if she's in it up to her pretty little neck she's one cool customer and I doubt I'll get anything substantive from her at all. Have any suggestions?"

Samuels sat back and put his feet up on the desk as he thought about the question.

"Honestly? I got nothin'. You got any ideas, Jeff?"

"Who me? I don't know nothin about interrogatin' no womens!" Minor answered in a horrible southern drawl. "Seriously guys, this woman makes up about five of me in the brains *and* looks department. If she were my age I'd be scared shitless of her. She's way out of my league."

"He's a lot of help, Robert. Why was it you keep him around?" John asked sarcastically.

"He always hits what he aims at?" suggested Samuels. "About all I can think of at this juncture is to keep playing it by ear. With the coverage of the asteroid impact so fresh, why not lead with that and see what you come up with. If the lab ever gets a positive match on the pilot's identity we may be able to backtrace some other connections."

General Kaminski refused to let fear of the separatists influence his retooling of the upper echelons of the military. He didn't care whose feathers he ruffled in his preparations for what he thought an inevitable confrontation.

The disquieting results of his personally motivated safeguards were reaching a climax. The rank and file members of the senior staffs, black and white, had registered their various objections to the CJCS's directives to no avail. The issue of race was polarizing the entire military establishment as nothing had since World War Two, with moderates and liberals left wondering what had set the clock back to the early 1900s. Their more bigoted brethren were seeing opportunity that had them salivating in anticipation of blacks losing postings to, in most cases, less qualified whites. This was a cracker's dream come true.

The news services were already quietly characterizing the upheaval as the precursor to a return to the turbulent conflict of the Sixties. More and more of the television news stations began carrying quotes from "unnamed sources" about the disturbing changes at the Pentagon.

America's black political machine was girding its loins for war. Word of boycotts and walkouts of civilian administrative and support personnel, not soldiers in the chain of command, were reaching the public. The White House was under constant pressure to explain the so far unexplainable goings on at the Pentagon.

The nation's African American gadflies were booking their flights, gassing up their cars and packing their bags for Washington, DC like sharks circling for the kill. The drought of rallying black-related issues in the last decade had the louder voices of the African American community thirsty for outrage.

Conservatives dismissed allegations as liberal alarmism, chiding the press for trying to turn rumor and innuendo into a firestorm of controversy to use against them. Liberals and moderates pointed to the reported changes at the Pentagon as a rollback of gains in equality at best, and at worst a return to the segregation of the forties with all its attendant civil rights issues. Scholars were divided over the legal implications of this kind of systematic exclusion.

The whole issue was feeding upon itself like the Worm of Ouroboros. Was the US capable of sustaining the kind of righteous indignation over inequities and institutionalized racism that would lead to its eventual repeal? Or, as so many agreed, had American culture become so dissipated and self-indulgent that few cared about the plight of others because their circumstance was the result of a wrong so obvious it signaled an end to what made America a haven of freedom and justice in the world?

America's youth had lived for a generation with little hope for their own future, a future of no jobs, no wealth, no hope for achieving status, lifestyle, or comfort equal to that of their parents. Could they rouse themselves from the self-indulgent pursuits television had conditioned them to covet so successfully as they grew into consumers separate from their parents? The systematic dumbing-down of America had virtually ensured that the government could pull off whatever underhanded business it wanted without comment or objection just as long as the talking heads on television fed everyone the proper words of safety, security and virtue for the country.

The administration was counting on several generations of apathy to keep events across the country from getting completely out of hand, the American Civil Liberties Union, Rainbow PUSH and the Nation of Islam notwithstanding.

The anticlimax of the collision of the Lancaster asteroid didn't do much in the way of distracting the nation. Hopefully the pictures transmitted by the probe of the impact zone would help slide the Pentagon debacle off the front pages, giving the administration a small respite.

The 101st Airborne Division stationed at Fort Campbell, Kentucky, was the lead assault group preparing for deployment to wherever in the world the separatists were located. The chain of command had been shuffled so every

African American above the rank of noncommissioned officer was reassigned for the duration.

The air assault division was at its highest level of alert, just short of actual deployment, to ensure that the bulk of their task force could be transported anywhere in the country in hours, most everyplace else in the world in forty-eight hours. However, they too were facing their own trials.

The membership of the assault force included African American troops in numbers that could not be eliminated or simply replaced. One out of four of the front-line troops were black, something that troubled the chairman greatly. During the expected invasion/pacification mission General Kaminski didn't want any members of the 101st to "go native", or find themselves conflicted about where their loyalties belonged. In closed-door meetings with the unit's commanding general, Kaminski disclosed the specifics of the air assault group's target. He also stressed that particular care was to be taken to acquire the technology held by the target group, admitting that there was a serious chance that the troops could find themselves outgunned by exotic weapons never before seen.

The 101st was shackled preparing for an operation against an enemy unknown while under specific orders to distrust over twenty percent of its personnel. The requirements sent down from the CJCS made planning the operation impossible.

The president's attention was only peripherally on the problems at the Pentagon and the entire loyalty versus race issue. He was concerned with the possible impact of the lunar probe's images scheduled to arrive late the next day. Although the satellite was built to air force specifications, NASA and JPL would receive the digitized images directly from the satellite as it traversed the side of the moon facing the earth. Pictures taken of the impact zone would be available when the probe was in direct line of sight of the earth. President Bender's concern was over any dissemination of these pictures without review. He was afraid of the fallout should the pictures show anything untoward at the point of impact.

The president requested Treasury to dispatch teams of agents to both locations where the satellite's images were to be received and processed to oversee the review of the images before they were released to the general public. Understandably both organizations resented and objected to restrictions to their operations, even in the name of national security. But the Bender administration knew it was going to have a tough row to hoe if there was something in the images they didn't want the public to see. And if past events were any kind of indication, any malfunction of the satellite just before it was scheduled to send pictures back to earth would only fuel the kind of conspiracy accusations surrounding the failure of the Mars probe at the end of the twentieth century.

NASA set up a direct, encrypted feed to the White House, so that as they received the pictures from the moon they could be instantly relayed to President

Bender. Simon Masters, at the president's request, called for the National Security Council to join the president when the first pictures were received.

No one knew what to expect, other than the resulting rubble of ice and rock dumped on the regolith-covered surface of the moon.

The commission was revising previous industrial and technical assessments made in light of the data Martin had recorded at impact. The tone of their revisions was considerably darker and took on an air of fear. Their reports were now more anxious about threat than enthusiastic about discovery.

The power the separatists demonstrated in reversing the momentum of millions of tons of rock and ice had humbled scientists who, until then, had only dealt in the realm of thousands of kilograms in terms of the capabilities of man's space program. The data showed they had the ability to manipulate objects that were so huge current scales were obsolete, and yet their means of manipulation were still unknown. They could easily have lifted the completely assembled International Space Station into high orbit many thousands of times over. That same power could have transported to the moon a habitat large enough to allow astronauts to live there for months, even years at a time, in one fell swoop. In fact, having millions of tons of lifting capability virtually ensured that the earth would never need to worry about collision with any space debris up to the size of a small moon if detected early enough.

Norma and the rest of the commission were busier than they had been at the beginning of their isolation, but now their work had begun to weigh on them emotionally. The White House's demands for them to provide comprehensive worst-case scenarios and the word reaching them through daily news broadcasts of the racial polarization of the military cast a depressive pall over their work.

America was the leading expert in the institutionalized punishment of nonwhites in the name of national security, giving no quarter, making no apology and passing off each such violation as a necessity of war, when in most cases the actions were only essential to the protection of the American economy. This propensity was not far from the minds of the nonwhite members of the commission, nor the nonwhite military and support personnel stationed at the shelter as they went about their daily routines. They couldn't help but wonder when they might be singled out for some sort of special treatment to ensure their loyalty to the country or as a preventative measure to minimize imagined harm to the United States of America.

Events at the shelter came to a head when two signs appeared over the twin water fountains just outside the commissary, one saying "White" and the other "Colored." Unfortunately, they were seen by several dozen people before someone tore them down. Word spread quickly, as did a tense hostility on the part of Dr. Roscoe and her fellow African Americans, which they aimed toward whomever put the signs up and every white person stationed there for tolerating the incident for even that brief time.

The black members of the commission and the scientific staff on all the other projects, led by Susan Roscoe, informed Dr. Milton and Commander Ames in writing that they would not continue their work in such an obviously hostile environment. That until they had the renewed assurance from the president of the United States they would be protected from any discrimination, slight or insult, they were all leaving. Additionally, they demanded that the person who posted the sign be removed from the installation and punished as promised.

Commander Ames and Dr. Milton were forced to call Diane Churchill and break the news.

Receiving her reassurance that the president would be immediately informed, they both impressed upon her that the situation had reached an untenable point underground and something drastic would have to be done. They realized the situation was a microcosm of what would occur in the general population in rather short order.

In the meantime, Milton and Ames were keeping things from spiraling out of control underground. They both knew that finding the culprit was unlikely and that they were largely helpless to prevent further such occurrences in the future. That was, until they approached Major Davis, the shelter's commanding officer.

When apprised of the problem of patrolling, informally of course, the corridors of the vast complex, he led them to an unused section of the administrative offices accessible only by swiping his ID card and using a key to unlock the door. The major stood silent, letting Ames and Milton absorb the room's contents.

From their position just inside the door, they saw over a hundred video screens, three command consoles and a wall full of what looked like video recorders.

"Jesus Christ, major. Does all this work?" asked Ames.

"Yes, commander, the function of that whole wall of VCRs was just replaced by this single unit here last month," the major replied, pointing a small, file-cabinet-sized unit next to the rack of recorders. "This computer can record the input from every camera in the complex and store it digitally without using those tape decks at all. The storage unit in this box can hold three months of continuous video from every camera down here and the few we have topside before we have to back it up."

"And so far you've never had occasion to use this room?" asked Milton. "I would hate to think that everything that goes on down here has been monitored and recorded by Big Brother."

"No, Doctor, currently this installation is unused. However, you must remember this complex was designed to operate under military discipline in the event of an atomic or biological attack that could destroy, or at least seriously compromise, normal operations of the country. There are no cameras in the individual rooms, but as you can imagine cameras do cover a majority of the common areas of the complex.

"If you want to keep an eye out for the anyone pulling the same kind of stunt that happened at the commissary, I can activate this center and begin round-the-clock coverage in here and alert you to anything that we catch."

Looking at Dr. Milton, Ames asked, "How do you feel about Big Brother keeping a lookout for mischief?"

"I hate like hell to have to go to this length in order to try to catch someone in the act, but we can't afford to alienate Dr. Roscoe and the rest."

Milton rubbed his eyes in frustration and asked, "Who else knows about this room, Major?"

"Probably no more than four or five of us, sir. I'm the only one down here, everyone else is topside."

"Can you do this, then? With your permission of course, commander, can you have this room manned by topside personnel only, without stretching your men too far?" Milton asked.

"Sure, why only people from topside, doctor?" inquired the major.

"As much as I hate to do this at all, I'm hoping to keep the fact that we are keeping an eye on the common areas quiet. I don't want whoever put up those signs to know they might be caught if they do something else. And I especially don't want some of the more sensitive types down here to get the idea that they're being spied on. How many people does it take to run this room, major?"

"It can be done with a single technician, it's mostly automated."

Ames then suggested, "Major, why don't we do this. Make up a roster of eight who can man the room in pairs rotating in six-hour shifts, and I suggest you integrate the pairs if you get my meaning."

"Great idea," added Milton.

Nodding his head, the major said, "That's the best idea I've heard in a while down here. I don't like the bullshit I'm hearing from Washington about excluding blacks from upper-level planning and operations. I'm not stupid and I've kept my ears open down here, but I don't see how a single group of separatists can imply guilt in a whole race. My wife's best friend has a brother-in-law posted in the Office of the Joint Chiefs and he's been telling her about this whole black/white thing going on there."

"That's the very thing we're trying to avoid here, Major. I'm glad you see things the way you do, it's going to make my job that much easier. When can you fire this room up?" Ames asked.

"I'll have a crew down here within the hour, Commander. I'll also make sure they don't talk to anyone down here about what they're doing. I'm going to key the door to your card and mine only, sir, if that's acceptable with you?" asked the major.

"Paul, is that all right or do you want to be able to get in here?" Ames asked Milton.

"No, Commander, the whole idea of this room is distasteful to me, though I do recognize the necessity. I ask only to be kept informed should some other incident be recorded."

"I'm only bringing the room online to help you keep everyone on the level down here, otherwise it would stay just like this. It helps no one if that kind of shit goes on unchecked, pardon my French, sir," said the major.

Laughing, Paul said, "Don't worry, major, I've already heard the word once or twice today. I appreciate your help."

"No problem, Doctor. Maybe our watching your back, so to speak, will let you get back to the important work you're doing down here, sir. From what I've been hearing, the people you and the rest of the government are looking for could put a serious dent in some of the bigger problems this country faces, *if* we can get them to share what they've got. For my wife and kid's sake I hope we don't get in a fight with them, I don't fancy looking up and seeing some hunk of the moon leveling my humble home."

"Neither do we, Major. Both the commander and I are on the same page there. I'm going back to the office to see what Diane's come up with. Again, thank you, Major. If you need anything from me don't hesitate to call." Milton left the two officers in the surveillance center to return to the other side of the complex.

"Major, can conversations be recorded here as well?" Ames asked, once Dr. Milton was out of earshot.

"In certain areas, sir. I don't really know how well the microphones work, we never really ran the system in its fully operational mode. Why do you ask?" asked the major, looking uncomfortable.

"Is there any way to disable the microphones from here or do they have to be done onsite?"

Looking visibly relieved, the major answered, "I thought you wanted . . . I mean to say, yes, sir. I can disable them and lock out the recording function in the computer. That way video only will be recorded."

"Do it. I don't want this to become a big hassle down the line. Do you understand, major?"

"Yes, Commander, I do," the major said as he crossed over to the center console. He flipped several switches and the monitors all powered up, each one focused on a common area of the complex. In moments the all consoles showed green status lights.

"I've locked out the audio circuits, Commander, and I also started the operator's log and set it to be accessed only by myself so no one can erase the record of anything that goes on down here. Uh, Commander?"

"Yes, major?"

"Do you want me to activate the camera in here? You know, to watch the watchers?"

"That's a great idea. Will they know they're being watched?" Ames asked.

"No, sir. That's part of the security system. Only you or I will be able to access that recording."

"That'll be fine then. Is there anything else I can help you with?"

"No, sir. I'll get the monitoring teams together and have the first team down here ASAP."

"Thank you, Major. I'll see you around then." Ames then left the major to finish his preparations.

Meanwhile, Norma was closeted in her room, joining the rest of the African American contingent's refusal to engage in any kind of work until reassured that their freedom and dignity were guaranteed while they were stationed there. Their strike also ensured that none of them would be in harm's way should some kind of racist nut be loose in the shelter. To them the signs were not just a joke; every one of them had suffered these same kinds of indignities and had experienced authorities everywhere universally minimizing such offenses.

To add insult to injury, they had been told that they shouldn't make a big deal about some small slight. Well, enough was enough.

Norma was half expecting the knock at her door, but instead of Susan Roscoe or any of the other senior personnel, she was surprised to see Alan standing nervously outside.

"Hey Alan, what's up?" she asked in subdued tones.

"I have no idea. I was just checking to see how you were doing. I heard what some asshole did at the commissary. Most everyone is trying to pass it off as a joke, but when I thought about it, it just made me mad."

"Come on in, no sense in standing out there in the corridor," Norma said, as she stood aside to let him in.

"So anyway," he began as he sat in the room's only chair, "I was all set to let it go as a joke, but then I began to rethink the whole thing and what you might be feeling. It was sort of a shock because I don't really think of you as black or African American – whatever. To me you're Norma, my friend, my workmate and sometimes when everything works right . . . you know, but I just don't think of you as black Norma, just Norma. Is that so wrong?"

"Oh, Alan, that's probably one of the nicest things you've ever said to me. And no, it's not wrong, but you're a member of a very small minority thinking like that. What happened here is the tip of the iceberg. Those kinds of feelings exist, mostly hidden, in everyone. What Susan Roscoe is concerned about is that we will end up having to live down here as second-class citizens or prisoners and not be able to do anything about it since the military is in control. Kind of like not having due process available to us by default."

"Hell, if they'd do it to Japanese Americans after Pearl Harbor then they'd damn sure do it to the separatists and maybe even you guys if they wanted to." Alan sat back and shook his head, his shoulders slumped in depression.

"She also mentioned that we could even be used as hostages if the government so desired and no one would be the wiser. No one knows this place exists, where better to hold us? Although to be honest, I'm not really worried too much about that possibility, who's going to want us back that bad? Personally, I just don't want things down here to degenerate into some sort of segregated, hostile community."

Norma was looking pretty glum and Alan wanted nothing more than to cheer her up. Unfortunately, this was something he felt helpless to do.

"Tell you what. Why don't I go and get us some lunch and bring it back here? That way you don't have to roam the halls," Alan suggested.

"I'm not very hungry."

"Did you have breakfast this morning? I'll bet not."

"No, I didn't. I just don't feel like eating, though," she persisted.

"That's fine. Tell you what, can I get something and come back and keep you company? I promise I won't force feed you!"

"Sure, I could use the company. Sitting around alone down here is kind of creepy."

"Great. I'll be back before you know it," he said, jumping to his feet. Leaning over and giving Norma a hug, Alan asked, "How about something to drink? Tea, coffee?"

"Some tea would be fine. You know what I like."

"Back in a flash!" Alan left the room, closing the door softly behind him. As he did, Norma hugged her knees to her chest and thought about the chain of events that brought her to this room nearly a mile underground. The letdown from the high of celebrity left her feeling somewhat empty now that her asteroid was no more, and she was so far from home. She wondered what her life would be like now, and more importantly, how life in these United States would be if there were some sort of conflict with the separatists.

Turning over and propping her head up on her scrunched-up pillow, Norma was treated to a symphony of noisy digestive objections to her missing dinner the night before and breakfast that morning. When she thought about it, maybe she could do with a bite to eat after all. Maybe Alan would be willing to share whatever he brought back.

When Alan returned and Norma saw that he had brought two of everything, she gave him a big hug and a kiss. When she saw the surprise in his eyes she said, "Down boy, don't read anything into it. I just realized how hungry I am. I'm just glad you ignored me when I said I couldn't eat anything now!"

"Yeah, that's what I thought. But you'll have to flip me for the pie," he said as he laid out the food on the bed between them.

Hundreds of miles to the east, Detective Mathews' lunch was being served up in much more elegant surroundings. He and Sydney had an unobstructed view of a picturesque stand of trees just outdoors. She had suggested someplace he'd never been for lunch. And, despite his reluctance to experiment with new, or what he called foo-foo establishments, because Sydney had suggested it he hadn't give their destination a second thought.

If you had asked John later what color the walls were or in what motif the dining room was decorated he wouldn't have a clue. He was completely enchanted by the woman sitting across from him. John was still a man of two minds. He still watched every move Sydney made, listened to every word she said, trying to spot anything that would reveal the existence of a hidden agenda. He knew he was infatuated with this beautiful creature before him, which made him uneasy and more than a little bit guilty.

More than once he considered laying all his cards on the table – the investigation, the FBI, the phone calls, everything, and taking whatever Sydney wanted to dish out. The one thing he couldn't stand to face was the possibility that she might exit his life forever because of his duplicity. In any case, he had come to lunch prepared for the accustomed keen insight Sydney had into his character, her razor-sharp wit and her uncanny ability to arouse him with the most innocent-seeming conversational repartee.

"A penny for your thoughts," John said, after they had placed their orders.

"Obviously you have an extremely undervalued opinion of my thoughts. Or have you decided my intellect is largely just smoke and mirrors?" she replied, smiling.

"Not at all. I was offering what a poor civil servant can afford, hoping you would take pity on me and advance me the necessary charity to make up the difference. Or, I could let you take the remainder out in trade," he replied.

"Hmm, that might be worth investigating, what have you got to offer?" Sydney asked, pinning him with a stare.

"I do windows and dishes. I've even been known to take out the garbage twice a year whether I need to or not."

She laughed as John felt her stocking-clad toes run up and down his leg.

"Why do you get so much pleasure out of teasing me?" John asked.

At the question, Sydney pull her foot back and her face turned serious. "Don't you like me to tease you? Does it really bother you? Because if it does I'll stop, but you're getting so good at giving it back to me I thought you were okay with it."

"It's not that at all, I just wondered what it is about me that makes you do it?" John asked. "Do I come off as such a pushover?"

"Not at all, it's because you can take it, and you know that it's all in fun. And, I guess with your job and your serious nature, I want to make our time together different from what you go through in a normal day. Kind of like a vacation from the realities of being a cop," she finished, looking closely at John's face, trying to read what he thought.

"Don't get me wrong," John began, "I really like it when you play around like that. I just hope it's not like teasing a cat with a piece of string. No, not really like that, I know it's nothing like that."

"John, do you know how few really decent men there are out there? Men who don't play silly games. Men who are capable of expressing honestly what they feel and what they want. In this neck of the woods there are practically none. And forget about finding a man who is capable of learning from his mistakes.

"So far you seem just a little too good to be true to me. And when I add in the fact that you are a police detective who doesn't bring his job into a relationship, the whole package seems too pat, almost unreal," Sydney explained.

John took in what she said, comparing her description of him to how he saw himself, considering how he must seem to someone on the outside. But then another thought percolated in his head. What if her behavior was *designed* to keep him off balance, to distract him from seeing something in her? What if she were deliberately keeping him emotionally and physically on the defensive to keep him from getting too close?

"In that case all I have to say is that the truth is far stranger than what you see. I confess to having given you a rather poor representation of my true nature. I hold back only to spare your health, my dear," John said, with unaccustomed confidence. "You see, my personality and skills normally render the average woman senseless. Judging by what I know about you, well, you may just survive."

Throwing her head back and laughing, Sydney was surprised by the remark from the normally self-effacing man before her. "Is *that* how it is now? So the Detective Mathews identity is your version of Clark Kent?"

Laughing as well, John answered, "Something like that, except I think capes are for men with gender issues. So, are you ready for the upcoming semester with a new batch of young women to mold, train and then set upon the men of America?"

"It's not like that at all, John. We've had this discussion before. We just show them that they do not have to settle for less than they want, no one does. Just like me, I'm not settling for less than I want, and certainly not less than I deserve. Can you give me that, seriously? I certainly hope so, I'd hate to believe that you're here under false pretenses."

John's heart froze, hoping nothing showed on his face. Did she know something was up, or was she fishing? Praying neither, John answered, "In that case I'm going to need a note from your doctor before we move on to the next step in this dance, ma'am. I can't be held liable for any and all mishaps that may result in your attempt to break this horse."

"Is that so? Well then mister, when should we schedule this momentous event? Bearing in mind that I have a quick trip to San Francisco Friday and I probably won't be back until Monday or Tuesday."

"Call me when you get back, I'll keep next weekend free. Maybe we can go away to some quiet bed and breakfast," John suggested.

"My, my. You're not going to waste any time, are you?"

"Should I? After all, as much as I like the dance, I think it's time we move along to the things more substantial. I don't want to lead you on any further just in case I'm not what you want. I'd hate to see you have to settle," John said with a grin.

Blowing John a kiss from across the table, Sydney said, "I hardly think that's possible at this point, John. Unless you are terribly deformed, or something equally emotionally debilitating, I can't imagine there'd be anything I'm not going to like . . . . Oh damn, look at the time! Can you run me back to the campus? I've got a meeting in less than thirty minutes that I can't miss."

"Sure, let me get the check and I'll have you there in no time, even if I have to use the siren and lights."

"Oh, would you? I've never been in hot pursuit before," Sydney gushed, mockingly.

"Bullshit, you're the first person I've ever met who can be in hot pursuit sitting still. Tell that lie to others, I know better," he said, signaling the waitress for the check.

The two drove back to Steddman in silence. When they turned into the gate Sydney sighed.

"What were you just thinking?" John asked.

"That sometimes life is just too demanding. I don't want to go to California Friday, I'd rather spend the weekend with you. In some ways I don't want to have to wait for what I want for the two of us, it would be great to be completely hedonistic and get whatever I want, whenever I want it."

"Yeah, I know what you mean, the problem is that we poor males of the species get such a bad rap when we're like that. The fairer sex calls us brutes, cavemen or worse. The better of us have learned that sometimes things other than what we want dictate the pace of what goes on Although, if I weren't so civilized I'd probably bite you on the butt as you got out of the car," John said, leering at her and licking his lips.

"Actually my dear sweet friend, that might be somewhat welcome, but not right now. Not while I have to do the bidding of others, but soon, I promise," her voice trailed off as she became distracted with something far off, her eyes focused on sights well away from the here and now.

When John pulled up in front of the administration building, Sydney released her seatbelt and surprised him by leaning over and kissing him with a passionate sense of urgency that was totally new. Before he could gather her into his arms to kiss her back, she was already getting out of the car. Leaning down Sydney said through the open door, "Rest up, cowboy, next week is going to put you through the wringer. Ta-ta." She closed the door and skipped up the steps of the building, waving at the car as she went in the door, leaving John befuddled once again. It always seemed that he just missed what was going on with Sydney by a hair, almost as if she was speaking in a language where he only knew every tenth word. Maybe as a man he wasn't *supposed* to know what was up with a woman. John had always had the feeling that men and women were completely different species and it was only by freak cosmic happenchance that they were able to reproduce together. Given how men and women "did it," perhaps sex was just a huge joke played on mankind by the universe's overmind.

John felt Sydney had revealed more of herself today than ever before. Her comment about doing the bidding of others might easily have meant something other than the work she did at the behest of the college. In some small way he actually began to feel like he was getting closer to the real Sydney. Unfortunately, the closer he got to knowing who she actually was, the less he wanted to find out she was something other what than she appeared. He felt if he could just hang on a little longer she'd finally reveal to him all the answers to her life, and then he would see exactly where he fit might in, if at all.

Riders on the storm
Riders on the storm
Into this house we're born
Into this world we're thrown
Like a dog without a bone
An actor out alone
Riders on the storm

Riders on the Storm

Written and performed by The Doors

CHAPTER 33

"WE HAVE A serious problem with the commission," President Bender said to his chief of staff. "There's been a racial prank, scratch that, it was more than a prank. And now all the African Americans, with the exception of the military, are on strike. They want some sort of guarantee that they will not be further subjected to any stupid behavior."

"What happened? Did they catch who pulled the stunt?"

"No, they didn't. Someone put up 'White' and 'Colored' signs over the water fountains."

"And they went on strike for that? What a bunch of babies, it was just a shitty joke, for Christ's sake."

"Was it? You weren't there. Hell, you're not black, you don't know how this affected them," the president said, softly chiding his long-time friend. "What looks like a joke to us obviously wasn't so funny to them. These people have provided us with the best advice and projections on every aspect of the acquisition of the separatists' technologies, and the best suggestions on how to handle them once they're located. I think they deserve better than to be the butt of some asshole's joke, don't you?"

"Of course, sir. I just don't see how something like this could get so blown out of proportion."

"They are not stupid, nor are they lightweights in their respective fields, and if they were offended or felt threatened enough to make a stand like this, shouldn't we give them their due? I'm considering going there and kicking some ass. I could be there for the download of the images from the lunar satellite tomorrow. What's on my schedule?" asked Bender.

"Not much, there's the National Security Council meeting that you called to coincide with the receipt of the images. It wouldn't be too big a deal to quietly move it to the shelter. We could take off at the crack of dawn and avoid the bulk of the press corps. I could have it announced as a schedule change after Air Force One is in the air."

"How about getting to the shelter, won't there be coverage in Utah when we land?"

"We could always leave tonight and get you to the shelter under cover of night. I'm afraid there's no way we can keep the whereabouts of Air Force One under wraps for long once it lands. You know that, sir. We can keep civilians from knowing the location of Shelter Fourteen, though. I'll put it out that you're touring some military bases. We can have you stop at NORAD on the way back to DC, the press can get at you then," Simon said, making some notes on his pad.

"Set it up. Tell Diane I want her to join me on the flight out tonight, and make sure that my arrival is a surprise. I'd love to scare the shit out of the bastard who posted those signs."

"Right away, sir. I'll also set up a relay to the shelter so you can get the images as soon as JPL does."

"Very good. I'm going to clear my desk and get ready to go," Bender said in dismissal.

Diane Churchill called Dr. Milton and Commander Ames and informed them that she would be arriving that evening and requested an all-staff meeting for first thing in the morning, omitting any mention of the president's arrival, per his order.

Masters made preparations for a direct video feed from NASA to Shelter Fourteen. The images would be received bit by bit, transmitted from lunar orbit by the reconnaissance satellite the next day. Telemetry from the satellite showed all systems working properly. NASA technicians tested all four cameras, taking pictures of the moon and of earth as the satellite sped to its rendevous with the moon. The controllers were overjoyed at the enhanced capabilities the satellite had for changing orbit because of the extra fuel it carried courtesy of the Russians. This would allow them to photograph and map the entire surface of earth's companion to an unprecedented extent. The optics in this satellite were much more advanced than those used by various Apollo flights to the moon. From low orbit the cameras could see objects as small as a pack of gum on the surface.

NASA was looking forward to finally proving to skeptics everywhere that the US landings on the moon had actually occurred and were not filmed on a secret soundstage in Nevada. The satellite was tasked with overflying each Apollo landing site and photographing the equipment left behind, the rovers, the lower stages of the landers and, hopefully, the American flags left behind at each site.

Various universities and colleges had made arrangements with NASA to receive every image in an effort to bolster studies in the sciences and, in some cases, the race to create virtual tours of the moon accessible via the Internet. Cal Tech and MIT were in an unofficial race to see who could produce the first complete digital model of the moon allowing virtual visitors to see the actual details of the ground as they overflew, hovered over and even landed on any part of the moon's surface. Given that the expected operational lifetime of the probe was over a decade, literally millions of images could be taken and transmitted back to NASA.

JPL had been working for the last week to plot the precise location of the impact of Norma's asteroid so that the satellite could photograph the site as closely as possible during its initial orbits. The news services were onsite at the Johnson Space Center and at the Jet Propulsion Laboratories, although not in the numbers as the actual impact had seen. This made various federal law enforcement officers nervous. With so much real-time coverage, should the cameras catch something, they could not cover it up without causing a major flap. Unfortunately, isolating the press or delaying the display of the pictures from the moon would only alert everyone to the administration's desire to conceal what the pictures might show.

When Diane entered Shelter Fourteen's theater, the polarization of the commission and the scientists from the other projects was shocking. The room was sharply divided along racial lines. The darker faces sat off to the left of the theater and whites, unwilling to cross the demarcation of the aisle separating the two groups, sat on the right.

Diane saw various expressions of hostility, suspicion and scorn; she knew the president had his work cut out for him.

"Since it looks like everyone who wants to be here is here, can we get started, ladies and gentlemen?" Taking a sip of water, Diane continued. "The purpose of this meeting is to resolve a serious problem that exists down here. A problem that President Bender made sure I addressed before the commission began its work. The very nature of the issues the commission is charged with studying precludes putting up with the kind of nonsense that occurred the other day.

Whoever posted those signs will probably never have the guts to admit they did it, but what the President said still stands. Anyone who is caught pulling anything like that stunt is in for some jail time."

By some unspoken agreement, the nonwhite contingent had chosen Dr. Roscoe to initially speak for them. Though her slight frame was scarcely imposing, the intensity of her personality could easily be seen in her face in the form of intense, dark eyes and sharp features.

"Good words, Dr. Churchill," Dr. Roscoe said formally, standing up to address Diane. "But what guarantee do we have that we will not have to put up with the same kind of crap as the military? The news reports are unsettling. What's to ensure we're not going to end up some kind of slave think tank down here? It's pretty obvious we aren't free to come and go as we please. Nor is there any protection from some white, racist nut just biding their time, waiting to catch one of us alone. What then, Doctor?"

Just then President Bender walked through an exit door at the front of the theater. An immediate buzz went through the crowd. When everyone saw who it was, the servicemen all jumped to their feet as Major Davis called them to attention.

"At ease everyone, please be seated. Thank you, Diane, for getting things started."

Looking around the stadium seating before continuing, President Bender began, "Dr. Roscoe, you had a question about what guarantees *I* will offer to keep things from degenerating into some schoolyard scuffle leaving you all picking my intellectual cotton, that sound about right?"

"Maybe not in those words, Mr. President, but yes," replied Dr. Roscoe, surprised at the president's sudden, unexpected appearance.

"Well, let's do this first. Who wants to own up to putting those signs up? Anyone?" President Bender asked, scanning the half of the theater where the whites sat.

"It's probably a good thing no one owned up because if I find out who did it they will spend the next five years or so in prison for their troubles. I wasn't kidding when I decreed that this kind of crime would not be tolerated. That's right, crime. As far as I'm concerned this country will no longer accept any racially motivated hate crime, no matter to what extent. We don't have the luxury to just let it go any more. No longer will boys being boys be accepted as an excuse for attacks on anyone's civil rights. Whether or not anyone likes it, it is my goal to do for civil rights violations that are racially motivated what this country has done for sexual harassment. I intend to back this up with legislation imposing both civil and criminal penalties."

The entire theater was silent, everyone trying to grasp the ramifications of such legislation.

Dr. Roscoe, still standing, asked, "That's all very noble, Mr. President, but until that happens, if in fact it does happen, what are we supposed to do in the meantime? Are we supposed to just look the other way, accepting whatever institutionalized indignity some closet cracker gets a hankering to pull next time, or the time after that? This country's record of catching white folks who pull that kind of crap is nonexistent, sir. How many people who burned black churches over the last two hundred years have your FBI caught, sir? How many of the domestic terrorists who were responsible for deaths, injuries, and thefts since we were made to row your folks over here from Africa have ever spent a day in jail, *sir*? As a mathematician let me help everyone in here out with the answer. Statistically speaking, none!

"With that kind of record, Mr. President, you will have to excuse us if we don't exactly have confidence in your legislation actually changing anything. And begging your pardon, we don't have the patience to wait for you to get something through Congress.

"Mr. President, anyone here with a lick of sense knows that until men were financially punished for groping women on the job we had to endure whatever they felt they could get away with. Nothing changes in this country until it starts to cost white folks money. So, Mr. President, we all know just how long it's going to take to make any kind of change, and by then this commission will have been long gone, for years maybe. Frankly I don't think the cracker contingent in the House and Senate are going to pass that kind of legislation anyway, so for all practical purposes your intent, noble as it sounds, amounts to nothing." Roscoe sat down to several hoots of support and a loud "damn straight" from someone on her side of the room, this in sharp contrast to the uncomfortable silence on the other side of the aisle.

"And another thing," Susan said, getting back to her feet. "How do you think what's going on at the Pentagon is looking to these so-called separatists, Mr. President? How do you think your administration's acceptance of that racist Kaminski looks to everyone on the outside? It's all over the news and it doesn't take rocket scientists to figure out what's happening there. Does he have your support for his actions? If so, that pretty much answers any question about your commitment to bringing a halt to the kind of discrimination we've had to endure all our professional lives." More than a few of Susan's group were angrily nodding their heads in agreement.

"And consider this Mr. President, and the rest of you sitting over there with your built-in, painted-on privilege. If this group we're looking for decides enough is enough with the crimes against blacks, with the institutionalized biases, with the embedded cultural disadvantages, and they demand that we finally be treated as equals, and that *all* the past wrongs be righted, they can make it stick. You know why? Because might makes right. He who has the biggest stick calls the shots. And the rest of you better think about this, the litmus test for whether or not you're going to reap the benefits of them beating America into submission might just be nothing more than the color of *your* skin. I don't know about the rest of Black America, but I can't wait."

"Right on," someone shouted as she sat down.

"Thank you, Dr. Roscoe, for your comments, but do you think they will help or hurt the situation we have here? Don't get me wrong, the whole US military apparatus is gearing up for just such a confrontation, and we will resist any attempt at putting undue pressure on this country. You are indeed right in your call for change, and I support equality for all, regardless of the blah, blah, blah . . . All of you know the rest of the platitudes politicians have mouthed through the years," he said, catching everyone by surprise. "However, in the final analysis the question still remains, as the Reverend Rodney King so eloquently asked, 'Can't we all just get along?'

"I think *that's* the issue we face down here today, and the question I'm here to answer to your group's satisfaction, one way or the other," President Bender finished to a smattering of snickers.

"What all of you are doing down here is helping me develop policy that will answer just these questions. Instead of seeing the glass half empty, try to look at it as half full, an opportunity to really get to the bottom of America's sickness about race. Use it. Help me figure out the best means of instituting changes to the fabric of our society that are fair, and with teeth."

"And in the meantime, if our glass is metaphorically empty, Mr. President? What then?" Susan asked, not bothering to stand this time.

"Fine, Dr. Roscoe, you tell me. What is going to satisfy your group at this point?"

"Is great wealth out of the question?" she asked, getting the first genuine laughs from both sides of the room.

Chuckling himself, President Bender replied, "That's a possibility, but only if you don't tell your white colleagues we slipped you something extra under the table.

"But seriously, I'm actually here for two reasons, the second is to view the images from the impact location of Ms. Lancaster's asteroid. The satellite is due to transmit the first batch around midday here and I thought we could all watch NASA's download from the satellite together. So that leaves us with the rest of the morning to come to some kind of accommodation, then all of us can have lunch and see the images come in together. Does anyone think we won't be able to find a way to work together again? Dr. Roscoe? What's the consensus of the group?"

Looking around and getting mostly nods from the others sitting around her, Susan stood up and answered, "Mr. President, I believe we can all be on the same page by then. We're at least willing to listen."

"That's all I ask. So we don't bring everything down here to a crashing halt, may I suggest that everyone who isn't directly concerned with the incident go and try to put at least some work in before lunch and then all meet back here to see the images come in. Major Davis? Where are you?"

Standing to be seen, the major raised his hand to get the president's attention.

"Good. Is there any reason we can't arrange to have lunch served in here, Major? I understand you set it up that way for the impact, is that correct?"

"Yes, sir. I'll see to it right away." Major Davis left through the same door through which the President had entered.

"Dr. Roscoe? Could you put together a smaller contingent of your people who can meet with myself, Diane, Dr. Milton and Commander Ames once the major returns?" the president asked.

Getting to her feet, looking around at those closest to her, Susan answered, "Would six of us be acceptable, Mr. President?"

"Absolutely, doctor. Commander, Dr. Milton, would the two of you secure a quiet place for us to meet and let's all get together in fifteen minutes,"

Dr. Milton stood up and suggested they meet in the private dining room off the commissary, looking over to Dr. Roscoe for approval.

In the back row of the theater seats, Alan caught up with Norma before she made it to the door and asked if she was going to join the group meeting with the president.

"I hadn't planned on it, why?" Norma asked.

"You might hear details of what's really going on topside and how the search is going, stuff like that," he answered brightly. "And, you know . . ."

"And you're dying to get the skinny on what's really going on aren't you?"

"Damn straight. Besides, who's gonna lead the jail break if the country decides to lock you darker types up for treason or something? I can't work in a vacuum!"

Laughing at Alan's enthusiasm and his way of letting the tension of the last couple of days drain away, she said, "You win, let me go and try to weasel my way into this meeting. If something really juicy comes up, I'll tell you about it at lunch."

"Cool, I'm heading back to the lab. Call me or come get me there if you get out early."

Norma went down to the bottom of the aisle and waited for Susan to finish talking with one of the other women on the commission. When Susan saw Norma she asked, "You want in on the meeting too?"

"Only if it doesn't cause a problem," Norma answered.

"Not at all, it would be good to have you along. How's that young man of yours?" Susan prodded.

"He's not exactly my young man. He's just concerned, no pissed is more like it, about the whole incident. He's got a good heart even if he's more like a playful puppy most ofthe time."

"I think he's a pretty lucky guy. He's got you to vouch for him," Susan said as she grabbed Norma's arm and the two of them left the theater together on their way to the commissary.

The meeting went pretty well, only getting somewhat heated when Major Davis, at the president's urging, revealed that the common areas were now under surveillance. It took both the commander's and Dr. Milton's assurances that this was only to watch for more incidents, not to keep tabs on anyone down there, to quiet the furor. Susan was somewhat mollified when Major Davis assured her that the monitoring teams consisted of one white and one black soldier and the fourth team consisted of an African American and an Asian.

Dr. Roscoe calmed down even more when President Bender asked her opinion on whether they should reveal the monitoring to the general public or not, leaving the decision to her. The consensus was that the best course of action was to get anyone who might be a problem out of the installation, and the only chance of catching them was to keep the monitoring a secret.

As time approached the noon hour there were still issues left on the table, but President Bender called a break so they could all eat, see the pictures from the satellite and let the others of their community know the progress they had already made. Agreeing to resume afterwards, the small group made their way back to the theater in time to see the real-time feed from JPL put up live on the big screen. Also at the foot of the screen were several computer monitors and a handful of telephones.

When President Bender entered the room he saw that Masters was on the phone in quiet conversation and two younger men in civilian dress were manning the keyboards in front of the computer screens.

The far wall had long tables of food and drink arrayed for the taking, and everyone, when they caught the aromas from the lunchtime fare, made a beeline to fill plates and dig in.

Norma looked around the theater, glad the room was fully lit, and saw Alan with a plate of food in deep conversation with Dr. Harris and one of the naval personnel. Waving to catch his attention she pointed to the food, letting him know she would get something to eat and join him. Susan Roscoe and Diane Churchill were making their way through the impromptu food line talking animatedly, their conversation punctuated with short bursts of laughter, looking all the world like two old friends meeting for lunch.

And watching the dynamic of so many different people brought together from so many different walks of life living in this isolated community was the president, wishing the real world, the world above ground, could be this easy. That the simple act of honest communication, which was curing most ills, could somehow translate to life above ground.

"Mr. President? Could I fix you a plate, sir?" one of the kitchen stewards asked.

"Thank you very much, but I think I'll just get in line with everyone else," he said.

The president went down to the front of the room, watched by a number of eyes as he did, and went to the end of the line, gracefully thanking everyone who offered to let him cut in. Striking up conversations with the others in line, he almost began to feel less like the head of the free world and more like a colleague, working along side these remarkable people.

While he was in line everyone looked up as the broadcast test pattern coming from JPL was replaced by a view of several blank windows and a running clock in the lower left hand corner of the screen. He headed to a table left open for senior administrators and honored guests, as a hand-lettered table tent proclaimed. He was delighted to see Paul, Diane, Susan Roscoe and the commander had grabbed seats together and were eating and talking like old colleagues. President Bender took notice of how handsome a couple the commander and Dr. Roscoe looked together.

Making room next to her, Susan patted the chair, saying to the president, "It's not every day that I get to have lunch with the president of the United States, plus you'll get a better view of the screens from here. We were speculating on what might happen if these people refuse to deal with us at all, if they completely reject any peaceful overtures and have the means of enforcing their isolation. The commander here rejects the idea that we're going to be able to take their technology by force, and I believe that with the apparent repudiation of families, friends and everything else from their past lives, there's nothing in the way of the carrot or the stick that's going to get them to engage us."

Just then Agent Bishop appeared and tapped President Bender on the shoulder, saying, "Mr. President, Dr. Lyons at JPL called and said they will be triggering the download of the first set of pictures in three minutes. You'll be able to see them on the big screen or over here on the monitor, sir."

"Thank you, Sam. Shall we table this until this afternoon's discussions everyone? I have a couple of things to check on before the pictures come in. Thanks."

Getting to his feet, he motioned Agent Bishop out of earshot of the table and asked, "Are our people in place in Houston and Pasadena?"

"Yes sir, but we may have a problem keeping everything on the QT. The signal is being received at the International Space Station and about half a dozen radio observatories outside the country, sir."

"Dammit, I didn't think about that. Do you know if the data is encrypted?" Bender asked.

"In a word, sort of. No one is going to be able to reconstitute the images without some knowledge of how NASA compresses and sends this kind of data back from their probes, but nearly everyone in the space industry appears to use the same protocols."

"I'm probably just being paranoid. The chances are that there's nothing really to see except a pile of rubble or a shallow hole, but I'm dying to know why the thing was tampered with in the first place. Maybe they were testing a new propulsion system," speculated the president.

"That's a hell of a kick in the pants, sir. If they could significantly affect something that big, what would they be going to use it for?'

"That, Sam, is the question. Heads up, there's something coming in."

Returning to his seat at the table with the others, President Bender peered over the technician's shoulder watching the picture build up on the nineteen-inch computer screen. The first pass showed a ghostly outline of a craggy, gray surface, and with each successive pass over the picture the details became sharper.

Once the first picture was complete another window opened up and the second image began to appear. The technician at the keyboard glanced back and addressed the group at the table, informing them that according to JPL, the impact zone probably wouldn't show up until the sixth or seventh image. He went on to add that all the images would be assembled into a single, larger picture once a number of orbits had been completed and they had a few hundred images to stitch together.

Several minutes later, when the eighth picture was building, an electronic circle was drawn on the image. The technician leaned back and said, "Mr. President, Dr. Lyons says that they believe this splash mark in the regolith and the rubble in this corner are from the asteroid. The probe took a series of about fifteen images from this quadrant. Pretty good guesswork, sir."

The big theater was nearly silent while everyone waited for the picture to fully display under the circle on the screen.

Alan reached over and squeezed Norma's hand when the splash of debris could easily be seen across the surface. "There's your contribution to history, kiddo," Alan said when the picture was complete. "Hey, maybe they'll name the crater after you!" Norma just squeezed his hand back and continued to watch the next picture build in silence.

The next two pictures missed showing the actual impact site, but they did show the splash debris from the impact.

The eleventh picture struck paydirt. Just off the center of the shot was a pile of rubble surrounded by a wall of debris.

"Bingo!" announced the technician at the keyboard, followed by several cheers around the room.

As the image began to build they saw, according to the scale along the bottom of the screen, that the crater was just over three kilometers in diameter, and although they could see a ghostly image of some debris inside the crater's walls, the ground looked pretty flat. A portion of the crater wall closest to the sunny side was slightly in shadow, but what could be seen in successively better detail showed the floor of the crater as fairly flat. When the picture was complete, the technician pulled it off to the side so it would remain uncovered when the next picture started to build.

The next few shots showed more views of the splash footprint, catching small portions of the crater wall off to the sides. When the nineteenth picture started to build, they saw a quarter of the impact crater in the upper left of the shot and splash debris along a rocky ridge cut diagonally from the crater to the lower right of the shot; the detail was fantastic. When the picture was complete, everyone was expecting the next picture to begin to build. Suddenly, the picture expanded to fill the entire screen.

Everyone stopped talking and looked at the huge screen to see what was happening. As they watched, the scene began to zoom in and the detail sharpen along the lower left edge of the picture, just underneath the southern crater wall. As the view zoomed in further, the whole room went silent. When the picture finally stabilized someone exclaimed, "Holy fuckin' shit!"

Everyone saw, clear as day, what looked like tire tracks in mud leading from the crater wall off the bottom edge of the picture.

CHAPTER 34

THE ENTIRE WORLD was in an uproar. The White House's efforts to prevent widespread distribution of the satellite photos failed miserably. The feed from the probe was received at the International Space Station, where the multinational crew viewed the pictures moments before they were received on earth. The images were copied and transmitted to France, Russia and Japan, viewed by government officials, then made their way to the people hours later.

The pictures had also been sent to over a dozen other receivers outside Houston and Pasadena. The damage was done. The world knew that something was on the surface of the moon.

Conspiracy theorists painted pictures of a super-secret US military base kept hidden for years or a joint US/Russian base from which the entire world was secretly ruled. Others revisited the scenario depicted in the movie *Independence Day*, fully believing that aliens from some other solar system were staging on the moon preparing for attack. One stubborn and particularly vocal contingent maintained that the base on the moon was the final destination of Adolf Hitler and his Third Reich, and the headquarters from which would burst the Fourth Reich.

The president wasn't all that surprised to find somebody operating on the moon and it didn't take a great leap in logic to assume their group of separatists had literally taken the high ground, against which all of General Kaminski's military planning was useless. It took little urging on the administration's part to convince the CJCS to reverse the actions he had previously implemented, restoring every African American officer to their original post.

Whatever craft made the tracks hadn't been photographed by the orbiting satellite. With no wind or rain to obscure the tracks over time, there was no way to determine the age of the markings, but nobody thought for a minute they weren't freshly made.

Suddenly, network and cable stations were running movies like *2001: A Space Odyssey* and *First Men on the Moon*, adding to the growing groundswell of opinion that human's must revisit earth's nearest neighbor to uncover what was there.

President Bender was being pressured from nearly every special interest group around the world, through their paid lobbyists, to authorize an immediate mission to the moon to confront the makers of the tracks. Every industrialized country wanted to obtain whatever information and technology could be begged, borrowed or stolen from those on the moon and bring it back for exploitation back home.

Russia's president coincidentally made a sojourn to the US, ostensibly to discuss issues in the still turbulent Middle East, but pledged technical and military support for a joint mission to the moon as long as whatever nuggets they mined would be shared equally with his country.

Unfortunately, NASA lacked the heavy-lifting capacity and the requisite spacecraft to make the trip to the moon and back, even if they modified and pressed into service a leftover lunar module over forty years old. There was no way that America could go it alone.

Russia's president revealed that they had the means of getting a dozen men down to the surface of the moon safely from orbit but lacked the means to get them off the surface once they had landed. At President Bender's suggestion the Russians flew a technical team from the Star City Space Program headquarters to Houston to see what kind of mission the two programs could cobble together.

The next hurdle for the NASA astronaut corps was the problem of selecting personnel who could pass astronaut training *and* perform as soldiers should such a mission be approved.

At Shelter Fourteen, moments after the surprise images had been received, Dr. Harris and his team were ordered to begin an extensive search of the moon to try to locate any evidence of gravitational control technology. Alan hadn't slept more than an hour or two since they received the picture showing the tire tracks. He and the naval technical crew were busy writing software that would enable the detector to act like a high-resolution scanner, sweeping the moon looking for the smallest deviation in its gravitational field.

Everyone worked through the weekend, trying to do something that, until a few short weeks ago, the scientific community considered impossible. Alan, on a sleep-deprived high, was as happy as a pig in slop. He was doing work no one had ever done before, he had the utmost respect of his elders and the US Navy. Most of all, he was doing this work in the presence of one of his best friends.

On Sunday, during the various news panel shows, every politician or pundit was asked to discuss the political, scientific and cultural ramifications of this new discovery. That was until Diane Churchill was ambushed live and asked to comment on the president's administration knowing that those discovered on the moon were a group of African American separatists who had successfully concealed their existence from the rest of the world for decades.

Almost literally struck dumb by the commentator's question, Diane covered poorly with a denial, begging off from answering with a "No comment." This lit a media frenzy for the rest of the day, sending the president's cabinet scurrying for cover like roaches when the lights came on.

The White House went into full defensive mode. For once, no one was concerned with how the information was leaked. The damage was done, Pandora's box was open. No amount of denials would suffice. General Kaminski's heavy-handed reassignments, clearly made along racial lines, and whispers concerning the FBI's secret investigation only confirmed to the nation what Diane denied on air.

In this new century fact, rumor and innuendo flowed with the speed and force of a deluge.

By the dinner hour, if you believed the cable and Internet news outlets, the president had all but admitted that a group of super-blacks were living in a permanent settlement on the moon in a city so advanced that the best industrial nations on earth couldn't compete with the wonders available to the lunar dwellers.

Polls showed the ambivalence of the American people, split almost equally among three factions. President Bender and his entire administration were wrestling with which of the three strategies to pursue. Should they leave well enough alone and let those on the moon live their lives unmolested? Should they try to make peaceful contact with them, coming hat in hand, so to speak, and asking them to share their largess with the world? Or, as a slight majority seemed to want, should they confront these people on their home turf as equals and demand to know just what was going on up there?

The stock market took a nosedive with technology, bioresearch, manufacturing and heavy industry taking the hardest hits. Consumer confidence in the economy dropped. Analysts pointed to the public's assumption that technological advances held by those living on the moon would invalidate much of the current research and make manufacturing capabilities at home obsolete.

An exhausted but exultant Dr. Harris was ready to test the new scanning capabilities of the detector Alan and the naval team had wrought. They began at the center of the moon, watching the indicators on screen. Alan moved the focus of the detector outward, watching the changes in the gravitational field.

When Dr. Harris announced that they had indeed created man's first gravity-based scanner, the room went wild, papers flung in the air like confetti. The tired team members forgot their fatigue as they all watched the coordinates and gravitational displacement figures being recorded by the lab's main computer.

"Settle down everyone, let's knock off and get something to eat or try to catch up on some sleep. The computer says that it's going to take at least six hours to scan the entire moon, I don't need anyone here to babysit. What I'll to do is slave one of the computers in the monitoring room to this one, they'll call me if something turns up," Dr. Harris announced.

Even though everyone on the development team had the rest of the day and night off, Alan and the rest couldn't help wandering intermittently into the lab or the Navy's monitoring room to take a peek at the results of the scan.

The next morning Martin was disappointed to see that the detector had recorded nothing unusual. He was hoping to find some evidence of the use of gravity-based technology on the moon, particularly on the far side, the perfect hiding place.

When Alan joined him in the lab after breakfast, they ran a quick scan of the data to see if the computer might have somehow missed the results of a reduction in the gravitational force on the moon. As their impromptu filters ran through the terabytes of collected data, Martin exclaimed, "Hold the phone, boys, I think I found the problem here!"

Gathering around Martin's chair, Alan and two technicians looked to where he was pointing on the screen. Drawing closer to see the tiny numbers Martin had highlighted, Alan said, "I see a displacement, why didn't the computer flag it?"

Then one of the naval guys said, looking closer at the numbers on the screen, "That's because they're not negative, the numbers are positive!"

"That means they've increased the local gravity, not reduced it. They're generating a denser gravity field over what looks like nearly a square kilometer of the moon, centered about forty feet below the surface according to these coordinates," Martin observed.

"How dense is the field? Does it approach one G?" asked the Navy tech as he sat down at his computer to copy the data for analysis.

"According to these readings," Martin began as he performed some swift calculations, "the field strength is within ninety-eight percent of the earth's gravity over the entire area. It appears there's some kind of habitat up there that has earth-strength gravity. This means anyone living up there won't have adapted irreversibly over time."

Alan leaned back and said, "That would help if they ever intended to come back to earth. No atrophy to fight, no adaptation to living back here if they come home. Also, if the gravity is so close to one G, it's a sure bet that whoever is living there is human. I mean, what are the odds they come from a planet that's got the exact same gravity as earth? That is, if they're some kind of aliens."

While Alan was speaking, Commander Ames arrived at the lab. Getting the gist of Alan's argument, Ames said, "Or they may just be acclimating themselves to our gravity so they don't have any period of adjustment when they invade."

"Jeeze, talk about the glass being half empty,"Alan remarked.

"He's right. We have to look at all of the possibilities and not go off half-cocked," Martin chided him. He turned to Ames and brought him up to date on what the data suggested.

"So this pretty much proves that there's some kind of long-term installation up there. Big enough to hold a couple of thousand people, Doc?" Ames asked.

"Easily. I can't really tell from the figures, but looking at the extent of the effect, this complex could be built like the shelter, with several vertical levels. If that's the case there's no telling how many people are up there. Why do you ask? Do you know something that you're not telling us?" Martin asked.

"You know the commission's working from the presumption that these people are black separatists, that they can control gravity and that they've made advances in medicine most of us would give our left nuts for. That's about all I know right now, except for your having located what looks like an artificial habitat on the moon."

"Yeah, not to mention Churchill blowing it on TV Sunday, eh?" Alan added.

Deliberately ignoring Alan's comment, Ames asked, "Martin, can you calculate the location of the base?"

"Already did, here's the latitude and longitude of the gravity field, and the offset from the impact crater made by Ms. Lancaster's rock," Martin replied, pulling several sheets of paper from the printer.

Ames took the papers, turned on his heel and quickly left the lab. His departure was unnoticed by Alan and the two technicians correcting the code in the scanning routine to give an alarm if either a decrease or increase in local gravity were detected while scanning.

Behind the scenes in Houston, the Star City and NASA mission planners were desperately trying to get an operations group to the far side of the moon and back. The Russians had escape capsules based on a modified Soyuz capsule from thirty years ago designed to get cosmonauts safely to the surface of the moon from an orbiting platform. Their original assumption was that there would be permanent colonies on the moon able to safely harbor any cosmonaut in need until they could be safely returned to earth. Unfortunately neither the Russians nor the Americans had a deep-space vehicle that would permit them to transport anyone to the moon's surface and back.

They began to get creative. The planning team divided the components to successfully complete the mission between the two programs.

The Americans had the space shuttle, the largest manned orbital craft currently in use, but it was only really capable of achieving low earth orbit about two hundred and fifty miles above the ground. For one of the shuttles to get to the moon and back it would have to be able to boost itself out of low orbit, breaking away from the earth's gravitational pull, and make its way to the moon. That would take many times the amount of fuel normally left in its tanks once it reached orbit.

The shuttle's large external fuel tank was usually jettisoned about seventy-five miles above the earth, only to fall back through the atmosphere and land in the Indian Ocean. The engineers reshuffled the deck, and decided that instead of detaching the tank on the way into orbit, the new mission would retain the tank and bring it into low earth orbit still attached to the shuttle. Then, the crew could refuel the tank so the shuttle could use its main engines to boost it out of the earth's orbit.

The Russians contributed to the mission the two escape pods modified to fit into the shuttle's cargo bay, making room for between eight and twelve soldiers to make the trip to the moon's surface. The Russians were also tasked with launching into orbit the additional liquid fuel to replenish the shuttle's depleted external tank.

The technical hurdles were huge. Both countries' personnel faced the herculean task of adapting thirty-year-old Russian technology with no hardware in common with the American shuttle and fitting it all safely into the shuttle's cargo bay. Further, the rescue pods were only equipped to sustain cosmonauts for three days, soft-landing them on the moon's surface using a combination of retro rockets and extremely strong air bags that would inflate to cushion the capsules on impact with the moon's surface.

The team struggled to equip the pods to share life support with the shuttle until deployment. One major problem remained. There was no space vehicle on earth that could get anyone stranded on the moon back into orbit for safe return home. The military mission plan called for the team to capture their own ride home once they landed on the surface of the moon. Publicly, General Kaminski remarked that they would be highly motivated by their lack of ability to get back in any other manner. Privately, he had all but written them off once they deployed to the surface, but hoped they got lucky.

The chairman's plan called for the ground team to convince those on the moon to return them home safely if they couldn't directly capture a suitable craft to do so. At worst, he hoped they would be returned home after throwing themselves on the mercy of the moon's inhabitants. The military's goals centered around the acquisition of any advanced technologies, any kind of weapons technologies being the top priority, no matter the cost. Already a team was being assembled for the mission, one that was probably the most dangerous the military had undertaken, ever.

Sydney's Steddman homecoming was marked by little fanfare. Her trip to California yielded promises from four more exceptional young black women to seriously consider Steddman College once they graduated next term, despite the chaos overrunning the country. She followed the news coverage with greater than average interest. She wondered when someone, either John or an agent from the FBI, would want to discuss with her the possibility that Jaylynn Williams might have ended up with the alleged separatists living on the moon. After all it was what she would do were she in their shoes.

John was wondering the same thing. He and Samuels also watched the news coverage hour by hour to see if anything they didn't know or suspect had made it into the eye of the public. Samuels was angrier that someone at FBI headquarters had obviously let the cat out of the bag about his investigation than he was about the extent of the news coverage. The breadth of the news coverage gave John the perfect opportunity to bring up the colony on the moon conversationally with Sydney.

Samuels' concern shifted from the paranoid concealment of his investigation from the rest of the world to trying to ferret out just where the leak had occurred. If someone at FBI headquarters was on to his secret investigation from the beginning, did they also pass that information on to those they sought? When he discussed this possibility with John they both wondered whether or not Sydney, if she were involved with the group, knew all along she was the subject of such scrutiny. If that was the case she had successfully hidden the connection so well that she frightened them with her cool, collected duplicity. In any case she was still no one to be taken for granted. Sydney Atkins was smart, and, short of being interrogated under drugs, would probably never let anything slip to give herself away.

If John managed to get away for the weekend with Sydney, he was sure it was going to be one of the most interesting experiences he'd ever had.

The pressure on President Bender to speak publicly became almost unbearable when the covert mission to Iraq was leaked to the press from an unnamed source on the Foreign Intelligence Committee. The details were hazy, but the time frame was correct, as was the fact that it was a joint US/British operation secretly planned and carried out with the assistance of the air force. That was enough to set the dogs barking once again.

Within hours, the Iraqi foreign minister lodged a formal complaint with the United Nations, demanding the matter be fully disclosed and the United States be censured for their transgression against the peace-loving people of Iraq. Meanwhile, behind the scenes a member of the Iraqi Foreign Ministry informed the State Department in complete confidence that perhaps one of their men might still be alive in Iraq. This same source asked directly what concessions the

US might be willing to make for the return of such a person if it turned out that this was the case.

"Whom do I have to screw to get out of this lousy job?" Bender asked Simon after calling a meeting with the director of the CIA and the top international legal expert from the Department of Justice. He wanted to know what their options were if their missing man was alive. Could they demand his return with any reasonable expectations? What were the odds he could be taken away by force? Did they, or MI-6, have the means of locating where he was being held? And, could they get anyone there to contact the man, or at the very least get enough intel to develop decent contingency plans?

The longer the president put off a press conference the lower his poll numbers dipped. His popularity slipped seemingly by the hour. His entire administration was under siege, being pressured on every front for information on the FBI investigation, the Pentagon's reassignments of African Americans, the mission to Iraq, the crashed UFO, and the cancellation of the next scheduled scientific shuttle mission.

So, when President Bender at last stepped up to the podium in the White House, the whole world was watching with keen interest.

President Bender's opening statement didn't surprise anyone. Most of what he said had been revealed in the press over the previous two weeks and contained the briefest recap of the major issues. He and Simon had decided that telling the public what they already knew, and then concluding without questions, though unsatisfying to the press in attendance, would at least give lip service to the idea of full disclosure.

His closer, an entreaty that America had passed the point where the prejudices of the past should no longer be tolerated if the country was to survive this current crisis, was delivered in a heartfelt, somber tone a father would use admonishing his child for knowingly committing a shameful act.

When he finished, President Bender turned and left the press room, ignoring the deafening cacophony of shouted questions.

We can never know about the days to come
But we think about them anyway.
And I wonder, if I'm really with you now
Or just chasing after some finer day.
Anticipation, Anticipation
Is making me late
Is keeping me waiting

Anticipation

Written and preformed by Carly Simon

CHAPTER 35

STEDDMAN'S FALL TERM was due to begin in a few short weeks and preparations were in full swing all over campus. Classrooms were spruced up, the grounds were looking extra inviting and the student activities calendar was filling in for the upcoming academic year.

Steddman College was coming alive after the sleepy pace of the summer session. Faculty and students who had stayed for the summer were looking forward to the hubbub and increased activity the fall always brought. Even Sydney was getting caught up in the anticipation and excitement. When she and John had opportunity for a quick lunch together, John found her mood infectious.

This time, Sydney opted to have lunch on campus, which surprised and delighted John. There was a validation of their growing relationship, he felt, if she was willing to be seen with him on her home turf. John took exceptional care with his appearance that morning, wanting to look his best for her and whoever might see the two of them together.

Despite the news from around the country, and the trials and tribulations of his ongoing assistance to Samuels' investigation, John was in a jaunty mood. He noticed he was whistling like a teenager during the drive to Steddman, seemingly just happy to be alive. Turning into the campus driveway, he was surprised to see so many young women so far in advance of the fall session beginning.

"How was your trip out west?" John asked when they were seated in the dining room.

"It wasn't too bad. The weather was great. I sometimes forget what summer weather without humidity can be like. The girls I think will be coming here next fall are exceptional and will make perfect little converts to our global conspiracy of female domination," she answered.

"Sometimes I'm not sure you're pulling my leg with that domination thing," John said with an easy laugh, "but things couldn't be run any worse than they are now."

"You have no idea. It looks like our esteemed president is determined to get us into some kind of alpha-male competition with these people on the moon. What's your take on all this?" Sydney asked.

"I think the whole idea of living on the moon is the most exciting and significant discovery to come along since the original Apollo landings. I'm dying to find out as much about them as possible, how they got there, why they went, everything. Unfortunately, it looks like instead of doing some friendly fact-finding, we're going to be knocking on their door with the barrel of a gun. Frankly, the whole idea of sending an armed mission up there makes me sick," John said, with a sour expression on his face.

"What makes you think any mission sent up is going to be armed?" Sydney asked, touching his arm in alarm.

"The rumor is that there's going to be some kind of special joint mission with the Russians. Scuttlebutt is that a special ops group is going to be included in the mission, but no real facts have been released yet," said John.

"But why? It's not like they've made any kind of aggressive moves against anyone down here. There's no sign that they have any hostile intent toward earth. They seem like they've gone out of their way to avoid notice," Sydney said, genuinely upset.

"You've been around long enough to know how things work. What we don't understand or makes us uneasy, we try to kill. It's the American way of life. Most of us aren't happy with it, but it's obvious whoever's up there is more advanced than us and that's scaring all those little men in Washington out of their shorts.

"Plus, taking into account that anyone who lives on the moon obviously has technology far more advanced than ours, the pressure to get that technology and financially exploit it must be huge. I'll bet every single corporation who gave the president and Congress money to get elected last time around is chomping at the bit to make sure they get first dibs on whatever they get from these people."

"It's just not right, John. What about what they want? What if they just want to be left alone? They're not hurting anyone by living up there and there's no reason they should share their resources with anyone, is there?"

"On the face of it, no. I would love for everyone to act like adults, but is that really a realistic expectation? Don't get me wrong, I don't agree with theft, or strongarming someone to give up what's theirs. I don't agree with the administration's sending guns into space either, but I understand. Most of what happens in these situations happens because of fear or greed; that's not about to change."

Sydney slouched in her seat and sighed. "I'm worried that if an armed mission is sent to the moon and they start shooting first the consequences are not going to be pleasant for anyone. Do we really want to go charging into someone else's backyard who might knock our own house down in retaliation? Has anyone given that prospect any thought?"

"I think *that* worry is the principal reason for sending an armed expedition in the first place, to kind of show we won't just lie down for anyone because they're bigger or better armed."

"But it's so unnecessary. No one has drawn a line in the sand, no one's put up a 'No Trespassing' sign or made any other hostile gestures to justify this kind of armed response. John, you of all people should know how just the sign of force, the threat of carrying a gun, polarizes the response police officers get. That's the same situation we have with America forcing its influence down the rest of the world's throat at the end of a gun. For you there's mistrust, there's the expectation that every cop is as bad as the worst of them.

"Cops are always complaining that the public doesn't respect them, and make doing the job more difficult by not helping. Part of it is because the police will never give credence to a citizen's complaint about another officer; they immediately go on the offensive and automatically blame the victim. Just like America blaming other cultures for their own bad press around the world."

"That's not fair," began John. "With cops there's no factual basis for the majority of the complaints. And by the way, aren't cops also innocent until proven guilty?"

"In a perfect world they would be, but unfortunately since they're in a position of authority the deck is almost impossibly stacked in their favor. When a cop is accused of breaking the law, the rest of the force, the unions and the fraternal orders protect them by trying to ruin the lives of those who make the accusations. Why not prosecute the bad apples as vigorouslyas you do the citizens who make the complaints?"

"I agree that the automatic response makes it seem patently unfair, but the system usually works," John said defensively.

"It does, but it also makes life more difficult for everyone. What would restore the confidence in the police, the courts and the government will never come to pass."

"What's that?" John asked.

"You may not like the answer."

"I'm a big boy, spill," John challenged.

"Think about this. The reason the general public hates the way crime is punished in this country is that the entire system is based on corruption and privilege. That is, if someone commits a white-collar crime, or even a murder and they've got enough money or influence, they get off. This same perception is shared in other countries regarding America and its behavior. Money and influence rule the day."

"But, but . . . ."

"Let me finish. The examples range from the public's perception of what really happens to the corporate thieves. The fact that judges, politicians, police officers, and anyone with the least bit of influence or money barely get a slap on the wrist when they're caught reinforces the negative beliefs about the whole system. The truth is everyone thinks that the entire legal system is run for the benefit of the wealthiest of Americans; perception is everything.

"The cure is simple. Anyone in a position of holding the public trust, an elected official, judge, lawyer, law enforcement officer, member of the military, city hall employee, *anyone* in such a position of public trust who commits a crime in the performance of their duties should automatically be charged with a capital offense. In other words, abuse the public trust while in a position of responsibility or privilege, then face the death penalty."

"Jesus Christ, Sydney. That's harsh."

"That's right, but in one stroke you bring the ultimate accountability to the courts, to the government, to every elected office. Crimes of this nature are the ultimate perversion of our country's system of freedom and equality. There is no equality when the playing field is tilted one way or another, it's as simple as that.

"A cop who takes a bribe to look the other way has violated the public trust. A judge who cuts an offender some slack because of the offender's ability to pay, or because of a friendly relationship with the defending attorney, violates the public trust. The congressman who sponsors legislation or amends a bill to favor a business in his district unfairly or to help a close friend in business has violated the public trust. They all deserve the harshest punishment available for two reasons. The first is that they undermined and destroyed that which is supposed to make this country the best possible place on this earth to live. Second, it will dissuade those who seek those positions of authority for their own personal gain from doing so if there's no percentage in it, and that they may lose their life if they stray.

"That's the ultimate accountability, and maybe the only means of restoring confidence in everything America really stands for. If you haven't let someone slide because they did you a favor in the past, or any other of the usual accommodations or compromises while on the job, you have nothing to worry about, and you bet your butt you'll see a change in the respect paid you.

"Do you think a congressman would take any of the myriad bribes they get in the way of trips, stock deals, jobs for their family members, book deals, real estate deals, whatever, if they thought discovery or disclosure would cost them their life? Think of the leverage a lobbyist would have over someone if they did take a bribe."

"Whew! You don't think small, do you?" John said. "How about someone who's unjustly accused? What then?"

"What happens to them now? The poor ones still rot in cells or get executed. Look how many death-row inmates have been released because of the availability of DNA testing. These men were going to be killed by the state! And in many cases it was because of corrupt cops, prosecutors or severely overworked public defenders. The whole thing straightens out when the system is clean. I take it from the look on your face you don't think so. Well then, what's your suggestion?"

"I'm not saying that the system doesn't stink . . ."

"Fine, but don't bother to give me that tired justification 'it's the best system out there,' because that won't wash, John. Does that mean that aspiring to mediocrity is good enough so don't rock the boat? Corrupt politicians are sending an armed mission to the moon to attack people who only want to be left alone. From all indications these are people who have never made an aggressive move against the earth, or this country. These so-called world leaders want nothing more than to get their hands on weapons technologies and whatever else they can steal. It's so wrong and it makes me angry." Sydney's mouth was tight, her breathing harsh and her knuckles whitening as she entwined her fingers together.

John paused a moment to let her calm down, then asked quietly, "What do you think is the best way to go about doing something about it? I don't like it any more than you do, although I don't think I feel as strongly as you."

Taking a deep breath, Sydney's face relaxed as she consciously brought herself back to her cooler, more detached demeanor. Opening her hands and dropping them into her lap, she said quietly, "Maybe we won't have to do anything. Maybe the people we're getting ready to confront will make something happen on their own."

Her words sent a chill down John's spine. Looking closely at Sydney's face, John thought he saw a brief glimpse of something in her eyes, a momentary flash of angry determination that passed so swiftly he wasn't even sure he really saw it.

"Anyway, the question is moot. Neither you nor I have any say in what's going to happen. I don't want to think about this for the whole weekend. By the way, what do you think about the call for a nationwide peace demonstration Saturday against going to war with the lunar inhabitants? Do you think you're going to be able to get away or will you have to stay in town? I'll understand if you do," Sydney said, changing the subject.

"The chief hasn't said yet. The demonstration is supposed to run from noon until four here; actually, it's supposed to be held in every big city in the country at the same time. I haven't seen who's pulled permits for the gathering or where things will be going on in town. Besides, aren't peace demonstrations supposed to be, well, peaceful?" John asked with a smile.

Seemingly back to her usual self, the cloud of anger dissipated, Sydney smiled and replied, "That's always the plan. Do you still have a tie-dyed t-shirt and a pair of bell-bottoms hiding somewhere in your closet?"

"If I do, that's where they're going to stay. Actually, for something like this we all have to wear our uniforms."

"Now seeing you dressed up in uniform would be worth the price of admission! If we have to stay in town, how about I cook us dinner Saturday night? You can stop by after you get off," she suggested.

"Shouldn't I be getting off *after* I get to your place?" he said, with a straight face.

"That all depends on you! I will admit though, I am a sucker for a man in uniform. Wear your blues and give it your best shot."

The two began to eat, falling into their favorite ongoing debate on the merits of each other's taste in music. Sydney showed nothing of the emotion from earlier in their conversation. John watched her carefully as they chatted, trying to detect any long-term fallout from their earlier discourse, but she seemed fine. John walked her back to her office, telling her he hoped that their lunch together wouldn't cause a stir or gossip.

Sydney laughed and said, "That's really no problem. Tell you what, I'll let you know if anyone asks me about that good-looking guy with the cute butt the dean had lunch with today."

Blushing slightly, John answered, "I don't think it's going to be about all that. I meant the other."

"You mean what we talked about? Don't worry about it. It sometimes feels good to let it go like that. Everyone has issues that set them off, but don't take it personally. That is, unless you've been taking money under the table or something like that," she said, pinching him on the butt.

"Hey, be careful there. I might just need that this weekend. You want me at my best, don't you?" he asked.

"If that little tiny pinch is enough to seriously sideline you, you probably won't live through what I have planned for you, officer." Standing on tiptoe to give John a kiss, she hugged him tightly and then let him go.

"Now shoo," she said, dancing just out of reach of the squeeze John aimed at her fanny as she dashed behind her desk.

On his way back to headquarters John had plenty of time to go back over their conversation. The argument for an automatic death penalty for people who violate the public trust wasn't really a bad idea. It actually made a weird kind of sense. The main hurdle of course was that those same corrupt legislators would never vote for something like that. Not to mention people never seem to get off their collective asses to force accountability in their own lives, let alone anyone else's.

The part of the conversation that interested John most was how Sydney seemed to argue the case for leaving the lunar inhabitants alone from their perspective, as if she personally shared their concerns. Not a very compelling bit of evidence upon which to hang one's hat, but it could be telling. He regretted not dropping into the conversation his thoughts, speculation really, on Jaylynn Williams. Perhaps he'd have the opportunity over the weekend, which kept him on an emotional high all the way back to the station.

Unknown to John, earlier that morning Agent Minor, sorting through data still trickling in from various far-flung electronic sources, was alerted by one of his network bugs watching the anonymous e-mail account that had sent Sydney the cryptic message several weeks back. Minor pulled up the message, simultaneously trying to see if his tracer had followed it back to the sender. The cryptic message said only:

"peek-a-boo red rover, red rover shoo fly, don't follow me"

He printed the message off for Samuels and sent a copy to Detective Mathews. Minor pulled up the tracer's log on the account and was shocked to see it showed a single hop from the e-mail host to one of the Internet backbone circuits and then disappeared without a trace. No second hop, no originating address, no host name, nothing. It was almost as if it was sent by a bunch of rogue electrons making mischief inside the wiring of the Internet itself. This was something he definitely didn't believe in, nor boogums or any other kind of electronic boogeymen.

This little fact alone was enough to raise his suspicions to a new level. The kind of hacker expertise this trick called for was beyond even Minor's considerable skills. He dialed a number in the 999 area code, laughing to himself because not even the telephone companies knew the number existed. No such call was ever recorded, or ever showed up on any long-distance telephone log. All calls to that particular telephone number were impossible to trace since the connection was switched every few seconds while the call was in progress.

The call was answered instantly. "This better be important, Jeff."

"I need some help on a problem. I need a trace on an e-mail message from an anonymous sender."

"Give me the address," the voice said.

He passed along the information and hung up the phone. If there was anything to find, the super-secret boys located several hundred feet under Fort Mead would be able to find it. Minor had only used the telephone number on two other occasions, helping him pull the proverbial rabbit out of the hat for a very important investigation.

The owner of the voice on the other end of the line was one of Minor's best friends in high school. His friend, after college graduation, disappeared into government service, pausing only to see if Jeff wanted to take a chance and join him working for the National Security Agency. Since then they hadn't seen each other in person again, not even for the holidays. Minor had been given the telephone number over Christmas when he went home to visit his folks and his friend called to wish him a Happy, Happy.

Four minutes later his phone rang. His friend started out asking if Minor was "yanking" him.

"What do you mean?" Minor asked.

"The back-trace went into a trunk shared by a bunch of Web TV, news and overseas corporate hosts and just disappeared. There's no incoming trace, it just leaves the trunk and goes into the e-mail account. What's the deal?"

"I don't know, I was hoping you would be able to tell me," Minor said.

"Can you tell me what you're working on?"

"I guess it's pointless to ask if this line is secure now, isn't it?"

Laughing, his friend replied, "If not, I'm working for the wrong team. What's up?"

"In a word, separatists." Minor waited for the next question, but was disappointed when all his running buddy said was, "No shit?"

"Yep, it might be something, it might not."

"This time I can't help you at all. I did put a trace on all the activity on the trunk for you, though. If something else comes through to the same account I'll buzz you."

"Cool enough. Thanks again."

"No problem. Say hello to the folks," and then the call was disconnected.

Minor sat back and thought about the implications of the message. It appeared someone on the Internet might be in coded contact with Dean Atkins, if the message wasn't just some kind of mail host computer screw-up or weird kind of spam. Unfortunately, there was no way to really tell, given the sheer number of messages crisscrossing the Internet every second of every day.

Minor was interrupted by the phone ringing just before lunch. He was disappointed when the person on the other end identified himself as the director of the forensics lab at FBI headquarters.

Minor took down the information on the identification of the owner of the foot recovered from the crash in Iraq. He brought the file up on the computer and quickly paged Samuels.

About two minutes later the phone rang with Samuels was on the line.

"What's up? Crack the case already?" Samuels asked.

"The lab called with the name of the pilot. They matched the footprint with a birth record. Do you want the info now, or can it wait until you get to the office?" Minor asked.

"Just give me the highlights," Samuels said.

"The foot belongs, er, belonged to one Byron Lane, born February 14th, 1939, in Brooklyn, New York. He served in the Air Force, went to Korea as a fighter pilot, blah, blah, blah. He disappeared from his home in Denver, Colorado in March of 1971, where he owned a helicopter charter business. His house, the business, the copters, two by the way, were left behind when he disappeared. No children, both parents dead, never married. Want anything else?" Minor asked.

"Nope. He sounds pretty typical of everyone on the list," said Samuels.

"Except for the lab guy going apeshit over the fact that the foot had every indication of belonging to a man twenty years younger than our boy."

"Oh, and what else did he say?"

"Uh, well. That's it really, although he asked if we might be needing anything else from him."

Samuels thought it over. "I'll give him a call and thank him for the effort. You come up with anything new?"

"Oh yeah. That blind e-mail account sent Dean Atkins a message again, but I can't make heads or tails of it."

"Really? What did the message say?" asked Samuels.

"Here it is. 'Peek-a-boo, red rover, red rover, shoo fly, don't follow me.' That's it."

"Is everything spelled right?" Samuels asked.

"Yes, as far as I can tell," Minor answered, double checking the text on the screen.

"What kind of punctuation was there?"

"Just commas, and no caps. Everything is in lower case."

"Shit. Beats the hell out of me," said Samuels. "Any luck tracing it back to the source?"

Minor decided that discretion was the better part of valor and answered, "Nothing. The message came from a backbone segment of the net that has a crapload of ISPs, Web TV, some government and overseas stuff. There was no originating header, it was like it came out of nowhere."

"That's no help. So far today we have a pilot who died twenty years younger than he lived and a phantom gremlin who can send messages through the Internet in such a way that even the famed Jeffrey Minor can't hack. Did I leave anything out, kid?"

Laughing at Samuels' characterization, Minor replied, "All except for the message itself. Maybe she's got a child somewhere who she only communicates with via e-mail. Red rover, shoo fly? This isn't the stuff of which great literature is made."

"You're right. If it is some kind of code, it's one that won't be cracked. If it's a mistake of some sort, its origin is pretty suspicious. Talk to John lately?"

"Not really."

"Do me a favor, collect everything you have on our foot guy and cook up a summary for me. I'm going to send it off to Washington and drop it in the director's lap. I'm tired of doing all the heavy lifting only to have someone come along and pull the rug out from under my feet."

"You know that in learned circles, that's a mixed metaphor, right?"

"Yeah, bite me. Just get that summary done, Mr. Manual-of-Style."

"No problem. I'll have it for you within the hour. Anything else?" Minor asked.

"Nope, that's it. Getting homesick for DC yet?" Samuels asked.

"Are you kidding? With all the crap going on back home, I'm way better off down here."

"I'll be back in the office this afternoon. We'll go over the memo on the pilot and I'll catch you up on what's been going on. See you then," Samuels finished and hung up.

By the time John returned from his lunch with Sydney, still feeling jazzed, it was midafternoon. Tossing a "Hey gang!" to the others in the squad, he sat down at his desk and began to sort through the handful of messages and requests in his in-box. Seeing that Agent Minor had given him a call, John picked up the phone and called the number on the message.

"Hey sport," said John. "Looking for a rematch?"

"Just the thing I was calling you for. What's your schedule look like for the rest of the week?" Minor asked.

"Not bad actually. Same time as before?"

"You really know how to hurt a guy," laughed Minor. "I don't normally get up that early, but maybe it'll give you an edge, what with me being still half asleep and all."

"Bullshit. I have it on pretty good authority that you shoot just as well in your sleep. Besides, you did pretty well the last time."

"Just lucky. What about Friday morning?" Minor suggested.

"Sounds great."

"I'll meet you out front. Oh yeah, I almost forgot. We IDed our pilot! You were right, he was in the crowd, so to speak," Minor added excitedly.

"Hey, that's great. Anyone we'd know?"

"No one special. I'll give you details Friday."

"Can't wait. If anything comes up just give me a call, Jeff. By the way, I'm probably seeing my special lady Saturday night."

"Really? Anything new there?"

"Other than the fact that I'm now convinced she makes about three of me in the brains department, nothing really. You find out anything new yourself?" John asked, more than half hoping nothing had turned up.

"Just an e-mail message. Nothing solid, nothing actionable. I'll bring you up to date at the range." Minor said goodbye and hung up, putting a big red X over Friday on the monthly planner hanging next to the desk. Not that he was likely to forget.

CHAPTER 36

NASA WAS UNDER a complete security lockdown. No nonessential personnel were allowed on the grounds of the Johnson Space Center or the Kennedy Space Center and all tours were temporarily cancelled due to security concerns. Public relations people cited the vague threat of terrorist action, although what kind of terrorist was deliberately left unsaid.

The Navy had selected twenty-four candidates to travel to Houston for preliminary training and testing for the mission to the moon. Of the initial twenty-four, only the top eight would make the trip. The final group would carry the new designation SEAL Team Omega; the unprecedented nature of the mission broke the tradition of numbering the teams.

The tests in physical conditioning, endurance, adaptation to increased g-forces and resistance to the various debilitating symptoms of weightlessness took place over the first three days of the SEALs' tenure in Houston. The team members all had differing reactions to the parabolic flights in NASA's Vomit Comet, the specially outfitted KC-135A that gave riders a taste of the weightlessness of space, thirty seconds at a time. Some took to the brief periods of weightless well, frolicking like children. A few couldn't seem to overcome the distress of being without weight, without the firm grounding of up and down. Those who couldn't adapt were dismissed without prejudice.

Next came a battery of psychological tests and interviews to determine sensitivity to the claustrophobic conditions of extended periods of time inside the pressure suits or in the Russian capsules.

Naturally, all the SEALS stood up very well. The only one who dropped out did so because of an ear infection, not because of any lack of performance on his part. However, small factors contributed to the elimination of twelve of the original candidates. Two of the Navy personnel previously had had minor cases of the bends from ascending from the depths of the ocean too rapidly for their bodies to adjust to the lessening pressure. This made them unsuitable for lowered air pressure. One SEAL had an earlier rupture of an eardrum and was downchecked, and two others had families with children and were disqualified in favor of those with no dependents.

The NASA technicians and trainers were joined by two armorers from MI-5, Britain's internal security service, who brought with them pistols and automatic weapons they promised would work in the airless environment of the moon. How they knew the arms would perform was left unsaid. The SEALs were drilled in the care and use of their custom-fitted $1.6 million dollar pressure suits. Once they had demonstrated mastery of their survival gear, the MI-5 amorers drilled them in the operation of the firearms while wearing the cumbersome gloves of the space suits.

Although appalled at the thought they were actively participating in the first armed mission into space, the NASA technicians fashioned harnesses and thigh packs to hold the weapons and ammunition the SEALs would carry. Additionally, they fitted each soldier's suit with a lipstick-sized, high-resolution camera that would broadcast real-time pictures of what each soldier saw to the escape pod's relay transmitter. The video signal would then be transmitted to the orbiting shuttle for direct transmission back to earth. The mission planners had also calculated the precise orbit the shuttle would have to take in order for it to remain above the SEALs down on the surface for the longest possible time.

The SEALs trained as a team beginning at dawn every morning, and then followed their PT with more drilling in their suits, often in NASA's huge underwater tank simulating the weightlessness of space, or on the lunar landscape simulator stage with massive helium balloons tethered to their suits to lighten their weight to the same one-sixth G as the moon. In every case, the training was designed to make their responses to any possible mishaps automatic, nearly reflexive, to give them the best possible chance of survival.

Every one of the SEALs died dozens of times in simulations, sometimes from the most minute or silly mistakes, but not one of them made the mistake of thinking that the harsh repetitions were unnecessary or excessive. They respected the difficulty of the trial ahead and the NASA trainers' devotion to making sure they had the best possible chance at the mission ahead.

Modifications to the shuttle were completed in record time. Testing of the Russian escape capsules, a cut-down copy of the standard Soyuz capsule, and the newly designed connections to the shuttle's internal environmental systems were to continue right up until the shuttle was rolled out to the launch site. The capsules were rigged with detachable panels, much like a soccer ball, under which inflatable airbags would deploy to cushion the impact with the moon's surface.

Unlike the Soyuz capsules used to return cosmonauts to earth, these capsules had no parachutes to slow their descent to the ground. Instead, the lunar landing capsules were attached to a thick, nine-foot-long pod consisting of a trio of retro rockets which would slow the capsule's drop to the lunar surface. The pod, attached to the capsule by steel and carbon fiber composite cables, was designed to slow the capsule to less than fifteen meters per second before running out of fuel. Once the fuel was depleted the pod would be jettisoned and the airbags deployed.

The NASA and Russian engineers were hard-pressed to configure the storage for weapons and consumables the SEALs needed. They were hampered by the need to stay under the designed weight limit of the retro pod and keep items from rattling around the inside of the pod like so many beans in a tin can, injuring or crushing those the capsules were supposed to protect.

The crew deck of the shuttle was not designed to carry eight additional men; therefore, the SEALs would have to endure the launch inside their pods, remaining inside for the duration of the rendezvous with the refueling tanks and the entire trip from earth to lunar orbit.

There was concern that the five days of isolation and inactivity might seriously debilitate the soldiers, making them ill-prepared to face the rigors of meeting their mission objectives. The final mission profile called for lightly sedating the SEALs right after launch and bringing them to full wakefulness just before achieving lunar orbit. Their in-suit supplies were modified to deliver, in addition to the prescribed sedative and supplies of low-residue food and water, and a light stimulant to assist in maintaining peak alertness for the duration of the mission once they reached the moon.

The mission commander, Air Force Colonel George Evers, was nearly overwhelmed by the additional procedures and protocols this mission required of him and his crew. Not only would they have to alter normal mission profile right off the bat and bring the main fuel tank into orbit, they would have to perform a low-orbit rendezvous with the Russian fuel tanks with the extra tank still attached. Four of the crew would exit the shuttle and connect the hoses from the Russian tanks to refuel the shuttle's main tank.

The next leg of the mission would alter the shuttle's trajectory to slingshot it around the earth, just like the lunar probe, and snap it out of earth orbit, aiming for where the moon would be three days later.

Once successfully inserted into lunar orbit, it would be the responsibility of the command crew to scan the lunar surface for any sign of the separatists' habitat. Then the most hazardous part of the mission would begin: the accurate deployment of the escape capsules close enough to the ground target so the soldiers wouldn't perish from lack of oxygen before reaching their objective.

Colonel Evers, as the highest ranking officer on site, insisted on having full tactical control of the mission. He didn't want to end up sending the SEALs down without being assured he wasn't sending them to certain death. He knew the whole mission was a crapshoot, and that the objectives relied on the flimsiest web of presumptions. However, if there was going to be a mission to the moon, not only did he want to be the commander of the mission, he wanted to be the one in the hot seat should anything go wrong.

The overinflation of the stock market prior to the turn of the century, and the subsequent corrections, left America with an economy in search of anything to energize a business model consisting mostly of a mad race to the bottom line.

Space-based industry looked attractive as a fount of new wealth, but the initial investment was always seen as too risky. Businesses looked to the government to make the initial inroads into developing the infrastructure of space travel and habitation, coming onboard only after the costs of developing the technology had been borne by someone else. Multinationals were watching very closely to see just how the president would play the mission to the moon.

Everyone with a dollar invested in the market was hoping for some kind of positive outcome from the mission, especially for a return of new discoveries and technologies that would revitalize the American economy.

The president's national security advisor announced to the nation that the country's military alert status had been elevated, provoking criticism from various groups and spokespersons, and a spate of jokes from the late night-comedians.

Black Entertainment Television ran a two-hour-long comedy retrospective showing clips from science fiction movies and television shows of the past in which black characters ended up dying or horribly disfigured, thus proving, tongue in cheek, that black folks couldn't possibly be living in outer space.

The president's commission was still hard at work, formulating contingency plans based on the few scenarios into which the current situation could evolve. The first plan assumed a peaceful integration of the separatists back into American society, with their technological, industrial and medical advances providing a renaissance of culture and explosive economic growth.

The second scenario assumed no desire on the part of the separatists to return to earth, but a willingness to open their colony to those of earth and help establish a peaceful beachhead on the moon.

The third plan, the one that caused dissension in the commission along racial lines, was based on the separatists wanting nothing to do with earth at all.

Every black member of the commission believed the president was going to put the worst possible light on the situation no matter what, that he would spin the commission's opinions to justify an armed and aggressive posture.

Dealing with Susan Roscoe was like trying to safely hold a porcupine having a seizure. People had to have their emotional and racial shit together before suggesting any course of action to her that was precautionary or defensive toward the separatists. The only members of the commission who had half a chance of getting her to cool out when she had her back up were Dr. Milton and Norma.

Dr. Harris, Alan and the naval personnel kept toe-to-heel watch on the moon base.

They were also treated to an onsite visit by General Kaminski, who toured the underground facility for little over an hour to inspect the apparatus responsible for the breakthrough in theoretical sciences.

Unfortunately, Dr. Harris got the distinct impression the chairman was more concerned about the fact that more than ten percent of those stationed down below were nonwhite. He demanded that new security procedures be implemented to prevent any unauthorized access to Martin's lab and the monitoring room, almost but not quite ordering all naval personnel on the project who might not be, in his words, appropriate, be reassigned. He later relented when he was bluntly reminded that he had to make a choice between keeping the current staff on site or facing the prospect of those relocated talking about what was going on at Shelter Fourteen, secrecy oaths and orders notwithstanding.

Fortunately, Commander Ames took it upon himself to conduct the impromptu tour of the facility, deflecting the general's attentions away from any kind of confrontation with Alan or Martin over the uses to which Martin's scientific technology would be put. He was secretly delighted that it was he, a member of the target minority, who was still in charge of the project by the president's direct orders. He was unfailingly polite to the general, and took pains to reassure him that the strength and effectiveness of the team stationed below, military and civilian, was based entirely on their differences. For his part, the chairman accepted the commander's running commentary in stoic silence.

The only other member of the underground community graced with General Kaminski's attentions was Dr. Milton, who was very uncomfortable with the assertion that the commission had done the country a great service in supporting the need for a decisive confrontation. Catching a warning glance from Ames, Dr. Milton held his tongue, thanked the chairman for his support of their efforts and left the room as quickly as politeness allowed.

It felt like the entire installation let out a sigh of relief when the chairman's entourage was in the lift headed for the surface. Although none of them said anything negative about the chairman, the military staff were conspicuously silent about the visit.

Commander Ames rode to the surface with the general, wanting to receive changes in the operation of the installation, if there were any, away from the below-ground staff. Surprisingly, the general was impressed with the entire operation and even praised Commander Ames on his maintaining discipline and security with the posting of so many civilians below. The only suggestion he had to offer was for Ames to keep particular watch over what Kaminski described as egghead liberals.

When they reached the surface, Ames thanked the general for taking time out to visit their installation, noticing immediately the general's undisguised expression of distaste when the elevator door was opened by a black noncom.

Ames was left to wonder how such a nakedly bigoted man could end up Chairman of the Joint Chiefs over a combined military force where nearly one out of every five men and women were not white.

On his flight back to Washington, General Kaminski called the military liaison officer at NASA in Houston for a detailed update on the mission. The shuttle Endeavour was completely outfitted and loaded with the Russian capsules, and would be rolled out of the Vehicle Assembly Building less than thirty-six hours before the scheduled launch. The Navy SEALs had passed their final space suit checkouts and were still practicing with their weapons. In the evenings they pored over the high-resolution photos of the area surrounding the gravitational anomaly. The CIA had greatly enhanced the images of the rocky terrain and had even found three possible locations for entrances to the hidden complex. The only puzzler was the complete lack of tracks in the immediate area. The nearest sign of any activity was nearly eight kilometers away in the direction of the asteroid impact site. So far, no surface vehicle had been spotted or photographed since the satellite achieved orbit.

While he was on the line, Kaminski queried the officer about the total weight of the mission. Puzzled, the Air Force colonel gave him the figures. The general then asked if an additional piece of equipment weighing seven hundred pounds could be added to the shuttle payload.

Checking the mission plan, the colonel answered in the affirmative.

Kaminski thanked him for the update and broke the connection. Activating the scrambled circuit to call the White House, he got the chief of staff on the line.

"Mr. Masters, I would like to request that we include an additional piece of equipment on the mission, one you will have to discuss with the president as soon as possible and have him up to speed on before I return to Washington," Kaminski began without preamble.

"What is the nature of this additional equipment, General?" Master's asked.

"It is my recommendation that we equip the mission with one neutron weapon in the event our men face an untenable situation up there. The use of this weapon as a final option would allow the neutralization of hostile forces without damaging the technology and habitat they hold."

"Son of a bitch, Isaac! Do you know what you're suggesting? Do you have any idea of the fallout this decision would cause if word of it got out?"

"Amusing choice of words, Mr. Masters. Unfortunately the situation isn't the least bit funny. I'm sending eight men directly into harm's way, not to mention the command crew of the shuttle and the shuttle itself. I want to have as many options open to me as possible. Sending along this device as insurance may well end up saving American lives."

"At what cost? I'll never be able to get the president to go along with this ridiculous idea, no sane man would," Masters hissed.

"I believe you are mistaken. Though a distasteful one, the idea is not so far-fetched that I'm sure he's never considered it. Word on the street is that you've already spoken to more than a few of his supporters in industry about the exploitation of the technology we bring back. Getting our hands on that technology without the interference of those who currently hold it would make everything so much easier, wouldn't it?" the general stated. "If my men get to the surface safely, and once there face weapons or defenses that they can't overcome, what then? Where's the stick to go with the carrot? How does the president propose we persuade these people to help get our men back to earth? I'd really like to know. As things stand right now, this entire trip is one big suicide mission if my men can't capture the means to get home . . ."

Masters cut off the general. "What about the UN resolutions forbidding nuclear weapons in space? How is that going to look?"

"Don't give me that load of crap. You know as well as I do that this country doesn't give a shit about the UN or their resolutions except when they serve our purposes. We use them or ignore them as the situation warrants. Besides, they aren't in command of this mission, now are they?"

"And what about what the American people think? Do you give a damn about them?"

"No, and neither do you. We're the ones who have to make the tough decisions, not the public. They don't want to concern themselves with the hard decisions of running a country and keeping it strong. Hell, they all want steak but don't want to be bothered with killing the cow. All they want is prepackaged, sanitized lives shielded from any hint of the ugly realities of the world around them. Now, you just trot down the hall and pass along my recommendation to the president. And set up an appointment for tonight. I want his authorization as soon as possible so NASA can integrate the weapon into the mission profile."

"Fuck you, Kaminski. You're not sending a nuke into space. I don't have to talk to the president to know what his answer is going to be," Masters shouted into the phone.

"Don't challenge me on this, Simon, one way or the other you *will* lose." Kaminski hung up. To his credit he did think further about adding nuclear capability to the mission. By the time they were on final approach into Washington, he had made up his mind to give his men on the ground any tools they might need to get the job done.

Masters hunted down the president in the residence, apologizing for interrupting lunch with his wife, but explaining that they were facing yet another crisis. The first lady, seeing the worried look on Masters' face and the questioning look on her husband's, excused herself, leaving the two alone.

"Sit down, Simon. Have you eaten?" Bender asked.

"No, sir. I'll get something later."

"All right, what is it now?"

"Sir. The chairman is requesting authorization to arm the mission with nuclear ordnance."

"What?" Bender said, standing up in shock, spilling his water across the table.

"God dammit. Has everyone gone mad around here? What the fuck is he thinking? Does anyone else know about this? Where is he?" Bender was off on an angry tear.

Masters stood and gently pushed Bender's arm, getting him to sit back down and gesturing to Agent Bishop, who had opened the door and stuck his head into the room, that everything was fine. When Bishop pulled the door shut, Masters continued.

"So far it's only a request, sir. He's inbound from Shelter Fourteen. He wants a meeting with you tonight to discuss it."

Mopping up the puddle of water on the table, Bender silently considered the situation. He tossed his sodden napkin across the table and collapsed into his chair.

"I didn't sign up for this. Why couldn't this have waited until I was out of office, marlin fishing somewhere?"

"No kidding. What do you want me to do? Should I set up the meeting?" Masters asked.

"Hell, yes. I want to nip this in the bud. That asshole is going to get stepped on, but good." He paused a second and continued quietly. "Doesn't he realize there's no justification for including a weapon of mass destruction on this mission? These people have done everything possible to avoid detection, to keep out of sight and out of mind. What is he thinking?"

"Sir, he did state that he wanted to ensure we had the necessary inducement to make sure our men get the kind of cooperation they'll need to get home safely."

"Speak softly and carry a big stick. Is that it?" Bender asked tiredly.

"I guess. What time do you want him here? And, do you want anyone else to attend the meeting, sir?"

"Quit 'siring' me to death, I'm not pissed at you. Get the corporate counsel in here and get Ames back here. I want some idea of the usefulness of deploying a neutron device in space and what kind of defense might be used against it. This meeting never happened, you understand me? The fewer who even suspect someone is considering sending up nuclear ordnance, the better."

When he got the call from Masters, Commander Ames was in a meeting with Harris and Milton. Ames took the call on Milton's phone, gesturing to the other two not to get up. They both half listened to what Ames was saying and went completely silent when Ames shouted "What? He wants to do what?"

When Ames concluded the call he had a full head of steam up.

"What?" said Martin.

"Kaminski is trying to get permission to bring a bomb to the moon."

"What kind of bomb, or need I ask?" Milton said.

"You don't mean . . ." Martin began, looking at Ames for the hoped-for denial. The commander just nodded.

"This is not good," began Dr. Milton. "Does he know what this means if he gets his way?"

"I don't think he cares about anything but what *he* wants," said Ames.

"He better seriously consider this," began Martin. "Any nuclear weapon onboard is going to be a bigger hazard to the shuttle from anyone who can control gravity."

Ames' eyebrow went up. "How so?" he asked.

"Think about it. How does a nuclear device explode? You jam a bunch of fissionables together over several microseconds until you get critical mass and the matter is converted into energy."

"Yeah, so?"

"What happens when you have a really dense gravitational field? What happens to the stuff inside the field?"

"Oh shit!" Ames said. "If they squeeze the materials in a bomb together they can make them cook off without using the triggering mechanism."

"That's right. Just think what would happen to the shuttle and the crew if they were enclosed in a gravitational field as strong as Jupiter's, for example. The wouldn't even need to detonate the bomb's materials to destroy the shuttle. Just squeeze it to death."

"You must convince the president to repudiate this act of madness," Dr. Milton implored.

"No sane person would want any weapon in space, let alone something like a nuclear bomb."

"He's right, Jim. This isn't the act of a sane person at all. All it does is guarantee that any peaceful consideration we might get from the lunar inhabitants goes right out the window. You m*ust* convince President Bender of the danger to the mission. Besides, I just don't see how a nuclear weapon is going to be much of a threat to anyone who can affect gravity over an area that size on the moon."

"Thank you, gentlemen. I will take your words to the president, I just hope he listens,"

Ames excused himself and left to prepare for his trip east. Just before he left Dr. Milton's office

Ames paused and said, "Let's just keep this among the three of us, shall we?"

Dr. Milton slouched in his chair and said, "Marty, I keep thinking about that perfect Chinese curse."

"You mean, 'may you live in interesting times'?"

"Exactly. I'm at a complete loss as to where we go now. I can't very well be expected to keep this from the rest of the commission. We can't develop any good policies or contingencies without taking this madness into consideration. Any ideas?"

Martin thought about it for a few seconds. "How about this. When you reconvene the steering committee, why don't you focus on the mission itself. You could postulate several scenarios, one of which would be an armed mission and its consequences. If you want I can even prepare a white paper on the probable uses of gravity as an offensive weapon against a manned space mission."

"Not bad." Milton sat up and began to make a few notes on the pad in front of him.

"What about defensive uses? How can they use gravity to defend against an attack?"

"Well, for one thing they could make it impossible to drop a bomb to the surface of the moon. They could redirect it away from the planet, even push the shuttle into the sun. If we intend to drop men to the moon's surface someone will have to make damn sure they actually get there."

"Good, write it up. I'll convene the committee around two this afternoon," Milton said.

When Commander Ames got to Washington he was rushed to the White House without delay. His military car was escorted by two motorcycle cops with sirens and lights blazing. When he arrived, he was ushered inside so fast he didn't take more than a handful of breaths before he was unceremoniously led into the Oval Office with President Bender and Masters.

"Sit down, commander," said the president, gesturing to the couch as he took a seat across from Ames. "This is a serious problem. Before we go on, I want your word nothing said here goes any further. On your word as a gentleman, I'm not going to make it an order."

"You have my word, Mr. President."

For the next fifteen minutes President Bender summarized the proposed mission to the moon and all the various scenarios that both the commission and the military planners at the pentagon had assembled. When he got to the part where he revealed that General Kaminski had requested room be made for a neutron bomb aboard the shuttle, the commander was on his feet before he even knew it.

When the president asked his opinion, Ames began pacing back and forth, so agitated he could not sit down. After a moment to organize his thoughts, Ames began, "If you ask me, I think the whole idea of sending an armed mission is foolish. It's like going up and taking a swipe at the biggest bully on the block. No, that's not right. These people haven't made any aggressive move against earth, there's nothing of the bully about them."

"Let me get this straight, commander," began Masters. "You're telling us that a nuke is useless against the capabilities of these people."

"If we're going to send our men up there I believe we have a better chance of opening a dialog if they don't go armed," Ames concluded.

"And if they're attacked?" Masters objected. "How do you expect those men to defend themselves if they are attacked?"

"Begging your pardon sir, but that's the fallacy of the whole defense by deadly force argument. Let's leave armies out of the equation for the moment. On the most basic level, sirs, cops don't defend anyone with deadly force. Their power is based on the premise that if you do something wrong or threaten someone they will kill you for your trouble. They aren't defending anything with their weapons unless they get fired on and return fire. But the concept of defending the public by carrying guns just doesn't exist, it's compliance through threat of injury or death."

The Ames and Masters waited for President Bender to speak. He got up and poured himself a glass of water, thinking over the commander's words. President Bender turned to face

Ames and said, "The chairman is due here by eight tonight. Can you get on the horn and have Dr. Milton summarize what you've just told us and have it here by seven-thirty?"

"Yes, sir. He may even have more than what I've thought of by then too," Ames answered.

"Oh? How so, Commander?" asked Bender.

"He was going to discuss the mission in committee this afternoon and advance the idea of an armed mission for discussion, sir."

"You didn't have anything to do with the agenda did you, Commander?" Bender asked, raising an eyebrow, a slight smile coming to his lips.

"No, sir! Dr. Milton decided to do it on his own. Well, maybe he sort of overheard my side of the conversation with Mr. Masters," Ames answered, a darkening blush coming to his cheeks. "I was in Dr. Milton's office when the call came through, sir."

"No harm done, son. That's what the commission was convened to do, cover the possibilities this situation may present and help keep us from overlooking something that just might end up biting us in the ass. Simon, where's Diane?"

"I believe she's returning from California sometime this evening. Why, sir? You don't want her to be in this meeting with Kaminski, do you?" Masters asked, somewhat alarmed at the prospect.

"Hell no, but I do want her to take a look at whatever Milton sends and add anything she thinks is germane. Commander, I'm going to save you the trouble of attending as well, no sense in killing off your career prematurely, is there?"

"Thank you, sir. If I you have nothing further for me I can call Dr. Milton and arrange for him to get that information to you ASAP," Ames said, rising to his feet.

Also getting to his feet, Bender shook hands with Ames before he could salute. "Thank you again, commander, for all your assistance. Agent Bishop will show you to an office where you can make whatever calls you require," Bender said as Agent Bishop opened the door, waiting patiently for the president to conclude his goodbye.

Resisting the impulse to, once again, try to salute his commander in chief, Ames shook hands with Masters and followed Agent Bishop past the president's secretaries and down the hall toward the Secret Service offices.

No one on the commission endorsed arming the mission to the moon, even the members of the military. They appended the entire text of all the UN resolutions passed through the years against the storage and detonation of nuclear weapons in space to their report.

With Diane Churchill's input on the information from the commission, President Bender had more than enough ammunition to deny the chairman's request. The meeting was short and to the point.

"General, I have given your request very serious thought. I have considered the lives we are putting at risk and all of the stated, and unstated, objectives of this very important mission. Having said that, I'm going to deny your request," President Bender said, holding Kaminski's gaze unflinchingly.

"May I ask why, Mr. President?"

"In consultation with Doctors Harris and Milton, and with the input of Ms. Churchill, I conclude that it is too dangerous to arm the shuttle with any nuclear weaponry. What you may not realize is that these devices can be triggered without using detonation codes by anyone with control of gravity," Bender said.

General Kaminski blinked his eyes in surprise.

"That's right, general. A compacted gravity field can squeeze the fissionables down to critical mass without resorting to using the detonation circuitry or my codes," said the president, pressing his point home. "I cannot allow a weapon of that magnitude to be sent where we can lose control of it. Sending it to the moon, in close proximity to a group that obviously has the ability to set it off regardless of the safeguards built into it, is an unacceptable risk to our men. I'm sorry, the answer is no."

"I see, Mr. President. So, do you and your advisors have any suggestions on how our soldiers are suppose to defend themselves up there? Are they just supposed to go knocking on the door with nothing but their dicks in their hands? Tell me how our boys are supposed to protect themselves," the general asked, sarcastically.

"General, there *is* no defense against what they're going to encounter up there. If these people don't want to be bothered with us they don't even have to let the shuttle reach the moon, they can send it right back home if they want. Don't you understand? They control gravity! They can destroy pretty much whatever they want, whenever they want! We're not going to get into a pissing contest with them without provocation, Isaac!" Bender said, jabbing his finger toward the general's chest. "This time you had better follow orders, General. We are not starting a war we so obviously can not win. Do you understand me?"

"Yes sir. I will follow your orders on this. However, I will not abandon my men to whatever threat they face up there. I want some kind of option that will ensure their safety."

"Don't be an ass. There is no guarantee of their safety. Anyone we send there is at risk in a way from which we cannot shield them. There is no safety net for them. Hell, we can't even get them back into orbit once they're on the surface. They're going to have to hitch a ride back up to the shuttle, or back home here, from the very people you want to threaten. Is that wise? Is that what they call considered planning from the Office of the Joint Chiefs?"

"All I want to do is make sure the men have every safeguard possible. We must be prepared for any contingency, including the need to use force to protect our men, our country, and now, our planet," replied Kaminski. "I will not go down in history as having sent men into harm's way without making every effort to protect the lives under my command."

Masters sat silent, letting the two men hash this out without his interference, watching and listening for any sign of the general's intention to commit treason. He knew that everything said in the Oval Office was recorded, as did the general. However, one never knew what might slip out.

"That's all very well and good. Let's say for the sake of argument my mind wasn't made up. What can you say, given that the control of these weapons is out of our hands the moment the mission is launched? How do you see the inclusion of a weapon that can be set off by the enemy whenever they get good and ready as protecting our troops lives?" Bender said, sitting back to listen to the general's arguments.

"First of all, the enemy's ability to detonate our ordnance is not a known fact, it's only speculation at this point. Secondly, we don't know the range of their gravity-based technology. High lunar orbit may keep us out of reach of their ground-based installations. And thirdly, there's no guarantee they know we're coming, and if they do suspect we are mounting a mission, they don't know exactly when it's due to arrive," Kaminski finished.

"Is that it? That's all you've got, Isaac? Did you forget that the rock that started this mess came from somewhere in the asteroid belt? We don't know where these people can go, where they've been or what they want from us other than leaving them alone. You don't know a damn thing about them. In terms of gathering intelligence, you're batting a big, fat zero, Isaac."

"Mr. President, I am operating in the dark as much as everyone else here. It's not fair to characterize my lack of direct intelligence that way. We're all working blind here, it's just in my case I have to try to support and protect our men without any knowledge of what they're going to face. Those darkies are not going to get the drop on my men up there, not if I can do anything at all to prevent it."

Pausing a moment to consider the chairman's statement, President Bender replied, " I hope I'm not going to get that kind of horseshit spewing forth in any public venue. Or did you think I was kidding when I stated I wasn't going to tolerate racist bullshit in my administration?"

Kaminski looked momentarily stricken by the president's reaction to his verbal gaffe. "I'm sorry, Mr. President, I meant no disrespect. It won't happen . . ."

Holding up his hand to silence the general, President Bender shook his head and said, "I am really tired of hearing that kind of crap from you. In any case, I believe we are finished here. No nuclear weapons on the mission. No orbital nukes either. Are we clear on this?"

"Crystal clear, sir. I will continue to send status reports on the mission preparations and stand ready to brief anyone you deem fit, sir."

"Thank you, Mr. Chairman. If there is anything else I can be of assistance on regarding the mission, don't hesitate to ask."

Getting to his feet along with the president and Masters, General Kaminski turned and left the office without a backward glance.

"Well, Simon? What do you think? Is our racist little warmonger going to behave?" Bender asked his longtime friend.

"I don't know what to think. I'm going to make damned sure nothing is smuggled aboard the bird before it takes off, just in case. Other than that, there's not much more we can do at this point except ask for his resignation or, worst case, bury him somewhere." Masters got up and poured himself a bourbon, straight.

"His kind of thinking scares me, Jim. Not just because it's him, but for the fact that more and more folks out there are thinking just like him every day."

"Why, what have you heard?" Bender asked tiredly.

"A couple of the senior senators have publicly hinted that if these people even look like they might be a threat that we should spend our last dime to wipe them out to preserve the American way of life. I don't have to tell you who they are, do I?"

"No, I can guess. What else?"

"A couple of my contacts on Wall Street want to know if I believe we have any chance at all of getting the separatists to share what they've got up there. The feeling is that the market is going to tank in a big way if anyone fires a shot." Masters gulped down the rest of his drink, grimacing in distaste. "Every one of them's just guessing of course, there's no precedent so no one knows what the fallout's going to be. My money's on another crash the country can little afford."

"Are you sure I can't talk you into trading jobs for the rest of the year?" Bender asked with a laugh.

"What? And take a cut in pay? Forget it, you're the pretty boy with delusions of grandeur. It's all yours, boss!" Masters took his glass back to the cart and picked up his folio. "I'm going home, I'm going to try to surprise the wife by getting home before midnight for a change."

Many a tear has to fall, but it's all . . . in the game
All in the wonderful game
That we know . . . as love
You had words with him
And your future's looking dim
But these things your heart can rise above
It's All In The Game
Written by Carl Sigman, composed by Charles Dawes and performed by Tommy Edwards

CHAPTER 37

THE MORNING OF the nationwide peace demonstration dawned sunny and warm in Atlanta, but the mood of the country was ugly. No one wanted war. No one could even imagine how the United States would wage a war against someone on the moon. None but a tiny minority wanted to see the country split along racial lines. Unlike previous administrations, President Bender's people knew that war would not bring prosperity, would not raise the Dow Jones average, and certainly wouldn't spark consumer confidence or promote any long–or short-term investment by the people.

The Congressional Black Caucus petitioned the United Nations to pass a resolution prohibiting the transportation of arms into space, which was endorsed by every member of the Security Council except the US, which used its veto power to kill the resolution. The international press was beginning to paint President Bender's administration as racist warmongers, questioning the motives of a country about to launch an armed expedition against people who had made every effort to be left alone.

The press uncovered a portion of Agent Samuels' list of those who had disappeared over the previous four decades. Family members, friends and former coworkers were being interviewed about the character and behavior of those believed to be living on the moon. Second-rate talking heads masquerading as experts in the various soft sciences were extolling profiles of the typical inhabitant of the lunar colony and the psychosociological basis for discarding their lives for an existence separate from earth.

From every perspective America was operating in full crisis mode. The feeling of unrest cast an uneasy pall over John and the rest of the off-duty officers called in to cover the streets during the planned peace demonstration.

John was paired with Jason for the day, assigned to a standard squad car with two other officers. They were to orbit around the rallying point of the peace demonstration, ready to deploy quickly should trouble erupt.

For John and Jason, it turned out to be a quiet day in the sun. When they returned to the station in the late afternoon to change out of their uniforms, John took the time to call Sydney at home to see if there was anything he could bring that evening.

He then went home to clean up. When he left for Sydney's place, he stopped along the way to pick up some flowers. He was unashamedly thrilled to be spending time with her again. The expectation of them spending the night together, finally sleeping together, added a measure of anticipation and a little bit of anxiety too.

By the time he got to her house, John was glad that the sun hadn't set yet. He recalled they'd be able to watch the sun go down through her dining room window while they ate. Once again, when she answered the door, Sydney gave John a warm hug and a not-so-quick kiss on the lips.

"Come on back, I was just tossing the salad." When they got into the kitchen, Sydney said, "Grab that bottle and open it will you? I could use a glass of wine."

Remembering where Sydney kept the corkscrew, John opened the bottle, poured both glasses, and then handed one to Sydney.

"So, officer, how was your day? Did you have to violate anyone's civil rights?" Sydney asked, eyebrow cocked.

Laughing easily, John answered, "Didn't even get to pull out my baton!"

"Is that code or something?" Sydney asked hopefully, the other eyebrow raised this time. "That begs the question just what does one have to do to provoke you into pulling out your baton in the first place?"

"Come on, that was too easy, you can do better than that. Not feeling well?" John teased.

Picking up the bowl of salad and flicking her head toward the dining room, she said, "Grab the glasses, everything's ready."

"How did the rally go? Did you see anyone of note?" she asked.

"Not really. We were too busy walking around to see much of the action. The mayor said a few words," said John.

"So, what was he saying?"

"Well, most of it was him advising calm and not to rush to judge the people on the moon, or the president's plan, so quickly."

"That's it? That's all you remember?" she said with a smile.

"Some of the spectators called him an Uncle Tom for fronting for the president. I guess they were thinking that anyone black should be unequivocally dead set against going to the moon. It was like he was supposed to be rabidly against anything white or something. It just didn't feel right, it's not supposed to be that way all the time."

Sydney quietly laid her hand over his, giving him a gentle squeeze. "I know. It's hard for anyone to understand anyone else, to walk a mile in their shoes."

"It's more than that. There's some an expectation that we're all supposed to behave like some kind of one-dimensional clone of the flavor of the day. Like I'm supposed to be whatever the rules say a white cop is supposed to be."

"Hey, before you get so depressed you can't move, why don't we eat."

Shaking himself out of his mood, John began to pick at his food. Before he knew it, his appetite was back and they were talking about music and film. Sydney took every opportunity to tease and cajole him.

When dinner was over and the dishes cleared, they settled down in the living room over coffee, John Coltrane playing softly in the background.

"I can see it's still on your mind. Want to talk about it?" Sydney asked.

"Not if it's going to put you off. I'm fine, really. What about you? What's your take on all this?" John asked.

Sydney looked John in the eye, paused several seconds and then said, "I think that the world is a very shitty place to live for about ninety-nine percent of the people here. Some of it's from their own personal dissatisfaction, but the larger portion of their misery is due to the daily trials and tribulations of living.

"These people on the moon have probably lived there for years, away from what *this* country specifically has to dish out. The fact that they're probably black is just incidental to their existence, but no one seems to see that. What *is* important is seeing what they have turned out to be like, to see what they have become away from here. *That's* what's important, not attacking them, not taking what they have away from them. In the mass hysteria that's been building for the last couple of weeks no one has focused on the most important point. Don't we want to see what these people are like, John? Wouldn't you like to find out if they have developed a culture that might lead us to the next social evolutionary change?"

"Yes, but what if they aren't benign like you think? What then? What if they have some sort of agenda that impacts the country? What if they are going to impose changes on the country regarding race relations and such?" John asked. "What are we supposed to do then?"

"Good question. Looking at the what-ifs is a good exercise, and we wouldn't be prudent if we ignored them. But, from watching the news and reading the paper all I'm seeing is fear and hostility. It stands to reason that anyone who's been living on the moon would have a lot to offer us. But all I see is preparation for a mission to steal what's theirs or to fire the first shot in a war that no one has been able to show the necessity for."

"I don't think it's been decided to attack them yet," John said. "I'm pretty sure that the mission is only supposed to take a look and try to make contact with them."

"What about the rumor that the president is sending nuclear weapons on the mission? Is this the equipment a reconnaissance mission calls for?" Sydney shot back.

"Hey! I don't know if they're sending those things along or not, and neither do you. If they are, I think it's wrong. It sends the wrong message." John took a sip from his cup, catching her glare at him out of the corner of his eye. "What? What did I say?" he asked, plaintively.

"That's it? Is that all you think it does? Send the wrong message? How about it's wrong to use or even own nuclear weapons at all? Or, why send weapons at all when no one has made the least aggressive move against the country? 'It sends the wrong message' seems a little weak, John. As a matter of fact, it sounds like you don't think that kind of behavior is the obscenity it is!" Sydney said, her lips thinning into a tight line of anger.

"That's not what I think at all. I'm just as curious as the next guy about the people up there. I *do* want to see how they live, but I don't know what they want. Apparently they've been there for a while now and they've been successful at keeping us from finding out they're there," said John. "How can we know what they think?"

"That's my point. No one in Washington or anywhere else in this world knows what these people are all about. Everyone else is willing to wait and see what comes of peaceful contact with them except for this country.

"According to the reports on the people the FBI says are up there, there's not one of them with a criminal record. They were all upstanding citizens before they disappeared. Where does anyone get off assuming they might be hostile? John, the chancellor of the college thinks that Jaylynn Williams might be up there. Did you ever think of that?" Sydney said, watching closely for any reaction on John's face.

"Yes, I did," John said softly.

"And what were you planning to do about it?" she asked.

"There's nothing I *can* do about it. I already wrote up my report and handed it in to the lieutenant and I'm sure he forwarded it on to the FBI. Why do you ask?"

"You see, that's my point exactly. There's nothing you or anyone else can really do about this situation. Those people have put themselves completely out of reach. But that's not going to keep us from trying, is it?"

"Trying what?" John asked

"Trying to hunt down those who left earth and squeeze them until everything they know of consequence has been wrung from them! It's wrong and there's no other way to describe it."

"For the most part I agree. But, and it's a big but, we still don't know if they're going to meet us peacefully or not. I feel we should be prepared for either eventuality. To some extent the mission needs to be prepared for a less-than-friendly reception when they reach the moon. I don't like it, but I understand and agree with the necessity." John could almost feel Sydney emotionally pulling away from him and felt stricken. The last thing he wanted was for anything to come between them; he knew just how much he had invested in the woman sitting across from him.

"I guess we know where *you* stand." There was pain in her eyes. Try as she might, she couldn't help feeling a sense of betrayal even though John hadn't really said anything other than he understood why the country was behaving as it was.

Sydney didn't know what she expected. She wasn't really angry with John, but in the futility of trying to find some grounding of sanity in her everyday world her frustrations continued to mount. The anger burned inside her, it had been smoldering for years, ever since she was a teenager. Anger at the unfair circumstance of being born black in a world where whites maintained the fiction that with hard work and perseverance, anyone could make it. Anger at the expectation that as a woman she was seen as only a second-rate intellect when she was working toward her Ph.D. in mathematics. Anger at her own expectations about John as a man, that somehow he was supposed to be able to use a lifetime of experiences to guide him to better understand her perspectives, her personal and cultural history. And she was angry at herself for putting such unfair expectations on the man before her, who had penetrated her careful defenses against getting involved. A man so different, so unlike her, and yet so compelling.

"That's not fair. I'm trained to be careful, to watch out for the what-ifs. It is essential for me to be able to see both sides of an issue. What do you want to hear from me? That I think the policies of this country in race relations suck? Damn straight they do. Do you want me to say that the whole idea of sending an armed mission to the moon when there's been no demonstrative need sickens me? Sure it does. But it's not fair for you to tell me that I have to proselytize against what's going on, because I can't. It comes with the fucking job, day in and day out."

"Then you have a shitty job, John. If you can't be who you are, if you can't even say what you feel, then what kind of existence do you call that?" Sydney asked.

"It's an imperfect existence. It's a compromise for what I think is a more important role I play. What I do is important to me. If Jaylynn Williams has been killed by some nutjob, or kidnaped and tortured by a racist shithole, I want to make damn sure the person who did it gets caught. If some pimp cruises the streets looking for kids who have lost all hope, or have fallen on some shitty circumstance, I want to be able to find them, get them away from the situation, and maybe, just maybe, return them safely home to their families.

"God damn it! I didn't ask for all the necessities of this role, but I'm going to play it the best way I know how. I don't know how you deal with what life hands out every fucking day because of your color, but I try to clean up my life the best way I know how.

"So don't preach to me about leaving those people alone. Because just like anyone else, I want to know how they could just drop everything, leave their families without a comforting word, let everyone think they were dead, and go off where they would never be heard from again. Don't forget, I've heard the pain in Jaylynn's parents voices, and seen the anguish in her boyfriend's eyes because she's gone. Especially so because none of them know what has happened to her, they have no idea, no closure. And, if it takes going up there and knocking on their door demanding an explanation, then dammit, let it be done," John finished with a shout. Then getting to his feet and picking up his sport coat laying on the chair next to the couch, he started for the door.

Sydney just sat there, stunned.

When he reached the living room door leading to the front hallway he turned back to her and said, "I don't know what to think about you, or about us. For a while there I thought we had managed to escape the kinds of things that keep people like us apart, but I was wrong. If it's not education, it's the careers. If it's not careers or money then it's religion. And if it's not religion it's race. Isn't there enough bullshit out there keeping people apart without you and me manufacturing things to get in the way?" John paused a second, as if he had more to say on the subject, instead he simply said, "Thank you for dinner . . . goodbye, Sydney."

Sydney just sat there, all the strength drained from her body. She was incapable of getting up, unable to utter a single word to bring him back. She was not able to recall any of the words just spoken except for John's "goodbye."

It wasn't until she heard John's car door slam that any change in her expression showed on her face, as a single tear, overflowing the corner of her eye, begin its slow journey down her cheek.

At the Kennedy Space Center in Florida, the shuttle Endeavour was just hours from beginning its final earthbound journey from the Vehicle Assembly Building to the launch pad. NASA and Russian technicians were continuing to test all critical components of the jury-rigged escape capsules in the cargo hold. The command crew and the Navy SEALs were asleep, having completed their last day of hectic training and then flying in from Houston. Both teams were in isolation, mostly to prevent catching anything as simple as a cold before the mission, and also to prevent any leaks to the news services.

Sunday morning, forgoing any worship services they may have otherwise attended, the entire launch apparatus of the Kennedy Space Center was devoting their every effort to getting Endeavour safely into space. The mobile launcher platform atop the crawler transporter, on which the shuttle was assembled and readying for launch, made its one-mile-per-hour trip to the launch pad. The command crew was undergoing their final mission profile go-round. The SEALs were being thoroughly checked over by the medical team.

The SEALs were informed, in the course of the mission briefing, that in case of an aborted launch, there was no way to get them out of the cargo bay. If conditions called for the crew capsule to be blasted free of the shuttle to save their lives, those in the cargo bay would be trapped. The SEAL team would share the fate of the shuttle. Because of this unprecedented danger they were offered one more chance to withdraw from the mission without prejudice. Predictably, no one dropped out.

Final suit fittings for the SEALS proceeded without incident. They also cleaned and checked their weapons for the last time before they were sealed inside the lockers inside the capsules.

NASA authorized the mission, and sent word to President Bender that, weather permitting, they were go for a launch.

President Bender immediately called a meeting of the National Security Council for first thing the next morning, including Diane Churchill, and flew in Doctors Milton and Harris from Shelter Fourteen for the meeting.

The meeting began with an undercurrent of hostility. The lines were clearly drawn between military and nonmilitary participants. When President Bender arrived he smiled at the polarized atmosphere reflected in the seating around the table.

"Good morning everybody, please be seated," President Bender began. "Last night I authorized the launch of the shuttle Endeavour for the mission to the moon. I also phoned the Russian president to formally request their launch of the unmanned refueling rocket which will rendezvous with the shuttle and refill the their main tank. I have also appointed Colonel George Evers commander of this mission, and placed the shuttle under military control. Make no mistake, ladies and gentlemen, this *is* a military mission. Are there any questions?"

Paul Milton immediately raised his hand. "Yes, Dr. Milton," said the president.

"Sir, I would like to ask, how is the mission armed?"

"Mr. Chairman, would you care to inform the group just what kinds of munitions the mission carries?" President Bender asked.

Clearing his throat, General Kaminski said, "The mission carries eight Navy SEALs, designated SEAL Team Omega. The are armed with personal hand weapons, fully automatic rifles and plastic explosives."

"Plastic explosives!? What in the world, pardon the expression, could they need with plastic explosives?" asked Dr. Milton. "Mr. President, I most strongly object. There is no room in an exploratory mission like this for any kind of weapons at all, let alone explosives."

The room erupted in a buzz of conversation. Holding up his hand for quiet, President Bender cut off General Kaminski's reply.

"Dr. Milton, while I sympathize with your position, I, and I alone, decided to take the simple precaution of arming our men with hand weapons and minimal explosives in the event their lives are in danger. This is a simple precaution, nothing more." President Bender said.

From the nonmilitary side of the room President Bender saw Diane Churchill gesture to him. "Yes, Diane. You have something to add?"

"Thank you, Mr. President. I want everyone at this table to understand just how ludicrous sending any weapons on this mission will be. According to the data gathered by Dr. Harris' studies in the area of gravitational control, those living on the moon have the resources to prevent anyone from ever reaching the moon. The control of gravity is fundamentally more powerful a force to be reckoned with than any we have been confronted with in history, and it's pointless to even consider armed opposition to those who wield that control.

"Mr. Chairman, Mr. President, it is my recommendation that we dispense with any futile pretense of carrying arms for defense and reconfigure the mission as an exploratory venture. And, by the way, if there are any thoughts of taking along special weaponry in secret, then scientifically I can state unequivocally that to do so would be a most foolhardy decision."

Dr. Milton broke in asking, "What do you mean by special, Ms. Churchill? You're not talking about nuclear weapons, are you? Didn't anyone read the commission's evaluation of that scenario? Not only is it a bad policy move, it puts the mission and the men involved directly at risk."

"Yes, Dr. Milton, we all read your commission's report," answered General Kaminski. "And, no, there are no nuclear weapons on board the shuttle. But I will not send American soldiers into potential harm's way without at least the minimum of defensive weaponry. Our men will not go up there unarmed."

"Besides, Dr. Milton, the decision to arm the mission is a strategic one. One on which I have the final say," added President Bender. "In this case the inclusion of small arms is not an unreasonable precaution to take. Remember, everyone, once these men descend to the moon's surface, they have no way back to orbit, or back to earth, on their own. They will have to convince those on the moon to return them safely home." President Bender looked around the table, catching the eyes of each participant before moving on. "Let's face it, if anything goes wrong, any little thing, they will not be coming home. If they cannot secure a ride from the separatists, they will run out of air, water and food. They will die as sure as I'm sitting here. That is the circumstance those brave men face. Now is it too much to ask that they have the bare minimum of protection or persuasion to shade the odds as much in their favor as possible?"

Dr. Milton was silent. General Kaminski was also silent, but everyone could see the smug satisfaction on his face. The rest of the group remained quiet, no one having anything else to add to a seemingly foregone conclusion.

President Bender directed his attention to Dr. Harris. "Dr. Harris. Would you brief the rest of us on your estimates on what our men will be looking at when they land?"

"Sure, Mr. President. If everyone will look at this chart over here, or if it's too far away, a copy is included on page three of the materials in front of you. As you can see right here, beginning at the impact crater here in the upper left hand corner as a starting point, the tracks lead down and to the right away from the impact site. From the scale along the bottom, it appears that the tracks extend four kilometers along this ridge here before they disappear under this rock formation. From our scan of the moon, using the gravity detector, we've located an area roughly one kilometer in diameter where the local gravity is earth-normal.

"Now, turn to the chart on the next page of your booklets, or look at this blowup of the area. The region where we measured the increased gravitational field corresponds with this area less than a kilometer from where the tracks disappear. Looking closely, within the circle the detector found, there are no visible features on the surface to indicate any artificial structures where the gravity field exists." Looking around the table, Martin continued, "Are there any questions before I go on?"

"Dr. Harris, do you have any idea how deep the field projects downward? In other words, how big do you think the habitat really is?" General Kaminski asked.

"Our measurements are not exact, General, we haven't been able to calibrate the detector to determine volume yet, but it looks like it does not extend any deeper than a hundred meters or so below the surface." Dr. Harris pulled up a third graphic showing a cutaway view of what the habitat might look like. "As best as we can tell, the area affected by the difference in gravity looks from the side like a stack of quarters, or a three-layer cake. That volume of space could hold quite a few people, I'm not exactly sure how many we're estimating are up there . . ."

"About eighteen hundred original inhabitants, and whatever offspring they may have had over the past four decades," answered the director of the FBI.

"The area covered is more than enough to hold nearly three times that number without any serious crowding. If we assume a certain amount of cubic footage devoted to life support, food and air treatment using plants and algae, some of Dr. Milton's people estimate there may be as many as twenty-five hundred inhabitants."

"Thank you, Dr. Harris, and my compliments to your team, Dr. Milton," said President Bender. "Dr. Milton, what's the word from NASA and the Russians on how close we can drop our men? I wouldn't want them to have to deploy too far from the objective."

"Mr. President, the word I received yesterday was that they are confident they can easily drop the men within five kilometers or less of this area here," Dr. Milton said, getting up and moving to the blowup of the ridge where the tracks disappeared. "They hope to drop the capsules north of this trench here to avoid having the men climb over any significant ridges. And, if you all direct your attention over here, this whole plain is fairly flat, with nothing over thirty meters in height. That's where the shuttle crew will be aiming when they release the capsules."

"Thank you, Dr. Milton. Are there any other questions?" Bender asked the group.

"I have one for Dr. Harris," the general said. "How closely are your people keeping an eye on that site?"

"General, we have twenty-four/seven coverage with the detector. The Navy has provided technicians to man the detector, and we have also developed programs that constantly scan the areas around the moon and the earth for any gravitational anomalies. If you're asking if we're going to be watching out for any sign of space–or aircraft using gravity manipulation during the course of the mission, you needn't worry. We are tapped into NORAD and the Pentagon networks. We'll give a shout at the first sign of trouble."

"Thank you, doctor. Is Commander Ames still in charge of the facility?" Kaminski asked.

"Yes sir, he is. Shelter Fourteen is still under military command, and all of my people and the commission are cooperating fully with your people, sir." Dr. Harris' hands began to sweat, not sure what the chairman was getting at. "Is there a problem, General?"

"None that I know of, why do you ask? Is there something going on we should all know about?"

Dr. Milton touched Dr. Harris on the arm. "General, is there some worry you have with either the staffing or the operations at the facility?"

Glancing over at President Bender before replying, General Kaminski said, "I have some concerns about so many civilians and possible sympathizers stationed at such an important strategic facility. This device of Dr. Harris' is the only early warning system we have that's able to alert us to any of the antigravity craft that might be operating in the area, or may be launched in some sort of attack against the US.

"Mr. President, I would like to request that all the civilians not directly working on Dr. Harris' project and any African American personnel stationed there be removed from the facility for the duration of this mission and until such time as this situation resolves itself, one way or the other," Kaminski asked.

Glancing at a shocked Dr. Milton and Diane Churchill, President Bender answered, "Denied. The facility is already under military supervision, the people stationed there have all been cleared by the FBI. There's no reason for any additional restrictions down there. Anyone who might possibly have a bone to pick with the decisions made in this administration has little they can do to disrupt the operation of Dr. Harris' systems."

"Mr. President, the possibility exists that there may be sympathizers down there. Maybe not overtly so, but when push comes to shove they may develop misguided loyalties toward the inhabitants on the moon once our men land. The situation is unprecedented, sir. Never have we had to confront a potential enemy who is comprised of a single subgroup of Americans."

"Mr. Chairman. Are you implying that any of the African Americans stationed at the shelter may in fact attempt to sabotage the efforts of the technicians stationed there?" asked Bender, hearing a mixture of gasps and snorts of derision from around the table.

"So what do you suggest? Should we pull everyone out who isn't white? What about Hispanics? Where do we place them on the racial scale?"

Stabbing his finger to the table, the general answered, "Can we afford to take any chances in protecting the lives of our men up there? What about the shuttle? It's going to be operating completely outside of its designed specifications. If anything happens up there our people are going to be five days away from the earth. There is no hope of rescue if our men are ambushed and the shuttle is damaged. The only means of keeping tabs on those on the moon is Dr. Harris' machine. I want it secured from any tampering," Kaminski insisted.

"I will take your request under advisement, Mr. Chairman. Is there anything else? Yes, Diane?" said the president.

"What is our contingency if they respond positively to our overtures?"

"In that case, Colonel Evers is our ambassador. He is going to be lead on communicating with the separatists. The shuttle will deploy two smaller relay satellites when the get into orbit to insure unbroken communications with the mission commander. We will also be able to see exactly what our men on the ground see just seconds after they see it. Each of the SEALs has a camera mounted on his helmet that will pick up whatever is in front of him for relay back to earth."

The director of the FBI got the attention of the president. "Sir, is this feed from the men on the ground going to be available to the public at large? I'm not sure that would be a good idea."

"Remembering what happened when other countries intercepted the data dump from the recon satellite," reminded Kaminski, "this time the feed is going to be encrypted and available on the defense networks only, unless countermanded by the commander in chief."

President Bender got everyone's attention once again. "Ladies and gentlemen, I don't think it's the height of hubris to state that this mission is going to be remembered for a good, long time after we're all gone. I want everyone here to make damn sure we are looking at every contingency, that we make every effort to ensure that what we do in the next few days does not lead to unnecessary conflict with these people, or the destruction of the American way of life.

"Once the shuttle Endeavour reaches orbit around the moon, I want the military defense condition to reflect the serious nature of the course we're undertaking. I also want our shadow government installations fully manned and ready to take over should any catastrophe befall Washington. If any of you so choose, you may be excused from your duties here in town to await the results of the mission in one of the protected locations outside of DC." President Bender paused to take a sip of water. "I will be moving my family out of town for the duration. I'm not going to tell any of you what to do, but I will understand whatever course of action you decide to take. Is there anything else before we adjourn?"

"Mr. President?" said CIA.

"Yes?"

"I would like a minute of your time after the meeting, sir," the director requested.

"Very well. Anyone else? Fine . . . thank you, everyone. We will reconvene tomorrow morning," the president finished.

As everyone filed out, a White House steward placed a fresh cup of coffee in front of the president as the director of the CIA came around the table and sat down in the chair next him.

"Mr. President, I have it on good authority that our man Kahill did not die during the mission in Iraq and he's being held incommunicado somewhere in Baghdad."

"Is this from the State Department? I heard something about this a little while ago. Do you have anything concrete?" President Bender asked.

"Not yet, sir. We're still trying to get some assets into the area to try to ferret out where they may be holding him. The person in the Iraqi delegation who passed the information along has not given us any additional details, probably because he doesn't know much more than one of our boys is being held. MI-6 is on it, sir. They're working their people as hard as they can to try to dig up any additional information."

"When you get anything we can use, I want to know about it immediately. I don't like that we might have left a man behind," stressed the President.

"Yes, sir. We'll stay on top of this. If he's still alive we will get him back."

"Good. Keep me posted." The director shook Bender's hand before he left the room. Waving away the steward, Bender leaned back in his chair, already exhausted, and the day wasn't half over yet.

CHAPTER 38

THE UNITED NATIONS met in emergency session. The subject under debate was the UN's disposition of the inhabitants on the moon and the US's alleged response to the discovery of the lunar inhabitants. Several nations called for immediately recognizing those on the moon as an independent nation should they so petition. Most called for the censure of the United States for their aggressive actions in launching an armed mission without cause. The resulting publicity around the world painted the US as a warmongering, imperialist bully.

In Atlanta, Detective Mathews was once again in the FBI's offices closeted with Agents Samuels and Minor, being brought up to date on where the bureau stood on their investigation.

"John, I have to ask you to do something, something like what came between us before. I want you to try to get something specific out of Dean Atkins. I have obscured her identity in Washington; however, the push is really on to try to locate anyone who may be in contact with the separatists. Their thinking is that in order to find and recruit candidates here, they have to have eyes and ears on the ground. It's not going to take too long before they sweat me for information on Atkins."

"I understand the need, but I have to warn you, I may have blown it Saturday night," John replied.

440

"How so? You didn't disclose any details about the investigation to her, did you?" Samuels asked in alarm.

"No, no, it wasn't anything like that. We had an argument about the whole separatist situation and how I felt about the mission to the moon. She jumped down my throat because I wasn't dead set against the aggressive posture the mission represented, and that I wasn't doing anything about it."

"What did she expect you to do?" Minor asked.

John threw up his hands in frustration. "I guess be more vocal about it. Hell, I don't know. She was just angry about the whole situation and I think I happened to be the closest target."

"John, let me ask you this," said Samuels, "Did she sound like she was closely identifying with the separatists? Like she felt personally on the defensive concerning our attempt to contact them?"

"You mean does she sound like she's one of them?" asked John.

"That's the question. What do *you* think?" prompted Samuels.

He went over the conversation in his mind, trying the recall the exact phrasing of her arguments and where she seemed to be most engaged, or angry. John replied, "Not directly. She was plenty pissed that it looks like the military is planning to shoot first and ask questions later. She never said anything like 'we' or 'they,' but she was impassioned in her condemnation of sending guns or nuclear bombs on the mission."

"I know that this is pretty unlikely but, did you see any sign that she might be getting ready to go on a trip? Could she be getting ready to run?" asked Samuels.

"Not that I saw. But given the care they took to conceal the departure of all the others, I doubt even I would get any clue or advance warning. That is, of course, assuming she's one of them, or at least in contact with them. Have you turned up anything new on her?" John asked Minor.

"Not really," Minor answered. "There was a funny message sent to one of her e-mail accounts, but it didn't make any sense to me. Bob thinks that if it's some kind of code, it's the kind we'd never be able to break." Minor turned to his computer and brought up the text of the message. "The message reads: peek-a-boo, red rover, red rover, shoo fly, don't follow me. And I wasn't able to locate the sender. As evidence it's so thin I couldn't even bring it to a grand jury."

John couldn't glean any content from the cryptic words. "Are you sure the message wasn't a mistake or some kind of spam?" John asked the computer expert.

"No, I'm not. As it stands now I can't tell *what* it is. The fact that it appeared out of nowhere with no sender information makes it suspicious, but that's about it."

"So we're still at square one then?" John asked.

"That's it. The only thing we have are the two phone calls made to her house by the Williams girl. Her travel itinerary over the last five years is just barely above what would be called statistically significant. We've got nothing, John," said Samuels.

"Even so, where's the bureau going to go once contact is made? Isn't her significance greatly diminished once that happens? What could she conceivably be charged with?" John asked.

"Obstruction of justice? Maybe concealing evidence in an investigation? After all, she did lie to you concerning her contact with the missing student." said Samuels.

"That's true. But there was no crime committed. You'd have a hard time making it stick," argued John.

"True, but it's enough to pull her in for questioning."

"Maybe, but what do you really think you'd get out of her? Believe me, she'd chew all of us up and spit us out. If she's involved, that would surely let the cat out of the bag about the fact that we have even this little bit of info on them and their operation."

John shook his head. "I'm thinking the only way we're going to get anything out of her is to wait until she's damn good and ready to spill whatever she knows. Of course that presupposes she knows anything at all."

"So what do you suggest? The ball's pretty much in your court, John. I don't want to haul her in, and I can't very well drop in, introduce myself and ask her a bunch of questions without tipping her to the fact that the FBI has taken more than a casual interest in her."

"My advice is to give it a day or so for things between us to cool down. If you can handle the wait, I will try to get her to open up on the issue. I'll come at her from the perspective of the missing girl. I may have to spill the fact we have the telephone records. If I do, I'm going to ask her point-blank to explain the calls."

"Sure, John, it's up to you to decide how to play this. I hate like hell that you're the one who has to do it, but I don't see any other way to go about it other than to bring her in officially. That alone will probably get this part of the investigation taken out of my hands," said Samuels. "Is there any way we can help *you* out, John? Do you want any kind of blanket over you?"

"No. That's not necessary. I have no reason to believe that I'm under scrutiny. There's definitely no reason to think I'm in any kind of danger. Is she still under surveillance?" John asked.

"As a matter of fact she is. John, we already knew about the argument the other night," Samuels said, a flush coming to his face. Minor chose that instant to find something of great interest on his computer screen.

"Son of a bitch! I completely forgot about that." John felt the heat of a blush rising to his face as well. Smiling ruefully he said, "I guess if there's something I want to keep private we'll have to go into the garage and talk underneath the car while it's running."

"My suggestion is to convince her you want to relive your youth and tell her you want to knock boots in the back seat of the car. You're safe from eavesdropping out there," Samuels promised.

"Let me ask you two a question. Will my relationship with Sydney jeopardize the investigation? Should we become . . . *intimate*, does that screw things up for you, and, more importantly, for me?" asked John.

"It does tend to muddy the waters, John. I won't lie to you about that. But you're a big boy, and you're a cop. You know where the lines have to be drawn. What you do with your pecker is your business, try not to let it get you in trouble." Samuels paused and then raised a cautionary finger. "On a personal note. If the two of you can find some kind of common ground on which to build a relationship, more power to you. I don't want to think that my investigation denied you the chance to find the one for you. Now get the hell out of my office before young Jeffrey here starts to cry," Samuels said, smacking Minor playfully across the back of the head.

The shuttle's command crew was still going over the mission profile, the bulk of the additional procedures centering around monitoring the SEALs in the cargo bay through the extensive medical sensors and monitors newly installed for the mission. Because of the mission's unique requirements, the command crew was carrying an Air Force physician familiar with both NASA's and the Air Force's astronaut training programs. He was responsible for monitoring the SEALs during their drug-induced slumber on the way to the moon, and it was his responsibility to remotely administer the drugs necessary to bring them to full wakefulness once they achieved orbit around the moon.

Commander Evers had worked with each member of his crew on previous missions, most tasked with the deployment of supersecret spy satellites for the nation's military and intelligence services.

For their part, the SEALs had to suffer through the indignity of cleaning out their colons before their final suiting up for the launch. Their mood was one of quiet determination. They clearly understood the dangers of the mission and put any thought of personal peril behind them to focus on the unique trial ahead.

The shuttle was situated at the launch pad. The main fuel tank was topped off. The SEALs were safely cocooned in the two escape capsules and the command crew was performing the final preflight checklist. A small pool of reporters was allowed into the press reviewing area, protected from the wind and rain. Even though there was an overcast sky with intermittent showers, the countdown proceeded. The launch wouldn't be aborted unless the winds picked up considerably, or the light rain became a downpour.

The fact that there was no real provision for the SEALs to return via the shuttle was never discussed outside of the heavily classified mission planning team. Most of the NASA support teams guessed the truth; however, none of them went to the press. None of them even considered exposing this aspect of the mission. They were proud of the fact that NASA had an unblemished safety record in space itself. Sending eight men on what any right-thinking man would call a suicide mission wasn't what NASA was all about. The chance of having an American die on the moon was far more disturbing than even the idea of bringing weapons into space. This aspect of the mission had laid a dark mood over the vast complex, only exacerbated by the gloomy weather lingering over Florida's coast. Fortunately, though wet, the weather remained relatively calm as the countdown continued to wind down.

By the time the president's press conference began, more people around the world were tuned to the news channels than for any other presidential press conference in history. The world's activities had all but come to a halt. Those who lived in countries where it was the dead of night were awake and watching. The media were disappointed to see the president giving his address from the Oval Office, knowing that there would be no opportunity for any questions from the press. The representatives of the national and international press were further discomfited when the White House did not release the text of the president's address beforehand, giving them nothing to debate or armchair quarterback prior to the broadcast.

"My fellow Americans, and all the citizens of the world watching and listening to the words I speak on this historic day, good evening and thank you for letting me into your homes.

"I come to you tonight to discuss the historic space mission we are about to undertake. In just under two hours the space shuttle Endeavour will be launching itself into history. The mission Endeavour undertakes tonight is simply to facilitate opening a dialog with people who live on a planetary body other than our own mother earth. And, although these people are thought to be friends and families who began their lives right here in this country, they have managed to build a home on earth's nearest neighbor, living there in secret for decades.

"We travel to their adopted home for many reasons. The foremost to begin a dialog, to open discussion between us and hopefully reacquaint ourselves with those who have lived apart from us for so long. We want to do this to understand the reasons behind their isolation from the world that spawned them, to try to understand their reasons for concealing their existence from us for so long. And finally, to extend the offer of friendship to allow those who have been left behind to rediscover their long lost friends and families. It is my sincere hope that families can be brought back together, and these brave and special Americans will rejoin America in its growth, in its scientific and technological achievements and in any cultural evolution in a spirit of peace and cooperation.

"The people we travel to meet have achieved much that all Americans can be proud of, achievements that speak to the limitless imagination and innovation of the human spirit. These accomplishments suggest a great wealth that, if shared with all of mankind, could conceivably lift more people out of poverty than any other period in the history of mankind. I also hope that those we go to meet today will be willing to help uplift all the peoples of the world, perhaps even bringing people everywhere into a new Renaissance.

"I would like to stress that this mission is one of peace and exploration and that none of the rumors of this mission being armed with nuclear weapons are true. America's exploration of space has always been peaceful. I believe that the kind of life we have here on earth, with its many current and historical conflicts, has no place in space. It is my hope that war between men will never spill off of this planet, contaminating other worlds with the worst that man has to offer, and that earthly man will eventually see the futility of war and mature past such destruction and terror.

"We will be watching very closely as events unfold on earth's nearest neighbor. My advice to everyone is to stay tuned and watch the launch, and to pray for the safe return of our brave astronauts. My message to the crew of the shuttle Endeavour is simply this: Go with God.

"May God bless America. Thank you, and good night."

President Bender waited a full thirty seconds after the "On Air" light went out above the television camera before he let out the breath he felt like he had been holding through the entire speech. Chief of Staff Masters came over from his post just off camera and handed President Bender a glass of fizzy liquid to drink.

"What's this?" he asked.

"Just a little something to settle your stomach. I though you might need it," Simon answered quietly.

"Thank you," Bender said, downing it in one long gulp.

"What's next?"

"Absolutely nothing. If you so desire, a few of us were going to watch the launch together in the Green Room. A big-screen television and a buffet have been set up for the evening. I think about twenty of the staff, along with a few spouses and significant others, are going to be there. It would be nice if you and the first lady could join us sir."

He took a deep breath and slowly let it out through his teeth, then said, "Perhaps, Simon. Let me talk to Sarah when I get upstairs."

"Very well, Mr. President. I hope to see you later on." Simon gathered up his papers and made his way out of the office.

Stopping only to grab the reading glasses he'd left on the desk, Bender headed back to the residence to shower and remove everything the White House makeup specialist had applied to his face and sprayed in his hair for the benefit of the television cameras. He took the elevator thinking that all he had to do was hold on for one more week. After that he wouldn't be called on to plot the world's course all on his own. He'd have the luxury of only having to follow, or counter, someone else's lead.

Standing there alone, the ship is waiting
All system are go, are you sure?
Control is not convinced,
But the computer, has the evidence.
No need to abort, the countdown starts.

Major Tom (Coming Home)
Written and performed by Peter Schilling

CHAPTER 39

"THIRTY SECONDS TO liftoff, winds are calm at eight knots. Downline tracking stations are online, all ground stations report ready. Twenty-five seconds to liftoff, all systems are go."

Martin and his team, along with every member of the commission and more than a handful of the military personnel, began to quiet as the clock ticked down. The atmosphere wasn't very partylike. Everyone seemed wrapped up in their own thoughts about what the mission meant to the country and the world, and yet no one really wanted to watch the liftoff alone.

Paul Milton, knowing exactly just how far the capabilities of the shuttle were being stretched to make this mission a reality, marked off in his mind the thousands of things that would have to go right in order to get the crew safely to the moon and back. His good wishes were with the crew of the shuttle, and even with the SEALs closeted away in the cargo hold of the orbiter.

Paul honestly didn't think anyone on earth would ever see those men alive again. In fact, a safe landing using untried Russian hardware for the first time was so unlikely he despaired of any part of the mission being successful at all. Paul feared that the death of so many Americans on such a foolhardy mission would immediately polarize Americans against space exploration. He truly felt that they were witnessing the beginning of the end of man's journey away from the planet, the end of that sense of curiosity and wonder that had fueled man's search for new worlds to conquer over the last fifty years.

"Twenty seconds to liftoff," the voice of mission control announced.

John, watching the live coverage of the launch, was home alone, his thoughts ping-ponging between his relationship with Sydney and the needs of the investigation. He had initially thought to go down to Pete's and watch the launch there, but knowing Pete as well as he did he knew even this historic mission wasn't going to get him to turn off his beloved music in favor of something as pedestrian as news on radio or television.

He wondered if those living on the moon were somehow able to watch the coverage of the launch from their vantage point. Then a vagrant thought floated through his head. If the message Sydney had received in her e-mail had been from those on the moon, how were they able to send it? And, if they could send messages via the Internet, could they tap into or receive radio and television programs up there as well? Even though the thought was barely more than a vague notion, he made a mental note to ask Jeff if any of these capabilities were easily available to people living a quarter of a million miles away on a planetary body that kept them turned away from earth at all times.

"Fifteen seconds to liftoff, all systems are go."

The president and first lady did make it down to the Green Room to mingle with the staff and other family members who managed to show up after all. There were far fewer people than would have shown up normally, probably due to the shadow government facilities being activated and fully manned in the preceding days. The impromptu gathering was subdued and somewhat less than festive. Still, everyone welcomed the chance to unwind after so many days of frantic work and the stress of trying to hold together a country in crisis.

"Ten seconds to liftoff . . ."

Agents Samuels and Minor were still at FBI headquarters, gathered in the common cafeteria with about forty other FBI personnel watching the launch coverage. The two agents had been busy writing a complete summary of every facet of their investigatory efforts with an eye toward closing the case, both hoping that arresting or detaining Dean Atkins would not become necessary. Samuels hoped the Bureau would be busy somewhere else in light of the probable dialog that would, one way or another, be opened up between the lunar inhabitants and earth.

Samuels had put a rotating detail on the dean, keeping an eye on her just in case she had a notion to bolt. It was a long shot, but if she ran, and she was going to rendezvous with one of the separatist's ships, they might have a shot at capturing the ship and its occupants before they they it got away.

"Nine . . ."

Sydney was at home, sitting cross-legged on her bed, her back against the headboard, the rain softly drumming on the roof above her. She was reading a book she was barely interested in.

She had picked it up in an effort to try not to think about her feelings toward John. She was trying, and failing, to convince herself that she had made the biggest mistake in her life when she allowed herself to fall in love with this man.

She was doggedly determined to read the book, pushing John from her thoughts as best she could. She was failing miserably. If there was one thing Sydney was no good at, it was lying to herself. When she took notice of the fact that she had begun, and read, the same page half a dozen times without remembering a single word or idea it contained, she realized what she had to do. Seeing the time, she got up off the bed and began to get dressed.

"Eight . . ."

General Kaminski was in his office along with his personal aide, watching the news feed of the nighttime launch. He still smoldered over the fact that he was denied the ability to deal with the lunar inhabitants from a position of superior strength and firepower. He had tried every means at his disposal to get some kind of orbital launch platform to the moon, even if it took additional rocket launches to get the weapons into orbit, but to no avail. He was relegated to sitting back, hoping the SEALs would be able to reach their objective and bring at least one of the separatists' spacecraft back home. Once back on earth the captured craft was to be torn apart, uncovering every secret of its construction and capabilities, come hell or high water.

In his mind, no bunch of *space niggers* were going to best the most powerful nation in the history of the world, nor were they going to be allowed to keep their technologies and medical advances a secret from the government of the United States of America. Not on his watch.

"Seven . . ."

Halfway around the globe, just before dawn, the former Iraqi fighter pilot known simply as Basra was in the office of the local military garrison in his adopted hometown. He, along with the sector commander and senior staff, were watching the British CNN coverage of the launch beamed down by satellite overhead. They were laughing and joking, placing mock bets on how long the shuttle would fly before exploding, sending the spacecraft, the crew and any cargo it carried crashing into the ocean. Although smiling to avoid notice or comment from the others, Basra kept his thoughts to himself. It hadn't taken any great leap in intelligence for him to believe the remarkable aircraft shot down months ago was somehow connected to this unprecedented American mission to the moon after thirty years of neglect.

He was also befriending as many of the officers as he could, hoping to overhear any discussion of an American spy being held somewhere in Baghdad. He was certain had the American operative been killed; the Great One would have publicly displayed the corpse as proof of the Americans' determination to destroy their country over nothing more than the oil on which it sat. No, the silence was telling. Something was being kept hidden. The only guess he had was that the American had been taken alive and was being tortured for whatever information the Great One could get from him, and maybe just for fun.

"Six . . ."

Colonel Evers was at the final go/no go point in the launch sequence. Once the solid rocket boosters were ignited, there would be no turning back. Should the flight have to be aborted before orbital insertion they would have to ride out the initial climb into the sky until the boosters and the main tank could be safely jettisoned, and guide the shuttle back to one of three emergency landing sites. Looking over the crowded forward and overhead instrument panels and seeing all greens, he committed the shuttle Endeavour to launch.

The SEALs stowed in the cargo bay inside the Russian capsules were barely aware of their surroundings, several gratefully so, as they had hung face down for the previous ninety minutes after being strapped in. Once they had been secured by the ground team, Air Force Dr. Sepin triggered the slow infusion of the sedative into their bloodstreams, watching the biomonitors carefully as the eight men slowed their respirations and slipped into unconsciousness. He too prayed for a successful launch, knowing that an aborted liftoff gave the men in the hold less than a fifty-fifty chance for survival. Pretty good odds given the danger, but unacceptable for a NASA that had lost astronauts only once during launch.

The command crew felt the vibration through their seats as hundreds of thousands of gallons of water were dumped below to prevent fire and heat damage to the launch platform. Each began making accommodation to whatever faith or superstition they harbored in the seconds before ignition.

"Five . . . four . . . three . . . two . . . one . . . ignition . . . liftoff . . . liftoff of the shuttle Endeavour on this historic mission to the moon."

Residents of southeastern Florida were treated to the sight of the dazzling flame of millions of pounds of thrust propelling the shuttle through the sound barrier and out of the envelope of air that sustained all life on earth.

The launch went off flawlessly. The trip into orbit was unremarkable for all its importance to mankind. The only tense moment came when the time came to normally jettison the main fuel tank, and no such jolt was felt throughout the crew deck. As the shuttle climbed into orbit, Colonel Evers carefully checked the status of the tank, quickly looking over temperature, pressure and electrical connections between the main tank and the shuttle. Everything was in the green.

Mission control was sending real-time positional data from ground stations, showing the estimated time until rendezvous with the Russian refueling rocket, already in orbit. In less than thirty minutes the bright reflection from the Russian rocket came into view.

You make me feel like a sticky pistil
Leaning into her stamen
You make me feel like Mr. Sunshine, himself
You make me feel like splendor in the grass
Where we're rollin'
Damn skippy baby
You make me feel like the Amazon's runnin' between my thighs
Feelin' Love
Written and performed by Paula Cole

CHAPTER 40

JOHN WAS WATCHING the shuttle rendezvous with the Russian fuel tank in orbit when his doorbell rang. Turning off the television, he went to the door and looked through the peephole to see who it was. Surprised, he threw open the door, letting both a cool, wet breeze and Sydney into his home.

"What? How . . . uh, hello," said John, completely nonplussed.

"Shhhh," she said, placing her fingertips over his lips. "I didn't want what happened last night to lie between us for another minute longer. I never should have treated you so unfairly." She paused to observe John's reaction.

"Where . . . I mean, how did you know where I live . . ." he began, but quieted immediately when he had a chance to take in how she looked standing there in his living room. Somehow she appeared smaller, more gentle and soft. He saw her hair was wet, tiny beads of water spread over her head like a diamond-laced veil. She wore a light pink wool sweater, also festooned with a covering of water droplets, pinpoints of light that sparkled in the glow of the single lamp. She wore leather sandals and a worn pair of form-fitting jeans. John felt as if he had had the wind knocked out of him: at that instant she was the most beautiful woman he had ever seen.

"That's not important John, *this* is," Sydney said, stepping in to embrace him.

She dropped her purse on the floor, reached up with one hand and drew his face down to her own. Their lips met, and John swore he felt a spark of electricity flow between. Her lips were soft and hot, and met his firmly as she held his head close to her own. Sydney moaned deep in her throat, her lips eagerly parted. Her breath warm in his mouth, her tongue slid against his lips, seeking his own, rubbing it in delicious sensation.

John pulled her body to him. He could feel that she wore nothing under her sweater as he ran his hands firmly along the sides of her body. One of his hands settled along the top of her firm behind. Submerged in sensation, Sydney's free hand went to John's own back and pulled his pelvis closer to her own, grinding herself against him, feeling him harden under the insistent friction.

The two continued their oral ministrations, their hands in constant motion pulling each other into as close a clinch as possible, when Sydney pulled back and said, "These clothes are beginning to piss me off. Are you going to take them off of me, or do I have to really get upset with you?" Having come to his home turf, Sydney was content to now let John lead, secure in the knowledge they both wanted the same thing.

John picked her up and carried her into the bedroom, setting her gently down on his bed. When she tried to sit up to take her shoes off, John firmly pushed her back down without a word.

Going to the foot of the bed, he took her closest foot in hand, unbuckled the sandal and took it off her foot, dropping it to the floor. Then reaching for the other foot, he repeated the action. Turning back to face her he then unbuttoned her jeans and slid the zipper down, the noise loud in the quiet of the room. He wiggled the jeans over Sydney's hips and tossed them into the nearby chair.

John took both her hands and helped her sit up. He then grasped the bottom of her sweater and pulled it up over her head. Sydney held her arms up over her head until he had peeled it off of her completely.

John's breath caught in his throat as he saw her naked for the first time. Her dark skin was unblemished, smooth and warm to the touch. When she lay back down he could see her face and chest in the light from the window. Her breasts were well rounded, just slightly larger than his hand, the nipples and areolae much darker than the flesh surrounding them. His gaze traveled down the smooth expanse of her belly to her lace-trimmed white panties. His hand, acting independently, ran softly from between her breasts, down her abdomen, feeling a slight ripple of response to his touch, and slid under the elastic band. Sydney arched her back in response to John's touch, her most sensitive flesh reaching for his fingers. John pulled his fingers out from under the elastic to Sydney's groan of frustration, got up, turned and grabbed both sides of the concealing garment. Sydney completely lifted her bottom off the bed, allowing him to slide her underwear over the swell of her thighs, past her knees and over her feet to join her sandals on the floor.

When he looked up to completely take her in, Sydney raised her far knee in a classic pose and held her arms out to John. When he returned to the head of the bed, she reached up to hug him close, then she pushed him back as she swung her feet to the floor. Standing close in front of him, she gave him a quick kiss on the lips.

"It's my turn now," she breathed toward his ear. She released each button until she reached the bottom of his shirt, pulled the tails from his pants and slid it off his shoulders. Kneeling down and untying his shoes, she pulled up on each foot, signaling John to raise each to allow her to remove his shoes. John reached out and steadied himself on her shoulder as she removed his socks and tossed them away. Slowly rising to her feet, Sydney ran both her hands up the material along the insides of John's legs, jolting him with pleasure when her hands met at the hard protrusion pushing against the confinement of his pants.

Laughing softly in sensual delight, she unbuckled John's belt and opened his pants. She let them drop to the floor, then tossed them aside. Looking up, smiling at John's face, she grabbed his shorts on both sides, pulling them down to the floor, his hardness now at eye level. Reaching out, Sydney enclosed him in her grasp, sending a jolt of pleasure through John, his leg muscles trembling. With her other hand she softly caressed the insides of his thighs, feeling the hairs, the warmth of his skin and the muscles beneath.

John couldn't help the moan that came from deep in his chest as he felt her grip him, and caress his skin. He gasped as he felt her lips kiss him, the sensual swirl of her tongue around his tip before she stood up. Overcome by feelings held in check for so long, John picked her up again and laid her down on the bed. As she moved over to give him room, he discovered anew the simple beauty of the woman before him. He took her in his arms, felt her smooth skin against his, the heat of her body warming him, the pulse of desire running between them.

Her hands reached up along the sides of his head, one moving to caress him along the side of his neck, the other pulling him to her. Her touch was pure pleasure, sending direct electrical stimulation to his brain. And when their mouths met once again, John's tongue rubbed her lips, the tip drawing a furrow down the center of her own. His hand traveling down the front of her body, his fingers combing through the tightly woven hair below her belly. His fingers were then sliding through the flesh of her hot, wet core, stroking, pleasure rapidly building urgent heat between her legs.

Her hand reached down and found him again, the rhythm of her stroking mirroring the stroke of his own fingers, her lips and tongue kissing his earlobe, drawing a hot, wet line down the side of his neck and then returning again to his mouth. Breaking the connection of their mouths, John's lips traveled down her neck across her chest to settle over a stiff nipple. His tongue momentarily painted broad strokes across her sensitive skin and then his lips encircled the hard rubbery protrusion of flesh. As his tongue scrubbed softly around the surface of her nipple, Sydney's whole body responded, pushing her pelvis even harder against his hand below with a sharp, "Yes," that trailed off in a hiss. John moved to the other nipple, increasing the urgency of her need for him.

When his head began to move lower she stopped him, saying, "No, I need you inside me. Please, John, now."

Raising himself up and over her, her legs already spread to accommodate him, he felt her hand guide him to her entrance. He was momentarily jolted by how hot her lips were as they spread to engulf him. As he slowly slid his length into her hot, velvety grip, they both groaned, their joining culminating the dance they'd begun so many weeks ago. Their pleasure merged, their movements synchronized, neither able to discern where they each left off and the other began.

John built a pressing rhythm, Sydney grinding from side to side below him, the friction of their joining pushing the intensity of their need even higher. Sydney pulled his head down to hers, thrusting her tongue into his mouth mirroring John's thrusts below, their breath and soft pleasured cries mingling together.

There was no intellect in their coupling, both surrendering to the animal need that had been building since they had first met. Sydney was meeting his every thrust, rubbing her hard little knot of nerves along the top of his equally hard shaft. Neither of them were going to be able to sustain this level of passion for long. John's movements were becoming faster, being urged on by Sydney's ragged breathing and soft moans every time he pushed fully inside her. John began to thrust faster, their bodies covered with a slippery sheen of perspiration, building, urging, and then he felt Sydney tighten around him as her voice rose in pitch until it was nearly inaudible. Her whole body tensed, arching up to pull him as deeply into her as possible. As John felt the ripple of her sheath of flesh squeeze him, preventing him from withdrawing, he too began to spasm, feeling as though his very life's essence was leaving him, shooting into the core of her being.

Waves of sensation, ripples of pleasure washed over the two, as John's arms, trembling from exertion, finally collapsed. Sydney wrapped her arms and legs around his body, as if trying to fuse them together, wanting to be as close as possible to him and loving the weight of him on top of her. He was pressing her into the bed, feeling the softening passage of her breath passing his ear as they began to slowly calm, both relaxing into postcoital bliss.

After several minutes had passed, when their breathing steadied, Sydney sighed and tweaked his butt.

"Easy, you could bruise a guy like that," John said softly in her ear, rolling off of her, pulling her to his side next to him.

Looking at John, Sydney chuckled. "Me? I'm ruined for any other man for life. I'll never be the same down there," she said, squeezing him where they remained joined together.

"Easy girl, I might need that thing later," he cautioned. When she laughed, she accidently pushed out his rapidly softening bit of formerly proud flesh with a barely audible plop, which set them both to laughing together.

"I forgot to ask you about something," John began.

"Don't worry about it, I don't have anything that will make your hair fall out, or anything else either," Sydney said, reaching down to softly stroke his most sensitive part. "I was counting on you to be safe as well. As for any other consequences? Let's just say that I'm not in the least bit worried about that, good enough?"

Vaguely disturbed, but trusting her judgment, John let it go.

"May I say for the record that we waited entirely too long to do this," Sydney said, stretching her legs and then kissing John on the nose. "What I can't understand is why you don't have a bevy of women lined up at your door every night if that's the kind of performance you turn out every time," she said, teasing him.

"I wouldn't say I'm all that, but thank you for the compliment. Really, though, it's all in your partner." His eyes crinkled in delight. "If it won't upset you, my I ask you what brought on this unexpected delight, this embarrassment of riches to me on such a rainy night?"

Sydney pushed him on his back and lay her head in the crook of his neck, softly caressing his chest and twining his sparse hairs. "When I left the house I was only thinking about apologizing for my behavior last night. I behaved abominably and you didn't deserve what I said to you. I was angry and you were the closest target on which I could vent. So, before we go any further, I'm sorry for the way I treated you last night."

"Apology accepted, say no more about it. Do you want to talk about some of the things that set you off? I've been told I have great listening skills."

"Is that so?" Sydney asked.

"I'm sorry, I was thinking about something else. What did you say?" He said, getting her back for some of the things she'd said in the past. "Ow!" he exclaimed as she sharply tugged on the hairs on his chest.

"Be glad my hand didn't go south on you there," she admonished him with a chuckle. "Anyway, you pretty much know what set me off. The whole injustice of treating people who just want to be left alone like some sort of enemy combatants. Xenophobia rears its ugly head, and the worst part of it is that these people are, or at least were, Americans. They grew up here, and there's no reason for knocking at their door armed to the teeth."

"I agree," John began, as he sat up and reached down to the top of the small chest at the foot of the bed, pulling a light cotton quilt over their cooling bodies. "But we have a long history of meeting the unknown over the barrel of a gun. It's the American way, you know. And these people living on the moon definitely fit the description of the unknown."

"Perhaps. But for the sake of argument let's say these people were discovered at the South Pole. I still think any expedition that went to investigate them would be armed. I just don't understand it." Reaching down between John's legs, cupping his sack in her hand she added, "I think bringing a set of these along would be enough." She laughed in the quiet of the bedroom, the sound of it musically blending with the quiet drumming of the rain falling on the roof.

"Easy, careful with the goods. Besides, we men don't normally lead with those. Have you ever seen guys wade in the water? We're all gung-ho until the water gets about midthigh, then we tiptoe until we just can't keep them dry anymore. If we're not willing to subject them to cold water, I don't think you're going to see us go into the great unknown without some sort of protection," he said, trapping her hand between his legs.

Raising her head off his chest, Sydney turned and kissed him, swiping her tongue across both his lips, sending an electrical jolt right to his scrotum. "Jesus, woman, what are you trying to do to me?"

"Committing the perfect murder. Is it really a crime to kill a man with pleasure? Besides, who'd want to prosecute? Everyone would be too busy thinking 'that lucky bastard.' I'm positive none of your real friends would feel the least bit sorry for you."

"Maybe not, but I'd be worried they wouldn't be able to close the lid of the coffin if I die like that. Besides, two can play that game," he said as he turned toward her, rapidly flicked his tongue back and forth across the cord of her neck, the sensation making a beeline right to her still sensitive genitalia.

"Oh, damn." Sydney shuddered as her pelvic muscles convulsed in sympathetic vibration to the thrumming on her neck. Pushing John on his back, she climbed on top of him, kissing him open-mouthed, her tongue teasing his, drawing it into her own mouth where she began to suck on it, making John moan into her mouth in desire. He began to harden at once, his hands clutching the bottom of her cheeks, grinding her against him, rolling himself back and forth against her before pulling her up and repositioning himself between her legs.

Sydney began to slide against him, wetting him, nerves firing again as their most sensitive flesh renewed pleasure so recently experienced. Sitting up astride John's midsection, she reached down and grabbed him firmly, rubbing the head against her much smaller protrusion, her breath once again hissing at the exquisite sensation the friction generated. She then lifted up and sank back down, engulfing him wholly, driving him fully inside her again.

John let go a deep, rumbling "Ohhh," as her heat spread throughout his body. His toes curled as Sydney began a slow, undulating rhythm over him, never raising more than a half inch or so, stirring him inside her.

John reached up, cupping her breasts, thumbs drawing slow circles around her nipples, adding to the sensations Sydney received from the joining of their parts below. Her mouth was dry from her breath ripping its way in and out. Her mind was trying to somehow catch up with the flood of sensory impulses keeping every nerve in her body alive, every touch sending her into new shuddering sensation.

Sydney knew it wasn't going to be long before she would explode. She reached behind her and gently clutched the twin orbs drawing tighter to the base of John's shaft. Stroking the sensitive skin below, she began to rise and fall, nearly dislodging him from inside her, more and more rapidly. She could feel his scrotum begin to draw even tighter, then she felt John pulsing inside her, the expansion pushing her over the edge into her own jolting release.

John, clutching her breasts as he tried to bury every inch inside her, felt her walls grip him again so tightly he couldn't withdraw if he tried. Sydney froze, fell forward on to his chest with a sigh, her face burying itself in the pillow next to his ear, still squeezing him rhythmically, gasping for breath, one hand sliding under his head, drawing his face up against her own.

They stayed like that for a minute or so, their heartbeats slowing, their only movement other than breathing, her squeezing him and him flexing inside her in response. He began to stroke her back, transiting from cheek to shoulder, gently massaging as he listened to her breathing slow.

Sydney turned her face to him, gently kissing him on the corner of the mouth, her hand slowly running through his hair. She looked at him, memorizing every feature, every line in his face so much so she felt she could recognize him just by touch.

John calmly returned her gaze, his hand squeezing her flank, eliciting another squeeze between her legs.

"I have never felt this good, ever," he said, brushing his lips across her neck.

"You have a gift of understatement," she replied, carefully disengaging herself and sliding to his side. "Is this why everyone speaks so highly of make-up sex?" she said, reaching up to wipe away a bead of sweat off of John's forehead. "We could have been doing this every time we argued over music. What were you thinking?"

"Me? You know as well as I do that it's always up to the woman to decide these sorts of things. I told you, women choose, men acquiesce."

"So that's how you guys get to duck responsibility all the time." She tucked herself comfortably in the crook of his arm, their faces inches apart.

"I knew you enjoyed teasing me, I just wasn't sure how you really felt. I wasn't sure if our differences were too great for us to be able to find common ground to ever really be together. Don't get me wrong, I was happy to share however much you wanted to give. But deciding when and where, and most of all 'if,' well, that's always been your sex's province."

Sydney's heart completely went out to John. "What differences are you referring to? Don't we have many similar likes and dislikes? Do we not have compatible body parts?" she asked with a smile. "And don't we have genuine affection for one another?"

"Yes, but I wasn't talking about those. You're far better educated than I, and there is the matter of race. Those sorts of things don't make much difference to me, and I'm not going to insult you by feeding you the 'some of my best friends are black' routine. My only friends right now are black, and you've met half of them," said John. "I can honestly say that in their own different way I care greatly for both of them. That small, exclusive group now includes you as well."

Sydney sharply drew in a breath, startled at the admission.

"I've never felt this way about a woman. I've been in love before, I got this close to getting married once," he said, holding his fingers a half an inch apart, "but nothing in life prepared me for how I feel about you." John stopped, seeing Sydney's eyes become shiny with unshed tears. "What? Did I say the wrong thing again?" John's heart began to flutter, a sinking feeling beginning to grow in the pit of his stomach, thinking he may have undone any progress they had made this night.

"No, it's nothing like that," she said, stroking his face. "You've said nothing wrong, I love and cherish every word you've spoken. Can't a girl well up out of sheer happiness?"

"Of course you can, I just thought you might find me wanting because of my job, or my belief that shit happens and sometimes screaming about it doesn't help. For me, I have never met anyone so perfect in all my life," John said, almost in a whisper.

"I'm hardly perfect. If you only knew the myriad of faults I carry around with me, the bloom would definitely be off the rose," Sydney said laughing.

"You're perfect for me. Your personality is perfect, your face is perfect, even your eyes are perfect, everything about you is perfect for me, regardless of what you see in yourself."

Laughing again despite herself, she touched her finger to his lips, shushing him, and said,

"You see, that goes to prove that sometimes things aren't always what they seem. As a matter of fact, my eyes come compliments of my mailman every three months. They aren't really green at all, they're brown just like most everyone else's. It just makes me feel like I have a little secret that no one else knows when I have these contacts in. See, I'm not so perfect, am I, now that you know my little secret about my eyes."

"Just how many secrets do you have? And more importantly, are any of them liable to shock my frail sensibilities?" John asked.

"I suppose that depends on your perspective. I'm not some secret axe murderer, at least not yet, and I'm not a stalker either. I don't think I even have any unpaid parking tickets. All in all, I'm a pretty boring college administrator by day and a secret agent by night. How about you? Is there a red cape and tights in your closet over there I should know about?" she asked, poking him in the ribs.

"Not me," he said, "I'm just an ordinary flatfoot by day, and couch potato by night. Other than going to Pete's every now and then, I don't really get out much. When my partner Jason got married, my going out and carousing days slowly faded into the sunset. Your coming into my life is like the sun coming out after the rain, everything seems more alive, colors brighter, the air cleaner. I love how you make me feel, but don't get me wrong. It's not some kind of puppy-love addiction. It's more like getting glasses after years of your eyes slowly going bad and you never really noticing it happen. Then, when you put them on all of a sudden you realize just how blind you were without them."

Sydney hugged him fiercely, not wanting to look him in the eye. Sensing something of this, John asked, "What's wrong? Sometimes I feel like I'm never saying the right words. That's what was so frustrating last night. No matter what I said, you had reasons why what I was saying wasn't right. I felt like you had all the answers and I was failing a test I hadn't had a chance to study for.

"The sad truth is that I don't have all the answers, not to what's going to happen to us or what's going to happen with the people on the moon. If you know the answers, just tell me. I want to be on the same page as you forever, if it can happen. But just let me know what's up." John wasn't angry, just a little bit frustrated. "I'm sure *you* have a pretty good idea what's going to happen with us. Do you have any insight into where this country's going when the shuttle gets to the moon, or what the people on the moon really want, what they're going to do when we get there? If you do then I'd really like to know, if for no other reason than to not sound so stupid about everything. Even if you're not ready to talk about what's going to happen with us, can you tell me what's up with them?" John said jokingly.

Drawing back and looking John right in the eye, Sydney said simply, "Yes, John, I can. As a matter of fact I'm one of only two people on the face of the earth who *can* tell you exactly what's going to happen."

"When you say one of two, you mean you and me, right? What's going to happen with us?" John asked.

"No, I meant I am one of only two people on earth who can tell you what's going to happen on the moon, because I am one of two people who are in contact with the people living there."

When he absorbed what Sydney had just said, John was dumbstruck; his mind went into a state of shock. "Hey, John! Snap out of it." Sydney shook him, feeling his skin go cool and clammy. She hugged him close to her own body and began to try to rub some warmth and circulation back into his torso, all the time calling his name. John began to register that she was calling him, but somehow he felt detached from his body. All the weeks of speculation, the vague suspicions and even the two tiny clues hadn't prepared him for the reality her words. His mind simply had had enough.

"God damn it, John, snap out of it," she said, slapping him across the face. At the fourth or fifth slap he suddenly reached out and grabbed her arm, his eyes slow to focus on her face.

Very slowly he asked, "What did you say?"

"Are you okay? Are you sure you can talk about this right now?" she carefully asked.

"More than anything I've ever needed to discuss in my entire life. Now. What. Did. You. Say?" John repeated, spacing the words out carefully.

"I said, I'm one of only two people on the face of the earth who knows exactly what the people on the moon want," she said, sitting up in the bed.

"What do you mean by that?" John asked. "Do you know someone who ended up going there? Did they tell you before they went what's going on up there?"

"John, I've spoken directly to just under fifty people who now live in the lunar colony. I've been responsible for finding and recruiting every woman who went to live there over the past eight years.

"Are you sure you want to hear this? Given your involvement in the investigation into Jaylynn, I certainly don't want anything bad to happen to you because of what I tell you tonight," she said.

"Bad happen to me? What do you mean? I'm not going to have to be killed after you spill what you know, am I? Or is someone going to spirit me off the planet to keep me from disclosing whatever you tell me?" John asked.

"Nothing like that, I promise you. Nothing will ever happen to you as far as I'm concerned. Besides, people on earth can barely get to the moon, let alone cause any mischief for us."

"Now it's *us?*" he asked.

"It's always been *us*, John," she said gently. "Even though I've never been off-planet myself, I am one of *them*. I believe in what they believe, I want what they want, and their dreams are my dreams."

"How does my loving you fit into *their* plans?" he asked. " How does it fare compared to what you and *they* want?"

"Don't be angry, John. Let me come to that later. Right now I owe you an explanation. Whatever you want to know, I'll tell you."

"How did you find out? When did you know?" he asked, anxious to hear it all.

"Lie back and get comfortable. Is it all right if I lie in your arms while I tell you the story? I need you to hold me, but I'll understand if you say no," she said, suddenly looking small and unsure of herself for the first time.

Scooting over and pulling her next to him, John pulled the quilt back over them The soft drumming of the rain on the roof once again intruded on the quiet of his room.

"Go back forty years. Back before the height of the peace movement, back to nineteen sixty-five. I'm not going to bore you with a review of the events of the day, or reminisce about simpler times. The time could have been any time, even now, it's the circumstances that sets this time apart.

"At a college campus not too different from Steddman, except that it's coed, and almost all white, a young black man working on his masters in astrophysics makes a discovery so fantastic that he can scarcely believe it at first."

"Does this man have a name?" John asked.

"His name is not important at this point, now don't interrupt. Anyway, he is so surprised by what he's found, he spends weeks confirming the nature of the discovery. Once he's satisfied that he has indeed discovered something no one else was even close to duplicating, he destroys his notes and even obscures the reference materials he used prior to making this discovery.

"Over the next few weeks, this man slowly withdraws from his classes, citing a slow, debilitating illness that's weakening his body, until he's little more than a vague memory in the minds of his advisors and former instructors. In the meantime he takes classes at a technical school in another nearby town. He learns welding, electronics, plumbing and more, all the time leaving his old academic life behind. His parents know nothing about the change he's made in his life, his friends see him less and less frequently until they all assume he's just moved on.

"About a year after withdrawing from college he rents a small garage not too far from the technical school and begins to build himself a vehicle. He makes up a cover story about building his own personal submarine for eventual sale to the Navy. As you've probably guessed, this man is building a craft capable of operating in the airlessness of space. When he is satisfied that it will hold up to the rigors of space, he adds a device that he'd built based on his discovery while working toward his masters degree in astrophysics.

"Guess what happened when he tried out this craft for the first time? Maybe you can't. I mean, how would you know? Well, the first time he turns on the device, it is a good thing he is inside of the craft and not standing outside because it shoots through the roof and is more than twenty miles above the earth before he can reduce the power and gain control of it. He had built, and flown, the world's first antigravity aircraft. Once he makes sure crashing through the garage roof hadn't damaged the integrity of his ship, he rises over one hundred miles above the earth."

"No one saw him make that first flight? Didn't anyone hear him go through the roof, actually see this ship rising?"

"Apparently not, John. Are you going to let me tell the story or not?"

"I'm sorry," he apologized. "Please continue."

"So, this man, let's call him Christopher so I don't have to keep calling him 'this man,' built the world's first private spacecraft, and had done it in secret. I won't bore you with the details of his experimenting with travel above the earth, or the improvements to his technology that the weeks after his initial flight wrought, but I will tell you that he moved his base of operations well away from the city so that his comings and goings wouldn't be observed. Remember, all this was taking place against the backdrop of the cold war, civil rights and anti-war movements ramping up in America and just before the government's establishment of its war on the intelligentsia in the late sixties.

"Christopher decides that one of the best things he can do for his people is to provide them with safe haven from the violence and segregation America visited on Negroes for centuries. So, with the help of a handful of like-minded followers, he moves his operation to a remote location out west and begins the construction of a much larger craft. His eventual goal, after many false starts, is what's now the colony that's been discovered on the far side of the moon.

"Our colony is populated by African Americans, no whites, no one from outside the country, just run-of-the-mill, ordinary black folks."

"I do have a question, though," John asked. "Why? Why not stay here on earth and maintain a separate community here?"

"For the simple reason that as long as he lived here someone would be after his discoveries and all the rest the colony has been able to accomplish. There would always be individuals, companies and governments willing to do whatever they deemed necessary to obtain Christopher's technologies. The sad thing about it was that he knew he had no legal recourse if a government coopted his invention. He always would lose to claims of national security. He would never get a fair shake anywhere here on earth.

"So once he and his followers, more like friends than disciples really, had perfected the tools they needed to begin building a habitat on the moon, it wasn't long before they had established a beachhead up there. Their first home away from home was little more than a cave, sealed to hold in air, with power being fed to it from crude solar cells and storage batteries. They constructed vehicles that transported them around the surface using the difference in gravitational effect from the front of the vehicle to the back. It wasn't long before they figured out a way to excavate and reseal larger and larger underground spaces, enlarging the habitat as the population grew."

John broke in with a flurry of questions. "How did they choose the people invited to live there? Wasn't there a problem with someone resenting that they had to completely give up their life here in order to go there? And what about those who were approached who decided not to go? What happened to them? They weren't, uh, 'eliminated' or anything, were they?" John asked.

"No, they weren't. At least they aren't now, I can't speak for what came before I came on the scene. I'm not sure if I would have been told in any case. Let's just say that for now, I have to make damn sure that anyone I approach isn't going to say no. We're not monsters," Sydney said, kissing him on the tip of his nose. "The long and the short of it was that over the years the colony grew and, obviously, no one here on earth was the wiser.

"When the people there were finally unencumbered from the strife they faced every single day of their lives here in America, they flourished. From what I've been able to piece together the scientific advances there are unbelievable, and they cover much more than just gravity research. The health of the people there is fantastic, about the only illness they seem to get are minor colds; we still haven't been able to completely eliminate them. There's none of the rampant factionalism you have down here, none of the 'every man for himself' that colors every decision, every law, every thought Americans have. Everything we do is done for the benefit of the community, especially for the good of the future generations. Our children, unlike those here in America or anyplace else on the globe now, will *always* grow up to live in a better world than their parents.

"Nowhere on this planet can that statement be made, at least not with any degree of honesty. We are a community of almost two thousand, families and individuals, just like most any community here. Unlike here, there's no keeping up with the Joneses, no getting over at your neighbor's or your coworker's expense, and best of all nobody is screwing anyone else over for a dollar."

"What I really want to know is, how did you get involved? And how does this affect us?" John asked quietly, not sure he wanted to hear the answer.

"I was approached by a woman at a conference. This woman knew much about me, my family, my schooling; too much information really. She said she wanted to talk to me about a job offer. At the time I was just beginning to work on my doctorate, the last thing I was looking for was a job. I was already teaching undergrads and wasn't too sure what kind of job she was talking about anyway. She had obviously done some pretty extensive research into my background, and it was unsettling, the factual data she'd been able to collect.

"She allowed me to get to know her over time. She told me about her work, not the part about the colony, just what she did here. She had business and academic contacts everywhere across the country, all black. She convinced me to let her introduce me to some possible employers who would be interested in me once I completed my degree. Eventually, she was the one who encouraged me to consider returning to Steddman. In all this time she never once mentioned the colony, or her role here on earth.

"After a while she became more of a mentor, and a genuine friendship began to develop between us. All the time she was watching me, evaluating me. Eight years ago she revealed to me who she really was and her responsibilities. That's when she offered me a choice; I could go there and forsake everything here on earth, or I could take her place as a recruiter for the colony. After some serious soul-searching I chose the latter, because I wasn't ready to give up life here yet. I hadn't traveled much, I hadn't really been in love yet. There was so much I hadn't seen and done. So, I chose the life I knew instead of the life I didn't know."

"Were you offered a chance to visit at least, so you could make an informed decision?"

"I wasn't. That's the rule. Once you go, you're gone. There's no coming back: a secret known by more than one person isn't a secret anymore. Am I curious? Of course. I know a little bit about what's gone on for the last few years, but not much. There was always the chance I would accidentally let the cat out of the bag. So nothing important was never told to me. Even if I'm somehow found out, there's nothing damaging that I can tell anyone, even against my will."

"Isn't that kind of harsh?" asked John.

"Not really, we're not in the habit of making mistakes that put the colony at risk. Each one of us believes that the community is far more important than the individual. We live that philosophy in a way that's not been seen here for centuries. We look out for our own." She paused to let John absorb what she'd said.

"So, how do you pick those you approach for recruitment?" John asked.

Sydney was silent for a second or two. "It's not a simple, straightforward process. We identify promising candidates from all industries, all walks of life. Nearly everyone we look at has achieved a measure of notable accomplishment, but not the level of notoriety that would cause a huge stir when they leave their lives here."

Shifting herself against him, Sydney tucked in closer as she continued. "In some cases we have to let the best of us get away because their disappearance would draw too much attention to what's been going on for the last few decades. Special people like Jaylynn Williams, who still have a small sphere of influence in life, are ideal for recruitment. And based on past experience, not much is normally done in disappearances like hers. Most of the time nothing's really done in the way of trying to find out what happened. Either the police are overworked, or they write off the absence of clues to a hate crime where the body will never be found. Truthfully, no one ever suspects that some missing person of color is actually living in a society so much better than here. Americans are so arrogant that they simply can't conceive of anywhere being a better place to live. And yet, there we are."

"And those who refuse to go? What then?" John asked carefully.

"In the eight years I've been approaching women to leave earth I haven't had a single one decide to stay behind. I'm not sure what I'd do, or be forced to do, should that happen. I will tell you this, though, I would never be a party to murder, nor would I sit by and condone that kind of act in another. I'm proud to say that we're better than that, we repudiate exactly that kind of sick behavior so common down here," she answered.

"So far, the whole thing sounds pretty good on the surface of it. I'm reserving judgement until I know more of what really exists up there. I guess what I really want to know is, will the colony still maintain such a wide separation from earth, even after the mission gets there? Do they know the mission is coming?"

"Yes, they do. They heard about it as soon as it was announced," Sydney answered.

"Sounds like they stay pretty well up-to-date on what's happening down here. How in the hell do they do that? Not with daily delivery of the *Wall Street Journal*, I'm guessing."

"Haven't you ever heard of television and radio? " Sydney said with a chuckle, seeing the startled expression on John's face.

"I'll be damned. Of course they would. Wait, if they're on the back side of the moon, how do they pick that stuff up? Isn't the moon's bulk in the way?" he asked.

"How hard do you think it would be to put satellites in orbit around the moon? The gravity's lower, and our spacecraft don't use any means of detectable thrust. There's always a relay satellite up there listening." Sydney let out a bark of strained laughter. "I almost said it wasn't like it was rocket science putting a satellite in orbit!"

"Funny. So they know nearly everything that goes on down here from TV and radio, but how do they communicate with you, and vice versa?"

"I'm not sure I can tell you that. I've already said too much already. The only reason I've told you what I have so far is because I feel you deserve an explanation for why I acted the way I did last night. I felt that you should know why I said what I said, and why I feel as I do. I wanted to see you face to face to explain everything, to apologize and to . . ." she trailed off with a saddened look on her face.

"To what?" John asked, alarmed. "To what!" he shouted.

Sydney briefly closed her eyes, then she looked him in the eye and said, "To say goodbye."

I won't ever leave while you want me to stay
Nothing you could do that would turn me away
Hanging on every word
Believing the things I heard
Being a fool
You've taken my life, so take my soul
That's what you said and I believed it all
I want to be with you as long
As you want me to
I won't move away
Ain't that what you said?
Ain't that what you said?
Ain't that what you said?
Liar, liar, liar

Liar

Written by Russ Ballard, performed by Three Dog Night

CHAPTER 41

AT FIRST JOHN was stunned; then a white-hot anger began to burn through him.

"Goodbye!? You came here to say goodbye? What the hell are you talking about? God damn it, I want an explanation and I want it right now!" he shouted.

John sat up and climbed over Sydney, getting off the bed. He began to pace back and forth, oblivious to the fact that he was naked.

"You say you came over here to apologize, you tell me you're involved with the separatists living on the moon, you make love to me, and now you tell me goodbye? That's unacceptable. Unless you're dying of some twenty-four-hour disease, a fucking 'goodbye' is totally unacceptable!" he shouted.

"Shhh, John, calm down. I'll explain everything, but come back here and lie down," Sydney said, her eyes pleading for him to give her a chance to explain.

Stopping in his tracks, John looked at her for a few seconds, unsure what he was going to do. His heart beat a mile a minute. Steeling himself for whatever she had to say, he came back to the bed and gestured her to move over. He sat down, his back against the headboard, refusing to lie down.

Seeing that he wasn't going to budge from his position, Sydney sat up, turned to face him, and leaned against the wall along side the bed, pulling the quilt up over her waist. "Are you ready to listen now? Can I tell you the truth and be able to count on your listening to everything before you go off half-cocked?" she asked. The last thing she needed was to have him go off the deep end, maybe even having her taken into custody, or worse yet, doing it himself.

Seething with anger, John replied curtly, "Fine, I'll listen. Go on."

Taking a deep breath, she began. "What happened here wasn't part of any plan. As much as I wanted us to get together these past few weeks, the last thing I wanted was for it to happen this way. It's not fair to either of us, and it makes what I have to do almost unbearable."

"Bullshit! I don't believe you. How could you let me fall in love with you? How could you make love to me, *then* tell me goodbye? That was . . . it was . . . . it was just wrong." John sounded so forlorn it broke Sydney's heart. "And I never saw it coming," he whispered.

"I don't have any choice . . ."

"Of course you do! There's no reason for you to go. No one has to know. I promise I won't tell. Hell, if you need some kind of assurance from me, I'll resign from the force."

"Oh, John," she sobbed, tears overflowing, running down her cheeks. "That's one of the main reasons I *have* to go," she said, barely in control of her voice. "I can't have you do that."

"I don't care. I don't want to be without you. This is not right!" John ended with a shout.

She looked down at her hands, twisting the edge of the quilt, her voice barely above a whisper. "How do you think I feel?"

"That's a damned good question! Just how *do* you feel?"

After a second she replied, "I would rather die than hurt you. Is that what you wanted to hear? Do you think I like this? That this is what I want?" A tear fell from her cheek, instantly absorbed by the quilt covering her lap. John's anger cooled slightly as he began to realize some of what she was feeling.

In his desperation, John's defenses were completely down. A measure of honesty was available to him that left him nearly without emotional censors. "Don't say anything for a minute, it's my turn to talk. I need to say this before I chicken out, before I try to show you how much of a man I am, how your saying goodbye doesn't hurt, or matter. None of what you're planning is right, it's not supposed to be this way.

"To me, what we have is what everyone wants in life, that special gift we all live for but forget to wish for when we blow out the candles. Being with you is the greatest feeling in the world. I can't exactly explain, I don't know all the right words, but this is what it's like for me.

"It's like the feeling you get when you see something wondrous for the first time. Like when you first see the Northern Lights, or when you see a newborn child's eyes focus on your face and then smile in recognition. It's like the feeling you get when meeting someone for the first time, talking for hours, and discovering a kindred soul, not wanting that day to end, ever. It's like spending time with an old friend and unexpectedly looking in their eyes, seeing something that neither of you suspected was there and being drawn into your first real kiss." John paused and took a couple of deep breaths. "It's like the first time you discover that the connection between you and another goes deeper than the joining of compatible body parts. That suddenly there's that unexplainable feeling of shared awareness that's like an electric spark in your brain, a thread of fire in your heart, and an oasis of calm in your soul. It's like a million other sensations, discoveries and dawning awarenesses that give meaning to life and make it the joy it is. You give me feelings like those, even more.

"And I just can't believe I finally had it all in the palm of my hand, and now, poof, it's gone. I just can't accept that, I won't accept it." When he finished, John looked over at Sydney and saw she was silently weeping. His own heart was like an open wound, she had hurt him worse than anyone ever had, but the reason it hurt so badly was of his own making, because of how much he had grown to love her. It was that simple.

His anger completely melted away. He then did something harder, and braver, than he'd ever done before. He crawled over next to Sydney, gathered her in his arms and held her while she cried.

John had a huge lump in his own throat. He didn't know *what* to do, he was just holding on, hoping against hope somehow he could change her mind.

"Look, there has to be a way to keep us together. What about if your people do develop some kind of dialogue or treaty with us down here? What if you can convince them that in order to keep the peace, and benefit other blacks here in the process, that they should work to uplift those who have been left behind? Isn't there a chance that it can work out for everyone?" John asked. "Why don't they use what they've built to deliver mankind from some of its bullshit narrow-minded shackles, and bring the wealth of knowledge they hold to everyone?"

"And risk that those who drove them off the earth in the first place use what we have for their own gain? To allow them to exploit our work and what our community represents to maintain their perverted hold over anyone different?" Sydney answered.

"Why not withhold whatever they've got until they exact the necessary concessions from those in power to make sure that doesn't happen?" John desperately suggested.

"And provoke the resentment and fears at the root of white America's institutional racism? This is a culture that aspires to mediocrity and does everything it can to destroy anything that threatens their exalted power. They systematically destroy anything that threatens to bring them down from their perch on high, that threatens to topple them from their mounds of stolen wealth, their stolen dignity, their stolen dreams, everything they took from the reds, browns, yellows, blacks, and every other culture they raped in their so-called manifest destiny, their white man's burden, as the history books call it?"

"You sound so bitter," John said sadly.

"Wouldn't you be? Wouldn't you harbor resentment over the daily reminder that you will never be granted the simple dignity of 'life, liberty and the pursuit of happiness' just because you have a different skin color than those who have demonstrated historically, time and time again, that they are your moral inferiors? How long would *you* be able to take it? How long would *you* be able to keep on living knowing that your efforts, as good as they might be, would do nothing to ensure a better life for your children? I've had it up to here with white entitlement.

"You're suggesting we bring our wealth of knowledge to a people whose children are so dissipated and selfish that they really believe that affirmative action is reverse racism? What assurance is there that our vast scientific and medical breakthroughs will be made available to all, regardless of race or culture? Don't bother answering, there is none.

"They deserve nothing from us, except to live forever with the knowledge that what we have exists, and they will never have it at *any* price. That's what they deserve, and that's what they'll get regardless of what they do to me if you turn me in." She angrily pulled away from John's embrace, got up from the bed and went into the bathroom across the hall, turned on the light and closed the door. Moments later Sydney came back into the bedroom and sat down at the foot of the bed, picking up her underwear from the floor and pulling it on.

Gazing at John across the bed, it seemed most of her anger had dissipated. "Perhaps it was wrong of me to let this happen. Believe me, this wasn't my plan at all when I left the house to come over here. I just came to apologize. I do care for you, more than any man who's ever been in my life. If there was some way we could be together, I would gladly spend the rest of my life with you. Making love to you was something I've wanted, something I've envisioned almost from the beginning, but I didn't think it would ever happen. But it did, and I cherish it for what it was."

John was sick at heart; he also felt sick to his stomach. He didn't even react to her state of undress as he watched her, it was simply the dread of losing this woman he loved. His throat and mouth were dry. He didn't know what else to say, except, "But I love you. I will do anything not to lose you. I will go away with you and keep them from finding you, I know how it's done. No one will ever find us, at least then we would be together."

"I would like that more than anything. Having to leave you, to never see you again is killing me. But I can't stay. If the authorities knew about my connection to the colony they'd never let me be."

"But they do, they already know," John said, before he could think.

Jumping to her feet, Sydney quickly retrieved her sweater from the chair and frantically pulled it over her head, she then began to pull on her jeans. "How do you know? Why didn't you tell me?" Then angrily, "Are you part of this? Was it your job to pump me for information, to try to get a confession out of me? Well, mister, you did one hell of a job on me. Oh, you're good, very good, Officer Matthews."

Swiftly rising from the bed, John grabbed her by both arms, forcing her to look him in the eye. "That's not true. No one made me love you, no one made me feel this way, and no one put me up to pumping you for information. If you'll just shut up a minute, I'll explain everything."

Her eyes wide, her breathing deep and ragged, Sydney quit trying to pull away from his grasp. Feeling her relax, John let her go and backed up to sit back down on the edge of the bed.

"Please, sit down. I'll tell you what they know, all right. You're not in any immediate danger of being arrested or anything like that, not as far as I know."

Sydney picked up her sandals, taking them over to the chair and sat down, her eyes never leaving John's face. "Fine, tell me what you know. How did you, or whoever, find out?"

"We never really 'found out,' as you put it. I uncovered something that didn't jibe with what you told me the first time I came to your office. When you got the Williams girl's file you said you hadn't had any recent contact with her; of course you knew her being dean and all, but you hadn't talked to her in a while. That wasn't unusual. With hundreds of students on campus, it wasn't out of character for you to tell me that.

"A few days later, when I got hold of her credit card bill, bank statements and her phone bills, I found something that didn't make sense. She had made two calls to your house from her cell phone in the days before she disappeared, both calls for several minutes. That's what put me on to you."

"Who did you tell and what was their reaction?" Sydney asked.

"Since the FBI had the ultimate oversight of the Williams girl's case, I passed the information on to the agent in charge. Because it was so thin, it was decided to wait to try to develop further leads before pulling you in as a material witness. However, it did start me looking into your travel and your phone calls, trying to see if there were any connections to other women who'd gone missing."

"And?" Sydney asked, tensing.

"No one, not a one. You were very careful, my compliments to you."

"So you've been on to me almost from the beginning. Having said so, do you really expect me to believe that you love me?"

"Don't think that. I was intrigued by you from the moment we met. As we spent more time together I was completely enchanted by you. Everything about you just pulled me closer and closer to you. I wanted nothing more than to be able to spend every minute of free time with you, grow old with you, however you wanted to share your life with me. I didn't lie to you, ever."

Sydney poked her finger at him in the dark. "A lie by omission is still a lie. That's not an excuse."

"I know, I know. I'm not trying to make any excuses for myself. But I just couldn't stay away from you, I kept falling in deeper and deeper. So fuckin' shoot me! And now, you tell me we can't be together. This whole situation is crazier than a shit-house rat. Isn't there any way this can work?"

Sighing deeply, and pulling on her sandals, Sydney leaned back, emotionally exhausted. "I've been thinking about this ever since I was told that I was going to be picked up and brought home. I thought about staying behind, but that would mean being completely severed from my people. I can't. It's too ugly down here, there's too much pain. This country is too sick for any black person in their right mind to want to stay here if they have a choice like mine."

"But what about us?" John sadly asked. "Is there even going to be an us?"

"Don't ask me that. How do you think I feel? I finally find a man I respect, a man who I could love for the rest of my life, and what happens? I have to leave him behind for no better reason than *his* skin is the wrong color. No one wins here, no one goes away happy, no one leaves here unhurt.

"I won't insult you by telling you to be happy with what we were able to share, there's not going to be any 'We'll always have Atlanta' as one of us bravely watches the other one leave. This is going to hurt for a long, long time."

"Do you love me?" John asked. "Just tell me that. Do you love me?"

"Please don't force me to answer that." Sydney put her head down, tears falling anew.

"Why can't you tell me? At least tell me why."

John felt himself go cold as the silence lengthened, suddenly feeling defenseless and naked, he pulled the quilt up over his lap.

"Look, even if you don't think there's anything in the future for the two of us, at least answer me this. What's going to happen when the shuttle gets to the moon? Are your people going to welcome them or not? I don't want to think you've thrown your lot in with someone who's going to kill those people." John was willing to do anything to keep her there, hoping he could say something, anything to change her mind.

"Don't worry, no one's going to harm those poor fools up there. By the time they get there, we'll be long gone," Sydney said.

"What do you mean? Gone where?" he asked.

"We're so far ahead of where America is on a technological scale there's no real comparison. Eventually, we're going to the stars. The moon, even the other planets in our solar system are just stopovers. Controlling gravity was just the beginning. What Christopher is working on now is a star drive," Sydney said, a tiny measure of animation returning to her voice. Coming back to the two of them, and John's original question she added, "So. As far as we're concerned there will be no grand confrontation. There will be no dialog with earth. There will be no sharing of technologies. We just want to be left alone, of that you can be assured."

John was relieved to know that the mission, and those in the shuttle, were safe.

Getting to her feet, Sydney said, "I have to go. I need to think. I need to go."

"Sydney, don't leave, please. Let's just talk about this, there has to be a way for it to work out between us. Please stay, just for the night." John got up, the quilt pooling at his feet. Without a look back, Sydney quickly left the room. John grabbed his underwear, hopping from one foot to the other to pull his shorts on, running after her. When he reached the living room, Sydney was picking up her purse and pulling out her keys. When she heard him coming down the hall she turned to him, waiting until he stopped in front of her, not touching, just waiting.

"I'm sorry, John. I *have* to go. Please don't ask me to stay, and please don't try to stop me, we don't want to have that be the last thing between us, do we?" With that Sydney flung herself in his arms and hugged him fiercely. Moments later she let go, and without a backward glance, opened the door and left the house, running through the rain to her car.

Before he could think, John ran after her, running across the lawn in just his shorts, getting soaked as he watched Sydney's car pull away.

John almost jumped out of his pants when a hand grabbed him by the shoulder, a familiar voice asking, "Are you all right there, John?" It took a moment for him to recognize Agent Minor in raincoat and hat. "Do you want me to stop her?" he added, reaching under his coat.

"NO!" he shouted. Then quieter, "No, let her go. She's just upset. I'll catch up with her in the morning. Son of a bitch. Come on, let's go inside."

Once the two of them were safely inside, drying themselves off, John pulled on a pair of pants and a t-shirt. Once decently dressed he asked, "Now, will you tell me what in the fuck you're doing lurking around my house? I'm not under surveillance am I?"

"No, not you. I'm supposed to be keeping an eye on her tonight. Everyone else was tied up," Minor answered.

"Well, shouldn't you be chasing after her?" John said, angrily.

"I could, but seeing you run out of the house in your Fruit of the Looms is what we call 'off profile.' I'm allowed some degree of latitude here, besides; her car's Lo-Jacked, I can pick her up anytime I want." Looking pointedly at John, Minor continued, "I guess I don't have to ask how things went here, do I? "

"Why, don't you have the place wired?" John shot back, praying for the right answer.

"Nope, not your place. At least, not by us." Minor grinned as he lay his finger along the side of his nose.

"I guess that's a relief. Did Samuels put you up to this? Is he thinking of pulling her in now?"

"Not that I know of. I got pulled for night duty because the regular agent's wife had to have her appendix out or something. Kind of funny, it happening when it's pouring down rain. What were the odds?"

"Yeah. Look, I'm fine here, and I don't think Sydney's going anywhere. All we had was a little falling out, I'm sure things will be fine in the light of day. What do you say we go get that drink we're always promising each other? I could use something to eat. Can you shake free for a couple of hours?" John said, hoping to give Sydney the opportunity to do whatever she was going to do, the casual smile on his face killing him inside.

Just as John was trying to distract Agent Minor from following Sydney away from his home, the monitoring room at Shelter Fourteen began to buzz with activity. The automated programs running on Martin's detector had spotted and homed in on an anomalous reading rapidly moving away from the surface of the moon.

Commander Ames, having been roused from his first decent night's sleep in more than a week, crashed into the monitoring room door, forgetting for the moment that he needed to swipe his card to gain entry.

"What's up, boys? What have you got?" he asked, noting the arrival of Alan, then Martin moments later.

The watch commander replied, "Bogey spotted about eight minutes ago, sir. Rising not far from the location of the underground installation and inbound at a hell of a clip. We're trying to get a read on the velocity but we aren't calibrated for that yet."

Seeing Alan fidgeting out of the corner of his eye, Ames turned to him and said, "What's on your mind, Mr. Richards?" The commander addressed Alan formally for the benefit of the cameras and microphones in the room.

Alan was sharp enough to answer in kind. "Commander, I can cobble up something to give you speed and distance in just a few minutes if I can use one of the terminals."

"Do it." Turning back to the watch commander, Ames asked, "Has NORAD been notified?"

"Yes sir, their repeaters are showing exactly what's on our screens here. They're notifying Washington and will coordinate everything from there, sir."

"Very well. Can anyone tell if this is a manned craft or not? I need to know as soon as possible if the inbound is a missile of some sort." Nodding to the WC, Ames asked, "What's your name, son?"

"Anson, Ensign Anson, sir."

"Anson, get on the horn and see what response the Pentagon has on tap. Do we have any idea whether or not they can track that thing on radar yet?"

"I don't know sir, I'll check," the ensign said, turning away, speaking urgently into the phone.

Not wanting to break Alan's concentration, Ames caught Martin's eye and gestured him over. "How's he coming?" he asked.

"This guy must speak binary as his birth language. I can't believe the things he's able to pull off. It looks like he'll have what you need in a few minutes." Martin shook his head at the reminder of Alan's remarkable programming abilities.

"Gotcha!" Alan shouted, as he savagely hit the Enter key in front of him. As he did every display in the room centered on the bogey, flipped colors, and changed scale to show the outline of the moon's and earth's surfaces with the incoming object circled in yellow. Looking closer, Ames could see the speed and distance from each planet rolling in a small box next to the circled object.

"Jesus Christ!" one of the ensigns said, looking at the figures on the screen.

"What's that, sailor?" Ames asked.

"Sorry, sir. According to the readout the bogey is heading directly for earth at just under one hundred thousand kilometers per hour."

Doing the math in his head, Commander Ames said out loud, "Somewhere around four hours until it arrives. Anson, inform everyone of the bogey's ETA."

"Yes, sir. They already know, Mr. Richards' update went out to them the same time he dropped it into the system here."

"Of course, thank you, Ensign. Dr, Harris, is there any way to calculate the size of the object with your device?" Ames asked.

"Not any way I can tell. Alan?"

"I can't think of any way to do that. We can't use mass; with gravity being manipulated there's no way to get a good measurement. The best bet is trying to get a visual on it."

"He's right," Martin agreed. "Without a reliable measure of the actual mass, there's no way to judge size."

Just as he finished his sentence the NORAD repeater display changed from DEFCON 4 directly to DEFCON 2, one step below maximum force readiness. This was only the second time in history the country had been placed on this level of alert, the other incident having occurred during the Cuban missile crisis. The room went silent.

Walking over to a locked safe in the corner of the room, Commander Ames quickly spun the twin dials on the door as the phone rang. Leaving the phone to Ensign Anson, Ames pulled a yellow binder out of the safe and carefully relocked the door, spinning the dials at random. Watching Commander Ames, both Alan and Martin backed up to the door, uncertain just what was going to happen. As Ames began paging through the emergency procedures manual, Anson cleared his throat.

"Commander? It's Major Franks topside. He needs to speak to you," he said, handing the instrument to Ames.

"Ames here. Yes, major. I was just going through the EPM when you called. Yes major, I understand. Yes, I authorize activation of Procedure One Zero One. Lock it down. Thank you, major, I will." Handing the phone back to the ensign, Ames turned to the back of the binder and pulled a compact disc out and handed it to Anson. "Ensign, please copy the alert files into the system and activate the in-house monitors. Dr. Harris, Mr. Richards, would you please remove yourselves to the lab and wait for me there? Thank you.

"Ensign, this facility is under direct military control for the duration of the alert. No civilians will be allowed in this wing, the Army will be posting guards outside the door here shortly. They *will* be wearing sidearms, gentlemen." Opening the binder to the inside of the cover, the commander signed the top of the sheet pasted inside and formally handed the binder to Anson.

"Ensign, you have the con," Ames said, smiling. "Relax, it's not as bad as all that. Call me if anything changes, and when the inbound gets within an hour of earth, beep me. I want to be here. Oh yeah, find out where the shuttle is out there. If that thing heads anywhere in its direction, I want to know about it before it happens, understand?"

Saluting Ames for the first time, Anson replied, "Yes, sir."

Topside, the gates to the above ground campus were closing. The grounds' lights, and the helipad's, were extinguished. The elevator shaft underwent some minor, but very important, changes as well. Steel baffles snapped halfway across the shaft every fifty feet to deflect and slow any over-pressured air resulting from an above-ground explosion. Steel shutters rolled down over the exterior windows of all the buildings: arms and munitions were being issued to the soldiers on duty. Two miles away, on the highest hill in the area, a camouflaged antenna mast rose out of the ground, permitting several military transceivers to lock onto communications satellites in orbit, and gave line-of-sight access to microwave repeaters in several directions just above the horizon. The same thing was happening simultaneously at four other distant locations surrounding the complex, greatly increasing the odds of remaining in contact with the rest of the world if any of the masts were taken out. Six mobile radar trucks were being deployed away from the Shelter Fourteen complex, intending to set up a wider perimeter, giving them total air coverage nearly two hundred and fifty miles in any direction.

The troops made their preparations for attack, ignorant of the threat for which they prepared, yet determined to protect their installation at all costs.

The increase in the United States' military preparedness didn't go unnoticed by the rest of the world. Allies were passed status information about the various forces abroad, but nothing of the nature of the threat. The gravity detector was classified, as was the data it collected.

Ships powered up their engines and left ports all over the world as quickly as they could get harbor clearance. All of the airborne command centers were quickly deployed.

Because of the data originating from Shelter Fourteen, the nation's ballistic missile defenses were activated in the event the incoming bogey was a missile. Fighters were warming up all around the country, ready to be sent up to intercept the bogey should it prove to be a manned craft.

General Kaminski was in the Pentagon situation room, sizing up the preparations, monitoring the status of the mightiest military machine on earth. He, at least, had the honesty and presence of mind to remind himself that neither the size of the force nor their location on earth in any way guaranteed he had the biggest stick in the game anymore. He was no fool. He knew absolutely nothing of the adversary he faced, their intentions, or what the ultimate goal was in this high-stakes game.

The shuttle Endeavour was still fifty hours from lunar orbit, nearly a lifetime in terms of combat; so much could happen in the span of a few hours, let alone a couple of days. His only source of on-the-spot intelligence on the moon's surface would be the eyes and electronic ears of Endeavour and the satellite still in orbit, and neither would be brought to bear anytime soon. At least the bogey didn't seem interested in the shuttle. Its vector sent it toward earth in a straight line.

CHAPTER 42

WHEN THE BOGEY was less than sixty minutes out, General Kaminski opened a direct line to President Bender's location, making sure that, should the necessity arise, he would have instant access to all nuclear unlock and release codes. At its current speed of over fifty thousand miles an hour, the bogey covered thirteen miles every second, unthinkable inside an atmosphere, and faster than anything ever devised by earthly man. It could literally outrun any missile the military could put up. The only hope of interception was a proximity burst from an extremely powerful explosion. A nuclear explosion.

Dawn was less than an hour away on the East Coast when the bogey began to slow its headlong plunge toward earth. Commander Ames and nearly everyone else up and down the command network breathed a short-lived sigh of relief. At least it appeared they were not facing some sort of a missile. Now the question was, what were the intentions of whoever might be traveling in the craft?

Ignorant of the events going on in the sky, Agent Minor had decided to take John up on his offer to grab a bite with his shooting buddy. Minor checked in to see where Dean Atkins' car was and was informed it was parked at her home. He figured he would swing by just before daylight and resume his surveillance.

Once they had shed their wet outerwear and were seated, coffee in hand, Jeff asked John in general terms what happened to send Sydney off like that, leaving John's romp out onto the lawn in his underwear unmentioned.

"Mostly it's her dissatisfaction with how the president is handling the separatist thing. She's pissed that we always seem to be trying to solve all the country's problems at gunpoint. My being a cop doesn't seem to be helping either," John lamented.

"Excuse me for saying so, but judging by the amount of time she spent at your place and your state of dress when I tapped you on the shoulder, the evening didn't seem to be a total loss," Minor said with a straight face.

"You have no idea," John replied, the hurt still fresh in his heart. A total loss was almost exactly how John scored the evening. He knew that keeping Minor occupied was probably the only thing that would allow Sydney to do whatever it was she needed to do to get away. It took John's best poker face and misdirection skills to keep from letting the young agent know anything of what went on or his feelings about his first, and probably last, night with Sydney.

"So did she let anything out of the bag? Did you get anything that you could use to tell if she's involved not?" Minor asked, hopefully.

Shaking his head, John looked down and took a sip of coffee. "Nothing that really matters." Adding, as he saw Minor's eyebrows raise, "What I meant to say is, we were kind of busy, at first, to chat about current affairs. Then what happened was she said some things, I said some things, then it just began to spiral downhill from there. Hell, you're lucky I even had my shorts on the way things degenerated so quickly."

"You always this lucky with the women, John? Or do you have to work at it?"

"Who, me? It took years of carefully crafted training as a lover to get this good," John replied ruefully. "You don't get this way without stepping in it time and time again." He paused a moment. "All joking aside, this is one woman I would give anything not to let get away."

John's sadness was a palpable thing hanging in the air. Jeff saw the regret over the evening's argument, and sympathized with his friend. Unfortunately for him, his sympathy for John kept him in the diner nearly until daybreak. Even as the two men were sitting back talking after the dishes had been cleared and coffee freshened, the incoming spacecraft was entering the atmosphere.

Commander Ames and his crew had been sharing positional data with NORAD in hopes that someone could get a visual on the craft, when all of a sudden the spacecraft seemed to explode.

"Wait one!" Ames said into his headset. "Bogey has exhibited a configuration change, stand by." Covering the microphone with his hand, Ames said to the monitoring crew, "Well?! What do we have, boys? Don't be shy!"

"Sir, the bogey has split into two, say again, two distinct objects. Both objects are under power and are entering the atmosphere," said the ensign. "Bearings on bogey designated as One show it heading for the eastern seaboard, sir. Bogey designated as Two is heading toward the Gulf of Mexico."

"Alert the air force. Keep sending them tracking data, we need to get our birds in the air," Ames ordered.

At his location underground, President Bender said aloud, "Are we under attack? Does anyone have any idea what's going on out there?"

Over the command network, General Kaminski answered, "Nothing is known, Mr. President. It appears the spacecraft has divided into two vehicles, possibly to enable atmospheric entry. The Air Force is attempting intercept right now, sir. The speed of the bogies over the upper atmosphere is still over mach six, they'll be tough to bring down, let alone keep an eye on if we can't track them by radar."

"General, are there any signs of additional craft coming from the moon? Two seem to be somewhat sparse for an invasion force, wouldn't you agree?" Bender asked.

"If that was their intention sir, I would agree. If they intend to attack Washington it's anyone's guess what kind of weaponry they'll be using, sir. I have ordered a full alert around Washington. All aircraft will be grounded in twenty-five minutes, sir, and DC airspace will be closed until further notice." Kaminski could be heard saying something to someone off-mic. When he came back he said, "Mr. President, the northernmost bogey is over Ohio, heading east. ETA to the DC area at its current speed is just under fourteen minutes. The only way we can track it is by Dr. Harris' equipment, still no sign on radar."

"And bogey two, General?" Bender asked.

"It appears to be headed south, sir. Perhaps to the Kennedy Space Center, we can't tell yet just where it's headed."

"No need to hold on this line, general, keep me posted of any changes."

"Yes, Mr. President. Are there any warnings or preparations you want issued for the city sir?"

"What? Wake the city and cause a panic? Until we're sure of any hostile intent I say we keep the military posture where it is and hope for the best."

"As you wish, sir. I'll be right here if you need me."

"Thank you, general," Bender answered. "Major? Can you switch that main display out there to this screen?" he asked the aide assigned to him.

"Right away, sir. Anything else, sir?" the major asked.

"I want to make sure we have wing-to-wing coverage around Washington. Get me the air force liaison on this line here," he said, pointing to the group of phones next to his chair.

"Right away, sir," the major replied, picking up the phone by the door.

Moments later one of the phones began to buzz softly, an amber light blinking to let the president know which line. Everyone in the room listened in without seeming to, waiting to see what the president had on his mind.

"This is the president. Yes, colonel, I do. I want you to make damn sure we're doing everything possible to ensure that if a bogey is vectoring in on the city we shoot the damn thing down before it gets anywhere near the outskirts. Do I make myself clear? I'm well aware of the difficulties you're experiencing by not being able to track the crafts conventionally. No, I don't care. Damn right. If that's what it takes. Washington, D.C. is to be protected at all costs. That is all." The president hung up the phone, and said under his breath, "And may God have mercy on all our souls."

Nearly everyone stationed at Shelter Fourteen was awake, watching the master display being piped to every public display screen in the installation. Those who went to sleep the night before were awakened by friends and associates as word spread about the military lockdown and the incoming spacecraft.

Most of the people stationed below ground were sitting or standing around quietly together in the commissary or in the other common areas. Watching, waiting to see events unfold.

The southernmost spacecraft slowed as it dipped lower and lower into the atmosphere, the dense air seemingly impeding its forward progress. The tracking data the shelter's computers were turning out indicated its vectoring away from Florida's Kennedy Space Center. Instead it was proceeding in a more southerly direction. In moments it dipped down to under twenty thousand feet above the ground. Fighters were converging on the projected flight path but continued to see nothing on radar. Sunrise was still an hour away, making seeing anything in the darkness of the predawn sky nearly impossible. Their only hope was that the craft's rapid, high-speed descent into the atmosphere might have heated the skin of it enough so that infrared sensors would be able to catch a glimpse of it.

The craft slowed even more as it entered Georgian air space. It lost altitude as it approached Atlanta. The Georgia Air National Guard was scrambled, pilots and crews already standing by on alert. Pilots were switched to E-3 control of their patrol patterns, everyone hoping for a chance to spot the craft before it could cause any harm.

The identical response was underway near the eastern seaboard, the action there centering just west of Boston.

Both spacecraft dipped below one thousand feet and almost immediately disappeared from the Shelter Fourteen monitors, the machinery controlling the crafts' gravitational resources obviously having been shut down. Helicopters were launched, ground troops directed to the area over highways and back roads. None of the hundreds of fighters criss-crossing the sky in standard search patterns, looking for any unusual signs that would point to the actual landing sites, could see anything.

Outside of Atlanta, two hundred fifty troops and law enforcement officers were quickly dispatched to investigate a possible downed aircraft, the cover story more than half believed in light of the national alert.

In the diner, both John's and Jeff's pagers went off within seconds of each other. Jeff pulled the pager off his belt and showed it to John. They were both being paged by Samuels.

Pulling out his mobile, Jeff dialed the number. The call was answered immediately. Once he identified himself, Jeff listened in silence for a few seconds and then said, "Don't bother, he's right here." He then handed the phone over to John.

"Yes, Robert? What's up" John said.

"A bogey from the moon just touched down west of town here. I know where Atkins' car is. What I want to know is, do you have any idea where she is? We checked and there's no one in her house. Did she say anything to you that would lead you to believe she's the reason the craft landed here?"

"Whoa. She came over to my place earlier to apologize for last night, and then one thing led to another. But as for her confessing some kind of outer-space heritage, she said nothing." John hoped his lie wouldn't be blown by the only means possible, a recording of what was said in his house. He didn't relish the idea of looking at an obstruction of justice charge for what he had decided not to tell Samuels, or anyone else for that matter. "The kind of things we said were more in line with lover chit-chat, not national security. Has the ship been located? We can head that way if you think we can help out," John offered.

Samuels paused a second before replying. "That won't be necessary, there're hundreds of people out there trying to locate the ship. Let me talk to Jeff."

Shrugging his shoulders, John handed the phone back, indicating Samuels was still on the line.

"Yes, sir. No, it's pretty much like John said. She left in a hurry." Giving John a "sorry" shrug, Jeff added, "That's right, he chased out of the house in his shorts. No. I don't think so. Very well. I understand." Closing the lid of his phone, he said to John, "Sorry, John. I'm to stick with you for the next few hours. I think somebody's going to want to talk to you about her."

"Shit. That's all I need at this point. Things between us are hard enough without people sticking their noses where they don't belong. Who's going to stick it to her? Better yet, who's going to interview her? That's one discussion I'd like to see, but only behind a bulletproof mirror. That woman doesn't pull any punches, and her tolerance for bullshit is nonexistent," John said.

Minor looked John in the eye. "Let me ask you something. Before I ask, I'm going to say up front, nothing you say will go any farther than you and me, I swear. You understand?"

Getting a careful nod from John, Minor asked, "Did you drag me here tonight to give her a chance to get away?"

Looking into the face of the younger agent across the table, John answered, "First of all, I understand the consequences of pulling a stunt like that. I am not a stupid man. If she is one of them, or at least knows something about the disappearances, or the people on the moon, she's probably the only material witness we're going to be able to dig up any time soon. If she's involved, I'm just as anxious to get the truth out of her as anyone else." John hoped Jeff wouldn't examine what he said too carefully. Perhaps the computer analyst wouldn't dig down into his words and find John hadn't answered the question at all.

"I will say this, though, I love her. She's probably the most perfect woman I've ever met, at least perfect for me. What kills me is that everything out there seems stacked against any two people getting together. With us, you add the fact that she's black and I'm white and it just doesn't look good. The last two times we've been together it's turned into a disaster, between the country going nuts about these people on the moon and our own personal problems, I'm seriously wondering how any of it works." John twirled his empty cup on the table. "How about you? How do you maintain any kind of relationship with the kind of job you have? You've been here for a couple of months now. Do you have a significant other back in DC?"

Grinning at John like he didn't have a care in the world, Jeff answered, "Only one? Just kidding. I do date, I see a couple of different women back home, both of them are in the Bureau so their schedules aren't any better than mine. It's hard sometimes, but I'm still pretty young so I'm not so anxious to commit to anything serious yet. But I do know what you're talking about. Mixed marriages just don't seem to work."

Seeing John's eyebrows shoot up, Jeff quickly added, "I meant agents and civilians. They have a hard time making it work. It's the same with cops too. Have you seen the divorce rate of sworn officers lately?" Shaking his head over the thought, Minor continued on about his love life in DC, not noticing John's lack of real interest.

John remained quiet in his own thoughts, his heartache a constant reminder of how much grief he'd buy himself if Sydney were picked up by the authorities and the truth came out.

To the west of Atlanta the search had been underway for a little over a half an hour. Without a reliable location of the spacecraft's landing site, the authorities were looking for a needle in a haystack. Almost as soon as a perimeter had been established, word came directly from Commander Ames, informing them that the spacecraft was powering up, probably preparing for departure. The fighters began to flood the sky with radar trying to find any trace of their target.

All of a sudden a dark object rose from the ground, climbing to twenty thousand feet in a matter of seconds. The early dawn's sunlight had just begun to appear. When the craft reached forty thousand feet it seemed to burst into brilliant light, startling several of the patrolling pilots. At the speed which the spacecraft was traveling, none of the fighters had any chance of intercept, although two managed to fire off missiles in the direction of the bogey. Unable to achieve any kind of lock on their intended target, they exploded harmlessly in the air when their fuel was exhausted.

The same scene played out a thousand miles away outside of Boston. The fighters there were a good deal closer to the craft than their southern counterparts when it took off skyward. The results of their effort was identical to that of the Georgia National Guard, no joy.

Later, when all the gun camera films were examined, they showed featureless saucers with no lights or visible means of propulsion. In times gone by the air force would have classified the tapes, to disappear into some hidden storage vault with the hundreds of others collected since the early forties. Now, everyone would want a copy to study. They would even be carefully leaked to the press by the Pentagon in the hope that someone else may have seen just such a craft in the past. As they amassed these reports the hope was to plot areas of interest the separatists may have visited in the past.

Detective Mathews was under informal arrest pending locating the Atkins woman. Wherever she had gone, she hadn't taken her car. There was no record of any taxi or limo pickup from her address. Had she taken the bus, it was a nine-block walk from her front door to get to one. None of the drivers on the nearest three bus lines could remember picking up such a woman the night before. A search of her house found nothing amiss. It looked exactly like she had left for work, fully expecting to return in the evening. Her clothes appeared to all be there, none of her matching luggage was missing and her bed was unmade. Her computer appeared to have been used recently and a check of her e-mail account showed nothing unusual.

To Special Agent Samuels, she appeared to be the eighteen hundred and fifty-first African American to have disappeared without a trace in the past four decades. After pumping John for every ounce of information concerning his and Sydney's evening together, he reluctantly released him, apologizing for the necessity of the questioning. He actually gave John his condolences if it was found that she had indeed left the planet. It didn't take a mind reader to divine the pain John was trying not to show.

The military personnel stationed at Shelter Fourteen were standing down. Fresh monitoring technicians had taken over for the overnight crew and the Army had returned their various support vehicles and personnel back to the base. Soldiers turned in their weapons and restored the communications antennae to their protected silos.

Commander Ames was asleep barely an hour when an urgent knocking at the door woke him. Staggering to the door, a bleary-eyed Ames saw a sergeant standing just outside the door with a large insulated cup in hand. Gesturing him into the room, Ames turned on the overhead light, shocking his eyes awake with the brightness of the fluorescent fixtures.

"What is it, Sergeant? This better be important, I left word not to be woken for anything short of death, blood, fire or flood."

"Yes, sir. You are wanted in Monitoring immediately. The ensign on duty suggested I bring you some coffee, sir."

"Is that black?" Ames asked.

"Yes sir," the sergeant replied, handing the cup over while Ames tried to remember if he had a fresh uniform to get into.

"Why didn't they just page me or call?"

Pulling the end of the phone cord from behind a pile of books on the desk, the sergeant answered, grinning, "Equipment malfunction, sir? There was also something uncharitable about you forgetting your pager over there."

"Very well. Give me five to shower and get into something decent. We have time for that, don't we?"

"I couldn't say, sir. Perhaps you should plug this back in and give them a call."

Gesturing to the man to plug the cable back into the wall, Ames didn't even get the chance to pick up the instrument before it began to ring. Stifling a laugh, Ames picked up the phone.

"Ames here. What's so damn important that you sent along a nanny to make sure I got up?

"What? I'll be right there." He pulled on his trousers from the night before and threw a sweatshirt over his undershirt. He then handed the cup of coffee to the sergeant saying,

"Eighty-six this for me, would you?" and bolted.

He took off for the monitoring center at a dead run. He was spared the search for his ID card; one of the crew opened the door for him.

"What do we have, gentlemen?" Ames asked, scanning the room. Seeing someone on the communications channel with NORAD, he took a beat to get a situation report.

"Sir. The installation on the moon has begun to exhibit unusual gravitational readings. There are broad, sweeping ripples in the gravitational constants around and under the entire extent of the installation. We're recording everything, NORAD and the Pentagon are online."

"Any change in alert status from the Pentagon?" Ames queried.

"No sir, since nothing is coming this way we're still at DEFCON Three."

"Where's Dr. Harris? Although I'm almost afraid to ask," Ames inquired.

"He's being sent for, sir. He's in his quarters. My guess is he was sacked out."

Walking over to the central display, Ames said, "Show me what happened."

Going back eleven minutes, the controller changed the orientation of the display to show side-by-side views of the area around the installation on the moon, one overhead and one from the side. Beginning the playback at double speed, the controller leaned back to give the commander a better view.

Pointing to the bottom of the display, the controller said, "Looking at these figures here, the gravitational displacement is not constant. The effect is rolling through the surrounding rock. The frequency is not like a pulse but more like a rolling wave. Maybe it's some kind of regularly scheduled maintenance routine. If you look at the extent of the coverage, it's pretty tightly focused."

"How far out is the shuttle, ensign?"

"They're about twenty-eight hours out. Do you think they might be warming up some kind of weapon, sir?"

"Who do I look like, ensign, Kreskin? I've got no idea. Patch me into NASA, I need to talk to the mission controller, right now."

The communications officer handed Ames a headset and clicked twice on the handset,

"Go ahead, sir."

"This is Commander Ames, who am I speaking with?"

"This is Colonel Tibbits, commander. What can I help you with?"

"Do you have an abort procedure that you can implement prior to orbital insertion, Colonel?" Ames asked.

"Yes, we do. It calls for a single passage around the moon to slingshot back. Why do you ask Commander?" Tibbits asked, sounding somewhat impatient.

"We are monitoring the installation on the back side of the moon and we have recorded gravitational readings sufficiently strong enough to pull that bird right out of orbit," Ames said, looking at the senior tech on duty for confirmation. Getting a nod, Ames turned his attention back to the colonel.

"Shit. Is the bird in imminent danger? Aborting the mission still puts them within line of sight of the installation once on the trip around. How confident are you of this threat?" Colonel Tibbits demanded.

"We have no direct indication of imminent danger to the mission. I'm only stating that the capability exists and has been confirmed. The power they are exhibiting right now could easily pull the shuttle down to the surface." The commander waited for Tibbits to respond, then added, "Is there anything we can provide you with, Colonel?"

"Not at this time. Your display is still being piped in to us here from last night's incident. The trouble is we don't have anyone here who understands the damn thing," Tibbits said in frustration.

"I'm going to assign an Ensign Decker to liaise with your people from here on out. The line will remain open to whomever you assign to us. I'm going to alert the Pentagon and bring them up to speed. My recommendation is to see if your boys there can plot an abort sequence that does not, repeat, does not traverse the far side of the moon, sir."

"Recommendation noted. Thanks for the heads-up."

"I'll be handing the line over to Ensign Decker. I'm going to get the Chairman of the Joint Chiefs up to speed."

Ames sat down at the desk and punched up the Pentagon. Finding the general was out, Ames left word for Kaminski to contact the shelter as soon as possible. When he hung up the phone, one of the techs called out, "Look at this!"

Rushing over to the central display, Ames saw that the readings inside the complex were still at earth-normal, but in the area immediately around the installation they were showing up as bright red. Just then a befuddled Dr. Harris entered the room. "What's up, Commander?" he asked.

"I haven't the foggiest. Take a look at this and tell me what you think."

"How long has this been going on?" Martin asked.

Looking at the clock, the controller replied, "Twenty-four minutes or so, sir."

"Has the displacement gotten any higher than this?"

"Not so far, sir. The readings are topping out at this level here. The focus of the field outside the habitat is getting sharper."

"What do you think that indicates, doctor?" Ames asked.

"I'm not sure. If I were a betting man I would say it looks like some kind of containment field. Maybe they are hardening the rock around the habitat, perhaps preparing for the arrival of the shuttle? Maybe it's some kind of defensive screen. Is it also above the habitat?" Martin queried.

"No sir, only in the surrounding rock." The screen changed perspective to a view from underneath the large installation. "See here. From underneath it looks like they're making some kind of shield covering the exterior of the entire shelter." Twisting a knob, the viewpoint changed to overhead. "There's nothing happening topside. Do you think it might be some kind of moon quake protection?"

"Your guess is as good as mine. Wait, what's that?" Martin said, pointing to the display.

"A third field has formed just outside of the one in the surrounding rock. The field strength is roughly double of that of the moon's, it's at about a third of a G." The tech began to type on the keyboard.

"Martin, what's happening up there?" Ames asked.

"You're not going to believe this, but it looks like the entire habitat is being lifted out of the ground. The surrounding rock is being sectioned by the two opposing gravitational fields."

Turning to the communications console, Ames ordered the ensign to contact the Pentagon. "Alert NASA that we may have another bogey in the sky very shortly. Decker, get Tibbits back on the line and bring him up to date. Please convey my compliments to the colonel and ask that he prepare the shuttle for evasive action."

The activity in the room kicked into high gear. Martin commandeered a console for his own use. He grabbed a phone and dialed Alan's room, trying to rouse him from his exhausted slumber. Getting no response, he beckoned Ames over. "Can you send someone over to get Richards out of bed? I need him to help me do a couple of things."

Overhearing the conversation, the watch commander picked up the phone and gave the order, nodding to Ames when he was done.

"Thanks," Martin said, immediately turning back to his screen, clearing it of the display and opening several windows with programming code flashing by.

"Holy shit!" shouted Decker. "Take a look at this!"

Everyone crowded around the various displays. Changing the aspect of the view to show the habitat from the side, the assembled spectators could clearly see that the bucket-shaped gravitational field was lifting out of the surface of the moon. "Holy mother of God!" someone whispered into the silence.

The entire habitat lifted clear of the surface of the moon and held stationary for several seconds. Then it began to smoothly climb ever higher above the surface of the moon.

"What's their speed?" Ames asked out loud.

"Around fifteen meters per second, sir, if I'm reading this right," Decker answered, repeating the information to Colonel Tibbits.

"Watch commander, inform the Pentagon. We're sending this out still, aren't we?" Ames asked.

"Yes sir, everyone on the net is getting it, sir."

"Doctor, is there any way to tell what course they're taking? Are they moving anywhere near the shuttle's path?" Ames queried.

"Not so far. The appear to be heading directly away from the sun," Martin answered.

"Speed increasing sir, the bogey is now passing fifty kilometers per hour. The increase is smooth, sir, now passing seventy-five KPH."

Martin turned from his screen. "Commander, do you have any idea how much power it takes to accelerate that kind of mass that quickly?"

"About the same as it takes to almost stop a mile-and-a-half-long asteroid from crashing into the moon?" Ames answered sarcastically.

Abashed, Martin turned back to his screen, initiating direct tracking of the habitat with the programs Alan had finished the week before.

"Any aspect change?" Ames asked Decker.

"No sir, direction is unchanged, speed increasing to two hundred KPH."

Just then the red phone, the direct line to the Pentagon situation room, rang once. Picking it up, Ames answered. "Yes, sir. The entire habitat seems to have lifted out of the surrounding rock sir. No, there's no sign of any other spacecraft in the area. The bogey is headed outbound. From the sun, sir, away from earth completely. Yes sir, right away." Hanging up the phone, Ames ordered a high-resolution scan of the flying habitat.

"The chairman wants to make sure that no smaller bogey gets by us and threatens the shuttle."

Picking up the phone, the Ames ordered additional personnel to the monitoring center. After they arrived, every screen in the room was live. The extra personnel were followed shortly by Alan, escorted by the same sergeant who had awakened Ames.

Martin got up and grabbed Alan by the sleeve. "Sit down, Alan. You awake? You need coffee?" At Alan's nod the watch commander called the commissary and ordered an urn as well as something to eat for everyone.

"Alan, pay attention. The entire habitat has lifted off from the surface of the moon and is heading out away from the sun." Pointing at the computer screen in front of the young programmer, Martin continued, "We need to be able to do a high-res scan around the main bogey here, and at the same time look for anything that splits off from the main mass."

Scrubbing his eyes to get them to focus better, Alan set his hands on the keyboard and transformed into a typing dervish. Everyone in the room stopped in amazement at the speed at which Alan attacked his keyboard. Moments later all of their screens updated as he added several tracking and scanning functions to the detector's already remarkable capabilities.

"Someone come here for a second," he said to the naval staff. "I need to explain what I just did, there's not going to be any online help for this thing for a while."

Two of the techs picked up pads and pencils, got up and went over to his screen. Alan began to explain what he had added, and how to access the new functions. While he was doing so, Ames sat down next to Martin. Glancing over at the two men listening to Alan's quick tutorial, Ames said, "This guy is a genuine strategic resource. Are you planning to keep him around for a while? Because if you're not, I'm going to find some way to snag him myself."

Chuckling softly, Martin said, "At this point in the game, you couldn't tear him away from this place at gunpoint."

Clapping Martin on the shoulder, Ames got up and stood behind the two techs trying to absorb the machine-gun delivery of Alan's directions. When they were satisfied they understood the new capabilities and controls, they began to circulate to the other consoles, showing their colleagues what they had just learned.

Alan was already putting something else together when coffee arrived along with a cart of juices, soft drinks, sandwiches, plates and napkins.

Ames went and drew a cup of coffee, setting it within Alan's line of sight, careful not to disturb the young man's concentration. Shaking his head, he returned and drew a cup for himself, wondering how long all of them were going to be able to keep up the killing pace the constant alerts were imposing on them. He went over to the watch commander and reminded him to make sure everyone took breaks along the way and got something to eat. Then he settled back into his chair and waited for any change in the situation that requiring his input. He almost laughed out loud when he thought about how General Kaminski was taking in this new development. If Ames' guess was correct, there probably wouldn't be much left behind on the moon by the time the shuttle got there.

President Bender, having taken the elevator down to the situation room under the White House, watched along with everyone else as the habitat traveled farther and farther away from the moon's surface. He listened in on the dialog between Ensign Decker and Colonel Tibbits in Houston. The news services were just beginning to break in with bulletins on the sighting of a large object coming out from behind the moon. Viewers on earth could see little more than a bright, shiny, starlike object visibly moving against the sky. Those in the US were unable to view the object directly in daylight. The pictures they saw on television originated from the International Space Station.

Suddenly, every cable and satellite television channel went dark; only local channels were broadcasting. All of the movie channels went dark. CNN, MSNBC, TBS and every other network that relied on satellites to distribute their signal went dark.

Moments later text saying simply, "Please stand by for a very important message" began to scroll across the world's television screens. The president, alerted to what was happening, had the main screen tuned to one of the satellite channels. General Kaminski, on his way back to the Pentagon, tuned in to one of the local news stations from the back of his limo. Commander Ames, having been alerted by Colonel Tibbits, had the media department switch every display in the shelter to the broadcast. The shelter staff, the commission members and the soldiers stationed below all came to a halt, waiting for whatever was to follow.

Detective Mathews, sitting in the squad room at the station, answered his phone, surprised to find Samuels on the other end. Almost immediately he slammed down the phone and ran to the cafeteria where the message was up on both televisions in the room.

Moments later, the screen cleared, and a message in English began to scroll up very slowly:

"To those of you living in the United States of America. We, who used to be your friends, your family members, your neighbors and coworkers, have lived apart from you for decades, wanting nothing more than to live in peace without interference from the culture in which we were birthed. We are not criminals, we have stolen nothing from you, we have asked nothing of you, and we want nothing from you. And yet, you send armed men to attack us.

"We have built a community free of greed, crime and self-interest. Within our community we have achieved a greatness of spirit absent from the lands of earth. We cherish every member of our community, we live for the aggrandizement of our future generations, each generation to be better off than the last. In this we have achieved a sense of community that you will not reach in any of your lifetimes.

"We have taken the lives we led on earth and lifted them up, marking achievements in science, medicine, and education unmatched anywhere on earth. We have done this in the absence of commerce, prejudice and selfishness, and yet we believe we have so much further to grow.

"We send this message, in part, to apologize to those we left behind who experienced pain and suffering at out departures over the years. We meant no harm, we wished to visit no hurts upon our families. However, simple prudence demanded our leavings take place in secret.

"The people running our country of birth are members of an immature, self-destructive species. You have so little regard for your own lives, we can only imagine what value you place on ours.

"What is ours is ours to keep. The sciences we master, the technologies we hold, they are also ours to keep. Without the constant assault on our beings and on our psyches, and without the vicious emotional violence constantly being perpetuated against black Americans, we have achieved so much more than your best are capable of. We hold the promise of a future free of want and need and yet your only response at discovery of us is to send weapons to try to beat us into submission.

"Your dissipated culture has nothing to offer us, even less so for yourselves. Your values are morally bankrupt and your entire society is structured to uplift the most wealthy at the expense of everyone else. There is little justice in the courts of America, especially for the black man, only a sick form of petty, destructive revenge. You imprison the sick and the mentally ill, and reward those with means who tapdance around the law. Your contemptible treatment of the colored peoples of the world continues to run unchecked. You squander lives for nothing better than goods or money. Your self-appointed moral compasses, your so-called religious leaders, especially those with political aspirations, are little better than perverts claiming to speak the word, or to know the mind, of God. That which you don't understand, you trivialize. That of which you are ignorant or fearful, you destroy.

"We have no hope that those we leave behind will live out their lives with any real measure of joy or peace. However, as with any diseased tissue, you have to excise it in order for the organism to thrive and survive. This is why we leave you behind.

"We leave our adopted home on the moon with regret. However, we refuse to involve ourselves in the petty concerns of terrestrial man. Your lives are of no consequence to us. We live *our* lives looking ever forward, not backwards to that which keeps *you* from greatness. You are welcome to the world which served as our first home away from home. It is our hope you will learn to live on it and use it well.

"To those we leave behind who did not know your loved ones are happier than they ever could have been on earth, we leave you with these words from Sir William Drummond:

"He who will not reason is a bigot, he who cannot is a fool, and he who dares not is a slave.

"Goodbye."

After the message replayed itself three times, a list of names began to scroll up the screen, obviously the names of those who were leaving the moon, and earth, behind.

It didn't take long for the alphabetical list to reveal Sydney's name among the others. John's heart was at once relieved and mortally pained as he realized she had made it safely home. Knowing Samuels and nearly everyone else in the world had seen the broadcast, and not wanting to talk to anyone about what had happened, John went back upstairs and checked out for the rest of the day. As he drove away from the station, for the first time in a long time, John wanted to do nothing more than to get stupefyingly drunk.

Thousands of families, friends and former associates were just as moved by the message and the roll call of names displayed afterwards.

In the commissary of Shelter Fourteen, as the list of the colony's citizens scrolled across the television screens scattered throughout the room, a sob was torn from the throat of one of their own. Everyone turned to see who it was, surprised, then dismayed to see Norma Lancaster collapse in a heap in her chair, her head down on the table, cradled in her arms as she was racked with heartbreaking sobs.

Seeing her distress, others sitting nearby converged on her table, trying to find out what had happened. When he heard the outcry and saw the names going by on the screen, Alan Richards pushed everyone aside as he made his way to Norma's table.

Kneeling at her side, gathering Norma in his arms, Alan gestured everyone away angrily.

"Leave her alone, I'll take care of her," he demanded.

Susan Roscoe and Paul Milton remained behind as the others slowly moved off. Paul put his hand on Alan's shoulder, and said quietly, "Let us help you get her out of here, okay, son?"

At Alan's nod, Paul went to her other side and helped Norma to her feet. With Susan Roscoe in the lead, her expression warning everyone well away, the three escorted Norma out of the room.

Alan lead them to Norma's room, gently pulling her ID card from around her neck and opening the door. Susan exchanged places with Paul, helping Alan get Norma into bed and covering her quietly sobbing form.

"You'll stay with her?" Susan asked Alan.

Alan nodded, then walked Susan to the open door. When she rejoined Paul, Alan explained, "Her parents were on that list."

"I though it might be something like that. Thank you for helping her, you're a good friend, Alan," Milton said. "If you need anything, if she needs anything, call me."

Nodding his thanks, Alan closed the door and turned off the overhead lights, leaving the small desk lamp to softly illuminate the room. He then got into bed behind her, gently hugging her to him spoon fashion, and just held her, knowing her heartbreak would not easily pass, but determined to be there for her, no matter what.

You can't always get what you want
You can't always get what you want
You can't always get what you want
But if you try sometimes you just might find
You'll get what you need

You Can't Always Get What You Want

Written by Mick Jagger and Keith Richards, performed by the Rolling Stones

CHAPTER 43

THE WORLD'S AIRWAVES degenerated into an impotent Tower of Babel as everyone scrambled to try to put their own spin on the numbing events they had just witnessed.

The demands for the shuttle mission to be recalled grew in strength. The recriminations over having squandered the hope for a better earth were legion, and criticism of the United States for having sent an armed mission to the moon came from every corner of the globe.

Telescopes tracking the space-borne colony showed it receding from earth orbit at such speed nothing launched by man could possibly reach it. It never came near the shuttle Endeavour, it presented no threat to anyone, which sent the worldwide chorus of anger at the President of the United States' decision to attack the colony even louder.

General Kaminski decided to continue the mission. The administration, if for no other reason than to see what the separatists might have left behind, agreed. As Endeavour passed the twelve-hour-to-orbit mark, the air force doctor brought the SEALs to full wakefulness by triggering the intravenous infusion systems to discharge a light stimulant into their bloodstreams.

In less than two hours all eight SEALs were fully awake and alert. They removed their space helmets and began the long checklist of medical and mechanical procedures prior to deployment. While they checked their suits and the capsules' minimal communications and life support gear, Commander Evers brought them up to date on the events of the past twenty-four hours. Evers warned CPO Pritchett, the SEAL team leader, that because of the departure of the entire colony, including their underground habitat, there might be little reason for them to deploy. In fact, given that the separatists had probably taken everything along with them, there would be no way the SEALs could return to the shuttle, let alone get back home to earth. Pritchett's only response was that they would cross that bridge when they came to it.

"First of all, does anyone have anything positive we can salvage from this entire fiasco?" the president asked the National Security Council.

The faces around the table were all noncommittal, all eyes sliding away from the president's as he looked around the room. In the uncomfortable quiet of the room General

Kaminski cleared his throat. "Yes, general?" Bender asked.

"Well sir, the shuttle mission could still bear fruit. I doubt seriously they took everything with them, Mr. President."

"And just how do you know that general? If they took their whole neighborhood, why not take the kitchen sink?" Bender challenged.

"Because, Mr. President, I have to believe that they were not prepared to leave at this time. I think we pushed them into doing so by sending the recon satellite and the shuttle mission there in the first place," Kaminski answered.

"You'd better be right. Strategically we've come up empty all the way around. The samples we got from the bird shot down in the Middle East still have our best baffled. I'm not confident we're ever going to get anything from those pieces, or the remains of the pilot's foot either. We're sucking hind teat here, ladies and gentlemen."

The director of the NSA raised a finger.

"Yes?" said the President.

"It's not much yet, but we're getting some pretty significant clues from the electronic components we've been testing. They seem to have perfected a means of doping glass in a way that allows the embedding of gated connections. Kind of like dropping rows of microscopic transistors into the glass substrate. The possibilities for building something tantalizingly close to quantum computers is very real, Mr. President. However, I can't give you any idea when a breakthrough will come."

"That's something at least." Fixing his eye on the FBI director, Bender asked, "And what of the investigation in Atlanta? Are you any closer to uncovering something substantive? Like how nearly two thousand people managed to disappear right under our noses without us ever being tipped off? Or how those hundreds of people were selected or recruited?"

"We have a little, Mr. President. Unfortunately the only person we had tentatively identified as being of interest never gave us anything concrete to go on." The director felt a cold bead of sweat begin to roll down his back.

"And is this person in custody?" asked Bender.

"No, Mr. President, she is not."

"And where's this woman now?" asked Bender.

The director paused a moment before answering. "She's somewhere between Earth's and Mars' orbits sir. We now know it was she who was picked up outside of Atlanta, if the roster of names broadcast is accurate."

Bender smacked his hand down on the table in front of him. "Dammit!" Everyone around him jumped in surprise. Visibly getting himself under control, Bender asked quietly, "And the names from the list? How many had you already identified before yesterday?"

"We had discovered all but forty or so, sir. The agent in charge compiled the list over the last six months. He didn't miss many."

"All black?" Bender queried.

"Yes sir, they were. And as near as we can tell, all from this country. I should have the relevant backgrounds on the whole group by tomorrow morning, sir."

Just then an aide came into the room carrying a stack of slim binders. He quickly went to the president and spoke in his ear. Getting a nod from Bender, he gave the president the top binder and distributed the rest.

"Ladies and gentlemen, we've just received high-res photos of the former location of the habitat on the moon from the first recon satellite. Go ahead and look through them." President

Bender paged through the dozen or so images. The best overhead shots showed a neat, perfectly round hole in the moon's landscape.

The room was silent, everyone awed at what the images showed and implied about the capabilities of the former lunar residents. The last few images showed extreme closeups of a handful of small, square objects scattered around the perimeter of the hole.

After a few minutes President Bender said, "Comments, anyone?"

The Secretary of Defense said, "If you look at the third from the last photo, Mr. President, down in the lower left hand corner, I'm wondering what those objects are. According to the scale here they appear to be about the size of a bus or semitrailer. If those are transports of some sort they might still contain equipment."

Everyone was silent, knowing what the secretary was suggesting.

"What if they don't? What then?" President Bender said quietly.

"Mr. President, I didn't mean to imply that there wouldn't be risks in examining them. However, if those are transports they might contain some clues on how they control gravity."

"What if they're just cargo containers? Without any means of getting our men back into orbit, sending anyone down there to check them out condemns them to death. Frankly I'm getting enough shit dumped on me for letting the separatists get away. If we drop anyone down there without means of getting them safely home, that's sending them on a suicide mission. I don't like it. Besides, the entire world knows we sent a team into orbit. It's going to be impossible to keep quiet the fact that we deployed the team to the surface." President Bender tossed the binder to the center of the table. "There's no harm in waiting until we can mount a mission that can get our men there and back safely. With those people gone it's not like there's any hurry."

In Shelter Fourteen, Dr. Harris was monitoring the progress of the huge, space-borne city. He studied the gravitational readings around the flying city, trying to divine something, anything, of the nature of its propulsion system. Martin was thinking that if he could better study the nature of the fields surrounding the perimeter of the vast space-borne complex he might get a clue. He had some tantalizing hints from the mathematical equations he used to design the detector in the first place, but would have given anything to discuss it with their scientists.

Things were winding down at Shelter Fourteen. The high military alert had been cancelled. The monitoring team was splitting its attention between the area immediately around the earth and the flying city. They scanned mostly for any smaller spacecraft trying to return to the moon or earth.

The commission was scheduled to disband in a couple of weeks, and they were preparing a comprehensive final report on everything they had covered. Dr. Milton decided to include a "Proposed First Contact Guideline" that would contain their guidelines on the makeup of a first contact team, and several proposed contingencies for dealing with the separatists from a psychosocial perspective.

Susan Roscoe, instead of railing against the status quo, was almost smug with satisfaction over America coming in second in the confrontation that never happened. There was more than a little fear in the minds of white Americans because of the color of people so obviously superior in technological capability.

They feared that the separatists might return to exact revenge on the country that sent soldiers to confront them at their front door. The heads of industry and those who held the chains of government were of two distinct minds. They wanted to make damned sure nothing threatened positions of power which fit quite well with their lust for those scientific and medical secrets the separatists may have left behind. They were willing to sacrifice anything for a chance to examine the moon, even the SEALs whom they would doom to death from oxygen starvation, if it meant they might find something. And more than a few of these powerful men had the ear of the Simon Masters.

Endeavour was only a few hours from orbit. The flight plan called for a close enough pass to use the moon's gravity to partially slow their flight. The main engines were due to fire for just over half a minute to slow the spacecraft and allow the moon's gravity to capture it into orbit.

The pictures from the recon satellite in lunar orbit had been transferred to the display screens inside the SEALs' capsules, showing the yawning hole in the surface and the large boxes strewn about.

CPO Prichett commanded the lead capsule. His second, Petty Officer Takahashi, commanded the second. They conferred with each other on overhead photos, spending the bulk of their time choosing way points on the surface. They identified three areas of interest, the large square things strewn around the hole on the surface, the point where the tracks leading to and from the impact zone of the asteroid vanished under the rock, and a small section of the crashed asteroid itself that looked like it could be broken machinery parts.

The ground team would have to cover just under thirty kilometers. Not an impossible distance, even burdened with space suits; the SEALs would carry only one-sixth of their actual weight due to the moon's reduced gravity. Still, the unfamiliarity of maneuvering on the moon would take its toll in the beginning as the men learned a new set of walking reflexes. Prichett worked out the coordinates for the landing zone with Colonel Evers, even though there was strong evidence there wouldn't be any landing at all. Should they deploy, the capsules could only provide minimal supplies needed to sustain life. The SEALs would be able to stretch their individual air supplies to about thirty-six hours, giving them a day and a half to breathe. The suits also supplied energy-giving supplements in addition to water.

Meanwhile, General Kaminski had co-opted the coordination of the various pieces of the mission's operational pie. A check of the Shelter Fourteen monitoring facility showed the space habitat still receding from earth at a steady pace, with no sign of any smaller spacecraft leaving the flying city.

As far as the general was concerned, those men were going to hit the ground, no matter what. He could barely wait, the deployment was less than three hours away.

Everything onboard Endeavour was stowed away, the spacecraft ready for the main engine burn. This final maneuver would put Endeavour into orbit around the moon, sixty miles above the lunar surface.

Everyone on board was keyed up, waiting to see how the shuttle would perform in this historic mission. There was every reason to expect the engines to fire on cue, but the bird was flying further than ever conceived and bringing the main fuel tank the whole way. There were more than a few upset stomachs at Houston Mission Control.

Colonel Evers and Captain Arden loaded the burn program into memory, checked the temperature of the fuel lines and pressure in the feeder system that would send the mixture into the bowels of the engine to be ignited, generating the thrust that would bend the shuttle's path into stable orbit around Earth's nearest neighbor.

The SEALs had secured all loose objects and replaced their helmets. Two minutes before burn, Pritchett and Takahashi signaled to the flight deck that both capsules were prepared for the burn.

The cable news networks were carrying coverage of the orbital insertion live, rotating between an over-the-shoulder view out the front windshield looking back toward earth, and a backward view of the lower deck, where the crew was seated in acceleration couches, helmets on. In the final seconds before burn, NASA showed an animated graphic describing the maneuver and the resulting orbital path Endeavour would take upon completion of the insertion burn.

The picture switched back to the forward camera view. The clock on the screen reached zero. There was a two-second delay and the camera began to vibrate, signaling the successful ignition of the shuttle's main engines. Colonel Evers read back to Houston the orbital figures off the navigation computer. Precisely thirty-eight seconds later the engines cut off automatically and the picture ceased its vibration.

Colonel Evers signaled that the burn was successful, and Endeavour had achieved orbit, precisely on track. His voice faded into the background as the announcer described the upcoming events, including radio blackout due shortly as the shuttle crossed behind the bulk of the moon. The announcer described how the mission had fallen into its own measure of luck, as the area on the surface of the moon where the colony had been located was still in direct sunlight, making inspection easy for the crew. Endeavour was scheduled to be out of radio contact with earth for less than an hour, after which Colonel Evers would transmit the first live images of the former site of the lunar colony.

When the shuttle passed behind the moon, the coverage from Houston switched to each network's own talking heads. Their discussions covered the prospect of deploying the landing crews. The resulting debate made for very lively television.

President Bender watched the coverage in the Oval Office. He muted the sound when NASA's animation of the landing showing how the air bags would cushion the capsules fall to the lunar surface showed for the ninth or tenth time.

He already knew, intimately, how once on the moon's surface, the men inside the capsules would have fired explosive bolts detaching the deflated bags from the exterior of the capsule, allowing them to open the hatch and exit to the surface. Had he approved deployment to the surface, the men would have ended up safely on the ground, perhaps shaken up, but alive and presumably uninjured.

He thought to himself, *too bad they're not going to have a chance to use the equipment*. He was still committed to the SEALs remaining aboard the shuttle and returning home with the rest of the crew. He was glad that for once the Secret Service was allowing him to watch the coverage right where he was, as no threat really existed to his safety.

The shuttle had completed its first few orbits around the moon by two o'clock in the morning, Washington time, photographing every area of interest several times. Americans were still glued to their television sets, waiting to get a look at the lunar surface where the colony used to be. President Bender had already ordered that all pictures be screened before public release. But, barring anything really unusual, the world would get to see the pictures moments after NASA.

By the time morning came to the eastern seaboard of the United States, the SEAL team had already sent their proposed mission plan back to earth for approval. The planned routes would take them to all three areas of interest in less than a day, making the most of their limited life support resources. They would split into two teams, each making its landing at the opposite ends of the exploratory route and meeting in the middle. Their rendezvous would take place at the point where the pipelines disappeared under the rock formation. Their hope was that whatever installation might be there would support them, with air, food and water left behind.

Looking the proposed mission over, General Kaminski and the secretary of defense tentatively approved it and forwarded their recommendations to the White House for President Bender's review.

President Bender also received a draft of a joint resolution due to come up for vote in full session of the United Nations stating that whatever the US exploration team uncovered on the moon would be shared with the entire world community. He was looking over the wording of the resolution when Simon made an appearance.

"Did you see this?" Bender asked.

"Yep, looked it over last night. If it had come out of the Security Council we just would have vetoed it, but everyone wanted an end-around us on this one. What are your thoughts?" Masters asked his boss.

"Since I've made up my mind to cancel the landing, they've got nothing," said the president. When Masters made no comment, Bender said, "Spit it out, Simon. What's going on under your hat?"

"Look, Jim, everyone out there is dying to get a look at what's been left behind up there. I believe your decision to abort the landing might have been premature," Masters said carefully.

The SEALs were impatiently waiting for authorization to deploy. In the shuttle's cockpit, Colonel Evers was fairly certain they wouldn't get that authorization. As much as he wanted to get an up close and personal look at what was down there, he didn't want to be responsible for sending those men to their deaths.

When the time came, Colonel Evers received notification from mission control that the president had put a hold on the drop. When he passed the hold order on to Pritchett and Takahashi, the SEALs took the information in silence. They hadn't put in all that training at NASA *and* flown two hundred and fifty thousand miles just for a quiet little vacation in space. As soon as Evers was off the intercom, everyone in the capsules began to speak at once. It took more than a few seconds for Pritchett to get them quieted down.

"Listen, girls. The president is our commander in chief. If he orders us to stand down, that's exactly what we're going to do, so pipe down." Pritchett then called Evers and requested to be put in contact with the military liaison at the Johnson Space Center.

"Wait one, chief," Evers answered. Moments later he came back and said, "Change to channel two, Colonel Tibbits is on the line."

"Thank you, colonel." Pritchett changed frequencies and said, "Colonel Tibbits, this is CPO Pritchett. I would like a SIT-REP on the status of our drop, sir." Pritchett waited for the signal to make its way to earth and for the Colonel's reply to return from a quarter of a million miles away.

"Chief Pritchett, your drop is currently on hold. I have no further information for you at this time," Tibbits answered.

"Understood, colonel. Would you be at liberty to divulge where the hold order originated?"

"Chief, I was informed that the order came from the commander in chief. It originally came through several hours ago." Colonel Tibbits waited a beat, then asked, "Is there anything else I can help you with, Chief?"

"No sir. Thank you, sir. Please advise the president that SEAL Team Omega is ready to deploy at this time."

"Thank you, Chief, I will pass your status up the ladder, but be advised that there has been no change since the hold came down."

"Understood, Colonel, Pritchett out."

Chief Pritchett announced to the other team members, "Listen up everyone. The president himself put the landing on hold. I wasn't given any reason for the hold, but my guess is that they're not going to send us down without a guarantee of us getting back. I know we discussed this very possibility from the beginning; even if those folks hadn't left, there was no reason to expect them to let us hitch a ride home with them in the first place."

"But Chief," came from the other capsule, "we never were counting on getting any help from them, or anyone else. We're here to do recon and get the intel back home."

"Before I radio our intentions, I want a roll call on whether to go, or no go." Pritchett called off.

"Anderson?"

"Go."

"Fisher?"

"Go."

"Hall?"

"Go."

"Takahashi?"

"I vote we go, sir."

"Davis?"

"Go!"

"Lane?"

"Go."

"Greenfield?"

"We're wasting air, sir, I say we go!"

"I concur. Everyone hang tight." Switching the intercom circuit to the command deck,

Pritchett called out, "Colonel Evers."

"Yes, Chief?"

"We're ready to deploy, sir. That is, we're ready to go even without a go from the C in C, sir."

Pausing for a second before replying, Evers finally said, "Chief, to deploy your team at this time would be against orders. Given the current circumstances, I agree with the president. You aren't suggesting mutiny, are you, Chief?"

Chief Pritchett didn't know how to answer the question.

"Colonel, permission to speak freely?"

"Granted, Chief, what's on your mind?"

"Sir, we all know why the president, and any right-thinking person in fact, doesn't want us to continue the mission. No one wants to be responsible. In fact, your cooperation in launching us against orders would probably end your career, sir."

Evers interrupted Pritchett, saying, "Get to the point, Chief."

"Well, sir. We've decided that we're ready to land and take our chances. Voluntarily, sir. We need eyes on the ground, if for no other reason than to confirm no one was left behind. We need to get that intel back home, sir. You know that just as well as I do, and there's never going to be a better chance, a more timely opportunity than right now. Colonel, we're the right men in the right place, at the right time." Chief Pritchett continued more formally. "Colonel Evers, we respectfully request you deploy us according to mission profile, sir. We're wasting time, and air. As it is, we barely have enough air to get all of us back to earth. The best possible use of our time and our training is to let us do the job we came to do."

"Are you through, Chief?" Evers asked.

"Yes, sir."

"Request denied."

"But . . ." began Pritchett.

"Denied, Chief. I'm sorry. I'm not prepared to go against a very specific order, not at this time." Colonel Evers clicked off the intercom, looking over at Captain Arden. "Shit!" he said.

"Sorry, sir?" Arden asked quietly.

"Pritchett's right, about everything. Those boys *are* in the right place at the right time."

"So?" Arden asked.

"So, regardless of what they want, I'm not letting them go." Just then, a transmission from mission control interrupted them.

"Endeavour, this is mission control."

"Mission control, Endeavour here."

"Be advised, Chairman of the Joint Chiefs is coming on the line. Wait one."

Evers and Arden looked across at each other. "Shit, this can't be good," Arden offered.

"Endeavour, this is General Kaminski. Do you copy?"

"This is Colonel Evers, general, I read you five-by."

"Colonel, prepare to copy new orders," the chairman said.

"Standing by to copy, general," Evers said, pulling his pad from his thigh pocket, seeing Arden prepared to copy as well.

Then the general asked, "Chief Pritchett, are you on the line as well?"

Breaking in with a click, Pritchett answered, "Standing by, General."

"Shuttle Endeavour is hereby ordered to proceed on mission with the deployment of SEAL Team Omega. Colonel Evers, prepare to copy. Chief Pritchett, you are hereby ordered to deploy to the surface of the moon."

"Yes sir. I acknowledge your order for SEAL Team Omega to deploy on mission to the surface of the moon. Is my read-back correct, general?" Pritchett inquired.

"Yes, Chief, I confirm the mission is a go. And chief, Godspeed."

"Thank you, general. We'll check in upon landing. SEAL Team Omega, over and out."

Chief Pritchett looked at the other three men in the capsule. Clicking over to the common channel, he said, "Takahashi, we are confirmed for deployment. I repeat, the mission is a go."

Cheers broke out in both capsules over the intercom.

"Understood, chief. We're ready to deploy, confirming all gear is stowed. We are awaiting launch, sir."

Switching to the command deck, Pritchett called out, "Colonel Evers?"

"Yes, Chief?" Evers answered immediately.

"Request immediate implementation of launch sequence, sir."

"Very well, chief." Entering the program into the flight computer and reading the results off the clock, Evers reported, "Chief, be advised that capsule one will launch in twenty-two minutes. Capsule two will follow twenty-five seconds later. Do you copy?"

"Yes, Colonel. Capsule one in two-two minutes, capsule two to follow two-five seconds later. Is that correct, sir?"

"Yes, Chief. Please make sure all helmets are secure and all gear is stowed for launch, we prepare for deployment immediately."

"Very good, sir. We're ready."

As the shuttle bay doors cycled open, Colonel Evers began to rotate Endeavour so that the cargo bay pointed directly toward the surface of the moon. Just before they moved into radio blackout, mission control wished the SEAL team good luck.

What goes up, must come down
What must rise, must fall
And what goes on in your life
Is writing on the wall

What Goes Up

Written by Alan Parsons and Eric Woolfson, performed by The Alan Parsons Project

CHAPTER 44

IN THE OVAL Office, the phone rang at President Bender's desk.

"Mr. President, I'm sorry to be making this call, but the Chairman of the Joint Chiefs just ordered SEAL Team Omega to deploy to the surface of the moon. Colonel Evers acknowledged the order and the mission clock has begun counting down for launch, sir."

Leaping to his feet, President Bender shouted into the phone, "God damn it, I authorized no such order. *My* orders were to abort the deployment of those men and to return the shuttle to earth once a detailed survey of the surface had been completed. I want the deployment aborted immediately! Do you understand me, Colonel?"

"Yes, sir, absolutely, sir! But it's too late to recall the team. Endeavour has moved into radio blackout. By the time we restore communications, sir, both capsules will be on their way to the surface."

Just then Masters rushed into the office. President Bender said, "Hold on, Colonel." Covering the mouthpiece of the phone, the President said, "That son of a bitch Kaminski ordered the SEAL team to launch. Did you know anything about this? If you did, I'll have your balls for breakfast, Simon!"

"Jim, I don't know what you're talking about. I have no knowledge of what the chairman has done," Masters said, beginning to sweat in fear. He had never seen James Bender this mad in all their years together.

Turning back to the phone, Bender said, "You're telling me, Colonel, there's no way to stop those capsules from launching? We have no way to contact Endeavour, no emergency or tactical data channel that we can use?"

"I'm sorry, sir. Until they come out from behind the moon, we've got nothing. According to the mission profile, they will be climbing into high orbit in the next thirty-three minutes, then we'll be able to communicate with them again."

"But by then the SEALs will be long gone?"

"Yes, Mr. President."

"Son of a bitch . . . Who allowed the chairman transmit the order to Endeavour, Colonel?"

"Sorry, sir, I did. I had no idea at first anything was out of the ordinary. It's just that when no one from the White House followed up with an authorization for a news release or even a request to be patched in to monitor the men once they were on the ground I began to smell a rat."

"If that's the case, why the hell did you wait until the shuttle was out of radio contact before calling for confirmation?" Bender demanded.

"I didn't really wait at all, sir, it's just that the general gave the order minutes before the shuttle went into communications blackout, sir. That was less than ten minutes ago, Mr. President, and I had a hell of a time getting through to you."

"Very well, colonel. There's nothing we can do about this now, is there? For now, keep this under your hat. Understand?"

"Yes, Mr. President."

Hanging up the phone, President Bender turned to the door where Simon and Agent Bishop were standing. "General Kaminski ordered the SEALs to deploy just before they went into radio blackout. There's no way to recall them before they launch. Agent Bishop, would you arrange for the general to be brought here immediately? And get Pascal at Justice over here too, I'm in the mood to have that son of a bitch charged with mutiny." As soon as he saw Bishop whisper into his mic, Bender turned his attention to Masters. Pointing to him, Bender said, "You, get on the horn and get Hughes to draft a statement."

"Saying what, Mr. President?" Masters asked.

"I don't know. No, wait. Tell Hughes to get over here too, he's going to have to short-stop the press until we figure this out."

"Yes, sir, Mr. President," said the agent.

"Simon, make sure we have a live hookup to those men downstairs, we're going to watch everything that happens up there. If anything at all happens to those men, our chairman is going to spend the rest of his years in Leavenworth."

"Yes, Mr. President, right away." Simon beat a hasty retreat from the office to get things set up.

Looking over to Agent Bishop, Bender said, "I've changed my mind, Sam. Have them put the general downstairs, he can cool his heels down there and await my pleasure."

"Very good, Mr. President. Mr. Pascal will be here in fifteen minutes, sir. Where would you like him brought?"

"Have him escorted here, would you please?"

"Yes sir." Sam called in, made the necessary arrangements and left the president alone in the office.

At that very moment, Colonel Evers was arming the explosive bolts that would release the capsules from the cargo bay. He announced over the radio, "All systems are green, sixty seconds to capsule one release. Chief Pritchett, you can call an abort at any time, otherwise, you and your men, go with God."

"Thank you, colonel, SEAL Team Omega is clear for launch."

Chief Pritchett and the rest of the team began to tense up. When the clock in the capsule reached zero, the men felt a sharp kick as the explosive bolts fired. They felt a brief sensation of weight as the spring-loaded launching system pushed them out of the cargo bay. Fifteen seconds later they were jolted again as the retro pod extended, pulling the support cables tight, slowly moving the capsule farther away from the shuttle.

Twenty-five seconds later, capsule two also rose from the cargo hold. The shuttle crew recorded the launch for later transmission to earth. Dr. Sepin, monitoring the vital signs of the SEAL team, saw that other than some elevated heart rates, all appeared fine.

As soon as the two capsules were safely away, Colonel Evers and Captain Arden initiated the orbital burn, slowing forward velocity and raising Endeavour into higher orbit. Endeavour remained in line of sight of the escape capsules, monitoring their progress all the way to the surface.

The retro packages attached to the capsules rotated and began to fire, slowing their orbital velocity. The computerized control of the burns separated them from each other in space. As they slowed, the moon's gravity began to pull them inexorably to the surface. The sensations the men inside felt were similar to those of an amusement park ride as they were forced deeper and deeper into their crash couches. When their forward motion had been arrested, both capsules dropped quickly toward the surface. As they fell, the distance between the two capsules widened. From the perspective of the shuttle, both appeared to be on target.

The ride to the surface was indescribable. When the capsule finally came to a stop and Chief Pritchett's eyes could finally focus, he noticed two things. One, the capsule was canted ninety degrees from vertical, and two, he felt heavy, weighted down for the first time in days.

"Is everyone okay?" the Pritchett asked in the dim light of the tiny compartment.

Getting positive responses from the other three, Pritchett began to figure out the sequence in which to deflate the bags to set the capsule level. Pulling the laminated instructions out of the pocket down by his feet, he chose the diagram that most closely resembled the capsule's attitude.

He then opened the panel underneath his left hand and flipped the safety cover off of the deflation switches. Double-checking the sequence one more time, the chief pressed the first button. After a second, everyone could feel the capsule slowly begin to settle upright. After a few minutes, the capsule stopped moving.

Seaman First Class Greenfield triggered the hoisting of the communications antenna, and activated the relay transmitter. At his circled finger signal, Chief Pritchett attempted to contact Endeavour.

"Shuttle Endeavour, this is SEAL Team Omega One, do you read me?"

Immediately, Colonel Evers voice filled their helmets. "SEAL Team Omega One, we read you loud and clear. How was the ride?" he said, the rest of the command crew cheering in the background easily heard down on the surface.

"Be advised colonel, the Russians were right, that last step is a doozy! We have sustained no apparent damage to the capsule, and everyone made it just fine. Please begin the mission clock, sir. Have you heard from the other capsule, colonel?" Pritchett asked.

"They're just coming in right now, chief. Arden says they're fine. I am activating the relay right now, SEAL Team Omega Two is now on Tact Two, chief."

"How long before you get out of comm blackout, Endeavour?"

"Eleven minutes, your transmissions are going to disc right now. Visual communications check, Chief. Please have your team activate their helmet cameras," Evers requested.

"Cameras activated, how do you read?"

Bending way over to peer into the crew deck, Evers got a thumbs-up from Sepin.

"Telemetry and visuals are five-by-five, Chief. Reading same from Team Two."

"Thank you, we will be tidying up here and exiting the capsule in five. Can you give us a heading from here?" Pritchett requested.

"We have you in sight, Chief. Once you exit, when you see a twin-peaked rock formation about seven clicks away, bear ten degrees to the left of the formation to way point one. You are less than ten kilometers from that big hole in the ground. "

"Got you, we'll be moving out shortly. Pritchett, out.

"SEALs, gear up, we move out in five. Lane, vent the capsule and get that hatch open. Once you're outside, deploy the sled. Davis, give him a hand." Clicking over to their own command frequency, Pritchett called out, "Team Two, this is Team One. How do you read?"

Takahashi answered, with just a trace of static coming over the transmission, "One, this is Two, we read you five-by."

"What's your status, Two?"

"We're down, we're tight, and we will be in the dirt in five minutes, chief."

"Take your time, two, make sure your men are acclimated before starting off. How far from the target did you touch down?"

"According to Endeavour, we're less than two kilometers from way point one. And you?"

Pritchett laughed, "We've got a ten-K hump before we get to the hole. Do me a favor, find us some air out there, will you?"

"Will do, Chief. We'll be checking in every fifteen minutes."

"Carry on, Two. Will look forward to hearing from you in fifteen. Out."

As he was talking, Chief Pritchett and the rest of the team were pulling equipment from their stowed locations. Davis was handing spare oxygen canisters out to Seaman Lane to attach to the sled. Greenfield was busy unloading the weapons locker and checking their arms. Pritchett thought in passing that he wanted to test the British-made machine guns and pistols to see if they would really fire in the airless environment, but nixed the idea.

"Greenfield, hand out the sidearms and get the rest of those things stowed on the sled. I want us on our way ASAP!"

"Yes, Chief. Hey, do you think these things will really work out here?" Greenfield asked, the other two pricking up their ears at the question.

"My guess is yes, but unless you see something we can eat scampering across the landscape, my orders are to leave them be. The last thing we need is an accident out here."

"Very good, sir. We should be loaded in just a couple of minutes. Anything else, sir?" Greenfield asked.

"No, I want everyone to get used to walking around. I'll be out in a second."

Once outside, he took a look around. He was almost aghast at the stark beauty of the lunar landscape. He could see for endless miles around the capsule, nothing moving other than his men. The world around him appeared as if he were inside a black and white film, the slanting sunlight casting sharp, deep shadows everywhere.

"Kind of gets to ya, eh, chief?" Lane offered.

"It does at that, Seaman. All right, men. We've got a hike ahead of us. Let's move out. We'll rotate pulling the sled, Greenfield and Lane take the first leg. We'll trade off every ten minutes until we get a handle on moving around out here." Bouncing up and down a few times to get his measure of how much his weight had changed from earth normal, Chief Pritchett was thankful that they wouldn't be lugging anywhere near their full weight across the landscape.

Pritchett took point, starting off, getting his bearings from the twin peaks Endeavour pointed out.

"Davis, take our six, and anyone having any problems, I want to hear about it immediately. No exceptions." As soon as he heard their acknowledgments, he started off at an easy, bounding walk.

Pritchett found that a loping gait was the best way to make time over the dusty lunar surface. He was reminded of the early footage of the Apollo astronauts bouncing around like a bunch of kids. It was exhilarating, the lack of weight along with the realization they were actually on the moon. The only really strange part was that when he looked up into the pitch black sky, Pritchett saw neither the earth nor moon.

As the men trekked across the lunar plain their conversation was sparse, the two on sled detail trying to match each other's stride to smooth the jerking and bouncing of their burden.

The march across the plain took a deeper toll on the energy reserves of the men than they had calculated. Unfortunately, this also increased their consumption of oxygen.

Seaman Lane broke the silence and said, "Hey guys, you know what this reminds me of?"

"No, what?" Pritchett answered.

"It reminds me of the two weeks we spent in the Antarctic. Crossing over that glacier. Remember?"

Davis decided to add his two cents. "That reminds me of a story my daddy told me. A few years ago he was stationed above the Arctic Circle and one day he got wind of this Eskimo who started off the day pushing his snowmobile across the tundra. He pushed it for miles and miles. He pushed it to the next town, and kept pushing it through town. He pushed it all the way through town to the mechanic's shop on the outskirts. He pushed it into the large garage door and stopped. When the mechanic saw him push the snowmobile into the shop he looked up and asked the Eskimo, 'What happened, did you blow a seal?' And the Eskimo replied, 'Nope, that's just frost on my mustache.'"

His radio was overloaded with the laughter of the others. After they all calmed down, the march improved as each of the four tried to top Davis' story.

Endeavour had risen from behind the moon's shadow and reestablished contact with mission control. The controllers let nothing of the confusion over Kaminski's deployment order slip as they began receiving telemetry from the capsules' relay transmitters. The controllers were determined to support the men the best they could, knowing all of NASA's resources could keep them alive for little longer than through the next day.

All eight helmet cameras were transmitting each SEAL's forward view, bouncing and jiggling enough to give more than one controller a case of vertigo.

Even so, the scenes from the helmet cameras were vastly better to look at than the secondary mission counter, ticking off the minutes until their air supplies would be exhausted.

When President Bender arrived at the situation room, accompanied Simon, his press secretary and David Pascal from Justice, General Kaminski was already there, fuming at his being summarily brought to the White House and told to cool his heels.

"Mr. President . . ." he began.

"Can it, Isaac. The next words out of your mouth will determine whether or not you are charged with mutiny and locked up or allowed to merely resign. So shut up and try not to live down to my expectations." He turned to the major in charge of the communications team. "Major, are we in touch with our men up there?"

"Yes sir. We have audio and visual, sir. Because of the distance sir, everything we see is a few seconds old," the major answered.

"Thank you, Major. Would you put the visuals up on the screen here? And pipe in the audio from the team leader," President Bender requested.

Once the display was to his liking Bender turned to the major and said, "Thank you, Major, give us the room, would you?"

The major gathered the communications personnel up and led them outside. Once Agent Bishop had closed the door, President Bender gestured for everyone to sit down around the conference table.

"Let's get this over with," Bender began. "General, you have a choice here. Mr. Pascal has laid out my options concerning your disobeying my direct order by launching the SEALs. You deliberately killed those men in violation of my direct order," Bender said, pointing to the screen above.

"You have engaged in mutinous activities which call for immediate court martial. If I get one word of bullshit out of your mouth you will be taken into custody and I will go upstairs and announce your crimes to the press and my intention to prosecute you in a military court.

"Your only alternative is to tender your resignation as Chairman, effective immediately, and to resign from the service, forfeiting all benefits and pensions. Furthermore, if you seek any position in the private sector having anything whatsoever to do with the government or the military of the United States or any other country, so help me God, I will see your head separated from your fucking body," Bender's voice turned completely cold, "or worse.

"So what's it going to be, Isaac? Prison or exile? There's no appeal here and I highly doubt anyone will be willing to take the side of a traitor."

Kaminski's face caved in defeat. All the strength left him as the enormity of what the president was prepared to do sunk in. When he looked up, he saw that he had no friends in the room. He looked at President Bender, eyes pleading, but took no comfort in what he saw.

Kaminski laid his shaking hands flat on the table in front of him and said, barely above a whisper, "Mr. President, I hereby tender my resignation as Chairman of the Joint Chiefs. I also resign from military service, forfeiting all accommodations and benefits due. I officially sever my working relationship with any and all branches of the United States government."

Kaminski couldn't speak for a moment, and when he regained his composure he added, "I am sorry, Mr. President. I believed I was acting in the best interests of my country. I offer no excuse, I have none."

President Bender turned away from Kaminski, disgusted, and said, "Agent Bishop, please arrange to have *Mr.* Kaminski escorted to his former office and allow him to remove his personal effects. I want him cashiered and out of that uniform by the end of the day. And please ask the major to return his people to duty." Bender didn't even look up as Kaminski was led to the door by Agent Bishop, who handed him off to two other members of the White House detail. Pascal quickly got to his feet and followed Kaminski out, taking charge of the duties severing Kaminski from government service.

"Now, Major, how are our men doing up there?" President Bender asked, once everyone was back at their stations.

"Well, Mr. President. Both capsules landed safely and the men are all fine. They've split into two teams and are here, and here," the major pointed on the overhead view of the area.

"Thank you. How long before the two teams meet up?"

"No more than seven or eight hours sir, depending on what they find. It might be longer if they stumble onto something." The major had the overhead view from Endeavour put up on the center screen. "Team One has a hike to the hole sir. They're going to be checking out the containers, or whatever they are, first. After that, they're going to rendezvous with Team Two at the rocks here," he said pointing to the screen.

"Simon, what do I have this afternoon?" Bender asked.

"Nothing that can't be pushed back, sir."

The waiting was much harder on the president than it was on the SEALs. Team One was making pretty good time, the only problem being that the trek in the open sunlight tended to keep their suits somewhat hot. Chief Pritchett made sure to take breaks in shelter from the sun where possible. All in all, they made very good time, reaching the vicinity of the empty hole in a couple of hours.

Once they reached the former site of the separatists' habitat, everyone began to focus on the scenes from the helmet cameras. As the SEALs approached the edge of the hole, everyone could see a small edging of rubble around the rim. With Greenfield bracing him, Chief Pritchett leaned over the hole, looking into the darkness. With nothing to see, Pritchett's camera looked briefly down to his feet before resuming a look into the hole. Suddenly the darkness was lit, even brighter than the lunar daylight. Over the audio everyone heard, " . . . dropped a magnesium flare into the hole. I don't know if anyone can see, but there's no holes or tunnels leading through the walls. It looks like they just scooped the whole installation out of the ground. The bottom is pretty smooth, and looks to be a couple of hundred feet deep, maybe more.

"We are now proceeding clockwise around the perimeter of the hole to those square boxes off to the side there."

The president took a look at the video stream from Team Two. It looked like they were traversing dirty ice. Team Two hadn't found any metal in the debris and they were crossing over the top of the rubble instead of taking the long way around. The footing was difficult, but they were saving time, an important consideration with their finite amount of air to breathe.

Meanwhile, the news channels were rehashing the same photos and speculating on whether or not the exploratory team would be allowed to land, despite the departure of the separatists. Then all hell broke loose. CNN broke in with the announcement that an unconfirmed source at NASA had disclosed that the Navy SEALs had landed on the moon. The other stations ran the same headline minutes later, and the phone rang for the president. It was Jim Hughes asking whether or not President Bender wanted to make a brief statement at that time.

"No, I have no comment at this time. You and Simon drafted a statement, you read it to them. I'm busy attending to affairs of national security," Bender said, and hung up just in time to see Team One reach one of the square containers.

As the audio was turned up, everyone in the room heard, " . . . appears to be made of some sort of ceramic material. There's no way into the container, but when I hit it on the side it feels hollow. There's no noise but . . . Wait, Davis is going to touch his helmet against the side while I hit it again. Stand by."

Seconds later a different voice said, "There was no echoing vibration. My guess is that they're empty of anything, even air, sir." Then Pritchett resumed his reporting.

"Mission control, be advised that I am going to attempt to breach the container. Stand by." The helmet views jerked around as Pritchett and the others moved back and forth, setting up a small explosive charge to try to open a hole in the end of the container. In just a couple of minutes, three members of the team had drawn away from the box while the screen labeled Davis was focused on a small device with large numbers on it. Davis' hand placed the object in the center of the smaller end of the of the box, around the corner from the rest of the team. Once the timer was set, Davis bounded away from the container, heading toward the others. The only sign of the detonation was a brief flash.

Everyone edged closer to the ends of their seats, anxious to see inside the box. Pritchett made his way to the end of the container and everyone held their breath. He flashed his light inside, looked around inside and announced, "The God damn thing is completely empty! The bottom of it is absolutely clean. The walls are about three inches thick and the interior is completely smooth. According to the overhead photos there's about thirty of these things scattered around. Mission control, please advise if anyone wants us to check each one."

"Roger that, Team One, stand by." The voices were turned down again as everyone sat back, disappointed.

President Bender picked up the phone next to his chair and said, "Put me through to mission control," and waited. When Colonel Tibbits answered, Bender said, "Colonel, please convey my compliments to Team One, but I want them to start off on their rendezvous with Team Two. I want to know if there's a chance any facility or shelter at Way Point Two can keep them alive. Thank you, Colonel." He hung up the phone, signaled a steward to come over and ordered a double scotch on the rocks. His stomach was in a knot, but he decided he needed a drink more than his stomach needed relief.

The minutes seemed to pass like hours, leaving President Bender and the rest with nothing better to do than rehash the events of the past week, or sit in quiet contemplation of their own thoughts.

When Team One was about midway to the rendezvous with the lagging Team Two, the phone at the president's elbow rang. Jim Hughes said, "Turn on CNN, Mr. President. Right now."

"Why, Jim, what's up?"

"It's better if you see for yourself."

Turning on the television at the end of the room, and finding the feed from CNN, President Bender was shocked to see a split screen showing the feed from several of the SEAL team members with the scroll along the bottom that said: "LIVE FEED FROM THE MOON." "How the fuck are they getting this?" Bender shouted into the phone.

"I'm not sure. We're looking into it, but word is that they're getting it from CNN in Tokyo. Someone over there is decoding the transmission and feeding it to CNN's bereau. They're feeding it to the satellite and it's going out worldwide," Hughes explained.

"Get them to pull the plug!"

"I'm trying, Mr. President. I'm not sure we're going to be successful. All they have to do is tell everyone how to decode the signal and anyone can pick it up. I'm thinking the best we can do is tell everyone here to cut the feed, but then everyone but the US will be seeing it. That's not going to go over . . ."

"I know, I know. How many of the press corps are upstairs right now, Jim?"

"It's a full house, sir. Actually, the joint is packed. I'd say about a quarter of them are new faces, and more are arriving every few minutes," said Hughes.

"You running the CNN feed up there?" Bender asked, dejectedly.

"I had to. As soon as it went up the cell phones began to ring off the hook. I had to tune it in, otherwise there would have been a riot," apologized Hughes.

"There's really nothing I can do about it now. According to what my people are finding out from calling around, there're more sets tuned into CNN than when the Gulf War started and that guy was reporting from under the table."

"Well, in for a penny, in for a pound. Keep them distracted, tell them I'm down here monitoring with the National Security Council and that I will make a statement later." President Bender sighed, wondering just when the high drama would die down enough to allow him to take a couple of days off.

The time passed glacially slow, and the real-time overhead map showed them teams still en route to their final way point.

A closer look showed that Team Two was running well behind their earlier pace. Pointing at the circle on the map, Bender said, "Major? What's going on with Team Two? They're barely moving."

"One of the men's suits is having trouble with its cooling system. With them in direct sunlight and trying to keep up a good pace, the suits are having a tough time keeping the men cool. That man's suit isn't cooling as well as it should be," the major answered.

"Is he in any danger?" Bender asked.

Looking at the president, not knowing what to say, the major just shrugged his shoulders, his expression speaking volumes.

"His internal temperature is about a hundred and one. They keep stopping wherever there's some shadow to let him cool down, but it's a crapshoot either way. They can push ahead and hope he doesn't fry, or they can keep stopping to let him cool down. If they do that too often they're running the risk of the whole team letting their oxygen get dangerously low."

After a few minutes of uncomfortable silence, the major called out, "Mister President?"

"Yes?"

"Team One just reported that they can see a red light under an overhang ahead. The location jibes with where the pipelines pass out of sight, sir."

"How far away are they?" Bender asked.

"Chief Pritchett thinks just under two kilometers sir. Endeavour concurs. They think they'll be at the light in about fifteen minutes sir," said the major as he donned a headset and plugged it into the console in front of him.

"Bring up the audio, major. I don't want to miss anything. And throw the chief's feed on the center screen."

"Yes, sir." The entire gallery was startled when the overhead map was replaced by the bobbing view from Pritchett's helmet.

The mood was electric, no one said a word. When he appeared to be about a hundred yards from the easily visible light, the chief said, "I can see the pipes. They look like they're flexible, about three feet in diameter. I can just make out a large silver panel, maybe a door into the rock."

The view steadied as the chief took smaller, slower steps. "Can you see this, mission control? The pipes disappear into a box sticking out from what looks like a wall with a door, or airlock. Christ, the box is huge, I count seven, eight, nine. Nine of these pipelines going into the box. Okay, I'm climbing over the nearest of the pipes. I'm going to get close to the door. My team is spreading out to cover me."

"Oops! Aw shit!" came over the radio as the view jerked around and the picture broke up into static, and then cleared, one of the silvery flexible hose like pipes came into view. "Sorry, slipped going over one of these things. No apparent damage to the suit. Mission control, do you still read my video?"

"Roger that, Chief."

"Okay," Chief Pritchett said, his breathing loud within the confines of his helmet. "I am approaching the door. It's about seven feet tall, about twice that wide. The ground is covered with boot prints. Something pretty heavy was dragged from over there by the box to just in front of the door."

Pritchett got on his knees for a closer look. The screen showed several of the tracks up close. "No markings in the tracks. I was half expecting Goodyear or Firestone," he said with a manic laugh, his breathing becoming even more rapid.

"Chief Pritchett, this is mission control. We advise you take a moment to rest. Our monitor is showing your respiration is a little fast and your heart rate is kind of high."

"Yeah? What does it say about my diapers? 'Cause thinking about knocking on this door is just about scaring the shit out of me." Everyone could hear the rest of the chief's team laughing in the background, momentarily overloading the audio.

"I'm walking over to the door," he said, consciously trying to slow his breathing. "There are two panels here beside the door itself. Are you getting this?"

"Roger that, Chief."

"All right. Looking around I can see no markings. The two panels are the same, with a red and a green light on each. The green lights are on. There's a recessed hole in a cutout below each panel. I'm going to try pulling the levers."

"Endeavour to Team One. Wait one, chief. Request you have another team member in close cover. We would like your camera on the panel and another on you."

"Roger that. Davis, front and center, Greenfield and Lane, split left and right. Stand by, Endeavour. Mission control, there is no vibration from the panel. I can't detect any heat through the gloves. The metal looks like brushed steel, the lights appear to be some kind of molded plastic or composite. Okay, Davis is standing to the right of me, I'm going to pull the lower of the two levers. Pulling . . . There's little resistance, kind of like opening a car door. No response on the panels, nothing appears to be happening. Okay, I'm now going to try the top lever. No joy. Nothing."

"Team One leader, suggest you try pulling both at the same time, it could be some sort of safety system to keep the door from being triggered accidentally."

"Got it, mission control, stand by. Okay, pulling both levers now."

The view from Seaman Davis' camera jumped and then centered on the edge of the door closest to the two astronauts. The camera views backed up as both moved away from the slowly opening door. The edge of the door was about a foot thick, with a smoothly rounded groove running in the middle of the inner edge from top to bottom. The door itself appeared to be made of steel. As the opening widened enough to see inside, the cameras revealed a chamber slightly wider than the door, about fifty feet deep, with a door on the far wall. Pritchett and Davis bracketed the door, covering both sides of the chamber inside, but it was empty.

Pritchett resumed his running monologue. "The chamber is empty, there is some of the regolith on the floor of the chamber, probably tracked in from normal in and out traffic. There is power here, overhead lights are on. I couldn't see whether or not they were triggered by the opening of the door. The outer door has come to a halt, it has opened slightly more than ninety degrees.

"There appear to be no visible sensors inside the doorframe, there's nothing hanging off the walls. At the far end, above the second door there's something that looks like a little window, maybe a camera behind it. I can see the panel on the far wall, its lights are also green. FYI, when this door opened there was no change in the lights on this panel. I'm going to proceed into the room. Davis, wait here, I'm not going far, I just want to see if there's a panel on the inside of this end of the room.

"Mission control, I'm walking into the room. The floor is textured metal, I can't feel any vibration through my boots. Okay. I'm inside, how do you read me, Endeavour? Is the rock blocking my signal any?"

"Endeavour to Team One. Your signal strength is the same, still reading you five-by-five."

"Roger, Endeavour. Mission control, do you have any suggestions on how to proceed? I want to get inside and see what we're dealing with here but I don't want to split up the team. I also don't want to take a chance that we can get in, but not get out. If so, I want to wait for Team Two so we're all inside together, please advise."

"Stand by, Team One," answered the mission controller.

"Mr. President, Colonel Tibbits wants to know what your suggestion is at this time," Major Adams asked.

"How far out is Team Two?" President Bender asked.

"At least an hour, sir. Seaman Fisher's suit is still running hot."

"Is Shelter Fourteen receiving this transmission?"

"Yes sir, both Ms. Churchill and Mr. Simon insisted," Adams answered. "Should I connect you to the installation sir?"

"Yes, major, I want to talk to Dr, Milton right away."

"One moment, sir."

Seconds later the phone by his side rang. "Dr. Milton, this is President Bender."

"Yes, sir. What do you need?" Milton asked.

"What's your read on this? What are the chances that those people might have left any booby traps behind?" President Bender asked.

"We were just talking about that, Mr. President. The consensus is that they wouldn't have bothered. We do, however, believe that anything left behind will be worthless to us, but not necessarily hostile. We're hoping the environmental infrastructure will still be intact so our men can live long enough for us to get them home," Dr. Milton said, leaving unsaid that it might be years before the US or any country would be able to do so.

"Thank you very much for your help, Dr. Milton. I'll be in touch," President Bender concluded.

"You're welcome, Mr. President, we'll be standing by."

Hanging up the phone, Bender said to Major Adams, "Inform Colonel Tibbits that the team is to proceed on its own initiative. Wait a minute, can I speak to them from here?"

"Yes, sir. NASA can patch you in by phone, sir."

"Do it. I want to speak to those boys before they go any farther."

"Yes, Mr. President," Major Adams said.

After exchanging a few terse sentences with Colonel Tibbits, the major sent the call to the president's phone.

The president heard, " . . . stand by for the President of the United States." Then the mission controller said, "Go ahead, Mr. President."

"SEAL Team Omega, this is the President of the United States. First of all, I want to express the nation's gratitude to you for your dedication to your duty. You also have my personal thanks for undertaking such an important mission on behalf of your country. Your efforts today will long be remembered by this nation, and I dare say, the entire world.

"As you have the best perspective on the situation at hand, as a matter of fact, you have the only perspective on the situation at hand, I am ordering you to proceed on your own initiative for the duration of the mission. You have conducted yourselves in the finest tradition of the United States Navy. Godspeed gentlemen, and from my heart, thank you."

Seconds later the president heard, "SEAL Team Omega One," "Two," "Yes sir, Mr. President. Thank you, Mr. President."

On the screen, everyone saw the two team leaders' cameras steady as Chief Pritchett turned to face the other three members of his team, lined up and standing at attention in their cumbersome suits. The same view was copied in front of Takahashi. Then Chief Pritchett's voice ordered, "Present arms." In the Chief's and Takahashi's views all six SEALs saluted, held the salute until Chief Pritchett said, "Order arms."

President Bender was speechless and every man and woman in uniform in the situation room sat a bit straighter at the unexpected display.

As Pritchett's view turned around to face the open door again, he resumed his running commentary. "Okay, I'm going to take Lane inside with me. Davis and Greenfield will wait outside. If something happens they may be able to blast the door open to get us out. Proceeding inside, still no sign of anyone home. Okay, Lane is covering the other door, I'm going to pull both inner levers. Pulling, now!

"Can you see this? The door is closing at about the same rate it opened, there's a slight vibration underfoot, probably the motors for the door . . . the door is almost closed." The helmet cams showed the door from three different perspectives, the fourth view was focused on the inner door. Everyone watching the view from Chief Pritchett's camera could also see that both men had holstered their sidearms and pulled out their machine guns.

"The outer door is shut, Endeavour, can you still read my signal?" Pritchett inquired.

"Endeavour to One, you're somewhat weak, but still reading you fine. How say you?" Colonel Evers asked.

"One to Endeavour, I read you slightly low, some static, but you're coming in fine.

Proceeding to the inner door. No change in panel lights. I'm pulling the levers now. The door is opening, no sign of atmosphere. Nothing is being stirred up around here. I can see lights on inside. From the little I can see there's a much larger room inside. Okay, I'm stepping back away from the door until it's fully opened. There's definitely a much bigger chamber inside, it's empty. I can see large blank walls, can't see much detail. Wait, are you getting this?

"There're two doors about the same size as this one on the far side of the chamber. I can see something written on the far wall. Proceeding, the chamber is about two hundred feet long, about the same in width."

The president, along with the rest of the people in the viewing gallery, was trying to catch details of the huge chamber through the bobbing helmet cams as Chief Pritchett was walking across the room to the far wall. The writing on the wall was hand written in bold red paint. As Pritchett and Lane got closer the whole world was watching, beginning to discern some of the writing. In the situation room, Major Adams uttered, "Well fuck *me!*"

As Chief Pritchett and Seaman Lane stopped, and held their helmets still, three-quarters of the world's population saw scrawled in huge, block letters: "WHITEY GO HOME."

EPILOGUE

TENS OF THOUSANDS mourned the departure of their family members and friends, and yet rejoiced in the fact that they were not dead. Travis Woodson saw that Jaylynn Williams' name was numbered among those in space. Good man that he was, he forgave her for leaving him so abruptly, and even understood her deliberately fighting with him on their last night together. He put in for a week's vacation and planned to travel to see Jaylynn's parents.

That night, as on the previous two, Alan was lying next to Norma in her room at Shelter Fourteen. However, this night both were lying entwined, sweat drying on their bodies after their exertions. Norma, though she didn't know the reason why, had come to understand that her parents were in a better place and she began to forgive them for their absence in her life. She embraced her own life, deciding to seize the day, for every moment is precious, as were the people who made a difference in one's life.

Team Two made it to the final way point on the moon safely, and with air to spare. SEAL Team Omega found that the installation had plenty of air and water, but little else. Further investigation showed that the installation was completely stripped of anything useful. There was no sign of any advanced technology, power being supplied by simple solar cells and storage batteries and environmental machinery running on automatic. Their only hope lay in the possibility NASA could launch and land food nearby until some means of getting them back to earth would manifest itself.

Detective John Mathews decided to remain with the Atlanta Police Department's Missing Persons Bureau once all the excitement died down. His friend Pete could tell that John was a changed man, more subdued and introspective. What Pete or anyone else didn't know was that the day after the events on the moon unfolded, John received an anonymous e-mail message simply saying, "I will always love you," giving him the only measure of comfort he would probably receive for the rest of his life. Later, Sydney wanted with all her heart to be able to say more, especially so since she discovered that her time with John yielded so much more than the momentary physical fulfillment of the love they shared. Sydney was pregnant, her single night of passion with John having produced a child, all the more precious for the circumstances of its parents.

Dr. Harris plotted the progress of the flying space colony until it reached the asteroid belt, and saw it halt its outward progress between the orbits of Mars and Jupiter. The powerful field that propelled it away from the moon had shut down, leaving it adrift in slow orbit around the sun. He was consumed with the intellectual challenge of divining the fundamental nature of the force of gravity. He believed that with the data he recorded from the colony in space, and a singular dedication to the science behind his own work, it wouldn't be long before he could meet with those living in space. This time there would be no coming to them hat in hand, or over the barrel of a gun. He was determined that he would be meeting them as an equal and coming to them in peace.

Don't miss *Conception*, Volume Two of the Darkside Trilogy

CHAPTER 1 BEGINS . . .

Somewhere, inside something
There is a rush of
Greatness. Who knows what stands in front of
Our lives. I fashion my future
On films in space
Silence tells me secretly
Everything . . . everything . . .

The Flesh Failures (Let the Sunshine In)
Written by James Rado, Gerome Ragni, and Galt MacDermot,
performed by the Broadway Cast of Hair

CHAPTER 1

H E SIMPLY COULDN'T believe what was plainly evident before his eyes. The six-hundred-pound laboratory bench, with its heavy stone top, was hovering over a foot off the ground without any visible means of support. The only movement in the room was the almost imperceptible slide of the bench toward the window, through which the early morning sun shown.

The only witness to the remarkable doings in the deserted lab was nearly struck dumb. He could scarcely credit what he had managed to accomplish, and yet the only thing he felt more strongly than wonder was fear. Just looking at the hovering lab bench, he knew that once anyone else found out what he had discovered, he would lose control of his work.

Christopher Benjamin Wright was a graduate student majoring in physics. He was one of a special few in the graduate program at Parsons University in Houston, Texas. What made him special was that he was one of only sixteen Negroes ever admitted to the advanced studies program at the university. Fall of 1964 had seen little acceptance of his kind in the South, especially in the halls of higher learning. In most cases Christopher would have been called "uppity" at best.

Christopher further differentiated himself from nearly all the rest of the Negroes attending the undergraduate and graduate programs at Parsons because he was there on an academic scholarship, not for playing football. His math and science scores throughout high school had marked him as having an exceptional mind, regardless of the color of the skin which housed it. Christopher even aced his college entrance exams with perfect math and science scores, and only missed four of the verbal questions. In fact, his scores were so good his high school counselor had to vociferously defend the scores when several members of the school board accused Christopher of cheating.

His straight As in his undergraduate classes and his serious focus on academic achievement so impressed his instructors that it was their unanimous support for him continuing his college career that got him a full-ride scholarship to the graduate program.

Now, he was standing awestruck at the crack of dawn in the school's physics lab, looking at the most amazing sight he could have imagined. As he began to regain his sense of self, Christopher noticed that the device in the middle of the lab bench was completely silent. There was no sign of the power it was consuming to do its remarkable feat. There was no glow or sign of electrical discharge. The only movement in the room was the slow drift of the bench toward the window.

Reaching over the edge of the floating bench, Christopher's heavily-gloved hand carefully touched the apparatus on the bench. Feeling nothing through the rubber-insulated glove, he turned the small knob on the face of the device. As he did so the bench slowly settled to the floor, displaced over two feet from its original position in the room. When the power to the device had been completely cut he let out a huge sigh, as if he had been holding his breath the whole time.

Realization of the predicament he would be in should anyone discover his device and its capabilities galvanized Christopher into action. He disconnected the plug that fed power to the device from the receptacle in the wall and unscrewed the clamp that secured the device to the tabletop. In mild panic, Christopher looked around for something large enough to conceal it from view so he could get it out of the building and off campus. His briefcase was too small, and there were no boxes in the room. He wasn't about to try to disassemble it for fear he wouldn't be able to put it back together again and have it work.

Gathering up his papers and shoving them in the briefcase, he tucked the unwieldy machine under his arm and left the lab. Looking both ways as he left the room, Christopher was relieved to see no one about. Quickly walking down the hall, and down the stairs a single floor, he made his way to his locker. Spinning the dial of the combination lock he opened his locker and, turning the device on end, squeezed it in to a space barely able to accommodate its width. Closing and locking the door, Christopher allowed himself to relax. Now all he had to do was wait. He would have a much better chance of getting it out of the building and to his small apartment under cover of darkness.

Though he was a student in good standing at Parsons, being caught trying to leave campus with something as unusual as a piece of lab equipment would arouse attention he now felt he could ill afford.

The day seemed to pass interminably slowly. When his final class was over in midafternoon he tried to lose himself in the library, reading science journals at first, then finally settling on rereading Jules Verne's First Men in the Moon. Though he periodically turned the pages, Christopher was paying no attention to the words before him. He was going over everything he'd done in the preceding weeks, retracing the steps he had taken in making his remarkable discovery. He began to list in his head the research materials he had borrowed from the library, the books and journals that would show up if someone took the time to see what he'd been up to in his studies. He needed to retrieve his lab notebooks from the past year as well, even those his faculty advisor had filed away in the department's main office.

It didn't take a genius to figure that anything a colored boy at an almost all-white university discovered wouldn't be left in his hands for very long.

Christopher's life was taking a turn completely away from any plans his parents had envisioned. The first thing on his agenda was to conceal as much of his research as he possibly could. That last thing he wanted was to leave behind a spore that could lead someone else down the path of discovery he had so recently traveled. Second, he needed to carefully craft a plan of withdrawal from the university that left no one suspicious of the true nature of his departure.

Now, the only thing he was thinking about was what he wanted – no, needed – to do to ensure his own future. Tonight he was going to get his device away from the university and figure out a safe place to become his new base of operations. Since he had nothing to do until the early spring sun set, Christopher pulled together the few things he had spread out on the table beside him and left the library to get a bite to eat.

Christopher's connections to his present life were few. He was indeed a well-liked student. His instructors were equally impressed with his academic acumen and his quiet, somewhat self-effacing manner. He had never been known to speak a word in anger, nor had he failed to act in anything but the most circumspect manner. Those coeds who overcame their natural reserve, or in a couple of cases, the de facto barriers of race, to approach him had been politely rebuffed, although said avoidance was accomplished in such a manner that not one of them ever took offense.

Leaving school was going to mean losing his financial support. His scholarship was not going to be there to sustain him once he severed his relationship with Parsons. A job would have to be found, preferably well away from his usual haunts, perhaps even in another town. Methodical, he was. By the time Christopher finished eating dinner he had assembled all the pieces of his immediate plan.

Walking home to the second-floor apartment above the neighborhood laundromat, he went into his dirty clothes hamper and pulled out several pairs of white socks, a pair of underwear and two t-shirts and packed them into his gym bag. Looking at it critically, he estimated there was more than enough room for the device hidden in his locker.

Once the sun had set, Christopher set off for the sciences building, setting a leisurely pace. Reaching campus, he felt better seeing a few students still about, mostly coming from the library. Entering the building and going up the stairs toward his locker he saw no one. Once he reached his locker his heart was pounding, the noise from the combination lock excruciatingly loud in his ears. Carefully opening the latch of the locker, he made sure the door didn't slip out of his hand to bang against the adjacent locker door. Setting the gym bag on the floor, he pulled out his soiled clothes and placed his device in the bottom of the bag, quickly replacing the clothes around the sides and on top. Zipping the bag, he carefully closed the locker and locked it once again.

As he drew close to home he realized he hadn't really thought of a safe place to hide his invention. The last place he wanted to keep it was in his room. The small apartment had little in the way of living space, let alone any real place to hide something the size of two phone books. There was no way he was going to trust it to the mail or a package delivery company and send it home to his mother. He was going to have to secret it somewhere close, but in a place unlikely to be discovered even with a fairly vigorous search.

Approaching the block on which he lived, Christopher scanned the area, looking for possible hiding places for his invention. Walking around to the back of the laundromat to climb the stairs to his apartment, the dark doorway to the basement caught his eye.

Casting an eye about and seeing no one, he carefully opened the door. A cool, moist wash of air enveloped him as he entered the dark cellar. Closing the door behind him, Christopher felt around for the light switch on the wall. Flicking the switch, Christopher could barely see to the other side of the room. The entire basement was lit by a single, naked light bulb just off the door.

Christopher looked around, there was little in the dank room but a huge gas-fired water heater hissing in the far corner. The body of the heater was about half a dozen feet deep, rounded on the top with the usual pipes and valves festooning the space between ceiling and tank. There was just enough space between the sides and the basement walls for Christopher to squeeze all the way through to the corner.

Looking up into the ceiling, he could see nothing but a yawning darkness between the joists of the floor above. Reaching into one of the dark recesses above the wall, all Christopher could feel was empty space. Pulling his hand back he came away with a thick coating of spider web strands, empty fly carcasses and a fine rain of dislodged dust and dirt.

Perfect, he thought. Bending down to lift the shirt-covered machine, Christopher carefully slid his precious invention into the shielding darkness.

Stepping back as far as he could, he could see no sign of the shirt wrapped around the device. Christopher knew that the hiding place was only temporary, but for now it was fine. Gently erasing his footprints in the dust behind the huge tank with a rag, he backtracked to the basement door, tossed the rag back behind the heater tank, turned off the light and made his way to his own apartment, finally able to relax.

Reliving those events of nearly forty years ago, Christopher mentally shook his head in amazement at the comparison of his circumstance between then and now. He was literally millions of miles from the Parsons campus, in a spacecraft flying parallel to a mile-long asteroid made up primarily of frozen water. The two objects were on course toward Earth's nearest neighbor in the sky. What a difference a few years makes, he thought as he flew silently through the void of space, further from the earth than any man had ever traveled.

Get Published, Inc!
Thorofare, NJ 08086
16 March, 2010
BA2010075